ALWAYS AND FOREVER

by

Betty Neels

*MILLS & BOON and MILLS & BOON with the Rose Device
are registered trademarks of the publisher.*

*First published in Great Britain 2001 by
Harlequin Mills & Boon Limited,
Eton House, 18-24 Paradise Road,
Richmond, Surrey, TW9 1SR*

THE CHRISTMAS COLLECTION © Harlequin Enterprises II B.V., 2001

The publisher acknowledges the copyright holders of the
individual works as follows:

Always and Forever © Betty Neels 2001
The Playboy's Mistress © Kim Lawrence 2001
Lady Allerton's Wager © Nicola Cornick 2001

ISBN 0 263 83303 8

101-1001

*Printed and bound in Spain
by Litografia Rosés S.A., Barcelona*

BETTY NEELS

spent her childhood and youth in Devonshire before training as a nurse and midwife. She was an army nursing sister during the war, married a Dutchman, and subsequently lived in Holland for fourteen years. She lives with her husband in Dorset, and has a daughter and grandson. Her hobbies are reading, animals, old buildings and writing. Betty started to write on retirement from nursing, incited by a lady in a library bemoaning the lack of romantic novels. Betty Neels has sold over 35 million copies of her books, world-wide.

KIM LAWRENCE

lives on a farm in rural Anglesey. She runs two miles daily and finds this an excellent opportunity to unwind and seek inspiration for her writing! It also helps her keep up with her husband, two active sons, and the various stray animals which have adopted them. Always a fanatical consumer of fiction, she is now equally enthusiastic about writing. She loves a happy ending!

NICOLA CORNICK

is passionate about many things: her country cottage and its garden, her two small cats, her husband and her writing, though not necessarily in that order! She has always been fascinated by history, both as her chosen subject at university and subsequently as an engrossing hobby. She works as a university administrator and finds her writing the perfect antidote to the demands of life in a busy office.

CHAPTER ONE

THERE was going to be a storm; the blue sky of a summer evening was slowly being swallowed by black clouds, heavy with rain and thunder, flashing warning signals of flickering lightning over the peaceful Dorset countryside, casting gloom over the village. The girl gathering a line of washing from the small orchard behind the house standing on the village outskirts paused to study the sky before lugging the washing basket through the open door at the back of the house.

She was a small girl, nicely plump, with a face which, while not pretty, was redeemed by fine brown eyes. Her pale brown hair was gathered in an untidy bunch on the top of her head and she was wearing a cotton dress which had seen better days.

She put the basket down, closed the door and went in search of candles and matches, then put two old-fashioned oil lamps on the wooden table. If the storm was bad there would be a power cut before the evening was far advanced.

This done to her satisfaction, she poked up the elderly Aga, set a kettle to boil and turned her attention to the elderly dog and battle-scarred old tomcat, waiting patiently for their suppers.

She got their food, talking while she did so because the eerie quiet before the storm broke was a little unnerving, and then made tea and sat down to drink it as the first heavy drops of rain began to fall.

5

With the rain came a sudden wind which sent her round the house shutting windows against the deluge. Back in the kitchen, she addressed the dog.

'Well, there won't be anyone coming now,' she told him, and gave a small shriek as lightning flashed and thunder drowned out any other sound. She sat down at the table and he came and sat beside her, and, after a moment, the cat got onto her lap.

The wind died down as suddenly as it had arisen but the storm was almost overhead. It had become very dark and the almost continuous flashes made it seem even darker. Presently the light over the table began to flicker; she prudently lit a candle before it went out.

She got up then, lighted the lamps and took one into the hall before sitting down again. There was nothing to do but to wait until the storm had passed.

The lull was shattered by a peal on the doorbell, so unexpected that she sat for a moment, not quite believing it. But a second prolonged peal sent her to the door, lamp in hand.

A man stood in the porch. She held the lamp high in order to get a good look at him; he was a very large man, towering over her.

'I saw your sign. Can you put us up for the night? I don't care to drive further in this weather.'

He had a quiet voice and he looked genuine. 'Who's we?' she asked.

'My mother and myself.'

She slipped the chain off the door. 'Come in.' She peered round him. 'Is that your car?'

'Yes—is there a garage?'

'Go round the side of the house; there's a barn—the door's open. There's plenty of room there.'

He nodded and turned back to the car to open its door and help his mother out. Ushering them into the hall, the girl said, 'Come back in through the kitchen door; I'll leave it unlocked. It's across the yard from the barn.'

He nodded again, a man of few words, she supposed, and he went outside. She turned to look at her second guest. The woman was tall, good-looking, in her late fifties, she supposed, and dressed with understated elegance.

'Would you like to see your room? And would you like a meal? It's a bit late to cook dinner but you could have an omelette or scrambled eggs and bacon with tea or coffee?'

The older woman put out a hand. 'Mrs Fforde—spelt with two ffs, I'm afraid. My son's a doctor; he was driving me to the other side of Glastonbury, taking a short-cut, but driving had become impossible. Your sign was like something from heaven.' She had to raise her voice against the heavenly din.

The girl offered a hand. 'Amabel Parsons. I'm sorry you had such a horrid journey.'

'I hate storms, don't you? You're not alone in the house?'

'Well, yes, I am, but I have Cyril—that's my dog—and Oscar the cat.' Amabel hesitated. 'Would you like to come into the sitting room until Dr Fforde comes? Then you can decide if you would like something to eat. I'm afraid you will have to go to bed by candlelight...'

She led the way down the hall and into a small room, comfortably furnished with easy chairs and a small round table. There were shelves of books on either side of the fireplace and a large window across which

Amabel drew the curtains before setting the lamp on the table.

'I'll unlock the kitchen door,' she said and hurried back to the kitchen just in time to admit the doctor.

He was carrying two cases. 'Shall I take these up?'

'Yes, please. I'll ask Mrs Fforde if she would like to go to her room now. I asked if you would like anything to eat…'

'Most emphatically yes. That's if it's not putting you to too much trouble. Anything will do—sandwiches…'

'Omelettes, scrambled eggs, bacon and eggs? I did explain to Mrs Fforde that it's too late to cook a full meal.'

He smiled down at her. 'I'm sure Mother is longing for a cup of tea, and omelettes sound fine.' He glanced round him. 'You're not alone?'

'Yes,' said Amabel. 'I'll take you upstairs.'

She gave them the two rooms at the front of the house and pointed out the bathroom. 'Plenty of hot water,' she added, before going back to the kitchen.

When they came downstairs presently she had the table laid in the small room and offered them omelettes, cooked to perfection, toast and butter and a large pot of tea. This had kept her busy, but it had also kept her mind off the storm, still raging above their heads. It rumbled away finally in the small hours, but by the time she had cleared up the supper things and prepared the breakfast table, she was too tired to notice.

She was up early, but so was Dr Fforde. He accepted the tea she offered him before he wandered out of the door into the yard and the orchard beyond, accompanied by Cyril. He presently strolled back to stand in the doorway and watch her getting their breakfast.

Amabel, conscious of his steady gaze, said briskly, 'Would Mrs Fforde like breakfast in bed? It's no extra trouble.'

'I believe she would like that very much. I'll have mine with you here.'

'Oh, you can't do that.' She was taken aback. 'I mean, your breakfast is laid in the sitting room. I'll bring it to you whenever you're ready.'

'I dislike eating alone. If you put everything for Mother on a tray I'll carry it up.'

He was friendly in a casual way, but she guessed that he was a man who disliked arguing. She got a tray ready, and when he came downstairs again and sat down at the kitchen table she put a plate of bacon, eggs and mushrooms in front of him, adding toast and marmalade before pouring the tea.

'Come and sit down and eat your breakfast and tell me why you live here alone,' he invited. He sounded so like an elder brother or a kind uncle that she did so, watching him demolish his breakfast with evident enjoyment before loading a slice of toast with butter and marmalade.

She had poured herself a cup of tea, but whatever he said she wasn't going to eat her breakfast with him...

He passed her the slice of toast. 'Eat that up and tell me why you live alone.'

'Well, really!' began Amabel and then, meeting his kindly look, added, 'It's only for a month or so. My mother's gone to Canada,' she told him. 'My married sister lives there and she's just had a baby. It was such a good opportunity for her to go. You see, in the summer we get quite a lot of people coming just for bed and breakfast, like you, so I'm not really alone. It's different in the winter, of course.'

He asked, 'You don't mind being here by yourself? What of the days—and nights—when no one wants bed and breakfast?'

She said defiantly, 'I have Cyril, and Oscar's splendid company. Besides, there's the phone.'

'And your nearest neighbour?' he asked idly.

'Old Mrs Drew, round the bend in the lane going to the village. Also, it's only half a mile to the village.' She still sounded defiant.

He passed his cup for more tea. Despite her brave words he suspected that she wasn't as self-assured as she would have him believe. A plain girl, he considered, but nice eyes, nice voice and apparently not much interest in clothes; the denim skirt and cotton blouse were crisp and spotless, but could hardly be called fashionable. He glanced at her hands, which were small and well shaped, bearing signs of housework.

He said, 'A lovely morning after the storm. That's a pleasant orchard you have beyond the yard. And a splendid view...'

'Yes, it's splendid all the year round.'

'Do you get cut off in the winter?'

'Yes, sometimes. Would you like more tea?'

'No, thank you. I'll see if my mother is getting ready to leave.' He smiled at her. 'That was a delicious meal.' But not, he reflected, a very friendly one. Amabel Parsons had given him the strong impression that she wished him out of the house.

Within the hour he and his mother had gone, driving away in the dark blue Rolls Royce. Amabel stood in the open doorway, watching it disappear round the bend in

the lane. It had been providential, she told herself, that
they should have stopped at the house at the height of
the storm; they had kept her busy and she hadn't had
the time to be frightened. They had been no trouble—
and she needed the money.

It would be nice, she thought wistfully, to have someone like Dr Fforde as a friend. Sitting at breakfast with
him, she'd had an urgent desire to talk to him, tell him
how lonely she was, and sometimes a bit scared, how
tired she was of making up beds and getting breakfast
for a succession of strangers, keeping the place going
until her mother returned, and all the while keeping up
the façade of an independent and competent young
woman perfectly able to manage on her own.

That was necessary, otherwise well-meaning people
in the village would have made it their business to dis-
suade her mother from her trip and even suggest that
Amabel should shut up the house and go and stay with
a great-aunt she hardly knew, who lived in Yorkshire
and who certainly wouldn't want her.

Amabel went back into the house, collected up the
bedlinen and made up the beds again; hopefully there
would be more guests later in the day...

She readied the rooms, inspected the contents of the
fridge and the deep freeze, hung out the washing and
made herself a sandwich before going into the orchard
with Cyril and Oscar. They sat, the three of them, on an
old wooden bench, nicely secluded from the lane but
near enough to hear if anyone called.

Which they did, just as she was on the point of going
indoors for her tea.

The man on the doorstep turned round impatiently as
she reached him.

'I rang twice. I want bed and breakfast for my wife, son and daughter.'

Amabel turned to look at the car. There was a young man in the driver's seat, and a middle-aged woman and a girl sitting in the back.

'Three rooms? Certainly. But I must tell you that there is only one bathroom, although there are handbasins in the rooms.'

He said rudely, 'I suppose that's all we can expect in this part of the world. We took a wrong turning and landed ourselves here, at the back of beyond. What do you charge? And we do get a decent breakfast?'

Amabel told him, 'Yes.' As her mother frequently reminded her, it took all sorts to make the world.

The three people in the car got out: a bossy woman, the girl pretty but sulky, and the young man looking at her in a way she didn't like…

They inspected their rooms with loud-voiced comments about old-fashioned furniture and no more than one bathroom—and that laughably old-fashioned. And they wanted tea: sandwiches and scones and cake. 'And plenty of jam,' the young man shouted after her as she left the room.

After tea they wanted to know where the TV was.

'I haven't got a television.'

They didn't believe her. 'Everyone has a TV set,' complained the girl. 'Whatever are we going to do this evening?'

'The village is half a mile down the lane,' said Amabel. 'There's a pub there, and you can get a meal, if you wish.'

'Better than hanging around here.'

It was a relief to see them climb back into the car and

drive off presently. She laid the table for their breakfast and put everything ready in the kitchen before getting herself some supper. It was a fine light evening, so she strolled into the orchard and sat down on the bench. Dr Fforde and his mother would be at Glastonbury, she supposed, staying with family or friends. He would be married, of course, to a pretty girl with lovely clothes—there would be a small boy and a smaller girl, and they would live in a large and comfortable house; he was successful, for he drove a Rolls Royce…

Conscious that she was feeling sad, as well as wasting her time, she went back indoors and made out the bill; there might not be time in the morning.

She was up early the next morning; breakfast was to be ready by eight o'clock, she had been told on the previous evening—a decision she'd welcomed with relief. Breakfast was eaten, the bill paid—but only after double-checking everything on it and some scathing comments about the lack of modern amenities.

Amabel waited politely at the door until they had driven away then went to put the money in the old tea caddy on the kitchen dresser. It added substantially to the contents but it had been hard earned!

The rooms, as she'd expected, had been left in a disgraceful state. She flung open the window, stripped beds and set about turning them back to their usual pristine appearance. It was still early, and it was a splendid morning, so she filled the washing machine and started on the breakfast dishes.

By midday everything was just as it should be. She made sandwiches and took them and a mug of coffee out to the orchard with Cyril and Oscar for company, and sat down to read the letter from her mother the postman had brought. Everything was splendid, she wrote. The baby was thriving and she had decided to stay another few weeks, if Amabel could manage for a little longer—*For I don't suppose I'll be able to visit here for a year or two, unless something turns up.*

Which was true enough, and it made sense too. Her mother had taken out a loan so that she could go to Canada, and even though it was a small one it would have to be paid off before she went again.

Amabel put the letter in her pocket, divided the rest of her sandwich between Cyril and Oscar and went back into the house. There was always the chance that someone would come around teatime and ask for a meal, so she would make a cake and a batch of scones.

It was as well that she did; she had just taken them out of the Aga when the doorbell rang and two elderly ladies enquired if she would give them bed and breakfast.

They had come in an old Morris, and, while wellspoken and tidily dressed, she judged them to be not too free with their money. But they looked nice and she had a kind heart.

'If you would share a twin-bedded room?' she suggested. 'The charge is the same for two people as one.' She told them how much and added, 'Two breakfasts, of course, and if you would like tea?'

They glanced at each other. 'Thank you. Would you serve us a light supper later?'

'Certainly. If you would fetch your cases? The car can go into the barn at the side of the house.'

Amabel gave them a good tea, and while they went for a short walk, she got supper—salmon fish cakes, of tinned salmon, of course, potatoes whipped to a satiny smoothness, and peas from the garden. She popped an egg custard into the oven by way of afters and was rewarded by their genteel thanks.

She ate her own supper in the kitchen, took them a pot of tea and wished them goodnight. In the morning she gave them boiled eggs, toast and marmalade and a pot of coffee, and all with a generous hand.

She hadn't made much money, but it had been nice to see their elderly faces light up. And they had left her a tip, discreetly put on one of the bedside tables. As for the bedroom, they had left it so neat it was hard to see that anyone had been in it.

She added the money to the tea caddy and decided that tomorrow she would go to the village and pay it into the post office account, stock up on groceries and get meat from the butcher's van which called twice a week at the village.

It was a lovely morning again, and her spirits rose despite her disappointment at her mother's delayed return home. She wasn't doing too badly with bed and breakfast, and she was adding steadily to their savings. There were the winter months to think of, of course, but she might be able to get a part-time job once her mother was home.

She went into the garden to pick peas, singing cheerfully and slightly off key.

Nobody came that day, and the following day only a solitary woman on a walking holiday came in the early evening; she went straight to bed after a pot of tea and left the next morning after an early breakfast.

After she had gone, Amabel discovered that she had taken the towels with her.

Two disappointing days, reflected Amabel. I wonder what will happen tomorrow?

She was up early again, for there was no point in lying in bed when it was daylight soon after five o'clock. She breakfasted, tidied the house, did a pile of ironing before the day got too hot, and then wandered out to the bench in the orchard. It was far too early for any likely person to want a room, and she would hear if a car stopped in the lane.

But of course one didn't hear a Rolls Royce, for it made almost no sound.

Dr Fforde got out and stood looking at the house. It was a pleasant place, somewhat in need of small repairs and a lick of paint, but its small windows shone and the brass knocker on its solid front door was burnished to a dazzling brightness. He trod round the side of the house, past the barn, and saw Amabel sitting between Cyril and Oscar. Since she was a girl who couldn't abide being idle, she was shelling peas.

He stood watching her for a moment, wondering why he had wanted to see her again. True, she had interested him, so small, plain and pot valiant, and so obviously terrified of the storm—and very much at the mercy of undesirable characters who might choose to call. Surely she had an aunt or cousin who could come and stay with her?

It was none of his business, of course, but it had seemed a good idea to call and see her since he was on his way to Glastonbury.

He stepped onto the rough gravel of the yard so that she looked up.

She got to her feet, and her smile left him in no doubt that she was glad to see him.

He said easily, 'Good morning. I'm on my way to Glastonbury. Have you quite recovered from the storm?'

'Oh, yes.' She added honestly, 'But I was frightened, you know. I was so very glad when you and your mother came.'

She collected up the colander of peas and came towards him. 'Would you like a cup of coffee?'

'Yes, please.' He followed her into the kitchen and sat down at the table and thought how restful she was; she had seemed glad to see him, but she had probably learned to give a welcoming smile to anyone who knocked on the door. Certainly she had displayed no fuss at seeing him.

He said on an impulse, 'Will you have lunch with me? There's a pub—the Old Boot in Underthorn—fifteen minutes' drive from here. I don't suppose you get any callers before the middle of the afternoon?'

She poured the coffee and fetched a tin of biscuits.

'But you're on your way to Glastonbury...'

'Yes, but not expected until teatime. And it's such a splendid day.' When she hesitated he said, 'We could take Cyril with us.'

She said then, 'Thank you; I should like that. But I must be back soon after two o'clock; it's Saturday...'

They went back to the orchard presently, and sat on the bench while Amabel finished shelling the peas. Oscar had got onto the doctor's knee and Cyril had sprawled under his feet. They talked idly about nothing much and Amabel, quite at her ease, now answered his carefully put questions without realising just how much she was telling him until she stopped in mid-sentence, aware that her tongue was running away with her. He saw that at once and began to talk about something else.

They drove to the Old Boot Inn just before noon and found a table on the rough grass at its back. There was a small river, overshadowed by trees, and since it was early there was no one else there. They ate home-made pork pies with salad, and drank iced lemonade which the landlord's wife made herself. Cyril sat at their feet with a bowl of water and a biscuit.

The landlord, looking at them from the bar window, observed to his wife, 'Look happy, don't they?'

And they were, all three of them, although the doctor hadn't identified his feeling as happiness, merely pleasant content at the glorious morning and the undemanding company.

He drove Amabel back presently and, rather to her surprise, parked the car in the yard behind the house, got out, took the door key from her and unlocked the back door.

Oscar came to meet them and he stooped to stroke him. 'May I sit in the orchard for a little while?' he asked. 'I seldom get the chance to sit quietly in such peaceful surroundings.'

Amabel stopped herself just in time from saying, 'You poor man,' and said instead, 'Of course you may, for as long as you like. Would you like a cup of tea, or an apple?'

So he sat on the bench chewing an apple, with Oscar on his knee, aware that his reason for sitting there was to cast an eye over any likely guests in the hope that before he went a respectable middle-aged pair would have decided to stay.

He was to have his wish. Before very long a middle-aged pair did turn up, with mother-in-law, wishing to stay for two nights. It was absurd, he told himself, that he should feel concern. Amabel was a perfectly capable young woman, and able to look after herself; besides, she had a telephone.

He went to the open kitchen door and found her there, getting tea.

'I must be off,' he told her. 'Don't stop what you're doing. I enjoyed my morning.'

She was cutting a large cake into neat slices. 'So did I. Thank you for my lunch.' She smiled at him. 'Go carefully, Dr Fforde.'

She carried the tea tray into the drawing room and went back to the kitchen. They were three nice people—polite, and anxious not to be too much trouble. 'An evening meal?' they had asked diffidently, and had accepted her offer of jacket potatoes and salad, fruit tart and coffee with pleased smiles. They would go for a short walk presently, the man told her, and when would she like to serve their supper?

When they had gone she made the tart, put the potatoes in the oven and went to the vegetable patch by the orchard to get a lettuce and radishes. There was no hurry, so she sat down on the bench and thought about the day.

She had been surprised to see the doctor again. She had been pleased too. She had thought about him, but she hadn't expected to see him again; when she had looked up and seen him standing there it had been like seeing an old friend.

'Nonsense,' said Amabel loudly. 'He came this morning because he wanted a cup of coffee.' What about taking you out to lunch? asked a persistent voice at the back of her mind.

'He's probably a man who doesn't like to eat alone.'

And, having settled the matter, she went back to the kitchen.

The three guests intended to spend Sunday touring around the countryside. They would return at tea time and could they have supper? They added that they would want to leave early the next morning, which left Amabel with almost all day free to do as she wanted.

There was no need for her to stay at the house; she didn't intend to let the third room if anyone called. She would go to church and then spend a quiet afternoon with the Sunday paper.

She liked going to church, for she met friends and acquaintances and could have a chat, and at the same time assure anyone who asked that her mother would be coming home soon and that she herself was perfectly content on her own. She was aware that some of the older members of the congregation didn't approve of her mother's trip and thought that at the very least some friend or cousin should have moved in with Amabel.

It was something she and her mother had discussed at some length, until her mother had burst into tears, declaring that she wouldn't be able to go to Canada. Amabel had said at once that she would much rather be on her own, so her mother had gone, and Amabel had written her a letter each week, giving light-hearted and slightly optimistic accounts of the bed and breakfast business.

Her mother had been gone for a month now; she had phoned when she had arrived and since then had written regularly, although she still hadn't said when she would be returning.

Amabel, considering the matter while Mr Huggett, the church warden, read the first lesson, thought that her mother's next letter would certainly contain news of her return. Not for the world would she admit, even to herself, that she didn't much care for living on her own. She was, in fact, uneasy at night, even though the house was locked and securely bolted.

She kept a stout walking stick which had belonged to her father by the front door, and a rolling pin handy in the kitchen, and there was always the phone; she had only to lift it and dial 999!

Leaving the church presently, and shaking hands with the vicar, she told him cheerfully that her mother would be home very soon.

'You are quite happy living there alone, Amabel? You have friends to visit you, I expect?'

'Oh, yes,' she assured him. 'And there's so much to keep me busy. The garden and the bed and breakfast people keep me occupied.'

He said with vague kindness, 'Nice people, I hope, my dear?'

'I'm careful who I take,' she assured him.

It was seldom that any guests came on a Monday; Amabel cleaned the house, made up beds and checked the fridge, made herself a sandwich and went to the orchard to eat it. It was a pleasant day, cool and breezy, just right for gardening.

She went to bed quite early, tired with the digging, watering and weeding. Before she went to sleep she allowed her thoughts to dwell on Dr Fforde. He seemed like an old friend, but she knew nothing about him. Was he married? Where did he live? Was he a GP, or working at a hospital? He dressed well and drove a Rolls Royce, and he had family or friends somewhere on the other side of Glastonbury. She rolled over in bed and closed her eyes. It was none of her business anyway…

The fine weather held and a steady trickle of tourists knocked on the door. The tea caddy was filling up nicely again; her mother would be delighted. The week slid imperceptibly into the next one, and at the end of it there was a letter from her mother. The postman arrived with it at the same time as a party of four—two couples sharing a car on a brief tour—so that Amabel had to put it in her pocket until they had been shown their rooms and had sat down to tea.

She went into the kitchen, got her own tea and sat down to read it.

It was a long letter, and she read it through to the end—and then read it again. She had gone pale, and drank her cooling tea with the air of someone unaware of what they were doing, but presently she picked up the letter and read it for the third time.

Her mother wasn't coming home. At least not for several months. She had met someone and they were to be married shortly.

I know you will understand. And you'll like him. He's a market gardener, and we plan to set up a garden centre from the house. There's plenty of room and he will build a large glasshouse at the bottom of the orchard. Only he must sell his own market garden first, which may take some months.

It will mean that we shan't need to do bed and breakfast any more, although I hope you'll keep on with it until we get back. You're doing so well. I know that the tourist season is quickly over but we hope to be back before Christmas.

The rest of the letter was a detailed description of her husband-to-be and news too, of her sister and the baby.

You're such a sensible girl, her mother concluded, *and I'm sure you're enjoying your independence. Probably when we get back you will want to start a career on your own.*

Amabel was surprised, she told herself, but there was no reason for her to feel as though the bottom had dropped out of her world; she was perfectly content to stay at home until her mother and stepfather should return, and it was perfectly natural for her mother to suppose that she would like to make a career for herself.

Amabel drank the rest of the tea, now stewed and cold. She would have plenty of time to decide what kind of career she would like to have.

That evening, her guests in their rooms, she sat down with pen and paper and assessed her accomplishments. She could cook—not quite cordon bleu, perhaps, but to a high standard—she could housekeep, change plugs, cope with basic plumbing. She could tend a garden... Her pen faltered. There was nothing else.

She had her A levels, but circumstances had never allowed her to make use of them. She would have to train for something and she would have to make up her mind what that should be before her mother came home. But training cost money, and she wasn't sure if there would be any. She could get a job and save enough to train...

She sat up suddenly, struck by a sudden thought. Waitresses needed no training, and there would be tips. In one of the larger towns, of course. Taunton or Yeovil? Or what about one of the great estates run by the

National Trust? They had shops and tearooms and house guides. The more she thought about it, the better she liked it.

She went to bed with her decision made. Now it was just a question of waiting until her mother and her stepfather came home.

CHAPTER TWO

IT WAS almost a week later when she had the next letter, but before that her mother had phoned. She was so happy, she'd said excitedly; they planned to marry in October—Amabel didn't mind staying at home until they returned? Probably in November?

'It's only a few months, Amabel, and just as soon as we're home Keith says you must tell us what you want to do and we'll help you do it. He's so kind and generous. Of course if he sells his business quickly we shall come home as soon as we can arrange it.'

Amabel had heard her mother's happy little laugh. 'I've written you a long letter about the wedding. Joyce and Tom are giving a small reception for us, and I've planned such a pretty outfit—it's all in the letter...'

The long letter when it arrived was bursting with excitement and happiness.

> *You have no idea how delightful it is not to have to worry about the future, to have someone to look after me—you too, of course. Have you decided what you want to do when we get home? You must be so excited at the idea of being independent; you have had such a dull life since you left school...*

But a contented one, reflected Amabel. Helping to turn their bed and breakfast business into a success, knowing that she was wanted, feeling that she and her mother were making something of their lives. And now she must start all over again.

It would be nice to wallow in self-pity, but there were two people at the door asking if she could put them up for the night…

Because she was tired she slept all night, although the moment she woke thoughts came tumbling into her head which were better ignored, so she got up earlier than usual and went outside in her dressing gown with a mug of tea and Cyril and Oscar for company.

It was pleasant sitting on the bench in the orchard in the early-morning sun, and in its cheerful light it was impossible to be gloomy. It would be nice, though, to be able to talk to someone about her future…

Dr Fforde's large, calm person came into her mind's eye; he would have listened and told her what she should do. She wondered what he was doing…

Dr Fforde was sitting on the table in the kitchen of his house, the end one in a short terrace of Regency houses in a narrow street tucked away behind Wimpole Street in London. He was wearing a tee shirt and elderly trousers and badly needed a shave; he had the appearance of a ruffian—a handsome ruffian. There was a half-eaten apple on the table beside him and he was taking great bites from a thick slice of bread and butter. He had been called out just after two o'clock that morning to operate on a patient with a perforated duodenal ulcer; there had been complications which had kept him from his bed and now he was on his way to shower and get ready for his day.

He finished his bread and butter, bent to fondle the sleek head of the black Labrador sitting beside him, and went to the door. It opened as he reached it. The youngish man who came in was already dressed, immaculate in a black alpaca jacket and striped trousers. He had a sharp-nosed foxy face, and dark hair brushed to a satin smoothness.

He stood aside for the doctor and wished him a severe good morning.

'Out again, sir?' His eye fell on the apple core. 'You had only to call me. I'd have got you a nice hot drink and a sandwich...'

The doctor clapped him on the shoulder. 'I know you would, Bates. I'll be down in half an hour for one of your special breakfasts. I disturbed Tiger; would you let him out into the garden?'

He went up the graceful little staircase to his room, his head already filled with thoughts of the day ahead of him. Amabel certainly had no place in them.

Half an hour later he was eating the splendid breakfast Bates had carried through to the small sitting room at the back of the house. Its French windows opened onto a small patio and a garden beyond where Tiger was meandering round. Presently he came to sit by his master, to crunch bacon rinds and then accompany him on a brisk walk through the still quiet streets before the doctor got into his car and drove the short distance to the hospital.

Amabel saw her two guests on their way, got the room ready for the next occupants and then on a sudden impulse went to the village and bought the regional weekly paper at the post office. Old Mr Truscott, who ran it and knew everyone's business, took his time giving her her change.

'Didn't know you were interested in the *Gazette*, nothing much in it but births, marriages and deaths.' He fixed her with a beady eye. 'And adverts, of course. Now if anyone was looking for a job it's a paper I'd recommend.'

Amabel said brightly, 'I dare say it's widely read, Mr Truscott. While I'm here I'd better have some more air mail letters.'

'Your ma's not coming home yet, then? Been gone a long time, I reckon.'

'She's staying a week or two longer; she might not get the chance to visit my sister again for a year or two. It's a long way to go for just a couple of weeks.

Over her lunch she studied the jobs page. There were heartening columns of vacancies for waitresses: the basic wage was fairly low, but if she worked full-time she could manage very well... And Stourhead, the famous National Trust estate, wanted shop assistants, help in the tearooms and suitable applicants for full-time work in the ticket office. And none of them were wanted until the end of September.

It seemed too good to be true, but all the same she cut the ad out and put it with the bed and breakfast money in the tea caddy.

A week went by, and then another. Summer was almost over. The evenings were getting shorter, and, while the mornings were light still, there was the ghost of a nip in the air. There had been more letters from Canada from her mother and future stepfather, and her sister, and during the third week her mother had telephoned; they were married already—now it was just a question of selling Keith's business.

'We hadn't intended to marry so soon but there was no reason why we shouldn't, and of course I've moved in with him,' she said. 'So if he can sell his business soon we shall be home before long. We have such plans…!'

There weren't as many people knocking on the door now; Amabel cleaned and polished the house, picked the last of the soft fruit to put in the freezer and cast an eye over the contents of the cupboards.

With a prudent eye to her future she inspected her wardrobe—a meagre collection of garments, bought with an eye to their long-lasting qualities, in good taste but which did nothing to enhance her appearance.

Only a handful of people came during the week, and no one at all on Saturday. She felt low-spirited—owing to the damp and gloomy weather, she told herself—and even a brisk walk with Cyril didn't make her feel any better. It was still only early afternoon and she sat down in the kitchen, with Oscar on her lap, disinclined to do anything.

She would make herself a pot of tea, write to her mother, have an early supper and go to bed. Soon it would be the beginning of another week; if the weather was better there might be a satisfying number of tourists—and besides, there were plenty of jobs to do in the garden. So she wrote her letter, very bright and cheerful, skimming over the lack of guests, making much of the splendid apple crop and how successful the soft fruit had been. That done, she went on sitting at the kitchen table, telling herself that she would make the tea.

Instead of that she sat, a small sad figure, contemplating a future which held problems. Amabel wasn't a girl given to self-pity, and she couldn't remember the last time she had cried, but she cried now, quietly and without fuss, a damp Oscar on her lap, Cyril's head pressed against her legs. She made no attempt to stop; there was no one there to see, and now that the rain was coming down in earnest no one would want to stop for the night.

Dr Fforde had a free weekend, but he wasn't particularly enjoying it. He had lunched on Saturday with friends, amongst whom had been Miriam Potter-Stokes, an elegant young widow who was appearing more and more frequently in his circle of friends. He felt vaguely sorry for her, admired her for the apparently brave face she was showing to the world, and what had been a casual friendship now bid fair to become something more serious—on her part at least.

He had found himself agreeing to drive her down to Henley after lunch, and once there had been forced by good manners to stay at her friend's home for tea. On the way back to London she had suggested that they might have dinner together.

He had pleaded a prior engagement and gone back to his home feeling that his day had been wasted. She was an amusing companion, pretty and well dressed, but he had wondered once or twice what she was really like. Certainly he enjoyed her company from time to time, but that was all…

He took Tiger for a long walk on Sunday morning and after lunch got into his car. It was no day for a drive into the country, and Bates looked his disapproval.

'Not going to Glastonbury in this weather, I hope, sir?' he observed.

'No, no. Just a drive. Leave something cold for my supper, will you?'

Bates looked offended. When had he ever forgotten to leave everything ready before he left the house?

'As always, sir,' he said reprovingly.

It wasn't until he was driving west through the quiet city streets that Dr Fforde admitted to himself that he knew where he was going. Watching the carefully nurtured beauty of Miriam Potter-Stokes had reminded him of Amabel. He had supposed, in some amusement, because the difference in the two of them was so marked. It would be interesting to see her again. Her mother would be back home by now, and he doubted if there were many people wanting bed and breakfast now that summer had slipped into a wet autumn.

He enjoyed driving, and the roads, once he was clear of the suburbs, were almost empty. Tiger was an undemanding companion, and the countryside was restful after the bustle of London streets.

The house, when he reached it, looked forlorn; there were no open windows, no signs of life. He got out of the car with Tiger and walked round the side of the house; he found the back door open.

Amabel looked up as he paused at the door. He thought that she looked like a small bedraggled brown hen. He said, 'Hello, may we come in?' and bent to fondle the two dogs, giving her time to wipe her wet cheeks with the back of her hand. 'Tiger's quite safe with Cyril, and he likes cats.'

Amabel stood up, found a handkerchief and blew her nose. She said in a social kind of voice, 'Do come in.

Isn't it an awful day? I expect you're on your way to Glastonbury. Would you like a cup of tea? I was just going to make one.'

'Thank you, that would be nice.' He had come into the kitchen now, reaching up to tickle a belligerent Oscar under the chin. 'I'm sorry Tiger's frightened your cat. I don't suppose there are many people about on a day like this—and your mother isn't back yet?'

She said in a bleak little voice, 'No…' and then to her shame and horror burst into floods of tears.

Dr Fforde sat her down in the chair again. He said comfortably, 'I'll make the tea and you shall tell me all about it. Have a good cry; you'll feel better. Is there any cake?'

Amabel said in a small wailing voice, 'But I've been crying and I don't feel any better.' She gave a hiccough before adding, 'And now I've started again.' She took the large white handkerchief he offered her. 'The cake's in a tin in the cupboard in the corner.'

He put the tea things on the table and cut the cake, found biscuits for the dogs and spooned cat food onto a saucer for Oscar, who was still on top of a cupboard. Then he sat down opposite Amabel and put a cup of tea before her.

'Drink some of that and then tell me why you are crying. Don't leave anything out, for I'm merely a ship which is passing in the night, so you can say what you like and it will be forgotten—rather like having a bag of rubbish and finding an empty dustbin…'

She smiled then. 'You make it sound so—so normal…' She sipped her tea. 'I'm sorry I'm behaving so badly.'

He cut the cake and gave her a piece, before saying

matter-of-factly, 'Is your mother's absence the reason? Is she ill?'

'Ill? No, no. She's married someone in Canada...'

It was such a relief to talk to someone about it. It all came tumbling out: a hotch-potch of market gardens, plans for coming back and the need for her to be independent as soon as possible.

He listened quietly, refilling their cups, his eyes on her blotched face, and when she had at last finished her muddled story, he said, 'And now you have told me you feel better about it, don't you? It has all been bottled up inside you, hasn't it? Going round inside your head like butter in a churn. It has been a great shock to you, and shocks should be shared. I won't offer you advice, but I will suggest that you do nothing—make no plans, ignore your future—until your mother is home. I think that you may well find that you have been included in their plans and that you need no worries about your future. I can see that you might like to become independent, but don't rush into it. You're young enough to stay at home while they settle in, and that will give you time to decide what you want to do.'

When she nodded, he added, 'Now, go and put your hair up and wash your face. We're going to Castle Cary for supper.'

She gaped at him. ' I can't possibly...'

'Fifteen minutes should be time enough.'

She did her best with her face, and piled her hair neatly, then got into a jersey dress, which was an off the peg model, but of a pleasing shade of cranberry-red, stuck her feet into her best shoes and went back into the kitchen. Her winter coat was out of date and shabby, and for once she blessed the rain, for it meant that she could wear her mac.

Their stomachs nicely filled, Cyril and Oscar were already half asleep, and Tiger was standing by his master, eager to be off.

'I've locked everything up,' observed the doctor, and ushered Amabel out of the kitchen, turned the key in the lock and put it in his pocket, and urged her into the car. He hadn't appeared to look at her at all, but all the same he saw that she had done her best with her appearance. And the restaurant he had in mind had shaded rose lamps on its tables, if he remembered aright...

There weren't many people there on a wet Sunday evening, but the place was welcoming, and the rosy shades were kind to Amabel's still faintly blotchy face. Moreover, the food was good. He watched the pink come back into her cheeks as they ate their mushrooms in garlic sauce, local trout and a salad fit for the Queen. And the puddings were satisfyingly shrouded in thick clotted cream...

The doctor kept up a gentle stream of undemanding talk, and Amabel, soothed by it, was unaware of time passing until she caught sight of the clock.

She said in a shocked voice, 'It's almost nine. You will be so late at Glastonbury...'

'I'm going back to town,' he told her easily, but he made no effort to keep her, driving her back without more ado, seeing her safely into the house and driving off again with a friendly if casual goodbye.

The house, when he had gone, was empty—and too quiet. Amabel settled Cyril and Oscar for the night and went to bed.

It had been a lovely evening, and it had been such a

relief to talk to someone about her worries, but now she had the uneasy feeling that she had made a fool of herself, crying and pouring out her problems like a hysterical woman. Because he was a doctor, and was used to dealing with awkward patients, he had listened to her, given her a splendid meal and offered sensible suggestions as to her future. Probably he dealt with dozens like her...

She woke to a bright morning, and around noon a party of four knocked on the door and asked for rooms for the night, so Amabel was kept busy. By the end of the day she was tired enough to fall into bed and sleep at once.

There was no one for the next few days but there was plenty for her to do. The long summer days were over, and a cold wet autumn was predicted.

She collected the windfalls from the orchard, picked the last of the beans for the freezer, saw to beetroots, carrots and winter cabbage and dug the rest of the potatoes. She went to the rickety old greenhouse to pick tomatoes. She supposed that when her stepfather came he would build a new one; she and her mother had made do with it, and the quite large plot they used for vegetables grew just enough to keep them supplied throughout the year, but he was bound to make improvements.

It took her most of the week to get the garden in some sort of order, and at the weekend a party of six stayed for two nights, so on Monday morning she walked to the villager to stock up on groceries, post a letter to her mother and, on an impulse, bought the local paper again.

Back home, studying the jobs page, she saw with regret that the likely offers of work were no longer in it. There would be others, she told herself stoutly, and she must remember what Dr Fforde had told her—not to rush into anything. She must be patient; her mother had said that they hoped to be home before Christmas, but that was still weeks away, and even so he had advised her to do nothing hastily…

It was two days later, while she was putting away sheets and pillowcases in the landing cupboard, when she heard Cyril barking. He sounded excited, and she hurried downstairs; she had left the front door unlocked and someone might have walked in…

Her mother was standing in the hall, and there was a tall thickset man beside her. She was laughing and stooping to pat Cyril, then she looked up and saw Amabel.

'Darling, aren't we a lovely surprise? Keith sold the business, so there was no reason why we shouldn't come back here.'

She embraced Amabel, and Amabel, hugging her back, said, 'Oh, Mother—how lovely to see you.'

She looked at the man and smiled—and knew immediately that she didn't like him and that he didn't like her. But she held out a hand and said, 'How nice to meet you. It's all very exciting, isn't it?'

Cyril had pushed his nose into Keith's hand and she saw his impatient hand push it away. Her heart sank.

Her mother was talking and laughing, looking into the rooms, exclaiming how delightful everything looked. 'And there's Oscar.' She turned to her husband. 'Our cat, Keith. I know you don't like cats, but he's one of the family.'

He made some non-committal remark and went to fetch the luggage. Mrs Parsons, now Mrs Graham, ran upstairs to her room, and Amabel went to the kitchen to get tea. Cyril and Oscar went with her and arranged themselves tidily in a corner of the kitchen, aware that this man with the heavy tread didn't like them.

They had tea in the sitting room and the talk was of Canada and their journey and their plans to establish a market garden.

'No more bed and breakfast,' said Mrs Graham. 'Keith wants to get the place going as soon as possible. If we can get a glasshouse up quickly we could pick up some of the Christmas trade.'

'Where will you put it?' asked Amabel. 'There's plenty of ground beyond the orchard.'

Keith had been out to look around before tea, and now he observed, 'I'll get that ploughed and dug over for spring crops, and I'll put the glasshouse in the orchard. There's no money in apples, and some of the trees look past it. We'll finish picking and then get rid of them. There's plenty of ground there—fine for peas and beans.'

He glanced at Amabel. 'Your mother tells me you're pretty handy around the house and garden. The two of us ought to be able to manage to get something started— I'll hire a man with a rotavator who'll do the rough digging; the lighter jobs you'll be able to manage.'

Amabel didn't say anything. For one thing she was too surprised and shocked; for another, it was early days to be making such sweeping plans. And what about her mother's suggestion that she might like to train for something? If her stepfather might be certain of his plans, but why was he so sure that she would agree to them? And she didn't agree with them. The orchard had always been there, long before she was born. It still pro-

duced a good crop of apples and in the spring it was so
beautiful with the blossom…

She glanced at her mother, who looked happy and
content and was nodding admiringly at her new husband.

It was later, as she was getting the supper that he came
into the kitchen.

'Have to get rid of that cat,' he told her briskly. 'Can't
abide them, and the dog's getting on a bit, isn't he?
Animals don't go well with market gardens. Not to my
reckoning, anyway.'

'Oscar is no trouble at all,' said Amabel, and tried
hard to sound friendly. 'And Cyril is a good guard dog;
he never lets anyone near the house.'

She had spoken quietly, but he looked at her face and
said quickly, 'Oh, well, no hurry about them. It'll take
a month or two to get things going how I want them.'

He in his turn essayed friendliness. 'We'll make a
success of it, too. Your mother can manage the house
and you can work full-time in the garden. We might
even take on casual labour after a bit—give you time to
spend with your young friends.'

He sounded as though he was conferring a favour
upon her, and her dislike deepened, but she mustn't allow it to show. He was a man who liked his own way
and intended to have it. Probably he was a good husband
to her mother, but he wasn't going to be a good stepfather…

Nothing much happened for a few days; there was a
good deal of unpacking to do, letters to write and trips
to the bank. Quite a substantial sum of money had been
transferred from Canada and Mr Graham lost no time in
making enquiries about local labour. He also went up to
London to meet men who had been recommended as

likely to give him financial backing, should he require it.

In the meantime Amabel helped her mother around the house, and tried to discover if her mother had meant her to have training of some sort and then changed her mind at her husband's insistence.

Mrs Graham was a loving parent, but easily dominated by anyone with a stronger will than her own. What was the hurry? she wanted to know. A few more months at home were neither here nor there, and she would be such a help to Keith.

'He's such a marvellous man, Amabel, he's bound to make a success of whatever he does.'

Amabel said cautiously, 'It's a pity he doesn't like Cyril and Oscar...'

Her mother laughed. 'Oh, darling, he would never be unkind to them.'

Perhaps not unkind, but as the weeks slipped by it was apparent that they were no longer to be regarded as pets around the house. Cyril spent a good deal of time outside, roaming the orchard, puzzled as to why the kitchen door was so often shut. As for Oscar, he only came in for his meals, looking carefully around to make sure that there was no one about.

Amabel did what she could, but her days were full, and it was obvious that Mr Graham was a man who rode roughshod over anyone who stood in his way. For the sake of her mother's happiness Amabel held her tongue; there was no denying that he was devoted to her mother, and she to him, but there was equally no denying that he found Amabel, Cyril and Oscar superfluous to his life.

It wasn't until she came upon him hitting Cyril and then turning on an unwary Oscar and kicking him aside that Amabel knew that she would have to do something about it.

She scooped up a trembling Oscar and bent to put an arm round Cyril's elderly neck. 'How dare you? Whatever have they done to you? They're my friends and I love them,' she added heatedly, 'and they have lived here all their lives.'

Her stepfather stared at her. 'Well, they won't live here much longer if I have my way. I'm the boss here. I don't like animals around the place so you'd best make up your mind to that.'

He walked off without another word and Amabel, watching his retreating back, knew that she had to do something—and quickly.

She went out to the orchard—there were piles of bricks and bags of cement already heaped near the bench, ready to start building the glasshouse—and with Oscar on her lap and Cyril pressed against her she reviewed and discarded several plans, most of them too far-fetched to be of any use. Finally she had the nucleus of a sensible idea. But first she must have some money, and secondly the right opportunity...

As though a kindly providence approved of her efforts, she was able to have both. That very evening her stepfather declared that he would have to go to London in the morning. A useful acquaintance had phoned to say that he would meet him and introduce him to a wholesaler who would consider doing business with him once he was established. He would go to London early in the morning, and since he had a long day ahead of him he went to bed early.

Presently, alone with her mother, Amabel seized what seemed to be a golden opportunity.

'I wondered if I might have some money for clothes, Mother. I haven't bought anything since you went away…'

'Of course, love. I should have thought of that myself. And you did so well with the bed and breakfast business. Is there any money in the tea caddy? If there is take whatever you want from it. I'll ask Keith to make you an allowance; he's so generous…'

'No, don't do that, Mother. He has enough to think about without bothering him about that; there'll be enough in the tea caddy. Don't bother him.' She looked across at her mother. 'You're very happy with him, aren't you, Mother?'

'Oh, yes, Amabel. I never told you, but I hated living here, just the two of us, making ends meet, no man around the place. When I went to your sister's I realised what I was missing. And I've been thinking that perhaps it would be a good idea if you started some sort of training…'

Amabel agreed quietly, reflecting that her mother wouldn't miss her…

Her mother went to bed presently, and Amabel made Oscar and Cyril comfortable for the night and counted the money in the tea caddy. There was more than enough for her plan.

She went to her room and, quiet as a mouse, got her holdall out of the wardrobe and packed it, including undies and a jersey skirt and a couple of woollies; autumn would soon turn to winter…

She thought over her plan when she was in bed; there seemed no way of improving upon it, so she closed her eyes and went to sleep.

She got up early, to prepare breakfast for her stepfather, having first of all made sure that Oscar and Cyril weren't in the kitchen. Once he had driven away she got her own breakfast, fed both animals and got dressed. Her mother came down, and over her coffee suggested that she might get the postman to give her a lift to Castle Cary.

'I've time to dress before he comes, and I can get my hair done. You'll be all right, love?'

It's as though I'm meant to be leaving, reflected Amabel. And when her mother was ready, and waiting for the postman, reminded her to take a key with her— 'For I might go for a walk.'

Amabel had washed the breakfast dishes, tidied the house, and made the beds by the time her mother got into the post van, and if she gave her mother a sudden warm hug and kiss Mrs Graham didn't notice.

Half an hour later Amabel, with Oscar in his basket, Cyril on a lead, and encumbered by her holdall and a shoulder bag, was getting into the taxi she had requested. She had written to her mother explaining that it was high time she became independent and that she would write, but that she was not to worry. *You will both make a great success of the market garden and it will be easier for you both if Oscar, Cyril and myself aren't getting under your feet,* she had ended.

The taxi took them to Gillingham where—fortune still smiling—they got on the London train and, once there, took a taxi to Victoria bus station. By now Amabel realised her plans, so simple in theory, were fraught with possible disaster. But she had cooked her goose. She bought a ticket to York, had a cup of tea, got water for Cyril and put milk in her saucer for Oscar and then climbed into the long-distance bus.

It was half empty, and the driver was friendly. Amabel perched on a seat with Cyril at her feet and Oscar in his basket on her lap. She was a bit cramped, but at least they were still altogether…

It was three o'clock in the afternoon by now, and it was a hundred and ninety-three miles to York, where they would arrive at about half past eight. The end of the journey was in sight, and it only remained for Great-Aunt Thisbe to offer them a roof over their heads. A moot point since she was unaware of them coming…

'I should have phoned her,' muttered Amabel, 'but there was so much to think about in such a hurry.'

It was only now that the holes in her hare-brained scheme began to show, but it was too late to worry about it. She still had a little money, she was young, she could work and, most important of all, Oscar and Cyril were still alive…

Amabel, a sensible level-headed girl, had thrown her bonnet over the windmill with a vengeance.

She went straight to the nearest phone box at the bus station in York; she was too tired and light-headed from her impetuous journey to worry about Great-Aunt Thisbe's reaction.

When she heard that lady's firm, unhurried voice she said without preamble, 'It's me—Amabel, Aunt Thisbe. I'm at the bus station in York.'

She had done her best to keep her voice quiet and steady, but it held a squeak of panic. Supposing Aunt Thisbe put down the phone…

Miss Parsons did no such thing. When she had been told of her dead nephew's wife's remarriage she had disapproved, strongly but silently. Such an upheaval: a strange man taking over from her nephew's loved memory, and what about Amabel? She hadn't seen the girl for some years—what of her? Had her mother considered her?

She said now, 'Go and sit down on the nearest seat, Amabel. I'll be with you in half an hour.'

'I've got Oscar and Cyril with me.'

'You are all welcome,' said Aunt Thisbe, and rang off.

Much heartened by these words, Amabel found a bench and, with a patient Cyril crouching beside her and Oscar eyeing her miserably from the little window in his basket, sat down to wait.

Half an hour, when you're not very happy, can seem a very long time, but Amabel forgot that when she saw Great-Aunt Thisbe walking briskly towards her, clad in a coat and skirt which hadn't altered in style for the last few decades, her white hair crowned by what could best be described as a sensible hat. There was a youngish man with her, short and sturdy with weatherbeaten features.

Great-Aunt Thisbe kissed Amabel briskly. 'I am so glad you have come to visit me, my dear. Now we will go home and you shall tell me all about it. This is Josh, my right hand. He'll take your luggage to the car and drive us home.'

Amabel had got to her feet. She couldn't think of anything to say that wouldn't need a long explanation, so she held out a hand for Josh to shake, picked up Oscar's basket and Cyril's lead and walked obediently out into the street and got into the back of the car while Aunt Thisbe settled herself beside Josh.

It was dark now, and the road was almost empty of traffic. There was nothing to see from the car's window but Amabel remembered Bolton Percy was where her aunt lived, a medieval village some fifteen miles from York and tucked away from the main roads. It must be ten years since she was last here, she reflected; she had been sixteen and her father had died a few months earlier...

The village, when they reached it, was in darkness, but her aunt's house, standing a little apart from the row of brick and plaster cottages near the church, welcomed them with lighted windows.

Josh got out and helped her with the animals and she followed him up the path to the front door, which Great-Aunt Thisbe had opened.

'Welcome to my home, child,' she said. 'And yours for as long as you need it.'

CHAPTER THREE

THE next hour or two were a blur to Amabel; her coat was taken from her and she was sat in a chair in Aunt Thisbe's kitchen, bidden to sit there, drink the tea she was given and say nothing—something she was only too glad to do while Josh and her aunt dealt with Cyril and Oscar. In fact, quite worn out, she dozed off, to wake and find Oscar curled up on her lap, washing himself, and Cyril's head pressed against her knee.

Great-Aunt Thisbe spoke before she could utter a word.

'Stay there for a few minutes. Your room's ready, but you must have something to eat first.'

'Aunt Thisbe—' began Amabel.

'Later, child. Supper and a good night's sleep first. Do you want your mother to know you are here?'

'No, no. I'll explain…'

'Tomorrow.' Great-Aunt Thisbe, still wearing her hat, put a bowl of fragrant stew into Amabel's hands. 'Now eat your supper.'

Presently Amabel was ushered upstairs to a small room with a sloping ceiling and a lattice window. She didn't remember getting undressed, nor did she feel surprised to find both Oscar and Cyril with her. It had been a day like no other and she was beyond surprise or questioning; it seemed quite right that Cyril and Oscar should share her bed. They were still all together, she thought with satisfaction. It was like waking up after a particularly nasty nightmare.

When she woke in the morning she lay for a moment, staring up at the unfamiliar ceiling, but in seconds memory came flooding back and she sat up in bed, hampered by Cyril's weight on her feet and Oscar curled up near him. In the light of early morning yesterday's journey was something unbelievably foolhardy—and she would have to explain to Great-Aunt Thisbe.

The sooner the better.

She got up, went quietly to the bathroom, dressed and the three of them crept downstairs.

The house wasn't large, but it was solidly built, and had been added to over the years, and its small garden had a high stone wall. Amabel opened the stout door and went outside. Oscar and Cyril, old and wise enough to know what was wanted of them, followed her cautiously.

It was a fine morning but there was a nip in the air, and the three of them went back indoors just as Great-Aunt Thisbe came into the kitchen.

Her good morning was brisk and kind. 'You slept well? Good. Now, my dear, there's porridge on the Aga; I dare say these two will eat it. Josh will bring suitable food when he comes presently. And you and I will have a cup of tea before I get our breakfast.

'I must explain…'

'Of course. But over a cup of tea.'

So presently Amabel sat opposite her aunt at the kitchen table, drank her tea and gave her a carefully accurate account of her journey. 'Now I've thought about it, I can see how silly I was. I didn't stop to think, you see—only that I had to get away because my—my stepfather was going to kill...' She faltered. 'And he doesn't like me.'

'Your mother? She is happy with him?'

'Yes—yes, she is, and he is very good to her. They don't need me. I shouldn't have come here, only I had to think of something quickly. I'm so grateful to you, Aunt Thisbe, for letting me stay last night. I wondered if you would let me leave Oscar and Cyril here today, while I go into York and find work. I'm not trained, but there's always work in hotels and people's houses.'

The sound which issued from Miss Parsons' lips would have been called a snort from a lesser mortal.

'Your father was my brother, child. You will make this your home as long as you wish to stay. As to work— it will be a godsend to me to have someone young about the place. I'm well served by Josh and Mrs Josh, who cleans the place for me, but I could do with company, and in a week or two you can decide what you want to do.

'York is a big city; there are museums, historical houses, a wealth of interest to the visitor in Roman remains—all of which employ guides, curators, helpers of all kinds. There should be choice enough when it comes to looking for a job. The only qualifications needed are intelligence, the Queen's English and a pleasant voice and appearance. Now go and get dressed, and after breakfast you shall telephone your mother.'

'They will want me to go back—they don't want me, but he expects me to work for him in the garden.'

'You are under no obligation to your stepfather, Amabel, and your mother is welcome to come and visit you at any time. You are not afraid of your stepfather?'

'No—but I'm afraid of what he would do to Oscar and Cyril. And I don't like him.'

The phone conversation with her mother wasn't entirely satisfactory—Mrs Graham, at first relieved and glad to hear from Amabel, began to complain bitterly at what she described as Amabel's ingratitude.

'Keith will have to hire help,' she pointed out. 'He's very vexed about it, and really, Amabel, you have shown us a lack of consideration, going off like that. Of course we shall always be glad to see you, but don't expect any financial help—you've chosen to stand on your own two feet. Still, you're a sensible girl, and I've no doubt that you will find work—I don't suppose Aunt Thisbe will want you to stay for more than a week or two.' There was a pause. 'And you've got Oscar and Cyril with you?'

'Yes, Mother.'

'They'll hamper you when you look for work. Really, it would have been better if Keith had had them put down.'

'Mother! They have lived with us for years. They don't deserve to die.'

'Oh, well, but they're neither of them young. Will you phone again?'

Amabel said that she would and put down the phone. Despite Great-Aunt Thisbe's sensible words, she viewed the future with something like panic.

Her aunt took one look at her face, and said, 'Will you walk down to the shop and get me one or two things, child? Take Cyril with you—Oscar will be all right here—and we will have coffee when you get back.'

It was only a few minutes' walk to the stores in the centre of the village, and although it was drizzling and windy it was nice to be out of doors. It was a small village, but the church was magnificent and the narrow main street was lined with small solid houses and crowned at its end by a large brick and plaster pub.

Amabel did her shopping, surprised to discover that the stern-looking lady who served her knew who she was.

'Come to visit your auntie? She'll be glad of a bit of company for a week or two. A good thing she's spending the winter with that friend of hers in Italy...'

Two or three weeks, decided Amabel, walking back, should be enough time to find some kind of work and a place to live. Aunt Thisbe had told her that she was welcome to stay as long as she wanted to, but if she did that would mean her aunt would put off her holiday. Which would never do... She would probably mention it in a day or two—especially if Amabel lost no time in looking for work.

But a few days went by, and although Amabel reiterated her intention of finding work as soon as possible her aunt made no mention of her holiday; indeed she insisted that Amabel did nothing about it.

'You need a week or two to settle down,' she pointed out, 'and I won't hear of you leaving until you have decided what you want to do. It won't hurt you to spend the winter here.'

Which gave Amabel the chance to ask, 'But you may have made plans...'

Aunt Thisbe put down her knitting. 'And what plans would I be making at my age, child? Now, let us say no more for the moment. Tell me about your mother's wedding?'

So Amabel, with Oscar on her lap and Cyril sitting

between them, told all she knew, and presently they fell to talking about her father, still remembered with love by both of them.

Dr Fforde, immersed in his work though he was, nevertheless found his thoughts wandering, rather to his surprise, towards Amabel. It was some two weeks after she had left home that he decided to go and see her again. By now her mother and stepfather would be back and she would have settled down with them and be perfectly happy, all her doubts and fears forgotten.

He told himself that was his reason for going: to reassure himself that, knowing her to be happy again, he could dismiss her from his mind.

It was mid-afternoon when he got there, and as he parked the car he saw signs of activity at the back of the house. Instead of knocking on the front door he walked round the side of the house to the back. Most of the orchard had disappeared, and there was a large concrete foundation where the trees had been. Beyond the orchard the ground had been ploughed up; the bench had gone, and the fruit bushes. Only the view beyond was still beautiful.

He went to the kitchen door and knocked.

Amabel's mother stood in the doorway, and before she could speak he said, 'I came to see Amabel.' He held out a hand. 'Dr Fforde.'

Mrs Graham shook hands. She said doubtfully, 'Oh, did you meet her when she was doing bed and breakfasts? She's not here; she's left.'

She held the door wide. 'Come in. My husband will be back very shortly. Would you like a cup of tea?'

'Thank you.' He looked around him. 'There was a dog…'

'She's taken him with her—and the cat. My husband won't have animals around the place. He's starting up a market garden. The silly girl didn't like the idea of them being put down—left us in the lurch too; she was going to work for Keith, help with the place once we get started—we are having a big greenhouse built.'

'Yes, there was an orchard there.'

He accepted his tea and, when she sat down, took a chair opposite her.

'Where has Amabel gone?' The question was put so casually that Mrs Graham answered at once.

'Yorkshire, of all places—and heaven knows how she got there. My first husband's sister lives near York—a small village called Bolton Percy. Amabel went there—well, there wasn't anywhere else she could have gone without a job. We did wonder where she was, but she phoned when she got there… Here's my husband.'

The two men shook hands, exchanged a few minutes' conversation, then Dr Fforde got up to go.

He had expected his visit to Amabel's home to reassure him as to her future; it had done nothing of the sort. Her mother might be fond of her but obviously this overbearing man she had married would discourage her from keeping close ties with Amabel—he had made no attempt to disguise his dislike of her.

Driving himself back home, the doctor reflected that Amabel had been wise to leave. It seemed a bit drastic to go as far away as Yorkshire, but if she had family there they would have arranged her journey. He reminded himself that he had no need to concern himself about her; she had obviously dealt with her own future in a sensible manner. After all, she had seemed a sensible girl…

Bates greeted him with the news that Mrs Potter-Stokes had telephoned. 'Enquiring if you would take her to an art exhibition tomorrow evening which she had already mentioned.'

And why not? reflected Dr Fforde. He no longer needed to worry about Amabel. The art exhibition turned out to be very avant-garde, and Dr Fforde, escorting Miriam Potter-Stokes, listening to her rather vapid remarks, trying to make sense of the childish daubs acclaimed as genius, allowed his thoughts to wander. It was time he took a few days off, he decided. He would clear his desk of urgent cases and leave London for a while. He enjoyed driving and the roads were less busy now.

So when Miriam suggested that he might like to spend the weekend at her parents' home, he declined firmly, saying, 'I really can't spare the time, and I shall be out of London for a few days.'

'You poor man; you work far too hard. You need a wife to make sure that you don't do too much.'

She smiled up at him and then wished that she hadn't said that. Oliver had made some rejoinder dictated by good manners, but he had glanced at her with indifference from cold blue eyes. She must be careful, she reflected; she had set her heart on him for a husband…

Dr Fforde left London a week later. He had allowed himself three days: ample time to drive to York, seek out the village where Amabel was living and make sure that she was happy with this aunt and that she had some definite plans for her future. Although why he should concern himself with that he didn't go into too deeply.

A silly impetuous girl, he told himself, not meaning a word of it.

He left after an early breakfast, taking Tiger with him, sitting erect and watchful beside him, sliding through the morning traffic until at last he reached the M1. After a while he stopped at a service station, allowed Tiger a short run, drank a cup of coffee and drove on until, mindful of Tiger's heavy sighs, he stopped in a village north of Chesterfield.

The pub was almost empty and Tiger, his urgent needs dealt with, was made welcome, with a bowl of water and biscuits, while the doctor sat down before a plate of beef sandwiches, home-made pickles and half a pint of real ale.

Much refreshed, they got back into the car presently, their journey nearing its end. The doctor, a man who, having looked at the map before he started a journey, never needed to look at it again, turned off the motorway and made his way through country roads until he was rewarded by the sight of Bolton Percy's main street.

He stopped before the village stores and went in. The village was a small one; Amabel's whereabouts would be known...

As well as the severe-looking lady behind the counter there were several customers, none of whom appeared to be shopping with any urgency. They all turned to look at him as he went in, and even the severe-looking lady smiled at his pleasant greeting.

An elderly woman at the counter spoke up. 'Wanting to know the way? I'm in no hurry. Mrs Bluett—' she indicated the severe lady '—she'll help you.'

Dr Fforde smiled his thanks. 'I'm looking for a Miss Amabel Parsons.'

He was eyed with even greater interest.

'Staying with her aunt—Miss Parsons up at the End House. End of this street; house stands on its own beyond the row of cottages. You can't miss it. They'll be home.' She glanced at the clock. 'They sit down to high tea around six o'clock, but drink a cup around half past three. Expecting you, is she?'

'No...' Mrs Bluett looked at him so fiercely that he felt obliged to add, 'We have known each other for some time.' She smiled then, and he took his leave, followed by interested looks.

Stopping once more a hundred yards or so down the street, he got out of the car slowly and stood just for a moment looking at the house. It was red brick and plaster, solid and welcoming with its lighted windows. He crossed the pavement, walked up the short path to the front door and knocked.

Miss Parsons opened it. She stood looking at him with a severity which might have daunted a lesser man.

'I have come to see Amabel,' observed the doctor mildly. He held out a hand. 'Fforde—Oliver Fforde. Her mother gave me this address.'

Miss Parsons took his hand and shook it. 'Thisbe Parsons. Amabel's aunt. She has spoken of you.' She looked round his great shoulder. 'Your car? It will be safe there. And a dog?'

She took another good luck at him and liked what she saw. 'We're just about to have a cup of tea. Do bring the dog in—he's not aggressive? Amabel's Cyril is here...'

'They are already acquainted.' He smiled. 'Thank you.'

He let Tiger out of the car and the pair of them followed her into the narrow hallway.

Miss Parsons marched ahead of them, opened a door and led the way into the room, long and low, with windows at each end and an old-fashioned fireplace at its centre. The furniture was old-fashioned too, beautifully kept and largely covered by photos in silver frames and small china ornaments, some of them valuable, and a quantity of pot plants. It was a very pleasant room, lived in and loved and very welcoming.

The doctor, treading carefully between an occasional table and a Victorian spoon-back chair, watched Amabel get to her feet and heaved a sigh of relief at the pleased surprise on her face.

He said, carefully casual, 'Amabel...' and shook her hand, smiling down at her face. 'I called at your home and your mother gave me this address. I have to be in York for a day or two and it seemed a good idea to renew our acquaintance.'

She stared up into his kind face. 'I've left home...'

'So your stepfather told me. You are looking very well.'

'Oh, I am. Aunt Thisbe is so good to me, and Cyril and Oscar are happy.'

Miss Parsons lifted the teapot. 'Sit down and have your tea and tell me what brings you to York, Dr Fforde. It's a long way from London—you live there, I presume?'

The doctor had aunts of his own, so he sat down, drank his tea meekly and answered her questions without telling her a great deal. Tiger was sitting beside him, a model of canine obedience, while Cyril settled near him. Oscar, of course, had settled himself on top of the bookcase. Presently the talk became general, and he made no effort to ask Amabel how she came to be so far from her home. She would tell him in her own good time, and he had two days before he needed to return to London.

Miss Parsons said briskly, 'We have high tea at six o'clock. We hope you will join us. Unless you have some commitments in York?'

'Not until tomorrow morning. I should very much like to accept.'

'In that case you and Amabel had better take the dogs for a run while I see to a meal.'

It was dark by now, and chilly. Amabel got into her mac, put Cyril's lead on and led the way out of the house, telling him, 'We can go to the top of the village and come back along the back lane.'

The doctor took her arm and, with a dog at either side of them, they set off. 'Tell me what happened,' he suggested.

His gentle voice would have persuaded the most unwilling to confide in him and Amabel, her arm tucked under his, was only too willing. Aunt Thisbe was a dear, loving and kind under her brusque manner, but she hadn't been there; Dr Fforde had, so there was no need to explain about Cyril and Oscar or her stepfather...

She said slowly, 'I did try, really I did—to like him and stay at home until they'd settled in and I could suggest that I might train for something. But he didn't like me, although he expected me to work for him, and he hated Cyril and Oscar.'

She took a breath and began again, not leaving anything out, trying to keep to the facts and not colouring them with her feelings.

When she had finished the doctor said firmly, 'You

did quite right. It was rather hazardous of you to undertake the long journey here, but it was a risk worth taking.'

They were making their way back to the house, and
although it was too dark to see he sensed that she was
crying. He reminded himself that he had adopted the role
of advisor and impersonal friend. That had been his intention and still was. Moreover, her aunt had offered her
a home. He resisted a desire to take her in his arms and
kiss her, something which, while giving him satisfaction
would possibly complicate matters. Instead he said
cheerfully, 'Will you spend the afternoon with me tomorrow? We might drive to the coast.'

Amabel swallowed tears. 'That would be very nice,'
she told him. 'Thank you.' And, anxious to match his
casual friendliness, she added, 'I don't know this part of
the world, do you?'

For the rest of the way back they discussed Yorkshire
and its beauties.

Aunt Thisbe was old-fashioned; the younger generation might like their dinner in the evening, but she had
remained faithful to high tea. The table was elegantly
laid, the teapot at one end, a covered dish of buttered
eggs at the other, with racks of toast, a dish of butter
and a home-made pâté. There was jam too, and a pot of
honey, and sandwiches, and in the centre of the table a
cakestand bearing scones, fruitcake, oatcakes and small
cakes from the local baker, known as fancies.

The doctor, a large and hungry man, found everything
to his satisfaction and made a good meal, something
which endeared him to Aunt Thisbe's heart, so that when
he suggested he might take Amabel for a drive the following day she said at once that it was a splendid idea.

Here was a man very much to her liking; it was a pity that it was obvious that his interest in Amabel was only one of impersonal kindness. The girl had been glad to see him, and heaven knew the child needed friends. A pity that he was only in York for a few days and lived so far away...

He washed the dishes and Amabel dried them after their meal. Aunt Thisbe, sitting in the drawing room, could hear them talking and laughing in the kitchen. Something would have to be done, thought the old lady. Amabel needed young friends, a chance to go out and enjoy herself; life would be dull for her during the winter. A job must be found for her where she would meet other people.

Aunt Thisbe felt sharp regret at the thought of the holiday she would have to forego: something which Amabel was never to be told about.

Dr Fforde went presently, making his goodbyes with beautiful manners, promising to be back the following afternoon. Driving to York with Tiger beside him, he spoke his thoughts aloud. 'Well, we can put our minds at rest, can we not, Tiger? She will make a new life for herself with this delightful aunt, probably find a pleasant job and meet a suitable young man and marry him.' He added, 'Most satisfactory.' So why did he feel so dissatisfied about it?

He drove to a hotel close to the Minster—a Regency townhouse, quiet and elegant, and with the unobtrusive service which its guests took for granted. Tiger, accommodated in the corner of his master's room, settled down for the night, leaving his master to go down to the bar for a nightcap and a study of the city.

The pair of them explored its streets after their breakfast. It was a fine day, and the doctor intended to drive to the coast that afternoon, but exploring the city would give him the opportunity of getting to know it. After all, it would probably be in York where Amabel would find a job.

He lunched in an ancient pub, where Tiger was welcomed with water and biscuits, and then went back to the hotel, got into his car and drove to Bolton Percy.

Amabel had spent the morning doing the small chores Aunt Thisbe allowed her to do, attending to Oscar's needs and taking Cyril for a walk, but there was still time to worry about what she should wear for her outing. Her wardrobe was so scanty that it was really a waste of time to worry about it.

It would have to be the pleated skirt and the short coat she had travelled in; they would pass muster for driving around the country, and Dr Fforde never looked at her as though he actually saw her. It had been lovely to see him again, like meeting an old friend—one who listened without interrupting and offered suggestions, never advice, in the friendliest impersonal manner of a good doctor. He was a doctor, of course, she reminded herself.

He came punctually, spent ten minutes talking to Miss Parsons, suggested that Cyril might like to share the back seat with Tiger, popped Amabel into the car and took the road to the coast.

Flamborough stood high on cliffs above the North Sea, and down at sea level boats sheltered in the harbour. Dr Fforde parked the car, put the dogs on their leads and walked Amabel briskly towards the peninsula. It was breezy, but the air was exhilarating, and they seemed to be the only people around.

When they stopped to look out to sea, Amabel said

happily, 'Oh, this is marvellous; so grand and beautiful—fancy living here and waking up each morning and seeing the sea.'

They walked a long way, and as they turned to go back Dr Fforde said, carefully casual, 'Do you want to talk about your plans, Amabel? Perhaps your aunt has already suggested something? Or do you plan to stay with her indefinitely?'

'I wanted to ask you about that. There's a problem. You won't mind if I tell you about it, and perhaps you could give me some advice. You see I was told quite unwittingly, by Mrs Bluett who owns the village shop, that Aunt Thisbe had plans to spend the winter in Italy with a friend. I haven't liked to ask her, and she hasn't said anything, but I can't allow her to lose a lovely holiday like that because I'm here. After all, she didn't expect me, but she's so kind and she might feel that she should stay here so that I've got a home, if you see what I mean.'

They were standing facing each other, and she stared up into his face. 'You can see that I must get a job very quickly, but I'm not sure how to set about it. I mean, should I answer advertisements in the paper or visit an agency? There's not much I can do, and it has to be somewhere Cyril and Oscar can come too.'

He said slowly, 'Well, first you must convince your aunt that you want a job—and better not say that you know of her holiday. Go to York, put your name down at any agencies you can find...' He paused, frowning. 'What can you do, Amabel?'

'Nothing, really,' she said cheerfully. 'Housework, cooking—or I expect I could be a waitress or work in a shop. They're not the sort of jobs people want, are they?

And they aren't well paid. But if I could get a start somewhere, and also somewhere to live…'

'Do you suppose your aunt would allow you to live at her house while she was away?'

'Perhaps. But how would I get to work? The bus service is only twice weekly, and there is nowhere in the village where I could work.' She added fiercely, 'I must be independent.'

He took her arm and they walked on. 'Of course. Now, I can't promise anything, Amabel, but I know a lot of people and I might hear of something. Do you mind where you go?'

'No, as long as I can have Cyril and Oscar with me.'

'There is no question of your returning home?'

'None whatever. I'm being a nuisance to everyone, aren't I?'

He agreed silently to that, but he didn't say so. She was determined to be independent, and for some reason which he didn't understand he wanted to help her.

He asked, 'Have you some money? Enough to pay the rent and so on?'

'Yes, thank you. Mother let me have the money in the tea caddy, and there is still some left.'

He decided it wasn't worth while asking about the tea caddy. 'Good. Now we are going to the village; I noticed a pub as we came through it—the Royal Dog and Duck. If it is open they might give us tea.'

They had a splendid meal in the snug behind the bar: a great pot of tea, scones and butter, cream and jam, great wedges of fruitcake and, in case that wasn't enough, a dish of buttered toast. Tiger and Cyril, sitting under the table, provided with water and any tidbits which came their way, were tired after their walk, and dozed quietly.

He drove back presently through the dusk of late autumn, taking side roads through charming villages—Burton Agnes, with its haunted manor and Norman church, through Lund, with its once-upon-a-time cockpit, on to Bishop Burton, with its village pond and little black and white cottages, and finally along country roads to Bolton Percy.

The doctor stayed only as long as good manners dictated, although he asked if he might call to wish them goodbye the following morning.

'Come for coffee?' invited Miss Parsons.

The stiff breeze from yesterday had turned into a gale in the morning, and he made that his excuse for not staying long over his coffee. When Amabel had opened the door to him he had handed her a list of agencies in York, and now he wanted to be gone; he had done what he could for her. She had a home, this aunt who was obviously fond of her, and she was young and healthy and sensible, even if she had no looks to speak of. He had no further reason to be concerned about her.

All the same, driving down the M1, he was finding it difficult to forget her. She had bidden him goodbye in a quiet voice, her small hand in his, wished him a safe journey and thanked him. 'It's been very nice knowing you,' she had told him.

It had been nice knowing her, he conceded, and it was a pity that their paths were unlikely to cross in the future.

That evening Amabel broached the subject of her future to her aunt. She was careful not to mention Aunt Thisbe's holiday in Italy, pointing out with enthusiasm her great wish to become independent.

'I'll never be grateful enough to you,' she assured her aunt, 'for giving me a home—and I love being here with you. But I must get started somewhere, mustn't I? I know I shall like York, and there must be any number of jobs for someone like me—I mean, unskilled labour. And I won't stop at that. You do understand, don't you, Aunt?'

'Yes, of course I do, child. You must go to York and see what there is there for you. Only you must promise me that if you fall on hard times you will come here.' She hesitated, then, 'And if I am not here, go to Josh and Mrs Josh.'

'I promise, Aunt Thisbe. There's a bus to York tomorrow morning, isn't there? Shall I go and have a look round—spy out the land…?'

'Josh has to take the car in tomorrow morning; you shall go with him. The bus leaves York in the afternoon around four o'clock, but if you miss it phone here and Josh will fetch you.'

It was a disappointing day. Amabel went from one agency to the next, and was entered on their books, but there were no jobs which would suit her; she wasn't a trained lady's maid, or a cashier as needed at a café, she had neither the training nor the experience to work at a crêche, nor was she suitable as a saleslady at any of the large stores—lack of experience. But how did one get experience unless one had a chance to learn in the first place?

She presented a brave face when she got back to her aunt's house in the late afternoon. After all, this was only the first day, and her name was down on several agencies' books.

Back in London, Dr Fforde immersed himself in his work, assuring Bates that he had had a most enjoyable break.

'So why is he so gloomy?' Bates enquired of Tiger. 'Too much work. He needs a bit of the bright lights—needs to get out and about a bit.'

So it pleased Bates when his master told him that he would be going out one evening. Taking Mrs Potter-Stokes to the theatre, and supper afterwards.

It should have been a delightful evening; Miriam was a charming companion, beautifully dressed, aware of how very attractive she was, sure of herself, and amusing him with anecdotes of their mutual friends, asking intelligent questions about his work. But she was aware that she hadn't got his full attention. Over supper she exerted herself to gain his interest, and asked him prettily if he had enjoyed his few days off. 'Where did you go?' she added.

'York...'

'York?' She seized on that. 'My dear Oliver, I wish I'd known; you could have called on a great friend of mine—Dolores Trent. She has one of those shops in the Shambles—you know, sells dried flowers and pots and expensive glass. But she's hopeless at it—so impractical, breaking things and getting all the money wrong. I had a letter from her only a few days ago—she thinks she had better get someone to help her.'

She glanced at the doctor and saw with satisfaction that he was smiling at her. 'How amusing. Is she as attractive as you, Miriam?'

Miriam smiled a little triumphant smile, the evening was a success after all.

Which was what the doctor was thinking...

CHAPTER FOUR

When Amabel came back from walking Cyril the next morning she was met at the door by her aunt.

'A pity. You have just missed a phone call from your nice Dr Fforde. He has heard of a job quite by chance from a friend and thought you might be interested. A lady who owns a shop in the Shambles in York—an arty-crafty place, I gather; she needs someone to help her. He told me her name—Dolores Trent—but he doesn't know the address. You might like to walk through the Shambles and see if you can find her shop. Most thoughtful of him to think of you.'

Josh drove her in after lunch. She was, her aunt had decreed, to spend as long as she wanted in York and phone when she was ready to return; Josh would fetch her.

She walked through the city, found the Shambles and started to walk its length. It was a narrow cobbled street, lined by old houses which overhung the lane, almost all of which were now shops: expensive shops, she saw at once, selling the kind of things people on holiday would take back home to display or give as presents to someone who needed to be impressed.

She walked down one side, looking at the names over the doors and windows, pausing once or twice to study some beautiful garment in a boutique or look at a display of jewellery. She reached the end and started back on the other side, and halfway down she found what she was looking for. It was a small shop, tucked between a bookshop and a mouthwatering patisserie, its small window displaying crystal vases, great baskets of dried silk flowers, delicate china and eye-catching pottery. Hung discreetly in one corner was a small card with 'Shop Assistant Required' written on it.

Amabel opened the door and went inside.

She supposed that the lady who came to meet her through the bead curtain at the back of the shop was Dolores Trent; she so exactly fitted her shop. Miss Trent was a tall person, slightly overweight, swathed in silky garments and wearing a good deal of jewellery, and she brought with her a cloud of some exotic perfume.

'You wish to browse?' she asked in a casual manner. 'Do feel free...'

'The card in the window?' said Amabel. 'You want an assistant. Would I do?'

Dolores Trent looked her over carefully. A dull little creature, she decided, but quite pleasant to look at, and she definitely didn't want some young glamorous girl who might distract customers from buying.

She said sharply, 'You live here? Have you references? Have you any experience?'

'I live with my aunt at Bolton Percy, and I can get references. I've no experience in working in a shop, but I'm used to people. I ran a bed and breakfast house...'

Miss Trent laughed. 'At least you sound honest. If you come here to work, how will you get here? Bolton Percy's a bit rural, isn't it?'

'Yes. I hope to find somewhere to live here.'

Several thoughts passed with quick succession through Dolores Trent's head. There was that empty room behind the shop, beyond the tiny kitchenette and the cloakroom; it could be furnished with odds and ends from the attic at home. The girl could live there, and since she would have rent-free accommodation there would be no need to pay her the wages she would be entitled to...

Miss Trent, mean by nature, liked the idea.

'I might consider you, if your references are satisfactory. Your hours would be from nine o'clock till five, free on Sundays. I'd expect you to keep the shop clean and dusted, unpack goods when they arrive, arrange shelves, serve the customers and deal with the cash. You'd do any errands, and look after the shop when I'm not here. You say you want to live here? There's a large room behind the shop, with windows and a door opening onto a tiny yard. Basic furniture and bedding. There's a kitchenette and a cloakroom which you can use. Of course you do understand that if I let you live here I won't be able to pay you the usual wages?'

She named a sum which Amabel knew was not much more than half what she should have expected. On the other hand, here was shelter and security and independence.

'I have a dog and a cat. Would you object to them?'

'Not if they stay out of sight. A dog would be quite a good idea; it's quiet here at night. You're not nervous?'

'No. Might I see the room?'

It was a pleasant surprise, quite large and airy, with two windows and a small door opening onto a tiny square of neglected grass. But there were high walls surrounding it; Cyril and Oscar would be safe there.

Dolores Trent watched Amabel's face. The girl needed the job and somewhere to live, so she wasn't likely to leave at a moment's notice if she found the work too hard or the hours too long. Especially with a dog and a cat...

She said, 'Provided your references are okay, you can come on a month's trial. You'll be paid weekly. After the month it will be a week's notice on either side.' As they went back to the shop she said, 'I'll phone you when I've checked the references.'

Amabel, waiting for Josh to fetch her in answer to her phone call, was full of hope. It would be a start: somewhere to live, a chance to gain the experience which was so necessary if she wanted to get a better job. She would have the chance to look around her, make friends, perhaps find a room where Cyril and Oscar would be welcome, and find work which was better paid. But that would be later, she conceded. In the meantime she was grateful to Dr Forde for his help. It was a pity she couldn't see him and tell him how grateful she was. But he had disappeared back into his world, somewhere in London, and London was vast...

Convincing Aunt Thisbe that the offer of work from Miss Trent was exactly what she had hoped for was no easy task. Aunt Thisbe had said no word of her holiday, only reiterating her advice that Amabel should spend the next few weeks with her, wait until after Christmas before looking for work...

It was only after Amabel had painted a somewhat overblown picture of her work at Miss Trent's shop, the advantages of getting one foot in the door of future prospects, and her wish to become independent, that Miss Parsons agreed reluctantly that it might be the chance of a lifetime. There was the added advantage that, once in

York, the chance of finding an even better job was much greater than if Amabel stayed at Bolton Percy.

So Amabel sent off her references and within a day or so the job was hers, if she chose to take it. Amabel showed her aunt the letter and it was then that Aunt Thisbe said, 'I shall be sorry to see you go, child. You must spend your Sundays here, of course, and any free time you have.' She hesitated. 'If I am away then you must go to Josh and Mrs Josh, who will look after you. Josh will have a key, and you must treat the house as your home. If you need the car you have only to ask...'

'Will you be away for long?' asked Amabel.

'Well, dear, I have been invited to spend a few weeks with an old friend who has an apartment in Italy. I hadn't made up my mind whether to go, but since you have this job and are determined to be independent...'

'Oh, Aunt Thisbe, how lovely for you—and hasn't everything worked out well? I'll be fine in York and I'll love to come here, if Mrs Josh won't mind. When are you going?'

'You are to start work next Monday? I shall probably go during that week.'

'I thought I'd ask Miss Trent if I could move in on Sunday...'

'A good idea. Josh can drive you there and make sure that everything is all right. Presumably the shop will be empty?'

'I suppose so. I'd have all day to settle in, and if it's quiet Cyril and Oscar won't find it so strange. They're very adaptable.'

So everything was settled. Miss Trent had no objection to Amabel moving in on Sunday. The key would be next door at the patisserie, which was open on

Sundays, and the room had been furnished; she could go in and out as she wished and she was to be ready to open the shop at nine o'clock on Monday morning. Miss Trent sounded friendly enough, if a trifle impatient.

Amabel packed her case and Miss Parsons, with brisk efficiency, filled a large box with food: tins of soup, cheese, eggs, butter, bread, biscuits, tea and coffee and plastic bottles of milk and, tucked away out of sight, a small radio. Amabel, for all her brave face, would be lonely.

Aunt Thisbe decided that she would put off her holiday until the following week; Amabel would spend Sunday with her and she would see for herself if she could go away with a clear conscience... She would miss Amabel, but the young shouldn't be held back.

She would have liked to have seen the room where Amabel was to live, but she sensed that Amabel didn't want that—at least not until she had transformed it into a place of which her aunt would approve. And there were one or two things she must tell Josh—that nice Dr Fforde might return. It wasn't very likely, but Aunt Thisbe believed that one should never overlook a chance.

Saying goodbye to Aunt Thisbe wasn't easy. Amabel had been happy living with her; she had a real affection for the rather dour old lady, and knew that the affection was reciprocated, but she felt in her bones that she was doing the right thing. Her aunt's life had been disrupted by her sudden arrival and that must not be made permanent. She got into the car beside Josh and turned to smile and wave; she would be back on Sunday, but this was the real parting.

There were few people about on an early Sunday

morning: tourists strolling along the Shambles, peering into shop windows, church goers. Josh parked the car away from the city centre and they walked, Amabel with the cat basket and Cyril on his lead, Josh burdened with her case and the box of food.

They knew about her at the patisserie; she fetched the key and opened the shop door, led the way through the shop and opened the door to her new home.

Miss Trent had said that she would furnish it, and indeed there was a divan bed against one wall, a small table by the window with an upright chair, a shabby easy chair by the small electric fire and a worn rug on the wooden floor. There was a pile of bedding and a box of cutlery, and a small table lamp with an ugly plastic shade.

Josh put the box down on the table without saying a word, and Amabel said, too brightly, 'Of course it will look quite different once I've arranged things and put up the curtains.'

Josh said, 'Yes, miss,' in a wooden voice. 'Miss Parsons said we were to go next door and have a cup of coffee. I'll help you sort out your things.'

'I'd love some coffee, but after that you don't need to bother, Josh. I've all the rest of the day to get things how I want. And I must take Cyril for a walk later. There's that park by St Mary Abbot's Church, and then I must take a look round the shop.'

They had their coffee and Josh went away, promising to return on the Sunday morning, bidding her to be sure and phone if she needed him or her aunt. She sensed that he didn't approve of her bid for independence and made haste to assure him that everything was fine…

In her room presently, with the door open and Cyril

and Oscar going cautiously around the neglected patch
of grass, Amabel paused in her bedmaking to reflect that
Miss Trent was certainly a trusting kind of person. 'You
would have thought,' said Amabel to Oscar, peering
round the open door to make sure that she was there,
'that she would have wanted to make sure that I had
come. I might have stolen whatever I fancied from the
shop.'

Well, it was nice to be trusted; it augered well for the
future...

Dolores Trent had in fact gone to Harrogate for the
weekend, with only the briefest of thoughts about
Amabel. The girl would find her own way around. It had
been tiresome enough finding someone to help out in the
shop. Really, she didn't know why she kept the place
on. It had been fun when she had first had it, but she
hadn't realised all the bookwork there would be, and the
tiresome ordering and unpacking...

If this girl needed a job as badly as she had hinted,
then she could take over the uninteresting parts and leave
Dolores to do the selling. It might even be possible to
take more time for herself; the shop was a great hin-
drance to her social life...

Amabel arranged the odds and ends of furniture to
their best advantage, switched on the fire, settled her two
companions before it and unpacked the box of food.
Aunt Thisbe had been generous and practical. There
were tins of soup and a tin opener with them, tins of
food for Oscar and Cyril, and there was a fruitcake—
one of Mrs Josh's. She stowed them away, together with
the other stores, in an empty cupboard she found in the
tiny kitchenette.

She also found a saucepan, a kettle, some mugs and

plates and a tin of biscuits. Presumably Miss Trent made herself elevenses each morning. Amabel opened a tin of soup and put the saucepan on the gas ring, then went to poke her nose into the tiny cloakroom next to the kitchenette. There was a small geyser over the washbasin; at least there would be plenty of hot water.

She made a list while she ate her soup. A cheap rug for the floor, a pretty lampshade, a couple of cushions, a vase—for she must have flowers—and a couple of hooks so that she could hang her few clothes. There was no cupboard, nowhere to put her undies. She added an orange box to the list, with a question mark behind it. She had no idea when she would have the chance to go shopping. She supposed that the shop would close for the usual half-day during the week, though Miss Trent hadn't mentioned that.

She made Oscar comfortable in his basket, switched off the fire, got Cyril's lead and her coat and left the shop, locking the door carefully behind her. It was mid-afternoon by now, and there was no one about. She walked briskly through the streets to St Mary's, where there was a park, and thought there would be time each morning to take Cyril for a quick run before the shop opened. They could go again after the shop closed. There was the grass for him and Oscar during the day; she could leave the door open...

And there were Sundays to look forward to...

On the way back she wondered about Dr Fforde; she tried not to think about him too often, for that was a waste of time. He had come into her life but now he had gone again. She would always be grateful to him, of course, but she was sensible enough to see that he had no place in it.

When she reached the shop she saw that the patisserie was closing its doors, and presently, when she went to look, the shop lights had been turned out. It seemed very quiet and dark outside, but there were lights here and there above the shops. She took heart from the sight of them.

After she had had her tea she went into the shop, turned on the lights and went slowly from shelf to shelf, not touching but noting their order. She looked to see where the wrapping paper, string and labels were kept, for she felt sure Miss Trent would expect her to know that. She wasn't going to be much use for a few days, but there were some things she would be expected to discover for herself.

She had her supper then, let Oscar and Cyril out for the last time, and got ready for bed. Doing the best she could with a basin of hot water in the cloakroom, she pondered the question of baths—or even showers. The girl at the patisserie had been friendly; she might be able to help. Amabel got into her bed, closely followed by her two companions, and fell instantly asleep.

She was up early—and that was another thing, an alarm clock, she thought as she dressed—opened the door onto the grass patch and then left the shop with Cyril. The streets were empty, save for postmen and milkmen, but there were signs of life when she returned after Cyril's run in the park. The shops were still closed, but curtains were being drawn above them and there was a delicious smell of baking bread from the patisserie.

Amabel made her bed, tidied the room, fed the animals and sat down to her own breakfast—a boiled egg, bread and butter and a pot of tea. Tomorrow, she promised herself, she would buy a newspaper when she went

out with Cyril, and, since the patisserie opened at half
past eight, she could get croissants or rolls for her lunch.

She tidied away her meal, bade the animals be good
and shut and locked the door to the shop. They could
go outside if they wanted, and the sun was shining...

She was waiting in the shop when Miss Trent arrived.
Beyond a nod she didn't reply to Amabel's good morning, but took off her coat, took out a small mirror and
inspected her face.

'I don't always get here as early as this,' she said
finally. 'Open the shop if I'm not here, and if I'm not
here at lunchtime just close the shop for half an hour
and get yourself something. Have you had a look round?
Yes? Then put the "Open" sign on the door. There's a
feather duster under the counter; dust off the window
display then unpack that box under the shelves. Be careful, they are china figures. Arrange them on the bottom
shelf and mark the price. That will be on the invoice
inside the box.'

She put away the mirror and unlocked the drawer in
the counter. 'What was your name?' When Amabel reminded her, she said, 'Yes, well, I shall call you
Amabel—and you'd better call me Dolores. There probably won't be any customers until ten o'clock. I'm going
next door for a cup of coffee. You can have yours when
I get back.'

Which was half an hour later, by which time Amabel
had dealt with the china figures, praying silently that
there would be no customers.

'You can have fifteen minutes,' said Dolores. 'There's
coffee and milk in the kitchenette; take it into your room
if you want to.'

Cyril and Oscar were glad to have her company, even

if only for a few minutes, and it made a pleasant break in the morning.

There were people in the shop by now, picking things up and putting them down again, taking their time choosing what they would buy. Dolores sat behind the counter, paying little attention to them and leaving Amabel to wrap up their purchases. Only occasionally she would advise a customer in a languid manner.

At one o'clock she told Amabel to close the door and lock it.

'Open up again in half an hour if I'm not back,' she said. 'Did I tell you that I close on Wednesday for a half-day? I shall probably go a bit earlier, but you can shut the shop and then do what you like.'

Amabel, while glad to hear about the half-day, thought that her employer seemed rather unbusinesslike. She closed the shop and made herself a sandwich before going to sit on the patch of grass with Oscar and Cyril for company.

She was glad when it was one o'clock on Wednesday; standing about in the shop was surprisingly tiring and, although Dolores was kind in a vague way, she expected Amabel to stay after the shop shut so that she could unpack any new goods or rearrange the windows. Dolores herself did very little, beyond sitting behind the counter holding long conversations over the phone. Only when a customer showed signs of serious buying did she exert herself.

She was good at persuading someone to buy the more expensive glass and china, laughing and chatting in an animated way until the sale was completed, then made no effort to tell Amabel how to go on, seeming content to let her find things out for herself. Amabel supposed that she must make a living from the shop, although it was obvious that she had very little interest in it.

It was a temptation to phone Aunt Thisbe and ask if Josh would fetch her for her half-day, but there were things she wished to do. Shopping for food and material for a window curtain, a new lampshade, flowers... Next week, when she had been paid, she would find a cheerful bedspread for the bed and a cloth for the table.

She did her shopping and took Cyril for a walk, and then spent the rest of her day rearranging her room, sitting by the electric fire eating crumpets for her tea and reading the magazine Dolores had left behind the counter.

Not very exciting, reflected Amabel, but it was early days, and there was Sunday to look forward to. She wrote a letter to her mother, read the magazine from end to end and allowed her thoughts to wander to Dr Fforde.

Sunday came at last, bringing Josh and the prospect of a lovely day and the reality of a warm welcome from Aunt Thisbe.

Warm as well as practical. Amabel was despatched to the bathroom to lie in a pine-scented bath—'For that is something you must miss,' said Miss Parsons. 'Come down when you are ready and we will have coffee and you shall tell me everything.'

Amabel, pink from her bath, settled before the fire in her aunt's drawing room with Oscar and Cyril beside her, and gave a detailed account of her week. She made it light-hearted.

'It's delightful working in such a pleasant place,' she pointed out. 'There are some lovely things in the shop, and Miss Trent—she likes to be called Dolores—is very kind and easygoing.'

'You are able to cook proper meals?'

'Yes, and I do—and the room looks so nice now that I have cushions and flowers.'

'You are happy there, Amabel? Really happy? You have enough free time and she pays you well?'

'Yes, Aunt. York is such a lovely city, and the people in the other shops in the Shambles are so friendly…'

Which was rather an exaggeration, but Aunt Thisbe must be convinced that there was no reason why she shouldn't go to Italy…

She would go during the following week, Miss Parsons told Amabel, and Amabel was to continue to spend her Sundays at End House; Josh would see to everything…

Amabel, back in her room with another box of food and a duvet her aunt had declared she didn't want, was content that she had convinced the old lady that she was perfectly happy; they would write to each other, and when Aunt Thisbe came back in the New Year they would review the future.

A week or two went by. Amabel bought a winter coat, a pretty cover for the duvet, a basket for Cyril and a cheap rug. She also saved some money—but not much.

After the first two weeks Dolores spent less and less time at the shop. She would pop in at opening time and then go and have her hair done, or go shopping or meet friends for coffee. Amabel found it odd, but there weren't many customers. Trade would pick up again at Christmas, Dolores told her.

Amabel, aware that she was being underpaid and overworked, was nonetheless glad to have her days filled. The few hours she spent in her room once the shop was closed were lonely enough. Later, she promised herself, once she felt secure in her job, she would join a club or go to night school. In the meantime she read and knitted and wrote cheerful letters home.

And when she wasn't doing that she thought about Dr Fforde. Such a waste of time, she told herself. But there again, did that matter? It was pleasant to remember... She wondered what he was doing and wished she knew more about him. Wondered too if he ever thought of her...

To be truthful, he thought of her very seldom; he led a busy life and time was never quite his own. He had driven to Glastonbury once or twice to see his mother, and since the road took him past Amabel's home he had slowed the car to note the work being carried out there. He had thought briefly of calling to see Mrs Graham, but decided against it. There was no point now that Amabel was in York and happy. He hoped that she had settled down by now. Perhaps when he had time to spare he would drive up and go to see her...

He was seeing a good deal of Miriam, and friends were beginning to invite them together to dinner parties. He often spent evenings with her at the theatre when he would much rather have been at home, but she was amusing, and clever enough to appear to have a sincere interest in his work. Hardly aware of it, he was being drawn into her future plans...

It wasn't until one evening, returning home after a long day at the hospital to be met by Bates with a message from Miriam—she—and he—were to join a party of theatregoers that evening, he was to call for her at seven-thirty and after the theatre he would take her out to supper—that he realised what was happening.

He stood for a moment without speaking, fighting down sudden anger, but when he spoke there was nothing of it in his voice.

'Phone Mrs Potter-Stokes, please, and tell her that I am unable to go out this evening.' He smiled suddenly as an idea drowned the anger. 'And, Bates, tell her that I shall be going away.'

There was no expression on Bates's foxy face, but he felt a deep satisfaction. He didn't like Mrs Potter-Stokes and, unlike the doctor, had known for some time that she was set on becoming Mrs Fforde. His 'Very good, Doctor,' was the model of discretion.

As for Dr Fforde, he ate a splendid supper and spent the rest of the evening going through his diary to see how soon he could get away for a couple of days. He would go first to Miss Parsons' house, for Amabel might have chosen to ignore the chance of working in a shop in York. In any case her aunt would know where she was. It would be interesting to meet again…

Almost a week later he set off for York, Tiger beside him. It was a sullen morning, but once he was clear of the endless suburbs the motorway was fairly clear and the Rolls ate up the miles. He stopped for a snack lunch and Tiger's need for a quick trot, and four hours after he had left his home he stopped before Miss Parsons' house.

Of course no one answered his knock, and after a moment he walked down the narrow path beside the house to the garden at the back. It appeared to be empty, but as he stood there Josh came out of the shed by the bottom hedge. He put down the spade he was carrying and walked up the path to meet him.

'Seeking Miss Amabel, are you? House is shut up.

Miss Parsons is off to foreign parts for the winter and Miss Amabel's got herself a job in York—comes here of a Sunday; that's her day off.'

He studied the doctor's face. 'You'll want to know where she's working. A fancy shop in the Shambles. Lives in a room at the back with those two animals of hers. Brings them here of a Sunday, spends the day at End House, opens the windows and such, airs the place, has a bath and does her washing and has her dinner with us. Very independent young lady, anxious not to be a nuisance. Says everything is fine at her job but she doesn't look quite the thing, somehow…'

Dr Fforde frowned. 'She got on well with her aunt? They seemed the best of friends…'

'And so they are. I'm not knowing, mind, but I fancy Miss Amabel took herself off so's Miss Parsons didn't have to alter her plans about her holiday.'

'I think you may be right. I'll go and see her, make sure everything is as it should be.'

'You do that, sir. Me and the missus aren't quite easy. But not knowing anyone to talk to about it…'

'I'm here for a day or two, so I'll come and see you again if I may?'

'You're welcome, sir. You and your dog.' Josh bent to stroke Tiger. 'Miss Amabel does know to come here if needful.'

'I'm glad she has a good friend in you, Josh.'

Dr Fforde got back into his car. It was mid afternoon and drizzling; he was hungry, and he must book in at the hotel where he had stayed before, but before doing so he must see Amabel.

She was on her hands and knees at the back of the shop, unpacking dozens of miniature Father Christmases in-

tended for the Christmas market. Dolores was at the hair-
dresser and would return only in time to lock the till,
tell her to close the shop and lock up.

She was tired and grubby, and there hadn't been time
to make tea. Dolores expected everything to be cleared
away before she got back. At least there had been no
customers for a while, but Amabel was becoming increasingly worried at the amount of work Dolores expected her to do. It had been fine for the first few weeks,
but Dolores's interest was dwindling. She was in the
shop less, and dealing with the customers and sorting
out the stock was becoming increasingly difficult. To
talk to her about it was risky; she might so easily give
Amabel a week's notice, and although she might find
work easily enough there were Oscar and Cyril to consider…

She unwrapped the last of the little figures and looked
up as someone came into the shop.

Dr Fforde stood in the doorway looking at her. His
instant impression was that she wasn't happy, but then
she smiled, her whole face alight with pleasure.

He said easily, 'Josh told me where you were. He also
told me that Miss Parsons is away.' He glanced round
him. 'You live here? Surely you don't run the place on
your own?'

She had got to her feet, dusting off her hands, brushing down her skirt.

'No. Dolores—that is, Miss Trent—is at the hair-
dresser. Are you just passing through?'

'I'm here for a couple of days. When do you close
this shop?'

'Five o'clock. But I tidy up after that.'

'Will you spend the evening with me?'

She had bent to stroke Tiger's head. 'I'd like that, thank you. Only I have to see to Oscar and Cyril, and take Cyril for a walk, so I won't be ready until about six o'clock.'

'I'll be here soon after five…'

Dolores came in then, assuming her charming manner at the sight of a customer. 'Have you found something you like? Do take a look round.'

She smiled at him, wondering where he came from; if he was on his own she might suggest showing him what was worth seeing in the city—the patisserie wasn't closed yet…

'I came to see Amabel,' he told her. 'We have known each other for some time, and since I am here for a day or two…'

'You're old friends?' Dolores asked artlessly. 'I expect you know York well? You don't live here?'

'No, but I have been here before. We met some time ago, in the West Country.'

Still artless, Dolores said, 'Oh, I thought you might be from London—I've friends there.' An idea—an unlikely idea—had entered her head. 'But I don't suppose you would know them. I came up here after my divorce, and it was an old schoolfriend—Miriam Potter-Stokes—who persuaded me to do something instead of sitting aimlessly around…'

She knew her wild guess had been successful when he said quietly, 'Yes, I know Miriam. I must tell her how successful you are.'

'Do, please. I must be off. Amabel, close at five o'clock. There'll be a delivery of those candlesticks before nine o'clock tomorrow morning, so be sure to be ready for it.' She gave the doctor a smiling nod. 'Nice to have met you. I hope you enjoy your stay here.'

She wasted no time when she reached her home, but poured herself a drink and picked up the phone.

'Miriam, listen and don't interrupt. Do you know where this Oliver of yours is? You don't? He's a big man, handsome, rather a slow voice, with a black dog? He's in my shop. On the best of terms with Amabel, the girl who works for me. It seems they've known each other for some time.' She gave a spiteful little laugh. 'Don't be too sure that Oliver is yours, Miriam.'

She listened to Miriam's outraged voice, smiling to herself. Miriam was an old schoolfriend, but it wouldn't hurt her to be taken down a peg. Dolores said soothingly, 'Don't get so upset, darling. He's here for a few days; I'll keep an eye on things and let you know if there's anything for you to worry about. Most unlikely, I should think. She's a small dull creature and she wears the most appalling clothes. I'll give you a ring tomorrow some time.'

When Dolores had gone the doctor said, 'Where do you live, Amabel? Surely not here?'

'Oh, but I do. I have a room behind the shop.'

'You shall show it to me when I come back.' He glanced at his watch. 'In half an hour.'

She said uncertainly, 'Well...'

'You're glad to see me, Amabel?'

She said without hesitating, 'Oh, yes, I am.'

'Then don't dither,' he said.

He came closer, and, looking down into her face, took

her hands in his. 'There is a Nigerian proverb which says, ''Hold a true friend with both your hands,''' he said. He smiled and added gently, 'I'm your true friend, Amabel.'

CHAPTER FIVE

CLOSING the shop, tidying up, feeding Oscar and Cyril, doing her face and hair, Amabel was conscious of a warm glow deep inside her person. She had a friend, a real friend. She was going to spend the evening with him and they would talk. There was so much she wanted to talk about...

He had said that he would be back at half past five, so at that time she shut her room door and went back into the shop to let him in, stooping to pat Tiger. 'I still have to take Cyril for a walk,' she told him as she led the way to her room.

He stood in the middle of it, looking round him, absently fondling Cyril. He didn't allow his thoughts to show on his face, but remarked placidly, 'Having access to space for Oscar and Cyril is an advantage, isn't it? They're happy here with you?'

'Well, yes. It's not ideal, but I'm lucky to have found it. And I have you to thank for that. I couldn't thank you before because I didn't know where you lived.'

'A lucky chance. Can we leave Oscar for a few hours?'

'Yes, he knows I take Cyril out in the evening. I'll get my coat.'

She was longing for a cup of tea; the afternoon had been long and she hadn't had the chance to make one. She was hungry too. He had told her that they were true friends, but she didn't know him well enough to suggest going to a café, and besides, Cyril needed his run.

They set off, talking of nothing much at first, but presently, walking briskly through the park, she began to answer his carefully put questions with equally careful answers.

They had been walking steadily for half an hour when he stopped and caught her by the arm. 'Tea,' he said. 'Have you had your tea? What a thoughtless fool I am.'

She said quickly, 'Oh, it doesn't matter, really it doesn't,' and added, 'It was such a lovely surprise when you came into the shop.'

He turned her round smartly. 'There must be somewhere we can get a pot of tea.'

So she got her tea, sitting at a very small table in a chintzy teashop where shoppers on their way home were still lingering. Since she was hungry, and the doctor seemed hungry too, she tucked into hot buttered toast, hot mince pies and a slice of the delicious walnut cake he insisted that she have.

'I thought we'd have dinner at my hotel,' he told her. 'But if you're not too tired we might take a walk through the streets. York is such a splendid place, and I'd like to know more of it.'

'Oh, so would I. But about going to the hotel for dinner—I think it would be better if I didn't. I mean, there's Cyril, and I'm not—that is—I didn't stop to change my dress.'

'The hotel people are very helpful about dogs. They'll both be allowed to stay in my room while we dine. And you look very nice as you are, Amabel.'

He sounded so matter-of-fact that her doubts melted away, and presently they continued with their walk.

None of the museums or historical buildings was open, but they wouldn't have visited them anyway; they walked the streets—Lendal Street, Davey Gate, Parliament Street and Coppergate, to stare up at Clifford's Tower, then back through Coppergate and Fosse Gate and Pavement and so to the Shambles again, this time from the opposite end to Dolores's shop. They lingered for a while so that she could show him the little medieval church where she sometimes went, before going on to the Minster, which they agreed would need leisurely hours of viewing in the daylight.

The hotel was close by, and while Amabel went away to leave her coat and do the best she could with her face and hair the doctor went with the dogs. He was waiting for her when she got back to the lounge.

'We deserve a drink,' he told her, 'and I hope you are as hungry as I am.'

It wasn't a large hotel, but it had all the unobtrusive perfection of service and comfort. They dined in a softly lit restaurant, served by deft waiters. The *maître d'* had ushered them to one of the best tables, and no one so much as glanced at Amabel's dowdy dress.

They dined on tiny cheese soufflés followed by roast beef, Yorkshire pudding, light as a feather, crisp baked potatoes and baby sprouts, as gently suggested by the doctor. Amabel looked as though a good meal wouldn't do her any harm, and she certainly enjoyed every mouthful—even managing a morsel of the lemon mousse which followed.

Her enjoyment was unselfconscious, and the glass of claret he ordered gave her face a pretty flush as well as loosening her tongue. They talked with the ease of two people who knew each other well—something which

Amabel, thinking about it later, found rather surprising—and presently, after a leisurely coffee, the doctor went to fetch the dogs and Amabel her coat and they walked back to the shop.

The clocks were striking eleven as they reached the shop door. He took the key from her, opened the door and handed her Cyril's lead.

'Tomorrow is Wednesday—you have a half-day?' When she nodded he said, 'Good. Could you be ready by half past one? We'll take the dogs to the sea, shall we? Don't bother with lunch; we'll go next door and have coffee and a roll.'

She beamed up at him. 'Oh, that would be lovely. Dolores almost always goes about twelve o'clock on Wednesdays, so I can close punctually, then there'll only be Oscar to see to.' She added anxiously, 'I don't need to dress up?'

'No, no. Wear that coat, and a scarf for your head; it may be chilly by the sea.'

She offered a hand. 'Thank you for a lovely evening: I have enjoyed it.'

'So have I.' He sounded friendly, and as though he meant it—which of course he did. 'I'll wait until you're inside and locked up. Goodnight, Amabel.'

She went through the shop and turned to lift a hand to him as she opened the door to her room and switched on the light. After a moment he went back to his hotel. He would have to return to London tomorrow, but he could leave late and travel through the early part of the night so that they could have dinner together again.

'Am I being a fool?' he enquired of Tiger, whose gruff rumble could have been either yes or no...

It was halfway through the busy morning when

Dolores asked casually, 'Did you have a pleasant evening with your friend, Amabel?'

Amabel warmed to her friendly tone. 'Oh, yes, thank you. We went for a walk through the city and had dinner at his hotel. And this afternoon we're going to the sea.'

'I dare say you found plenty to talk about?'

'Yes, yes, we did. His visit was quite unexpected. I really didn't expect to see him again…'

'Does he come this way often? It's quite a long journey from London.'

'Well, yes. He came just before I started work here—my mother told him where I was and he looked me up.'

She had answered readily enough, but Dolores was prudent enough not to ask any more questions. She said casually, 'You must wrap up; it will be cold by the sea. And you can go as soon as he comes for you; I've some work I want to do in the shop.'

She's nicer than I thought, reflected Amabel, going back to her careful polishing of a row of silver photo frames.

Sure enough, when the doctor's large person came striding towards the shop, Dolores said, 'Off you go, Amabel. He can spend ten minutes in the shop while you get ready.'

While Amabel fed Oscar, got Cyril's lead and got into her coat, tidied her hair and made sure that she had everything in her handbag, Dolores invited the doctor to look round him. 'We're showing our Christmas stock,' she told him. 'It's always a busy time, but we close for four days over the holiday. Amabel will be able to go to her aunt's house. She's away at present, Amabel told me, but I'm sure she'll be back by then.' She gave him a sly glance. 'I dare say you'll manage to get a few days off?'

'Yes, I dare say.'

'Well, if you see Miriam give her my love, won't you? Are you staying here long?'

'I'm going back tonight. But I intend to return before Christmas.'

Amabel came then, with Cyril on his lead. She looked so happy that just for a moment Dolores had a quite unusual pang of remorse. But it was only a pang, and the moment they had gone she picked up the phone.

'Miriam—I promised to ring you. Your Oliver has just left the shop with Amabel. He's driving her to the sea and spending the rest of the day with her. What is more, he told me that he intends returning to York before Christmas. You had better find yourself another man, darling!'

She listened to Miriam raging for a few minutes. 'I shouldn't waste your breath getting into a temper. If you want him as badly as all that then you must think of something. When you have, let me know if I can help.'

Miriam thought of something at once. When Dolores heard it she said, 'Oh, no, I can't do that.' For all her mischief-making she wasn't deliberately unkind. 'The girl works very well, and I can't just sack her at a moment's notice.'

'Of course you can; she's well able to find another job—plenty of work around before Christmas. When he comes tell Oliver she's found a better job and you don't' know where it is. Tell him you'll let him know if you hear anything of her; he won't be able to stay away from his work for more than a couple of days at a time. The girl won't come to any harm, and out of sight is out of mind…'

Miriam, most unusually for her burst into tears, and Dolores gave in; after all, she and Miriam were very old friends…

The doctor and his little party had to walk to where he had parked the car, and on the way he marshalled them into a small pub in a quiet street to lunch upon a sustaining soup, hot crusty bread and a pot of coffee—for, as he explained, they couldn't walk on empty stomachs. That done, he drove out of the city, north through the Yorkshire Moors, until he reached Staithes, a fishing village between two headlands.

He parked the car, tucked Amabel's hand under his arm and marched her off into the teeth of a strong wind, the dogs trotting happily on either side of them. They didn't talk; the wind made that difficult and really there was no need. They were quite satisfied with each other's company without the need of words.

The sea was rough, grey under a grey sky, and once away from the village there was no one about. Presently they turned round, and back in the village explored its streets. The houses were a mixture of cottages and handsome Georgian houses, churches and shops. They lingered at the antiques shops and the doctor bought a pretty little plate Amabel admired before they walked on beside the Beck and finally turned back to have tea at the Cod and Lobster pub.

It was a splendid tea; Amabel, her cheeks pink, her hair all over the place and glowing with the exercise, ate the hot buttered parkin, the toast and home-made jam and the fruit cake with a splendid appetite.

She was happy—the shop, her miserable little room, her loneliness and lack of friends didn't matter. Here she was, deeply content, with someone who had said that he was her friend.

They didn't talk about themselves or their lives; there were so many other things to discuss. The time flew by and they got up to go reluctantly.

Tiger and Cyril, nicely replete with the morsels they had been offered from time to time, climbed into the car, went to sleep and didn't wake until they were back in York. The doctor parked the car at his hotel, led the dogs away to his room and left Amabel to tidy herself. It was no easy task, and she hardly felt at her best, but it was still early evening and the restaurant was almost empty.

They dined off chicken *à la king* and lemon tart which was swimming in cream, and the doctor talked comfortably of this and that. Amabel wished that the evening would go on for ever.

It didn't of course. It was not quite nine o'clock when they left the hotel to walk back to the shop. The girl who worked in the patisserie was still there, getting ready to leave. She waved as they passed and then stood watching them. She liked Amabel, who seemed to lead a very dull and lonely life, and now this handsome giant of a man had turned up...

The doctor took the key from Amabel, opened the shop door and then gave it back to her.

'Thank you for a lovely afternoon—Oliver. I feel full of fresh air and lovely food.'

He smiled down at her earnest face. 'Good. We must do it again, some time. When she looked uncertain, he added, 'I'm going back to London tonight, Amabel. But I'll be back.'

He opened the door and pushed her inside, but not before he had given her a quick kiss. The girl in the patisserie saw that, and smiled. Amabel didn't smile, but she glowed from the top of her head to the soles of her feet.

He had said that he would come back…

Dolores was in a friendly mood in the morning; she wanted to know where Amabel had gone, if she had had a good dinner, and was her friend coming to see her again?

Amabel, surprised at the friendliness, saw no reason to be secretive. She gave a cheerful account of her afternoon, and when Dolores observed casually, 'I dare say he'll be back again?' Amabel assured her readily enough that he would.

Any niggardly doubts Dolores might have had about Miriam's scheme were doused by the girl in the patisserie who served her coffee.

'Nice to see Amabel with a man,' she observed chattily. 'Quite gone on her, I shouldn't doubt. Kissed her goodbye and all. Stood outside the shop for ages, making sure she was safely inside. He'll be back, mark my words! Funny, isn't it? She's such a plain little thing, too…'

This was something Miriam had to know, so Dolores sent Amabel to the post office to collect a parcel and picked up the phone.

She had expected rage, perhaps tears from Miriam, but not silence. After a moment she said, 'Miriam?'

Miriam was thinking fast; the girl must be got rid of, and quickly. Any doubts Dolores had about that must be quashed at once. She said in a small broken voice,

'Dolores, you must help me. I'm sure it's just a passing infatuation—only a few days ago we spent the evening together.' That there wasn't an atom of truth in that didn't worry her; she had to keep Dolores's sympathy.

She managed a sob. 'If he goes back to see her and she's gone he can't do anything about it. I know he's got commitments at the hospital he can't miss.' Another convincing lie. 'Please tell him that she's got another job but you don't know where? Or that she's got a boyfriend? Better still tell him that she said she would join her aunt in Italy. He wouldn't worry about her then. In fact that's what she will probably do…'

'That cat and dog of hers—' began Dolores.

'Didn't you tell me that there was a kind of handyman who does odd jobs for the aunt? They'll go to him.'

Put like that, it sounded a reasonable solution. 'You think she might do that?' Dolores was still doubtful, but too lazy to worry about it. She said, 'All right, I'll sack her—but not for a day or two. There's more Christmas stock to be unpacked and I can't do that on my own.'

Miriam gave a convincing sob. 'I'll never be able to thank you enough. I'm longing to see Oliver again; I'm sure everything will be all right once he's back here and I can be with him.'

Which was unduly optimistic of her. Oliver, once back home, made no attempt to contact her. When she phoned his house it was to be told by a wooden-voiced Bates that the doctor was unavailable.

In desperation she went to his consulting rooms, where she told his receptionist that he was expecting her when he had seen his last patient, and when presently he came into the waiting room from his consulting room she went to meet him.

'Oliver—I know I shouldn't be here. Don't blame your receptionist; I said you expected me. Only it is such a long time since we saw each other.'

She lifted her face to his, aware that she was at her most attractive. 'Have I done something to annoy you? You are never at home when I phone; that man of yours says you're not available.' She put a hand on his sleeve and smiled the sad little smile she had practised before her mirror.

'I've been busy—am still. I'm sorry I haven't been free to see you, but I think you must cross me off your list, Miriam.' He smiled at her. 'I'm sure there are half a dozen men waiting for the chance to take you out.'

'But they aren't you, Oliver.' She laughed lightly. 'I don't mean to give you up, Oliver.' She realised her mistake when she saw the lift of his eyebrows, and added quickly, 'You are a perfect companion for an evening out, you know.'

She wished him a light-hearted goodbye then, adding, 'But you'll be at the Sawyers' dinner party, won't you? I'll see you then.'

'Yes, of course.' His goodbye was friendly, but she was aware that only good manners prevented him from showing impatience.

The sooner Dolores got rid of that girl the better, thought Miriam savagely. Once she was out of the way she would set about the serious business of capturing Oliver.

But Dolores had done nothing about sacking Amabel. For one thing she was too useful at this busy time of the year, and for another Dolores's indolence prevented her from making decisions. She was going to have to do something about it, because she had said she would, but later.

Then an ill-tempered and agitated phone call from Miriam put an end to indecision. A friend of Miriam's had mentioned casually that it was a pity that Oliver would be away for her small daughter's—his goddaughter's—birthday party. He'd be gone for several days, he had told her. The birthday was in three days' time…

'You must do something quickly—you promised.' Miriam managed to sound desperately unhappy, although what she really felt was rage. But it wouldn't do to lose Dolores's sympathy. She gave a sob. 'Oh, my dear, I'm so unhappy.'

And Dolores, her decision made for her, promised. 'The minute I get to the shop in the morning.'

Amabel was already hard at work, unwrapping Christmas tree fairies, shaking out their gauze wings and silky skirts, arranging them on a small glass shelf. She wished Dolores good morning, the last of the fairies in her hand.

Dolores didn't bother with good morning. She disliked unpleasantness if it involved herself, and the quicker it was dealt with the better.

'I'm giving you notice,' she said, relieved to find that once she had said it it wasn't so difficult. 'There's not enough work for you, and besides, I need the room at the back. You can go this evening, as soon as you've packed up. Leave your bits and pieces; someone can collect them. You'll get your wages, of course.'

Amabel put the last fairy down very carefully on the shelf. Then she said in a small shocked voice, 'What have I done wrong?'

Dolores picked up a vase and inspected it carefully.

'Nothing. I've just told you; I want the room and I've no further use for you in the shop.' She looked away from Amabel. 'You can go back to your aunt, and if you want work there'll be plenty of casual jobs before Christmas.'

Amabel didn't speak. Of what use? Dolores had made herself plain enough; to tell her that her aunt was still away, and that she had had a card from Josh that morning saying that he and Mrs Josh would be away for the next ten days and would she please not go and visit them as usual next Sunday, would be useless.

Dolores said sharply, 'And it's no use saying anything. My mind's made up. I don't want to hear another word.'

She went to the patisserie then, to have her coffee, and when she came back told Amabel that she could have an hour off to start her packing.

Amabel got out her case and began to pack it, explaining to Cyril and Oscar as she did so. She had no idea where she would go; she had enough money to pay for a bed and breakfast place, but would they take kindly to the animals? There wouldn't be much time to find somewhere once she left the shop at five o'clock. She stripped the bed, packed what food she had in a box and went back to the shop.

When five o'clock came Dolores was still in the shop. She gave Amabel a week's wages, told her that she could give her name for a reference if she needed to, and went back to sit behind the counter.

'Don't hang about,' she said. 'I want to get home.'

But Amabel wasn't going to hurry. She fed Oscar and Cyril and had a wash, made a cup of tea and a sandwich, for she wasn't sure where the next meal would come from, and then, neatly dressed in her new winter coat, with Cyril on his lead, Oscar in his basket and carrying her case, she left the shop.

She didn't say anything. Good evening would have been a mockery; the evening was anything but good. She closed the shop door behind her, picked up her case, waved to the girl in the patisserie, and started off at a brisk pace, past the still lighted shops.

She didn't know York well, but she knew that she wasn't likely to find anywhere cheap in and around the main streets. If she could manage until Josh and his wife got back...

She reached the narrow side streets and presently saw a café on a street corner. It was a shabby place, but it had a sign in its window saying 'Rooms to Let'. She went inside and went to the counter, where a girl lounged reading a magazine.

The place was almost empty; it smelled of fried food and wasn't too clean, but to Amabel it was the answer to her prayers.

The girl was friendly enough. Yes, there was a room, and she could have it, but she didn't know about the dog and cat. She went away to ask and came back to say that there was a room on the ground floor where the animals could stay with her, but only at night; during the day she would have to take them with her. 'And since we're doing you a favour we'll have to charge more.'

A lot more. But at least it was a roof over their heads. It was a shabby roof, and a small ill-furnished room, but there was a wash handbasin and a window opening onto a window box which had been covered by wire netting, and that solved Oscar's problems.

Amabel handed over the money, left her case, locked the door and went out again, intent on finding a cafeteria. Presently, feeling all the better for a meal, still accompanied by Oscar in his basket and Cyril, she bought a take away meat pie and milk, carrying them to her room.

Oscar, let out of his basket at last, made a beeline for the window box, and then settled down to eat the meat in the pie while Cyril wolfed the crust, washing it down with the milk before climbing onto the bed.

Amabel washed in tepid water, cleaned her teeth, got into her nightie and then into bed. She was tired, too tired to think rationally, so she closed her eyes and went to sleep.

She was up early, asked for tea and toast from the girl at the counter and took Cyril out for five minutes. Since she didn't dare to leave Oscar he went too, grumbling in his basket.

Assuring the girl they would be back in the evening, she locked the door and set off into the cold bright morning.

It was apparent by midday that a job which would admit Cyril and Oscar was going to be hard to find. Amabel bought a carton of milk and a ham roll and found a quiet corner by St Mary's, where she fed Oscar and Cyril from the tin she had in her shoulder bag before letting a timid Oscar out to explore the flowerbeds. With a cat's good sense he stayed close to her, and soon got back into his basket and settled down again. He was a wise beast and he was aware that they were, the three of them, going through a sticky patch...

The afternoon was as disappointing as the morning, and the café, when Amabel got back to it, looked uninviting. But it spelled security of a sort, and tomorrow was another day.

Which turned out to be most unfortunately, just like the previous one. The following morning, when Amabel went to her frugal breakfast in the café, the girl at the counter leaned across to say, 'Can't put you up any longer. Got a regular booked the room for a week.'

Amabel chewed toast in a dry mouth. 'But there's another room I can rent?'

'Not with them animals. Be out by ten o'clock, will you? So's I can get the bed changed.'

'But just for a few nights?'

'Not a hope. The boss turned a blind eye for a couple of nights but that's it. Tried the Salvation Army, have you? There's beds there, but you'd have to find somewhere for that dog and cat.'

It was another fine morning, but cold. Amabel found a sheltered seat in the park and sat down to think. She discarded the idea of going home. She had escaped once; it might not be as easy again, and nothing was going to make her abandon Cyril and Oscar.

It was a question of waiting for eight days before Josh and his wife returned, and, however careful she was, there wasn't enough money in her purse to buy them bed and board for that time. She would try the Salvation Army—after five o'clock the girl had said—and hope that they would allow Cyril and Oscar to stay with her.

She had bought a local paper, so now she scanned the vacancies in the jobs columns. She ticked off the most promising, and set off to find the first of them. It was a tiresome business, for her suitcase was quite heavy and Oscar's basket got in the way. Each time she was rejected. Not unkindly, but with an indifference which hurt.

It was after four o'clock when she finally gave up and started on her way to the Salvation Army shelter. She had to pass the end of the Shambles to reach it, and on an impulse she turned aside and went through the half-open door of the little church she had sometimes visited. It was quiet inside and there was no one there. It was cold too, and dimly lighted, but there was peace there…

Amabel sat down in one of the old-fashioned high-backed pews, put Oscar's basket beside her, and, with her case on the other side and Cyril at her feet, allowed the tranquillity of the little church to soothe her.

She said aloud, 'Things are never as bad as they seem,' and Cyril thumped his tail in agreement. Presently, tired from all the walking, he went to sleep. So did Oscar, but Amabel sat without moving, trying to make plans in her tired head which, despite her efforts, was full of thoughts of Oliver. If he were there, she thought dreamily, he would know exactly what to do…

The doctor had reached York shortly after lunch, booked a room at the hotel and, with the faithful Tiger loping beside him, made his way to Dolores's shop. She was sitting behind the counter, reading, but she looked up as he went in and got to her feet. She had known that sooner or later he would come, but she still felt a momentary panic at the sight of him. Which was silly of her; he stood there in the doorway, large and placid, and his quiet greeting was reassuring.

'I've come to see Amabel,' he told her. 'Will you allow her to have an hour or two off? Or perhaps the rest of the afternoon? I can't stay in York long…'

'She's not here…'

'Oh, not ill, I hope?'

'She's gone. I didn't need her any more.' There was no expression on his face, but she took a step backwards. 'She's got an aunt to go to.'

'When was this? She had a week's notice, presumably?'

Dolores picked up a vase on the counter and put it down again. She said again, 'There's this aunt…'

'You sent her packing at a moment's notice?' The doctor's voice was quiet, but she shivered at the sound of it. 'She took the cat and dog with her?'

'Of course she did.'

'Did you know that her aunt was away from home?'

Dolores shrugged. 'She did mention it.' She would have to tell him something to make him see that it was useless looking for the girl. 'Amabel said something about going to stay with friends of her mother—somewhere near…' She paused for a moment, conjuring up names out of the back of her head. 'I think she said Nottingham—a Mrs Skinner…'

She heaved a sigh of relief; she had done that rather well.

He stood looking at her, his face inscrutable, his eyes cold. 'I don't believe you. And if any harm comes to Amabel I shall hold you responsible.'

He left the shop, closing the door quietly behind him, and Dolores flew to the kitchenette and reached for the bottle of whisky she kept hidden away there. Which meant that she missed seeing the girl at the patisserie go to the door and call to the doctor.

'Hi—you looking for Amabel? Poor kid got the sack

at a moment's notice—told she wasn't wanted by that Dolores, I suppose...'

'You spoke to her?'

'Didn't have a chance. Had me hands full of customers. She waved though—had her case and that dog and cat, going heaven knows where. Haven't seen hair nor hide of her since...'

'How long ago?'

'Two days?'

'Dolores said that she had gone away to friends.'

The girl sniffed. 'Don't you believe it—that woman will tell you anything she thinks you want to hear.'

'Yes. You think Amabel is still in York? I'm going to drive to her aunt's house now; there's a man, Josh...'

'I've seen 'im once or twice of a Sunday—brings her back here—she goes there on her free day.'

The doctor thanked her. 'Probably she is there—and thank you. I'll let you know if I find her.'

'You do that—I liked her.'

She watched him go. He was a man to satisfy any girl's dreams, not to mention the money. That was a cashmere coat, and a silk tie costing as much as one of her dresses...

Of course there was no one at Miss Parsons' house, and no response from Josh's cottage when he knocked. He was equally unsuccessful at the village shop—Josh was away, he was told, and there had been no sign of Amabel.

The doctor drove back to York, parked the car once more at the hotel and set off with Tiger to scour the city. He was worried, desperately concerned as to Amabel's whereabouts. He forced himself to think calmly as he systematically combed the streets of the inner city.

He didn't believe for one moment that Amabel had left York, and he thought it unlikely that she would have had enough money to get her home. And to go home was the most unlikely thing she would do. She was here, still in York. It was just a question of finding her...

He stopped at several of the smaller shops to ask if anyone had seen her and was told in one of them—a shabby little café—that there had been a girl with a dog. She had bought a roll and had coffee two days ago. A slender clue, but enough to take the doctor through the streets once more.

It was as he reached the lower end of the Shambles for the second time that his eye lighted on the little church close by. He remembered then that Amabel had told him that she had gone there from time to time. He went through its open door and stood just inside, aware of the quiet and the cold, and he saw Amabel, a small vague figure in the distance.

He heaved a great sigh and went quietly to where she was sitting. 'Hello, Amabel,' he said in a calm voice, 'I thought I might find you here.'

She turned her head slowly as Cyril got to his feet, wagging his tail and whining with pleasure. 'Oliver— Oliver, is it really you?'

She stopped because she was crying, and he went and sat down beside her and put a great arm around her shoulders. He sat quietly and let her weep, and when her sobs became sniffs offered a handkerchief.

'So sorry,' said Amabel. 'You were a surprise—at least, I was thinking about you, and there you were.'

He was relieved to hear that her voice, while still watery, was quite steady.

'Are you staying in York?' she asked politely. 'It's nice to see you again. But don't let me keep you.'

The doctor choked back a laugh. Even in dire circumstances, Amabel, he felt sure, would always be polite. He said gently, 'Amabel, I went to the shop and that woman—Dolores—told me what she had done. I've spent hours looking for you, but we aren't going to talk about it now. We are going to the hotel, and after a meal and a good night's sleep we will talk.'

'No,' said Amabel quite forcibly. 'I won't. What I mean is, thank you, but no. Tomorrow...'

He had Oscar's basket, and her case. Now he said, 'One day at a time, Amabel.'

CHAPTER SIX

SEVERAL hours later Amabel, fed and bathed and in bed, with Cyril curled up on the floor and Oscar stretched out on her feet, tried to sort out the evening so that it made sense. As it was, it had been a fairy tale dream. In no other way could she account for the last few hours.

How had Oliver been able to conjure a private sitting room out of thin air? A tray of tea, food for Oscar and Cyril? Her case had been unpacked and its contents whisked away to be washed and pressed, she was in a bedroom with a balcony where Oscar could feel free, had had a delicious meal and a glass of wine, and Oliver urging her to eat and drink and not ask questions but to go to bed since they must leave early in the morning.

She had obeyed sleepily, thanked him for her supper and said goodnight, then spent ages in the bath. And it had all seemed perfectly normal—just as a dream was always normal. In the morning she must find a way of leaving, but now she would just close her eyes...

She opened them to thin sunshine through the drawn curtains and a cheerful girl with a tray of tea.

'Dr Fforde asks that you dress quickly and meet him in the sitting room in twenty minutes—and I'm to take the dog with me so that he can have a run with the doctor's dog.'

Amabel drank her tea, put Oscar on the balcony and went into the sitting room. She showered and dressed with all speed, anxious not to keep Oliver waiting, so her hair didn't look its best and her make-up was per-functory, but she looked rested and ready for anything.

The doctor was at a window, looking out onto the street below. He turned round as she went in and studied her. 'That's better. You slept well?'

'Yes. Oh, yes, I did. It was like heaven.' She bent to stroke Cyril's head. 'Thank you for taking him out. And thank you for letting me stay here. It's like a dream.'

Breakfast was brought in then, and when they had sat down at the table she said, 'I expect you are in a hurry. The maid asked me to be quick. I'm very grateful, Oliver, for your kindness.' She added, 'There are several jobs I shall go and see about this morning.'

The doctor loaded toast with marmalade. 'Amabel, we are friends, so let us not talk nonsense to each other. You are a brave girl, but enough is enough. In half an hour or so we are leaving York. I have written to Josh so that he will know what has happened when he comes back home, and we will let Miss Parsons know as soon as possible.'

'Know what?'

'Where you will be and what you will be doing.'

'I'm not going home.'

'No, no, of course not. I am hoping that you will agree to do something for me. I have a great-aunt recovering from a slight stroke. Her one wish is to return to her home, but my mother hasn't been able to find someone who will live with her for a time. No nursing is needed, but a willingness to talk and be talked to, join in any small amusement she may fancy, help her to make life enjoyable. She is old, in her eighties, but she loves her garden and her home. She has a housekeeper and a housemaid who have both been with her for years. And don't think that I'm asking you to do this because you happen to be between jobs…'

Which sounded so much better, reflected Amabel, than being out of work, or even destitute. He was asking for her help and she owed him a great deal. Besides, he was her friend, and friends help each other when they were needed.

She said, 'If your great-aunt would like me to be with her, then I'll go to her. But what about Cyril and Oscar?'

'She has a house in the country; she likes animals and they will be welcome there. I should point out that she is a very old lady and liable to have another stroke, so the prospect for you is not a permanent one.'

Amabel drank the last of her coffee. 'Well, I expect for someone like me, with no special skills, it would be hard to find permanent work. But I must write to Aunt Thisbe and tell her.'

'Better still, if you have her phone number you can ring her up.'

'May I? When we get to wherever we are going?'

He crossed the room to the telephone on a side table. 'You have the number with you?' He held out a hand and she handed him the grubby slip of paper she had carried everywhere with her. He got the receptionist and waited for her to get the number, then handed Amabel the phone.

Aunt Thisbe's voice was loud and clear, demanding to know who it was.

'It's me. Amabel. There's nothing wrong, but I must tell you—that is, I must explain—'

The phone was taken from her. 'Miss Parsons? Oliver Fforde. Perhaps I can set your mind at rest. Amabel is with me and quite safe. She will explain everything to you, but I promise you that you have no need to worry about her.' He handed the phone back. 'I'll take the dogs for a quick walk—tell Miss Parsons that you will phone again this evening.'

Aunt Thisbe's firm voice begging her to take her time and tell her what had happened collected Amabel's wits for her. She gave a fairly coherent account of what had been happening. 'And Oliver has told me that he has a job waiting for me with an old aunt and has asked me to take it. And I've said I would because I should like to repay his kindness.'

'A sensible decision, child. An opportunity to express your thanks and at the same time give you a chance to decide what you intend to do. I heard Oliver saying that you will phone again this evening. This has changed things, of course. I was thinking of returning for Christmas, so that you would have somewhere to come over the holiday period, but now that there is no need of that and so I shall stay here for another few weeks. But remember, Amabel, if you need me I will return at once. I am very relieved that Oliver has come to your aid. A good man, Amabel, and one to be trusted.'

Amabel put down the phone as Oliver returned. He said briskly, 'I've put the dogs in the car. If you will get your coat, we'll be off.'

He shovelled Oscar into his basket. 'I must be back at the hospital by three o'clock, so I'll drop you off on the way.' He added impatiently, 'I'll explain as we go.'

Since it was obvious to her that he had no intention of saying anything more until it suited him, Amabel did as she was told.

Consumed by curiosity, and a feeling of uncertainty about her future, Amabel had to wait until they were travelling fast down the M1 before the doctor had anything to say other than enquiries as to her comfort.

'We are going to Aldbury in Hertfordshire. It's a small village a few miles from Berkhamsted. My mother is there, arranging for my aunt's return, and she will explain everything to you—time off, salary and so on—and stay overnight to see you settled in. She is very relieved that you have agreed to take the job and you will be very welcomed, both by her and by Mrs Twitchett, the housekeeper, and Nelly.'

Amabel said, 'Your great-aunt might not like me.'

'There is nothing about you to dislike, Amabel.'

A remark which did nothing for her ego. She had never had delusions about herself, but now she felt a nonentity…

The doctor glanced at her as he spoke, at her unassuming profile as she looked steadily ahead. She looked completely unfazed, accepting the way in which he had bulldozed her into an unknown future. He/had had no chance to do otherwise; there had been no time, and to have left her there alone in York would have been unthinkable. He said, 'I've rushed you, haven't I? But sometimes one has to take a chance!'

Amabel smiled. 'A lucky chance for me. I'm so grateful, and I'll do my best with your great-aunt. Would you tell me her name?'

'Lady Haleford. Eighty-seven years old, widowed for ten years. No children. Loves her garden, birds, the country and animals. She likes to play cards and cheats. Since her stroke she has become fretful and forgetful and at times rather peevish.' He added, 'No young society, I'm afraid.'

'Well, I have never gone out much, so that doesn't matter.'

When he could spare the time, he reflected, he would take her out. Dinner and dancing, a theatre or concert. He didn't feel sorry for her, Amabel wasn't a girl one could pity, but she deserved some fun and he liked her. He was even, he had to admit, becoming a little fond of her in a brotherly sort of way. He wanted to see her safely embarked on the life she wanted so that she would have the chance to meet people of her own age, marry… He frowned. Time enough for that…

They travelled on in silence, comfortable in each other's company, and after a while he asked, 'Do you want to stop? There's a quiet pub about ten miles ahead; we can let the dogs out there.'

The pub stood back from the road and the car park was almost empty. 'Go on inside,' the doctor told her. 'I'll see to the dogs and make sure Oscar's all right. We can't stay long.'

As long as it's long enough to find the Ladies' thought Amabel, wasting no time.

They had beef sandwiches and coffee, saw to the dogs and got back into the car. Oscar, snoozing in his basket, was hardly disturbed. Life for him had had its ups and downs lately, but now he was snug and safe and Amabel's voice reassured him.

Travelling in a Rolls Royce was very pleasant, reflected Amabel, warm and comfortable and sliding past everything else on the road. And Oliver drove with relaxed skill. She supposed that he was a man who wasn't easily put out.

When he turned off the motorway he said, 'Not long now,' and sure enough, a few miles past Berkhamsted, he took a side turning and then a narrow lane and slowed as they reached Aldbury. It was a charming village, having its origin in Saxon times. There was a village green, a duck pond and a pub close by, and standing a little apart was the church, and beyond the village there was a pleasing vista of parkland and woods. Amabel, staring round her, knew that she would like living here, and hoped that it might be in one of the brick and timber cottages they were passing.

The doctor drove to the far side of the pond and stopped before a house standing on its own. Its front door opened directly onto the pavement—and it was brick and timber, as the others. It had a thatched roof, just as those did, but it was considerably larger and yet looked just as cosy.

He got out and opened Amabel's door. 'Come in and meet my mother again,' he invited. 'I'll come for the dogs and Oscar in a moment.'

The house door had been opened and a short stout woman stood there, smiling. She said comfortably, 'So here you are, Master Oliver, and the young lady…'

'Miss Amabel Parsons. Amabel, this is Mrs Twitchett.'

He bent to kiss her cheek and Amabel offered a hand, aware that as it was being shaken she was being studied closely. She hoped that Mrs Twitchett's smiling nod was a good sign.

The hall was wide with a wood floor, handsomely carpeted, but Amabel had no time to look around her for a door was thrust open and Mrs Fforde came to meet them.

The doctor bent to kiss her. 'No need to introduce

you,' he said cheerfully. 'I'll leave you for a moment and see to the dogs and Oscar.'

'Yes, dear. Can you stay?'

'Ten minutes. I've a clinic in a couple of hours.'

'Coffee? It'll be here when you've seen to the dogs. What about the cat?'

'Oscar is a much-travelled beast; he'll present no problems and the garden is walled.'

He went away and Mrs Fforde took Amabel's arm. 'Come and sit down for a moment. Mrs Twitchett will bring the coffee; I'm sure you must need it. I don't suppose Oliver stopped much on the way?'

'Once—we had coffee and sandwiches.'

'But it's quite a drive, even at his speed. Take off your coat and come and sit down.'

'My husband's aunt, Lady Haleford, is old and frail. I expect Oliver has told you that. The stroke has left her in need of a good deal of assistance. Nothing that requires nursing, you understand, just someone to be there. I hope you won't find it too arduous, for you are young and elderly people can be so trying! She is a charming old lady, though, and despite the fact that she can be forgetful she is otherwise mentally alert. I do hope that Oliver made that clear to you?'

Mrs Fforde looked so anxious that Amabel said at once, 'Yes, he did. I'll do my best to keep Lady Haleford happy, indeed I will.'

'You don't mind a country life? I'm afraid you won't have much freedom.'

'Mrs Fforde, I am so grateful to have a job where Cyril and Oscar can be with me—and I love the country.'

'You will want to let your mother know where you

are?' asked Mrs Fforde gently. 'Presently, when you are settled in, phone her. I shall be staying here overnight and will fetch Lady Haleford in the morning.'

The doctor joined them then, and Mrs Twitchett followed him in with a tray of coffee, Tiger and Cyril sidling in behind her.

'Oscar is in the kitchen,' he observed. 'What a sensible animal he is. Mrs Twitchett and Nelly have already fallen for his charms.' He smiled at Amabel and turned to his mother. 'You'll go home tomorrow? I'll try and get down next weekend. You will discuss everything with Amabel before you go? Good.' He drank his coffee and bent to kiss her cheek. 'I'll phone you...'

He laid a hand on Amabel's shoulder. 'I hope you will be happy with my aunt, Amabel. If there are any problems, don't hesitate to tell my mother.'

'All right—but I don't expect any. And thank you, Oliver.'

He was going again out of her life, and this time it was probably for the last time. He had come to her aid, rescued her with speed and a lack of fuss, set her back on her feet once more and was now perfectly justified in forgetting all about her. She offered her hand and her smile lighted up her face. 'Goodbye, Oliver.'

He didn't reply, only patted her shoulder and a moment later he was gone.

'We will go upstairs,' said Mrs Fforde briskly. 'I'll show you your room, and then we will go over the rest of the house so that you will feel quite at home before Lady Haleford arrives. We should be back in time for lunch and I'll leave soon after that. You're sure you can manage?'

'Yes,' said Amabel gravely. 'I'm sure, Mrs Fforde.'

It might not be easy at first, but she owed Oliver so much…

They went up the staircase, with its worn oak treads, to the landing above, with several doors on either side and a passage leading to the back of the house.

'I've put you next to my aunt's room,' said Mrs Fforde. 'There's a bathroom between—hers. Yours is on the other side of your room. I hope you won't have to get up in the night, but if you are close by it will make that easier.'

She opened a door and they went in together. It was a large room, with a small balcony overlooking the side of the house, and most comfortably furnished. It was pretty chintz curtains matching the bedspread, thick carpeting and a dear little easy chair beside a small table close to the window. The small dressing table had a stool before it and there was a pink-shaded lamp on the bedside table.

Mrs Fforde led the way across the room and opened a door. 'This is your bathroom—rather small, I'm afraid…'

Amabel thought of the washbasin behind the shop. 'It's perfect,' she said.

'And here's the door to my aunt's bathroom…' They went through it, and on into Lady Haleford's room at the front of the house. It was magnificently furnished, its windows draped in damask, the four poster bed hung with the same damask, the massive dressing table loaded with silver-backed brushes and mirror, little cut-glass bottles and trinkets.

'Has Lady Haleford always lived here?'

'Yes—at least since her husband died. They lived in the manor house before that, of course, but when her son inherited he moved there with his wife and children and she came here. That was ten years ago. She has often told me that she prefers this house to the manor. For one thing the garden here is beautiful and the rooms aren't too large. And, being in the village, she can still see her friends without having to go too far. Until she had her stroke she drove herself, but of course that won't be possible now. Do you drive?'

'Yes,' said Amabel. 'But I'm not used to driving in large towns.'

'It would be driving Lady Haleford to church and back, and perhaps to call on local friends.'

'I could manage that,' said Amabel.

They went round the house in a leisurely manner. It was, she considered, rather large for one old lady and her two staff, but it was comfortable, rather old-fashioned, and it felt like home. Downstairs, beside the drawing room, there was a dining room, the morning room and a small sitting room—all immaculate. The kind of rooms, reflected Amabel, in which one could sit all day.

The last room they went into was the kitchen, as old-fashioned as the rest of the house. Something smelled delicious as they went in, and Mrs Twitchett turned from the Aga to warn them that dinner would be on the table in half an hour. Nelly was doing something at the table, and sitting before the Aga, for all the world as though they had lived there for ever, were Cyril and Oscar, pleased to see her but making no effort to rouse themselves.

'Happen they're tired out,' said Mrs Twitchett. 'They've eaten their fill and given no trouble.'

Amabel stooped to pat them. 'You really don't mind them being here?'

'Glad to have them. Nelly dotes on them. They'll always be welcome in here.'

Amabel had a sudden urge to burst into tears, a foolishness she supposed, but the relief to have a kind home for her two companions was great. They deserved peace and quiet after the last few months…

She smiled uncertainly at Mrs Twitchett and said thank you, then followed Mrs Fforde out of the kitchen.

Over dinner she was told her duties—not onerous but, as Mrs Fforde pointed out, probably boring and tiring. She was to take her free time when and where she could, and if it wasn't possible to have a day off each week she was to have two half-days. She might have to get up at night occasionally, and, as Mrs Fforde pointed out, the job at times might be demanding. But the wages she suggested were twice as much as Dolores had paid her. Living quietly, thought Amabel, I shall be able to save almost all of them. With a little money behind her she would have a chance to train for a career which would give her future security.

The next morning, buoyed up by high hopes, she waited for Mrs Fforde's return with Lady Haleford. All the same she was nervous.

It was a pity that she couldn't know that the doctor, sitting at his desk in his consulting rooms, had spared a moment to think of her as he studied his next patient's notes. He hoped that she would be happy with his great-aunt; the whole thing had been hurriedly arranged and even now she might be regretting it. But something had had to be done to help her.

He stood up to greet his patient and dismissed her from his thoughts.

Mrs Fforde's elderly Rover stopped in front of the door and Amabel went into the hall, standing discreetly at a distance from Mrs Twitchett and Nelly, waiting at the door. She and Cyril had been out early that morning for a walk through the country lanes; now he stood quietly beside her, and Oscar had perched himself close by, anxious not to be overlooked.

Lady Haleford was small and thin, and walked with a stick and the support of Mrs Fforde's arm, but although she walked slowly and hesitantly there was nothing invalidish about her.

She returned Mrs Twitchett's and Nelly's greetings in a brisk manner and asked at once, 'Well, where's this girl Oliver has found to look after me?'

Mrs Fforde guided her into the drawing room and sat her in a high-backed chair. 'Here, waiting for you.' She said over her shoulder, 'Amabel, come and meet Lady Haleford.'

Amabel put a cautionary finger on Cyril's head and went to stand before the old lady.

'How do you do, Lady Haleford?'

Lady Haleford studied her at some length. She had dark eyes, very bright in her wrinkled face, a small beaky nose and a mouth which, because of her stroke, drooped sideways.

'A plain girl,' she observed to no one in particular. 'But looks are only skin-deep, so they say. Nice eyes and pretty hair, though, and young...' She added peevishly, 'Too young. Old people are boring to the young.

You'll be gone within a week. I'm peevish and I forget things and I wake in the night.'

Amabel said gently, 'I shall be happy here, Lady Haleford. I hope you will let me stay and keep you company. This is such a lovely old house, you must be glad to be home again, you will get well again now that you are home.'

Lady Haleford said, 'Pooh,' and then added, 'I suppose I shall have to put up with you.'

'Only for as long as you want to, Lady Haleford,' said Amabel briskly.

'Well, at least you've a tongue in your head,' said the old lady. 'Where's my lunch?'

Her eye fell on Cyril. 'And what's this? The dog Oliver told me about? And there's a cat?'

'Yes. They are both elderly and well-behaved, and I promise you they won't disturb you.'

Lady Haleford said tartly, 'I like animals. Come here, dog.'

Cyril advanced obediently, not much liking to be called dog when he had a perfectly good name. But he stood politely while the old lady looked him over and then patted his head.

Mrs Fforde went home after lunch, leaving Amabel to cope with the rest of the day. Oliver had advised her to let Amabel find her own feet. 'She's quite capable of dealing with any hiccoughs,' he had pointed out, 'and the sooner they get to know each other the better.'

A remark which hadn't prevented him from thinking that perhaps he had made a mistake pitching Amabel into a job she might dislike. She was an independent girl, determined to make a good future for herself; she had only accepted the job with his great-aunt because she had to have a roof over her head and money in her pocket. But he had done his best, he reflected and need waste no more time thinking about her.

But as he had decided not to think any more about Amabel, so Miriam was equally determined to think about him. Dolores had phoned her and told her of his visit. 'I told him that she had left York—I invented an aunt somewhere or other, a friend of her mother's...' She didn't mention that he hadn't believed her. 'He went away and I didn't see him again. Is he back in London? Have you seen him?'

'No, not yet, but I know he's back. I rang his consulting rooms and said I wanted an appointment. He's been back for days. He can't have wasted much time in looking for her. You've been an angel, Dolores, and so clever to fob him off.'

'Anything for a friend, darling. I'll keep my eyes and ears open just in case she's still around.' She giggled. 'Good hunting!'

As far as she was concerned she didn't intend to do any more about it, although she did once ask idly if anyone had seen Amabel or her visitor when she had her coffee in the patisserie. But the girl behind the counter didn't like Dolores; she had treated Amabel shabbily and she had no need to know that that nice man had gone back one evening and told her that Amabel and her companions were safe with him.

Miriam had phoned Oliver's house several times to be told by Bates that his master was not home.

'He's gone away again?' she'd asked sharply.

'No. No, miss. I assume that he's very busy at the hospital.'

He told the doctor when he returned in the evening. 'Mrs Potter-Stokes, sir, has been ringing up on several occasions. I took it upon myself to say that you were at the hospital. She didn't wish to leave a message.' He lowered his eyes. 'I should have told you sooner, sir, but you have been away from home a good deal.'

'Quite right, Bates. If she should phone again, will you tell her that I'm very busy at the moment? Put it nicely.'

Bates murmured assent, concealing satisfaction; he disliked Mrs Potter-Stokes.

It was entirely by chance that Miriam met a friend of her mother's one morning. A pleasant lady who enjoyed a gossip.

'My dear, I don't seem to have seen you lately. You and Oliver Fforde are usually together...' She frowned. 'He is coming to dinner on Thursday, but someone or other told me that you were away.'

'Away? No, I shall be at home for the next few weeks.' Miriam contrived to look wistful. 'Oliver and I have been trying to meet for days—he's so busy; you would never believe how difficult it is to snatch an hour or two together.'

Her companion, a woman without guile and not expecting it in others, said at once, 'My dear Miriam, you must come to dinner. At least you can sit with each other and have a little time together. I'll get another man to make up the numbers.'

Miriam laid a hand on her arm. 'Oh, how kind of you; if only we can see each other for a while we can arrange to meet.'

Miriam went home well satisfied, so sure of her charm and looks that she was positive that Oliver, seeing her again, would resume their friendship and forget that silly girl.

But she was to be disappointed. He greeted her with his usual friendly smile, listened to her entertaining chatter, and with his usual beautiful manners evaded her questions as to where he had been. It was vexing that despite all her efforts he was still no more than one of her many friends.

At the end of the evening he drove her home, but he didn't accept her invitation to go in for a drink.

'I must be up early,' he told her, and wished her a pleasantly cool goodnight.

Miriam went angrily to her bed. She could find no fault in his manner towards her, but she had lost whatever hold she'd thought she had on him. Which made her all the more determined to do something about it. She had always had everything she wanted since she was a small girl, and now she wanted Oliver.

It was several days later that, an unwilling fourth at one of her mother's bridge parties, she heard someone remark, 'Such a pity he cannot spare the time to join us; he's going away for the weekend...'

The speaker turned to Miriam. 'I expect you knew that already, my dear?'

Miriam stopped herself just in time from trumping her partner's ace.

'Yes, yes, I do. He's very fond of his mother...'

'She lives at such a pleasant place. He's going to see an old aunt as well.' She laughed. 'Not a very exciting weekend for him. You won't be with him, Miriam?' The speaker glanced at her slyly.

'No, I'd already promised to visit an old schoolfriend.'

Miriam thought about that later. There was no reason

why Oliver shouldn't visit an old aunt; there was no reason why she should feel uneasy about it. But she did.

She waited for a day or two and then phoned him, keeping her voice deliberately light and understanding. There was rather a good film on; how about them going to see it together at the weekend?

'I'll be away,' he told her.

'Oh, well, another time. Visiting your mother?'

'Yes. It will be nice to get out of London for a couple of days.'

He was as pleasant and friendly as he always had been, but she knew that she was making no headway with him. There was someone else—surely not that girl still?

She gave the matter a good deal of thought, and finally telephoned Mrs Fforde's home; if she was home, she would hang up, say 'wrong number', or make some excuse, but if she was lucky enough to find her out and the housekeeper, a garrulous woman, answered, she might learn something...

She was in luck, and the housekeeper, told that this was an old friend of the doctor's, was quite ready to offer the information that he would be staying for the weekend and leaving early on Sunday to visit Lady Haleford.

'Ah, yes,' said Miriam encouragingly, 'his great-aunt. Such a charming old lady.'

The housekeeper went on, 'Back home after a stroke, madam told me. But they've got someone to live with her—a young lady, but very competent.'

'I must give Lady Haleford a ring. Will you let me have her number?'

It was an easy matter to phone and, under the pretext

of getting a wrong number, discover that Lady Haleford lived at Aldbury. It would be wise to wait until after Oliver had been there, but then she would find some reason for calling on the old lady and see for herself what it was about this girl that held Oliver's interest.

Satisfied that she had coped well with what she considered a threat to her future, Miriam relaxed.

Amabel, aware that fate was treating her kindly, set about being as nearly a perfect companion as possible. No easy task, for Lady Haleford was difficult. Not only was she old, she was accustomed to living her life as she wished—an impossibility after her stroke—so that for the first few days nothing was right, although she tolerated Cyril and Oscar, declaring that no one else understood her.

For several days Amabel was to be thoroughly dispirited; she had done nothing right, said nothing right, remained silent when she should have spoken, spoken when she was meant to be silent. It was disheartening, but she liked the old lady and guessed that underneath the peevishness and ill-temper there was a frightened old lady lurking.

There had been no chance to establish any kind of routine. She had had no free time other than brief walks round the garden with Cyril. But Mrs Twitchett and Nelly had done all they could to help her, and she told herself that things would improve.

She had coaxed Lady Haleford one afternoon, swathed in shawls, to sit in the drawing room, and had set up a card table beside her, intent on getting her to play two-handed whist. Her doctor had been that morning, pronounced himself satisfied with her progress and suggested that she might begin to take an interest in life once more.

He was a hearty man, middle-aged and clearly an old friend. He had taken no notice of Lady Haleford's pee-vishness, told her how lucky she was to have someone so young and cheerful to be with her and had gone away, urging Amabel at the same time to get out into the fresh air.

'Nothing like a good walk when you're young,' he had observed, and Mabel, pining for just that, had agreed with him silently.

Lady Haleford went to sleep over her cards and Amabel sat quietly, waiting for her to rouse herself again. And while she sat, she thought. Her job wasn't easy, she had no freedom and almost no leisure, but on the other hand she had a roof—a comfortable one—over her head, Oscar and Cyril had insinuated themselves into the household and become household pets, and she would be able to save money. Besides, she liked Lady Haleford, she loved the old house and the garden, and she had so much to be thankful for she didn't know where to begin.

With the doctor, she supposed, who had made it all possible. If only she knew where he lived she could write and tell him how grateful she was...

The drawing room door opened soundlessly and he walked in.

Amabel gaped at him, her mouth open. Then she shut it and put a finger to it. 'She's asleep,' she whispered unnecessarily, and felt a warm wave of delight and content at the sight of him.

He dropped a kiss on her cheek, having crossed the room and sat down.

'I've come to tea,' he told her, 'and if my aunt will invite me, I'll stay for supper.'

He sounded matter-of-fact, as though dropping in for tea was something he did often, and he was careful to hide his pleasure at seeing Amabel again. Still plain, but good food was producing some gentle curves and there were no longer shadows under her eyes.

Beautiful eyes, thought the doctor, and smiled, feeling content in her company.

CHAPTER SEVEN

LADY HALEFORD gave a small snort and woke up.

'Oliver—how delightful. You'll stay for tea? Amabel, go and tell Mrs Twitchett. You know Amabel, of course?'

'I saw her as I came in, and yes, I know Amabel. How do you find life now that you are back home, Aunt?'

The old lady said fretfully, 'I get tired and I forget things. But it is good to be home again. Amabel is a good girl and not impatient. Some of the nurses were impatient. You could feel them seething under their calm faces and I can sympathise with them.'

'You sleep well?'

'I suppose so. The nights are long, but Amabel makes tea and we sit and gossip.' She added in an anxious voice, 'I shall get better, Oliver?'

He said gently, 'You will improve slowly, but getting well after illness is sometimes harder than being ill.'

'Yes, it is. How I hate that wheelchair and that horrible thing to help me walk. I won't use it, you know. Amabel gives me an arm...'

The old lady closed her eyes and nodded off for a moment, before adding, 'It was clever of you to find her, Oliver. She's a plain girl, isn't she? Dresses in such dull clothes too, but her voice is pleasant and she's gentle.' She spoke as though Amabel wasn't there, sitting close to her. 'You made a good choice, Oliver.'

The doctor didn't look at Amabel. 'Yes, indeed I did, Aunt.'

Nelly came in with the tea tray then, and he began a casual conversation about his mother and his work and the people they knew, giving Amabel time to get over her discomfort. She was too sensible to be upset by Lady Haleford's remarks, but he guessed that she felt embarrassed...

Tea over, Lady Haleford declared that she would take a nap. 'You'll stay for dinner?' she wanted to know. 'I see you very seldom.' She sounded peevish.

'Yes, I'll stay with pleasure,' he told her. 'While you doze Amabel and I will take the dogs for a quick run.'

'And I shall have a glass of sherry before we dine,' said the old lady defiantly.

'Why not? We'll be back in half an hour or so. Come along, Amabel.'

Amabel got up. 'Is there anything you want before we go, Lady Haleford?' she asked.

'Yes, fetch Oscar to keep me company.'

Oscar, that astute cat, knew on which side his bread was buttered, for he settled down primly on the old lady's lap and went to sleep.

It was cold outside, but there was a bright moon in a starry sky. The doctor took Amabel's arm and walked her briskly through the village, past the church and along a lane out of the village. They each held a dog lead and the beasts trotted beside them, glad of the unexpected walk.

'Well,' said the doctor, 'how do you find your job? Have you settled in? My aunt can be difficult, and now, after her stroke, I expect she is often querulous.'

'Yes, but so should I be. Wouldn't you? And I'm very

happy here. It's not hard work, and you know everyone is so kind.'

'But you have to get up during the night?'

'Well, now and then.' She didn't tell him that Lady Haleford woke up during the early hours most nights and demanded company. Fearful of further probing questions, she asked, 'Have you been busy? You haven't needed to go to York again?'

'No, that is a matter happily dealt with. You hear from your mother and Miss Parsons?'

'Yes, Aunt Thisbe is coming home at the end of January, and my mother seems very happy. The market garden is planted and they have plenty of help.' She faltered for a moment. 'Mother said not to go home and see her yet, Mr Graham is still rather—well, I think he'd rather that I didn't visit them...'

'You would like to see your mother?' he asked gently.

'Yes, but if she thinks it is best for me to stay away then I will. Perhaps later...'

'And what do you intend to do later?'

They turned for home and he tucked her hand under his arm.

'Well, I shall be able to save a lot of money. It's all computers these days, isn't it? So I'll take a course in them and get a good job and somewhere to live.' She added anxiously, 'Your aunt does want me to stay for a while?'

'Oh, most certainly. I've talked to her doctor and he thinks that she needs six weeks or two months living as she does at present, and probably longer.'

They had reached the house again.

'You have very little freedom,' he told her.

She said soberly, 'I'm content.'

They had supper early, for Lady Haleford became easily tired, and as soon as the meal was finished the doctor got up to go.

'You'll come again?' demanded his aunt. 'I like visitors, and next time you will tell me about yourself. Haven't you found a girl to marry yet? You are thirty-four, Oliver. You've enough money and a splendid home and the work you love; now you need a wife.'

He bent to kiss her. 'You shall be the first to know when I find her.' And to Amabel he said, 'No, don't get up. Mrs Twitchett will see me out.' He put a hand on Amabel's shoulder as he passed her chair, and with Tiger at his heels was gone.

His visit had aroused the old lady; she had no wish to go to bed, she said pettishly. And it was a pity that Oliver could visit her so seldom. She observed, 'He is a busy man, and I dare say has many friends. But he needs to settle down. There are plenty of nice girls for him to choose from, and there is that Miriam...' She was rambling a bit. 'The Potter-Stokes widow—been angling for him for an age. If he's not careful she'll have him.' She closed her eyes. 'Not a nice young woman...'

Lady Haleford dozed for a while so Amabel thought about Oliver and the prospect of him marrying. She found the idea depressing, although it was the obvious thing for a man in his position to do. Anyway, it was none of her business.

A week went by, almost unnoticed in the gentle routine of the old house. Lady Haleford improved a little, but not much. Some days her testiness was enough to cast a blight over the entire household, so that Mrs Twitchett burnt the soup and Nelly dropped plates and Amabel had to listen to a diatribe of her many faults.

Only Cyril and Oscar weathered the storm and her fierce little rages, sitting by her chair and allowing her peevish words to fly over their heads.

But there were days when she was placid, wanting to talk, play at cards, and walk slowly round the house, carefully hitched up under Amabel's arm.

Her doctor came, assured her that she was making steady progress, warned Amabel to humour her as much as possible and went away again.

Since humouring her meant getting up in the small hours to read to the old lady, or simply to talk until she drowsed off to a light sleep, Amabel had very little time for herself. At least each morning she took Cyril for a walk while Lady Haleford rested in her bed after breakfast before getting up, and she looked forward to her half-hour's freedom each day, even when it was cold and wet.

On this particular morning it was colder and wetter than it had been for several days, and Amabel, trudging back down the village street with Cyril beside her, looked rather as though she had fallen into a ditch and been pulled out backwards. Her head down against the wind and rain, she didn't see the elegant little sports car outside Lady Haleford's gate until she was beside it.

Even then she would have opened the door and gone inside if the woman in the car hadn't wound down the window and said in an anxious voice, 'Excuse me—if you could spare a moment? Is this Lady Haleford's house? My mother is a friend of hers and asked me to look her up as I was coming this way. But it's too early to call. Could I leave a message with someone?'

She smiled charmingly while at the same time studying Amabel's person. This must be the girl, reflected

Miriam. Plain as a pikestaff and looks like a drowned rat. I can't believe that Oliver is in the least bit interested in her. Dolores has been tricking me… She spent a moment thinking of how she would repay her for that, then said aloud, at her most charming, 'Are you her granddaughter or niece? Perhaps you could tell her?'

'I'm Lady Haleford's companion,' said Amabel, and saw how cold the lovely blue eyes were. 'But I'll give her a message if you like. Would you like to come back later, or come and wait indoors? She has been ill and doesn't get up early.'

'I'll call on my way back,' said Miriam. She smiled sweetly. 'I'm sorry you're so wet standing there; I am thoughtless. But perhaps you don't mind the country in winter. I don't like this part of England. I've been in York for a while, and after that this village looks so forlorn.'

'It's very nice here,' said Amabel. 'But York is lovely; I was there recently.'

Her face ringed by strands of wet hair, she broke into a smile she couldn't suppress at the remembrance of the doctor.

Miriam said sharply, 'You have happy memories of it?'

Amabel, lost in a momentary dream, didn't notice the sharpness. 'Yes.'

'Well, I won't keep you.' Miriam smiled and made an effort to sound friendly. 'I'll call again.'

She drove away and Amabel went indoors. She spent the next ten minutes drying herself and Cyril and then went to tidy herself before going to Lady Haleford's room.

The old lady was in a placid mood, not wanting to

talk much and apt to doze off from time to time. It wasn't until she was dressed and downstairs in her normal chair by the drawing room fire that she asked, 'Well, what have you been doing with yourself, Amabel?'

Glad of something to talk about, Amabel told her of her morning's encounter. 'And I'm so sorry but she didn't tell me her name, and I forgot to ask, but she said that she'll be back.'

Lady Haleford said worriedly, 'I do have trouble remembering people… What was she like? Dark? Fair? Pretty?'

'Fair and beautiful, very large blue eyes. She was driving a little red car.'

Lady Haleford closed her eyes. 'Well, she'll be back. I don't feel like visitors today, Amabel, so if she does call make my apologies—and ask her name.'

But of course Miriam didn't go back, and after a few days they forgot about her.

Miriam found it just impossible to believe that Oliver could possibly have any interest in such a dull plain girl, but all the same it was a matter which needed to be dealt with. She had begun to take it for granted that he would take her to the theatre, out to dine, to visit picture galleries, and even when he had refused on account of his work she had been so sure of him…

Her vanity prevented her from realising that he had merely been fulfilling social obligations, that he had no real interest in her.

She would have to change her tactics. She stopped phoning him with suggestions that they should go to the theatre or dine out, but she took care to be there at a mutual friend's house if he were to be there, too. Since

Christmas was approaching, there were dinner parties and social gatherings enough.

Not that he was always to be found at them. Oliver had many friends, but his social life depended very much on his work so that, much to Miriam's annoyance, she only saw him from time to time, and when they did meet he was his usual friendly self, but that was all. Her pretty face and charm, her lovely clothes and witty talk were wasted on him.

When they had met at a friend's dinner party, and she'd asked casually what he intended to do for Christmas, he'd told her pleasantly that he was far too busy to make plans.

'Well, you mustn't miss our dinner party,' she'd told him. 'Mother will send you an invitation.'

The days passed peacefully enough at Aldbury. Lady Haleford had her ups and downs—indeed it seemed to Amabel that she was slowly losing ground. Although perhaps the dark days of the winter made the old lady loath to leave her bed. Since her doctor came regularly, and assured Amabel that things were taking their course, she spent a good many hours sitting in Lady Haleford's room, reading to her or playing two-handed patience.

All the same she was glad when Mrs Fforde phoned to say that she would be coming to spend a day or two. 'And I'm bringing two of my grandchildren with me— Katie and James. We will stay for a couple of days before I take them to London to do the Christmas shopping. Lady Haleford is very fond of them and it may please her to see them. Will you ask Mrs Twitchett to come to the phone, Amabel? I leave it to you to tell my aunt that we shall be coming.'

It was a piece of news which pleased the old lady mightily. 'Two nice children,' she told Amabel. 'They must be twelve years old—twins, you know. Their mother is Oliver's sister.' She closed her eyes for a moment and presently added, 'He has two sisters; they're both married, younger than he.'

They came two days later; Katie was thin and fair, with big blue eyes and a long plait of pale hair and James was the taller of the two, quiet and serious. Mrs Fforde greeted Amabel briskly.

'Amabel—how nice to see you again. You're rather pale—I dare say that you don't get out enough. Here are Katie and James. Why not take them into the garden for a while and I will visit Lady Haleford? Only put on something warm.' Her eyes lighted on Cyril, standing unexpectedly between the children.

'They are happy, your cat and dog?'

'Yes, very happy.'

'And you, Amabel?'

'I'm happy too, Mrs Fforde.'

Oscar, wishing for a share of the attention, went into the garden too, and, although it was cold, it was a clear day with no wind. They walked along its paths while the children told Amabel at some length about their shopping trip to London.

'We spend Christmas at Granny's,' they explained. 'Our aunt and uncle and cousins will be there, and Uncle Oliver. We have a lovely time and Christmas is always the same each year. Will you go home for Christmas, Amabel?'

'Oh, I expect so,' said Amabel, and before they could ask any more questions added, 'Christmas is such fun, isn't it?'

They stayed for two days, and Amabel was sorry to see them go, but even such a brief visit had tired Lady Haleford, and they quickly slipped back into the placid pattern of their days.

Now that Christmas was near Amabel couldn't help wishing that she might enjoy some of the festivities, so it was a delightful surprise when Lady Haleford, rather more alert than she had been, told her that she wanted her to go to Berkhamstead and do some Christmas shopping. 'Sit down,' she commanded, 'and get a pen and some paper and write down my list.'

The list took several days to complete, for Lady Haleford tended to doze off a good deal, but finally Amabel caught the village bus, her ears ringing with advice and instructions from Mrs Twitchett, the list in her purse and a wad of banknotes tucked away safely.

It was really rather exciting, and shopping for presents was fun even if it was for someone else. It was a long list, for Lady Haleford's family was a large one: books, jigsaw puzzles, games for the younger members, apricots in brandy, a special blend of coffee, Stilton cheese in jars, a case of wine, boxes of candied fruits, and mouth-watering chocolates for the older ones.

Amabel, prowling round the small grocer's shop which seemed to stock every luxury imaginable, had enjoyed every minute of her shopping. She had stopped only briefly for a sandwich and coffee, and now, with an hour to spare before the bus left, she did a little shopping for herself.

High time too, she thought, stocking up on soap and toiletries, stockings and a thick sweater, shampoos and toothpaste. And then presents: patience cards for Lady Haleford, a scarf for Mrs Twitchett, a necklace for Nelly, a new collar for Cyril and a catnip mouse for Oscar. It was hard to find a present for her mother; she chose a blouse, in pink silk, and, since she couldn't ignore him, a book token for her stepfather.

At the very last minute she saw a dress, silvery grey in some soft material—the kind of dress, she told herself, which would be useful for an occasion, and after all it was Christmas... She bought it and, laden with parcels, went back to Aldbury.

The old lady, refreshed by a nap, wanted to see everything. Amabel drank a much needed cup of tea in the kitchen and spent the next hour or so carefully unwrapping parcels and wrapping them up again. Tomorrow, said Lady Haleford, Amabel must go into the village shop and get coloured wrapping paper and labels and write appropriate names on them.

The village shop was a treasure store of Christmas goods. Amabel spent a happy half-hour choosing suitably festive paper and bore it back for the old lady's approval. Later, kneeling on the floor under Lady Haleford's eyes, she was glad of her experience in Dolores's shop, for the gifts were all shapes and sizes. Frequently it was necessary to unwrap something and repack it because Lady Haleford had dozed off and got muddled...

The doctor, coming quietly into the room, unnoticed by a dozing Lady Haleford and, since she had her back to the door, by Amabel, stood in the doorway and watched her. She wasn't quite as tidy as usual, and half obscured by sheets of wrapping paper and reels of satin ribbon. Even from the back, he considered, she looked flustered...

The old lady opened her eyes and saw him and said,

'Oliver, how nice. Amabel, I've changed my mind. Unwrap the Stilton cheese and find a box for it.'

Amabel put down the cheese and looked over her shoulder. Oliver smiled at her and she smiled back, a smile of pure delight because she was so happy to see him again.

Lady Haleford said with a touch of peevishness, 'Amabel—the cheese…'

Amabel picked it up again and clasped it to her bosom, still smiling, and the doctor crossed the room and took it from her.

'Stilton—who is it for, Aunt?' He eyed the growing pile of gaily coloured packages. 'I see you've done your Christmas shopping.'

'You'll stay for lunch?' said Lady Haleford. 'Amabel, go and tell Mrs Twitchett.' When Amabel had gone she said, 'Oliver, will you take Amabel out? A drive, or tea, or something? She has no fun and she never complains.'

'Yes, of course. I came partly to suggest that we have dinner together one evening.'

'Good. Mrs Twitchett told me that the child has bought a new dress. Because it's Christmas, she told her. Perhaps I don't pay her enough…'

'I believe she is saving her money so that she can train for some career or other.'

'She would make a good wife…' The old lady dozed off again.

It was after lunch, when Lady Haleford had been tucked up for her afternoon nap, that the doctor asked Amabel if she would have dinner with him one evening. They were walking the dogs, arm-in-arm, talking easily like two old friends, comfortable with each other, but she stopped to look up at him.

'Oh, that would be lovely. But I can't, you know. It would mean leaving Lady Haleford for a whole evening, and Nelly goes to her mother's house in the village after dinner—she's got rheumatism, her mother, you know—and that means Mrs Twitchett would be alone...'

'I think that something might be arranged if you would leave that to me.'

'And then,' continued Amabel, 'I've only one dress. I bought it the other day, but it's not very fashionable. I only bought it because it's Christmas, and I...really, it was a silly thing to do.'

'Since you are going to wear it when we go out I don't find it in the least silly.' He spoke gently. 'Is it a pretty dress?'

'Pale grey. Very plain. It won't look out of date for several years.'

'It sounds just the thing for an evening out. I'll come for you next Saturday evening—half past seven.'

They walked back then, and presently he went away, giving her a casual nod. 'Saturday,' he reminded her, and bent to kiss her cheek. Such a quick kiss that she wasn't sure if she had imagined it.

She supposed that she wasn't in the least surprised to find that Lady Haleford had no objection to her going out with the doctor. Indeed, she seemed to find nothing out of the ordinary in it, and when Amabel enquired anxiously about Nelly going to her mother, she was told that an old friend of Mrs Twitchett's would be spending the evening with her.

'Go and enjoy yourself,' said that lady. 'Eat a good dinner and dance a bit.'

So when Saturday came Amabel got into the grey dress, took pains with her face and her hair and went

downstairs to where the doctor was waiting. Lady
Haleford had refused to go to bed early; Mrs Twitchett
would help her, she had told Amabel, but Amabel was
to look in on her when she got home later. 'In case I
am still awake and need something.'

Amabel, the grey dress concealed by her coat, greeted
the doctor gravely, pronounced herself ready, bade the
old lady goodnight, bade Oscar and Cyril to be good and
got into the car beside Oliver.

It was a cold clear night with a bright moon. There
would be a heavy frost by morning, but now everything
was silvery in the moonlight.

'We're not going far,' said the doctor. 'There's rather
a nice country hotel—we can dance if we feel like it.'

He began to talk about this and that, and Amabel, who
had been feeling rather shy, lost her shyness and began
to enjoy herself. She couldn't think why she should have
felt suddenly awkward with him; after all, he was a
friend—an old friend by now...

He had chosen the hotel carefully and it was just right.
The grey dress, unassuming and simple but having style,
was absorbed into the quiet luxury of the restaurant.

The place was festive, without being overpoweringly
so, and the food was delicious. Amabel ate prawns and
Caesar salad, grilled sole and straw potatoes and, since
it was almost Christmas, mouthwatering mince pies with
chantilly cream. But not all at once.

The place was full and people were dancing. When
the doctor suggested that she might like to dance she got
up at once. Only as they reached the dance floor she
hesitated. 'It's ages since I danced,' she told him.

He smiled down at her. 'Then it's high time you did
now,' he told her.

She was very light on her feet, and she hadn't forgotten how to dance. Oliver looked down onto her neat head of hair and wondered how long it would be before she discovered that she was in love with him. He was prepared to wait, but he hoped that it wouldn't be too long…!

The good food, the champagne and dancing had transformed a rather plain girl in a grey dress into someone quite different. When at length it was time to leave, Amabel, very pink in the cheeks and bright of the eye, her tongue loosened by the champagne, told him that she had never had such a lovely evening in her life before.

'York seems like a bad dream,' she told him, 'and supposing you hadn't happened to see me, what would I have done? You're my guardian angel, Oliver.'

The doctor, who had no wish to be her guardian angel but something much more interesting, said cheerfully, 'Oh, you would have fallen on your feet, Amabel, you're a sensible girl.'

And all the things she suddenly wanted to say to him shrivelled on her tongue.

'I've had too much champagne,' she told him, and talked about the pleasures of the evening until they were back at Lady Haleford's house.

He went in with her, to switch on lights and make sure all was well, but he didn't stay. She went to the door with him and thanked him once again for her lovely evening.

'I'll remember it,' she told him.

He put his arms round her then, and kissed her hard, but before she could say anything he had gone, closing the door quietly behind him.

She stood for a long time thinking about that kiss, but presently she took off her shoes and crept upstairs to her room. There, was no sound from Lady Haleford's bedroom and all was still when she peeped through the door; she undressed and prepared for bed, and was just getting into bed when she heard the gentle tinkling of the old lady's bell. So she got out of bed again and went quietly to see what was the matter.

Lady Haleford was now wide awake, and wanted an account of the evening.

'Sit down and tell me about it,' she commanded. 'Where did you go and what did you eat?'

So Amabel stifled a yawn and curled up in a chair by the bed to recount the events of the evening. Not the kiss, of course.

When she had finished Lady Haleford said smugly, 'So you had a good time. It was my suggestion, you know—that Oliver should take you out for the evening. He's so kind, you know—always willing to do a good turn. Such a busy man, too. I'm sure he could ill spare the time.' She gave a satisfied sigh. 'Now go to bed Amabel. We have to see to the rest of those Christmas presents tomorrow.'

So Amabel turned the pillow, offered a drink, turned the night light low and went back to her room. In her room she got into bed and closed her eyes, but she didn't go to sleep.

Her lovely evening had been a mockery, a charitable action undertaken from a sense of duty by someone whom she had thought was her friend. He was still her friend, she reminded herself, but his friendship was mixed with pity.

Not to be borne, decided Amabel, and at last fell asleep as the tears dried on her cheeks.

Lady Haleford had a good deal more to say about the evening out in the morning; Amabel had to repeat everything she had already told her and listen to the old lady's satisfied comments while she tied up the rest of the parcels.

'I told Oliver that you had bought a dress...'

Amabel cringed. Bad enough that he had consented to take her out; he probably thought that she had bought it in the hope that he might invite her.

She said quickly, 'We shall need some more paper. I'll go and buy some...'

In the shop, surrounded by the village ladies doing their weekly shopping, she felt better. She was being silly, she told herself. What did it matter what reason Oliver had had for asking her out for the evening? It had been a lovely surprise and she had enjoyed herself, and what had she expected, anyway?

She went back and tied up the rest of the presents, and recounted, once again, the previous evening's events, for the old lady protested that she had been told nothing.

'Oh, you spent five minutes with me when you came in last night, but I want to know what you talked about. You're a nice girl, Amabel, but I can't think of you as an amusing companion. Men do like to be amused, but I dare say Oliver found you pleasant enough; he can take his pick of pretty women in London.'

All of which did nothing to improve Amabel's spirits.

Not being given to self-pity, she told herself to remember that Lady Halcford was old and had been ill and didn't mean half of what she said. As for her evening out, well, that was a pleasant memory and nothing more. If she should see the doctor again she would take care to let him see that, while they were still friends, she neither expected nor wanted to be more than that.

I'll be a little cool, reflected Amabel, and in a few weeks I expect I'll be gone from here. Being a sensible girl, she fell to planning her future...

This was a waste of time, actually, for Oliver was planning it for her; she would be with his aunt for several weeks yet—time enough to think of a way in which they might see each other frequently and let her discover for herself that he was in love with her and wanted to marry her. He had friends enough; there must be one amongst them who needed a companion or something of that sort, where Cyril and Oscar would be acceptable. And where he would be able to see her as frequently as possible...

The simplest thing would be for her to stay at his house. Impossible—but he lingered over the delightful idea...

He wasn't the only one thinking about Amabel's future. Miriam, determined to marry Oliver, saw Amabel as a real threat to her plans.

She was careful to be casually friendly when she and Oliver met occasionally, and she took care not to ask him any but the vaguest questions about his days. She had tried once or twice to get information from Bates, but he professed ignorance of his employer's comings and goings. He told her stolidly that the doctor was either at his consulting room or at the hospital, and if she phoned and wanted to speak to him at the weekend Bates informed her that he was out with the dog.

Oliver, immersed in his work and thoughts of Amabel,

dismissed Miriam's various invitations and suggestions that they might spend an evening together with good-mannered friendliness; he didn't believe seriously that Miriam wanted anything more than his company from time to time; she had men-friends enough.

He underestimated her, though. Miriam drove herself to Aldbury, parked the car away from the centre of the village and found her way to the church. The village shop would have been ideal ground from which to glean information, but there was the risk of meeting Amabel. Besides, people in the village might talk.

The church was old and beautiful, but she didn't waste time on it. Someone—the vicar, she supposed—was coming down the aisle towards her, wanting to know if he could help her…

He was a nice elderly man, willing to talk to this charming lady who was so interested in the village. 'Oh, yes,' he told her, 'there are several old families living in the village, their history going back for many years.'

'And those lovely cottages with thatched roofs—one of them seems a good deal larger than the rest?'

'Ah, yes, that would be Lady Haleford's house. A very old family. She has been ill and is very elderly. She was in hospital for some time, but now I'm glad to say she is at home again. There is a very charming young woman who is her companion. We see her seldom, for she has little spare time, although Lady Haleford's nephew comes to visit his aunt and I have seen the pair of them walking the dogs. He was here recently, so I'm told, and took her out for the evening…! How I do ramble on, but living in a small village we tend to be interested in each other's doings. You are touring this part of the country?'

'Yes, this is a good time of year to drive around the countryside. I shall work my way west to the Cotswolds,' said Miriam, untruthfully. 'It's been delightful talking to you, Vicar, and now I must get back to my car and drive on.'

She shook hands and walked quickly back to her car, watched by several ladies in the village shop, whose sharp eyes took in every inch of her appearance.

She drove away quickly and presently pulled up on the grass verge the better to think. At first she was too angry to put two thoughts together. This was no passing attraction on Oliver's part; he had been seeing this girl for some time now and his interest was deep enough to cause him to seek her out. Miriam seethed quietly. She didn't love Oliver; she liked him enough to marry him and she wanted the things the marriage would bring to her: a handsome husband, money, a lovely home and the social standing his name and profession would give her.

She thumped the driving wheel in rage. Something would have to be done, but what?

CHAPTER EIGHT

QUIET though the routine of Lady Haleford's household was, Christmas, so near now, was not to be ignored. Cards were delivered, gifts arrived, visitors called to spend ten minutes with the old lady, and Amabel trotted round the house arranging and rearranging the variety of pot plants they brought with them.

It was all mildly exciting, but tiring for the invalid, so that Amabel needed to use all her tact and patience, coaxing callers to leave after the briefest of visits, and even then Lady Haleford exhibited a mixture of lethargy and testiness which prompted her to get the doctor to call.

He was a rather solemn man who had looked after the old lady for years, and he now gave it as his opinion that, Christmas or no Christmas, his patient must revert to total peace and quiet.

'The occasional visitor,' he allowed, and Amabel was to use her discretion in turning away more than that.

Amabel said, 'Lady Haleford likes to know who calls. She gets upset if someone she wishes to see is asked not to visit her. I've tried that once or twice and she gets rather uptight.'

Dr Carr looked at her thoughtfully. 'Yes, well, I must leave that to your discretion, Miss Parsons. Probably to go against her wishes would do more harm than good. She sleeps well?'

'No,' said Amabel. 'Although she dozes a lot during the day.'

'But at night—she is restless? Worried…?'

'No. Just awake. She likes to talk, and sometimes I read to her.'

He looked at her as though he hadn't really seen her before.

'You get sufficient recreation, Miss Parsons?'

Amabel said that, yes, thank you, she did. Because if she didn't he might decide that she wasn't capable enough for the job and arrange for a nurse. Her insides trembled at the thought.

So Amabel met visitors as they were ushered into the hall and, unless they were very close old friends or remote members of Lady Haleford's family, persuaded them that she wasn't well enough to have a visitor, then offered notepaper and a pen in case they wanted to write a little note and plied them with coffee and one of Mrs Twitchett's mince pies.

Hard work, but it left both parties satisfied.

Though it was quite quiet in the house, the village at its doorstep was full of life. There was a lighted Christmas tree, the village shop was a blaze of fairy lights, and carol singers—ranging from small children roaring out the first line of 'Good King Wenceslas' to the harmonious church choir—were a nightly event. And Mrs Twitchett, while making sure that Lady Haleford was served the dainty little meals she picked at, dished up festive food suitable to the season for the other three of them.

Amabel counted her blessings and tried not to think about Oliver.

*   *   *

Dr Fforde was going to Glastonbury to spend Christmas
with his mother and the rest of his family. Two days
which he could ill spare. He had satisfied himself that
his patients were making progress, presented the theatre
staff with sherry, his ward sister and his receptionist and
the nurse at the consulting rooms with similar bottles,
made sure that Bates and his wife would enjoy a good
Christmas, loaded the car boot with suitable presents
and, accompanied by Tiger, was ready to leave home.

He was looking forward to the long drive, and, more
than that, he was looking forward to seeing Amabel, for
he intended to call on his aunt on his way.

He had been working hard for the last week or so,
and on top of that there had been the obligatory social
events. Many of them he had enjoyed, but not all of
them. He had found the dinner party given by Miriam's
parents particularly tedious, but he had had no good reason to refuse the invitation—although he had been relieved to find that Miriam seemed no longer to look upon
him as her future. She had been as amusing and attractive as always, but she had made no demands on his
time, merely saying with apparent sincerity that he must
be glad to get away from his work for a few days.

It was beginning to snow when he left, very early on
the morning of Christmas Eve. Tiger, sitting very upright
beside him, watched the heavy traffic. It took some time
to get away from London but the doctor remained patient, thinking about Amabel, knowing that he would be
seeing her in an hour or so.

The village looked charming as he drove through it
and there was a small lighted Christmas tree in the cottage's drawing room window. He got out of the car,
opened the door for Tiger, and saw Amabel and Cyril

at the far end of the village street. Tiger, scenting friends, was already on his way to meet them. Oliver saw Amabel stop, and for a moment he thought she was going to turn round and hurry away. But she bent to greet Tiger and came towards him. He met her halfway.

There was snow powdering her woolly cap and her coat, and her face was rosy with cold. He thought she looked beautiful, though he was puzzled by her prim greeting.

He said cheerfully, 'Hello. I'm on my way to spend Christmas with the family. How is my aunt?'

'A bit tired,' she told him seriously. 'There have been a great many visitors, although she has seen only a handful of them.'

They were walking back towards the house. 'I expect you'd like to see her? She'll be finishing her breakfast.' Since he didn't speak, the silence got rather long. 'I expect you've been busy?' Annabel finally ventured.

'Yes, I'll go back on Boxing Day.' They had reached the front door when he said, 'What's the matter, Amabel?'

She said, too quickly, 'Nothing. Everything is fine.' And as she opened the door added, 'Would you mind going up to Lady Haleford? I'll dry the dogs and tidy myself.'

Mrs Twitchett came bustling into the hall then, and Amabel slipped away. Oliver wouldn't stay long and she could keep out of his way…

The dogs made themselves comfortable on either side of Oscar in front of the Aga, and when Nelly came in to say that Mr Oliver would have a cup of coffee before he went away Amabel slipped upstairs. Lady Haleford would be ready to start the slow business of dressing.

'Go away,' said the old lady as Amabel went into her room. 'Go and have coffee with Oliver. I'll dress later.' When Amabel looked reluctant, she added, 'Well, run along. Surely you want to wish him a happy Christmas?'

So Amabel went downstairs again, as slowly as possible, and into the drawing room. The dogs and Oscar had gone there with the coffee, sitting before the fire, and the doctor was sitting in one of the big wing chairs.

He got up as she went in, drew a balloon-backed chair closer to his own and invited her to pour their coffee.

'And now tell me what is wrong,' he said kindly. 'For there is something, isn't there? Surely we are friends enough for you to tell me? Something I have done, Amabel?'

She took a gulp of coffee. 'Well, yes, but it's silly of me to mind. So if it's all the same to you I'd rather not talk about it.'

He resisted the urge to scoop her out of her chair and wrap her in his arms. 'It isn't all the same to me...'

She put down her cup and saucer. 'Well, you didn't have to take me out to dinner just because Lady Haleford said that you should— I wouldn't have gone if I'd known...' She choked with sudden temper. 'Like giving a biscuit to a dog...'

Oliver bit back a laugh, not of amusement but of tenderness and relief. If that was all...

But she hadn't finished. 'And I didn't buy a dress because I hoped you would take me out.' She looked at him then. 'You are my friend, Oliver, and that is how I think of you—a friend.'

He said gently, 'I came to take you out for the evening, Amabel. Anything my aunt said didn't influence me in any way. And as for your new dress, that was something I hadn't considered. It was a pretty dress, but you look nice whatever you are wearing.' He would have liked to have said a great deal more, but it was obviously not the right moment. When she didn't speak, he said, 'Still friends, Amabel?'

'Yes—oh, yes, Oliver. I'm sorry I've been so silly.'

'We'll have another evening out after Christmas. I think that you will be here for some time yet.'

'I'm very happy here. Everyone in the village is so friendly, and really I have nothing to do.'

'You have very little time to yourself. Do you get the chance to go out—meet people—young people?'

'Well, no, but I don't mind.'

He got up to go presently. It was still snowing and he had some way to drive still. She went with him to the door, and Tiger, reluctant to leave Cyril and Oscar, pushed between them. Amabel bent to stroke him.

'Go carefully,' she said, 'and I hope that you and your family have a lovely Christmas.'

He stood looking down at her. 'Next year will be different!' He fished a small packet from a pocket. 'Happy Christmas, Amabel,' he said, and kissed her.

He didn't wait to hear her surprised thanks. She stood watching the car until it was out of sight, her mouth slightly open in surprise, clutching the little gaily wrapped box.

The delightful thought that he might come again on his way back to London sent a pleasant glow through her person.

She waited until Christmas morning before she opened the box, sitting up in bed early in the darkness. The box contained a brooch, a true lover's knot, in gold

and turquoise—a dainty thing, but one she could wear
with her very ordinary clothes.

She got up dressed in the grey dress and pinned the
brooch onto it before getting into her coat and slipping
out of the house to go to church.

It was dark and cold, and although the snow had
stopped it lay thick on the ground. The church was cold
too, but it smelled of evergreens and flowers, and the
Christmas tree shone with its twinkling lights. There
weren't many people at the service, for almost everyone
would be at Matins during the morning, but as they left
the church there was a pleasant flurry of cheerful talk
and good wishes.

Amabel made sure that Lady Haleford was still asleep,
had a quick breakfast with Mrs Twitchett and Nelly and
took Cyril for his walk. The weather didn't suit his elderly bones and the walk was brief. She settled him next
to Oscar by the Aga and went to bid Lady Haleford good
morning.

The old lady wasn't in a festive mood. She had no
wish to get out of her bed, no wish to eat her breakfast,
and she said that she was too tired to look at the gifts
Amabel assured her were waiting for her downstairs.

'You can read to me,' she said peevishly.

So Amabel sat down and read. *Little Women* was a
soothing book, and very old-fashioned. She found the
chapter describing Christmas and the simple pleasures of
the four girls and their mother was a sharp contrast to
the comfortable life Lady Haleford had always lived.

Presently Lady Haleford said, 'What a horrid old
woman I am...'

'You're one of the nicest people I know,' said

Amabel, and, quite forgetting that she was a paid companion, she got up and hugged the old lady.

So Christmas was Christmas after all, with presents being opened, and turkey and Christmas pudding and mince pies, suitably interposed between refreshing naps, and Amabel, having tucked Lady Haleford into her bed, went early to bed herself. There was nothing else to do, but that didn't matter. Oliver would be returning to London the next day, and perhaps he would come and see them again...

But he didn't. It was snowing again, and he couldn't risk a hold-up on the way back to London.

The weather stayed wintry until New Year's Day, when Amabel woke to a bright winter's sun and blue sky. It was still snowy underfoot, and as she sloshed through it with a reluctant Cyril she wondered what the New Year would bring...

As for the doctor, he hardly noticed which day of the week it was, for the New Year had brought with it the usual surge of bad chests, tired hearts and the beginnings of a flu epidemic. He left home early and came home late, and ate whatever food Bates put before him. He was tired, and often frustrated, but it was his life and his work, and presently, when things had settled down again, he would go to Amabel...

Miriam waited for a few days before phoning Oliver. He had just got home after a long day and he was tired, but that was something she hadn't considered. There was a new play, she told him, would he get tickets? 'And we could have supper afterwards. I want to hear all about Christmas...'

He didn't tell her that he was working all day and

every day, and sometimes into the night as well. He said mildly, 'I'm very busy, Miriam, I can't spare the time. There is a flu epidemic…'

'Oh, is there? I didn't know. There must be plenty of junior doctors…'

'Not enough.'

She said with a flash of temper, 'Then I'll get someone who will enjoy my company.'

The doctor, reading the first of a pile of reports on his desk, said absent-mindedly, 'Yes, do. I hope you will have a pleasant evening.'

He put the phone down and then picked it up again. He wanted to hear Amabel's voice. He put it down again. Phone conversations were unsatisfactory, for either one said too much or not enough. He would go and see her just as soon as he could spare the time. He ignored the pile of work before him and sat back and thought about Amabel, in her grey dress, wearing, he hoped, the true lover's knot.

Miriam had put down the phone and sat down to think. If Oliver was busy then he wouldn't have time to go to Aldbury. It was a chance for her to go, talk to the girl, convince her that he had no interest in her, that his future and hers were as far apart as two poles. It would be helpful if she could get Amabel away from this aunt of his, but she could see no way of doing that. She would have to convince Amabel that she had become an embarrassment to him…

There was no knowing when Oliver would go to Aldbury again, and Miriam waited with impatience for the snow to clear away. On a cold bright day, armed with a bouquet of flowers purporting to come from her mother, she set out.

The church clock was striking eleven as she stopped before Lady Haleford's cottage. Nelly answered the door, listened politely to Miriam's tale of her mother's friendship with Lady Haleford and bade her come in and wait. Lady Haleford was still in her room, but she would fetch Miss Parsons down. She left Miriam in the drawing room and went away, and presently Amabel came in.

Miriam said at once, 'Oh, hello—we've met before, haven't we? I came at the wrong time. Am I more fortunate today? Mother asked me to let Lady Haleford have these flowers...'

'Lady Haleford will be coming down in a few minutes,' said Amabel, and wondered why she didn't like this visitor.

She was being friendly enough, almost gushing, and Lady Haleford, when Nelly had mentioned Miriam's name, had said, 'That young woman—very pushy. And I haven't met her mother for years.' She had added, 'But I'll come down.'

Which she did, some ten minutes later, leaving Amabel to make polite conversation that Miriam made no effort to sustain.

But with the old lady she was at her most charming, giving her the flowers with a mythical message from her mother, asking about her health with apparent concern.

The old lady, normally a lady of perfect manners, broke into her chatter. 'I am going to take a nap. Amabel, fetch your coat and take Mrs Potter-Stokes to look round the village or the church if she chooses. Mrs Twitchett will give you coffee in half an hour's time. I will say goodbye now; please thank your mother for the flowers.'

She sat back in her chair and closed her eyes, leaving

Amabel to usher an affronted Miriam out of the room. In the hall Amabel said, 'Lady Haleford has been very ill and she tires easily. Would you like to see round the church?'

Miriam said no, in a snappy voice, and then, mindful of why she had come, added with a smile, 'But perhaps we could walk a little way out of the village? The country looks very pretty.'

Amabel got into her coat, tied a scarf over her head and, with Cyril on his lead, led the way past the church and into the narrow lane beyond. Being a friendly girl, with nice manners, she made small talk about the village and the people who lived in it, aware that her companion hadn't really wanted to go walking—she was wearing the wrong shoes for a start.

Annoyed though Miriam was, she saw that this was her chance—if only there was a suitable opening. She stepped into a puddle and splashed her shoe and her tights and the hem of her long coat, and saw the opening…

'Oh, dear. Just look at that. I'm afraid I'm not a country girl. It's a good thing that I live in London and always shall. I'm getting married soon, and Oliver lives and works there too…'

'Oliver?' asked Amabel in a careful voice.

'A nice name, isn't it? He's a medical man, always frightfully busy, although we manage to get quite a lot of time together. He has a lovely house; I shall love living there.'

She turned to smile at Amabel. 'He's such a dear— very kind and considerate. All his patients dote on him. And he's always ready to help any lame dog over a stile. There's some poor girl he's saved from a most miserable life—gone out of his way to find her a job. I hope she's grateful. She has no idea where he lives, of course. I mean, she isn't the kind of person one would want to become too familiar with, and it wouldn't do for her to get silly ideas into her head, would it?'

Amabel said quickly, 'I shouldn't think that would be very likely, but I'm sure she must be grateful.'

Miriam tucked a hand under Amabel's arm. 'Oh, I dare say—and if she appeals to him again for any reason I'll talk to her. I won't have him badgered; heaven knows how many he's helped without telling me. Once we're married, of course, things will be different.'

She gave Amabel a smiling nod, noting with satisfaction that the girl looked pale. 'Could we go back? I'm longing for a cup of coffee...'

Over coffee she had a great deal to say about the approaching wedding. 'Of course, Oliver and I have so many friends, and he's well known in the medical profession. I shall wear white, of course...' Miriam allowed her imagination full rein.

Amabel ordered more coffee, agreed that four bridesmaids would be very suitable, and longed for her unwelcome visitor to go. Which, presently, she did.

Lady Haleford, half dozing in her room, opened her eyes long enough to ask if the caller had gone and nodded off again, for which Amabel was thankful. She had no wish to repeat their conversation—besides, Oliver's private life was none of her business. She hadn't liked Miriam, but it had never entered her head that the woman was lying. It all made sense; Oliver had never talked about his home or his work or his friends. And why should he? Mrs Twitchett had remarked on several occasions that he had given unobtrusive help to people.

'He's a very private person,' she had told Amabel. 'Lord knows what goes on in that clever head of his.'

There was no hope of going to see Amabel for the moment; the flu epidemic had swollen to a disquieting level. The doctor treated his patients with seeming tirelessness, sleeping when he could, sustained by Mrs Bates's excellent food and Bates's dignified support. But Amabel was always at the back of his mind, and from time to time he allowed himself to think about her, living her quiet life and, he hoped, sometimes thinking about him.

Of Miriam he saw nothing; she had prudently gone to stay with friends in the country, where there was less danger of getting the flu. She phoned him, leaving nicely calculated messages to let him see that she was concerned about him, content to bide her time, pleased with herself that she had sewn the seeds of doubt in Amabel's mind. Amabel was the kind of silly little fool, she reflected, who would believe every word of what she had said. Head over heels in love with him, thought Miriam, and doesn't even know it.

But here she was wrong; Amabel, left unhappy and worried, thought about Oliver a good deal. In fact he was never out of her thoughts. She *had* believed Miriam when she had told her that she and Oliver were to marry. If Lady Haleford hadn't been particularly testy for the next few days she might have mentioned it to her, but it wasn't until two o'clock one morning, when the old lady was sitting up in her bed wide awake and feeling chatty, that she began to talk about Oliver.

'Time he settled down. I only hope he doesn't marry that Potter-Stokes woman. Can't stand her—but there's no denying that she's got looks and plenty of ambition. He'd be knighted in no time if she married him, for she knows all the right people. But he'd have a fashionable practice and turn into an embittered man. He needs to be loved…'

Amabel, curled up in a chair by the bed, wrapped in her sensible dressing gown, her hair neatly plaited, murmured soothingly, anxious that the old lady should settle down. Now was certainly not the time to tell her about Miriam's news.

Lady Haleford dozed off and Amabel was left with her thoughts. They were sad, for she agreed wholeheartedly with the old lady that Miriam would not do for Oliver. He does need someone to love him, reflected Amabel, and surprised herself by adding *me*.

Once over her surprise at the thought, she allowed herself to daydream a little. She had no idea where Oliver lived—somewhere in London—and she knew almost nothing about his work, but she would love him, and care for him, and look after his house, and there would be children…

'I fancy a drop of hot milk,' said Lady Haleford. 'And you'd better go to bed, Amabel. You looked washed out…'

Which effectively put an end to daydreams, although it didn't stop her chaotic thoughts. Waiting for the milk to heat, she decided that she had been in love with Oliver for a long time, accepting him into her life as naturally as drawing breath. But there was nothing to be done about it; Miriam had made it plain that he wouldn't welcome the prospect of seeing her again.

If he did come to see his aunt, thought Amabel, pouring the milk carefully into Lady Haleford's special mug, then she, Amabel, would keep out of his way, be coolly pleasant, let him see that she quite understood.

These elevating thoughts lasted until she was back in her own bed, where she could cry her eyes out in peace and quiet.

The thoughts stood her in good stead, for Oliver came two days later. It being a Sunday, and Lady Haleford being in a good mood, Amabel had been told that she might go to Matins, and it was on leaving the church that she saw the car outside the cottage. She stopped in the porch, trying to think of a means of escape. If she went back into the church she could go out through the side door and up the lane and stay away for as long as possible. He probably wasn't staying long...

She felt a large heavy arm on her shoulders and turned her head.

'Didn't expect me, did you?' asked the doctor cheerfully. 'I've come to lunch.'

Amabel found her voice and willed her heart to stop thumping. She said, 'Lady Haleford will be pleased to see you.'

He gave her a quick, all-seeing look. Something wasn't quite right...

'I've had orders to take you for a brisk walk before lunch. Up the lane by the church?'

Being with him, she discovered, was the height of happiness. Her high-minded intentions could surely be delayed until he had gone again? While he was there, they didn't make sense. As long as she remembered that they were friends and nothing more.

She said, 'Where's Tiger?'

'Being spoilt in the kitchen. Wait here. I'll fetch him and Cyril.'

He was gone before she could utter, and soon back again with the dogs, tucking an arm in hers and walking her briskly past the church and up the lane. The last time she had walked along it, she reflected, Miriam had been with her.

Very conscious of the arm, she asked, 'Have you been busy?'

'Very busy. There's not been much flu here?'

'Only one or two cases.' She sought for something to talk about. 'Have you seen Lady Haleford yet? She's better—at least I think so. Once the spring is here, perhaps I could drive her out sometimes—just for an hour— and she's looking forward to going into the garden.'

'I spent a few minutes with her. Yes, she is making progress, but it's a long business. I should think you will be here for some weeks. Do you want to leave, Amabel?'

'No, no, of course not. Unless Lady Haleford would like me to go?'

'That is most unlikely. Have you thought about the future?'

'Yes, quite a lot. I—I know what I want to do. I'll go and see Aunt Thisbe and then I'll enrol at one of those places where I can train to use a computer. There's a good one at Manchester; I saw it advertised in Lady Haleford's paper.' She added, to make it sound more convincing, 'I've saved my money, so I can find somewhere to live.'

The doctor, quite rightly, took this to be a spur-of-the-moment idea, but he didn't say so.

'Very sensible. You don't wish to go home?'

'Yes. I'd like to see Mother, but she wrote to me just after Christmas and said that my stepfather still wasn't keen for me to pay a visit.'

'She could come here...'

'I don't think he would like that. I did suggest it.' She added, 'Mother is very happy. I wouldn't want to disturb that.'

They had been walking briskly and had passed the last of the cottages in the lane. The doctor came to a halt and turned her round to face him.

'Amabel, there is a great deal I wish to say to you...'

'No,' she said fiercely. 'Not now—not ever. I quite understand, but I don't want to know. Oh, can't you see that? We're friends, and I hope we always will be, but when I leave here it's most unlikely that we shall meet again.'

He said slowly, 'What makes you think that we shall never meet again?'

'It wouldn't do,' said Amabel. 'And now please don't let's talk about it any more.'

He nodded, his blue eyes suddenly cold. 'Very well.' He turned her round. 'We had better go back, or Mrs Twitchett will be worried about a spoilt lunch.'

He began to talk about the dogs and the weather, and was she interested in paintings? He had been to see a rather interesting exhibition of an early Victorian artist...

His gentle flow of talk lasted until they reached the cottage again and she could escape on the pretext of seeing if the old lady needed anything before lunch. The fresh air had given her face a pleasing colour, but it still looked plain in her mirror. She flung powder onto her nose, dragged a comb through her hair and went downstairs.

Lady Haleford, delighted to have Oliver's company,

asked endless questions. She knew many of the doctor's friends and demanded news of them.

'And what about you, Oliver? I know you're a busy man, but surely you must have some kind of social life?'

'Not a great deal—I've been too busy.'

'That Potter-Stokes woman called—brought flowers from her mother. Heaven knows why; I hardly know her. She tired me out in ten minutes. I sent her out for a walk with Amabel…'

'Miriam came here?' asked Oliver slowly, and looked at Amabel, sitting at the other side of the table.

She speared a morsel of chicken onto her fork and glanced at him quickly. 'She's very beautiful, isn't she? We had a pleasant walk and a cup of coffee—she couldn't stay long; she was on her way to visit someone. She thought the village was delightful. She was driving one of those little sports cars…' She stopped talking, aware that she was babbling.

She put the chicken in her mouth and chewed it. It tasted like ashes.

'Miriam is very beautiful,' agreed the doctor, staring at her, and then said to his aunt, 'I'm sure you must enjoy visitors from time to time, Aunt, but don't tire yourself.'

'I don't. Besides, Amabel may look like a mouse, but she can be a dragon in my defence. Bless the girl! I don't know what I would do without her.' After a moment she added, 'But of course she will go soon.'

'Not until you want me to,' said Amabel. 'And by then you will have become so much better that you won't need anyone.' She smiled across the table at the old lady. 'Mrs Twitchett has made your favourite pudding. Now, there is someone you would never wish to be without!'

'She has been with me for years. Oliver, your Mrs Bates is a splendid cook, is she not? And Bates? He still runs the place for you?'

'My right hand,' said the doctor. 'And as soon as you are well enough I shall drive you up to town and you can sample some of Mrs Bates's cooking.'

Lady Haleford needed her after-lunch nap.

'Stay for tea?' she begged him. 'Keep Amabel company. I'm sure you'll have plenty to talk about…'

'I'm afraid that I must get back.' He glanced at his watch. 'I'll say goodbye now.'

When Amabel came downstairs again he had gone.

Which was only to be expected, Amabel told herself, but she would have liked to have said goodbye. To have explained…

But how did one explain that, since one had fallen in love with someone already engaged to someone else, meeting again would be pointless. And she had lost a friend…

Later that day Lady Haleford, much refreshed by her nap, observed, 'A pity Oliver had to return so soon.' She darted a sharp glance at Amabel. 'You get on well together?'

'Yes,' said Amabel, and tried to think of something to add but couldn't.

'He's a good man.'

'Yes,' said Amabel again. 'Shall I unpick that knitting for you, Lady Haleford?'

The old lady gave her a thoughtful look. 'Yes, Amabel, and then we will have a game of cards. That will distract our thoughts.'

Amabel, surveying her future during a wakeful night, wondered what she should do, but as events turned out she had no need to concern herself with that.

It was several days after Oliver's visit that she had a phone call. She had just come in with Cyril, after his early-morning walk, and, since Nelly and Mrs Twitchett were both in the kitchen, she answered it from the phone in the hall.

'Is that you, Amabel?' Her stepfather's voice was agitated. 'Listen, you must come home at once. Your mother's ill—she's been in hospital and they've sent her home and there's no one to look after her.'

'What was wrong? Why didn't you let me know that she was ill?'

'It was only pneumonia. I thought they'd keep her there until she was back to normal. But here she is, in bed most of the day, and I've enough to do without nursing her as well.'

'Haven't you any help?'

'Oh, there's a woman who comes in to clean and cook. Don't tell me to hire a nurse; it's your duty to come home and care for your mother. And I don't want any excuses. You're her daughter, remember.'

'I'll come as soon as I can,' said Amabel, and took Cyril to the kitchen.

Mrs Twitchett looked at her pale face. 'Something wrong? Best tell us.'

It was a great relief to tell someone. Mrs Twitchett and Nelly heard her out.

'Have to go, won't you love?' Nelly's eye fell on Cyril and Oscar, side by side in front of the Aga. 'Will you take them with you?'

'Oh, Nelly, I can't. He wanted to kill them both; that's

why I left home.' Amabel sniffed back tears. 'I'll have to take them to a kennel and a cattery.'

'No need,' Mrs Twitchett said comfortably. 'They'll stay here until you know what's what. Lady Haleford loves them both, and Nelly will see to Cyril's walks. Now, just you go and tell my lady what it's all about.'

Lady Haleford, sitting up in bed, sipping her early-morning tea and wide awake for once, said immediately, 'Of course you must go home immediately. Don't worry about Cyril and Oscar. Get your mother well again and then come back to us. Will she want you to stay at home for good?'

Amabel shook her head. 'No, I don't think so. You see, my stepfather doesn't like me.'

'Then go and pack, and arrange your journey.'

CHAPTER NINE

THE doctor had driven himself back to London, deep in thought. It was obvious that Miriam had said something to Amabel which had upset her and caused her to retire into her shell of coolness. But she hadn't sounded cool in the lane. The only way to discover the reason for this was to go and see Miriam. She had probably said something as a joke and Amabel had misunderstood her...

He had gone to see her the very next evening and found her entertaining friends. As she had come to meet him he had said, 'I want to talk to you, Miriam.'

She, looking into his bland face and cold eyes, said at once, 'Oh, impossible, Oliver—we're just about to go out for the evening.'

'You can join your friends later. It is time we had a talk, Miriam, and what better time than now?'

She pouted. 'Oh, very well.' Then she smiled enchantingly. 'I was beginning to think that you had forgotten me.'

Presently, when everyone had gone, she sat down on a sofa and patted the cushion beside her. 'My dear, this is nice—just the two of us.'

The doctor sat down in a chair opposite her.

'Miriam, I have never been your dear. We have been out together, seen each other frequently at friends' houses, visited the theatre, but I must have made it plain to you that that was the extent of our friendship.' He asked abruptly, 'What did you say to Amabel?'

170

Miriam's beautiful face didn't look beautiful any more. 'So that's it—you've fallen in love with that dull girl! I guessed it weeks ago, when Dolores saw you in York. Her and her silly pets. Well, anyway, I've cooked your goose. I told her you were going to marry me, that you had helped her out of kindness and the sooner she disappeared the better...'

She stopped, because Oliver's expressionless face frightened her, and then when he got to his feet said, 'Oliver, don't go. She's no wife for you; you need some-one like me, who knows everyone worth knowing, en-tertains all the right people, dresses well.'

Oliver walked to the door. 'I need a wife who loves me and whom I love.' And he went away.

It was a pity, he reflected that his next few days were so crammed with patients, clinics and theatre lists that it was impossible for him to go and see Amabel. It was a temptation to phone her, but he knew that would be un-satisfactory. Besides, he wanted to see her face while they talked.

He drove back home and went to his study and started on the case notes piled on his desk, dismissing Amabel firmly from his thoughts.

Lady Haleford had summoned Mrs Twitchett to her bed-room and demanded to know how Amabel was to go home. 'I don't know where the girl lives. Didn't some-one tell me that she came from York?'

'And so she did, my lady; she's got an aunt there. Left home when her mother brought in a stepfather who don't like her. Somewhere near Castle Cary—she'll need to get the train to the nearest station and get a taxi or a bus, if there is one.'

Mrs Twitchett hesitated. 'And, my lady, could we keep Oscar and Cyril here while she's away? Seeing that her stepfather won't have them? Going to put them down, he was, so she left home.'

'The poor child. Arrange for William down at the village garage to drive her home. I've already told her that of course the animals must stay.'

So Amabel was driven away in the village taxi, which was just as well, for the journey home otherwise would have been long and tedious and she had had no time to plan it.

It was late afternoon when William drew up with a flourish at her home.

There were lights shining from several windows, and she could see a large greenhouse at the side of the house. As they got out of the car she glimpsed another beyond it, where the orchard had been.

The front door opened under her touch and they went into the hall as she saw her stepfather come from the kitchen.

'And about time too,' he said roughly. 'Your mother's in the sitting room, waiting to be helped to bed.'

'This is William, who brought me here by taxi,' said Amabel. 'He's going back to Aldbury, but he would like a cup of tea first.'

'I've no time to make tea…'

Amabel turned to William. 'If you'll come with me to the kitchen, I'll make it. I'll just see Mother first.'

Her mother looked up as she went into the sitting room.

'There you are, Amabel. Lovely to see you again, dear, and have you here to look after me.' She lifted her face for Amabel's kiss. 'Keith is quite prepared to let bygones be bygones and let you live here…'

'Mother, I must give the taxi driver a cup of tea. I'll be back presently and we can have a talk.'

There was no sign of her stepfather. William, waiting patiently in the kitchen, said, 'Not much of a welcome home, miss.'

Amabel warmed the teapot. 'Well, it all happened rather suddenly. Do you want a sandwich?'

William went very soon, feeling all the better for the tea and sandwiches, and the tip he had accepted reluctantly, and Amabel went back to the sitting room.

'Tell me what has been wrong with you, Mother. Do you stay up all day? The doctor visits you?'

'Pneumonia, love, and I went to hospital because Keith couldn't possibly manage on his own.'

'Have you no help?'

'Oh, yes, of course. Mrs Twist has been coming each day, to see to the house and do some of the cooking, and the hospital said a nurse would come each day once I was back home. She came for a day or two, but she and Keith had an argument and he told them that you would be looking after me. Not that I need much attention. In fact he's told Mrs Twist that she need not come any more, now that you are back home.'

'My stepfather told me that there was no one to look after you, that he had no help…'

Her mother said lightly, 'Oh, well, dear, you know what men are—and it does seem absurd for him to pay for a nurse and Mrs Twist when we have you…'

'Mother, I don't think you understand. I've got a job. I came because I thought there was no one to help you. I'll stay until you are better, but you must get Mrs Twist back and have a nurse on call if it's necessary. I'd like to go back to Aldbury as soon as possible. You see, dear, Keith doesn't like me—but you're happy with him, aren't you?'

'Yes, Amabel, I am, and I can't think why you can't get on, the pair of you. But now you are here the least you can do is make me comfortable. I'm still rather an invalid, having breakfast in bed and then a quiet day here by the fire. My appetite isn't good, but you were always a good cook. Keith likes his breakfast early, so you'll have all day to see to the house.'

She added complacently, 'Keith is doing very well already, and now he won't need to pay Mrs Twist and that nurse he can plough the money back. You'll want to unpack your things, dear. Your old room, of course. I'm not sure if the bed is made up, but you know where everything is. And when you come down we'll decide what we'll have for supper.'

Of course the bed wasn't made up; the room was chilly and unwelcoming and Amabel sat down on the bed to get her thoughts sorted out. She wouldn't stay longer than it took to get Mrs Twist back, see the doctor and arrange for a nurse to visit, whatever her stepfather said. She loved her mother, but she was aware that she wasn't really welcome, that she was just being used as a convenience by her stepfather.

She made the bed, unpacked, and went back downstairs to the kitchen. There was plenty of food in the fridge. At least she wouldn't need to go to the shops for a few days...

Her mother fancied an omelette. 'But that won't do for Keith. There's a gammon steak, and you might do some potatoes and leeks. You won't have time to make a pudding, but there's plenty of cheese and biscuits…'

'Have you been cooking, Mother?'

Her mother said fretfully, 'Well, Keith can't cook, and Mrs Twist wasn't here. Now you're home I don't need to do anything.'

The next morning Amabel went to the village to the doctor's surgery. He was a nice man, but elderly and overworked.

'You're mother is almost fit again,' he assured Amabel. 'There is no reason why she shouldn't do a little housework, as long as she rests during the day. She needs some tests done, of course, and pills, and a check-up by the practice nurse. It is a pity that her husband refuses to let her visit; he told me that you would be coming home to live and that you would see to your mother.'

'Has Mother been very ill?'

'No, no. Pneumonia is a nasty thing, but if it's dealt with promptly anyone as fit as your mother makes a quick recovery.'

'I understood from what my stepfather told me on the phone that Mother was very ill and he was without help.' She sighed. 'I came as quickly as I could, but I have a job…'

'Well, I shouldn't worry too much about that. I imagine that a few days of help from you will enable your mother to lead her usual life again. She has help, I believe?'

'My stepfather gave Mrs Twist notice…'

'Oh, dear, then you must get her back. Someone local?'

'Yes.'

'Well, it shouldn't be too difficult to persuade Mr Graham to change his mind. Once she is reinstated, you won't need to stay.'

Something which she pointed out to her stepfather later that day. 'And do please understand that I must go back to my job at the end of week. The doctor told me that Mother should be well by then. You will have to get Mrs Twist to come every day.'

'You unnatural girl.' Keith Graham's face was red with bad temper. 'It's your duty to stay here…'

'You didn't want me to stay before,' Amabel pointed out quietly. 'I'll stay for a week, so that you have time to make arrangements to find someone to help Mother.' She nodded her neat head at him. 'There was no need for me to come home. I love Mother, but you know as well as I do that you hate having me here. I can't think why you decided to ask me to come.'

'Why should I pay for a woman to come and do the housework when I've a stepdaughter I can get for nothing?'

Amabel got to her feet. If there had been something suitable to throw at him she would have thrown it, but since there wasn't she merely said, 'I shall go back at the end of the week.'

But there were several days to live through first, and although her mother consented to be more active there was a great deal to do—the cooking, fires to clean and light, coal to fetch from the shed, beds to make and the house to tidy. Her stepfather didn't lift a finger, only coming in for his meals, and when he wasn't out and about he was sitting by the fire, reading his paper.

Amabel said nothing, for eventually there was only one more day to go…

She was up early on the last morning, her bag packed, and she went down to cook the breakfast Keith demanded. He came into the kitchen as she dished up his bacon and eggs.

'Your mother's ill,' he told her. 'Not had a wink of sleep—nor me neither. You'd better go and see to her.'

'At what time is Mrs Twist coming?'

'She isn't. Haven't had time to do anything about her…'

Amabel went upstairs and found her mother in bed.

'I'm not well, Amabel. I feel awful. My chest hurts and I've got a headache. You can't leave me.'

She moaned as Amabel sat her gently against her pillows.

'I'll bring you a cup of tea, Mother, and phone the doctor.'

She went downstairs to phone and leave a message at the surgery. Her stepfather said angrily. 'No need for him. All she needs is a few days in bed. You can stay on a bit.'

'I'll stay until you get Mrs Twist back. Today, if possible.'

Her mother would eat no breakfast, so Amabel helped her to the bathroom, made the bed and tidied the room and then went back downstairs to cancel the taxi which was to have fetched her in an hour's time. She had no choice but to stay until the doctor had been and Mrs Twist was reinstated.

There was nothing much wrong with her mother, the doctor told her when he came. She was complaining about her chest, but he could find nothing wrong there, and her headache was probably due to the sleepless nights she said she was having.

He said slowly, 'She has worked herself up because you are going away. I think it would be best if you could arrange to stay for another day or two. Has Mr Graham got Mrs Twist to come in?'

'No. He told me that he had had no time. I thought I might go and see her myself. You don't think that Mother is going to be ill again?'

'As far as I can see she has recovered completely from the pneumonia, but, as I say, she has worked herself up into a state—afraid of being ill again. So if you could stay…'

'Of course I'll stay until Mother feels better.' She smiled at him. 'Thank you for coming, Doctor.'

He gave her a fatherly pat. He thought she looked a bit under the weather herself he must remember to call in again in a day or two.

Amabel unpacked her bag, assured her mother that she would stay until Mrs Twist could come, and went to see that lady…

Mrs Twist was a comfortable body with a cheerful face. She listened to Amabel in silence and then said, 'Well, I'm sorry to disoblige you, but I've got my old mum coming today for a week. Once she's gone home again I'll go each day, same as before. Staying long, are you?'

'I meant to go back to my job this morning, but Mother asked me to stay until you could arrange to come back.' She couldn't help adding, 'You will come, won't you?'

'Course I will, love. And a week goes by quick enough. Nice having your ma to chat to.'

Amabel said, yes, it was, and thought how nice that would have been. Only there was precious little time to chat, and when she did sit down for an hour to talk it was her mother who did the talking: about how good Keith was to her, the new clothes she had bought, the holiday they intended to take before the spring brought all the extra work in the greenhouses, how happy she was... But she asked no questions of Amabel.

She said, 'I expect you've got a good job, darling. You were always an independent girl. You must tell me about it one day...I was telling you about our holiday...'

It was strange how the days seemed endless, despite the fact that she had little leisure. She had written a note to Lady Haleford, saying that she would return as soon as she could arrange help for her mother. Since her mother seemed quite well again, it was now just a question of waiting for Mrs Twist's mother to go home. Her mother, however, was disinclined to do much.

'There's no need for me to do anything,' she had said, half laughing, 'while you're here.'

'Mrs Twist does everything when she comes?'

'Oh, yes. Although I do the cooking. But you're such a good cook, love, and it gives you something to do.'

One more day, thought Amabel. She had missed Cyril and Oscar. She had missed Oliver too, but she tried not to think of him—and how could she miss someone she hardly ever saw?

Amabel had been gone for almost two weeks before the doctor felt free to take time off and go to Aldbury. His aunt greeted him with pleasure. 'But you've come to see Amabel? Well, she's not here. The child had to go home; her mother was ill. She expected to be gone for a week. Indeed, she wrote and told me she would be coming back. And then I had another letter saying that she would have to stay another week. Can't think why she didn't telephone.' She added, 'Mrs Twitchett phoned and a man answered her. Very abrupt, she said, told her that Amabel wasn't available.'

It was already late afternoon, and the doctor had a list early on the following morning, a clinic in the afternoon and private patients to see. To get into his car and go to Amabel was something he wanted to do very much, but that wasn't possible; it wouldn't be possible for two days.

He thought about phoning her, but it might make matters worse and in any case there was a great deal he could do. He went back home, sat down at his desk and picked up the phone; he could find out what was happening...

Mrs Graham's doctor was helpful. There was no reason, he said over the phone, why Amabel should stay at home. She had told him very little, but he sensed that her mother's illness had been used to get her to return there. 'If there is anything I can do?' he offered.

'No, no, thanks. I wanted to be sure that her mother really needs her.'

'There's no reason why she shouldn't walk out of the house, but there may be circumstances which prevent her doing that.'

The doctor picked up the phone and heard Miss Parsons' firm voice at the other end.

'I hoped that you might be back...' He talked at some length and finally put the phone down and went in search of Bates. After that, all he had to do was to possess his soul in patience until he could go to Amabel.

He set off early in the morning two days later, with Tiger beside him and Bates to see him on his way.

Life was going to be quite interesting, Bates thought as he went in search of his wife.

Once free of London and the suburbs, Oliver drove fast. He hoped that he had thought of everything. A lot was going to happen during the next few hours, and nothing must go wrong.

It was raining when he reached the house, and now that the apple orchard had gone the house looked bare and lonely and the greenhouses looked alien. He drove round the side of the house, got out with Tiger, opened the kitchen door and went in.

Amabel was standing at the sink, peeling potatoes. She was wearing an apron several sizes too large for her and her hair hung in a plait over one shoulder. She looked pale and tired and utterly forlorn.

This was no time for explanations; the doctor strode to the sink, removed the potato and the knife from her hands and folded his arms around her. He didn't speak, he didn't kiss her, just held her close. He was holding her when Mr Graham came in.

'Who are you?' he demanded.

Oliver gave Amabel a gentle push. 'Go and get your coat and pack your things.' Something in his voice made her disentangle herself from his embrace and look up at his quiet face. He smiled down at her. 'Run along, darling.'

She went upstairs and all she could think of then was that he had called her darling. She should have taken him into the sitting room, where her mother was… Instead she got her case from the wardrobe and began to pack it, and, that done, picked up her coat and went downstairs.

The doctor had watched her go and then turned to Mr

Graham, who began in a blustering voice, 'I don't know why you're here, whoever you are—'

'I'll tell you,' said Oliver gently. 'And when I've finished perhaps you will take me to Amabel's mother.'

She looked up in surprise as they went into the sitting room.

'He's come for Amabel,' said Mr Graham, looking daggers at Oliver. 'I don't know what things are coming to when your daughter's snatched away and you so poorly, my dear.'

'Your doctor tells me that you are fully recovered, Mrs Graham, and I understand that you have adequate help in the house…'

'I'm very upset—' began Mrs Graham. Glancing at the quiet man standing there, she decided that a show of tears wouldn't help. 'After all, a daughter should take care of her mother…'

'And do the housework and the cooking?' From the look of her Amabel has been doing that, and much more besides.

'She ought to be grateful,' growled Mr Graham, 'having a home to come to.'

'Where she is expected to do the chores, cook and clean and shop?' asked Oliver coolly. 'Mr Graham, you make me tired—and extremely angry.'

'Who is going to see to things when she's gone?'

'I'm sure there is adequate help to be had in the village.' He turned away as Amabel came into the room. 'Everything is satisfactorily arranged,' he told her smoothly. 'If you will say goodbye, we will go.'

Amabel supposed that presently she would come to her senses and ask a few sensible questions, even ask for an explanation of the unexpected events taking place around her, but all she said was, 'Yes, Oliver,' in a meek voice, and went to kiss her mother and bid her stepfather a frosty goodbye.

She said tartly, 'There's a lot I could say to you, but I won't,' and she walked out of the room with Oliver. Tiger was in the kitchen, and somehow the sight of him brought her to her senses.

'Oliver—' she began.

'We'll talk as we go,' he told her comfortably, and popped her into the car, settled Tiger in the back seat and got in beside her. Presently he said in a matter-of-fact voice, 'We shall be home in time for supper. We'll stop at Aldbury and get Oscar and Cyril.'

'But where are we going?'

'Home.'

'I haven't got a home,' said Amabel wildly.

'Yes, you have.' He rested a hand on her knee for a moment. 'Darling, *our* home.'

And after that he said nothing for quite some time, which left Amabel all the time in the world to think. Chaotic thoughts which were interrupted by him saying in a matter-of-fact voice, 'Shall we stop for a meal?' and, so saying, stopping before a small pub, well back from the road, with a lane on one side of it.

It was dim and cosy inside, with a handful of people at the bar, and they had their sandwiches and coffee against a background of cheerful talk, not speaking much themselves.

When they had finished the doctor said, 'Shall we walk a little way up the lane with Tiger?'

They walked arm in arm and Amabel tried to think of something to say—then decided that there was no need; it was as though they had everything that mattered.

But not quite all, it seemed, for presently, when they stopped to look at the view over a gate, Oliver turned her round to face him.

'I love you. You must know that, my dear. I've loved you since I first saw you, although I didn't know it at once. And then you seemed so young, and anxious to make a life for yourself; I'm so much older than you...'

Amabel said fiercely, 'Rubbish. You're just the right age. I don't quite understand what has happened, but that doesn't matter...' She looked up into his face. 'You have always been there, and I can't imagine a world without you...'

He kissed her then, and the wintry little lane was no longer a lane but heaven.

In a little while they got back into the car, and Amabel, with a little gentle prompting, told Oliver of her two weeks with her mother.

'How did you know I was there?' she wanted to know, and when he had told her she said, 'Oliver, Miriam Potter-Stokes said that you were going to marry her. I know now that wasn't true, but why did she say that?' She paused. 'Did you think that you would before you met me?'

'No, my darling. I took her out once or twice, and we met often at friends' houses. But it never entered my head to want to marry her. I think that she looked upon me, as she would look upon any other man in my position, as a possible source of a comfortable life.'

'That's all right, then,' said Amabel.

She looked so radiantly happy that he said, 'My dearest, if you continue to look like that I shall have to stop and kiss you.'

An unfulfilled wish since they were on a motorway.

There was no doubt about the warmth of their welcome at Lady Haleford's cottage. They were met in the hall by Mrs Twitchett, Nelly, Oscar and Cyril, and swept into the drawing room, where Lady Haleford was sitting.

She said at once, 'Amabel, I am so happy to see you again, although I understand from Oliver that this visit is a brief one. Still, we shall see more of each other, I have no doubt. I shall miss you and Oscar and Cyril. Oliver shall bring you here whenever he has the time, but of course first of all he must take you to see his mother. You'll marry soon?'

Amabel went pink and Oliver answered for her. 'Just as soon as it can be arranged, Aunt.'

'Good. I shall come to the wedding, and so will Mrs Twitchett and Nelly. Now we will have tea...'

An hour later, once more in the car, Amabel said, 'You haven't asked me...'

He glanced at her briefly, smiling. 'Oh, but I will. Once we are alone and quiet. I've waited a long time, dear love, but I'm not going to propose to you driving along a motorway.'

'I don't know where you live...'

'In a quiet street of Regency houses. There's a garden with a high wall, just right for Oscar and Cyril, and Bates and his wife look after me and Tiger, and now they will look after you three as well.'

'Oh—is it a big house?'

'No, no, just a nice size for a man and his wife and children to live in comfortably.'

Which gave Amabel plenty to think about, staring out of the window into the dark evening through rose-coloured spectacles, soothed by Oliver's quiet voice from time to time and the gentle fidgets of the three animals on the back seat.

She hadn't been sure of what to expect, and when she got out of the car the terrace of houses looked elegant and dignified, with handsome front doors and steps leading to their basements. But Oliver gave her time to do no more than glimpse at them. Light streamed from an open door and someone stood waiting by it.

'We're home,' said Oliver, and took her arm and tucked it under his.

She had been feeling anxious about Bates, but there was no need; he beamed at her like a kindly uncle, and Mrs Bates behind him shook her hand, her smile as wide as her husband's.

'You will wish to go straight to the drawing room, sir,' said Bates, and opened a door with a flourish.

As they went in, Aunt Thisbe came to meet them.

'Didn't expect to see me, did you, Amabel?' she asked briskly. 'But Oliver is a stickler for the conventions, and quite right too. You will have to bear with me until you are married.'

She offered a cheek to be kissed, and then again for Oliver.

'You two will want to talk, but just for a moment there is something I need to do…' he murmured.

Aunt Thisbe made for the door. 'I'll see about those animals of yours,' she said, and closed the door firmly behind her.

The doctor unbuttoned Amabel's coat, tossed it on a chair and took her in his arms. 'This is a proposal—but first, this…' he bent his head and kissed her, taking his time about it.

'Will you marry me, Amabel?' he asked her.

'Will you always kiss me like that?' she asked him.

'Always and for ever, dearest.'

'Then I'll marry you,' said Amabel, 'because I like being kissed like that. Besides, I love you.'

There was only one answer to that…

THE PLAYBOY'S MISTRESS

by

Kim Lawrence

*Kim Lawrence is already an
established star of Modern Romance™.
Now we're delighted*

*to bring you her first
Medical Romance™!*

Coming soon:

Partners by Contract
by
Kim Lawrence

*Don't miss this intensely
emotional story . . .*

CHAPTER ONE

DARCY slid her pink feet—the bath had been *very* hot—into a pair of slippers and padded through the quiet flat to the phone. It was nice to have the flat to herself for once. Jennifer was a great flatmate, but she thought silence was something you filled with noise—preferably the loud, throbbing variety! Music-wise the two were not compatible.

Propping the phone against her ear, Darcy hitched the towel wrapped sarong-style, around her slender body a little tighter and waited for someone to pick up. She was just about to hang up when Jack Alexander answered the phone.

'Hi, Dad,' she called cheerfully down the line. 'Is Mum around?' She eased her bottom onto the table-top, anticipating a nice long natter.

'I'm afraid you can't speak to your mother, Darcy...she...she isn't here...'

It wasn't the news that her hyperactive mother wasn't at home that struck Darcy as strange—her community-minded parent was on more village committees than she had fingers to count them on—it was the peculiar note that bordered on panic in her phlegmatic stepfather's voice.

Her post-warm-bath, pre-glass-of-wine, mellow holiday mood evaporated. Darcy wasn't psychic, but she did know Jack, and she had the nasty suspicion that the icy fingers tap-dancing up her spine knew what they were about.

Her heart was thudding as she lightly asked, 'What is it tonight? Practice for the carol concert or the church roof committee...?'

Jack would tell her what was up in his own good time—he wasn't the sort of man who could be hurried. An affectionate smile briefly curved her lips as her thoughts rested on the man who had married her mother—Darcy loved him to bits.

Darcy had been five and her elder brother, Nick, seven when Jack entered their lives. After a couple of years Clare had come along and then, much to everyone's surprise, the unplanned but much loved twins. The Alexanders were a tight-knit family.

'Neither,' came back the strangled response.

The line between Darcy's straight, well-defined, darkish eyebrows deepened; Jack sounded perilously close to tears. This, she reminded herself, is the man who delivered his own grandchild in the back of a Land Rover without breaking sweat. She immediately ditched tactful reticence in favour of the upfront approach.

'What's up, Dad?' she asked bluntly.

'It's your mother…'

Anxiety grabbed Darcy's quivering tummy muscles in an icy fist; eyes wide in alarm, she shot upright from her perch on the console table. All sorts of awful scenarios ran through her head and with some trepidation she put the most alarming of these into words.

'Is Mum *ill*…?'

'No…no, nothing like that; she's…she's…'

A noisy sigh of relief expelled, Darcy slid to the floor.

'She's gone away.'

'Away as in…?'

'She's spending Christmas in a…a *retreat* in Cornwall.'

'But that's the other end of the country!' Darcy heard herself exclaim stupidly—as if the *where* mattered! It was the how and why that were infinitely more important. Her spinning head struggled to make sense of what she was hearing and failed miserably. No matter what else was wrong in her life, there had always been a solid, reliable, constant…Mum… No, this just didn't make sense—no sense at all!

'It wouldn't matter if it was down the road; they don't even have a phone,' her stepfather came back in a heavy, doom-laden tone. 'I don't know what I'm going to do! Everyone's asking after her. She's making the costumes for the school Nativity play, the WI want two-hundred mince pies by Thursday… How do you make mince pies, Darcy…?' he asked pathetically.

'We've got more important things than mince pies to worry about.' As if he needed reminding of that! 'Have you any idea at all why has she done this, Dad? Did you have a row or something?'

'No, nothing like that; she'd been a bit quiet lately…but you're right; it must be my fault.'

'*Nonsense!*' Darcy meant it. The day she found a man who was half as marvellous as Jack Alexander she was going to stick to him like superglue!

'Apparently she needs time alone. Are you still there…? Darcy…Darcy…?'

'Sorry, Dad, I dropped the phone.' There was a distinctly surreal feel about the entire situation. People like Cathy Alexander didn't suffer from identity crises, they didn't walk out on their family with no proper explanation!

'God, Darcy, what am I going to do…?' She could hear the escalating panic in her stepfather's gruff voice. 'Sam, Beth and the children arrive from the States on Friday. It's too late to put them off.'

'No, you mustn't do that!' Darcy replied swiftly. Since Jack's daughter from his first marriage had moved to the States the opportunities for Jack to see her and his only grandchild were few and far between.

'Nick rang to say to expect him at the end of the week, and no doubt Clare will show up some time.'

Darcy permitted herself a wry smile—it was so like Clare not to commit herself to a date.

'Your grandmother is likely to drop in on us at any moment. Can you imagine what she's going to make of this...? At the last count we were doing Christmas dinner for fifteen people that I know of, and the Aga's gone out and I can't light it! I never did have the knack with the darned thing like your mother has...'

Darcy could hear him gulp down the line. She took a deep breath; desperate circumstances required drastic solutions.

'Don't panic,' she instructed her harassed stepfather with shameless hypocrisy. 'If I pack now I should be there about... There shouldn't be too much traffic at this time of night, should there...?'

'Your skiing holiday, Darcy!'

Darcy recognised a token protest when she heard it.

'I know how much you've been looking forward to it...'

Darcy allowed herself a final indulgent moment to wistfully visualise crisp snow-covered slopes, twinkling mountain villages and the hunky outdoor type she had been destined to meet amidst the après-ski *gluwein* before she squared her slight shoulders.

'With my luck I'd probably have come back with several limbs in plaster.' You had to be philosophical about these things.

Did her cancellation insurance cover family crises caused by the parent of the policy-holder unexpectedly needing to find herself...? Somehow Darcy didn't think so.

'You can't cancel,' Jennifer insisted a little later that evening as she sat on Darcy's bed. Darcy smiled and continued to replace the skiing gear in her suitcase with clothes more suited to Christmas in a remote corner of the Yorkshire

Dales. 'You've been looking forward to it all year. I don't see why it has to be you; why can't Clare go home to help?'

Darcy laughed. 'I don't think domesticity is really Clare's scene,' she responded wryly. Her beautiful, talented and slightly spoilt half-sister had a heart of gold, but she needed therapy to recover from a broken fingernail.

'And it's yours…?'

Darcy couldn't deny this. 'I'll have to learn, won't I?'

Jennifer, seeing her friend wasn't to be dissuaded, sighed. 'Well, I think you're being a fool.'

Darcy shrugged. 'So what's new?'

Jennifer's expression darkened. '*That*,' she said angrily, 'wasn't your fault!'

'Tell that to Michael's wife and children.'

This year Reece Erskine wasn't taking any chances. He was going to lose himself in the wilds of deepest, darkest Yorkshire until the so-called *festive* season was well and truly over!

So he didn't like Christmas… Why was it considered a crime when a man refused to participate in the manic few weeks that culminated in several days of gluttony in the company of people you avoided for the rest of the year?

Of course, the most insupportable part was the fact that everyone was so *understanding*. He refused to put on a paper party hat and suddenly he was failing to come to terms with his loss. He'd had it with pop psychology, no matter how well-intentioned!

After the debacle last year, when the girlfriend—and he used the term in the loosest possible sense—of the moment, armed with champagne, sympathy and a criminally sexy nightie, had tracked him down to the hotel he'd holed up in, he wasn't leaving any clues. She'd proved to be a scarily tenacious woman! She'd had her revenge, though; she'd sold the story of their so-called 'stormy relationship' to a tabloid.

Whether he would have been quite so keen to avail himself of Greg's hospitality if he'd known that the renovations of the big Victorian pile had been at such an early stage was questionable, but that was academic now he was here.

'God, man, you're getting soft,' he told himself in disgust. His deep voice sounded eerily loud in the empty lofty-ceilinged room. 'What's a rat or two between friends...? A bit of good old-fashioned frontier spirit is what's called for here. Who wants to call Room Service when he could pump up the old Primus stove?' His tone lacked conviction even to his own ears.

Having unrolled his sleeping bag, he made his way into the overgrown garden that stretched down towards what sounded like a river in full spate. He tightened the collar of his leather jacket around his neck; it was almost as cold out here as inside.

From the bone-chilling temperature in the old place even after he'd lit that smoky fire in the cavernous grate, he suspected he'd need to invest in a few thick blankets to supplement his state-of-the-art bedding, which might well live up to its press and be able to withstand a night in the North Pole, but the Yorkshire Dales in December—forget it!

He looked around in distaste at the bleak landscape. God, the place was so *grey*—grey and extremely wet! It was baffling when you considered how many people waxed lyrical about the area.

The periphery of his vision picked on something that broke the dismal grey monotony. Something suspiciously like a human voice raised in song drifted across from the general direction of that fleeting glimpse of scarlet. Reece immediately felt indignant. Greg had sworn on his very alive grandmother's grave that Reece wouldn't see another human being unless he wanted to—and even then it wouldn't be easy!

Reece had come away with the distinct and very welcome impression that the natives were hostile to strangers.

Eager to defend his solitude against intruders, Reece followed the melody to its source, wrecking his shiny new boots in the process. He discovered the clear, pure sounds actually came from just beyond the boundary of the sprawling grounds. He could no longer eject the songbird, but his curiosity was piqued.

His days as a choirboy enabled him to correctly identify the number as *The Coventry Carol*. How very seasonal; how very corny, he thought, his lip curling.

Acting on impulse—which wasn't something he made a habit of—Reece swung himself up onto the lower bare branch of a convenient oak tree. The identity of the owner of the bell-like tones was going to bug him unless he satisfied his curiosity. Besides, if he was going to be carolled on a regular basis it was as well to be forewarned.

From his lofty vantage point he could now see into what must be the garden of the sprawling stone-grey house that sat at the bottom of the lane that led up to Greg's investment.

In the summer the green-painted summer-house was a magical place, where wisteria tumbled with vigorous old-fashioned roses up the clapboarded walls and over the roof. In Darcy's childhood it had been the place her knight in shining armour was going to propose. However, the romance was purely a seasonal thing; in the winter it became a cold, unfriendly place her childish imagination had peopled with ghouls and similar nasties—it was still private, though, hence the bit of impromptu choir practice.

Her voice, never in her view solo material at the best of times, was every bit as rusty as she'd expected.

'I can't do it!' she groaned.

That new vicar, she decided darkly, was a dangerous man, who had shamelessly used his spaniel eyes and a judicious amount of moral blackmail until she had almost been falling over herself to volunteer to stand in for her musical mother and perform the solo in the Christmas carol concert.

It wasn't until she'd been halfway down the lane from the church that the full horror of what she'd done had hit Darcy. She'd suffered from terminal stage fright since that awful occasion in infants' school when, after she'd been given the linchpin role of the donkey in the nativity play, the strain had proved too much! She'd frozen and had held up proceedings until she had been carried bodily off the makeshift stage.

What's the worst that could happen...? What's a bit of public humiliation between friends...?

A loud noise like a pistol shot interrupted her gloomy contemplation of her future as a figure of fun. If she hadn't automatically taken a startled step backwards the large individual who along with a piece of rotten branch had fallen at her feet would have landed directly on top of her.

As it was, the summer-house didn't escape so lightly—the jagged end of the branch penetrated the roof, ripping off several tiles, and travelled downwards, gouging a nasty big hole in the side of the structure. But at that moment Darcy's concerns were reserved for the man lying in a crumpled heap at her feet.

She dropped down on her knees beside him; phrases like 'recovery position' and 'clear airway' were running through her head. Despite the first aid course she'd completed early that year, she felt completely unprepared to cope with an actual emergency now that one had fallen at her feet.

'Please, please, don't be dead,' she whispered, pressing her fingers to the pulse spot on his neck. To her immense relief, she immediately felt a steady, reassuringly strong beat.

Grunting with effort, Reece rolled onto his back. For only the third time in his life he was literally seeing stars. He ruthlessly gathered his drifting senses, the halo vanished and he realised he wasn't seeing an angel but a golden-headed schoolboy. Given the clear soprano of his singing voice, the lad had a surprisingly low, pleasing speaking voice.

'I'll do my level best,' the leather-clad figure promised, much to Darcy's relief.

'I live just over there.' The scarf she wore wrapped twice around her neck prevented her turning her head to indicate the overgrown path behind them. 'I'll go and get help.'

Darcy froze with shock when a large hand curled firmly around her forearm.

'No, don't do that.' He hadn't figured out the extent of his injuries yet, and if the boy disappeared who knew if he'd ever come back or get help? The kid looked scared half to death.

'Give me a hand to get up.'

He seemed determined to get up with or without her help, so Darcy shrugged philosophically and helpfully slid her arm under the shoulders of the tall, dark-headed figure.

It wasn't as easy as she'd expected; he might be lean, but her unexpected visitor was endowed with a generous share of muscle and there wasn't a single useful roll of excess flesh or fat to grab onto.

'Ahh...!'

The involuntary grunt of pain that escaped his firmly clamped lips made Darcy jerk back with a squeamish squeak.

'Did I hurt you...? I...I'm *so* sorry.'

If all he'd done was bust his shoulder he'd got off pretty lightly. Reece supported his injured arm with his healthy arm and hauled himself upright, ignoring the sharp, burning pain in his shoulder as best he could. Nostrils flared, he spared the hovering boy a brief glance. The kid had a soft round face, snub nose and big blue eyes, and he looked as if he was going to throw up—which made two of them.

'Not your fault,' he gritted. The knowledge that he couldn't blame anyone but himself for his present situation wasn't doing anything to improve Reece's frayed temper.

'Should you be doing that?' Darcy wondered fretfully, watching the tall figure get slowly to his feet.

The stranger ignored her query. 'Listen, I think I might have hurt my shoulder.'

From where Darcy was standing there didn't seem much 'might' about it. It was obvious he was in pain; it was also obvious he was more good-looking than any man had a right to be.

Her slightly awed gaze was tinged with vague resentment as she took in the impressive overall effect of the combination of square jaw, sharp high cheekbones, wide, firm mouth and straight, strong, patrician nose. Even if you took that rich, thick dark hair complete with auburn highlights and those stunning, thickly lashed green eyes out of the equation, he was knockout material; with them he became almost *too* handsome.

Those spectacular eyes were at that moment slightly dazed as he looked around, obviously trying to get his bearings.

'I've got a phone in my pocket.' Lifting his arm gingerly from his chest, Reece nodded towards the breast pocket of his leather jacket. 'Could you fish it out for me…?'

The kid was looking at him as if he had two heads, which, given the cautionary tales that were drummed into the youth of today about strangers, was hardly surprising. He attempted a strained smile.

'I'm quite harmless.' He used the tone he normally reserved for frightened animals—perhaps it would work on kids too?

Darcy almost laughed at this preposterous claim—no man with a mouth like his could be classed as harmless! She withdrew her gaze from the said mouth with some difficulty—it was, after all, rude to stare.

She took a deep breath; she felt oddly reluctant to touch him, which was strange because she usually had to repress her naturally tactile nature—men especially could take a spontaneous hug the wrong way, as she'd learnt to her cost!

'Inside pocket.'

Darcy swallowed and for some reason got a lot clumsier. Her nostrils twitched, and her tummy muscles went all quivery, her twitching nose detected a faint whiff of expensive masculine cologne, but most of all she got a noseful of freshly scrubbed *male*. He felt warm, and despite the sub-zero temperatures she suddenly felt uncomfortably hot; she averted her flushed face as her fingers skated lightly over the surface of a broad, solid chest.

The sad thing was this was the closest she'd been to a male since Michael—*How sad is that?* Perhaps I'll be reduced to tripping up sexy strangers so I can grope them, she reflected with an angry self-derisive sniff.

It was a relief when she finally retrieved the phone and held it up for his inspection. They could both see straight away that the mangled mess was never going to work again.

The stranger swore; considering the circumstances, Darcy thought he was quite restrained. She had no inkling that he was restraining himself in deference to the presence of an impressionable youth.

'You must have fallen on it,' she said sympathetically.

He turned his head stiffly, his green eyes gazing directly down into her face. 'Brilliant deduction,' he observed nastily.

Darcy coloured angrily; so what if it hadn't been the

most intelligent thing in the world to say? *She* wasn't the one who'd been stupid enough to climb up a rotten tree. Which reminded her. Why had he been climbing a tree…? His clothes, which she had noticed straight off were extremely expensive-looking, were not what she'd call accepted tree-climbing gear.

Some people never lost touch with the inner child, but somehow she didn't think this man was one of them—in fact, it was hard to imagine that he'd *ever* been a child. He gave the impression of having emerged into this world complete with cynicism and raw sex appeal.

Reece bit back the blighting retort that hovered on the tip of his tongue and forced himself to smile placatingly at the boy.

'Are there any grown-ups around, lad…? Your parents…?'

Lad! Darcy blinked incredulously. 'What did you…?'

She'd be the first to admit that she was no raving beauty, but although she'd never brought traffic to a halt, or reduced a crowded room to awed appreciative silence like Clare, she had turned a head or two in her time. *Lad…!* Nobody had ever implied she was butch before!

True, she hadn't put on any make-up this morning, and add to that the fact the yellow cagoule she wore was a cast-off from one of the twins and was thickly padded enough to disguise her unchildlike curves completely, then just *maybe* his mistake was understandable; especially if he'd fallen on his head.

Her lips pursed; for a moment she couldn't actually decide whether or not she was insulted, then her ready sense of humour came to her rescue.

I've always said I don't want concessions made for my sex, that I don't want to be treated as a sex object—well, now's my chance!

Having three brothers, she'd learnt at an early age it was better to laugh at herself before they had the chance.

'My dad's at home.' She couldn't resist the naughty impulse to raise her normal husky tone to her approximation of a reedy boyish treble.

She gestured towards the path half-hidden by a massive holly bush smothered with red berries. 'It's not far; can you manage?' she wondered, her eyes travelling with an increasingly doubtful frown up and down his tall frame; underneath that naturally olive skin-tone he didn't look a good colour.

'You'll be the first to know if I can't,' came the dry response.

'But your head's bleeding.'

'It's nothing.'

Darcy shrugged; if he wanted to play the macho hard man it was nothing to her.

'Be careful of the...' Darcy waited like a worried little mother hen as her unlikely charge avoided the motley collection of dirty boots, Wellingtons and trainers which always seemed to breed in the back porch. 'Dad!' she yelled lustily, preceding him into the rustic surroundings of the kitchen.

If he hadn't been clutching his arm Reece would have clutched his head—the kid's piercing tone had increased the throb in his head to the point where he found it difficult to focus.

Her three brothers were already in the kitchen, and her yell brought Jack in matter of seconds.

'Good God, what's happened...?' her stepfather gasped, staring in horror at the blood smeared all over her jacket.

'Don't worry, it's not mine,' Darcy assured him.

The stranger swayed gently; it was a development that alarmed Darcy. 'It's his,' she explained, placing a supportive hand beneath the tall man's elbow. 'Part of that oak tree next door fell through the roof of the summer-house.' She gently led her white-faced charge properly inside.

Reece bided his time, waiting for the tidal waves of nausea to pass.

'I've been telling the new owner's agent since the summer that thing was dangerous!' Jack exclaimed. 'Are you sure you're all right, Darcy?' He scrutinised her healthy-looking, pink-cheeked face worriedly. 'Hurt anywhere?'

'I'm fine.' Darcy unwrapped the looped scarf from around her throat.

'And you, Mr...?'

The dazed-looking stranger with blood running down the side of his face closed his eyes and leaned heavily against the wall. An anxious Jack looked to Darcy to supply the information.

Her shoulders lifted. 'Don't ask me—I've no idea who he is.'

'How come you were in the summer-house with a guy and you don't know his name?' Nick wondered, regarding the stranger with a suspicious light in his hostile blue eyes.

'I wasn't in the summer-house; I was outside.' Darcy kept her impatience in check—Nick always chose all the wrong moments to play the protective big brother; he was the most infuriatingly inconsistent person she knew.

'Doing what?' Nick persisted doggedly.

Darcy rolled her eyes in exasperation before returning her attention to the man beside her. 'You should sit down,' she said in soft aside to the object of her brother's suspicions.

'Give me a minute,' the stranger responded tersely, resisting her efforts to point him in the right direction. Darcy was a strong girl but she knew right away that moving this man against his will was beyond her capabilities.

'Harry, Charlie, could you give me a hand?' she called to her younger brothers.

The twins shook their identical heads in unison.

'We'd like to, but…' Harry began.

'There's blood…' Charlie completed with a shudder of disgust.

Darcy, in no mood on this occasion to see the amusing side of a pair of strapping, beefy specimens who came over 'funny' at the sight of blood, gave a snort of exasperation. 'You're hopeless, the pair of you!'

'Wimps,' Charlie agreed cheerfully.

Harry nodded his agreement. 'Maybe he's one of those contractors working on the Hall.'

'Nah! They've all gone home for the holiday,' his identical twin pointed out. 'Besides, does he look like a builder to you…? He's obviously loaded.'

Darcy was inclined to agree with Charlie, but she couldn't help but reflect that the injured stranger looked more than physically capable of the odd bit of manual labour. Her mind drifted back to the way the hard, muscular contours of his lean torso and broad chest had felt— With a muffled snort of dismay she brought her reflections to an abrupt halt mid-drool.

The tiny sound drew Jack's concerned attention.

She flushed uncomfortably, shook her head and silently mouthed 'I'm fine', which she was, if you discounted the fact she was sleazing over a total stranger who was bleeding on their kitchen floor. She grabbed a clean tea towel from the dresser drawer to stem the flow.

'Maybe he's the bloke that bought the place,' Darcy heard Harry suggest.

Reece, who was feeling less awful, noticed a little hazily that the notion seemed to afford amusement all round.

'My God, mate, but you've been done,' the instigator of the theory sniggered, digging his twin in the ribs.

Darcy gave a long-suffering sigh. 'I hardly think now is the right time for a cross-examination,' she told them repressively.

At first it had felt as if the room was full of a lot of people. On closer examination Reece now realised there were actually only four besides himself and the choirboy, all male. The two youngest, despite being almost his own height, were scarcely more than boys, and either they were identical twins or he was seeing double.

'Shut up!' With enviable lung power the diminutive figure beside him silenced the assembly. 'Let's not get sidetracked here; it doesn't matter who he is—he's had an accident. Charlie, go get the First Aid kit.'

'I don't know…'

Darcy, wise to male helplessness ploys, was ahead of him. 'First shelf down in the bathroom.' She turned to the younger—by five minutes—of her twin brothers. 'Harry, get the dogs out of here.' With a lot of noisy encouragement the dogs eventually removed themselves from the chairs.

Reece remained mildly disorientated while his youthful rescuer continued to throw out a steady stream of orders as if they were going out of fashion to everyone, including himself. The hell of it was he found himself obeying the kid and meekly sitting down in the larger of the two armchairs. The small figure was arguing with the dark-haired male around his own age.

'How should I know why he was up a tree? Maybe he's a tree surgeon…?' Her elder brother had a very suspicious nature and seemed to have jumped to the deeply embarrassing and bizarre conclusion that she was trying to cover up some sort of secret assignation.

Darcy couldn't help but wistfully wonder what life was like with a few secret assignations—alas, unless she could rid herself of her wholesome image and get herself a bit of glamour it seemed unlikely that she would ever find out!

'My name's Reece Erskine.' So much for anonymity.

Nobody started in recognition at the sound of his name— Maybe I'm not as famous as I think, he wondered. A self-deprecating little smile made his mobile lips quiver as he relaxed a little.

'I don't need to trouble you; if I could just use your phone...' His firm words only elicited a few fleeting glances of benevolent dismissal.

Reece wasn't used to having his opinion dismissed and he found the novel experience irritating. It was even more irritating that he didn't have enough functioning brain cells to demonstrate to them how very much in control he really was.

'Shouldn't we call an ambulance?' a worried Jack Alexander appealed to his eldest stepchildren.

'Was he out long?' Nick asked his sister.

'I'm not sure...'

'I wasn't unconscious at all.' Reece's jaw tightened; he might just as well have spoken to the brick wall beside him for the notice anyone was taking.

'It would probably be quicker to take him to Casualty ourselves.' Darcy held out her hand expectantly as young Charlie returned conspicuously empty-handed.

'I can't find it.'

She gave a sigh of exasperation and glared up at her tall young brother. 'Do I have to do everything myself?' she wondered witheringly.

To Reece's amazement, the big guy shifted uncomfortably and looked sheepish before he joined his twin at the far end of the room. He was finding the family dynamics of this noisy household deeply confusing. Maybe it's me...? Maybe I'm concussed, he thought. He closed his eyes and the room continued to spin.

Darcy took the stairs at the far end of the room two steps at a time. She tore along the narrow upper hallway, shedding her layers as she went—the First Aid kit was exactly where she'd said it would be. Why couldn't men find something when it was right under their noses…?

'Learnt helplessness,' she snorted in knowledgeable disgust, and Mum let them get away with it, she thought disapprovingly as she rapidly retraced her steps. Her respect for what her mother accomplished on the home front had increased by leaps and bounds since she'd arrived home.

She ripped the scrunchy thing that had slid down to the slippery end of her shiny pony-tail free and shoved it in her pocket before she gave her head a little shake and lifted her fine hair free of the collar of her ribbed polo-necked sweater.

'I'll just clean up this head wound first.' He endured her cleaning the small but deep head wound with stoicism. 'I think it might be your collar-bone.' Darcy bent over the chair, bringing her face almost on a level with his.

He didn't know where she'd come from but he wasn't complaining; she was a major improvement on all the brawn. He watched her narrow, slender hands as she set about her task. They were nice hands, and it was an even nicer face. A roundish face with a pointy little chin, a hint of sultriness about the full lower lip…? No more than a hint, he decided, revising his original estimate as she raised the big blue kitten eyes to his face and murmured… 'Sorry. I broke mine once,' she continued in a slightly husky, oddly familiar voice. 'I know how much it hurts. I think it'll be less painful if it's supported, but if I hurt you too much, yell.'

'I will.'

Darcy's eyes lifted; under the scrutiny of those wide-spaced blue eyes, Reece got that strange feeling of familiarity again as she gave an unconvinced little smile.

'A fine little nurse our Darcy is,' the fatherly-looking figure remarked fondly.

Darcy; where had he heard that before…?

'They'll want to X-ray you in the hospital, I expect.'

She was halfway through tying the supportive sling gently around his neck before a stunned Reece saw what had been blindingly obvious all along.

The schoolboy and the slender, but very obviously *feminine* blonde were one and the same person!

'You're a girl!' he blurted out unthinkingly.

The note of resentment in the shocked cry made Darcy's lips twitch and her stepfather's expression grow concerned.

'Perhaps I ought to call that ambulance.'

Darcy put the final twitch to the knot around his neck and straightened up, brushing her hands down the gentle curve of her thighs.

'I'm Darcy.'

'Reece,' he gulped, not meeting her eyes. Since discovering the gender of his rescuer Reece seemed unable to stop looking at her breasts; they were full, rounded and at that moment strained against the tight sweater she wore.

She bent a little closer. '34 C,' she whispered.

His head came up with a jerk; predictably she was smiling.

In someone more fair-skinned the deepening of colour beneath that even olive tone of his skin would have been a full-scale blush.

'Mr Erskine thought I was a boy,' she explained solemnly to her family. Having been the victim of this mortifying case of mistaken identity, she didn't feel inclined to spare her patient's embarrassment.

After a startled pause, this announcement was greeted

with predictable hilarity. The twins cracked up; even Jack looked amused.

'Now, there's a novelty.' Nick lost his habitual sardonic sneer as he grinned in malicious delight at his sister.

Not wanting to come over as someone totally without humour, Reece smiled—it wasn't the easiest thing he'd ever done.

Darcy wasn't a vindictive girl—she'd made her point, and she had no wish to see him squirm excessively. She decided to take the spotlight off his mistake.

'Wasn't it you, Nick who gave up your seat on the train to the pregnant lady who *wasn't*…?'

Nick winced. 'Don't remind me.'

Reece's eyes did another unscheduled detour—this time in the direction of her flat midriff. There was no possibility that anyone would make that particular mistake in her case. Her jeans were cinched in around an impossibly narrow waist by a wide leather belt, and the blue denim clung to a nicely rounded bottom and slender thighs… The more details he took in, the more he felt inclined to think he really was concussed—nothing else could explain the fact he'd mistaken her for a boy!

'I'll take him to the hospital.'

'That's all right, Darce, I'll do it,' Nick offered.

Darcy reached up and ruffled his hair affectionately. 'No, you've just had a long drive—I'll do it. Always supposing you two filled up my car last night after you used it.'

The blond-haired seventeen-year-olds looked innocently hurt that she'd raised the possibility they might have found a better use for her twenty quid.

'As if we would.'

The three older members of their family snorted.

'It's really not necessary…' Reece began, getting to his feet. 'I've no wish to impose.'

The pocket-sized blonde looked amused by his attempt to regain a bit of dignity. 'You've already imposed, Mr Erskine,' she responded bluntly. 'So you might as well get your money's worth.'

CHAPTER TWO

REECE levered himself into the cramped front seat of the Beetle. He rapidly discovered there was a soggy patch in the worn upholstery. A quick survey revealed the half-open window was the most likely culprit. He tried to close it, but it seemed as though the ventilation was permanent.

Reece, who liked his cars the same way he liked his women—sleek, racy and maintenance-free—gritted his teeth and settled back to make the best of it.

'I'll be with you in a minute,' the diminutive blonde promised, bending down to peer with concern at him through the window.

Reece saw she'd discarded the yellow cagoule thing in favour of more feminine garb—a dark ankle-length trench coat that billowed as she ran off down the steep path towards the grim-faced big brother, who, it seemed to Reece, was the only one of the family with enough common sense to view him, a total stranger, with even a hint of suspicion.

A heated conversation ensued and, thanks to the broken window and prevailing icy wind, Reece could hear snatches of what they were saying.

'Give me the keys, Darcy.'

'Don't be stupid, Nicky, you're shattered.'

'And you're not?'

A blustery gust snatched away the next section of the conversation but it involved a considerable amount of gesticulation—it seemed to Reece that his colourful neighbours favoured extravagant body language.

'What if he's a homicidal psychopath...or a sex maniac? Or worse?'

Reece's muzzy, throbbing head didn't immediately make the connection between the sinister character they were discussing and himself until the brother continued in a suspicious growl, '...And I'm sure I've seen his face somewhere before. Erskine...Erskine...why does that sound familiar...? Don't laugh, Darce, I'm serious. Your trouble is you're too damned trusting.'

Under the circumstances, it seemed more than legitimate to eavesdrop. Reece leant casually towards the open window but unfortunately a large dog chose that particular moment to poke his nose through the gap and lick him affectionately on the forehead. He withdrew swiftly to avoid any more displays of overt affection.

'See!' he heard the girl cry triumphantly. 'Wally likes him.'

He assumed the canine approval finally swung it because a few moments later the blonde came jogging energetically down the path towards the car. She fended off the affections of the dog, who bounded over as he saw her coming, and only clicked her tongue in irritation as she brushed off the large muddy paw-prints on her coat.

'No, Wally, you can't come today.'

Reece didn't think he'd miss the large, slobbering dog.

'Sorry I was so long.' Darcy's smile faded as her eyes collided with the large stranger's green eyes and their gazes meshed. His stare had a heady, narcotic quality, and for a moment Darcy was physically incapable of looking away.

A breathless, confusing moment later she was free of that mesmeric gaze, and other than a heart that was still thudding too fast and loud and a dryness in her throat there were no lasting side-effects. It all happened so fast she wasn't really sure in retrospect if anything unusual had happened—he certainly wasn't acting as if it had.

Naturally she was relieved to see that the clouded vagueness had gone from his eyes, but she didn't consider the cool, analytical detachment that had replaced it to be an unqualified improvement!

'I'm not in any position to complain…?' The fleeting smile might have softened his hard eyes but Darcy was making a point of not looking—she didn't want a repeat performance of that silliness! The little shudder that chased its chilly pathway up her slender spine had nothing to do with the weather.

'Darcy.' For a fleeting, selfish moment she almost regretted not letting Nick, even in his exhausted condition, drive him.

'Of course…*Darcy*. I'm in your debt, Darcy.'

Darcy could almost hear him thinking, Outlandish name…outlandish family. She had a strong suspicion that had this man not considered himself in her debt he would have had no qualms about complaining; he didn't give her the impression of someone who had a particularly high patience quotient. She just couldn't see him suffering in silence.

'I'm not keeping score.' She decided to make allowances for his attitude. I probably wouldn't want to smile either if I'd just bashed my head and bust my arm, she reasoned.

'You're just being neighbourly, I suppose?'

This time it was impossible to misinterpret the acerbic scepticism in his voice. She twisted the excess moisture from the ends of her wet hair as she slid in beside him. With a wet splat the hair was casually flicked over her shoulder. There was a faint puzzled line between her feathery eyebrows as she turned in her seat and levelled her thoughtful gaze at him.

'Is that so unusual?' she asked, unable to keep the edge from her voice.

'Only slightly less so than an honest politician.'

Reece had noticed straight off that at some point during the last few minutes she'd paused to anoint those wide lips with a covering of glossy lipstick, and the soft colour clung stubbornly to the damp outline. This evidence of female vanity amused Reece; it also drew his attention to the soft lushness of her mouth.

Through the miasma of dull pain he felt his libido drowsily stir. It was the sort of mouth it was a crime not to kiss. Reece shifted uncomfortably as she gazed trustingly over at him. That was definitely one for the modern-man-is-a-myth school.

'Well, it looks like your cynicism has survived the crack on the skull intact—congratulations.'

'You sound disapproving…?'

Darcy shrugged; she didn't fight with people who were in urgent need of medical attention—even if they were misguided.

'In my experience people rarely do anything for nothing,' he announced, authoritatively doling out some more of his homespun cynicism.

This was a man who had very definite opinions, she decided, and a strong belief in his own infallibility. Darcy was beginning to suspect it might be mixed blessings that Reece Erskine had recovered his wits—he was one seriously joyless individual. In a different situation she might have been tempted to put up a strong argument against this jaundiced slant on life, but under the circumstances she contented herself with a gentle, 'I promise you, I have no hidden motives.'

Despite her assurance, his silent response—this man could do things with an eyebrow that defied belief!—made it abundantly clear that he wouldn't have taken her words at face value if she'd had her hand on a stack of Bibles.

She found it increasingly hard to hide her growing antipathy as she carefully scraped a clear area in the condensation on the windscreen in a businesslike manner.

Reece couldn't decide if he was being reprimanded or

not. However, there was nothing ambiguous about her disapproval—the stuff was emanating from her in waves! He caught the full force of it almost as clearly as the light perfume that pervaded her smallish person—his nostrils twitched; it was light, flowery and vaguely distracting, but it made a pleasant change from the wet-dog smell that wafted every so often from the direction of the old blanket flung over the back seat.

He watched as she wiped the excess moisture from her face with the back of her hand; her skin was remarkably clear, creamy pale and very lightly freckled.

'She doesn't like wet weather,' Darcy explained defensively as the engine spluttered and fizzled on the first three attempts.

'Who doesn't…?'

'Bingo!' Darcy gave a gentle sigh of relief when the engine eventually came to life. 'She's temperamental sometimes,' she explained, banging the dashboard affectionately.

Reece wasn't really surprised that she endowed the rusty pile of metal with human characteristics—it was entirely in keeping with the sentimental, mawkish traits this girl had displayed so far.

'The heater will warm up in a minute,' she promised with another trusting beam in his direction—she wasn't the type to hold a grudge, it seemed. 'I'll take the back road and we'll be there in no time at all.'

'Good,' he said, turning his face deliberately to the dismal view through the window. He hoped she'd take the hint and leave him in peace, since there wasn't any place he could escape if she didn't.

The snub was deliberate enough to bring a flush of annoyance to her cheeks. There was nothing Darcy would have liked more than to let her moody passenger brood in peace; he wasn't her idea of the ideal travelling companion—not by a long chalk!

The problem was he'd had a bump on the head; for all she knew, he might have a fractured skull! If he dozed off, how was she to know if he'd just fallen asleep or lapsed into a coma? This alarming possibility made her search his face surreptitiously for signs of imminent collapse—she found none.

But she did discover that in the subdued light her passenger's to-die-for bone-structure had an almost menacing quality. Nick's outlandish hypotheses were still fresh in her mind, and Darcy reasoned that this explained the small bubble of anxiety which she sensibly pushed aside—at least she *thought* it was anxiety that was responsible for the adrenalin surge that had her body on red alert.

The idea of being stuck miles away from medical assistance with an unconscious man had limited appeal for Darcy. No, the fastidious and reserved Mr Erskine was going to stay awake whether he liked it or not!

Trying to keep her growing uneasiness from her voice, she asked, 'What brings you to this part of the world?' Only a comment on the weather, she decided, could be less innocuous—not that you'd think so by his tight-lipped, rude response.

'Solitude.' *Surely* she'd take the hint now.

With anyone else Darcy would have felt inclined to put down this display of boorish bad manners to pain and discomfort—*with anyone else…*!

He considered himself a tolerant, patient sort of bloke, but ten minutes and what felt like several hundred questions later Reece was having trouble controlling his temper.

'You can't possibly be spending Christmas at the Hall!'

He hadn't come right out and said so—actually the gorgeous but tight-lipped Mr Erskine hadn't come right out and said *anything* without prompting, and then it had been as vague and uninformative as he could make it—but by a process of elimination Darcy was now pretty sure the injured hunk was actually staying at the semi-derelict Hall for the duration of the holiday.

'Oh…?' Reece wasn't about to let on that he'd been thinking much the same thing himself. After all his furtive planning he was going to end up holed up in some tinsel-decked hotel again this year.

Darcy felt encouraged to pursue her point—by his standards, this response had been positively garrulous.

In the cramped conditions—the car hadn't been constructed with his length of leg in mind—he lost all feeling in his right foot. Reece slowly shifted his right leg, rotating his ankle. His muscle-packed thigh nudged against the blonde's leg.

A startled, gusty breath snagged in Darcy's throat. A sensation that was all fizzing sexual awareness and no common sense dramatically surged through her, coalescing in a squirmy mess low in her belly.

Help, where had that come from?

The momentary distraction almost had disastrous consequences.

'*Hell!*' She braked sharply to allow the bedraggled cat dazed by the headlights to cross from one side of the narrow lane to the other. The feral creature disappeared into the dark undergrowth. 'Whew! Close call.' Her heartbeat slowed down to a steady canter as they accelerated away.

You could say that again! The abrupt halt had sent Reece's head on a collision course with the windscreen—the seat restraint was the only thing that had stopped him making contact. The pressure against his damaged ribs was exquisitely painful. It was becoming obvious to Reece that his chauffeur was the type of bleeding heart who saw no conflict in risking life and limb to save a dumb animal—probably the less appealing the better.

'Are you all right?'

Now she asks! 'I'm fine!'

Darcy's dark brows shot quizzically towards her fair hairline; his taut tone had been several degrees to the right of brusque.

'You're obviously not.' No doubt such stoicism was admirable but in this instance not really practical. 'Have you hurt yourself some more…? Shall I stop the car…?'

And prolong the agony of sharing space with Miss Sweetness and Light? *Anything*, he decided, was better than that—even replying to her incessant questions for another five minutes.

She obviously wasn't going to be satisfied until he owned up to something. 'I jarred my shoulder. *Why* can't I be staying at the Hall…?' he asked before she could press the point any further.

'Well, leaving aside your injuries…'

'Yes, let's do that…'

Repressing the angry retort that hovered on the tip of her tongue, Darcy jammed her foot on the brake as the lights ahead turned red. 'And the fact that the place is uninhabitable…'

'I found it quite cosy.'

'It's Christmas!'

'Your point being…?'

'Time of good cheer and loving your fellow man… Does that ring any bells…?'

The cynical light in his hooded, secretive eyes intensified. 'And come the New Year I can go back to screwing the bastards…?' he queried hopefully.

The sound of an impatient car horn brought her attention to the green light. 'Are you always unpleasant just for the hell of it?'

'It does give me a nice glow,' he admitted glibly.

'I don't think you've got the hang of the Christmas-spirit thing, Mr Erskine.'

'It's Reece, and as far as I'm concerned, Darcy, Christmas is just like any other day of the year…'

'But…'

'…except, of course, for the exceptionally high hypocrisy factor.'

'You mean you don't celebrate at all?' Darcy knew that it was none of her business how this man celebrated or didn't during the festive season, but for some reason she just couldn't let it go. 'What about your family…?'

'I don't have a family.' Reece hardly even felt a twinge of guilt as he brutally disposed of his numerous relatives.

'Oh!' Darcy, who was pretty blessed in that department, felt guilty at her abundance. 'That's sad, but even someone like you must have friends,' she insisted earnestly. She heard his startled intake of breath. Oh, dear, that hadn't come out quite as she'd intended.

'Are you *trying* to wind me up?'

'Why would I?' Even if it was exhilarating in a dangerous sort of way.

'Sins of a previous life catching up with me…?'

Darcy repressed a grin. Sarcastic pig…!

'Maybe you *don't* have any friends,' she countered nastily.

'I have friends,' he confirmed tightly. 'The sort who respect my privacy,' he added pointedly.

'Then it's a religious thing…?'

Her swift change of subject made him blink. 'What is…?'

'Ignoring Christmas.'

'It's a personal-choice thing,'

'There's no need to yell,' she remonstrated gently.

Reece's nostrils flared. 'Hard as this might be for you to comprehend, I don't *like* the festive season.'

'It must be pretty spartan inside,' Darcy mused, thinking about the bleak aspect of the old Hall.

An image of walls stripped back to bare brick ran through his mind; the draught from the open window whistling down his neck wasn't the only thing that made him shudder.

'Depends on what you're used to,' he responded evasively.

He looked to her as if he was used to the best—of everything. In fact, Darcy thought, shooting another covert glance in his direction, she didn't think she'd ever met a man who looked *more* accustomed to the good life and all its trimmings than him.

That wasn't to say there was anything *pampered* or soft about him—in fact, the opposite was true. Even in his present battered and bruised condition it was obvious he was in peak physical condition, and he had the indefinable but definite air of a man who would be ruthless to achieve his own ends.

Of course looks weren't everything, and for all she knew he might be afraid of the dark and give generously to charities. Either way, why would a man like him choose to spend any time, let alone Christmas, alone in a dump like…? It made no sense…unless he was hiding out, or running away…? Perhaps Nick's suspicions weren't so crazy after all!

Well, even if he is a sex maniac I should be safe; he doesn't come over as the type who goes for women who can be mistaken for boys—*lucky me*!

Darcy gave herself a mental shake and shrugged off the self-pitying direction of her reflections. Whilst there wasn't much point pretending that physically this man hadn't seriously unnerved her, there was no point advertising the embarrassing fact—though no doubt he was used to women making fools of themselves over him. As the feeling was *obviously* one-sided, and they were going to stay strangers, there didn't seem much point getting bogged down with uncomfortable self-analysis.

'Well, obviously I don't know what the Hall is like inside at the moment, but I would have—'

Reece was not used to explaining his actions, and he decided it was time to call a halt to her interminable speculation once and for all.

'You do surprise me,' his acid drawl interrupted. 'I was under the impression the locals keep fairly up-to-date with *all* the developments around here. I imagined I'd discovered the net-curtain-twitching capital of Yorkshire.'

Two pink spots appeared on Darcy's smooth cheeks; she sucked in an angry breath and crunched her gears. The faintly amused condescension in his voice made her see red. Why not just call us nosy yokels with nothing better to do than gossip and be done with it? She'd have liked to bop him one on his superior nose.

'You'll have to make allowances for me— I'm only home for the holiday, so I'm not completely up to speed yet.'

'That accounts for it, then.'

Darcy's eyes began to sparkle dangerously; the man had a very nasty mouth and there were limits to how much she was willing to make allowances for his delicate condition.

'*We're* nosy? That's pretty rich coming from someone who was spying on me from up a tree!' She hadn't been going to mention it because of his injuries, but he was asking for it...

Reece, who hadn't been in a situation that made him blush for years, felt his colour rise for the second time today.

'I wasn't spying.'

'That's what all the peeping Toms say,' she cut back with a provoking little smile.

Reece gritted his even white teeth.

'I've been demoted from sex maniac, then?'

'You were eavesdropping!' she exclaimed accusingly, a rush of colour flooding her cheeks. Her memory in play-back mode, she tried to recall exactly how bad what they'd said had been.

'It was hard not to, the way you were yelling.'

'Yelling is better than spying,' she countered with undeniable accuracy.

'I was investigating the noise pollution,' he gritted with the air of a man on the brink of losing his temper.

At that moment they approached a particularly savage bend in the road. His knuckles whitened as he braced his good hand against the dashboard.

'Will you do me a favour and keep your eyes on the road?' he pleaded grimly as her smouldering eyes showed a tendency to linger indignantly on his face.

'It's so hard,' she confessed apologetically, 'when there's you to look at.' She sighed soulfully, placing a hand mo mentarily over her strongly beating heart.

Actually it was getting increasingly hard to treat the fact she was a long way from immune to his raw brand of physical magnetism as a joke.

He shifted in his seat once more, as if trying to alleviate some discomfort, and his broad shoulders nudged against hers in the restricted space of the small car.

Darcy was conscious of a fleeting feeling of guilt that she was being so mean to someone who was injured and in pain. The other feeling the brief contact created was less fleeting and much more disturbing; the fluttery sensation low in her belly went into overdrive, and pulses had started hammering a loud tattoo in places she didn't know she had pulses! Her palms felt uncomfortably damp as she grimly gripped the cold steering-wheel.

'Ha ha.' Reece's nostrils flared as he watched the provoking little witch toss her bright head. 'You were making a racket and I came out here for peace and quiet.'

She'd never claimed to be Kiri Te Kanawa, but a *racket*—charming! What a great confidence-boost just when she needed it.

'If this is a sample of your usual behaviour I think I can guarantee you that,' she promised him drily. 'It's true that in the country we do take an interest in what our friends and neighbours are doing; perhaps it can be intrusive sometimes…' she conceded.

Reece found his wandering attention captured and held by the dramatic rise and fall of her well-formed bosom. The fascination bothered him—it was totally irrational: he'd seen bosoms a lot more spectacular. He worriedly recalled reading somewhere that head injuries could totally alter someone's personality.

'…but I'd prefer that to indifference…'

'God!' Reece groaned as if in pain and rolled his head from side to side in an effort to alleviate the increasing stiffness in his neck. 'I knew I should have taken a taxi.'

'My driving's not that bad,' Darcy muttered truculently. The fact he was treating the journey like a white-knuckle ride hadn't escaped her notice.

'I'm very grateful for what you've done,' he ground out. He sounded as if each syllable hurt.

'Save it! I don't want your gratitude.' With an airy gesture that caused the car to lurch slightly towards the centre of the road she brushed aside his protest. 'We may be nosy in the country, but we don't step over sick people yet, or ask for payment when we pick them up!'

She shot a disgusted glance at his perfect, slightly bruised profile; anyone would think his movements were front-page news, the way he was acting!

'I wouldn't like you to run away with the impression I give a damn if you get triple pneumonia. I was just making polite neighbourly conversation to take your mind off your pain.'

'I'm not in pain.'

With a lofty sniff Darcy dismissed this transparent untruth. 'You don't have to tell me anything if you don't want to.' An expression of fierce concentration on her face, she stared unblinkingly through the rain-washed windshield.

'No, I don't, do I?'

Another five minutes and the hospital came into view. Even as he broke the silence, Reece couldn't understand what made him do so.

'I'm being a great deal of trouble.'

As much as he liked to give the impression he didn't have one, it looked to her as if the cranky Mr Erskine's conscience was giving him trouble—she was in no hurry to ease it.

'Yes,' she agreed sweetly.

Reece was gripped by an urgent and irrational desire to make those wilful lips smile once more.

'And behaving like an ungrateful monster.' His efforts were rewarded: her lips twitched.

'Such perception.'

Truly kissable lips; shame about the sharp tongue that went with them. A nerve along the chiselled edge of his strong jaw began to throb.

'I came here to escape Christmas…'

'You should have said.'

'Should have said what?' he demanded in a driven voice.

Darcy drew up beside the Casualty doors with her engine running. 'Christmas has bad associations for you, doesn't it?'

He stiffened.

She had spoken on impulse; now she wished she hadn't. For an unguarded moment there she'd seen something in his eyes that made her feel like an intruder. The moment was gone; now there was only hostility and suspicion as he scowled at her.

'What the hell are you talking about?'

Darcy shook her head. 'I just got the impression… Forget it; I obviously got the wrong end of the stick. I'll drop you off here—less far to walk.' She thought about leaning across him to open the door but, recalling what she had experienced the time she'd touched him, she changed her mind.

When he'd gone Darcy drove around looking for a parking space, and even when she found one she wasn't sure whether or not her presence would be appreciated. But, personality clashes aside, it didn't seem quite right somehow to drive off without even finding out how he was. The family would certainly think it very odd if she returned with no news.

It was with mixed feelings she finally presented herself at the reception desk.

'I'm enquiring about a Mr Erskine,' she began tentatively as she approached the smart-looking female who presided over the empty waiting area. 'I came in w—'

'Did you really?' The young woman blushed and continued in voice absent of wistful envy this time. 'I mean, they're expecting you.'

Darcy looked blank. 'They are?' she said doubtfully. It occurred to her this was a case of mistaken identity.

'They said to send you right on in. Rob!' The receptionist flagged down a white-jacketed young nurse. 'Will you take Mrs Erskine through to cubicle three?'

Mrs…? God, they thought…!

'I'm not!' Darcy denied hoarsely, but nobody seemed to be listening to her as she trotted obediently along beside the young nurse.

My God, this was so embarrassing. She just hoped Reece Erskine didn't think the mistake any of her doing.

'I think there's been a mistake,' she began firmly as the young man drew back a curtain and stood to one side.

'Here she is…Darcy, *darling*.'

Darling…?

'Oh, God!' she breathed, her eyes riveted on the bare torso of the man who had greeted her with such a highly deceptive degree of warmth.

He was standing there, stripped to the waist, in the process of zipping up his trousers one-handed; her makeshift sling had been replaced by a more professional-looking collar and cuff arrangement.

Darcy didn't make a habit of mentally stripping casual acquaintances, but it seemed she must have made an exception with him because she found herself comparing the reality to that mental image stored in her head and finding it had hardly done him justice. With wide shoulders, amply endowed with muscle in a lean, athletic, unbulky way, his body was way better than good—it was sensational!

Her tongue clove to the roof of her mouth as her hot eyes went into exploration mode. No wonder her emergency stop had made him cranky—there were spectacular darkish-blue bruises all the way down one side of his ribcage.

'It looks a lot worse than it is,' he comforted her.

Blushing wildly, Darcy tore her eyes from his body. 'Good,' she croaked hoarsely.

'I could do with a hand here.'

Darcy almost choked when she realised he was talking about his zip. Eyes wide, she mutely shook her head. The alarmed backward step she took brought her into abrupt contact with a second person in the tiny cubicle, who until that moment she hadn't even been aware of. No, I was too busy leching over Reece Erskine, she thought shamefully.

'Sorry,' she mumbled incoherently.

'No harm done,' the white-coated figure assured her cheerfully. 'Just a few cracked ribs, lots of bruising and the dislocated shoulder, of course.'

'What?'

The doctor looked bemused for a moment by her alarm, then he grinned. 'I see what you mean…no, I'm talking about your husband, not me.' Chuckling over their crossed lines, the doctor held an X-ray film up to the light.

There was that husband thing again. Darcy waited expectantly, sure that Reece would take this opportunity to correct the error—he didn't, and her confusion deepened.

She felt obliged to respond. 'A *few* seems a bit vague.' Even as she spoke, she was overpoweringly aware of the tall, scantily clad figure who had moved up behind her.

'Point taken.' With an unoffended grin, the medic clipped the film onto an illuminated screen and pointed out the defects with his pen. 'One, two and here's number three.'

'I thought he might have broken his collar-bone.'

'I can see how you might, but no. It was a dislocation. Agony to pop back, of course.' The disgusting, bloodthirsty *popping* noise he made to illustrate the point made Darcy shudder.

'It sounds awfully painful,' she protested.

'It was,' Reece volunteered.

'We offered him an anaesthetic, but your husband *insisted* we do it right away.' The doctor hastily defended his actions. 'A few days and the shoulder should be back to normal,' he promised. 'Actually, it's on account of the head injury we'd like to keep him in overnight, Mrs Erskine, but he doesn't seem too keen.'

'I'm not…'

'She's not surprised, are you, darling?'

The warm, caressing note froze her to the spot without

the added trauma of hearing her addressed again as 'darling'. 'She knows how much I hate hospitals.'

She felt a large competent hand push aside the hair from the nape of her neck. Darcy's hair was plentiful and incredibly silky, but very fine and inclined to go kinky when exposed to moisture—it had definitely been exposed and right now it was a mass of crinkly curls.

Her breath expelled in a soft hiss as she felt the unmistakable touch of cool lips against the sensitive flesh of her exposed nape. Her eyes closed and the strength drained from her body.

The doctor only gave a slightly benevolent smile as he watched them. 'Of course, if he hadn't been going home in the care of an experienced nurse I'd have insisted...'

Darcy's eyes flickered open. He's married, married to a nurse, was her first thought. Then it clicked— Me, he's talking about me!

'Where are you working at the moment, Mrs Erskine?'

'I...I'm...' It was bad enough realising she had a whole new identity created by this madman without being expected to act in character too!

'Darcy is staying at home. Making a home is a full-time job as far as we're concerned, isn't it, darling...?' A firm hand beneath her jaw turned Darcy's head so that she was exposed to the full intensity of his green eyes. No desperate appeal for her co-operation there—on the contrary; if anything, there was a hint of challenge.

'*You're* a full-time job!' she breathed incredulously.

The doctor laughed. 'I'll send a nurse in to suture up that head wound,' he explained, scribbling rapidly on the sheet in front of him.

Darcy waited until he'd gone before she exploded.

'*Are you mad?*' she seethed. Why hadn't she just told the doctor he was lying through his teeth when she'd had the chance?

'Hush, *darling*, or they'll hear you.'

She saw that he was looking well pleased with himself—and why not? Her anger escalated rapidly as he calmly began to shrug on his shirt as if nothing had happened. The man had the gall to stand there looking as if butter wouldn't melt in his mouth, when... Her train of thought skittered to an abrupt full stop—it had been a bad mistake to think *mouth*; she could still feel the tingling area on her neck where his lips had been moments before.

'Let them!'

He directed a mildly irritated glance in her direction.

'I don't know what you're playing at...'

'Sure you do; you're not that stupid.'

Darcy's eyes narrowed. 'Let's pretend for the sake of argument that I am,' she suggested sweetly.

'I think I can just about make that giant leap. They were highly reluctant to discharge me without assurances I have someone responsible to take care of me. Whilst I could have just walked out of here, it seemed less stressful all round if I was married.' The longer he was here, the more likelihood there was of someone recognising him and then it was only a matter of time before the local Press showed up...in his experience these things snowballed pretty fast.

'And you thought of me. Naturally I'm *deeply* flattered,' she spat sarcastically. 'Why on earth did I have to be a nurse...?' she wailed.

'I thought that was a nice touch,' he agreed complacently. 'If the doc had been on the ball he'd have realised you're not old enough to be experienced.'

'You're mad...quite mad!' she announced with conviction.

'You're not a nurse, then?'

'Of course I'm not a nurse!'

'Just when your father said you were a great little nurse I thought...'

'I've got brothers—I can stick on a plaster. I'm not Florence Nightingale…!'

'True. Nobody with an ounce of caring in their body could stand there watching me struggle like this.' He stood there, one arm inserted in his shirt, wondering what to do next.

'If that was a hint, you're really pushing it!' she growled. 'What if someone asks me to do something…*nursey*?' she worried hoarsely.

'Is that likely?' he drawled, managing to project the distinct impression he found her complaints slightly hysterical.

It occurred to Darcy that they were drifting away from the real cause of her simmering anger. 'Don't try and change the subject,' she growled.

One slanted dark brow quirked. 'Which was…?'

'I'm not your wife!'

'This is true,' he conceded with an expression that suggested he was mightily relieved about this. 'I didn't think you'd mind—it's not like I'm actually asking you to marry me or anything drastic.'

'For your information, I've been proposed to *several* times!' she felt goaded into unwisely boasting.

'Congratulations,' he drawled, looking amused.

Darcy's cheeks were burning with humiliation as she discovered a major flaw in his manipulations. 'What were you going to do if I'd driven straight off?'

'I knew you wouldn't do that,' he stated confidently.

'How could you possibly…?'

'You'd be eaten up by guilt if you did. You're deeply into doing the right thing.' He made it sound like a flaw in her character. 'Be a sport, Darcy,' he cajoled.

'I'm not lying for you.'

He sighed. 'Just don't say you're not, that's all I'm asking. It's no skin off your nose. Walk out of here with me and then you'll never have to see me again.'

Darcy's shoulders slumped in defeat. 'I must be mad…'

A wolfish grin split his lean, dark face. 'Good girl,' he approved.

Further comments were made impossible by the arrival of the nurse who'd directed Darcy here originally.

'I've come to suture your head wound,' the young man explained.

Darcy took the opportunity to excuse herself. 'I'll wait outside.' Halfway through the curtain, she paused. 'Are you going to give him a local anaesthetic?' she asked the young nurse.

He looked confused. 'Well, yes,' he admitted.

'Pity!' Darcy declared maliciously.

The sound of husky laughter followed her down the corridor.

CHAPTER THREE

'GOODBYE, Mrs Erskine…Mr Erskine,' the young receptionist gushed breathily as she left them with obvious reluctance at the swing-doors.

Darcy gave a sigh of relief as the doors swung shut. The red carpet was about the only thing that had been missing and, given enough time, she had the impression the smitten young woman would have produced that too. At least she could drop the wifey act now.

'What are we?' Darcy grouched, intensely relieved to be out of the place and out of her role. 'Visiting royalty? Do you always have this effect on people?'

'What effect is that?'

Darcy raised a sceptical brow. 'Like you didn't notice!' she hooted. 'The woman was deferential, bordering on obsequious.'

Despite the enigmatic smile she received in reply, Darcy got the impression he was even less pleased than she was by the VIP treatment.

The rain had stopped, but it had started to freeze, making the pavement underfoot lethally slippery. Darcy moved cautiously past the men who were gritting the entrance to the hospital, smiling in a distracted way at them as she passed. The gravel was crunchy underfoot as they passed the tall, twinkly Christmas tree, and a layer of sparkling frost added to the festive look in a way that expensive ornaments never could.

She only just stopped herself mentioning how much she loved the smell of pine to the wet blanket beside her.

'Where are we parked?'

Even though she hadn't forgotten the tall, commanding presence at her side—chance would be a fine thing—she started when he spoke. It made her realise how uptight and wound up the whole play-acting thing in the hospital had made her. Her fellow conspirator, on the other hand, had seemed almost to relish his role, or maybe it was her discomfort he enjoyed…? Considering the glimpses she'd had of his warped sense of humour, the latter seemed the most likely explanation.

'*We…?*' She lifted her eyes to his face, but not for long—for some reason she felt oddly reluctant to maintain contact.

Like a silly, lust-struck teenager afraid to look the unattainable object of her fantasies in the eyes! Self-disgust curled in her belly. Grow up, Darcy!

By the time she had sternly told herself to stop acting so *wet*, he had paused under the blue-white beam of an overhead light and was making a careful minor adjustment to the jacket draped over his broad shoulders. His head was bent forward at an angle; she couldn't see his face, just the strong curve of his jaw and the sharp angle of his cheekbones, but even these sketchy details were enough to proclaim him as something pretty special to look at indeed.

'Are you going to abandon me…?' He contemplated his abandonment with what seemed to her unnatural composure.

'That was my plan, yes.' She could see the flaw in this plan even before he came over all pathetic and helpless.

'No wallet, no money or plastic. See for yourself.' He opened his jacket, inviting her to disprove his claim.

No way—she'd been there, done that and felt her hormones riot! She was not conscious of placing her tightly clenched hands firmly behind her back.

'There's no need to act like an endangered species; I believe you,' she told him gruffly. Her sigh of defeat had a long-suffering sound to it. 'Do I look like a soft touch?' she wondered, wearily running a harassed hand through her dampish curls.

Dark head on one side, he regarded her in a considering fashion. To add insult to injury, it took him bare moments to come to a decision.

'Actually, yes, you do.' She also looked extremely young, still full of youthful ideals, a soft target for unscrupulous operators—a student home for the holiday possibly…?

His own innocence and youth seemed a long way off at that moment. It seemed an opportune time, given the direction of his wayward thoughts, to remind himself how far removed she was from the females who temporarily lent a bit of variety to his solitary existence— Reece wasn't looking for anything other than temporary.

His candour made Darcy's face darken in annoyance.

'And you're the type to take advantage,' she accused rattily.

Taken advantage of by Reece Erskine—now, there was a thought! She was too busy being angry, flustered and ashamed of her thoughts to notice that a new expression had filtered into his eyes.

Soft… His mind seemed determined to explore this avenue and there was no lack of appropriate material to feed his interest—soft lips, soft curves. The compulsive nature of his speculation had none of the objectivity Reece took for granted in sexual matters.

Don't go there, he urged himself, repressing the sudden strong inclination to lean closer to all that *softness*, smell the flowery scent that enveloped her small person.

Darcy set off purposefully, reluctant to invite ridicule by admitting she'd forgotten where she'd left the car. She was too damned spooked at the prospect of being enclosed in a small space with him once more to think straight or accept defeat graciously. She heard his soft but firm footsteps shadowing her.

'You *said* I'd never have to see you again,' she reminded him crankily.

'I'm a great believer in telling people what they want to hear if that gets the job done.'

'Lying, you mean.'

Reece winced. 'I wouldn't have put it that way.'

'That I never doubted!'

Despite the fact she wasn't making any allowances for his delicate condition, his long long legs seemed to be having no problem keeping up with the cracking pace she was setting—*pity*!

'I'm not exactly thrilled to find myself obliged to beg a lift either,' he rasped huskily.

Of all the ungrateful rats! Darcy came to an abrupt halt and turned her wrathful gaze upon the tall figure who had almost collided with her.

'That makes two of us!' she retorted sharply.

Their eyes met.

It was at that moment Darcy felt *it*—*it* was a tense excitement so thick the air quivered with it, so thick her limbs were all but immobilised by it.

It didn't seem to be a one-sided situation. His burning eyes kept moving back to her parted lips as though they were being dragged there against his will. She felt as if she was being drawn in by that raw expression in his hungry eyes. The tightness in her chest finally found release in a fractured sigh.

The compulsion to reach up and press her lips to his was so strong her head spun. Would they be cold, warm…firm…? Wondering sent delicious little shivers skating along her spine.

She wouldn't do it, of course, because she wasn't the sort of girl who gave in to lustful base instincts…all the same, *thinking* about it—and she discovered her embarrassingly lurid imagination had a mind of its own—made her body temperature soar despite the sub-zero temperature around them. Her dry-throated excitement mounted with dizzying rapidity as her knees began to literally shake.

Seconds probably carried on ticking relentlessly away in the few moments after speculative green eyes had met startled blue—but Darcy was unaware of the passing time as they stood stock-still in a silence broken only by the distant wail of an ambulance.

No good will come of this, a sensible voice, to which she paid no heed, forecast in her head.

Reece felt his breath perceptibly quicken. Her mouth was just sensationally lush. The uneven sound of her breath catching in the back of her throat was driving him slightly crazy. He watched as her clenched fingers unfurled and she began to reach out...he thought about them touching his face...his hair...his...!

With a mumbled expletive he took a step backwards. 'Darcy...!'

It was a verbal warning, the sort an adult gave a reckless child about to indulge in dangerous exploration.

Mortified, Darcy let her extended hand fall away, and she stood there feeling stupid and confused by what had just occurred—whatever that was... He had wanted to kiss her too—hadn't he...? It hadn't been a figment of her overheated imagination, had it?

The uncertainty only lasted a split-second; she hadn't imagined anything—it had been real. She thrust her softly rounded chin forward defiantly. As unlikely as it seemed, Reece Erskine had wanted to kiss her just as much as she'd wanted to kiss him! She raised her eyes stubbornly to his stony face and her heart sank—only he didn't now!

So he had gone off the idea; she was damned if she was going to let him make her feel ashamed!

'Darcy what?' She sniffed angrily. 'Darcy, don't kiss me…?' she suggested shrilly.

She watched his eyes widen as she gave an appalled gasp—*I can't believe I said that!*

'Were you going to?'

I asked for that, didn't I? What was she supposed to say…? Given a little bit of encouragement, *probably*…?

Darcy served up a withering look. 'What a tactless thing to ask,' she observed, resorting to disgust to disguise the extent of her dismay.

Spontaneous and asking for trouble would have been closer to the mark in his estimation. No wonder the brother wanted to keep her at home—if she was his sister he'd never let her out of his sight!

For the first time Darcy noticed the lines of strain around his sensual mouth—as if not kissing her hadn't been the easy option…then why…? A horrifying possibility occurred to her. 'Are you married?'

Unprepared for the tense, accusing query, Reece blinked, his jaw tightening. 'That's not relevant.'

Her mouth hardened with contempt; that meant he was. Not again! She didn't know who she despised the most at that moment—him or herself. 'To me it is!' she choked bitterly.

Reece gave an exasperated sigh; he could cope with a lot of things but he discovered—rather to his surprise—that being looked at as if he was some sort of moral derelict by those big blue eyes was not one of them.

'If it matters so much to you, I was, but I'm not now.' He saw her slender hunched-up shoulders slump in relief. 'Though why it should be so important to you I don't understand…'

And Darcy wasn't about to explain. Having an affair with a married man—even if she hadn't known he was at the time—was not the sort of thing she felt like sharing.

'I'd introduce the subject of morals if I thought you'd understand.'

'I don't see where morals come into it,' he drawled. 'You didn't do anything…'

'If I had…would you have…?' Cheeks flaming, she struck her forehead with the palm of her hand. 'Oh, God!' she wailed. 'Me and my mouth…!' How to take an embarrassing situation and make it ten times worse in one easy-to-follow lesson!

His eyes automatically moved to the object of her contempt. The muscles in his strong throat worked overtime.

'Yes, I'd have kissed you back,' he admitted throatily. The words seemed drawn from him against his will.

Her eyes widened. 'You would…?' She saw his lips twitch at the incredulity in her voice. 'I knew that.' A puzzled frown crinkled her smooth brow. 'Then why didn't you…?'

Reece's bark of rueful laughter brought her back to her senses—and not before time. He stared at her flushed face for a couple of moments before replying.

'You don't kiss married men; I don't kiss girls young enough to be my…kid sister.'

It was the very last explanation Darcy had expected to hear. 'How quaint that you've got principles.'

'It comes as as much of a shock to me as it does to you,' he assured her drily. 'It's getting cold out here.' He spoke abruptly now, as if the humour of the situation was wearing thin. 'If you really can't stomach the idea of giving me a lift back I should be able to make alternative arrangements.'

Darcy touched his arm; he didn't flinch but his rigidity didn't suggest relaxed and carefree—was it possible he was not entirely immune to the contact? This not unflattering possibility was heady stuff.

'How old exactly do you think I am?' Repressing a smug smile, she worked her way towards her grand finale.

Whilst it might have been wiser to leave him in ignorance, given the dangerous sexual chemistry in the air, she wanted the satisfaction of establishing herself as a mature woman of the world in his eyes. Perhaps for once in her life she wanted danger…? Her eyes slid over his tall, rangy frame before coming to rest on his face, and she gulped; he registered high enough on the danger scale to satisfy the most reckless risk-taker, she conceded.

'Nineteen…twenty maybe.'

'I'm twenty-seven.'

His chin came up and the dark veil of lashes lifted from his high, chiselled cheekbones. His narrowed eyes raked her face. 'Not possible.'

'Furthermore,' she continued, breathless after his intense scrutiny, 'I'm not some teenage virgin.' Like he really wanted to know that, Darcy.

'What are you, then?'

'Your best hope of getting home, mate.'

His mobile lips quirked; his expression was still rapt. 'I'd not forgotten that. I was actually wondering what you do when you're not doing the angel-of-mercy act.'

A wistful expression flitted across her face. 'At this moment I should be skiing.'

'But you were lured away by the glamour of deepest, darkest Yorkshire?'

His sneering irony brought an annoyed frown to her face. She took any criticism of her beloved Dales very personally.

'There was a family crisis,' she told him tersely.

'So they called you.' That would figure.

Darcy resented his tone. 'I don't mind,' she flared. 'Who else would they call?'

'You tell me. My recollection is a bit cloudy, but there didn't seem any shortage of family members from what I saw.'

'You don't know the half of it,' she mumbled. 'I get a panic attack every time I think about how many people I'm meant to be cooking Christmas lunch for.'

'Is this the same girl—sorry, *woman*, who considers every strand of tinsel sacred…?' he taunted gently.

'This is the woman,' she countered angrily, 'who is trying to step into her mother's shoes and failing miserably!' The instant the impetuous retort emerged from her lips she regretted it; she regretted it even more when she saw the curiosity on his face.

'Your mother's ill…?'

'No, she's not. She's…*away*.'

His dark brows lifted. 'Another man…' It might have been a trick of the light but Darcy thought his hard eyes actually softened. 'Bad luck, kid. It happens.'

Darcy was furious and horrified by his casual assumption that her mother would have an affair. 'Not to my family! My mother has gone to a retreat to recharge her batteries, that's all…' Tears prickled the backs of her eyelids and her voice thickened emotionally. 'And I'm not a kid.'

Reece looked down into her stormy upturned face. 'Want to talk about it?' he was surprised to hear himself offer; he wasn't prone to encouraging soul-baring.

'Not to you.' Darcy thought he looked relieved rather than disappointed by her blunt response.

'Fair enough.'

She eyed him suspiciously before she eventually nodded and blew on her icy fingertips. 'If the interrogation's over, perhaps we should get along before hypothermia sets in.'

Face burning with embarrassment and humiliation, she turned abruptly on her heel. She deliberately turned her face to the icy embrace of the cold north wind and, as luck would have it, found the car almost immediately.

'I can't find the keys,' she admitted after turning her pockets and handbag inside-out and upside-down.

Reece, who had watched her feverish attempts silently, walked around the car to join her.

'Might these be what you were looking for?'

Relief was mingled with chagrin as she saw he was indicating the familiar bunch of keys inserted in the driver's door. He pulled them out, and instead of dropping them into the palm she held out he placed them in a way that meant his fingers brushed against her wrist. The tingle that shot up her extended arm was neat electricity.

'Thanks,' she mumbled without looking at him. She couldn't decide whether or not that touch had been as artless as it had appeared.

He inclined his glossy head graciously. 'My pleasure.'

The fit inside the car was even snugger than she remembered. His head brushed the top of the car and in order to accommodate his legs he had to draw his knees up towards his chest at an awkward angle.

She went to turn the ignition key but he reached out and covered her hand with his, and if anything this time the sensation was even stronger.

Her eyes, wide and startled, lifted to his. 'What's wrong?'

Besides the state of imminent collapse of my nervous system, that is?

'This kissing thing.'

Darcy wriggled her hand from beneath his and clasped it protectively to her heaving chest. 'What kissing thing?' she asked, desperately affecting amnesia.

'You wanting to kiss me.'

'*You* wanting to kiss me.'

'That too,' he agreed. 'The point is, now that you know I'm not a married man and I know you're not a teenager...or for that matter a virgin...' A choking sound emerged from Darcy's throat. 'Incidentally we have that much in common. There's no actual reason we shouldn't.'

'Shouldn't…?' She hoped he wasn't going to say what she thought he was going to say—he did.

'Kiss.'

She almost kept the wobble from her cool response. 'Other than the fact I'd scream blue murder, probably not.' She sent up a silent prayer that her claim would never be put to the test.

'Ah…! You've gone off the idea… Maybe it's for the best,' he conceded casually, before leaning back in his seat and closing his eyes.

Just like that! Heavens, she didn't expect him to get suicidal because she'd said she didn't want to kiss him, but he could at least have the decency to look as if he cared! It was, she decided, eyeing his profile with loathing, a matter of simple good manners!

Darcy knew straight off she'd not fall back to sleep for some time—her feverishly active mind was racing like an overwound clockwork toy. She glanced at the illuminated fingers of the clock on the bedside table and groaned: it was only two a.m.

Her tiny bedroom set beneath the eaves faced due north, and the wind was battering against the window-panes, sneaking through every odd crack or cranny in the well-insulated room. The Hall wouldn't be well-insulated…

'Oh, hell, why did I go and think that…?' She rolled onto her stomach and pulled a pillow over her head to drown out the noise. I will not think about him, she told herself angrily.

Trouble was, she did.

Her family had been surprised when on her return she hadn't brought home the invalid to eat with them. Their collective comments to this effect had served to add to the burden of her own guilty conscience until she'd eventually exploded.

'If you want to feed him, feel free, but don't expect any thanks. Me, I've had enough of him for one evening!' she'd announced.

After that they'd let it alone, but she'd been able to tell that they thought she was being mean and she'd caught Nick regarding her speculatively several times during the evening.

Thirty minutes after she'd woken from her restless sleep Darcy, armed with a torch, blanket and a flask of coffee, made her way up the lane towards the Hall.

There was no front door to knock. The beam of her torch feebly illuminated a very sorry state of affairs. Horrified, Darcy explored further; things didn't get any better.

'And I didn't even offer the man a cup of tea,' she moaned, stepping over a pile of ladders that lay across her path. 'And why…? Just because he accepted no means no. If I find him dead from hypothermia or in a coma it'll be my fault.' The knowledge increased the urgency of her search for signs of life.

A room with a door seemed a logical place to look. Her efforts were rewarded with the sight of the smouldering embers of a large fire in the wide inglenook.

Tentatively she approached the large human-sized bundle on the floor. She put down everything but the torch and knelt down beside the figure. Her ears were straining for signs of healthy breathing—in her present frame of mind she'd have welcomed the odd wheeze or two!

One minute she was shuffling a little closer to the figure with her hand raised, the next she was flat on her back, pinned beneath a heavy figure. An ungentle hand was pressed over her mouth.

'If you don't want to get hurt, stop struggling,' an ugly growl advised her. 'Are you alone?'

How the hell did he expect her to reply with a dirty great

paw over her mouth…? It seemed her assailant's thoughts were running along similar lines.

'I'm going to take away my hand, but if you try and yell to your mates you'll regret it. Understood…?'

Heart pounding, Darcy shook her head as vigorously as her position would allow. If she hadn't known this was Reece she'd have already died of heart failure. To her relief the suffocating hand lifted.

'For heaven's sake, get off me, you idiot; I can't breathe!' she gasped.

'Darcy!'

The pressure across her ribs eased but he didn't shift completely. 'Of course Darcy,' she grumbled crossly. 'Who did you think it was?'

'A burglar.'

She heard sounds of him searching for something just before a strong light was shone in her face.

'Will you take that out of my eyes?' she pleaded, screwing her watering eyes up tight. 'I can't see a thing.'

She felt a hand tug at the knitted cloche she wore on her head and pull it off. The same hand ran gently through the soft waves that had been crammed beneath. Suddenly the pressure over her middle was gone, as was the hand… Disturbingly she had mixed feelings about her release; there had been something very soothing about those probing fingers—no, that wasn't quite the right word…

She struggled to sit up and managed it with both hands braced behind her for support on the dusty floor.

'I had a torch but I lost it when you leapt on me like that.' She squinted into the dusty corners, hoping to relocate it.

Reece regarded her incredulously. 'Well, what did you expect, woman, creeping up on a man in the middle of the night?'

Fair question if you stopped to look at it from his point

of view—something that Darcy hadn't done up to this point. She realised how foolish her impulsive behaviour might seem.

She watched nervously as he got to his feet and moved towards the fire, pausing to choose a couple of dry logs. The fire immediately began to sizzle as the flames licked the wood. Picking up a box of matches from the shoulder-high age-darkened oak mantel, he began to light half a dozen or so candles which were laid out there in various stages of demise. As they took hold he switched off the torch and slid it into his pocket—it came as no surprise that he'd been sleeping fully clothed.

'Don't you just love candlelight?' he drawled.

'Not especially.' His dark hair was mussed up and what had been the suggestion of a shadow over his strong jaw earlier was now a well-developed dark stubble. Neither of these factors altered the fact he looked devastatingly attractive—well, looking at him made her feel fairly devastated at any rate.

'Now,' he said in a don't-muck-me-about sort of voice, 'you can tell me what you thought you were doing.'

What had seemed a perfectly logical step to take at the time suddenly seemed extremely difficult to explain to her critical audience.

'If you don't speak I'll just have to assume you couldn't bear to be parted from me any longer...' he warned.

The satiric taunt made the colour flare in Darcy's pale cheeks. 'In your dreams,' she grunted, catching her lower lip between her teeth.

'Talking of dreams, you owe me one—you rudely interrupted a particularly...'

'I don't want to know anything about your dreams,' Darcy assured him, drawing herself up on her knees and dusting the seat of her trousers with a vigorous hand.

'Even if you were involved...?'

He seemed to take a malicious delight in winding her up. '*Especially* if I was involved.' Thank goodness she had a thick sweater and a windcheater over her pyjama top, because things were happening to her nipples that couldn't be blamed on the temperature.

Reece laughed then and went to sit down on an upturned packing case. 'I'd offer you a seat, only this is the only one.' He fingered the rough surface. 'It's the only table too, for that matter.'

Darcy gathered the drifting threads of her wits—she hadn't come here to talk furniture. 'I only came to look at you,' she gritted, wondering why she had ever cared if he expired in his sleep.

'Not touch…?' he muttered.

'Will you stop interrupting me?'

'Sorry,' he responded meekly.

Meek, him…? That was the best joke she'd heard in ages.

'I shouldn't have let you spend the night alone just because you irritated me.'

Now that she had his complete attention, Darcy wasn't sure that was what she wanted… She didn't trust that innocent expression in those green eyes either.

He rapidly proved her distrust was well-placed!

'So you decided to spend the night with me after all, Darcy. I don't know what to say…'

Her jaw locked tight as she tried to act as if his wolfish grin didn't do anything to her at all.

'I'm sure you'll manage to come up with something suitably smutty,' she predicted acidly, rubbing her sweaty palms against her jeans.

His low chuckle was not only genuinely amused, it was also deeply, devastatingly sexy.

'The doctor said you needed to be carefully observed. I just thought I'd pop round and see if you were all right.'

'You thought you'd *pop round* at,' he glanced down at the slim-banded wristwatch on his wrist, 'three a.m.,' he read incredulously.

'I didn't know if you could cope, with your ribs and the shoulder…' She gave an exasperated sigh. 'If you must know,' she said, gathering up the flask and blanket and thrusting them out to him, 'I was worried about you.'

Reece looked from her angry, flushed face to the offerings in her hand and back again. 'I'm touched.'

'There's no need,' she said with dignity, 'to be sarcastic.'

'I'm not.'

Darcy tapped a pearly fingertip nervously against a white tooth and eyed him with an exasperated frown. 'It's perfectly simple,' she began to explain patiently. 'I was lying there, listening to the wind, thinking about you…'

'Snap.'

It took two seconds' exposure to his wickedly explicit eyes to extinguish the innocent look of enquiry on her face. 'I wasn't doing *that* sort of thinking,' she gasped, horrified.

'What sort of thinking would that be, Darcy…?'

'If you'd got ill in the night nobody would have known. I would have felt responsible.'

'You've got a thing about responsibility, haven't you, Darcy?' he mused softly. 'Don't you ever get the urge to do something irresponsible?' The humour faded abruptly from his eyes.

Darcy swallowed, and waited for the worst of the spasms in her belly to pass. It must be the candles, she reasoned desperately. 'No, never.' Her stern denial emerged as a hollow whisper.

Her fingers, still curled around the blanket and Thermos, trembled. It didn't occur to her to release her grip on them as he pulled them—and her—slowly towards him. Finally he removed them from her weak grasp and placed them on the floor. His eyes never left hers all the time.

An image of the livid bruising she'd seen on his body came into her head, but her imagination didn't limit itself to damage; it conjured up some impressive muscles, smooth olive-toned flesh and crisp body hair too. She ran the tip of her tongue over her dry lips to lubricate them and gave her head a tiny shake, but neither act totally dispelled the disturbing image.

'Did I hurt you?' she asked hoarsely. She knew she hadn't been a submissive victim.

He touched the side of her face softly and sent an illicit little shiver through the tense body. Darcy couldn't afford the time to worry if the tremor had been transmitted through his fingertips—it was taking all her energy convincing her knees they didn't want to fold under her. To make matters infinitely worse, the debilitating weakness wasn't just affecting her limbs…at best, her brain was functioning on a very basic, fuzzy level.

'Do you want to?' Finger on the angle of her jaw, he tilted her face up to his.

Darcy shook her head—she didn't want to think about what she'd like to do to him; it wasn't decent. His face was swimming in and out of focus as she stared back at him.

'I don't like hurting people. Do you…?'

Reece didn't reply; he simply took her by the shoulders and drew her unresisting body towards him, parting his thighs to let her rest within their confining circle.

'Are you quite sure that concern for my health was the only reason you came here, Darcy…?'

She had to do something to throw cold water on the escalating intimacy and danger of a situation that was fast getting out of hand.

'What other reason could there be?'

Underneath the faint antiseptic hospital scent and a distinctive male fragrance she could smell him—not just his soap or cologne, but *him*! Panic was just a heartbeat away—or was it capitulation she could sense…?

'This one…' His intention was written clear on his dark, impassioned features.

Desperation and panic flared in her wide eyes just before they reflexly closed. The uncoordinated flailing movements of her hands brought them in contact with the iron-hard thighs pressed either side of her hips; she froze and her fingers spasmed, relaxed, then tentatively spread out over the hard-muscled expanse.

'That's good,' he approved.

Darcy gave a sigh; it was. She felt his breath as it moved over her cheek, felt it tease the quivering line of her trembling lips in the moment before his lips purposefully parted hers. The sensual, silken, smooth stab of his tongue melted her last resistance.

Darcy gave a lost little cry and sank deeper into the seductive velvet blackness inside her head. The explosive force of his hunger was something she'd never encountered before. Almost more shocking was the equally unexpected raw response that uncoiled within her. She gave herself up totally to the seductive exploration, only stopping when she could no longer breathe.

They drew apart, but not very far. Her forehead was resting against his, her fingers were twisted in the glossy strands of his dark hair.

'I forgive you totally for waking me up.'

And, given he kissed like an angel, she was prepared to forgive him for sounding so smug. He knew all the moves all right; even now Darcy didn't want to admit even to herself that it wasn't simple slick technique that had made her respond to him that way.

'Ever undressed inside a sleeping bag?'

Darcy stiffened slightly but didn't draw back. She only

had herself to blame for this situation—if she hadn't kissed him back like that...

'Isn't that a bit of a leap from a kiss?'

'There are kisses and then again there are *kisses*.'

Again he was right. Until that particular moment Darcy hadn't known how great the gap between the two was. She was pink all over already, and the shade deepened perceptively as she encountered the sensuous warmth of his eyes.

'It's a challenging proposition...' she admitted, a responsive smile in her voice. Yesterday she would have laughed her socks off if someone had suggested she would be seriously considering sleeping with a man she barely knew.

'I can hear a "but" coming on,' Reece predicted gloomily.

Reluctantly Darcy released her hold on his hair and straightened up. She became aware for the first time that at some point during the embrace Reece had removed her windcheater. She stood there shivering, but not from cold.

'I think it would be a safer bet all round if you invest in a heated blanket,' she explained regretfully.

'No electricity.' His gesture caused the candles to flicker and dance in the draught he created. 'And if you're worried on a safety basis I'm a prepared sort of guy.'

'I wasn't.'

'You ought to be; you don't know me.'

She blinked. Is he lecturing *me* on safe sex...? 'Which is one of the reasons I'm not about to sleep with you.'

'The others being...?'

'You have several broken bones.'

Reece impatiently disposed of this objection. 'We can work around that.'

Just imagining what 'working around' might involve made her skin burn.

'You know you want to.'

Darcy gasped. 'That,' she bit back with tremulous contempt, 'is an incredibly arrogant thing to say.'

'Maybe, but it's true,' he returned imperturbably.

'What are you doing…?' she squawked as he got to his feet.

'I can't make love to you if we're on opposite sides of the room.'

This would have been even truer if I had stayed safely tucked up in my own bed—only I didn't. Why didn't I…? Did I want this to happen…? She shook her head in feverish denial but the idea clung stubbornly on.

'I find you quite incredibly exciting.'

His honeyed drawl froze her to the spot, the dark reckless glow in his eyes liquefied her bones, and held her there. Eyes a little wild, she tilted her head to maintain eye contact as he came closer…and closer.

'I think you must be thinking of someone else…'

'You smell like summer.'

'I do…? When you said we could work around it…are you sure…?'

Reece took her small face between his big hands. 'I don't say things I don't mean.'

'You're quite sure…' Darcy felt his low laughter against her ear, smelt the male muskiness of his arousal.

'Shut up and kiss me, woman.'

CHAPTER FOUR

THE impetus of the kiss made them stagger backwards into the makeshift table. A small bottle of tablets fell onto the dusty floor; Darcy automatically tried to avoid stepping onto the contents.

'Your painkillers...' Fortunately the bottle of whisky set beside it on the table hadn't fallen.

The arm around her waist didn't slacken.

'To hell with them,' he slurred.

'Good God!' she gasped. 'You've mixed tablets with booze, haven't you?' she accused hoarsely. 'That explains it.'

'Explains what?' He didn't sound terribly interested in her reply.

'This!' she indited shakily, stabbing a finger at her chest and discovering in the process that at some point during the kiss he'd managed to remove her sweater.

If undressing women ever became an Olympic event he would win gold with one hand tied behind his back—quite literally, she thought, her eyes sliding to his immobilised arm.

Flushing deeply, she gathered the lightly elasticated neckline of her pyjama top in one fist, which didn't so much conceal what was going on underneath the thin, silky fabric as draw his hot-eyed attention to it.

'I've no idea what you're talking about, but hell, you taste good.' He pushed a hank of her silky hair aside to press an open-mouthed kiss to the pulse point on her neck.

Darcy's head fell back and she groaned, the sensual shock of his touch juddering through her responsive body.

'You don't understand.' She valiantly struggled past the passion barrier to make him listen.

'Reece, I think it's probable you're having a reaction to your medication.' Depressing as it was, it did perfectly explain away the inexplicable—a man like him being so deeply in lust with an average type like herself.

'So that's what this is.' He firmly unglued her fingers and peered down the open neckline; what he saw seemed to afford him considerable pleasure.

She got even hotter. 'I don't think you're taking this seriously.'

'Believe me,' he grated hoarsely, 'I'm taking this very seriously.'

'You don't really want me,' she whimpered.

Reece's jaw tightened. 'Is that a fact...?' He slid the silky fabric clear down her shoulders and with a muffled groan pressed his lips to the heaving contours he'd revealed. 'Absolutely incredible...'

'Sweet...sweet...mercy...' Darcy tried to regroup but it was an uphill battle. His tongue had begun to travel very slowly over the slope of one breast. Did it really matter that he wasn't in full possession of his senses...? *'Listen!'* Fingers in his hair, she pulled his head back.

'What the hell's wrong now?' There was a light sheen of sweat covering his taut, lean features, the dampness extending down the glistening column of his throat. His hot eyes kept sliding from her face in the general direction of her heaving breasts.

'It's the medication. I think you've had some sort of reaction to it. You can't take alcohol with some sorts of analgesia. That's why you're acting like this.' Miserably Darcy brushed a strand of hair from her damp face and found she couldn't look him in the eyes—it was too humiliating... Her body was literally throbbing with arousal, aching for his touch.

'You can't think of any other reason…?' The blood in her temples roared as his eyes slid in hot, sensual appraisal over her body. 'A reason like I'm sexually attracted to you!' She audibly caught her breath. 'A reason like I've been lying here alone all night, wondering what it would be like to have you beside me, warm and soft, to be inside you. Then you're here…' His throat muscles worked. 'And you want to stay.' He smiled with grim satisfaction when she didn't respond to the challenge.

Darcy couldn't speak; the sound of his low, vibrantly masculine voice saying things no man had ever said to her was like a fist tightening inside her belly. She felt light-headed and dizzy and her blood seemed to hum hotly, pooling; the ache between her thighs was so intense she could hardly stand up, and, her breathing shallow and fast, she stared breathlessly up at him.

'But the—'

'Paracetamol. You can buy it anywhere over the counter.' His sensuous lips curled contemptuously as her eyes widened. 'The doc wanted to give me something stronger but I've never been keen on having my senses dulled.'

'Then this is…'

Reece nodded. 'The real thing. Unless you're going to tell me you're taking hallucinogenic drugs?'

The dazed look still in her eyes, she shook her head vigorously.

'Does this feel real enough for you?' he asked, pressing his lean, hard body tight against hers.

Darcy could feel him, thick and hard, pressing into the softness of her belly. 'It…you feel incredible,' she gasped.

'Take my shirt off, Darcy?'

'Because of your shoulder.'

'Because I want you to.'

That seemed a good enough reason to Darcy.

Her hands were shaking as one by one she slid free the buttons and pushed the soft cord fabric aside to reveal his broad chest and flat belly. Expression rapt, she spread her fingers and felt the fine muscles just beneath the surface of his taut skin twitch and tighten.

Her hair looked silver by candlelight and all Reece could see of her as she leant closer was the top of her head and the exposed nape of her slender neck. It wasn't an area he'd previously considered erotic—was it napes in general or this nape in particular…? That was a question for later—right now he needed to assuage the fire in his blood, the ache in his loins.

A deep line bisected her smooth brow as she examined the bruised area. 'Tell me if I hurt you,' she whispered, tracing a line across his belly with her fingernail.

'I'm hurting,' he told her thickly.

Alarmed, she raised her eyes questioningly to his. 'Where…?' she began. She saw the expression on his face and her voice faded away.

'Here…' he took her hand and showed her '…here and here,' he elaborated thickly.

Darcy whimpered, the last remnants of her control evaporating.

'I want to see you. Take your clothes off for me. All of them.'

Not doing as he requested—or was it a demand?—was never an option. Like someone in a dream she crossed her arms and began to lift the hem of her top up over her smooth stomach.

'And, Darcy…?'

She paused.

'Look at me.'

Darcy did. She could hear the harsh, uneven sound of his breathing, loud in the quiet room. Even in this light she could make out a definite flush of colour along his slashing cheekbones and the fire in his eyes— Did I really put it there…? How strange…how marvellous.

Their eyes locked, and her anxiety was instantly soothed; he looked just as needy as she felt. Despite the new confidence, her hands trembled uncontrollably as she did as he had bid. It was no slow, seductive striptease because even with a fire now blazing in the hearth it didn't seem such a good idea to linger over disrobing.

'You're beautiful.' She almost believed him.

He closed the small gap between them. Where he touched her Darcy's skin tingled, and pretty soon she tingled all over. 'And cold.' He began to briskly massage her cold extremities. 'Come on, get in here.' Taking her by the hand, he led her towards the sleeping bag and blankets.

The cotton lining still retained the last remnants of his body heat. Darcy drew her knees up to her chin and waited for him to join her, anticipation pumping darkly though her. She watched as he shed his clothes, ripping the shirt as he tried to ease it too quickly over his injured arm; he was lean, lovely and very, *very* aroused.

He was actually so beautiful she wanted to cry—she *was* crying, hot tears sliding over her cheeks. He wiped away the dampness with his thumb when he finally came to join her but didn't question their presence.

'Come here,' he whispered.

Darcy did; there wasn't very far to go. They lay side by side, close but not touching, until with a hoarse groan he reached across with his good arm and drew her on top of him. His mouth reached hungrily for hers.

Darcy responded joyfully to the demands of his lips and thrusting tongue. It was intoxicating to have nothing to separate them any longer. Darcy wriggled to fully appreciate the sensation. His skin was warmer than hers; it was harder, and she discovered it had a deliciously smooth texture roughened by drifts of body hair that prickled against her breasts and thighs. Every detail delighted her and increased the pressure of excitement building inside her to detonation point.

'For a one-handed man,' she remarked a hundred or so gasps later, 'you manage pretty well.'

A savage grin split Reece's face as he looked into her flushed, aroused face. 'If you think that was good, wait until you get a taste of no hands.'

A confused frown drew Darcy's feathery brows together as she puzzled over his words, the meaning of which was brought crashing home to her seconds later.

Shock tensed her muscles for a split-second before she gave a languid sigh and relaxed. She moaned his name out loud and writhed restlessly as his tongue flickered lower over the soft curve of her abdomen. The excitement built to fever pitch as he continued his merciless ministrations.

The zip on the sleeping bag gave way as he brought her knees up and knelt between them, but Darcy didn't register the blast of cold air. The pleasure was so intense it bordered on pain; she cried out in protest but she cried out even louder when he stopped.

He kissed her, stilling her inarticulate protests.

He tasted and smelt of her and sex; it was a mind-shattering combination.

'I want you so badly!' she moaned, leaning her face into his neck.

'Then take me, sweetheart,' he urged throatily. 'Take me.'

Darcy lifted her head. 'I can. Can I…?' she gasped wonderingly. He whispered things in her ear that convinced her she could—she could do anything she wanted to.

Darcy stared down gloatingly at the magnificent man beneath her—his eyes were closed, his skin glistened with sweat. Her muscles tensed, she bore downwards. The cry of relief and triumph that was wrenched from her throat as she lowered herself upon him echoed around the room.

Reece's eyes snapped open. 'Oh, my God, sweetheart!' he groaned. 'You are…' A red mist danced before his eyes; he couldn't speak, he couldn't think, he could just thrust and thrust…

She rubbed her gritty-feeling eyes. Someone had carefully tucked the sleeping bag around her while she slept. Someone nothing. Her eyes went to the only other person in the room.

'Sleep well?' The fully clad figure bent over a portable keyboard didn't lift his dark head, but seemed to sense her wakefulness.

'Yes, thank you.' She tucked her nose below the covers. So this was that embarrassing morning-after feeling. 'What are you doing?'

'Sending a few e-mails.'

What sort of person sent e-mails at this time of the morning…? The sort of person you slept with last night—a *stranger*, her mental critic added, just in case she didn't feel bad enough already, a beautiful stranger.

'Right…' She cleared her throat. 'What time is it…?' she asked, more out of a desire to fill the yawning gap in their conversation than a genuine desire to know.

'Almost seven.'

'Seven!' she yelped, shooting upright. 'Oh, God!' she groaned, clasping her hands to her bare breasts.

Reece closed the lid of the laptop with a click and turned to face her. His gently ironic expression made her even more aware of the absurdity of displaying inhibitions the morning after the night before—especially when the night before was the one they'd shared!

'Is that a problem?'

'Dad and the boys will be up for breakfast,' she agonised.

'Can't they do *anything* without you to take charge?'

'Of course they can,' she responded, exasperated. 'And I don't "take charge".' Did she really strike him as a bossy, *organising* female? 'I just want things to be...' A frown puckered the smooth skin across her broad, seamless brow.

'The same?' he put in gently, drawing her startled gaze.

'I don't know what you mean.'

'Sure you do—you're trying to step into your mother's shoes. Has it ever occurred to you, Darcy, that maybe she wants her absence to be noticed...?'

A flicker of uncertainty made the soft corners of her mouth droop for a few tell-tale seconds before her expression hardened. 'You know nothing about it,' she blustered angrily. 'Mum isn't a frustrated housewife and she isn't menopausal.'

'Is that what the menfolk think...?'

Nick had put forward this theory but Darcy had soon put him right. 'Anyway, you're missing the point.'

He looked mildly perplexed. '*I* am...?'

'They'll wonder where I am.'

She watched his sensual lips twist. 'And you don't want to broadcast the fact you spent the night with me.'

The sad part was her reputation could probably survive intact. She'd learnt a long time ago that people didn't think of her and steamy sex in the same thought. She was doomed to be the eternal Mary Poppins figure. Which was pretty ironic when you had an almost ruined marriage on your conscience.

'Do you blame me?' she asked him scornfully. He didn't respond but a nerve along his jaw-line did some flexing. 'Relax,' she sighed disconsolately. 'Even if I did want to tell, nobody would believe me.'

Reece got to his feet and strolled towards her. 'Put this on—you look ridiculous.' He handed her her pyjama top.

His scornful contempt of her maidenly modesty was even more infuriating because she shared his opinion; even so, she couldn't bring herself to expose herself to the full glare of his scrutiny, which was, she reasoned gloomily, bound to be a whole lot more objective than it had been last night.

'If you're waiting for me to turn my back you'll be waiting a long, long time,' he drawled, taking up a grandstand seat on the packing case. He stretched out his long legs and casually crossed his booted feet at the ankle.

'You're no gentleman.'

He seemed to find her accusation amusing.

With an angry toss of her tousled hair she pulled the garment over her head.

It was a classic case of more haste, less speed. With her head halfway through the arm-hole she took a deep breath and told herself to calm down. So she didn't have the best boobs in the world—they were more than adequate…some might even say ample…what did it matter if he didn't grade them in the top ten per cent…? After all, they were only ships that had passed—and collided—in the night.

The rest of the manoeuvre was performed with a bit of belated dignity. She smoothed the fabric into place.

'I'm perfectly at ease with my body,' she declared defiantly. Why not just give him a list of your insecurities to peruse at his leisure and be done with it, you *idiot*!

'Oh, it shows, sweetheart, it shows,' came the bone-dry response.

Whilst his facial muscles didn't budge an inch, the sardonic amusement in his eyes said it all. Then suddenly he wasn't smiling any more and something was added to the atmosphere that hadn't been there a second before—something that made her heart-rate pick up tempo.

'Last night…' he began heavily.

Here was the point where he explained it had been great *but*... She jumped in to beat him to the punchline; no way could she endure the big brush-off she sensed was heading her way!

'Last night!' For some reason she found herself grinning in a manic kind of way across at him. 'Yes, mad wasn't it...?' She shrugged in a way that suggested that kind of madness came her way on a regular basis.

'Mad, bad...' his deep voice lovingly caressed each syllable and became diamond-hard as he continued '...mind-blowingly great sex...is that what you are trying to say?'

Darcy wasn't trying to say anything; she was trying to remember how to breathe! Not only did he sound as if he meant it, he looked it too. In fact, that mean, hungry look on his rampantly male features made her shudder inside and blush hotly on the outside—she wished she could have reversed the scenario; it would have shown less.

Now, here was something she hadn't bargained for. Was it a good or bad thing...?

With a rush she got to her feet and tugged the pyjama top down as far as it would go over her thighs.

'I'm glad you enjoyed yourself.' Of all the *moronic*... With a sigh of relief she located her clothes folded in a neat pile—Darcy retained a very definite memory of throwing them along with her inhibitions to the four winds the previous night. She found the thought of Reece retrieving and carefully folding her clothes somehow strangely unsettling.

'Did you?'

'You know I did,' she choked.

'I seem to recall your mentioning something to that effect,' he agreed.

Darcy choked some more.

'Why are you running away?' His languid tone suggested

casual curiosity rather than a driving desire to discover the reason.

Darcy zipped up her jeans, swearing softly as the zip snagged in the fabric of the pyjama trousers she had on underneath. 'That's rich coming from you!' she said, going into attack mode.

There was a tense silence.

'Meaning…?' Darcy had never heard that dangerous note in his voice before but she didn't doubt he used it often—and no doubt it had the desired effect of cowing the recipient. Well, not this time, mate…!

A mulish expression settled on her soft features as she planted her hands on her hips and laughed. 'You've got to be kidding…? You're holed up here; what's that if it's not running away?'

She watched the anger slowly fade from his eyes. 'Christmas. I'm running away from Christmas…'

A startled laugh was drawn from her. 'There's a lot of it around.' If all Mum was running away from was Christmas she'd be delighted—the complications arose if it was her life or, nasty thought, her family that had made her flee!

'Pardon…?'

Darcy shook her head. 'Nothing,' she prevaricated, her eyes sliding from his.

'Then why are you looking so shifty?' he wondered, displaying an unforgivable and highly worrying degree of perception.

'I've got that sort of face,' she snapped back bad-temperedly.

'You wouldn't make a poker player,' he agreed.

'I was just thinking.'

'Dare I ask what?'

'If you must know, I was thinking you don't strike me as the sort of man who runs away from anything. And even if you did, why on earth would you run away here…?' Her eyes did a quick, highly critical circuit of the room.

He shook his head and clicked his tongue. 'Don't let the Yorkshire Tourist Board hear you say that,' he chided.

'I meant this house.'

'Why not…?' he drawled.

'No electricity, I'm guessing poor plumbing…?' She began to tick off the reasons on her fingers.

'Diabolical,' he conceded ruefully. 'If you want the bathroom I'd wait until you get next door if I were you.'

'Thanks for the advice.' She refused to be sidetracked. 'You still haven't told me why.'

The imperious angle of his head made it seem as though he was looking down his masterful nose at her—Darcy didn't relish the sensation.

'Could that be because I don't think it's any of your business…?'

Darcy relished this sensation even less! She caught her breath angrily at the calculated rebuff.

'Well, that put me in my place, didn't it?'

A spasm of something close to regret flickered across Reece's features.

'Hold on.' He moved to intercept her before she reached the door. 'My friend's builders have been a little less than truthful with their reports to him,' he explained abruptly. 'I'd say they've fallen behind schedule by a couple of months. I was expecting something less…basic.'

'Then you're not staying?' Of course he's not, dumbo. 'I wasn't…'

Sure she must have misheard his soft response, Darcy raised her startled eyes to his face. 'What's changed?'

He was watching her with that infuriatingly enigmatic smile that told her absolutely nothing. 'I like the neighbours.'

Their eyes met and a great rush of sexual longing

crowded out sensible coherent thought. She never figured out how long she stood there staring at him like a drooling idiot.

Does he think all he has to do is click his fingers and I'll…? Why not, Darcy, girl, that's all he had to do last night! Her face flushed with mortification.

'Like the idea of sex on tap, you mean!'

His mouth tightened.

'Well, let me tell you, if you think last night was anything other than a one-off, think again!' she advised hotly.

'Does the idea of a relationship based on sex frighten you, Darcy?'

'No,' she told him candidly, 'it appalls me!'

'And excites you,' he interjected slyly.

'No such thing!' she blustered.

'Liar…you want me and we both know it.'

Darcy gave a hoarse, incredulous laugh—talk about Neanderthal. 'Why not just thump your chest and drag me off to your cave?'

Reece thought the general idea was sound, although he was thinking more along the lines of a nice hotel room with good plumbing and Room Service.

'It may not be a particularly politically correct thing to say, but—'

'*May?*' she squeaked. 'There's no ''may'' about it!'

'Tell me, do you regret last night happened? Do you regret we made love, Darcy?'

She lifted her chin, met his eyes scornfully, and opened her mouth. 'You bet I…' The blood drained dramatically from her face. 'I…*no*,' she admitted with the utmost reluctance—now would have been a good time to lie.

'As I was saying, from the first moment I saw you…'

Perhaps the significance of her confession was wasted on him…? Then again, perhaps this was wishful thinking on her part.

'The first moment you saw me you thought I was a boy. Is there something you're not telling me…?'

He eyed her with signs of irritation. 'So, not the *first*,' he gritted. 'We're not talking about *then*, we're talking about *now*.'

Darcy didn't want to talk about now—actually, she didn't want to talk about anything with this infuriating man who seemed to have the knack of making her say incriminating things.

'And now,' she announced coldly, 'I'm going home—or I would be if you'd shift yourself.' She looked pointedly past his shoulder at the door.

Reece immediately stepped to one side with a fluid grace that made her stomach muscles quiver; perversely she found herself reluctant to take the escape route offered.

Whilst she hovered indecisively he moved to her side. 'I'll walk you home.'

Darcy's eyes widened. 'You're joking—right?'

'Actually,' he confessed, 'I was hoping you'd let me have the use of your shower, or, better still, a long, hot bath.'

'My God, but you've got a nerve!' she gasped.

'I've also got several broken ribs, extensive bruising and a bust shoulder, but don't let that influence your decision.'

Despite herself, Darcy felt a smile forming. 'We're not a hotel!' she told him severely.

'Is that a no?'

Darcy's eyes narrowed. 'It should be.' He didn't look surprised by her capitulation, but then, why would he, when you've already proved you're a push-over in every sense of the word? 'If you say *anything* to my family about…you know what…'

'So, Darce…?'

'So what?' Darcy waved her secateurs in her brother's

face. 'If you're going to get in my way you might as well carry this lot.' She indicated the large pile of freshly cut holly at her feet.

'*Me!*'

My God, but men were hopeless. 'I suppose you'd just stand there and watch me shift the lot.' They'd certainly stand by and watch her decorate the house with boughs of festive greenery, not to mention decorate the enormous tree that by family tradition they collected from the local garden centre owned by her godparents.

'It's sharp.'

'It's holly, Nick; of course it's sharp.'

'This sweater cost me a fortune,' he grumbled, preceding her up the garden path. 'Where do you want it?' he asked when they eventually reached the house.

'Leave it in the porch. Feel like a cup of coffee?' she asked as her brother followed her into the house.

'I feel like some answers.'

Darcy, her expression suspicious, watched as he plucked a couple of stray glossy leaves from the fine rib of his sweater.

'About what?' she asked, trying not to sound defensive.

'About what you were doing with our neighbour. I thought you couldn't stand him.'

'I can't,' Darcy asserted stoutly. 'The man had a serious accident. What was I supposed to do—say he couldn't take a shower?' She turned away, crashing the cups and saucers. 'Did you say you wanted tea or coffee?'

'Neither. It would be when you bumped into him while you were walking the dogs that he asked to use our facilities, would it, Darce…?'

'Yes, that's right,' she agreed quickly, not turning around.

'Since when, little sister, did you take the dogs for a walk wearing your pyjamas?'

Darcy started and spilt the milk over the work surface.

'Language!' her brother reproached.

She shot him a withering glance and wiped her clammy palms on the seat of her jeans before she picked up the cup; the faint tremor in her fingers was barely noticeable—though eagle-eyed Nick had probably spotted it.

'Since when did you become Miss Marple?' She laughed lightly as she planted herself on a chair and raised the scalding drink to her lips. Playing it down was the best way to go…

'Since I looked into your room after I took the dogs for a walk around seven and found you weren't there.'

All the colour bar a small pink circle over either cheek fled Darcy's guilty face. 'What were you doing in my room?'

'Fetching you a cup of tea.'

It was typical of Nick to discover his considerate side at the worst possible moment. 'Oh…' What else could she say? She certainly wasn't going to volunteer any more information if she could help it!

'What is a guy like him with that sort of serious money doing hanging around someone like you?' Nick wondered suspiciously. 'No offence intended, Darce…' he added casually.

Darcy wondered what he'd say if she told him she took offence—serious offence. She was about to quiz her tactless sibling on the 'serious money' statement when his next comment distracted her.

'Has he followed you here, Darcy, is that it? I'm assuming you'd already met before yesterday.'

'Why on earth would you think that?' There was no way he could have picked anything up from her attitude when she'd brought Reece back earlier. She'd been very careful about that—so careful, in fact, that her behaviour had bordered on the catatonic, before she'd swiftly excused herself and nipped off to the church to do the flowers—it was Mum's turn on the rota; Adam would probably have a fit when he saw her efforts.

'I think that because I didn't think you were the sort of girl who would spend the night with a complete stranger.' If what he had said wasn't bad enough, Nick had to go and make it even worse by adding, 'Even if he is rich and powerful.'

For several moments Darcy didn't do anything, but when she finally lifted her eyes from the rim of her coffee-cup they were sparkling with anger.

'How dare you?'

Nick looked taken aback by the rancour in his sister's shaking voice. 'Come on, Darce, you must admit it was pretty sus...'

'I don't have to admit anything!' she said in a low, intense voice that throbbed with emotion. Carefully pushing her seat back, she rose to her feet. 'Not to you at least.' She ran her tongue over the bloodless outline of her pale lips. 'Just for the record, Nick, you're the biggest hypocrite I know.'

His eyes filled with concern, Nick rose to his feet. 'Darce, I didn't mean—'

Darcy cut him off with a flash of her narrowed eyes. 'Incidentally, I'll sleep with who the hell I like!' she yelled, sweeping from the room.

Her dramatic exit was ruined by the fact she narrowly avoided colliding with the solid bulk of Reece Erskine on her way out.

'Whoa there.' She'd have fallen rather than accept the arm he tried to offer her; it wasn't easy, as he was carrying a large wicker hamper balanced on the crook of his functioning elbow, and his solicitous action almost sent it to the floor.

'What are you doing here?' The tense, scratchy thing

didn't sound like her voice at all. Making a superhuman effort, she pulled herself together and stepped back away from his chest—and the temptation to lay her head on it. Even holding her breath, she could still smell the fresh male fragrance that emanated from his warm skin, so she gave up on what was not really a practical long-term solution to her problem to begin with.

'That's no way to greet a guy carrying gifts, Darce.'

Darcy hadn't even noticed the twins and Jack, who had entered the kitchen behind Reece—when he was around she didn't tend to notice much else.

'Cool!' Harry cried, holding up a large box of Belgian chocolates and adding them to the pile of luxury items he and his twin were extracting from the hamper they'd set down on the table.

Darcy glanced at the growing pile—there was no way he'd got that little lot from the village shop.

'This is mine,' Charlie crowed, discovering a bottle of champagne.

Clicking his tongue tolerantly, his father removed the bottle from his crestfallen son's hand. 'This is really very generous of you, Reece…'

'A small thank-you for everything you've done for me.'

'It really wasn't necessary,' Jack insisted.

'Dad, you're not going to give it back, are you?' Charlie asked in alarm.

'How did we raise two such avaricious little monsters…?' The twins exchanged rueful grins. 'What the boys are trying to say, Reece, is the gift is much appreciated. Can we offer you a drink—it looks like there's one on the go… Darcy…?'

'In case nobody noticed, I'm busy,' she responded shortly.

If her stepfather had looked annoyed by her unneighbourly response she could have coped, but no, he had to go and look hurt and guilty.

'I suppose,' he responded worriedly, 'we have let a lot of things fall on your shoulders.' He turned to Reece. 'It's just my wife usually…'

'I enjoy it, Dad,' Darcy interrupted hurriedly, hating the forlorn expression on her stepfather's face and despising herself for putting it there. 'Actually, I was just off to pick up the tree. Anyone like to come?' she enquired. She was predictably underwhelmed by the response. 'Right, I'll be off, then.'

'If you don't mind, I wouldn't mind coming along for the ride.'

Darcy spun around, horror etched on her pale features. 'You!'

'I'm getting a bit stir-crazy, unable to drive,' Reece explained glibly to the room in general.

'You'd be bored,' she said several shades too emphatically.

'I think it's an excellent idea,' Jack responded firmly, reproach in his eyes.

Nick spoke for the first time. 'I'm sure Darcy will enjoy having company.'

Darcy shot her treacherous narrow-minded brother a seething look from under the sweep of her lashes. 'There will be lashings of mud.' Nobody paid her any heed.

'Borrow some Wellingtons—the twins look about the same size as you.'

With a sigh Darcy subsided into a resentful silence whilst her eager family—with the notable exception of Nick—equipped their neighbour.

'You look awfully pale, Darcy.'

Thanks, bro, she thought as Nick's contribution to the conversation brought her a lot of highly undesirable attention.

'Yes, she does, doesn't she?' her stepfather agreed. 'Are you feeling all right?'

'Absolutely fine.'

'It's probably sleep deprivation,' Nick continued smoothly. 'She's not been sleeping too well.' He wasn't looking at his sister as he spoke but at the tall figure who stood beside her. The two men exchanged a long look.

'Is that right? You didn't say so, Darcy.'

'Lot on my mind, Dad...' she muttered. 'Holidays are always the same—it takes me the first week to wind down.'

'Darcy is a computer analyst,' her proud stepfather explained to Reece. 'She has a *very* responsible job.'

Darcy cringed. 'Give the man a break, Dad,' she laughed uncomfortably. 'I'm sure Mr Erskine doesn't want to know about my work.'

Nick, of course, couldn't resist stirring the pot. 'You mean, he doesn't already?'

'If you've got nothing better to do, Nick, you could take a look at the Christmas lights for me.' She felt a surge of satisfaction as her brother looked suitably horrified at the prospect. 'They don't seem to be working.'

'I think,' Nick announced hopefully, 'that it's time we bought some new ones.'

'You can't do that, Nick!' Charlie protested. 'We've had them for ever...'

'My point exactly,' Nick muttered. 'It's the same every year—they never work.'

'I remember the time the cat—that one that had no tail—' Harry began.

'Oscar,' his twin supplied.

Nick decided to inject a little reality into this trip down memory lane. '*I* remember the time they fused the electrics while Mum was cooking Christmas dinner...'

There was a collective subdued gasp of dismay and all eyes turned to Jack.

'Far be it from me to break with tradition,' Nick put in quickly. 'I'll fix the damned things.'

'You all seem pretty protective of your father,' Reece observed as he trailed Darcy outside.

'Stepfather, actually, but yes, I suppose we are.'

'Stepfather; that makes the twins your...?'

Darcy gave a resigned sigh. 'Jack adopted Nick and me when he married Mum—I was five. Not that it's any of your business.' She stood beside the Land Rover, jingling the keys. 'You can't *want* to come...' Please...please, let him say he doesn't. She always had been a hopeless optimist!

CHAPTER FIVE

'DID you have to bring this thing?' Reece scowled as the big dog, his paws planted on the back of the passenger seat, licked his face ecstatically.

'I wanted *him* to come,' Darcy, tight-lipped, pointedly replied. 'Sit down, Wally!' Reluctantly the big animal curled up on the back seat of her stepfather's Land Rover, his eyes reproachful.

Reece wiped the excess canine saliva off his neck with a pained grimace. 'A man could get to feel unwanted.'

'Not by Wally.' The dog's ears pricked up at the sound of his name. 'Or my family,' she reflected with a frustrated little snort. 'You've certainly weaseled your way into their affections,' she hissed nastily. 'It was a master stroke to appeal to the twins' stomachs.'

Reece, who wasn't really interested in the direct route to the twins' hearts, responded with a slightly distracted smile.

'I take it the way to your elder brother's heart is not through his stomach...'

'You noticed that, did you?' Darcy had not yet forgiven Nick. How dared he lecture her on morality, she fumed— the man who had had, much to his parents' dismay and her awe, an affair with a thirty-year-old divorcee when he was just seventeen?

'Let's just say I didn't feel warm and welcome when he looked at me,' Reece responded drily. His eyes narrowed. 'Is he giving you a hard time?' he wondered suspiciously.

'I don't give a damn what Nick thinks!'

'Yeah, I heard that bit.'

A deep tide of colour washed over her fair skin as she

worked out what he must have heard. 'Don't go reading anything into that. I was establishing a principle. Sex isn't a high priority for me.'

Darcy knew she was wasting her breath; the man obviously had her down as some sort of sex junkie—I could always refer him to Michael, she thought. He would set the record straight. Not that Michael had ever come right out and complained about her sex drive, or lack of it, but that was probably because the man had still had a wife at home to keep happy. From his point of view, the fact she hadn't made excessive demands had probably been a godsend!

'You got many other prospects lined up?'

'Has anyone ever told you you've got a very crude mouth, and a one-track mind?' He wasn't the only one, she thought, struggling hard to banish the image of his big, sexy body shifting beneath her…his skin glistening…the ripple of muscle… The heat travelled like a flash-flood up her neck and bathed her face. The empty feeling in the pit of her belly got emptier and achier.

Despite her determination to think of anything else but the man beside her, Darcy couldn't have stopped her eyes from furtively fluttering to the mouth she'd criticised if her life had depended on it. Perfection didn't seem too extravagant an adjective for that wide, mobile curve which intriguingly managed to combine both sensuality and control.

'Actually,' she mused, her voice husky, 'the new vicar did ask me to the Christmas dance.' She'd almost forgotten this unexpected event, which had occurred only this morning, but then she had other things on her mind. How her little sister would laugh if she ever discovered what a man-magnet the sister she despaired of had become.

'New vicar…' Reece didn't look as though he was taking the opposition seriously. 'I'm seeing tweed jackets, maybe a goatee—looks aren't everything, of course…'

'Actually, Adam played rugby for Oxford,' she was pleased to announce.

'In the Sixties…?'

'I'd say he's thirty…'

'Broken nose…?' Reece suggested hopefully.

Darcy's lips twitched. 'No, he was a back-row man. It was a toss-up between male modelling and the church,' she lied outrageously. Her expression sobered. 'Reece, are you?' she began.

'Am I what?'

'Nick said…' she began.

'Nick said what?' Reece thought he could guess.

'He said you were rich—super-rich, actually. Is that true?'

Reece didn't prevaricate. 'Yes.'

Deep down she'd always known he didn't live in the same world as she did. Darcy tried not to let her disappointment show; she'd been secretly hoping that Nick might have got it wrong. Now there was no point even dreaming this thing might be anything other than a one-night stand.

'I suppose you're famous too?' she accused bitterly.

She made it sound as though he'd been concealing the fact he was wanted by Interpol. Reece had never met a female who had reacted in quite this way to his social position and wealth before.

'Obviously not,' he drawled, amusement in his voice.

'Don't be offended,' she soothed absently. 'I don't read the financial pages.'

'But Nick does?'

'Hardly; he's a sports journalist.'

Reece laughed. 'I think you're being a bit severe; I knew a sports writer once who had read a book.'

Darcy couldn't summon the necessary smile to respond

to his raillery. 'Are you involved in property development? Is that why you came to the Hall?'

'My company is involved in property development,' Reece agreed, not mentioning that this property development didn't include small country houses being renovated on a shoestring.

It did involve a string of brand-new hotels in various capitals of the world which the leisure arm of his empire now ran. A good many office complexes and several sports stadiums which had popped up all over Europe had also begun their existence on a drawing board in the Erskine Building—he didn't mention this either.

'Then you're some sort of property developer...?' she prodded.

'That was one of the areas we've diversified into during the last few years.'

'*We?*'

'Well, it's not a one-man show; my sister Kate is heavily involved in the running of the hotel chain, and my cousin Declan has just joined us. My kid brother has just finished his stint at Harvard, so hopefully he'll—'

'You told me you didn't have a family!' Darcy twitched her rear-view mirror and saw an almost comical grimace of dismay register on his drop-dead gorgeous features.

'*I did...?*' he echoed evasively.

'Yes, you did.'

'They're a lovely bunch but a bit...overwhelming *en masse*—like at Christmas time. Don't you ever wish you were an only child...?'

The encounter with Nick still fresh in her mind, Darcy found herself nodding. 'When I'm around Nick, yes, I do.'

'The guy's only trying to protect you.' Reece had a sister of his own, and a real headache she was too.

Darcy could hardly believe her ears—Reece, defending Nick of all people! 'This male bonding is all very sweet but have you forgotten it's you he wants to protect me from?' she reminded him.

'I'd not forgotten. I have this nasty feeling when he gets me alone he's going to ask me what my intentions are.'

Did he really expect her to appreciate the humour of this remark? 'He already knows. That's the problem.'

She sensed his looking at her, and couldn't stop herself taking her eyes off the road for a split-second…he was pushing an unruly hank of glossy almost black hair from his eyes. Did he always have to look so damned pleased with himself? she wondered, resenting the way just looking at him sent her temperature rocketing.

Reece would have been astonished if he'd been privy to her thoughts. He had rarely felt less complacent in his life; things were happening to him that he didn't want or need— his eyes were drawn to the shell-like shape of her ear— cancel 'didn't need'. Every time he looked at this woman he *needed* with a capital N.

'Perhaps he could tell me,' he muttered under his breath.

'Pardon?'

She wanted to know; well, he'd tell her! 'I can't look at your ear without wanting to whisper in it. I can't look at your mouth—'

'Stop!' Darcy yelled, her stressed heart pumping out adrenalin like a pneumatic drill. 'If you say things like that I'm likely to crash the car.'

'In that case, wouldn't it be far safer if you parked somewhere? Somewhere quiet and secluded would be good.' From what he'd seen, that shouldn't be too difficult— they'd barely passed another car.

Darcy broke out in a cold sweat. 'You can't say things like that to me!' She could hardly hear herself speak above the frantic clamour of her heart.

Reece sighed. 'I can't *not* say things like that to you. Do you think it's possible they've put something in the water…?'

'I think it's possible you've got nothing better to do than harass me,' she responded weakly in a strangulated version of her own deep, husky voice.

'Actually, I brought a heap of paperwork with me.'

'I'm flattered no end.'

'Do your boyfriends always have to work so hard?'

She could have said What boyfriends? but she didn't want to reveal the disgraceful lack of sexual encounters in her work-orientated life. 'You're not a boy or my friend.'

'I'm your lover.'

This man was the master of the one-liners; there was no doubt about it. Darcy dabbed the beads of sweat from the full outline of her upper lip with the tip of her tongue and tried to coax her respirations into a more manageable rate.

'You're my one-night stand,' she bit back coldly. He would never know that this admission hurt her more than it did him. 'Listen, I can see why you might think I'm up for…that I might want you to…' Darcy's voice dropped to an agonised whisper. 'You know what I mean.' Still he didn't respond. 'Last night wasn't me…'

Even though her eyes remained rigidly fixed on the road, she could feel his eyes travelling over her body, her skin prickling in response to the unseen scrutiny.

'I have to dispute that.'

The low rasp of his voice was like a caress, and she could picture his slow, sensual smile in her head. She ground her teeth in frustration.

'I don't normally act like that,' she insisted.

'Then last night was special…?'

'Last night was mad, a mistake!' she yelled. 'I'm not passing judgement on people that do act like that, but it's just not me.'

'I think it is you.'

'Haven't you heard a thing I've said?' she asked shrilly.

'You've made a lot of noise but you haven't come right out and said no.'

She gave a contemptuous laugh. 'And I'm supposed to believe that's all it takes…?'

'Believe it or not, it's true.'

You could have taken a chainsaw to the tension in the air.

'Will you fasten your seat belt?'

Reece smiled, but didn't push his advantage. 'It hurts the bust ribs,' he explained mildly.

So would being thrown through the windscreen. 'Don't be such a sissy!' she admonished sternly.

'You're the boss.'

If only, she thought wistfully. I should have said no—why didn't I say it…? 'If the word "mouth" crosses your lips once more I'll make you walk back,' she warned him sternly. Darcy had no intention of becoming a rich man's plaything—no matter how tempting the notion was.

'Last night—'

Darcy cut him off. 'That too.'

'I have a very extensive vocabulary, Darcy.'

'And I have a very low tolerance level.' Her angry sneer morphed into a weak scowl. 'Why the hell did you come here?' If he hadn't been doing so she'd never have met him and her life would have been a lot simpler.

'Maybe I got tired of well-meaning people trying to rehabilitate me.'

Darcy puzzled over his obscure reply. 'I don't understand.'

'That's the way I'd like to keep it for the moment.'

There was only a handful of people in the garden centre, but Reece suspected they'd have come in for personal attention even if the place had been packed out. As if he'd been expecting them, the guy Reece assumed ran the place appeared as soon as they drew up. He greeted Darcy warmly and enfolded her in a bear-like hug. When she emerged she reluctantly acknowledged his presence.

'This is Richard Stenning, my godfather. Uncle Rick, this is Reece, and, before you say anything, he's *not* my boyfriend.'

'But I'm working on it.'

Both men seemed to find this crack amusing; Darcy didn't.

'I was thinking between six feet and six feet six…?' she said briskly, eyeing up the swathes of green pine.

'I'm six four and a half actually.'

'Not you, *stupid*, the tree.'

The older man looked at the bickering couple with a benevolent smile. 'Come along this way, Darcy, I think I've got just what you want.'

Darcy doubted this very much unless he had a supply of six-foot-four-and-a-half males with fascinating green eyes, black hair and sex appeal that went off the scale! Despite this, she stomped obediently after him.

Despite Reece's unhelpful contributions, she eventually selected one that was neither too bushy nor too straggly and didn't have any bare bits. The tree was bagged in a net and installed in the back of the Land Rover beside Wally.

'You'll have a mince pie, of course?'

Reece bent downwards to enquire in her ear, 'Is this another family tradition?'

Darcy ignored him and the tantalising male scent of him that teased her receptive nostrils—she was partially successful.

'Wouldn't miss it for the world,' she agreed, following their host into the shop area, which was dripping with both tasteful and gaudy Christmas decorations—not the place for a man who was trying to avoid Christmas, although Reece seemed to be taking the festive surroundings in his stride. 'But no sherry for me,' she added hastily, with an expression of regret, 'I'm driving.'

'But you'll have some, Mr Erskine?'

'Reece. Yes, I'd love some.'

Darcy was watching from under the protective sweep of her lashes, so she had the satisfaction of seeing his eyes widen in shock as he took a robust bite from his innocent-looking pie. Her lips twitched; she was far more tentative in her approach.

'Delicious as usual,' she mumbled, chewing away valiantly; Uncle Rick must have a stomach of cast iron, she decided, watching him munch his way through two for her one. The problem with Aunty Grace's mince pies was that they looked totally delicious and had the consistency of concrete. 'Aunty Grace has surpassed herself this year.'

'Delicious,' she heard Reece agree faintly after he very visibly swallowed.

'Would you like another, Reece?'

Reece patted his stomach. 'Love to, but I don't want to take the edge off my appetite—I'm taking Darcy to lunch,' he explained glibly.

'First I've heard about it.'

'It was meant to be a surprise, darling.' He glanced at the steel-banded watch on his wrist. 'Talking of which, we should be making a move—I've booked a table for twelve.'

'Where would that be…*darling*?' she wondered innocently. The man was entirely too slick.

'Why, where else but your favourite, *daaarling*?' Reece drawled smoothly.

'Twelve…? You'd better get a move-on, Darcy; it'll take you twenty minutes to get to the Bull's Head. You give my best to the family.'

Darcy bent forward and kissed the older man's cheek. 'I will, Uncle Rick. Why, Reece!' she exclaimed, picking up the glass carefully secreted behind a potted palm. 'You've forgotten your sherry,' she reminded him spitefully.

'So I have.' He met her eyes and, nostrils flared, tipped back the glass, downing the contents in one gulp—like taking nasty medicine, she thought, stifling the urge to giggle.

'Was that a test, or an initiation ceremony?' he muttered under his breath as they walked together back to the Land Rover.

If it had been he'd have passed with flying colours. 'Uncle Rick only hands out the mince pies and sherry to valued friends and customers.'

'I'm surprised he still has any.'

'Shut up,' she hissed, waving through the window. 'He'll hear you.'

'What was that I just drank?'

'Sherry.'

'I've tasted sherry, sweetheart, and that wasn't it.'

Darcy, who had sampled the sweet, syrupy concoction in the past, had some sympathy with his view. 'It's probably safer to call it fortified wine,' she conceded.

'How about we head for the Bull's Head, your favourite watering hole?' he reminded her drily.

'How about I drop you at the nearest bus station? Oh, sorry, I forgot I'm talking to limo man.'

'Helicopters are my preferred mode of transport. Do you realise that nearly all our conversations have taken place while you're at the wheel of a car—?'

'Is there anything wrong with my driving?' she asked belligerently.

'Not a thing—when you're looking at the road. It would make a nice change to be able to have a conversation that doesn't prohibit the odd physical gesture.'

Darcy swallowed nervously and decided it would be safer to never relinquish her place at the wheel. 'Your problem,' she announced scornfully, 'is you think I'll agree to anything if you kiss me.'

'From where I'm sitting that's a revelation not a problem.'

It was one revelation too many for Darcy; she couldn't concentrate on the road when her mind was full of forbidden images. The battle of words, at times undeniably stimulating, had lost all appeal. With a muffled plea for heavenly intervention she brought the Land Rover to an abrupt halt on the grassy verge. Without even bothering to switch off the engine, she leapt from the driver's seat.

Reece switched off the engine and pocketed the keys before following her.

Darcy, who was hunched over, her hands braced against her thighs, turned her head to look at him.

'Go away!' she pleaded hoarsely. She didn't actually hold out much hope of his doing as she requested.

'Are you all right?'

'Very obviously not.' She took another deep breath and slowly straightened up. She brushed a few stray strands of hair from her face; it was an intensely weary gesture. 'If you must know, I couldn't stand being in that car with you any longer.' She was past caring what he thought.

Reece didn't seem to take offence in her anguished observation. 'It's pretty intense, isn't it?' he commiserated.

Darcy's brows drew into a suspicious line above her wide, startled eyes. 'Are you saying that *you*...?' She moved her head in a scornful negative gesture, rejecting the idea that Reece could be similarly affected by her proximity.

'I can't stop thinking about last night or wanting it to happen again.' His tone might have been matter-of-fact bordering on rudely abrupt, but the lick of flames in his deep-set eyes was not!

Darcy was shaking so hard she had to fold her arms tight

across her middle to hide the tremors. In the process she unwittingly drew attention to her full, heaving bosom. 'That was sex.'

'That was *exceptional* sex,' Reece contradicted firmly. 'A relationship has to start somewhere.'

Darcy looked at him blankly. 'Relationship...? You don't want a relationship.'

'How do you know what I want?' he demanded.

'Well, do you?'

'Maybe not. Well, actually, no, I don't want a relationship. I don't want to be celibate either.'

He didn't even have the guts to look her in the eye when he said it, she thought wrathfully. The perversity of the average male was simply breathtaking. But it had shut up the voice in her head, the one recklessly shrieking 'Go for it! Go for it!', and a good thing too, she decided glumly.

'The only thing I know for sure I want is you.'

She couldn't legitimately complain about eye-contact now—an earthquake couldn't have broken the grip his dark-lashed eyes had on her. The air escaped her lungs in one long, sibilant hiss; her eyes, huge in her pale face, were glued to his face. Her thoughts were in total chaos. You can't let yourself be seduced by someone saying he wants you—even if that someone is Reece Erskine, she told herself angrily.

'Naturally I'm flattered,' she drawled, giving a scornful, unnatural little laugh that implied just the opposite.

His jaw tightened. 'I'm not trying to flatter you.' Reece, who prided himself on self-control, discovered he couldn't take his eyes from the lush curve of her lovely lips, even though the looking caused the distant buzzing in his head to increase significantly.

'What are you trying to do, then?' Other than drive me out of my mind, that is...? It just didn't seem possible for a man to walk into her life and turn everything upside-down. 'You may be in the mood for some sort of holiday romance, but I simply don't have the time, energy or inclination.' Well, the first two at least were true.

'I thought you were on holiday too.'

Some holiday! 'My mum's gone walkabout, my stepfather, who I happen to be crazy about, needs constant reassurance, several hundred members of the family are likely to descend on us at any second and I can't even bake a mince pie, let alone feed and entertain them!' Stupidly it was the last deficiency that made her eyes fill with tears.

Reece moved towards her and she ached to throw herself into his arms. With a stiff little gesture that shrieked rejection she swayed backwards; it stopped Reece in his tracks.

'Are you trying to tell me this isn't a good time for us?' There was no smile to match the flippancy of his tone.

Darcy wanted to cry from sheer frustration, but she didn't have the luxury. As right as it felt to have his arms close around her, she knew it was all an illusion created by her overactive hormones. If she had been after casual sex she wouldn't have looked any further than this man: he fulfilled every criteria for the role.

The problem was she couldn't be that casual about sex, and when she got involved serious disaster usually followed—she was thinking about the rat Michael here, the one who had forgotten to mention his wife and children. His wife with kids in tow landing up on her doorstep pleading with Darcy not to take her husband away was one of her least favourite memories. Just recalling Michael's defence made her blood boil— 'I wanted to tell you, Darce, but I didn't want to hurt you'.

'There is no us!'

'There could be if you let it happen.'

And letting it happen would be so easy. Darcy sighed; his voice had a dangerously mesmeric quality…it was so hypnotic and attractive, in fact, that a person was inclined to forget just how outrageous the sentences formed by these perfect lips were.

'You're really worried about your mother, aren't you…?'

This observation brought her back to reality with a resounding thump.

'Am I supposed to believe you care about what I'm worried about?' she sneered, eyeing him with open contempt. 'The only thing you care about as far as I can see is getting me back into your bed!'

It was true, but that didn't alter the fact her words made him mad as hell. The flare of something close to fear in her eyes made him realise that his feelings must have been reflected on his face, so he made a conscious effort to control his anger.

'Listen, sweetheart,' he said after he'd counted to ten a couple of times, 'I've absolutely no idea if this thing is going to run its course in a matter of days, weeks or months but I think for both our sakes we should find out. If we don't we'll always wonder…' He paused long enough for her to appreciate the truth of what he was saying. 'I know you've some sort of guilt trip about sleeping with me last night, but it happened and I don't see much point beating yourself up over it.'

'Maybe I wouldn't if you didn't keep throwing it back in my face. Just for the record, I'm not…easy!'

'Just for the record,' he retorted drily, 'I don't think you're *easy*…anything but, as a matter of fact,' he added in a wry aside. 'This isn't the sort of attraction you can pretend isn't there, Darcy.'

That was true.

'I may want to get you into bed,' he continued with a candour that made her mouth grow dry and started up the distressing palpitations once more, 'but it doesn't mean we can't communicate outside the bedroom.' Darcy had no way of knowing how extraordinary this statement was coming from Reece Erskine, and Reece wasn't about to tell her—the truth was, it made him uneasy to acknowledge it. 'You're obviously worried about your mother and I thought it might help to talk to someone not personally involved. I may be shallow but I'm not totally insensitive.'

He sounded genuine. She searched his face—he looked genuine. 'I was only talking to her the day before; she didn't give a clue anything was wrong.' Her fingers clenched tightly.

'And you think you've done something?'

'Not me personally maybe—but us, the family. Why else would she walk out like this just before Christmas? She's made sure we can't contact her...' She gnawed away silently on her lower lip as she puzzled over the bizarre, bewildering behaviour of her parent.

'It's possible this is *her* problem.'

Darcy regarded him with disdain. 'Families are there to help you with your problems; you don't shut them out when you most need them.' An expression she didn't understand flickered across his handsome face. 'It's not at all like her—she's so *responsible*. Poor Jack is convinced it's something he's done.'

'But you don't think so.'

Darcy shook her head jerkily; now she'd started to talk it was hard to stop. 'Why couldn't she talk to us...?' she wondered unhappily.

'I expect you'll be able to ask her yourself when she comes home.'

In front of Jack and even her brothers she had to act optimistic and upbeat, and it was a relief almost to stop being so damned cheerful. 'Whenever that might be.'

'You've no idea at all how long she's likely to be away?'

Despondently Darcy shook her head. 'I'm really trying hard to make everything the same as it usually is...' It seemed important somehow not to let things slip, to keep a sense of continuity.

'And driving yourself into an early grave in the process,' he observed disapprovingly. 'The secret of a successful manager is delegation, Darcy.' She looked so transparently touched by his comment that he felt impelled to add, 'You ought to try it; you might even find you've got time for a personal life, and, as you already know, I have a vested interest in that.'

She stared wonderingly up into his face. It sounded as if he was saying he wanted to be part of her personal life, which didn't fit with what he had said about not wanting a relationship—in fact, it seemed to directly contradict it. The warmth in his eyes made her lose track for a few moments. 'How would I go about doing that?'

'You really want to know?'

Darcy gave a rueful smile. 'I wouldn't have asked otherwise.'

'Make a list of things you need to do and halve it.' She opened her mouth to protest but he didn't give her the opportunity. 'Divide the remaining tasks amongst the others. And don't tell me you can't give orders because I've been on the receiving end. Actually,' he admitted, his firm tone gentling, 'I quite liked it. Some of the time I quite like you…'

Darcy gulped. 'And the rest…?' she prompted huskily.

'I want to throttle you.'

'Which is it now?'

'Neither. It's been a hell of a long time since I wanted to wake up beside someone.'

'You're not trying to tell me you're celibate?'

'No, I'm not,' he agreed tersely. 'Sex is one form of recreation that I've made a point of including in my schedule,' he explained casually.

There was an appalled silence.

'That sounds pretty cold-blooded.' If she'd any sense she'd get back into the Land Rover and drive away. Darcy knew she wouldn't—she *couldn't.*

'It's an accusation that has been levelled at me before.'

'You want to kiss me.' It was a statement, not a question—it was the sort of statement that a girl who didn't want to be kissed didn't make.

'For starters,' he growled.

'Then for God's sake,' she pleaded in an agonised whisper, '*Do it!*'

My God, but the man could move fast with the right motivation. She barely had time to draw breath let alone change her mind before his mouth was hard on hers, and his tongue began to make some electrifying exploratory forays into the warm, moist interior.

The sheer pleasure of his touch as his fingers slid surely under the woollen jumper she wore made her whimper and sag, weak-kneed, against him. His hand worked its way smoothly up the slender curve of her back. Darcy grabbed for support and then remembered his injuries.

'I forgot.'

Reece's mouth came crashing back down on hers and stole away the rest of her words.

Eyes closed, she gave a long, blissful sigh when his head eventually lifted. 'I've hurt you.' She made an agitated effort to pull back, but he had other ideas.

'If I can't cope I'll tell you,' he breathed into her mouth.

'I don't think I can cope with much more of this!' she breathed back, touching her tongue to the fleshy inner part of his upper lip. She shuddered—they both did.

'Cope with what?'

Darcy laid her hand flat against his chest, feeling his heart beat through the layers of clothing. She'd known him for less than forty-eight hours and already he'd taken over her thoughts. If she had any sense she'd call it a day now before things got any worse.

'Cope with…*wanting*.' She put all the aching longing in the one word.

What was happening to her—where had this wilful recklessness come from? After Michael she'd been cautious—pathologically so, Jennifer had said. Would Jennifer approve of the new Darcy? The one who saw the flare of fierce possession in his eyes and felt the heat melt her bones and didn't even once contemplate running for cover? Hell, what did it matter? She needed action not analysis, and she needed Reece.

'Does that mean you've stopped trying to push me away?'

'I don't recall doing much pushing.' Grabbing, that was another matter.

'Why fight…?'

'My thought exactly.'

'It'll burn itself out soon enough.' Wasn't that the way with hot things? 'And I can get back to normal.'

Though his own thoughts had been running much along the same lines, Reece found that her sentiments filled him with a sense of discontent. He was perfectly aware that for a man who had a policy of never spending the entire night with a woman this was a pretty perverse response. Knowing it made no sense didn't lessen the gut feeling.

'And normal is…?' He slid his thumb down the soft curve of her cheek.

There was danger and raw, unrefined charisma in his smile. Without waiting for her to reply, he dipped his head and parted her lips with masterful ease.

'This normal…?' His tongue stabbed and she moaned low in her throat and pressed herself tight against his hips. She wondered vaguely if he was permanently aroused—not

that she had any major objections if this should be the case.
'Or this…?' He withdrew.

Darcy gave a whimper of protest as he lifted his head.

'I preferred the first,' she admitted huskily.

'That being the case, perhaps we should…' He dangled
the Land Rover keys in front of her. 'Can you drive…?'

Darcy nodded her head vigorously. So fierce was her
need that if flying had been the only way to get into bed
with him she'd have sprouted wings!

CHAPTER SIX

DURING the afternoon there had been several flurries of snow, and by the time Darcy got back home complete with the Christmas tree and a slightly guilty conscience a little of the powdery whiteness had begun to stick to the damp ground.

She stamped her feet to loosen the snow on her boots and lifted the old-fashioned iron latch on the kitchen door, hoping as she did so that there was nobody about; it wasn't that she intended to be *furtive*, exactly. 'Furtive' implied she had something to hide or be ashamed of, and, whilst Darcy acknowledged she was deeply confused and wildly exhilarated by what had happened to her, shame didn't feature at all. It was just that there were some things you couldn't share with your family, no matter how close you were, and Darcy didn't see much point in drawing unnecessary attention to her extended absence.

'Where have you been?'

So much for subterfuge.

Her entire family minus only one important member were seated around the long farmhouse table, but that absence brought an aching lump to her throat—if there was ever a time she'd needed her mum it was now. Darcy swallowed; she didn't need this, not when her mind was still full of the passionate coupling which had just taken place next door. She felt as if the evidence of her abandoned behaviour was written all over her face.

'Clare, you're home.' If Clare noticed her half-sister's greeting was lacking a certain warmth she didn't show it.

'Finally,' Nick contributed drily. 'Had trouble choosing the right tree, did you?' he wondered guilelessly.

Unexpectedly it was Clare who came to her rescue. 'Never mind about that, Nick.'

I'll second that, Darcy thought, pulling off her mittens. 'Good journey, Clare?'

'In case you hadn't noticed, it's snowing.' Clare's expression suggested that Darcy was in some way to blame for this.

I didn't notice because I've spent the afternoon making wild, passionate love to a gorgeous man. How, Darcy wondered, would that explanation go down…?

Clare shook back her rippling waist-length mane of hair and looked impatient. Like her half-sister, she was blonde and blue-eyed, but that was where the resemblance ended.

'I arrive to find that my mother…' she choked tearfully.

'She's ours too.'

'Shut up, Harry! Why didn't anyone tell me what was happening?'

'We didn't want to upset you, darling,' Jack soothed.

Nobody, Darcy reflected, feeling a twitch of resentment, ever wanted to upset Clare.

'Well, I'm upset now.' Clare sniffed.

'Did you remember to pick up the order from the farm, Nick?' Darcy asked, shaking her hair free of a few stray snowflakes, which were rapidly melting in the warm room. She hung her damp coat on the peg behind the door.

'How can you act as if nothing has happened?' Clare tearfully accused Darcy.

The implication that she didn't give a damn made Darcy turn angrily on her sister. 'What do you expect me to do, Clare?' she snapped. 'Mum's a grown woman; we can't bring her back against her will. We just have to wait.' Patience never had been one of her younger sister's most obvious qualities—when Clare wanted something she wanted it *now*, and more often than not she got it! 'Sitting about whining isn't going to help anyone!'

There was an almost comical look of shock on Clare's face as she recoiled from her sister's anger—Darcy was a bit surprised herself, as she rarely raised her voice to her sister. Instantly she regretted her outburst, not to mention her ungenerous thoughts. Clare could be thoughtless and selfish, but her kid sister could also be generous and loving, and not nearly as hard-bitten as she liked to make out.

There was a scraping sound as the younger girl rose gracefully to her feet. Darcy was happy being herself, but she wouldn't have been human if she hadn't felt the occasional touch of wistful envy when she looked at her spectacularly beautiful sister. Occasionally on bad days, when her hair was particularly unruly and the bathroom scales told her things she'd rather not know, she couldn't help but think that it would be nice if—just once—someone took notice of *her* when she walked into a room beside her gorgeous sister.

Seeing her sister stand there, tall, willowy and with a face and figure that would have stood out as exceptional on any catwalk, Darcy knew this was only going to happen in her wildest dreams.

Clare had no qualms about using her looks when it suited her, but she'd never had any intention of making her living out of them. Thanks to a big injection of capital from her parents, her dreams of becoming a fashion designer were well on the way to becoming a reality. She'd started her own business straight from art college and she had ambitious plans for her fashion label.

'We're all missing her, Clare,' Darcy said quietly. From the corner of her eye, she saw Harry reach across and hug his dad and the emotional lump in her throat ached.

'I know,' Clare admitted huskily. 'Sorry. Is the other thing true, or is Nick winding me up…?'

'Is what true…?' Darcy responded cagily. What had Nick the wind-up artiste been saying this time? she wondered, shooting her brother a suspicious glance. She didn't have to wait long to find out.

'Nick says that *Reece Erskine*…' Clare murmured the name in a dreamy, reverential way that made Darcy stiffen in alarm '…is staying next door—which is very obviously impossible,' she added quickly. 'I suppose he *is* having me on…?' Despite her conviction that this was a wind-up, there was a gleam of hope in her eyes as she appealed to her big sister.

'Yes, he is staying next door,' Darcy disclosed reluctantly. She watched her sister go pale with excitement.

'Why would…?' Clare began. 'No, it doesn't matter. Let me think… This is too marvellous…!'

Darcy thought so, but she had mixed feelings—no, actually, they weren't mixed at all; she didn't like the idea of Clare thinking Reece's proximity was marvellous one little bit.

'It is?'

'Of course it is, silly!' Clare exclaimed. 'Did you invite him for dinner, Darce…?' Her lovely face creased with annoyance. 'Of course you didn't,' she predicted critically. Her exasperation increased as the jerky little movement of Darcy's head confirmed her suspicions. 'Honestly, Darcy! What were you thinking of?'

Reece's tongue sliding smoothly skilful over her stomach…his burning eyes devouring her, the tiny quivering contractions that tightened her belly as she was overwhelmed by an almost paralysing desire to have him deep inside her.

'Are you listening to me, Darcy?'

The shrill, indignant sound of her sister's voice broke through the sensual thrall of her recollections. Darcy was appalled and slightly scared by her lack of self-control.

Sweat trickled damply down her stiff spine, and her cheeks felt as if they were on fire.

'I haven't got the time to have a dinner party, Clare,' she told her sister gruffly.

Her words fell on selectively deaf ears.

'Better still!' Clare, the bit firmly between her pearly teeth, enthused excitedly, 'We could invite him to stay. Yes, why not…? According to Dad, the Hall is not fit for human habitation.' She clapped her hands, her eyes glowing with enthusiasm. 'Yes, that would be perfect! Is anyone going to answer that?' she exclaimed, irritated by the persistent ring of the phone in the hallway.

Jack rose from his chair and put his hand on Darcy's shoulder. 'I'll go.'

'Perfect for what?' asked Charlie, who was growing bored with the subject, when his father had left the room. 'I don't see what's so great about the guy next door. You haven't even met him.'

Clare turned to her young brother, her expression one of supreme scorn for his ignorance.

'Don't you know anything…? He's one of the richest men in the country—he inherited a fortune from his grandfather and he's doubled it, or trebled it, whatever.' With a graceful flick of her wrist Clare dismissed the odd million or ten.

'That would explain the Merc in the shed,' Harry remarked thoughtfully to his brother.

'Have you two been spying?' Darcy exclaimed in a horrified tone.

'No harm done, Darce,' Harry soothed. 'Nobody was around. We saw some guys delivering this bed, though— gigantic thing it was, so he must be thinking about staying.'

Darcy, who knew all about the bed, tried to blend in with the furniture. If anyone looked at her now they would know—they'd just *know*…!

'Is he as good-looking as he looks in the photos I've seen of him?'

'I thought it was his money you were interested in.' Harry received an annoyed glare for his insensitive comment. 'I suppose you think he's going to take one look at you and propose you share his bed and bank account,' he sniggered.

'It has been known,' Clare confirmed calmly.

The awful part was that her sister's complacence was perfectly understandable—Darcy could see it all: Reece blinded by Clare's beauty, wondering what he'd ever seen in the dowdy little sister with the funny nose. Why hadn't she foreseen this? she wondered bitterly.

If the loud, realistic gagging noises Harry made as he headed for the door dragging his twin with him were anything to go by, her comment made him feel sick too.

Charlie seemed perfectly willing to follow his twin but he couldn't resist a taunting parting shot. 'What makes you think he's not already got a girlfriend or a wife even…?'

'Those boys get worse!' Clare exclaimed angrily as the door slammed behind them. 'He hasn't, has he, Darce?' she added worriedly.

'How should I know?' Helping her sister seduce her own lover was above and beyond the call of sisterly duty.

'Well, you have seen more of him than everyone else.'

'Something gone down the wrong way, Darce?' Nick asked solicitously.

'Do you want a drink of water?' Clare asked

Darcy wiped the moisture from the corner of her eye. 'I'm fine,' she protested hoarsely. The image in her mind of Reece's powerful body slick with sweat, his powerful thighs quivering with need and power, made it difficult for her to formulate a suitable reply. 'He didn't discuss his personal life with me, Clare.'

The indentation between her brows deepened as it struck

her forcibly just how adept he'd been at distracting her when their conversation had begun to touch on personal areas, but then his methods of distraction were in a class of their own. Married men acted like that…what if he'd been lying all along…? Clammy perspiration broke out along her brow as her tummy tied itself in knots of apprehension.

Darcy took a deep breath and firmly pushed aside her fears; this was her own insecurity at work. Reece wasn't the type to resort to subterfuge—let's face it, she thought, he doesn't need to! He'd been upfront enough—he wanted sex and nothing more.

'I can't believe you wasted all that time.'

'I wouldn't call it wasted exactly.' The way she recalled it, there hadn't been a second they hadn't filled with touching or tasting or *taking*… Darcy was confused on any number of matters but one thing was clear to her—she was glad they'd been lovers. She would always treasure the memory and no matter what the outcome that much at least wouldn't change.

'Oh, you're hopeless, Darcy!'

Hopelessly in love. Darcy felt as though a large fist had landed a direct hit on her solar plexus. Suddenly the missing pieces of the emotional jigsaw fell into place. Her mouth opened and closed several times as she gasped for air like a land-locked fish. If anyone had noticed her condition they would no doubt not have considered it attractive—but nobody did.

'I have made some enquiries…'

Clare squealed and gave her older brother her immediate approving attention. 'Why, you clever old thing, you. And…?'

'He's a widower.'

'Excellent!' Clare exclaimed gleefully; unlike Darcy, she didn't detect any undercurrent in Nick's words.

'*Clare!*' Darcy exclaimed, unable to hide her shocked disapproval.

'There's no more edifying sight,' Nick drawled to nobody in particular, 'than a woman in full pursuit.'

'I thought hunting was your favourite pastime, Nick…? But, silly me, you're a man, so that makes it all right, doesn't it?' Darcy heard herself perversely defending her sister.

Nick grinned. 'Sexist down to my cotton socks,' he conceded good-naturedly. 'I can't help myself any more than you can help yourself being scrupulously fair, Darce—even when it's not in your best interests,' he added in an amused but not unsympathetic undertone.

'Thank you, Darce. There's no need for either of you to look like that,' Clare insisted with a moody little pout. 'It's just such an excellent opportunity for me. It's not as if I'm going to marry him or anything.' A naughty grin flickered across her face. 'Unless, of course, the opportunity arises,' she added with a husky laugh. She shrugged when neither of her siblings showed any appreciation of her joke. 'Can you imagine how much free publicity I'd get being seen with Reece Erskine? It could really be the break I've been waiting for. It's perfectly legitimate,' she announced, a shade of defiance entering her voice.

Darcy couldn't help but wonder if her sister actually believed that. 'Dad would go spare if he could hear you.'

'Well, he can't, can he?' Clare pointed out unrepentantly. 'And what he doesn't know won't harm him—unless you tell him…'

'I can see it would put the spotlight on a brilliant new designer who is just starting out if she was seen in all the right places with someone the media love to write about,' Nick agreed.

'Don't encourage her!' Darcy pleaded.

'At last, someone who understands!' Clare sighed in a long-suffering 'nobody understands me' sort of way.

'But doesn't it rather spoil your plan if the guy in question bends over backwards to avoid the spotlight?' Nick wondered.

'These things have a way of leaking out—you of all people should know that, Nick.'

Darcy, who knew how ambitious her sister was for her business, was shocked by this display of casual ruthlessness.

'You mean you'd leak things to the Press…? Plant a story…?'

'Don't you worry your head about the details, Darce.'

The patronising comment brought an angry flush to Darcy's cheeks. 'I think you're getting a little bit ahead of yourself, Clare,' she bit back coldly. 'You haven't even met the man yet.' If she had her way that situation was not about to change. 'And there's no question at all of his staying here. Once Beth and the children arrive, not to mention Gran, we'll all be doubling up, if not trebling up!'

'I've thought about that,' Clare replied smoothly. 'You could share with the children in the attic room, and I suppose under the circumstances I could share with Gran.'

'That's mighty big of you.'

'There's no need to be like that, Darcy. I think it's the least you could do—'

'Whatever gave you the impression that I want to help you? I think what you're planning to do is callous and calculating…'

Clare looked blankly astonished by her placid sister's fresh outburst. 'But you said to Nick…' She was starting to think Darcy might be sickening for something—it wasn't like her to be so belligerent.

'I pointed out that Nick is a sexist pig.' She paused to glare at her unmoved brother. 'Which he is. But that doesn't mean I don't basically agree with him. What you're planning to do is cold-blooded and unethical.'

Clare's lips tightened. 'I think you're being very selfish. Mum and Dad invested a lot of money in my business, and I owe it to them to make it a success. I'm not trying to trap the man, but if meeting him happens to oil a few wheels, where is the problem?' Slow tears began to form in her lovely eyes; she sniffed and one slid artistically down her smooth cheek.

Even though she knew her sister could cry on cue, Darcy knew that it wouldn't be long before she'd be saying soothing things to drive that tragic expression from her lovely face. The pattern of behaviour had been laid down early on in childhood and was nigh on impossible to break at this stage in their lives. Somehow Darcy always ended up stiffly apologising and in her turn Clare would accept it and emerge looking gracious and generous.

'Maybe I don't have your lofty principles, Darcy,' she added huskily, 'but I do have fun…and so will he.'

The thought of Clare having fun with Reece made Darcy lose all desire to pour oil on troubled waters.

'What is it, Dad?' It was Nick who had noticed Jack's return.

'It was your mother.' Jack smiled a little dazedly at their expectant faces. 'She's coming home.'

Darcy closed her eyes. 'Thank God,' she breathed. Only just blinking back the emotional floods, she opened her eyes and saw Clare hugging their father while Nick, an imbecilic grin on his face, was pounding him on the back.

'Did she say why she…?' Darcy began huskily.

Jack shook his head. 'No, she said she wanted to talk. That's good, isn't it…?'

'Very good,' Darcy said firmly, hoping with all her heart that she was telling the truth.

Jack nodded. 'She'll be here tomorrow morning.'

Darcy had reached the point when she couldn't hold back the tears of relief any longer. 'I'll go get the tree in,' she announced huskily.

She was struggling with the evergreen when Nick joined her.

'Good news…?' He stood, his back against the garage door, watching her efforts and making no reference to her puffy eyes.

'The best,' she agreed.

'Personally I'm keeping all extremities crossed just in case.'

'A wise precautionary measure,' Darcy agreed with a tired smile.

'About Clare…'

'I don't want to talk about Clare.'

'You know she doesn't mean half of what she says.'

'The half she does mean is enough sometimes,' Darcy responded drily.

'Things aren't going as well as she'd hoped with the firm. I don't know the details, but I do know it's not good.'

Darcy's eyes widened in sympathy. 'I didn't know.'

'Only knew myself because she was in a bit of a state when I dropped in the other week. It does explain the conniving-bitch act.'

'You don't think she's desperate enough to…?'

'Sleep her way out of trouble?' Nick considered the idea. 'Shouldn't think so.'

Darcy was torn; she knew she ought to be more concerned about her sister's welfare than the possibility that Clare might find the solution to her problems in the bed of her own lover. Jealousy was not a nice feeling.

'Do you think you could give me a hand with this?'

Nick took the tree off her. 'All you had to do was ask. There's never a twin around when you want one,' he added, hefting it into his arms.

'And there's always two around when you don't want one,' Darcy added with feeling.

They were halfway up the driveway when Nick planted the rootball on the ground. His expression as he turned to face her suggested he'd come to a decision about something.

'I didn't tell Clare all the things I learnt about Erskine.'

'From a reliable source, no doubt.'

'It's all on file, Darce. Do you want to know?'

She shrugged her shoulders, affecting uninterest, while she was just bursting to shake the information out of him.

'Well, in that case…' he began, balancing the tree against his hip.

'I'm interested!' she snapped, grabbing his shoulder and spinning him back to her.

'Apparently the guy married his childhood sweetheart. Five years ago this Christmas Day she was killed.'

Darcy closed her eyes. Now she had the answer to his distaste of all things Christmassy. How awful to have such a powerful reminder year after year of his personal tragedy. Her tender heart ached for him.

'That's not all. She was pregnant…'

Oh, God, there was more to come! She could hear it in Nick's voice. Her eyes flickered open; she met her brother's eyes—not only more but *worse*. Darcy didn't see how that was possible but she waited tensely, her stomach tied in knots for him to deliver the clincher.

'A motorbike mounted the pavement—it was crowded with people coming out of midnight mass. They were holding hands, but it didn't touch him, just her.'

Darcy was seeing the horror of it; her chest felt so tight she could hardly breathe. 'He saw her die.' She blinked back the hot sting of tears; she ached with empathy. She turned away from her brother and fought to master her

emotions. Losing a wife he loved and his unborn child—
how did a person come back after a cruel blow like that?

'She died instantly, but he tried to revive her. When the
paramedics got there eye-witness reports said that it took
five guys to eventually persuade him to let her go, and,
Darcy...' he touched her arm '...he made the biggest deal
of his life on New Year's Eve. Makes you think, doesn't
it...?'

'What are you suggesting—?' she began, hotly defensive.

'I'm not suggesting anything. I'm just saying that a man
like that needs handling with care...'

Darcy's eyes slid from her brother's. 'Shouldn't you be
telling Clare that?' she muttered evasively.

'Clare thinks she's a lot more irresistible than she is.'

'You only think that because you're her brother,' Darcy
retorted. Jealousy tightened its grip on her—Reece wasn't
Clare's brother.

Darcy tucked her hair behind her ears and stood back to
get the full effect of her decorative efforts. She heard the
door open behind her.

'Switch on the lights, will you?' she called without turning around. She gave a satisfied sigh as the tree was illuminated. 'It's a bit lopsided.'

'It's got character,' a very familiar deep voice replied.

Darcy gave a startled yelp and dropped the bauble in her
hand as she swung around. 'What are you doing here?' Her
body temperature seesawed wildly at the sight of the tall
figure, as did her emotions.

'Do you give all your lovers receptions this warm and
welcoming?'

Lovers. A sensual shudder rippled down her spine.
'Hush!' she hissed, reaching up and pressing her hand to
his lips. 'Someone will hear.'

His disdainful expression was that of a man who didn't care what other people thought. Darcy would have taken her hand away, but he caught hold of her wrist and held it there against his mouth. The giddiness that had begun to recede came rushing back with a vengeance as his lips moved along her flexed fingertips, then equally slowly returned to the starting point.

Reece couldn't get over how incredibly fragile her bones were as he circled her wrist with his fingers. With the utmost reluctance he removed her hand from his lips, but not before he'd touched the tip of his tongue to the palm of her hand and felt her shiver with pleasure.

'And that matters…?' The shiver inclined him towards indulgence.

'How did you get here?'

He got the impression from the way her eyes were darting wildly around the room that she wouldn't have been surprised if he had announced he had materialised out of thin air. The truth was far more prosaic.

'I knocked on the door and was kindly directed this way.'

'Who by?'

'A twin; which one, I wouldn't like to say.'

'Oh, I thought maybe Clare had brought you?'

'I brought myself, and who might Clare be?'

'She's my sister.'

His eyes narrowed. 'Tall, blonde, persistent…?'

He'd missed out 'beautiful', which was tactful of him. 'You've met.' Of course they had—when Clare set her mind on something she didn't hang around.

'Not *met* precisely. I saw her through the window; she was knocking on the door.'

'You don't have a door.'

The bed to make love to her in, the door to keep out the world—he was a man who believed in prioritising.

'I do now.' A few phone calls had improved the conditions to bearable. 'I also have electricity. If I'm staying around I see no reason to suffer unnecessarily.'

How big an 'if' are we talking about here, she wondered, and do I have any influence on it?

'Why didn't you answer the door?' she puzzled abruptly. One sight of Clare would have most men tripping over themselves to let her in.

'I came here to escape people.'

Darcy knew what he'd come to escape, and she also knew that memories were not so easy to shake as flesh and blood people. It wasn't her place to share this with him—if he'd chosen to confide in her it might have been different, but he hadn't.

'I thought it was just Christmas,' she reminded him as with a grin she draped a strand of tinsel around his neck.

'Slip of the tongue.'

It could slip in her direction any time. 'Freudian…?'

'You tell me; you seem very well-versed.' His expression didn't suggest his opinion of psychoanalysis was high.

'This is Christmas.' Her gesture took in the room. 'And I'm people,' she reminded him.

He reached out and cupped her chin in his hand. 'You're a special person,' he contradicted firmly.

The breath caught in her throat. It didn't mean anything; there had only been one special person in Reece's life and he had lost her.

Darcy had promised herself she wouldn't allow herself to fall into this trap. When he wasn't here it had been easy to tell herself she wasn't going to see desire in his face and read love. Now he was here she had to keep reminding herself he was out for a good time and that was all; she had to accept that because the only alternative to not seeing him at all was even less acceptable—wasn't it…?

'Why are you here, Reece?'

An alertness flickered into his eyes. 'Here as in this

room? Or are we talking bed…life…?' His voice hardened. 'What's happened, Darcy?'

'Nothing.' Nervously she withdrew the hand he held and nursed it against her chest.

'Then why won't you look at me?' He took her chin in his hand and forced her face up to him. 'Look at me, Darcy,' he commanded. His eyes scoured her face, reading each line and curve. 'Someone's told you about Joanne.'

Joanne…so that had been her name. It struck her afresh that his perception was nothing short of spooky.

'Nick,' she admitted, half-relieved. 'I'm so sorry, Reece.'

'And now you want to comfort me, offer me solace and make me forget…'

It was hard not to recoil from the arid harshness in his voice.

'You'll never forget; why would you want to? I'm sure you have a lot of precious memories.' She could almost see the barriers going up—she had to do something to stop him retreating behind them. 'And actually,' she improvised wildly, 'I'm concerned about getting…*involved* with some-one who has so much unresolved…' Her underdeveloped lying skills deserted her.

'Angst…? Baggage…?' he suggested with a quirk of one dark brow.

Darcy had the distinct impression he was relieved by what she'd said.

'I don't mean to be callous.' It horrified her that he found it so easy to believe she was that shallow.

'Don't apologise for being honest, Darcy.'

Ouch!

The lines bracketing his sensual mouth suddenly relaxed. 'Sorry.'

Her eyes widened. 'What for?'

'I get defensive.'

And I'm not defensive enough, she thought, staring longingly up into his strong-boned face—she loved every inch of it.

'I was afraid at first you might be the sort of girl on the look-out for marriage and children.'

It was coming over loud and clear that he didn't want either—at least, not with her!

'*Me…?*' she gave a jaunty laugh and shook her head. 'That's not on my agenda for years and years yet!'

'It's hard to timetable these things. Sometimes it happens when you least expect it.'

'Is that how it happened…with you and your wife?' She seemed to have tapped into some hitherto unsuspected streak of masochism in her nature. 'Sorry, I didn't mean to pry.'

His taut jawline tensed. 'Jo and I were as good as brought up together; her parents and mine were… You know the sort of thing.' Darcy nodded. 'She proposed to me when we were seven.' For a moment his expression softened and grew distant. 'I did the proposing the next time. Keep your eyes wide open, sweetheart,' he recommended gently. 'It would be a shame to miss a once-in-a-lifetime experience because you were concentrating on your career.'

The irony was exquisitely painful. 'You think it only happens once?'

'I *know* it only happens once.'

Darcy's thoughts drifted to her mother and Jack; they might not seem to be the world's most perfect couple just now but she had total faith in their love for one another. And significantly both of them had had previous marriages. It was hard to bite back the retort that hovered on the tip of her tongue.

'And if, like you, something happens to…?' she probed clumsily.

'Then that part of your life is over,' he bit back abruptly.

'There are other things…' his restless eyes wandered hungrily over her trim figure '…like *sex*.'

He was condemning himself to a very bleak future—not to mention herself. Despite the rebellion which she sensed building up inside her, Darcy had no control over her physical response to the smoky, sensual invitation in his eyes.

'And that's enough for you?' How sad—how horribly sad. Is that what she wanted to be? A distraction to temporarily fill the gaping hole in his life?

'You sound like my mother.'

A person that Darcy was beginning to have a lot of sympathy for. How did you help someone who didn't think he needed helping?

'It's not enough for me, Reece.' Fundamentally you couldn't change yourself, not even for love. It was a relief to recognise that she'd only be pretending to let him think otherwise, and, as tempted as she was to take what he had to offer, she knew that in the long run it would be more painful.

With a sinking heart she watched his expression shifting, growing harder and more remote.

'I thought you enjoyed uncomplicated sex.'

His tone wasn't quite a sneer but it was painfully close to it. Darcy flushed and lowered her eyes. Letting her mind drift back over her recent uninhibited behaviour, she wasn't surprised he'd arrived at this conclusion.

'At the time, but not later on.'

'That morning-after-the-night-before feeling—you're very frank.'

'It's no reflection on you, on your…'

His mobile lips curled as she floundered. 'Technique?' he suggested. 'Don't fret, Darcy, I'm not plagued with doubts in that direction.'

'You might be a nicer person if you were!'

'Would it make any difference to your decision if we were to put this arrangement on a more formal footing?'

'Formal!' she echoed, startled.

'Formal as in exclusive.' He hadn't planned to say this and in fact had been almost as surprised to hear himself say it as she appeared to be. Now he had, he could see the practical advantages of the idea—the idea of her being with other men was one he'd been having major problems with.

'As in, you don't sleep with anyone else?'

'As in, neither of us sleep with anyone else,' he corrected blandly. Darcy's eyes widened. Was that a hint of possessiveness she was hearing, and, if it was, what did that mean?

'That would be a major sacrifice.' Did the man think she cruised the single scene in a bid to add fresh scalps to her belt?

He seemed to find her sarcasm encouraging. 'It makes sense; we both want the same things…you're not at the stage where you want a commitment, and I'm past it.'

Darcy gazed up at him, speechless with incredulity. You dear, delicious, *deluded* man, she thought bleakly.

'Are you still worried I'm a loose cannon, emotionally speaking?'

I'm the only emotional basket case around here. 'You seem to have got your life on track very successfully,' she choked. 'Your work-life, anyhow.'

Reece's eyes narrowed shrewdly. 'Nick again…'

'He mentioned you didn't take any time off after the…accident.'

'Very tactfully put,' he congratulated her. 'A certain section of the Press never forgave me for ruining a great tragic story by not falling apart in public. I'm not comfortable with the role of tragic hero,' he explained, a spasm of fastidious disgust crossing his face. 'After Joanne died the Press had a field-day. The public appetite for the personal tragedy of people who have a high public profile is almost limitless. They wheeled out the experts to pontificate on the grieving process, interviewed every person I'd ever said good morning to...'

Darcy could feel the pain behind his prosaic words. It must have been agony for a very private man to have his grief dissected and analysed.

'And when you were working you weren't thinking.'

Reece shot her a startled look. 'That was the theory—it didn't always work,' he admitted wryly. 'After Jo's death the Press pack were their usual rabid selves, and my lack of co-operation only increased their appetite. Of course when I didn't oblige them by drowning my sorrows in a gin bottle they were even less happy. Chequebook journalism being what it is, any ex of mine can look forward to making a tidy profit—several have.'

Darcy's face froze. 'Is that meant to be an incentive?' she breathed wrathfully.

'Hell, no, I didn't mean you!' he exclaimed—she seemed to be remarkably lacking in avarice.

Darcy's hands went to her hips as she tossed back her hair. 'You'd better not.'

'I've made you mad, haven't I?'

'Whatever gave you that idea?' she snapped sarcastically.

'Let me take you to dinner; we can talk more.'

Darcy didn't want to talk more—she'd already had more *talk* than she could cope with. 'I c-can't go to dinner with you,' she stuttered.

'Why not?'

'Well, I've got a lot to do.'

'You have to eat.'

'And it's Clare's first night home.'

He looked palpably unimpressed by her clinching argument. 'The table's booked for eight-thirty.' He consulted his watch. 'That gives you twenty minutes to get ready.'

'Do people always do what you say?'

The lines that fanned out from his eyes deepened as if he found her futile resistance amusing—Darcy couldn't shake the uneasy notion that pursuit had a lot to do with his interest; perhaps his interest would cool rapidly once she'd settled for his terms.

'Nineteen minutes,' he said, not taking his eyes off her face.

'I don't react well to ultimatums,' she told him, smiling grimly through clenched teeth. 'Anyhow, you can't drive and I've promised the car to the boys tonight.'

'Nice try, but I've hired a driver.'

'Doesn't the driver think it's bit sus that his employer is sleeping in a derelict mansion?'

Reece's dark brows moved in the general direction of his dark hairline. 'I didn't ask him,' he replied. 'Eccentricity is only frowned upon if you don't have money, Darcy.'

'That's a cynical way of looking at things.'

'Whether you like it or not, that's the way the world works.'

'I don't have to like it,' she snorted.

'No,' he agreed, 'you don't have to like it—just me. *Do you?*'

The clipped abruptness of his question was unsettling, but not as unsettling as the peculiar intensity of his expression.

'Like you...?' Was this a trick question? 'I...I don't know you,' she blurted awkwardly. For a moment she thought he was going to push it, but much to her relief he dropped the subject.

'You're cutting things fine, and I'm hungry—in case you've forgotten, you did me out of lunch.' A slow, sensual smile curved his lips. 'Not that I'm complaining,' he added huskily.

Reece wondered if all her skin had turned the deep shade of crimson that her face had—he made a mental note to test the theory some time soon…very soon.

She looked just about everywhere but his face. It was while she was looking at the Christmas tree she thought of another excuse—feeble, but a drowning person wasn't fussy.

'I haven't finished decorating the tree.'

His attention was promptly diverted to the twinkling tree set beside the window.

'It looks as though it will collapse under the weight if you add another thing,' he commented after a moment's silent contemplation of the overladen branches.

Darcy rushed to defence of her efforts; it might not be fashionably minimalist, and it was light-years away from being colour co-ordinated, but every item that adorned it had sentimental value.

'Mum never threw away any of the things we made at school, not a thing; everything on that tree has a history.' She grabbed the fairy that had been gracing the top of the tree for as long as she could remember.

'There's a limit to how much *history* one little evergreen can take.'

There was also a limit to how much proximity she could take, Darcy thought as his hand brushed her shoulder—it was electric. The fizzling surge of sexual desire stole her breath. She took a stumbling step backwards.

'I can't…' she began stiltedly. Her eyes, which had been fixed on his expensively shod size twelves, started to travel upwards as if obeying an unspoken command. Long legs, more than a suggestion of muscle in the thigh area, and the loose cut of his tailored trousers couldn't disguise the fact he was aroused…as was she…*help*!

No benevolent force came to her aid. She could feel the glazed expression sliding into her eyes, feel the prickle of heat travelling over her body, and the worst part was being totally incapable of preventing it.

'Not touch—me neither.' His low-pitched voice carried an indecent amount of sensual suggestion.

She fought hard to master her seething emotions. 'I wasn't going to say that,' she managed to protest weakly. Her throat closed up as her wide, fearful eyes meshed with hot, determined green.

'You didn't need to.'

'That obvious, am I?' she asked, her throat clogged with shame. His thumb moved slowly down the extended column of her throat. Darcy, her eyes still melded with his, shivered and swayed far more violently than the overladen tree. She shook her head in an attempt to clear the sexual lethargy that had permeated her entire body.

'I'm not coming to dinner with you.'

His indulgence had a feral quality to it. 'Of course you are.'

Darcy bared her teeth. 'I'm not coming,' she continued, trying to keep a grip on both her temper and determination—at the last second she lost her nerve. Telling him she was in love with him would have the desired effect of sending him running, but it would also leave her without a shred of pride. 'Because we have nothing to talk about,' she finished limply.

'Fine; we won't talk,' he responded amiably. 'We'll do this instead.'

Darcy closed her eyes as his mouth came down hard on hers, and the wild wave of longing that washed over her sent her spinning out of control. She gave a discontented sigh when he lifted his head.

Finally Darcy heard what he obviously already had; she

recognised the click-clack of the ridiculous high-heeled mules that Clare wore around the house.

'Darcy… Sorry, I didn't know we had company.'

Sure you didn't, Darcy thought as her sister made a graceful attempt to pull together the sides of the gossamer wrap she wore, so graceful in fact that they were granted several tantalising glimpses of what was underneath; Darcy didn't actually feel very tantalised—she felt as mad as hell! She cringed at her sister's painful *obviousness*.

As you could see right through the wrap and she wasn't wearing a stitch underneath, Darcy didn't see why she'd bothered to put it on in the first place. In fact, she didn't see why she'd bothered to put on anything at all—surely a towel dropped at the right moment would have achieved her purpose just as well. Reece had got an eyeful of the celestial body. She gritted her teeth and felt anger bubbling within her.

He was staring… major surprise—*not*! It was the moment that Darcy had been subconsciously dreading; now it was here it was even worse than she'd imagined. In that moment she knew what it would feel like if she accepted his offer and became—for want of a better word—his mistress. There would be the constant fear that he would tire of her, or cheat, or… No, she couldn't cope on his terms.

'Your hair's sticking up,' she snapped abruptly. And I mussed it up, she wanted to shout at her sister.

'Thanks.' Reece smoothed down his dark hair with his good hand and turned to smile at Clare.

Clare, who had looked a little startled by Darcy's abrupt tone, began to look more confident.

'You must be Clare. Run along and get changed, Darcy.' The man had the unmitigated gall to absently pat her on the behind. 'Clare will entertain me.'

I just bet she will!

'Darcy missed her lunch on account of me, so I thought

the least I could do was take her to dinner,' he explained smoothly.

'What's wrong with the way I look now?' Darcy asked mutinously.

It occurred to Darcy too late that to invite a man to look at her when he'd only just feasted his eyes on Clare was a bad move—the comparison was hardly likely to do her any favours. She'd invited the scrutiny, though, and she was getting it; it took all her will-power not to drop her gaze under the searching intensity of that raw sexual appraisal.

'Not a thing.'

A gratified glow spread through her electrified body, but she didn't let herself respond—she couldn't.

'Here you are.' Nick strolled past the frozen figure of his younger sister in the doorway, apparently oblivious to the electric atmosphere.

Darcy gave a sigh of exasperation. 'I suppose you didn't know we had a visitor either?'

'As a matter of fact, Charlie mentioned Reece had come here to snog you.' He picked up an apple from the selection in the fruit bowl and polished it on his jumper.

'He mentioned *what*?' she yelped.

Reece cleared his throat. 'He asked me whether I was going to,' he admitted. 'What was I supposed to do—lie?'

'Yes!' Darcy responded with feeling.

Nick did some more apple-polishing. 'I suppose you know you can see right through that thing, Clare?'

Clare shook her head like someone emerging from a trance. 'What? I...' With a muffled sob she ran, clicking and clacking, from the room.

'Was it something I said?' Nick wondered innocently.

'Don't be facetious, Nick!' Darcy snapped. 'I should go after her...'

'And rub salt in the wound...?'

'What wound?'

Brother and sister looked at one another but didn't reply.

'I'm taking your sister for a meal.'

Nick bit down hard into his apple. 'So long as you don't take her for a ride, mate, be my guest.'

'He won't be your guest, because I'm not going, and I'm sure you mean well but I don't need a chaperon, Nick.'

Nick looked from his sister to the tall man at her side, but didn't budge.

'For heaven's sake, Nick!' she cried, totally exasperated. 'I'm quite capable of taking care of myself.'

'Not always, you weren't,' Nick reminded her quietly.

'What did he mean by that?' Reece asked the moment they were alone again.

'I got involved with someone who forget to mention he was already married.' If he despised her for what she'd revealed he was hiding it well; maybe he was reserving judgement, which was more than most people did. 'I thought he wanted a wife, but he wanted a mistress…is this ringing any bells?'

There was a guarded expression in his lushly lashed eyes. 'Do you still see him?' he fired abruptly.

'Who?'

'The married guy!'

The implication that she would knowingly continue an affair with a married man brought a furious sparkle to Darcy's eyes.

'I don't know why,' she gritted, her voice dripping sarcasm, 'but once I've broken up a marriage the excitement goes clear out of a relationship.' Her icy blue gaze swept contemptuously over his face. *'You're as bad as him!'*

'I haven't lied to you…I haven't asked you to marry me…'

You haven't fallen in love with me, she wanted to wail.

'But you have asked me to be your mistress—not in so many words, but it amounts to the same thing.'

'But you're holding out for a ring?' he speculated scornfully.

Darcy shook her head and smiled sadly. 'No, I'd settle for a lot less than that.'

'Such as…?'

She met his eyes, her own gaze steady and clear, and, holding her breath, jumped in with both feet. 'Love.'

His big chest rose sharply. 'You know—'

'I know you loved your wife and you'll never love anyone else, or that's what you tell yourself. I think the truth is you're too afraid to look forward, so you keep on looking back—'

Reece, who'd been holding his breath, exhaled noisily. 'And you'd know all about it…'

'The only thing I know for sure,' she returned with an emotional catch in her husky voice, 'is that I'm in love with you.' There, I said it.

'You're *what*…?' For once his effortless air of command had totally deserted him.

There was no way she was going to say it again. 'You heard me.'

He opened his mouth, closed it again and then abruptly turned on his heel and left her standing there beside the sparkling Christmas tree.

She made it to her room before she started crying in earnest. This orgy of misery was interrupted by her sister's entrance.

'Go away, Clare!' she begged gruffly without looking around.

'Are you getting ready to go out?'

'The dinner date's off,' Darcy explained with a quiver of high-pitched hysteria.

'I wanted to explain about the way I acted… I had the most awful interview with the bank manager yesterday and…I didn't know that you and Reece…'

'There is no me and Reece!' Darcy sobbed, lifting her downcast face.

'Darcy, have you been crying?' Clare exclaimed, lifting the tissue from her own pink nose. 'Oh, Darce, what's wrong?' she cried, wrapping her arms around her sister's shaking body. 'He's not worth it!' she cried soothingly.

If Darcy could have brought herself to truly believe that, she'd have felt a lot happier.

CHAPTER SEVEN

'THAT'S it. I'm going in!'

Darcy caught hold of her sister's arm. 'No, Clare,' she hissed urgently. 'We can't barge in—Mum and Dad need to talk...'

'They've been talking for over an hour!' Clare pointed out. 'How long can it take?' she wailed, wringing her slender hands. 'Darcy, I just can't take not knowing what the hell is going on for another minute.'

There was a murmur of general assent from their brothers.

Darcy sighed. 'Well, actually,' she admitted, letting go of Clare's arm, 'neither can I.'

Nick placed his hand on the doorknob to the sitting room, where their parents had been ensconced since Cathy Alexander had returned home earlier that morning, and looked questioningly at his siblings.

Darcy shrugged and Nick, taking this as encouragement, pushed the door open. The twins and Clare pressed from behind, sending Darcy headlong through the door with a precipitate rush.

'Come along in, children,' Jack said drily as his family stood there, all displaying varying degrees of sheepishness and a uniform level of anxiety.

Darcy looked at her parents' faces and gave a sigh of relief—everything was going to be all right! Until that moment she hadn't known how apprehensive she'd been. Jack looked dazed—but good dazed, like a man who'd just won the lottery as opposed to one who'd just been told his marriage was over. As for her mother, Cathy was positively glowing.

'Your mother's got some marvellous news for you all.'

'Jack, they might not think it's so marvellous.'

Jack Alexander clasped his wife's hand as if he was never going to let go. 'Of course they will. Your mother is going to have a baby.'

His news was greeted by a stunned silence.

'You're joking, right...?' Darcy heard Nick say, his tone suggesting he was just as gobsmacked as she felt.

'This is no joke, Nick,' his mother said quietly. 'It was a shock to me too...'

Darcy recognised an understatement when she heard it. Take what I'm feeling and times it by the odd million or so... No wonder Mum bolted!

'...and it's taken some time for me to get used to the idea,' Cathy admitted, casting an apologetic sideways look at her husband. 'I know it will mean a lot of changes...'

'Not to us—we'll be at university... But you know, Mum, I thought you were past that sort of thing.' Charlie winced as his twin kicked him in the shin.

'She's only forty-seven, idiot!' Harry hissed.

Clare was the first to recover. 'Why, Mum, that's marvellous!' she cried, running gracefully forward to embrace Cathy. *'Isn't it...?'* she said pointedly to Nick and Darcy.

Her words seemed to shake Nick out of his trance-like state. 'It's a relief, is what it is!' he sighed, surging forward to join his sister.

Cathy looked at her elder daughter over their heads, and there were tears in her eyes. 'And you, Darcy...? Do you mind...?'

'Mind...?' Darcy echoed hoarsely. *'Mind...?'* She saw for the first time what Clare had seen right off—their mother was desperately embarrassed by the situation and seeking their approval.

'She means no, Mum,' said Nick, directing a playful punch at his sister's shoulder, which almost knocked her off her feet.

Darcy rubbed her shoulder. She knew she was grinning like an idiot but couldn't seem to stop; the relief was so intense she felt weak.

'God, Mum, it's so good to have you home. Now tell us, what has the doctor said…?'

'Yes, you'll need a hospital with all the facilities,' Clare began thoughtfully, perching herself on the arm of the sofa to let Darcy move forward and get in on the hugs.

'Because of my age…?'

'Age nothing!' Clare denied robustly. 'If it was me I wouldn't set foot in a place that didn't offer every pain-killing device known to man, and don't let Beth brainwash you with all that stuff about natural childbirth when she gets here,' she warned. 'Just keep in mind that it was Beth who ended up giving birth in the back of the Land Rover.'

'I never knew you were so clued up, Clare!' Darcy exclaimed. 'I'd sort of assumed—'

'Just because my career is important it doesn't mean I don't like babies, Darcy, and wouldn't mind having a few—when the time is right.'

That put me in my place and quite right too, Darcy conceded, aware she'd been guilty of pigeon-holing her sister.

The males of the Alexander family began to drift away as the discussion on modern childbirth got increasingly technical—or, as Harry put it, *yucky*!

The piped music in the lift was working its way through a Christmas medley and Reece was working his way through the enamel on his white teeth. Having taken the penthouse suite—thanks to a last-minute cancellation—he had no option but to endure the agony longer than anyone else.

He reached the foyer and was immediately spotted by the assistant manager, who hastened discreetly to his side.

'I hope everything—'

'Fine, fine…' Reece murmured without slackening his pace. He seemed genuinely oblivious to the fact that his tall, distinguished person was a magnet for numerous curious and admiring eyes.

'Will your wife…?'

This stopped Reece.

'I have not got a wife!' Without raising his voice above a low murmur he managed to give his words the impact of a blood-curdling yell.

It might have been that his ears had become supersensitive, but the more often he denied it the less convincing it seemed to sound. Perhaps that was what happened when you were forced to repeat yourself ad nauseam to disbelieving people all morning—first his mother, then his sister. The rest of the family would no doubt have got in on the act too if he hadn't instructed the switchboard to say he wasn't taking calls from *anyone*!

He didn't know what was worse—their initial reproaches that he'd slunk off to marry someone they'd never met and cheated them out of a wedding, or their bitter disappointment when he'd finally convinced them it was all lies.

He wouldn't have had the ear-bashing at all if he hadn't allowed himself to weaken and ring home to tell them where he was—and that weakness too could be laid at the door of Miss Darcy Alexander, with all her idealistic claptrap of families and sharing!

'No, sir.' The poker-faced individual couldn't stop his eyes from straying to the newspaper poking out of Reece's pocket which had announced very authoritatively that he was:

Billionaire head of the Erskine Empire secretly wed.
Honeymooners involved in accident.

'Damn you!' Reece said without any particular conviction as he strode off.

'Where are we going, boss?' his driver asked as he produced the Mercedes—as requested, fully fuelled—in front
of the hotel.

'We're not...I am.'

'The arm—'

'Is fully functioning,' Reece snarled belligerently.

'If you say so.' The driver, who had found his employer
to be punctiliously polite, looked startled.

'I do,' Reece replied in a more moderate tone as he slid
into the driver's seat. 'Take Christmas off.'

'Thanks very much.'

'And, Andy...' he picked up the newspaper spread out
at the appropriate page on the front seat and screwed it into
a tight bundle before pressing it firmly into the driver's
hand '...take a different newspaper while you're at work.'

'Does this mean that job with your mother is off?' the
young man asked with a rueful grimace.

'Do I look like the vindictive type? No,' he said, ad-
justing the mirror, 'don't answer that.'

'I wasn't going to.'

'If you can put up with my mother the job is yours,'
Reece yelled over his shoulder just before the window slid
silently down and the car drew smoothly away.

Cruising in the outside lane of the motorway, the man
without a vindictive bone in his body contemplated the awful retributions he was going to visit on Darcy Alexander.

Having so-called 'friends' leak stories to the Press was
an occupational hazard as far as he was concerned—even
when that stupid kiss-and-tell story had appeared last
Christmas he'd been able to shrug it off; this was different,
though. He'd *believed* in those big blue eyes—hell, he'd

even believed it when she'd said she loved him; that fact was largely responsible for the fact he hadn't had a moment's peace since. And now she turned out to be the sort of girl that ran to the newspapers with a fake but eye-catching story... Why...? Was she deluded enough to think that this would in some way obligate him to actually marry her...?

Before long he'd find out—even if he had to wring the truth out of her!

'I don't know what the fuss is about; in my day plenty of women had babies well into their forties.'

'Yes, Gran,' Darcy replied meekly, deciding on reflection that this probably wasn't the moment to point out the lamentably high maternal death-rate enjoyed by women of that rosy bygone era. When Gran was in full nostalgia mode it was better to let her run on...and on...and on...uninterrupted.

'If anyone had seen fit to ask my advice...but of course they didn't...'

'You won't believe how much little Jamie has grown, Gran!'

'Grown into what, is the question,' the old lady retorted, suitably diverted but not placated. 'I told that girl of Jack's she was making a rod for her own back, picking the child up every time he whimpered. Worn to a frazzle she looked, last time I saw her.'

'Well, she looks pretty marvellous now,' Darcy replied uncooperatively, 'and Jamie is a dear little boy, so why don't you stop being such a grouch, Granny Prue,' she coaxed gently, 'and get into the Christmas spirit?'

The lady, who was neither particularly old nor infirm, but a modern-minded, sprightly sixty-nine, sniffed.

'In *my* day I wouldn't have dared speak to my elders that way, young lady. You always did have far too much to say for yourself,' she mused, unable to totally disguise her approval of this character flaw in her granddaughter.

The entire clan, minus little Jamie, who, Darcy assumed, was taking a nap, was dutifully lined up to greet Prudence Emery. It was a noisy, boisterous occasion, during which the lady in question hid her pleasure by criticising the new décor in the room and offending Nick by falsely claiming he was losing his hair.

Taking advantage of a lull in the clamour, Cathy drew her daughter to one side. 'You've got a visitor, Darcy,' she explained quietly. 'He's in the sitting room, if you want to slip away.'

'He…! Who he…?' Darcy demanded, grabbing hold of Cathy's sleeve.

Aware of her mother's startled response to her shrill reaction, Darcy took a deep breath and tried to regain her serenity—actually she'd never been particularly serene to begin with, and lately not at all! Contemplating the way she'd been lately wasn't going to improve her mental wellbeing, so Darcy wisely decided not to go there.

With a self-conscious grimace she released her mother's sleeve and brushed down the creased fabric. If she couldn't manage serene she could at least rise to sane! People lost out in the love stakes every day of the week and they still carried on functioning as useful members of society; only wimps curled up in a corner and moaned about their tough break.

There wasn't even any reason to assume that this visitor was Reece, and even if it was that wasn't necessarily significant. He could have come calling for any number of reasons—none of which she could bring to mind at that particular moment. The 'he's discovered he can't live without me' reason was one she forbade herself to think about even in the hypothetical sense.

'Is it anyone special?' she asked, overdoing the languid

unconcern like mad to compensate for her previous behaviour.

'You tell me, dear.'

Darcy gave her mother a pained look; it was a burden having a parent who could read you like a book.

'I'd be surprised if he wasn't special to someone,' Cathy volunteered innocently.

'Does this *special* man have a name?' Darcy wasn't in the mood for enigmatic; her brain was aching.

'It's the gentleman who I believe was staying next door—Reece Erskine; a nice boy,' Cathy mused innocently.

Nice! Darcy choked with quiet restraint; her heart felt as if it was trying to climb up her throat. The anticipation rushing through her veins made her head buzz loudly.

'Right.' She made a vague fluttery motion with her hand. 'Well, I suppose I'd better… Couldn't you just say I'd gone away, Mum?' She blushed deeply and lowered her eyes. 'No, of course you couldn't,' she mumbled, shamed by her display of cowardice. 'The sitting room, you said…? I'll just go and…' Darcy made a hasty dive for the door; her mother was quite capable of asking any number of uncomfortable questions if she hung around any longer.

He didn't hear the door open, which, considering the racket they were making, wasn't entirely surprising. Darcy had taken the intervening minutes to compose herself sufficiently to avoid looking a total fool when she came face to face with him.

Her mental preparations had not, however, prepared her for the sight of Reece, sharply dressed in a beautifully cut mid-grey suit, crouched down on all fours with her small nephew riding on his back. It was only a matter of forty-eight hours since she'd last seen him but the wave of longing that hit her was so intense that for several seconds it drove all other considerations from her mind.

He had the sort of earthy sex appeal that a memory could

not fully do justice to, or maybe she'd made some subconscious effort to spare herself pain by playing down the details. In the flesh he was bigger, leaner and more good-looking than any male had a right to be—definitely more good-looking than a girl in love could be expected to cope with.

As she watched an excited Jamie grabbed a hank of Reece's dark hair and ordered him to stop in his baby treble. Reece promptly fell down flat on his belly, flipped over and with straight arms lifted the laughing little boy above his head. She only just stopped herself crying out a warning for his poor shoulder, or maybe she didn't because his head suddenly turned. Their glances clashed warily.

In that second all Darcy's hopes faded and died. The world had become an even more confusing place—why anger...? Well, at least I know why he *hasn't* come to visit—a look of love that was not.

'Hello, Reece; your shoulder's better?' She nodded her head towards his arm, unable to take her eyes off his face.

'Full working order,' he agreed, flexing his shoulder to illustrate the range of movement. Underneath the commonplace response she was deeply aware of his seething anger.

'Aunty Darcy!' Jamie cried, catching sight of his favourite aunt. 'Come and play with us.'

'Not now, Jamie, darling. Granny has arrived—why don't you go and see her?'

'Has she got me a present?' the little boy wondered with innocent avarice.

Darcy smiled in a distracted manner and patted his curly head. 'It's very possible,' she told him drily. As she spoke she was very aware of Reece agilely leaping to his feet, and the room suddenly felt too compact for comfort—far too compact to take all the turbulent emotions seething around them.

'I'll go, then,' the child agreed graciously. 'Don't go

away!' he added imperiously to Reece, who was smoothing his sleek black hair away from a broad heroic-looking forehead.

Reece smartly saluted the little boy, who solemnly saluted back after a fashion.

'You can play with Darcy while I'm gone,' Jamie announced in a spirit of generosity before he left.

A choking sound emerged from Darcy's throat as her cheeks fairly exploded with mortified colour.

Reece's eyes ran insolently over her slender figure from head to toe. A muscle leapt in his rigid jaw and disturbed for a moment the smooth, sardonic mask he wore.

'I'll pass, if you don't mind,' he drawled with languid contempt as he slid the loose knot on his tasteful silk tie up to his brown throat.

The deliberate insult made the colour ebb from Darcy's cheeks. An expression of hurt confusion appeared on her face as she watched him refasten a single button on his jacket with equal precision. This was the first time she'd seen him dressed formally; perhaps he donned a hostile personality along with the suit...?

Reece saw the hurt and the bewilderment—both were hard to miss; fortunately he knew what a duplicitous little creature she was, otherwise he might have been foolish enough to respond to the urge to kiss away the hurt.

The icy glitter in his eyes was pure, unadulterated contempt—to put it mildly, Darcy was disconcerted. She responded accordingly.

'Mind...?' she laughed. 'I *insist*.' She bit back further retorts; they'd get nowhere if this thing degenerated into a childish round of insults. 'You've come a long way just to be nasty, Reece...'

He thrust his hands deep into the pockets of his loosely tailored trousers and viewed her from under the protective shield of lush dark lashes.

'I've had to wait a long time to be nasty.' He looked pointedly at his wristwatch as if she'd deliberately kept him waiting—an attitude which struck Darcy as being perverse in the extreme, considering she hadn't known his plans.

Maybe he didn't like children? Perhaps Jamie had driven him crazy…? It wasn't likely, considering the fact the atmosphere had been pretty convivial until she'd walked in, but she couldn't think of anything else to explain his hostility.

'You met my mum…?'

'She was very kind.' So much so that it had been hard to maintain his crusading rage in the face of such genuine warmth. 'You must be relieved she's home. I'm happy for you.'

She'd rarely heard or seen anyone displaying fewer symptoms of happiness.

'I don't mean to be blunt, but why exactly are you here, Reece? It's not that I'm not over the moon to see you…' Irony was an excellent disguise for the truth.

'Like you don't know…?' he drawled.

Darcy had the uncomfortable feeling she'd walked into this conversation halfway through.

'I've not the faintest.'

He shook his dark head, regarding her with disdainful distrust. 'What I don't understand is what you thought you'd gain by it.'

Her bewilderment increased. *'It?'*

Reece breathed heavily, his nostrils flaring, before he turned abruptly away, dragging both hands viciously through his hair.

'If what I've done is so awful that you can't even look at me, it only seems fair I get to know what it is.'

He'd have thought better of her if she'd not tried to pretend, if she'd been frank about it. 'You want to play it like that—fine.'

Something inside Darcy snapped; this was the man she'd fallen in love with, the man she'd spent every miserable second they'd been apart craving for. The sound of his voice brought her out in goosebumps, the touch of his hand or, for that matter, any part of his body set her nervous system into meltdown, and here he was, treating her as if she was public enemy number one! Surely this couldn't all be because she'd said she loved him—surely walking away had been punishment enough for that transgression.

She planted her hands on the gentle curve of her hips and raised the angle of her chin an aggressive few degrees.

'Don't take that tone with me!' Unless he considered falling in love with him to be a betrayal of trust, Darcy's conscience was clear.

'What tone did you expect me to take after you fed that ridiculous story to that filthy rag?' he spat in disgust.

'What story?' For that matter, what filthy rag? She now knew that Reece, who might well be the financial genius everyone said he was, could mess up like everyone else. Human fallibility could be charming in a way, but not on this occasion.

He produced a screwed-up newspaper from his pocket and waved it in front of her. 'I expect you've had your copy framed. Did you get a kick out of seeing your name in print?' he asked, ignoring for the moment the fact her name hadn't appeared in the article.

'You can carry on talking in riddles if you like, but we'll get nowhere fast, and if you think I'm going to oblige you by being intimidated by this pathetic display, think again!' she flung for good measure.

Reece surveyed her through disillusioned eyes. 'You fed the paper a story about me being married—to you.'

The accusation was so ridiculous that she couldn't even be angry any more. 'Don't be stupid.' With a frown she impatiently snatched the paper from his hand.

'Page five,' he told her curtly. 'Have you any idea what havoc you've caused…?' he ranted. 'It took me three-quarters of an hour to convince my mother I haven't got married, and even after I'd managed to do that she still wanted to know what you were like…'

Darcy was bewildered but intrigued by these revelations. 'What did you say?'

Reece shot her a murderous glare. 'As for my sister, she insisted on giving me the number of the lisping idiot who designed her friend's wedding dress…! I wouldn't let that fawning creep within ten miles of my inside leg!'

Darcy giggled; it was inappropriate but she couldn't help herself, he looked so outraged. A blast of raw wrath from his spectacular eyes had her hurriedly spreading out the paper on the floor and squatting down beside it.

'You didn't make the front page—I can see why you're so miffed,' she mocked flippantly. 'I'm pretty miffed myself,' she added, solemnly quoting, '"Witnesses tell us that the distraught young bride temporarily separated from her husband was comforted by the hospital staff after she collapsed." *How wet!*' she exclaimed in disgust. 'I might sue.'

'Get in line.' It was slowly dawning on Reece that she wasn't reacting like the guilty party here—in fact, nothing had gone as he'd envisaged so far. He'd sailed in here, determined to deal out a retribution that was both swift and awful—the details of which he hadn't quite worked out—and he'd been taken to the family bosom and treated like a long-lost son.

Darcy tucked her hair behind her ears as she bent over the paper. The grainy picture didn't do him justice. Rapidly she scanned the rest of the print beneath. It only took her a few moments to digest the salient details. She sat back on her heels and lifted her face to his.

'Well, you've only yourself to blame.'

'Me!'

'Well, you're the one who made up that stupid story about me being your wife, and it was obvious that that girl on the hospital reception recognised you…'

She saw his eyes widen fractionally as he absorbed what she was saying.

'You're saying that *she's* the source of this story…?' My God, why hadn't he thought of that? It was so damned *obvious*. It made no sense…it was entirely out of character for him to jump to a conclusion the way he had.

Darcy shrugged. 'Well, let's face it, she's a hell of a lot more likely a candidate than me. If I did want my five minutes of fame I can think of better ways to get it than that!'

There was a startled silence.

If she'd been the sort of girl to gloat, now would have been the time to do it. The expression on Reece's taut face revealed he had accepted her explanation and accepted the fact he had egg all over his handsome face, and Darcy suspected this wasn't a situation he'd had much experience in dealing with. In her opinion a dose of humility wouldn't do the man any harm at all—loving him didn't stop her recognising the character flaws in his personality.

She held up her hand and after a fractional pause he grabbed it and hauled her to her feet.

'I might,' he conceded slowly, 'have been a trifle…*hasty*.'

'You weren't a *trifle* insulting and rude?' She withdrew her hand from his firm grasp even though every instinct told her to cling for all she was worth.

'I suppose you want me to apologise,' he growled belligerently, his colour slightly heightened.

'Grovelling would be a start,' she conceded, symbolically wiping the fingers that had moments ago been enfolded in his on the seat of her skirt. 'I thought you were supposed to be clever—even Jamie could have figured it out. I had no reason to plant a story; if you recall, I wasn't too keen on the idea of being Mrs Erskine to begin with.'

'I was under the impression that was exactly what you wanted. No ring, no sex—classic case of carrot-dangling.'

'How like a man!' she gasped contemptuously. 'I didn't propose to you, I just told you how I felt.' She glared bitterly at the outline of the broad back he presented her with. It struck her as representative of his attitude. 'I only wanted a relationship where both parties are open to the possibility of natural development. We're talking *possibility* here, Reece! Is that so outrageous? I suppose it is,' she mused thoughtfully, 'if you're an emotional coward.'

In the act of pacing over to the opposite side of the room, as though he couldn't bear to be close to her, Reece stopped and spun back towards her.

'What exactly do you mean by that?' he demanded, his pent-up frustration clearly illustrated in every tense, dangerous line of his lean body.

'You loved your wife, and what happened was a terrible tragedy, but it isn't loyalty to her memory that prevents you from having feelings for anyone else.'

'Is that a fact?'

'Yes, it is,' Darcy reiterated bravely in the face of his simmering displeasure—she'd given the matter a lot of thought and had promised herself that if she ever saw Reece again she would share her conclusions with him. 'You're afraid to feel in case you get hurt again—it's only natural for you to be wary...'

'So it's a simple matter of cowardice?' He released a short incredulous gasp as his dagger-sharp glare bored into her.

Darcy refused to be intimidated—after all, what did she have to lose by speaking her mind? 'After my experience with Michael I could have decided to mistrust all men, but I didn't.'

'You're an example to us all. You asked me if it's outrageous for you to be so uncomfortable with your sexual desires that you dress them up with socially acceptable labels like *love* and *relationship*.' He skimmed her pale face with a provocative sneer.

Indignation shot through Darcy, who barely recognised this translation of her earlier appeal to him.

'I'll tell you what's outrageous, shall I?' He didn't wait for her to respond but plunged furiously onwards. 'You playing amateur shrink… Of all the glib…!' The fire died from his eyes as abruptly as it had ignited, leaving a bleakness that swiftly delivered an emotional ache to her throat.

He groaned suddenly and, with the appearance of a man in acute pain, brought his hands up to his head. She watched his long fingers curl deep into his hair as if he was contemplating tearing out the odd fistful or two.

'God, but I hate the way you make me feel.'

Whilst she empathised wildly with his pain, she couldn't help but be cheered by this news—at least he wasn't indifferent to her.

'Sorry,' she murmured softly.

Reece lowered his hands. 'What for?'

'For not planting the story.'

Her neutral calm was beginning to irritate him deeply.

'If I had you'd have a legitimate reason to dislike me,' she explained. 'And that would be very convenient for you, wouldn't it, Reece?'

'I *do* dislike you.' There was a shade of helplessness in his strong face as he watched her catch her full lower lip between her teeth and gnaw thoughtfully on the softness.

Darcy shook her head. 'No, you like me—you *definitely* like me,' she added firmly, raising her clear blue eyes to his. 'And I think you're afraid you could get to like me more. That's why you skipped town.'

'What town?'

He sounded amused by her claim—on balance she preferred hostility. Amusement opened the possibility she'd badly misjudged the strength of his feelings. It had been a calculated risk to directly challenge him and she was beginning to wonder if it hadn't backfired; she might emerge from this looking a total fool.

'A figure of speech.' What possessed me…? Why didn't I keep my big mouth shut…?

'Have you always considered yourself irresistible?'

A wry laugh was wrenched from her throat. 'With a sister like Clare? Do me a favour.'

'Clare is a clothes horse.' Darcy stood, her mouth slightly ajar, whilst he casually dismissed her beautiful sister. His glorious eyes sought, found and clung to hers. 'You're a *woman*.'

The hoarse observation was uttered with total conviction.

'*Reece*.' Darcy hadn't even been conscious of moving towards him like a heat-seeking missile until his big hands came up on her shoulders, preventing her from pressing herself closer.

This close she could see the beads of sweat across his upper lip and feel the fine febrile tremors that were running through his greyhound-lean frame.

'You were right, Darcy, there's no future for someone like you with someone like me.'

'What's someone like me…?'

'Warm, giving…' His big, capable, clever hands left her shoulders and slid all the way down the smooth curve of her back before closing over the tight swell of her buttocks. Darcy quivered as hard as a highly strung thoroughbred and pressed closer.

'In that case,' she murmured huskily into his mouth, 'why did you just kiss me…?' Her head was tilted backwards, exposing the long, graceful line of her pale throat.

'Because I have no moral backbone at all.' His hot eyes

lingered smoulderingly on her slightly parted lips. 'And you have the world's most sexy mouth.'

'I do?' she exclaimed, lifting a hand to her lips and provocatively tracing the full outline. She could almost hear the satisfying sound of his control snapping.

'You know you do,' he ground out savagely before he kissed her again, bending her backwards from the waist with the raw force of the embrace. She felt one arm steal around her waist, hauling her upwards until their hips were level. His free hand slid under the hem of her skirt and moved confidently underneath.

The frantic flood of feeling generated by the intimate contact sent her spiralling out of control. She started babbling—she had no accurate recall later of what she said, which was possibly a good thing, but she knew it featured his name and 'please', and both more than once.

It was a major shock to her system when he suddenly released her and placed her back on her feet.

'I can't give you what you want, Darcy.'

She shook her head, refusing to hear what he'd said, refusing to hear the horrid coldness in his voice. Stretched up on tiptoe, she let her tongue slide along the firm, sensual line of his lower lip. A husky little laugh rolled off her tongue.

'You can give me some of the things I want,' she assured him, plastering herself sinuously up against him in a manner that left no doubt to her meaning.

'Darcy, stop that!' he rapped unsteadily as she slid her hand between the buttons of his shirt. He grabbed her wrist and firmly removed it.

Darcy gazed indignantly up at him as he moved her bodily away from him. The heat of arousal died from her eyes, leaving a bemused, resentful expression.

'You stopped!' she wailed.

'I stopped what?' he snapped, making unnecessary adjustments to his tie.

'Kissing me,' she elaborated disapprovingly. Her body had responded to the promise of sensual satisfaction; now it responded just as swiftly and equally violently to being so rudely deprived.

Reece's eyes slid to her face long enough to take in the sexy pout but didn't linger. 'You don't want me to kiss you; I'm not husband material and I'm emotionally stagnant—remember...?'

Darcy remembered but somehow it didn't seem so important any longer. Glutting her hungry senses on the taste, touch and scent of him was.

'What if I can live with that?' She caught hold of the lapels of his jacket and forced him round to face her. 'What if I want to be your mistress...?' This wasn't a perfect world; a girl had to take what she could get, she told herself, rationalising her about-face.

'I don't want you for a mistress, Darcy.' He delivered the uncompromising verdict with a stony face.

There was a period of total, disbelieving silence.

Darcy felt the hot blood rush into her cold face. Now would be the time to retire, beaten, but with a token degree of dignity intact—Darcy never had known when to quit.

'I don't believe you,' she whispered.

'You make too many demands.' She flinched as if he'd struck her. That look in her eyes was one that would haunt him to his dying day. 'You were right—I need a low-maintenance mistress, and frankly that's not you.' He had to get out of here before this bout of selflessness wore off.

Darcy's stomach was a churning mess of misery. Pride was the only thing that enabled her to lift her head and look him bravely in the face; he looked interestingly pale, she noted irrelevantly.

'I'm sure you're right.'

'Yeah, right,' he agreed with a noticeable lack of enthusiasm.

'It's probably best you go now; I'll explain to Jamie.' Perhaps someone will explain to me why I keep inviting rejection. Perhaps someone will explain to me how a person is meant to cope with humiliation on this mega scale.

'Great kid,' Reece observed flatly as she led the way to the front door.

Darcy, normally a besotted aunt, couldn't even manage a smile.

'So this is your young man, Darcy.'

Darcy only just stopped herself pushing his solid bulk through the front door and slamming it safely shut as her grandmother, who had an honours degree in making awkward situations worse, materialised as if by magic.

'This is Reece Erskine, Gran, and he's not my man, young or otherwise,' she explained quietly. 'This is my grandmother.' She pressed her back against the exposed stone wall in the hallway to allow Reece an uninterrupted view of her grandmother, and the support the cold stone afforded was actually quite welcome.

'Mrs…?' He looked to Darcy to help him out and wished he hadn't, she looked so desperately pale.

'Prue.' Prudence Emery held out her hand. 'You can always tell a lot about a man from his handshake.'

Reece wondered if it had told her he was the sort of man who played fast and loose with lovely young women just because he didn't have the self-control to keep his lust under control.

'Mr Erskine was just going, Gran.'

'I read that article you wrote in the *Economist*—the one about ethical investments; very interesting. Though I thought you were a little unrealistic when you said—'

'*Gran!*' Darcy wailed, unable to contain herself any longer.

'Well, really, Darcy!' Her grandmother was not slow to express her disapproval at this interruption. 'I don't often have the opportunity to speak with someone who actually—'

'Actually, Prue, I do have to be going; it was very nice meeting you...'

'Is he always so abrupt?' Prudence asked her granddaughter.

'Only when he's just had to fend off the amorous advances of stupid women!' Darcy explained before excusing herself.

CHAPTER EIGHT

'ISN'T this just perfect?' Clare exclaimed, holding up a cute baby-blue sleepsuit.

'But is it entirely practical?' Darcy wondered, fingering the velvet teddy bears.

Her half-sister gave a sigh of exasperation as Darcy diligently searched for the wash label. 'Does it matter? It's cute, it's gorgeous—I'm going to buy it.'

Darcy grinned. 'I give in. Perhaps we should pick up some of those nice little vests…'

'Nice *practical* little vests. You're hopeless,' Clare complained, adding the sleepsuit to their overladen shopping basket. 'Don't you ever just throw caution to the winds and buy something totally frivolous, or do something you'll definitely regret?'

Would falling for the wrong man qualify? Darcy wondered bleakly. 'Let's be really silly and get the pink dungarees with elephants.'

'What if it's a boy?'

'He can blame his big sisters for any gender issues that arise in later life.'

'While you're about it,' Clare said, catching on to this reckless mood quickly, 'why don't we go back and buy that dress?'

'I'd never dare wear it in public.'

It was only her sister's pushiness that had got her into the designer shop—it had taken the joint persuasive powers of Clare and the elegant assistant to get her into the dress. Strapless black and deceptively simple. Darcy was inclined to think their flattering reaction had been a put-up job by

Clare to boost her flagging ego—besides, there was no way she could wear something that could be fitted in her wallet.

'Who'd want to?' Clare scorned. 'If you play your cards right, it's not the sort of dress that would see the outside of a bedroom—private viewings only,' she giggled huskily.

Darcy's expression drew taut. If she thought bedrooms she thought Reece.

'Let's pay for these.'

'You're changing the subject, Darce.'

Darcy changed it some more. 'If we want to find a table for lunch we'd better get a move-on.'

The streets of York were crowded with shoppers buying last-minute gifts, but even in the mêlée the couple drew a lot of attention—they were an extremely handsome pair. This man was the rare breed that people didn't barge into and bustle, and the girl by his side benefited from the invisible exclusion zone around them.

'Hold up—progress check.' The girl placed her list on the broad back of her companion and began to tick off the list she carried.

'Mum'll love that pashmina. She'd love it even more if you came home for Christmas,' she added slyly.

'Kate, don't push it...'

The young woman straightened her felt hat to a jaunty angle. 'It was worth a try,' she explained with a philosophical shrug. 'And stranger things have been known to happen.'

Stranger things like her brother ringing her up two days before Christmas to ask her to help him buy Christmas gifts for the family. The fact that her brother was intending to buy Christmas presents *personally* definitely constituted strange, if not miraculous.

Displaying tact and restraint she wasn't renowned for, Kate had only asked, 'Why York?'

She was still, however, eaten up with curiosity to discover what had brought about this dramatic thaw in her big brother's attitude to the festive season. He did after all have more reason than most to be cynical and disillusioned about this time of year.

'Who's Jamie?' she asked, consulting the list once more.

'A kid I know.'

'How old is he?'

Reece leaned down and drew a tentative line about knee-level.

'You don't know how old he is?'

'Not old.'

'I know I make shopping look easy…but *really*, Reece.'

'I thought you liked shopping.' He looked nonplussed by her attitude.

Kate was unable to deny this. 'Perhaps we should take a lunch-break——*Reece*!' she called out, hurriedly grabbing the bundles of brightly wrapped gifts he'd left on the cobbled pedestrianised road before plunging through the crowd after him. If he hadn't been so tall she'd have lost him almost immediately.

'What on earth are you doing?' she cried, as panting, she eventually caught up with him.

Her brother didn't reply, and she'd have laid odds he hadn't even heard her——he was gazing with a fixed, hungry expression at a point across the street. She automatically checked out what had caught his attention.

'Oh, my!' she exclaimed once she had zeroed in on his target——a tall, willowy blonde dressed in an outfit that had 'designer' written all over it. A dedicated follower of fashion, Kate couldn't place the distinctive style. 'She is incredibly gorgeous,' she conceded reluctantly, 'if you like blondes.' She touched the deep copper tendrils of hair that artistically surrounded her face a shade defensively.

Reece, it seemed, obviously did like blondes——or at least

this one—because, ignoring her completely, he was crossing over the street with scant regard for the traffic flow.

'Heavens!' she exclaimed when she realised her brother was going to approach the young woman. This was a major departure for him! For the past few years Kate hadn't seen her big brother so much as raise a finger to make a woman notice him—of course they noticed him when he did nothing! 'This is not typical behaviour,' she explained to a startled-looking passer-by before she gathered up the parcels and resignedly followed him.

Kate's amazement escalated when her brother walked straight past the drop-dead gorgeous blonde as if he didn't see her and right up to the girl she was with, a girl that Kate hadn't noticed until now.

As she got closer Kate could see that the girl wasn't unattractive, and in fact if she hadn't been with the stunner you'd have thought she was a very pretty young woman, though at that moment she looked as if she wouldn't have minded being invisible. The way Reece was behaving, Kate didn't really blame her; he was her brother but even she could recognise he could be pretty intimidating on occasion.

Darcy retreated into the doorway as the large, life-like mirage moved steadily towards her. Her stomach muscles spasmed painfully and the blood drained from her face.

'Hello, Darcy. How are you…?' The mirage spoke; his voice was deep and vibrant, and it made the hairs on the nape of her neck stand on end. Either this was a cruel coincidence or he'd been following her, which, given the way they'd parted, seemed extremely unlikely.

Kate saw the expression on the young woman's face and her own eyes widened—she wasn't screaming for help, but she did look as if she was about to faint. Not strangers—not by a long way!

It was no surprise to Darcy that he was with a beautiful young woman; Reece and beautiful women went together naturally. She couldn't help but notice he appeared to have overcome his qualms about very young women because there was no way this redhead was more than twenty. Presumably if she was low maintenance he was willing to overlook the age-gap.

By avoiding directly meeting the bone-stripping blaze of his emerald scrutiny, Darcy managed to respond stiltedly.

'What a surprise, Reece; how are you…?' She was beginning to understand how relatively mild-mannered creatures could turn feral and dangerous if cornered.

'I'm fine.' A spasm of irritation crossed his patrician features. 'No, I'm not fine, not fine at all!' he bellowed harshly. 'In fact I'm awful.'

I'm not so crash-hot myself, Darcy wanted to yell back. She drew herself up to her full height; it alarmed her that, despite the fact her defences were on full red alert, her skin prickled with sexual awareness and it smothered her like a rash. After the emotional mauling she'd received at their last encounter she didn't fancy a repeat performance. The nasty truth was she didn't trust herself in his company. It wasn't as if she'd planned to act like some willing sex slave last time! She squirmed, recalling that awful moment of rejection.

'Well, don't look at me like that—it's not my fault!' she yelled. '*I* didn't run away.' She bit down hard on her lip, hating the *needy* sound of this last tellingly bitter comment.

Kate was aware that the tall blonde, just as curious a witness to this exchange as she was, had moved beside her to get a better view.

'Kate,' she whispered, thrusting out her hand. 'Sister.' She nodded towards Reece.

There was barely a pause before the other girl responded.

'Clare,' came the hushed, hurried response. 'Sister.' She nodded towards Darcy.

'I want to look at you…!' Reece announced defiantly. The line etched above his nose deepened. 'I need to look at you…I *have* to look at you!' he finished on a startled note of discovery.

Darcy was more shaken by this announcement than she was prepared to admit even to herself. 'Well, you've looked,' she sniffed. 'So now you can go away, and if you follow me,' she added rebelliously, 'I'll call the police. They take a very dim view of stalkers. *Clare!*' She looked around wildly for her sister.

'Coming, Darce!'

'Darcy, you can't go!' Reece began urgently.

I can't *not* go! Darcy ignored his plea and made a neat side-step around him; unfortunately his elbow caught the parcels she carried and sent them flying.

'Let me.' Reece joined her on his hands and knees and began to place the tiny items back in the numerous bags. 'We should talk…' The steady stream of busy people divided, leaving the couple to form an island as the flood moved around them.

'Talk…?' Darcy responded in a low, bitter voice. 'Aren't you afraid I'll embarrass you by doing something silly like offering myself up to you unconditionally…?' Gulping back the tears, she continued to feverishly ram tiny baby items back in the bags any which way.

For once in his life when he really needed to say something Reece was speechless. When you heard it put like that it was pretty hard to escape the conclusion that he'd been a prize fool. What had seemed like noble self-sacrifice now seemed like cowardly caution.

'What's the point?' she added, snatching the last item from his hand and getting to her feet. 'Nothing's changed.' If he'd denied it she might have hung around to hear what he had to say, but he didn't, he remained on his haunches, staring blankly at the hand she'd ripped the soft booties from. 'Come on, Clare.'

'Reece,' Kate murmured after she'd endured several curious stares of passers-by. 'It might be a good idea to get up some time soon unless you want to be charged with causing an obstruction.'

Prone to clumsiness, Kate felt a brief surge of envy as her brother, who, even in moments of extreme stress—and this was obviously one of them—was beautifully co-ordinated, rose to his feet.

'Kate, what do you know about babies...pregnancy...that sort of thing?'

'Well, I read the book Mum gave me, and I attended all the classes at school, but...' She paused; there was no flicker of answering humour in her brother's eyes. 'Could you be more specific?'

'How long does it take before you'd know you were pregnant?'

'Well, I suppose that would depend on when in your cycle you conceived, but I do know you can tell almost straight away these days with the kits they've got. Never had call to try them out myself but I hear they're pretty accurate.'

'Oh, my God!'

At moments of emotional crisis in her life Reece had always stood out as a comforting figure of calm authority to Kate. Now she was shocked to discover that even her self-contained brother knew what panic felt like.

'What is it, Reece? What's wrong?'

He raised a distracted hand to his forehead, his skin deathly pale and clammy to the touch. 'All those bags were filled with baby clothes,' he said in a voice wiped clean of all emotion.

'Then you think...and it's yours...*hell's bells*!' No wonder he looked stunned. 'Anyone can buy baby clothes—it doesn't mean she's pregnant. They're probably presents.'

'There were dozens of them.'

Kate wondered whether now would be the right time to say congratulations.

Reece turned to his sister, a zealot-like gleam of purpose in his eyes. 'I've got to go.'

'I thought you might,' she responded drily. 'What shall I—?'

'See you later.'

No 'when' later, no 'where' later; how typical, Kate thought, watching her tall sibling weave his way skilfully through the shoppers.

There were no signs of life at the Alexander house. Frustrated but not deterred, Reece pondered his next move—he could wait, but inactivity didn't recommend itself to him in his present frame of mind. He decided to drive down the road to the nearby village to see if there was any clue to their whereabouts.

There was a noticeably large collection of cars in the cobbled village square; Reece joined them. Leaving the car, he shadowed the handful of recent arrivals. Their destination proved to be a small hall with a tin roof set just behind the church.

'Two pounds fifty, please,' the large female at the door demanded, blocking his way into the glorified tin shed.

Impatiently he handed her a ten-pound note from his wallet. His impatient direction of 'Keep it' as she began to meticulously count out the correct change seemed to shock her Yorkshire thriftiness, but he got in, that was the main thing—into what, he wasn't quite sure, but instinct told him there was a strong possibility, given the scarcity of social occasions in the area, that Darcy would be here.

The place was heaving, but thanks to their height he spotted the twins almost immediately; their blond heads were easy to identify above the audience, who were seated in rows of uncomfortable wooden-backed chairs. He slid into the back row and waited.

He waited all the way through the infants' nativity play and the resonant recitation by a large bearded individual. His patience was rewarded when the choir trouped onto the small makeshift stage. In the front row, looking angelically sexy and terrified, was Darcy.

'You were marvellous, Darcy.'

'I think I'm going to throw up.'

'What you need is a drink.'

'What I need is several,' Darcy, whose knees were still shaking, informed the pushy cleric firmly. 'And, considering it's your fault I was up there to begin with, you're buying.'

Adam Wells grinned. 'Sounds reasonable to me.' He gave her a quick hug. 'You're a trouper.' With a display of sensible caution he moved away. 'Not still feeling sick, are you?' he enquired warily.

'That's passed, but it was a close call. I'll hold you to that drink.'

'How about now?' Adam suggested, looking around the dimly lit empty hall.

Darcy, who hadn't really taken the offer seriously, looked surprised. 'Mum and Dad are waiting.'

'They're not the only ones.'

Thanks to the excellent acoustics, the words uttered by the tall, sinister figure who rose from the shadows at the back of the hall reached the front with no problem.

'That's excellent voice projection you have there…?' Adam commented as the tall figure came to a halt just in front of the low stage.

'Reece Erskine.'

The vicar leant down to offer the newcomer with the unfriendly expression his hand. 'Adam Wells.'

After a pause Reece responded. A closer inspection confirmed his suspicions that this Adam chap was far too young and flashily good-looking to project the right sort of gravitas required for his chosen career.

'Hello, Darcy.'

Darcy's only reason for grabbing Adam's sleeve was a desire to stay on her feet. The expression in Reece's eyes as they rested on her slender fingers curved tightly over the dark sleeve suggested he wasn't considering extenuating circumstances—he was considering homicide! This example of male perversity brought a spark of rebellion to Darcy's face. It seemed he didn't want her but he didn't want anyone else to have her either! 'What are you doing here?'

'I'm a music-lover.'

Darcy snorted. 'I thought your opinion of my voice would have been a good enough reason to give the place a wide berth!' She stopped short, her eyes widening. 'Were you sitting there all the way through?' she asked hoarsely.

Reece nodded.

Darcy swallowed and went cold all over; it was just as well, she reflected, that she hadn't known that. The idea of Reece watching her made her feel ridiculously exposed and vulnerable. No, that would definitely have been one critical pair of eyes too many. She turned to Adam.

'Reece thinks I have a terrible voice,' she informed him, sparing an unfriendly glare for the figure standing just below them.

'I'm sure that's not true, Darcy.'

'It does lack a certain depth and power...'

Darcy took an outraged gasp. 'See, I told you! Who made you a music critic...?' she demanded, squaring her shoulders aggressively. The fact he was essentially right was no excuse in her eyes for his comment.

'But if you set aside technique,' Reece continued as if she hadn't spoken, 'it was the most moving thing I've ever heard.'

Darcy's aggressive stance wobbled. *'It was…?'*

'Of course, I'm not what you could call objective.'

The hunted, furtive expression on Darcy's face got more pronounced as his warm, caressing glance came to rest squarely on her face.

'You're not?' she squeaked.

'There comes a time in a man's life when he has to admit defeat.'

Darcy's heart skipped a couple of beats and she promptly forgot that only earlier that day she'd sworn that if he ever came crawling back it would afford her great pleasure to laugh scornfully in his face—at the time she hadn't actually expected the opportunity to arise.

'What are you saying, Reece?' she squeaked without the trace of a scornful laugh. She slid her bottom onto the edge of the makeshift stage and dropped hastily to the floor. A person couldn't hear something like what she suspected—*hoped*—he was about to say perched on this ridiculous platform.

For some inexplicable reason Reece seemed to find her action extremely alarming; he shot forward and clamped his hands around her waist, lowering her the last inch or so as though she were delicate china.

'You shouldn't be doing that,' he reproached huskily, as if she'd just done something wildly reckless.

Despite the distracting warmth of the hands circling her waist and the deliciously weak, tingling feeling that permeated her body, she had to ask. 'Why not?'

'I'd have thought that was obvious.'

The only obvious thing to Darcy was that she was destined to love this man for better or worse, in the for ever after sense. She shook her head in bewilderment. Amidst the emotional turmoil she clung to the tenderness she saw shining in his marvellous eyes—everything was going to be all right. Her vision blurred as she stared, mesmerised by that warmth, into his dark, strong-boned face.

'I'll let your parents know you're making your own way home, shall I, Darcy...?' Adam didn't act as if he expected a response—he wasn't disappointed.

'You should have told me,' Reece reproached throatily, running a finger over the soft curve of her cheek. His smile was strained as he tweaked a strand of her blonde hair.

'I thought I did,' Darcy murmured, turning her cheek into his open palm. He hadn't told her he loved her yet but surely that was only a matter of time.

It occurred to Reece that they were at cross purposes. 'What are we talking about here?'

'I did tell you I loved you...I even had a crack at hinting that you might love me too, but,' she brooded darkly, 'that wasn't a big success.' The humiliation of that occasion was still too recent not to hurt.

'Poor baby,' he crooned, placing a warm, wonderful kiss on her parted lips. 'I was an idiot.'

'I think so,' she agreed breathlessly.

'You should have told me about the baby,' he murmured, stroking the side of her diminutive nose with his.

Darcy shivered as his lips made sensual progress towards her ear. 'How did you know? Did Mum tell you?' she wondered, sinking her fingers into the marvellous lushness of his hair.

'Does she know? I'm glad you told her.' He hated the idea of her having no one to share the news with, no one to soothe her worries.

'Told her?' Darcy echoed, pulling a little away. 'I didn't have to *tell* her, silly.' She bit down gently on his lower lip before sliding the tip of her tongue inside. The judder that ran through his body was highly satisfactory.

'I suppose a mother just knows these things,' Reece agreed, breathing in the warm, fresh scent that rose off her skin and hair.

'Well, she was shocked to begin with,' Darcy conceded. 'But I think the idea's starting to grow on her.'

'And you, how do you feel about becoming a mother?'

'Oh, I feel…' Her dreamy smile faded; she stiffened. 'What did you say…?' A quiver of apprehension shivered down her spine.

'I know how you feel,' he sympathised, misreading her expression. 'I was pretty shocked myself to start off with, but I'm delighted, really I am.'

Darcy firmly detached herself from his arms. 'What exactly are you delighted about, Reece…?' A terrible suspicion was forming in her mind—and it was so horrible she didn't want to contemplate it. But she had no option.

'Becoming a father, of course.'

The suspicion solidified.

'You think I'm pregnant?'

His indulgent smile was tinged with a hint of concern; her skin had acquired a worrying, greyish tinge. 'Isn't that what we've just been discussing?' He pulled a chair forward. 'Perhaps you should sit down.'

'Maybe you should.' So this was what his sudden change of heart had been about—for some reason he'd got the idea she was carrying his child. That was what happened when you allowed wishful thinking to take the place of common sense! She felt as if a lump of ice was lodged behind her breastbone as she lifted her chin to face him.

'It might have been what you were discussing, Reece, but I wasn't.'

'There's no need to pretend, Darcy; I saw the baby clothes—I know.'

'You know!'

For some reason Reece couldn't fathom she seemed to find this comment hilarious. His expression was sombre and guarded by the time her wild laughter had died away.

'I'm not pregnant, Reece.'

'You mean it was a false alarm?' Reece was amazed at how bad this made him feel, but was determined not to let her see his disappointment.

'I mean that I never have been. I was buying the clothes for Mum—*she's* expecting the baby; that's what brought about her emotional crisis.'

'Then you're not...?'

'Not even a little bit,' she confirmed, shaking her head from side to side.

'But I thought...' His eyes moved to her flat midriff and the blood drained from his face. There was a lengthy pause. 'I did some jumping to conclusions, didn't I...?' he remarked ruefully. He didn't mention the degree of wishful thinking that had made him reach such a rash conclusion.

'You're not the only one.' Her smile was grim as she recognised the extent of her wilful self-delusion. 'I thought you came here because you'd realised you loved me—how silly is that?' She laughed bitterly. There came a time in a girl's life when she really ought to stop setting herself up for rejection—humiliation aside, it hurt too damned much!

'Don't look so concerned, Reece, I'm not about to hold you to anything you said while overcome by paternal feelings. Though actually I think you'll find you didn't actually say anything too incriminating.'

'I did come here because I love you, Darcy.'

Darcy backed away, evading the hand that tried to grasp her wrist. 'So the fact that you thought I was carrying your child had nothing whatever to do with it.'

His broad shoulders lifted; he knew how this was going

to sound. 'That was a factor, certainly, but only in that it acted as a catalyst.'

'So you mean you'd be here if you hadn't thought I was pregnant?'

The expression in his eyes said it all. At least he wasn't lying—that was something. Though it wasn't enough to make her feel anything less than deliriously unhappy.

'Not this soon maybe.' The cynical little twist of her lips escalated his growing sense of frustration.

'Don't panic, Reece; as entertaining as the spectacle of you trying to talk yourself out of this might be, I won't make you sweat. You didn't actually say anything that could be construed as a concrete proposal of any variety.' No need for that when I'm so eager to hear what I want. 'And if you feel a fool you can take comfort from the knowledge that I feel much worse.'

'I'm not trying to talk my way out of anything,' he grated.

'If you say so,' she drawled.

'I *do* say so.' She smiled again with faint, damning disbelief. 'Listen, Darcy, I was *happy* when I thought you were carrying my child. Don't you see what that means…?' he appealed, his taut expression urgent.

Her normally animated face was blank as stone. 'It means you want to be a father.'

'If it was that simple I could have done something about it years ago. When Jo and the baby died I swore I'd never…' His rich voice cracked and Darcy began to sweat with the effort of not rushing to comfort him—it was following impulses like that which had got her in this mess to begin with. 'Before today I thought the very last thing I wanted—other than to feel responsible for another human—was a child.'

His emotions when he spoke of his wife were obviously genuine, but anything else was suspect as far as Darcy was concerned—or at least her interpretation of them was. She could no longer trust her own judgement.

'I suppose I'm responsible in my own small way for this breakthrough.'

'Will you stop talking like that?' he bellowed.

'Like what?'

Reece took several deep breaths and when he replied it was with a calm he was far from feeling. 'I only want a child if you're the mother...' he said slowly, as if he was explaining something simple to a very small child.

'You expect me to believe that!' Darcy gasped, her face crumbling.

This reaction hadn't been the one he'd hoped for. In the face of her tears, his hard-fought-for calm deserted him totally.

'This is just plain ridiculous. I love you!' he yelled in a very un-lover-like manner as he advanced purposefully towards her. If words wouldn't convince her of his sincerity, maybe actions would.

'Don't touch me!' she breathed venomously, batting his extended hand away. She refused to be swayed by the flicker of pain in his deep-set eyes. 'I'm not interested in what you've got to say, not now, not ever!' She ran down the central aisle, knocking several chairs over as she went.

For a long time after the door had slammed shut Reece stood there in the dimly lit hall, thinking. By the time he left he had the outline of a plan in his mind.

CHAPTER NINE

'LET me get this straight,' Clare said, her smooth brow wrinkling in an incredulous frown. 'The man said he loved you, and you ran away? And this is because…you love him? Am I getting this right?'

Darcy hadn't confided in her sister in the hope of being mocked—where was a bit of sisterly solidarity when a girl needed it?

'He was lying.' The explanation emerged as hopelessly feeble with an unattractive hint of petulance. Even before she heard it Darcy had already been wishing she hadn't, in a moment of weakness, revealed the disaster that was her love-life to her half-sister.

'Don't talk!' Clare remonstrated sharply. 'You'll crack the mask. How do you know he was lying?' She picked up the damp ends of Darcy's hair. 'Have you ever thought of trying some of that serum that helps frizziness?'

'I like frizz!' Darcy snapped.

Unable to bear being the passive target of her sister's subtle but searching questioning technique for another second—first a hint on skin care, the next a 'Did you sleep with him that first night?' Darcy gave a grunt of exasperation and flung off the towel that was draped around her shoulders.

Her sister followed her to the bathroom and waited while she rinsed off the greenish face mask which had set hard as concrete.

'You won't get the full benefit—you didn't leave it on long enough,' she predicted as Darcy scrubbed at her tingling face with a towel. 'So what about Reece, then?'

Darcy scowled. 'What about him?' she said unencouragingly—problem was, when Clare had the bit between her teeth she didn't need any encouragement. 'I wish I hadn't told you!' she cried, throwing the damp towel at Clare's head.

'Let's say, just for the sake of argument, that he was telling the truth.'

Darcy buried her head in her hands. 'I've already told you he only turned up because he saw the baby clothes and got this stupid idea that I was pregnant!'

'So when you told him you were about to be a sister, not a mum, he did what any man who was only reluctantly doing the right thing by a casual lover he'd accidentally impregnated would…'

Darcy winced. 'You've got such a delicate way of putting things.'

Clare's grin broadened. 'He hung around saying he loved you…?' She gave a bark of laughter. 'Come off it, Darcy, why would he do that? If he really only cared about the baby he'd have been out of there as fast as his Merc would take him.'

'Reece has more style than that! Oh, don't look at me like that!' Darcy snapped. 'You didn't see his face when he realised—he was devastated. He was only trying to spare my feelings. If he was in love with me he's had plenty of opportunities to say so.'

'Perhaps he didn't know then?'

'I thought you were meant to be the realist.'

Clare shook her head. 'Listen, Darcy, I'm playing devil's advocate here because to be quite frank if you end up with him I'd be green with envy, and if you don't I might just feel inclined to… I don't suppose you could call it rebound if he never was in love with you.'

'You're so smart,' Darcy hissed. 'What about the redhead?'

'I told you, she's the sister. Go on—admit it; the idea of me making a move on your man makes you want to tear my hair out!'

'I'm not in the mood for mind games, Clare; I've fallen in love with him, that's no secret—*unfortunately*,' she added gloomily. It seemed that her love-life was the main topic of conversation in the locality.

'This isn't like you, Darcy…'

'What isn't like me…?'

'Wimping out isn't like you. You're not totally convinced he isn't in love with you, are you? Be honest.' She gave a crow of triumph as her sister's eyes slid away. 'I thought as much. You'll always wonder if you don't find out for sure.'

'How do you propose I find out?'

'Go next door and ask him.'

'What?' Darcy exclaimed, dropping the comb she'd been running through her damp hair.

'He's next door waiting right now,' Clare explained smugly.

'This is a set-up!' Darcy accused wrathfully. 'You've been got at,' she fumed. 'How much did it cost him?' The flicker of pain on her sister's face brought her back to her senses. 'I didn't mean that, Clare; I was mad. He's next door, you say…?'

'Waiting,' Clare agreed.

The shiny new door complete with a Christmas wreath swung open when she placed her hand on it. Chin high— Darcy didn't want anyone to get the idea this was one of the scariest things she'd ever done—she stalked towards the brand-new living-room door and pushed it open.

She opened her mouth to announce herself and it stayed that way as she took in the decor—actually it was hard to miss. Just about every possible surface had been draped with strings of twinkling, blinking fairy lights, there were singing Santas and clockwork reindeer, and the tree was so tall she decided it must have been erected with the aid of heavy-duty lifting equipment.

'Good God!' she gasped. 'What have you done?'

'Do you like it? All courtesy of Uncle Rick. I bought his entire stock.' Reece's tall figure moved out from behind the bulk of the towering fir. He was wearing dark jeans and a lighter cashmere sweater; the sleeves were pushed up to his elbows and she could see the fine mesh of dark hairs on his strong, sinewed forearms.

Darcy tore her eyes clear of this disturbing spectacle and focused her gaze on the very top of the towering Christmas tree. She briskly began to rub her own forearms, which, like the rest of her body, were covered by a layer of goose-bumps. She was incapable of disentangling the earthy sex appeal from the rest of the man, which meant she couldn't look at him and think pure, chaste thoughts.

It took her several dry-throated seconds to get on top of her steamy, impure thoughts.

'I take it you were working on the theory that more is better,' she remarked hoarsely.

'I was making a point.'

'If the point was you have no taste, congratulations—it worked.'

'I'm a changed man. I'm not running any more—not from anything.'

The same couldn't be said of Darcy, whose wary glance finally strayed to his face and refused to budge. 'Could you make that any more oblique if you tried...?' she croaked. If he wanted to say something, why didn't he just say it?

'I could have made it more tasteless, only they didn't have a Santa costume to fit me, which was a pity because they had this one number with strategically placed Velcro.

One quick flick and the whole thing was off.' He inscribed a sweeping motion with his hand.

The image his words and action conjured up reduced her to a stuttering wreck. 'That's d-disgusting!' she choked, going a deeper shade of pink.

'Ingenious, I thought.' He moved towards her, but his stride was lacking the flowing animal grace she realised she associated with him. It was then she saw what she'd been too self-absorbed to notice earlier—the screaming tension behind his mocking grin. 'So you came.' His eyes were acting very hungry as they moved restlessly over her slender figure.

'Clare can be very persuasive,' she croaked drily.

'Nice girl.'

'*Beautiful* girl.'

'Really…? I hadn't noticed.' His grin invited her to share the joke. It was an invitation she tried very hard to refuse. Reece sighed noisily. 'Listen, Darcy, I'm not interested in beautiful girls, I'm interested in *you*!' he announced forcibly. '*Oh, God!*' He struck his forehead with the heel of his hand.

Reece's relief was palpable when she started to laugh. The laughter didn't remove the high tension between them but it did reduce it slightly.

'Can we start again?'

She gave a jerky little nod and shot a covetous peek at his profile—it was perfect, but then she hadn't expected it not to be.

'Thanks. The thing is, I'm so damned nervous I don't know what I'm saying.'

'*You're* nervous!' The sneaky peek was in danger of turning into a transfixed stare.

'You look shocked.'

Darcy was shocked. 'I just never thought of *you* as….'

It wasn't the fact he was vulnerable that shocked her, it was the fact he was letting her see it!

'*Human?*' A surge of colour travelled along the slashing crests of his slanted cheekbones and his ironic gaze drilled into her. 'The rest of my life is hanging on my getting this right, Darcy. I think under the circumstances I've got every right to be nervous.' He dragged an unsteady hand through his hair, his raw frustration clearly evident in his voice and tense stance.

She raised her eyes slowly to his, and her heart began banging noisily against her ribs. 'Perhaps you ought to get on with it,' she suggested gruffly.

Darcy had the sort of optimism that wouldn't lie down and play dead for long. It was making a spectacular comeback at that precise moment and she was trying hard not to show it.

Reece nodded. He folded his long frame down onto the bed, and patted the spot beside him. 'Sit…?'

Darcy shook her head emphatically—if she did as he suggested they'd never get any talking done.

'You're probably right,' he conceded, apparently arriving pretty swiftly at the same conclusion she had. 'You said you loved me, and I ran away. I said I loved you, and you ran away. Have you wondered what would happen if we both said it at the same time…?'

Her throat was so dry she could hardly form the words. 'I don't waste my time on pointless speculation…'

He smiled; it wasn't a safe kind of smile.

'Neither do I, sweetheart.' There was a very predatory look in his eyes as he explained this—the sort of look which should have offended her sense of political correctness; hormones being what they were, it actually sent a surge of sexual excitement so intense through her that she felt dizzy.

'I reacted badly when you said you loved me, so any

scepticism on your part when I announce I feel the same way is kind of understandable—up to a point...'

'What point is that?'

'The point where you ruin both our lives, Darcy.' He paused as if he expected her to protest. 'I won't let you do that,' he warned forcefully.

'Then what are you waiting for? Talk. I'm listening.'

'I did come back because I got it into my head that you were pregnant...'

'Which I'm not...'

'...but that only speeded things up; I'd have come back eventually—how could I not...?' The wondering expression in his eyes as they came to rest on her made her eyes widen...she hardly dared believe what she was seeing was real. 'It just speeded the process up.'

'What process...?'

'The one that made me see that if you're a lucky sod you do get to be in love twice in one lifetime. Joanna died...' His head dropped so she could no longer see his expression, but she could see the strong muscles of his throat work.

'I know how she died, Reece,' Darcy cut in quietly. It was an awful feeling, standing there seeing how much he was hurting and being utterly impotent to help.

'Then you'll know she died and I couldn't do a damned thing—I was standing there and I...' At that moment he lifted his head, his expression more composed than she'd expected—as if he was telling a story and not reliving it, something she instinctively knew he'd done many times before. 'She was so damned happy about the baby—I couldn't do a thing to help her, Darcy.'

'I know,' she cried, dropping down onto the floor at his feet and taking his big hands in hers. She spread her small fingers out against his and she sealed their palms together. 'I was her husband; I was meant to protect her and I didn't. There wasn't a scratch on me.' While staring at their conjoined hands, hers so ridiculously small by comparison with his, he experienced a great surge of protectiveness that was primitive in its intensity.

Darcy closed her eyes and a single tear slipped out between her tightly closed lids. Reece had scars—they just weren't the sort that showed.

'I never wanted to be in a position to let down someone I loved ever again. Can you understand that?'

Darcy opened her eyes; her lashes were wet but her gaze was clear and composed. She nodded.

'It was arrogance, really,' he conceded with a self-derisive sneer, 'that emotional-control thing. I was remote from all that messy emotional crap. Then you came along and you challenged all that just by being there—then to add insult to injury you used the L word; I was mad as hell with you about that!'

'I was mad as hell with myself about that,' she confided huskily.

'I didn't want to believe what was happening. But even I couldn't ignore what had happened to me for long, and I squirmed out of that by telling myself you deserved something better than an emotional cripple. I know I was brutal.' There was an expression of bitter self-recrimination on his face as he recalled the events. 'And I'm desperately sorry for it, but at the time it felt like the right thing to do.

'The truth is, Darcy, running away gets to be a habit after a while. In a way thinking you were pregnant suited me—gave me an excuse; I didn't need to think too much about why I needed to be with you. Didn't need to face up to my own feelings. I never believed in love at first sight—lust at first sight, sure, but not love.'

He hadn't known then that love came in many guises and not just in the form of a gentle, slowly growing bond. He'd finally come to accept that sometimes the strongest bonds were forged in fire. He just prayed he hadn't left it too late.

'It wasn't like that with…Jo…*sorry*.'

The man had just said he'd fallen in love her with on sight and he was *apologising*!

'I'm all right with your past, Reece—I've got one myself. It's your future I might get a bit possessive about.'

During the stark, shocked silence that followed Darcy felt his big body stiffen.

'Does that mean…?' he asked, his darkened eyes searching her face with unconcealed urgency.

Her fingers curled tight against his and the pressure he offered in return was so emphatic she almost winced. She only broke the contact in order to press her splayed fingers to either side of his strong face. He did the same thing to her, his own long fingers curling round the softly rounded outline of her jaw.

Darcy blinked rapidly, her head still reeling from his impassioned confessions. 'When you open up, lover, you *really* open up.'

'Pretty disillusioning stuff, I suppose…?'

His eyes didn't leave hers for an instant. Darcy could almost physically feel the waves of tension emanating from his lean frame.

'I suppose it might be for someone who has put the man she loves on some sort of pedestal. In case you're wondering—I didn't and I don't.' He continued to look blankly at her. 'Stupid,' she crooned lovingly. 'I'm saying I love you—not,' she added drily, 'for the first time, and I'm warning you, if you do what you did last time I'll…'

She never did get the chance to tell him what she'd do because the tight control he'd had on his emotions slipped. Darcy saw the fierce glitter of his emerald eyes just before his mouth came down hard and hungry on hers.

Darcy's arms snaked up around his neck as he lifted her

onto the ridiculously opulent bed and plunged deeper into the sweet, welcoming darkness of her mouth. For long moments they kissed and touched with frantic urgency.

'God, but I love you.' He continued to nuzzle her neck.

Darcy nodded in languid agreement; his hand was under her sweater, running over the warm skin of her stomach, and the other was fiddling with the zip on her skirt.

Thinking skin on skin made her dizzy and hot, but blissfully happy. In fact it was possible, she reflected dreamily, that this much happiness was illegal.

'Say you love me, Darcy,' he insisted.

'I...' His fingers chose that moment to correctly locate one shamelessly engorged nipple, and Darcy let out a long sibilant sigh of pleasure and threw one arm over her head.

Reece's eyes darkened as he studied the enraptured expression on her aroused face. 'You were saying...?' he prompted throatily.

'Was I...?' she asked languidly, forcing her heavy eyelids open.

He brushed the silvery strands of hair back from her forehead before kissing the tip of her nose. Their eyes collided and Darcy smiled a slow, languorous smile that oozed satisfaction—he loved her, he really loved her!

'I remember now. I love you, Reece.'

'Too right you do!' her forceful lover gritted back, a smile of triumph curving his sensual mouth. 'And don't you ever forget it.'

Somehow Darcy didn't think that was likely.

'What,' she asked, shooting a flirtatious little look at him through the spiky fringe of her eyelashes, 'would you do if I did have some problem remembering...?'

'I'd do this.' She let out a startled shriek as he lifted her jumper over her head and impatiently flung it aside. 'And this.' Her bra swiftly followed suit.

Breathing hard, he gazed, transfixed momentarily by the

spectacle of her heaving, pink-tipped breasts. The warmth low in her belly sizzled into a full-scale conflagration.

'Isn't that a bit…excessive…?' she wondered huskily.

'No,' he contradicted confidently. '*This* is excessive, and this, and this…'

'Menace me some more,' she whispered brokenly as he divested her of her last stitch of clothing.

'Like this?' he asked, settling between her parted thighs and thrusting up hard.

Darcy expelled her breath very slowly and turned her hot cheek against the cool pillow. 'Exactly like that,' she moaned feverishly. To feel him inside, all the way inside her, filling her so perfectly. 'Is there more?' She managed to force the husky question past her parched vocal chords.

She felt the laughter rumble deep in his powerful chest.

'As much as you can take,' he boasted—actually, it didn't turn out to be a boast at all.

'You know,' Darcy said some time later, 'I should be going.'

Reece's hand, which was stroking her hair, stilled.

She lifted her head from his chest. 'I don't want to.' She felt him relax.

'Then don't.'

'I wish I could stay, but there's loads to do for tomorrow and I should get back. Mum is quite likely to get an attack of superwomanitis, and it's important she doesn't over-exert herself.

'In that case,' Reece remarked, throwing aside the covers and exposing her toasty warm body to a blast of cooler air, 'you'd better move your lovely little butt.'

Darcy rolled onto her side and propped herself up on one elbow. 'You're kicking me out of bed?' she asked indignantly.

'You'd prefer a display of unreasonable possessiveness...?'

She laid a loving hand on his chest and tweaked a curly strand of dark hair. 'Well, a sign or two that you'd miss me wouldn't go amiss,' she responded tartly.

'I won't miss you.' The extra-hard tweak she gave made him wince. 'Because I'm coming with you.'

'You are?' she echoed, her eyes growing round with wonder.

'Unless you have any objections.'

'Are you quite sure?' she wondered doubtfully.

'A man could get to feel unwanted...'

'Oh, no,' she purred lazily, 'you're wanted all right,' she assured him, allowing her wickedly lascivious stare to wander over his sleek, powerful body. Her smile grew smugly content as he responded instantly and pretty blatantly to her teasing. 'I just wasn't sure you'd be into our full-on, no-holds-barred, traditional sort of Christmas.'

'I just want to be with you,' he responded simply.

There was such naked, unconditional love in his face that Darcy's eyes filled with tears of sheer happiness. 'And I want to be with you,' she sniffed.

'Then let's get moving before we catch pneumonia.' Darcy let out a startled shriek as he tipped her off the bed. All thoughts of retaliation faded from her mind as she lifted her head in time to see Reece, completely at ease with his naked state, strut panther-like across the room.

Reece caught her looking and grinned. 'If you really want to go, Darcy, don't do that.'

'I'm only looking,' she complained.

'There's looking and then there's what you're doing...'

'If you don't like it, put some clothes on.'

'I will, but not because I don't like it...'

It took them longer to get dressed than expected because several items of essential clothing had gone missing. The silky pair of pink knickers were eventually discovered draped over a branch of the Christmas tree.

'It seems a pity to remove them,' Reece remarked indelicately as she snatched them free. 'You have to admit they'd be a talking point.'

'I know exactly what I'm going to buy you for Christmas,' Darcy confided as he slid her jacket over her shoulders. 'It'll be a bit late, of course, but you won't mind,' she predicted confidently.

'Is it a secret?' he asked, watching the play of emotions on her face with indulgent pleasure.

'No, it's a dress.'

He laughed low in his throat. 'Is it in my size?'

'No, it's in mine,' she giggled.

'It sounds promising.'

'You'll love it,' she promised.

The laughter died from his eyes. '*I love you.*'

The memory of the lonely ache in her heart receded even further.

He bent his head down towards her and Darcy stroked the strong edge of his jaw. 'You know,' she sighed, 'I'm going to miss this place.' She leaned backwards into his body and gave a contented sigh as his arms drew her closer still.

'You won't have to.'

'How's that…?' she murmured absently as she rubbed her cheek lovingly against his sleeve.

'I spent so much cash on the place that I thought I might as well buy it,' he explained casually.

'You what?' Darcy twisted out of his arms and gazed up at him, a stupefied expression in her wide eyes.

'Well, I'm as flexible as the next man, but I don't fancy sharing a bedroom with the twins every time we come to visit your parents.'

'And are we likely to be doing that often?' she enquired

wonderingly. It sounded as if Reece had been giving the matter a lot of thought.

'Well, obviously we will be after we're married, and, as fond as I am of your brothers, can you imagine trying to get a baby to sleep with them in the house?'

'Do you mind backtracking a bit there...?' Darcy pleaded hoarsely. 'You did say *married*?'

'I know we haven't discussed it, but *obviously*... What did you think I wanted from you, Darcy?' he demanded, looking mightily offended by her response.

'A baby...?'

'Naturally I'll cut back on my work commitments for the first year or so.'

'Do I have any say in this...?' she felt impelled to ask.

'You don't want a baby?' He accepted the news stoically. 'That's not a problem.'

'Of course I want babies!' she exclaimed.

'Whose?' he came back, quick as a flash.

Darcy blinked. 'Whose what?'

'Babies.'

'Yours, of course.'

'Then you'll have to marry me!' he responded with a smugly complacent smile.

'People get married for that reason but not me!' Her words carried the cool ring of total conviction.

The warm laughter fled his eyes, leaving a defiant wariness. 'What would make you want to get married?' He thrust his hands deep into his pockets and gave the impression of a man ready to argue her into submission.

'Finding a man I didn't want to live without, a man I wanted to share everything with, a man...'

'Like me.'

'Was that a statement or a question?'

'You little witch—you really had me going there for a minute!'

Still holding his eyes, she thrust out one slender hand. 'Shake on it...?'

'Don't be silly, woman,' he cried, hauling her into his arms. 'We'll kiss on it.'

'We don't have any mistletoe.'

'Who needs it...?' he growled, tilting her head back.

Who indeed? Darcy thought, melting with a blissful sigh into his masterful embrace.

LADY ALLERTON'S WAGER

by

Nicola Cornick

In *Lady Allerton's Wager* we meet
Kit and Eleanor . . . Now they
have their very own story!

Look out for

The Notorious

Marriage

by
Nicola Cornick

Coming soon in
Historical Romance™.

Chapter One

The Cyprians' Ball was scarcely an event that featured on the social calendar of any of the debutantes of the *ton*, although more than one bitter chaperon had observed that it was the only place outside the clubs where all the eligible bachelors could be found. The most unobtainable of gentlemen, who would scorn to step inside the doors of Almack's Assembly Rooms for fear of ambush, showed far greater alacrity in striking up an intimate acquaintance of quite another sort, and a masquerade was ripe with all sorts of possibilities.

It was late in the evening when Marcus, sixth Earl of Trevithick, joined the crowds of revellers milling in the Argyle Rooms. Being neither a callow youth nor particularly requiring an *inamorata*, he had seen no need to hurry to be first through the door.

The room, with its elegant pillars and lavish decoration, seemed as gaudy as the birds of paradise that flocked there. Marcus knew that he was already drawing their attention. With his height, stature and wicked dark good looks it was inevitable, but he felt little pride in the fact. Once his name was whispered amongst the Cyprians he knew that some would lose interest and hunt for bigger game, for they were motivated by cupidity rather than lust. He had the looks and the title but he had little money, for he had inherited estates that had gone to rack and ruin.

'Been rusticating, Marcus? I had heard you were still in northern parts!'

It was his cousin, Justin Trevithick, who had clapped Marcus on the shoulder. Justin, the only child of a scandalous second marriage between Marcus's Uncle Freddie Trevithick and his housekeeper, was a couple of years younger than his cousin. The two had never met as children, for Marcus's father, Viscount Trevithick, had disapproved of his brother's morals and had steadfastly refused to acknowledge his nephew. When Marcus was twenty-two he had bumped into Justin at White's and they had hit it off at once, to the amusement of the *ton* and the despair of the strait-laced Viscount and his wife. Now, eleven years later, they were still firm friends.

Marcus and Justin shared the distinctive lean Trevithick features, but whilst Marcus's eyes and hair were the sloe-black of his pirate forebears, Justin's face was lightened by the fair hair and green eyes that in his mother had captured the attention of Lord Freddie. He turned and took two glasses of wine from a passing flunkey, handing one to his cousin. Marcus grinned, inclining his dark head.

'I have just returned from Cherwell,' he said, in answer to Justin's enquiry. 'I was there longer than I had intended. The tenant there has been fleecing the estate for some time, but—' he gave a sardonic smile '—it won't be happening again!'

Justin raised his eyebrows. 'I don't believe our grandfather ever visited that house. Towards the end he never even left Trevithick. It led the unscrupulous to take advantage.'

Marcus nodded. He had inherited from his grandfather a bare fifteen months before and had swiftly discovered that people had indeed taken advantage of the late Earl's infirmity in his last years. It seemed ironic that his grandfather, whose soubriquet had been the Evil Earl, had himself been cheated in his old age. The Trevithick estates were huge and the subsequent confusion had taken until now to sort out. There were still places that Marcus had not had the time to visit, business that remained unfinished.

'Do you intend to stay in London for the little Season?' Justin asked.

Marcus pulled a face. 'I should do, as it's Nell's debut. I would like to, but—'

'Lady Trevithick?' Justin enquired.

Marcus took a mouthful of his wine. 'It is damnably difficult to share a house with one's mother after an absence of fifteen years!' He grimaced. 'I have already asked Gower to find me a set of rooms—preferably on the other side of town!'

Justin smothered a grin. 'I saw Eleanor at Almack's earlier this evening,' he said, tactfully changing the subject. 'Pershore and Harriman were dancing attendance, to name but two! She seems to have taken well, which is no surprise since she has all the Trevithick good looks!'

Marcus laughed. 'I do believe that Mama is uncertain which of us to make a push to marry off first, though I believe she will have more success with my sister! I don't look to take a wife just yet!'

'Well, you certainly won't find one here,' Justin said,

turning back to scan the crowds. 'Women of another sort, perhaps…'

'Perhaps.' Marcus allowed his gaze to skim over the ranks of painted faces. 'It is a complication I could do well without, however.'

Justin grinned. 'There's one that would be worth it!'

Marcus turned to follow his cousin's gaze. The ballroom was packed and the dancers were executing a waltz, which was the excuse for much intimate and provocative behaviour. Yet in the middle of the swirling crowds, one couple stood out, for they danced beautifully but with total decorum. The gentleman was tall and fair, but he did not have much of Marcus's attention. The lady in his arms was another matter, however.

She was taller than most of the women present and only a few inches short of his own six foot. She wore a silver mask and her silver domino swung wide as she danced, revealing beneath it a dress in matching silk that clung to a figure that Marcus could only describe as slender but voluptuous. Her face was pale with a hint of rose on the cheekbones and her ebony black hair was piled up on top of her head in a complicated mass of curls that was just asking to be released from its captivity. Marcus grinned. Her hair was not the only thing that looked as though it would benefit from being given its freedom—the silk dress hinted at all sorts of delightful possibilities and he was already entertaining the idea of peeling it off her like the skin of a ripe fruit. Glancing around, he realised that at least half the men in his vicinity were thinking along the same lines and his grin broadened. Perhaps they had tasted the fruit already, for the very fact that she was at the Cyprians' Ball marked her as no lady. Marcus shrugged. It mattered little to him who had been before him, but he had every intention of being next in succession.

'Setting your sights, Marcus?' Justin Trevithick enquired, a smile in his voice. Like the Earl, he was watching the dancing couple. 'From what I've just overheard, you are at least tenth in the queue!'

'I don't like waiting in line,' Marcus murmured, not taking his gaze from the girl's face.

'Who is she, Justin?'

'Damned if I know!' Justin said cheerfully. 'No one does! The guesses are inventive and range wide, but no one can put a name to the face!'

'What about the lady's escort?'

Justin was laughing at his cousin's persistence. 'Now, there I can help you! The fortunate gentleman is Kit Mostyn! A shame we are not on terms with the Mostyns and cannot beg an introduction!'

Marcus gave his cousin an incredulous look, then laughed in his turn. 'Mostyn! How piquant! Then it will be doubly enjoyable to take the lady away from him...'

Justin raised his eyebrows. 'Is this love or war, Marcus?'

'Both!' his cousin replied promptly. 'They say all is fair, do they not? Well, then...'

The dancers were circling closer to them now. Marcus thought that the lady looked very comfortable in Lord Mostyn's arms, for she was talking eagerly and smiling up at him. Marcus's eyes narrowed. He had nothing against Kit Mostyn personally, but there had been a feud between the Mostyn and Trevithick families for centuries. Marcus knew little of the detail of it, and just at the moment he had no interest in healing the breach. He waited until the couple were directly beside him, then made a slight movement that attracted the lady's attention. She looked up and their eyes met for a long moment before she deliberately broke the contact. Marcus had the impression of a wide, smoky gaze, a slightly deeper silver colour than her dress. A moment later, she looked back at him over her shoulder, with what he could only interpret as a gesture of invitation.

Justin laughed. 'A result, I think, Marcus!'

Marcus thought so too. He watched as the music ended and the lady and her partner strolled to the edge of the dance floor, then, without haste, he made his way towards them through the crowd.

'Your servant, Mostyn.' There was a mocking edge to Marcus's drawl and he saw the younger man stiffen slightly before he returned his bow with the very slightest one of his own. Marcus's attention had already moved to the lady, which was where his real interest lay. At close quarters she looked younger than he had imagined, but then he realised that it was not so much a youthful quality but an impression of innocence. Her eyes lacked the knowing look that characterised so many of her profession. Marcus reflected cynically that that air of innocence must be worth a great deal of money to this particular lady. Gentlemen would pay over the odds to possess so apparently unspoilt a beauty. It amused him, for in his youth he had become entangled with a Cyprian who had pretended to a naïveté she simply did not possess and had tried to sue him for breach of promise. Such candour was appealing but ultimately an illusion.

He held out his hand to her and after a moment she took it in her own.

'Marcus Trevithick, at your service, ma'am. Would you do me the honour of granting me a dance?'

Marcus felt rather than saw Kit Mostyn flash the girl

a look of unmistakable warning. She ignored him, smiling at Marcus with charm but absolutely no hint of coquetry. Grudgingly, Marcus had to admit that she might have been at a Dowager's ball rather than a Cyprian's masquerade. She had an inherent dignity. As she smiled, a small, unexpected dimple appeared at the corner of her mouth.

'Thank you, my lord. I should be delighted.'

He bowed slightly and led her on to the floor, where a set was forming for a country dance.

She carried herself with a poise that contrasted starkly with the flirting and ogling that was going on all around them and Marcus found it oddly touching—until he thought that this was no doubt all part of the act. Innocence, dignity… It was a clever way to set herself up as out of the ordinary. Nevertheless, her artfulness mattered little to him and he was confident that they could come to an understanding. Sooner rather than later, he hoped. He was beginning to want her very much. He studied her bent head and the way that the ebony curls brushed the nape of her neck. He wanted to touch her. Her mouth was as sultry as her figure, promising sensuous delight. He felt a powerful impulse to kiss her where they stood.

'Will you give me a name for a name?' he asked softly. 'You already know who I am.'

Her smoky grey gaze brushed his face and made him feel suddenly heated. She smiled a little, the dimple flashing. 'My name is Elizabeth, my lord. In fact, I am known as Beth.'

'Yes? And…?'

She considered. 'That is all I wish to tell you. There are no names at a masquerade. You have already broken the rules once by telling me your own identity.'

Marcus laughed. He had no problem with breaking any of society's rules that he did not agree with.

'What is Mostyn to you?' he asked, as the music brought them together again. 'I would like to know—before I attempt a trespass.'

He felt her fingers tremble in his before she freed herself and stepped away from him. She danced most gracefully.

'Kit is very dear to me,' she said, when eventually they came back together.

'I see.'

'I doubt it.' Once again that silver gaze pierced him. 'He is a friend. Closer than a friend—but that is all.'

An old lover, Marcus thought, with a vicious rush of envy. That would explain why they looked so comfortable together, yet had none of the heat of sensuality between them. Old passions had burned themselves out, leaving only the flame of friendship. It made him jealous to think of their past relationship, yet it also implied that there might be a vacancy...

'And is there anyone else?' Foolish question, when she probably had a dozen admirers paying for her favours! Yet her cool gaze searched his face and she answered quietly.

'I do not care to discuss such matters here, my lord.'

Marcus allowed his gaze to hold hers for several long seconds. 'Then may we discuss it in private? I confess that would suit me very well...'

He felt that he might reasonably have expected some encouragement at this point, even if it was only a smile, but Beth gave his suggestion thoughtful consideration, and then inclined her head.

'Very well. There is a study off the hallway—'

'I know it.'

She nodded again. The dance was finishing anyway, but no one paid any attention as she slipped from the line of dancers and went out into the entrance hall. Marcus waited a few moments before following her, pausing to see if he was observed. It seemed that everyone was too preoccupied with their own *amours* to be concerned about his.

He picked his way through the entwined couples and crossed the checkerboard black and white tiles of the hall. He vaguely remembered that the study was the third door on the left and he was just in time to catch the faintest swish of material as Beth whisked through the door, leaving it ajar for him.

Marcus smiled to himself. The situation was most promising and, despite his cynicism, he had to admit that there was something intriguing about the lady's air of aloof mystery. Perhaps it was all assumed simply to whet jaded appetites, but it was working on him and he was more world-weary than most. He quickened his step, went into the study and closed the door behind him.

It was a small room with a mahogany card table and chairs in the middle and matching mahogany bookcases about the walls. Long amber curtains shut out the night and the only light came from one lamp, standing on a side table.

Beth was standing beside the window. She had taken the dice from their box on the table and was tossing them lightly in one hand. She did not look up when Marcus came in and for a moment he thought he sensed something tense and wary in her stance, though the impression was fleeting.

He took a step forward. 'Would you care to indulge in a game of chance, sweetheart?' he asked.

She looked at him then, a stare as straight and protracted as the one she had first given him in the ballroom. Marcus was amused. He knew of few men and even fewer women who were so direct. Her eyes were a shadowed silver behind the mask, her gaze as deliberate and fearless as a cat.

'If you are sure that you wish to play, my lord.'

They were talking in *double entendres* now and Marcus appreciated her quick wit. It made the pursuit even more enjoyable. He wondered if she knew who he was, even though he had given only his name and not his title. It was entirely possible. She had focused on him from the first and he did not flatter himself that it was simply because she was attracted to him. She might well consider that his status and physical attributes outweighed a lack of fortune. And fortune was relative anyway. He could pay her well enough.

He kept his eyes on her face and smiled slowly. 'I'm sure. Which game do you prefer?'

The lady smiled too, the dimple quivering again at the corner of her deliciously curved mouth. Marcus suddenly wished he could cut to the chase and simply kiss her. It was a high-risk strategy and might backfire, but it was very tempting. He took a step closer. She took one back.

'Hazard might be appropriate,' she said coolly, tossing the dice from one hand to the other. 'One throw of the dice. The winner takes all.'

Marcus hesitated. It was clear from her words that she would be his prize if he won and he considered it very sporting of her to offer her services for free. The reckoning would come later, of course, if they suited each other: the villa, the carriage, the jewels…

But if she won the wager…

'I like your terms, but first I need to know what you

want from me if I lose,' he drawled. 'I do not have a fortune to offer. What would you settle for, sweetheart?'

He waited confidently for her to name her price. A necklace of diamonds, perhaps, to outclass the exquisite but tasteful grey pearls already around her neck.

She moved closer until he could smell her perfume. It was a subtle mix of jasmine and rose petals, warm as the sun on the skin, and it sent his senses into even more of a spin. Damn it, whatever the price, it had to be worth it.

'I don't want a fortune,' she said sweetly, 'just a small part of your patrimony. I want Fairhaven Island.'

Marcus stared. It comprehensively answered the question of whether or not she knew who he was, but it seemed an extraordinary suggestion. Fairhaven fell in the part of his estate that he had not yet had time to visit, but as far as he was concerned, it was a storm-swept isle in the middle of the Bristol Channel that supported a few people, a flock of sheep and nothing else. There was no earthly reason he could see why it should appeal to a courtesan. It was worth absolutely nothing at all.

Part of his mind prompted him to ask a few questions and get to the bottom of the mystery. The other part, tantalised by her perfume, suggested that there was no need to cavil and he was bound to win the bet anyway. Even if he lost he was fairly certain that he could persuade her to humour him. The time for a discussion on land and property was not now, when he wanted to sweep her into his arms, but later and best left to the lawyers.

'Very well,' he said, adding slowly, 'Do you always honour your bets?'

She looked away for the first time. 'I do not usually gamble, my lord. Do you honour yours?'

Marcus laughed. No man would have dared ask him that question but, after all, he had questioned her integrity first. And she still had not really answered him.

'I never renege,' he said. He took her hand in his and felt her tremble slightly. Her skin was very soft; he turned the hand over and pressed a kiss on the palm. 'But you did not answer my question.'

There was a flash of something in her eyes that almost looked like fear but it was gone as swiftly as it had come. She raised her chin.

'I will pay my debt, my lord—if I lose.'

Marcus nodded. He drew her closer until one of her palms was resting against his chest.

'And if I wish to take something on credit?' he asked, his voice a little rough.

'Then you might find yourself even further in debt since there is no guarantee that you would win.' She looked him straight in the eye. 'If you are willing to take the risk—'

It took Marcus only a split second to decide that he was. He bent his head and brought his mouth down on hers.

He was experienced enough not to try to take too much too soon. Even a Cyprian liked to be courted and he was no naïve boy to pounce without finesse. He kissed her gently, exploratively, holding her like china until he felt the tension slide from her body and she started to respond to him. She tasted soft and sweet and very innocent. She even trembled in his arms. It had to be an illusion, but it was such a beguiling one that Marcus felt his self-control slipping dangerously. He deepened the kiss and, after a moment's hesitation, she kissed him back tentatively, pressing a little closer to him. Desire surged through his body, so powerful it pushed all other thoughts aside and he pulled her to him fiercely, careless now of gentleness. But it was too late—she was withdrawing from him, as elusive as she had ever been. Marcus stifled a groan of frustration.

'The game, my lord?' Her voice was husky.

The game. He had forgotten. Intent on a different game of his own devising, he had not been certain that she would persist in their wager. Still, he was quite willing to indulge her.

'If you wish.' Marcus shrugged. 'All on the one throw.' He gave her a slight bow. 'I will concede you the honour of calling the main, madam.'

Beth threw him one swift glance. 'Then I call a nine.'

She took the dice up and cast them on to the walnut table. Marcus watched them spin and settle on the polished wood. A five and a four. She really had the devil's own luck. He could not believe it. He smiled a little. 'Will you play for the best of three?'

'Certainly not.' She sounded breathless and as she turned into the light he saw the expression on her face. He had expected triumph or greed. What he saw was relief.

'Fairhaven,' she said, on a questioning note. 'You will honour your bet, my lord?'

Marcus did not reply. For the first time, doubt surfaced in his mind, faint but troubling. She had come close to him again; her skirt brushed against his thigh. Part of him responded to her proximity, but he clamped down hard on his desire and tried to concentrate.

'Why do you want it?' he asked.

She laughed then and he saw the triumph that had been missing a moment before. 'Your question comes a little late, my lord! Surely that is academic now.' She took a step back and her silken skirts rustled. 'My man

of business will call on yours on the morrow. Goodnight,
my lord!'

She turned to go, but Marcus caught her arm in a tight
grip and spun her round to face him. He tore the mask
from her face with impatient fingers. Without it she was
even more striking than he had supposed. Her face was
a pure oval, the smoky eyes set far apart beneath flyaway
black brows, the nose small and straight, the sultry
mouth that was not smiling now. She was breathing very
quickly and he could tell that she was afraid. And that
she was not the courtesan she pretended to be. For some
reason that took all the anger out of him.

'One of us is in the wrong place, I believe,' he said
slowly.

'It is I,' she said simply. 'Did you truly believe me a
Cyprian, my lord?'

Marcus started to laugh. He could not help himself.
'Assuredly. Until I kissed you.'

That gave him the advantage. He saw the colour come
up into her face and she tried to free herself from his
grip. He stood back, letting her go with exaggerated
courtesy. No, indeed, this was no courtesan, but even so
he still wanted her. He had no idea whom she was, but
he intended to find out.

'You will honour your bet?' she asked again.

Marcus grinned, folding his arms. 'I will not.'

He saw the fury come into her eyes and held her gaze
steadfastly with his own.

'I will *make* you do so!' she said.

'How?' Marcus shifted slightly. 'Are you telling me
that you would have honoured yours had I won? If so,
I would press you to play me for the best of three!'

She blushed even harder at that but her mouth set in

a stony line. 'What I would have done is immaterial, my lord, since you lost. You claimed never to renege!'

Marcus shrugged. 'I lied.'

'A liar and a cheat,' Beth said, in a tone that dripped contempt. 'I repeat, my man of business will call upon yours on the morrow, my lord, and will expect you to have ready the title to Fairhaven to hand over.'

The study door closed behind her with a decided snap and Marcus heard the quick, angry tap of her footsteps receding across the marble hall. He picked the dice up casually in one hand and sat down in one of the chairs. A whimsical smile touched his lips. He could not believe that his judgement had been so faulty. To mistake a lady for a Cyprian, even given the circumstances... He had been thoroughly misled by his desire, like a youth in his salad days. Led by the nose—or some other part of his anatomy, perhaps. It had never happened to him before.

He tossed the dice absent-mindedly in his hand. So he had been richly deceived and for an intriguing reason. He wanted to know more about that. He wanted to know more of the lady. Damn it, he still wanted *her*. Marcus shifted uncomfortably in his chair. And he needed a drink. Urgently.

Justin found him in the refreshment room after he had already downed a glass of brandy in one swallow. Justin watched him take a refill and despatch it the same way, and raised his eyebrows.

'Unlucky in love, Marcus?'

'Unlucky in games of chance,' Marcus said feelingly. He took Justin's arm and drew him into the shelter of one of the pillars, away from prying gossips. 'Justin, you know more of West Country genealogy than I! Tell me, does Kit Mostyn have a sister?'

Justin nodded. 'He has a widowed younger sister, Charlotte. Allegedly a blonde beauty, but she lives retired so it is difficult to say with certainty.'

Marcus frowned. Beth had never been a blonde and she could scarcely be described as retiring. Perhaps she was Mostyn's mistress after all. Yet something in him rebelled at such a thought.

'What is all this about, Marcus?' Justin was asking, looking puzzled. 'I thought you were about to make a new conquest, old fellow, not indulge in a mystery play!'

'So did I,' Marcus said thoughtfully. His face lightened and he held up the glass. 'Only find me the bottle and I will tell you the whole story!'

'I cannot believe that you just did that, Beth.'

Christopher Mostyn sounded mild, but his cousin knew full well that he was angry. She had known him well enough and long enough to tell.

Beth sighed. 'It was your idea to escort me there, Kit—'

'I may have escorted you to the Cyprians' Ball, but I did not expect you to behave like one!'

Now Kit's voice sounded clipped, forbidding further discussion. Beth sighed again. Kit was head of the family and as such she supposed he had the right to censure her behaviour. The fact that he seldom did owed more to his easygoing nature than her obedience.

Beth rested her head back against the carriage's soft cushions and closed her eyes. Truth to tell, *she* could not believe that she had behaved as she had. And she had only told Kit half the story, the half relating to the wager. She knew that if she had told Kit that Marcus Trevithick had kissed her, very likely he would have stormed back and challenged the Earl to a duel and matters would be immeasurably worse.

Beth opened her eyes again and stared out of the window. They were travelling through the streets of London at a decorous pace and the light from the lamps on the pavement skipped across the inside of the carriage in bars of gold and black. It hid her blushes and a very good thing too, for whenever she thought of Marcus Trevithick, she felt the telltale colour come into her face and the heat suffuse her entire body.

Not only had she overstepped the mark—by a long chalk—but she knew that she had been completely out of her depth with such a man. She had a lot of courage and, allied to her impulsive nature, she knew it could be her downfall. However, her nerve had almost deserted her in that secluded room. If he had won the bet... Beth shivered. Like as not he would have demanded his prize there and then on the card table or the floor... But he had not won. She took a deep, steadying breath.

Marcus Trevithick. Children of her family were taught to hate the Trevithicks from the moment they were born. There were tales told at the nursemaid's knee—stories of treachery and evil. The Earls of Trevithick were jumped-up nobodies, whereas the Mostyns could trace their ancestry back to the Conquest and beyond. The Trevithicks had stolen the Mostyn estates during the Civil War and had wrested the island of Fairhaven from them only two generations back, taking the family treasure and the Sword of Saintonge into the bargain. No good had come to the Mostyns ever since—their fortunes had fallen whilst the Trevithicks had flourished like an evil weed.

Marcus Trevithick. Beth shivered again. She could not believe that he was evil, but he was certainly dangerous.

He was also the most attractive man that she had ever met. Having been a child bride, her experience was necessarily small, but even so she was certain that he could stand comparison in any company.

The carriage drew up outside the house in Upper Grosvenor Street that she had rented for the little Season. Kit descended and helped her out with cold, studied politeness. He did not say a word as he escorted her up the steps and into the entrance hall. Beth bit her lip. She knew she was well and truly in disgrace.

Charlotte Cavendish, Kit's sister, was sitting in the red drawing room, her netting resting on the cushion beside her. She was reading from Oliver Goldsmith's *The Vicar of Wakefield* but cast the book aside with a smile as they came in. Like her brother, she was very fair with sparkling blue eyes, slender and tall. A scrap of lace was perched on her blonde curls as a concession to a widow's cap.

'There you are! I had almost given you up and gone to bed…'

Her smile faded as she looked from her brother's stony face to Beth's flushed one.

'Oh, dear. What has happened?'

'Ask your cousin,' Kit said shortly, stripping off his white gloves. 'I will be in the book room, enjoying a peaceful glass of brandy!'

Charlotte's gaze moved round to Beth. 'Oh, dear,' she said again, but there was an irrepressible twinkle in her eyes. 'What have you done, Beth?'

Beth wandered over to the big red wing-chair opposite and curled up in it. She was beginning to feel annoyed as well as guilty.

'It is all very well for Kit to act the moralist, but it

was his idea to go to the Cyprians' Ball in the first place—'

Charlotte gave a little squeak and clapped her hand to her mouth. 'Beth! You told me you were going to Lady Radley's rout!'

'Well, so we did, but then Kit had the idea of the Cyprians' Ball!' Beth wriggled uncomfortably under her cousin's horrified stare. 'We were masked, so I thought there would be no harm…' She looked defiant. 'Very well, Lottie, I admit it! I was curious!'

'Oh, Beth,' Charlotte said in a failing voice. 'I know I cannot accompany you about the town, but I thought you would come to no harm with Kit!'

'Well, you were wrong!' Beth said mutinously. It suddenly seemed much easier to blame the whole thing on her cousin. 'None of this would have happened if Kit had not decided to have some fun!'

'None of what?' Charlotte asked, in the tone of someone who was not entirely sure they wanted to know the answer.

Beth yawned. She was very tired and suddenly wanted her bed, but equally she wanted someone to confide in. Her cousin had been as close as a sister this year past, closer than they had ever been in childhood when Charlotte's five years' seniority had put Beth quite in awe of her.

Beth, Kit and Charlotte had grown up together, but time and differing fortunes had scattered them. Charlotte had married an officer and followed the drum, Kit had spent several years in India and Beth had been orphaned at seventeen and left penniless. Friends and relatives had murmured of schoolteaching or governessing, but two days after her bereavement, Sir Frank Allerton, a widower whose estate marched with that of the Mostyns, had called to offer her an alternative future. He had not been a friend of the late Lord Mostyn, but Beth knew that her father had esteemed him as an honest man, and so she had accepted.

She had never regretted her decision, but she did regret the lack of children of her marriage. Her home and parish affairs had given her plenty to do, but when Frank had died, leaving her a widow at nineteen, she had been lonely. Though Kit had inherited Mostyn Hall and the title he was seldom at home, and it was Beth who kept an eye on the estate. Then, a year into Beth's widowhood, Charlotte had lost her husband during the retreat from Almeira and had come back to Mostyn. Fortunately she and Beth had found that they got on extremely well. Charlotte was cool and considered where Beth was impetuous and tempered some of her cousin's more madcap ideas. Beth's liveliness prevented her cousin from falling into a decline.

'So what has happened?' Charlotte asked again, recalling Beth's attention to the lamp-lit room. 'You went to the Ball...'

'Yes. We only intended to stay for a little, although I think Kit might have lingered if he had been there alone!' Beth said, with a sudden, mischievous grin. 'At any rate, it was not as I had imagined, Lottie! There was the most licentious behaviour—'

Charlotte looked exasperated. 'Well, what did you expect, Beth? You were at the Cyprians' Ball, not a Court Reception!'

Beth sighed. 'Yes, I know! Everyone was staring at me—no doubt because they thought me a demirep!' she added, before her cousin could make the observation herself.

'Yes, well, it was a reasonable assumption—' Charlotte

looked at her frankly '—and you do have a lovely figure, Beth! The gentlemen—'

'Spare me,' Beth said hastily, remembering the disturbing heat in Marcus Trevithick's eyes. 'I thought you wished to hear what had happened, Lottie?'

'Yes,' her cousin said obligingly, 'what did?'

'Well, Kit and I had a few dances and, as we were waltzing, the behaviour was becoming more and more uninhibited so I decided it would be wise to come home. Then a gentleman came up to us and asked me to dance.'

Beth looked away. When Marcus Trevithick had first approached her she had been amused and some dangerous imp of mischief had prompted her to play along. She had not known his identity then, but she had been tempted by the atmosphere, tempted by *him*…

She looked back at Charlotte, who was waiting in silence. 'We danced a country dance together and he introduced himself as Marcus Trevithick. I had had no notion—I have never met Trevithick before, and although he knew who Kit was he did not know me, though he made strenuous attempts to find out my name…'

'I'm sure he did,' Charlotte said drily. 'Did he proposition you, Beth?'

'Lottie!' Beth looked shocked, then smiled a little. 'Well…'

'Well, who could blame him?' Charlotte seemed torn between disapproval and laughter. 'The poor man, thinking you Haymarket ware and no doubt getting a setdown for his trouble!'

'It was not quite like that,' Beth admitted slowly. 'Yes, he did…make his interest plain, but I did not discourage him exactly…' Suddenly, foolishly, it seemed difficult to explain. Or at least difficult to explain without

giving some of her feelings away, Beth thought hopelessly. And Charlotte was no fool. She would read between the lines and see all the things that Beth had not
admitted.

'It is just that I thought of Fairhaven,' she said, in a
rush. 'You know that I had been intending to make
Trevithick a financial offer for the island! Suddenly I
thought how much more fun it would be to make a wager...' She risked a glance at her cousin from under her
lashes and saw that Charlotte was frowning now, all hint
of amusement forgotten.

'So I suggested that we step apart, and then I challenged him to a game of Hazard, with Fairhaven as the
stake—'

'Beth!' Charlotte said on a note of entreaty. 'Tell me
this is not true! What did you offer against his stake?'

Beth did not reply. Their eyes, grey and blue, met and
held, before Charlotte gave a little groan and covered
her face with her hands.

'Do you wish for your smelling salts, Lottie?' Beth
asked, uncurling from her armchair and hurrying across
to the armoire. 'You will feel much more the thing in a
moment!'

'I feel very well, thank you!' Charlotte said, although
she looked a little pale. 'I feel better, in fact, than you
would have done if Trevithick had claimed his prize! I
take it he did *not* win?'

'No, he did not!' Beth felt the heat come into her face.
'I won! And if I had lost I should not have honoured
the bet! It was only a game—'

'No wonder Kit cut up rough!' Charlotte said faintly.
'Stepping aside with a gentleman who already thought
you a Cyprian, challenging him to a game of chance,
offering yourself as the stake...' She took the smelling

salts and inhaled gratefully. The pale rose colour came back into her face.

'I have shocked you,' Beth said remorsefully.

'Yes, you have.' Charlotte's gaze searched Beth's face before she gave a slight shake of the head. 'Each time you do something outrageous, Beth, I tell myself that you could not possibly shock me more—and yet you do!'

'I am sorry!' Beth said, feeling contrite and secretly vowing not to tell Charlotte any more of the encounter. 'You know I am desperate to reclaim Fairhaven!'

'Not so desperate, surely, that you would do anything to take it back!' Charlotte sat back and patted the seat beside her. 'This obsession is ridiculous, Beth! The island was lost to our family years ago—leave it in the past, where it belongs!'

Beth did not reply. She had learned long ago that Charlotte was practical by nature and did not share the deep mystical tug of their heritage. Beth could remember standing on the cliffs of Devon as a small child and staring out across the flat, pewter sea to where a faint smudge on the horizon signified the island that they had lost. The tales of her grandfather, the dashing Charles Mostyn, and his struggle with the dastardly George Trevithick, had captured her child's imagination and never let it go. Lord Mostyn had lost the island through treachery and, fifty years later, Beth had vowed to take it back and restore the family fortunes. In her widowhood, a woman of means, she had twice offered George Trevithick, the Evil Earl, a fair price for the island. He had rejected her approach haughtily. But Beth was persistent and she had fully intended to repeat the offer to his grandson, the new Earl. It was one of the reasons that she had come up to London. Fate, however, had intervened…fate, and her own foolish impulse.

But perhaps it had not been so foolish, Beth thought. Whatever the circumstances Fairhaven was hers now, won in fair play. And she intended to claim it.

'What sort of man is Marcus Trevithick, Beth?' Charlotte asked casually. 'What did you think of him?'

Beth jumped. She was glad of the lamp-lit shadows and the firelight, for in the clear daylight she did not doubt that her face would have betrayed her.

'He is perhaps of an age with Kit, or a little older,' she said, glad that she sounded so casual herself. 'Tall, dark… He has something of the look of the old Earl about him.'

'The Evil Earl,' Charlotte said slowly. 'Do you think that his grandson has inherited his character along with his estates?'

Beth shivered a little. 'Who knows? I was scarce with him long enough to find out.'

'Yet you must have gained some impression of his nature and disposition?' Charlotte persisted. 'Was he pleasing?'

Pleasing? Who could deny it? Beth remembered the strength of Marcus's arms around her, the compelling demand of his lips against hers. He was a man quite outside her experience. But he was also a liar and a cheat. She saw again his mocking smile. She turned her hot face away.

'No, indeed. He was a proud, arrogant man. I did not like him!'

Charlotte yawned and got to her feet. 'Well, I am for my bed.' She bent and dropped a soft kiss on Beth's cheek, pausing as she straightened up. 'You did not tell Lord Trevithick your name?'

'No,' Beth said, reflecting that that at least was true.

'And though you were with Kit, you were masked.' Charlotte sounded satisfied. 'Well, at least he will not know your identity. For that we must be grateful, I suppose, for it would cause the most monstrous scandal if it were known that you had attended the Cyprians' Ball! People would assume—' She broke off. 'Well, never mind. But perhaps you will think twice in future before you play such a hoyden's trick again!'

The door closed softly behind her. Beth lay back on the cushions and let out her breath in a huge, shaky sigh. Charlotte was in the right of it, of course—it would be very damaging for it to become known that she had been at the Cyprians' Ball. And what Charlotte did not know was that whilst she had not given Trevithick her name, he had seen her face without the mask. Beth stared into the fire. Well, it mattered little. She would send Gough to call on the Earl's man of business in the morning, and once the title to Fairhaven was in her pocket, she would leave for Devon without delay.

Even though he had said he would not honour his bet, Beth could see no reason why Marcus Trevithick would decline to surrender the island to her, for it could not be worth much to him. He had lands and houses far more valuable and there was no sentimental reason for him to hold on to the least important part of his estate. If he persisted in his refusal, however, she was still prepared to pay him, and, Beth thought with satisfaction, one could not say fairer than that. She had heard that his pockets were to let and she was certain that he would see the sense of the matter.

She raked out the embers of the fire, doused the lamp and went upstairs to bed. It should have been easy to put the matter out of her head but for some reason the memory of the encounter—the memory of Marcus Trevithick—still lingered as she lay in her bed. She told herself that she had seen the last of him, but some unnerving instinct told her that she had not. Then she told herself that she did not wish to see him again and the same all-knowing voice in her head told her that she lied.

Chapter Two

'A gambler, a wastrel, a rake and a vagabond!' the Dowager Viscountess of Trevithick said triumphantly, ticking the words off on her fingers.

There was a short silence around the Trevithick breakfast table. The autumn sun shone through the long windows and sparkled on the silver. There were only three places set; one of Marcus's married sisters was coming up from the country for the little Season but had not yet arrived, and the other had gone to stay with friends for a few weeks. Only Marcus, his youngest sister Eleanor and the Dowager Viscountess were therefore in residence at Trevithick House.

'A vagabond, Mama?' Marcus enquired politely. 'What is the justification for that?'

He thought he heard a smothered giggle and looked round to see Eleanor hastily applying herself to her toast. Although she appeared to be the demurest of debutantes on the surface, Marcus knew that his sister had a strong sense of humour. It was a relief to know that the Viscountess had not crushed it all out of her during Marcus's years abroad.

'Traipsing around the courts of Europe!' the

Viscountess said, giving her son a baleful glare from her cold grey eyes. 'Drifting from one country to another like a refugee…'

Marcus folded up his newspaper with an irritable rustle. He had a headache that morning, no doubt from the brandy that he and Justin had consumed the night before, and Lady Trevithick's animadversions on his character were not helping. In fact, he was surprised that she had not added drunkard to the list.

'I scarce think that a diplomatic mission accompanying Lord Easterhouse to Austria constitutes vagabondage, Mama,' he observed coolly. 'Your other charges, however, may be justified—'

'Oh, Marcus, you are scarcely a wastrel!' Eleanor protested sweetly. Her brown eyes sparkled. 'Why, since your return from abroad I have heard Mr Gower say that the estates are already better managed—'

'Enough from you, miss!' the Dowager Viscountess snapped, chewing heavily on her bread roll. 'You are altogether too quick with your opinions! We shall never find a husband for you! As well try to find a wife for your brother! Why, Lady Hutton was saying only the other day that her Maria would be the perfect bride for Trevithick were it not that Hutton would worry to give her into the care of someone with so sadly unsteady a character! So there is no prospect of *that* fifty thousand pounds coming into the family!'

Marcus sighed. It was difficult enough having a parent who was so frank in her criticism without her holding the view that he was still in short coats. How Eleanor tolerated it, he could not imagine. He knew that if he had been in her shoes he would have taken the first man who offered, just to escape Lady Trevithick. Marcus was also aware that his friendship with Justin did not help either. The Dowager Viscountess had never got over her disapproval of her nephew and barely acknowledged him in public, a sign of displeasure that Justin cheerfully ignored. Families, Marcus thought, could be damnably difficult.

As if in response to that very thought, Penn, the butler, strode into the room.

'Mr Justin Trevithick is without, my lord, and enquiring for you. Shall I show him in?'

Marcus grinned. 'By all means, Penn! And pray send someone to set another cover—my cousin may not yet have partaken of breakfast!'

The Dowager grunted and hauled her massive bulk from the chair. 'I have some letters to write and will be in the library. There is the possibility that Dexter's daughter may be a suitable wife for you, Marcus, but I have some further enquiries to make!'

'Well, pray do not hurry on my account, Mama!' Marcus said cheerfully, gaining himself another glare from his parent and a covert smile from his sister. 'Miss Dexter would need to be very rich indeed to tempt me!'

'Marcus, you make her much worse!' Eleanor whispered, as the Dowager Viscountess left the room. 'If you could only ignore her!'

'That would be difficult!' Marcus said drily. 'I curse the day she appointed herself my matchmaker!' His expression softened as it rested on his sister. 'How you tolerate it, infant, I shall never know!'

Eleanor shook her head but did not speak and, a second later, Justin Trevithick came into the room. He shook Marcus's hand and gave Eleanor a kiss.

'Eleanor! I'm glad that Lady Trevithick did not whisk you away—'

The door opened. 'Her ladyship requests that you join

her in the library, Miss Eleanor,' Penn said, in sonorous tones. 'Lord Prideaux has called and is with her.'

Eleanor gave her cousin and brother a speaking glance, then dutifully followed Penn out of the room. Marcus gestured towards the coffee pot. 'Can I offer you breakfast, Justin? And my apologies for my mother's transparently bad manners at the same time?'

Justin laughed. 'Thank you. I will take breakfast—and for the rest, please do not regard it! The only thing that concerns me is that Lady Trevithick considers Prideaux more suitable company for Eleanor than myself! He is a loose fish, but then, I suppose his parents were at least respectably married!'

'So were yours,' Marcus commented.

'Yes, but only after I was born!' Justin leant over and poured some coffee. 'How do you feel this morning, old fellow? Must confess my head's splitting! That brandy was nowhere near the quality it pretended!'

'The coffee will help,' Marcus said absently, reflecting that the brandy had proved to be the opposite of his mysterious adversary of the previous night. She had been Quality masquerading as something else and today he was determined to get to the bottom of that particular mystery. He had told Justin an expurgated version of the whole tale the previous night over the maligned brandy bottle, and his cousin had been as curious as he as to the lady's motives. Justin had been closer to the fifth Earl than Marcus because their grandfather had taken Justin up deliberately to spite his elder son, but despite his far greater knowledge of the old man's estates and fortune, he could throw no light on why anyone would want the island of Fairhaven.

The door opened for a third time as Penn came in.

'Mr Gower is here to see you, my lord. He says that it is most urgent.'

Marcus frowned, checking the clock on the marble mantelpiece. It was very early for a call from his man of business, but if Gower had managed to find him rooms well away from Albemarle Street, then the earlier the better. Remembering the previous night, his frown deepened. There was another reason why Gower might have called, of course...

'Thank you, Penn, I will join Mr Gower in the study shortly,' he said.

The door closed noiselessly as Penn trod away to impart the message. Justin buttered another roll. 'Shall I wait here for you, Marcus, or do you prefer to join me at White's later?'

Marcus stood up. 'Why don't you come with me to see Gower?' he suggested. 'I have the strangest suspicion that this relates to the business last night, Justin, and I would value your advice.'

His cousin raised his eyebrows. 'Your mysterious gamester, Marcus? Surely she does not really intend to claim Fairhaven!'

'We shall see,' Marcus said grimly.

Mr Gower was waiting for them in the study, pacing the floor with an impatience that set fair to wear a track through the rich Indian rug. He was a thin, aesthetic-looking man whose pained expression had come about through years of trying to make the irascible old Earl see sense over the running of the Trevithick estates. There was a thick sheaf of papers in his hand.

'My lord!' he exclaimed agitatedly, as the gentlemen entered. 'Mr Trevithick! Something most untoward has occurred!'

Marcus folded himself negligently into an armchair.

'Take a seat and tell us all, Gower!' he instructed amiably. 'What has happened—has one of the housemaids absconded with the silver?'

Mr Gower frowned at such inappropriate levity, but he took a seat uncomfortably on the edge of the other armchair, placing his shabby leather briefcase at his feet. Justin strolled over to the window, still eating his bread roll.

'This morning I had a call from a gentleman by the name of Gough who has chambers close to mine,' Mr Gower said, still agitated. He shuffled his papers on the table. 'He is a most respected lawyer and represents only the best people! He came to tell me of an agreement between one of his clients and yourself, my lord, an agreement to cede the title deeds to the island of Fairhaven, which is—'

'I know where it is, thank you, Gower,' Marcus said coolly. He exchanged a look with Justin. 'Gough, is it? Did he tell you the name of his client?'

'No, sir,' the lawyer said unhappily. 'He told me that his client expected—*expected* was the precise word used, my lord—that I would have the deeds to the island ready to hand over immediately. Naturally I told him that I could do no such thing without your consent, my lord, and that you had issued no such authorisation. He therefore suggested...' Mr Gower shuddered, as though the suggestion had been made with some force '...that I call upon you to gain your approval forthwith. Which I am doing, sir. And,' he finished, apparently unable to stop himself, 'I do feel that I should protest, my lord, at the cavalier manner in which this transaction appears to have been handled, putting me in a most difficult position with a fellow member of my profession!'

There was a long silence. 'You are right, Gower,'

Marcus said slowly. 'The whole matter is damnably out of order and I apologise if it has put you in a difficult situation.'

'But the island, my lord!' Gower said beseechingly. 'The deeds! If you have an agreement with Mr Gough's client—'

'There is no agreement,' Marcus said. He heard Justin draw breath sharply, but did not look at him. 'Tell Gough,' he said implacably, 'that there is no agreement.'

'My lord...' Gower sounded most unhappy. 'If there is any way that such a contract could be proved, I do beg you to reconsider!'

Marcus raised one black eyebrow. 'Do you not trust me, Gower?' he asked humorously. 'At the very most it could be construed as a verbal contract and there were no witnesses.'

Gower blinked like a hunted animal. 'None, my lord? Can you be certain of that?'

A smile twitched Marcus's lips. 'Perfectly.'

'But even so...' Gower glanced across at Justin. 'A verbal contract, my lord...'

'I think Mr Gower feels that you should honour your pledges, Marcus,' Justin said, with a grin. 'Even in a game of chance—'

'A game of chance!' Gower looked even more disapproving. 'My lord! Mr Trevithick! This is all most irregular!'

'As you say, Gower,' Marcus murmured. 'Have no fear. Gough's client will never sue. I would stake my life on it!'

Justin grimaced. 'Can you be so sure, Marcus? She sounds mighty determined to me!'

Gower, who was just shuffling his papers into his briefcase, scattered them on the carpet. 'She, sir, *she*?'

he stuttered. 'Good God, my lord, not even the old Earl would have indulged in a wager with a female!'

'He was missing a trick then,' Marcus said coolly, 'for I found it most stimulating!' He rose to his feet. 'Good day, Gower. Give Gough my message and if you find his instructions are that he persists in his claim, refer him direct to me. Penn will show you out!'

'Marcus,' Justin said, once they were alone, 'do you not consider this a little unsporting of you? After all, the girl won the bet, did she not?'

'She did,' Marcus conceded. He met Justin's eyes. 'Truth is, Justin, I would like to meet her again, find out about this passion she has for Fairhaven. It intrigues me.'

'And this is how you intend to flush her out?'

'Precisely!' Marcus grinned suddenly. 'I could go to Kit Mostyn and ask for his help, of course, but I would wager he will not grant it! So…if I refuse to honour the bet, my mysterious opponent may show her hand again!'

Justin's lips twisted. 'You're a cunning devil, Marcus! But what is your interest in the lady herself?'

Marcus's grin deepened. 'That depends—on the lady and who she turns out to be!'

'And you would recognise her again?'

'Oh, yes,' Marcus said slowly. 'I would recognise her anywhere, Justin.'

'Pull your chair up a little closer, my love,' Lady Fanshawe instructed her goddaughter, gesturing her to move to the front of the theatre box. 'Why, you will not be able to see anything at all from back there! But do not lean out too far! It is not good to lean excessively, for the gentlemen will stare so! Oh, pray do look, Beth!' Lady Fanshawe leant as far out of the box as she could without falling. 'It is Mr Rollinson and Lord Saye! I do believe they will call upon us in the interval!'

Beth edged her chair forward an inch and leant backwards at the same time. She had every intention of effacing herself until she was practically invisible. The invitation to the theatre was a longstanding one and could not be avoided, for Lady Fanshawe had been her mother's closest friend. That was the only reason why Beth had come to Drury Lane that evening, although the play, Sheridan's *The Rivals*, would normally have been sufficient to tempt her out. Normally, but not now. The matter of Marcus Trevithick and her ill-conceived wager with him had suddenly become so very difficult that she had no desire to risk meeting him again.

Beth chanced a glance over the edge of the box at the crowded auditorium below. Fortunately it would be easy to be inconspicuous in such a crush. People were milling around and chattering nineteen to the dozen: dandies, ladies, courtesans… Beth drew back sharply as a passing buck raised his quizzing glass at her in a manner she considered to be odiously familiar. Lady Fanshawe did not notice for she was waving excitedly to an acquaintance in the crowd.

It was already very hot. Beth fanned herself and looked around idly. Kit had escorted her again that evening but as soon as they had arrived he had left her in Lady Fanshawe's company and could now be seen in a box to the left, chatting to a very dashing lady in green silk with nodding ostrich feathers. Lady Fanshawe had taken one look and remarked disapprovingly that one met with any old riff-raff at the theatre and that Kit need not think to foist his *chère amie* on their attention! Beth had been a little curious, but had tried not to stare. She thought that the dashing lady looked rather fast but, given her own performance at the Cyprians' Ball, she was scarcely in a position to comment.

As time wore on without mishap, Beth started to relax a little. She felt comfortably nondescript in her rose muslin dress. She had chosen it deliberately because it was so unremarkable and she had tried to disguise herself further with a matching rose-pink turban, but Charlotte had positively forbidden her to leave the house looking such a dowd. Beth sighed. It was a terrible shame that Charlotte could never accompany them, but her cousin had had a fear of crowds ever since she was a girl and the glittering hordes that thronged the *ton*'s balls and parties terrified her. It was odd, for Charlotte was perfectly comfortable in society she knew, and could travel and visit amongst friends quite happily, but she was never at ease with strangers.

Beth watched as Kit took a fond farewell of his companion and turned to rejoin them for the start of the play. He was just making his way back to their box when Beth saw that his attention had been firmly caught by a slender young lady, very much the debutante, who was just taking her seat opposite. Intrigued, Beth watched as the young lady saw Kit and faltered in her conversation. For a long moment the two of them simply gazed at each other, then the girl gave Kit a half-smile and turned hesitantly away. Beth smiled to herself. Kit seemed smitten and she must remember to quiz him on the identity of the young lady...

She froze, all thought of Kit and his romantic entanglements flying from her mind as she saw the gentleman who had entered the box behind the girl. She recognised his height, the arrogant tilt of his head. She could even imagine those smooth, faintly mocking tones that she had last heard at the Cyprians' Ball, but which had positively leapt from the page of the letter he had sent her via Gough earlier in the week:

'My dear lady adventuress…'

Beth's fan slipped from her shaking fingers and she leant down to retrieve it, trying to shrink into the shadows. Bent almost double, she groped around on the floor and tried to think quickly at the same time. How was she to avoid Marcus Trevithick seeing her when their boxes were almost opposite each other? If she tried to leave now, would she be able to slip away or would she only draw more attention to herself? She cursed the pale pink dress, which had seemed such a good idea earlier but in the dim light seemed to glow like a beacon.

'What are you doing down there on the floor, Beth, my love? Are you feeling unwell? Do you wish to return home?'

Beth straightened up hastily as Lady Fanshawe's carrying tones threatened to attract the notice of the whole theatre.

'I am very well, I thank you, dear ma'am. I had only dropped my fan…' Her words trailed away as, under some strange compulsion, she looked across the theatre and directly into the dark eyes of Marcus Trevithick. There could not be the slightest doubt that he had recognised her. He held her gaze for a long moment, a smile starting to curl the corners of his mouth, then he inclined his head in ironic salutation

The play started at last and Beth forced herself to look at the stage and nowhere else. This proved difficult as a wayward part of her seemed to want to look across at the Earl of Trevithick all the time and she had to fix her gaze firmly on the actors instead. She soon discovered that she was one of the few people in the whole theatre who was giving their undivided attention to the stage.

The chatter about her scarcely faltered and it seemed that most of the fashionable crowd viewed the play as a diversion from the main business of the evening. Eventually the noise began to grate on Beth, who inevitably found her concentration interrupted. After that it was easy for her thoughts to wander back to the tangle in which she found herself.

When Gough had come to her five days before and told her that the Earl was refusing to honour his bet and give Fairhaven to her, she had been annoyed but not particularly surprised. She had sent the lawyer back to offer a price that she felt was more than fair and had waited, confident that Trevithick would agree this time. It had come as a nasty shock when Gough returned the next day, out of countenance, to relate that he had seen the Earl in person and that her offer had been spurned. Further, the Earl was demanding in no uncertain terms that his client identify herself and discuss the matter with him face to face. This Beth declined to do, but she sweetened her refusal with a far more tempting sum of money. She could afford it and he... Well, she had thought that he would seize the chance to make such a profit. Instead, Gough had delivered the letter.

My dear lady adventuress,

Your offers intrigue me but you should know that I will only do business with you directly. If you choose not to identify yourself it makes no odds; I shall soon know your name and your direction. Then, even if you do *not* choose it, I shall seek you out...

After that, Beth had not set foot outside the house for two days. Glancing across at Marcus Trevithick now, she acknowledged that she had not felt afraid, precisely, more angry and outmanoeuvred. She had won the wager, but he held all the cards. He was not only refusing to give her Fairhaven, but he was also refusing to *sell* it to her, and if he discovered her identity he could ruin her by having it whispered abroad that she, a respectable lady, had attended the Cyprians' Ball. She knew that the wisest thing was to withdraw her offer and retire from the lists, but it seemed that Marcus Trevithick was not prepared to let her do so. She was angry with him, but she was furious with herself for giving him the advantage.

'Do you care to take a walk during the interval, Beth?' Kit enquired, from beside her. 'It might be pleasant to stretch our legs…'

Beth came back to the present, looked around and realised that the curtain had come down at the end of the first act. She glanced across at Marcus Trevithick and saw that he was already moving purposefully towards their box. So much for her half-formed hope that he would not dare accost her there! She took a quick breath.

'A walk? Yes! No…I am not sure… Yes!'

Kit looked understandably confused. 'What the deuce is the matter with you, Beth? You're as edgy as a thoroughbred mare!'

Beth grabbed his arm. She could see that Marcus had been delayed by an acquaintance, but he was still watching her with the concentrated attention of a predator. There could be no question that he meant to approach her.

Beth took one last look and hurried out of the box. 'Yes, by all means! Let us walk! This way!'

She steered her cousin out of the doorway and

plunged into the corridor outside, making for the place where the crowd was thickest.

'Steady on, Beth!' Kit protested, as he was buffeted on all sides. 'You'll have us trampled in the crush!'

It was inevitable that such tactics, whilst they might delay matters, could not put them off forever. It was only a matter of minutes before someone recognised Kit and stopped him for a word, whilst the pressure of the crowd pulled Beth from his side before she had even noticed. Seconds later she looked round and realised that her cousin was nowhere in sight. Marcus Trevithick was, however.

He was leaning against a pillar just a few feet away from her, arms folded, as though he were prepared to stay there all night. His black gaze was watchful and faintly amused. Beth felt her breath catch in her throat. For one moment it seemed as though the press of people would whisk her past him, but then he stretched out one hand in a negligent gesture and caught her arm, pulling her to his side.

'Well, well! My mystery lady—at last! Have you any idea of the balls and routs I have endured these past few days in the hope of catching sight of you, ma'am?'

There were prying eyes and ears all around them. Beth strove to keep her face blank and give nothing away, though her heart was hammering.

'Good evening, my lord! I am sorry that you have put yourself to such trouble on my account!'

Marcus gave her a look of brilliant amusement. 'Thank you! It was worth it, however, for now I have found you again!' He tucked her hand through the crook of his arm and steered her out into the corridor. The crowd had lessened now and they could stroll along without too much difficulty. Beth looked around for rescue, but none was immediately forthcoming.

'I only wanted to speak with you, you know,' Marcus said reproachfully. 'I was utterly intrigued by your offer and wished to discuss the matter with you—'

'Is that not why you employ a man of business, my lord?' Beth asked, keeping her bright social smile in place. 'To relieve you of such onerous tasks?'

'Generally. But this would hardly be onerous.'

Beth found the warmth in Marcus's tone difficult to resist. She glanced up through her lashes and saw that he was smiling at her. It made her feel strangely hot and cold at the same time and she almost shivered. She made an effort to gather her scattered senses.

'If you had but honoured your wager, my lord, such a situation would not have occurred!'

'True.' Marcus bent closer and she felt his breath stir the tendrils of hair by her ear. 'But that would have defeated my object—of seeing you again, sweetheart!'

Beth stopped dead and glared at him. 'Do *not* call me that!' she hissed. 'You must know I am no…no lightskirt for your tumbling!'

Marcus grinned. 'Then why behave like one, ma'am? A dignified request to buy Fairhaven might have elicited a more dignified response!'

Beth could have wept with frustration. What had started as a light-hearted idea—to visit the Cyprians' Ball—had caused more trouble than she could ever have imagined. She wondered what on earth had possessed her to dance with Marcus Trevithick and to further the masquerade. At the time the opportunity to trick him out of Fairhaven had seemed too good to miss, amusing, clever even. She had congratulated herself on her ingenuity—and on her courage! Now she could see that the wager had been the product of too much wine and excitement. She tightened her lips in exasperation.

'It was an impulse! Which I now bitterly regret!'

'Understandably. If you are indeed the lady you pretend to be, what could be worse than a version of the events of that night circulating amongst the *ton*? Dear me, ma'am, it does not bear thinking about!'

Beth coloured up furiously. 'You would not do such a thing!'

'Why not?'

Marcus's tone was mild, but when she glanced up at his face Beth saw that he was watching her intently. It was exactly the problem that Charlotte had hinted at, the one that Beth had not even anticipated. If the Earl of Trevithick let it be known that he had had an encounter with a lady indecorously disporting herself at the Cyprians' Ball, no one would believe in her innocence. And yet some instinct told her that he would not do that to her. Her troubled grey gaze scanned his face and she saw the hard lines soften a little as a smile came into his eyes. Suddenly she was acutely aware of him; of the smooth material of his sleeve beneath her fingers and the hard muscle of his arm beneath that, of the warmth of his body so close to hers and the disturbing look in his eyes.

'Just tell me your name,' he said softly, persuasively.

'Beth, my dear! There you are!' Beth jumped and swung round, tearing her gaze from Marcus. Lady Fanshawe was bearing down on them, her good-natured face wreathed in smiles. Her gaze moved from her goddaughter to the Earl of Trevithick and her smile faltered slightly in surprise, but she recovered herself well.

'Oh! Lord Trevithick, is it not? How do you do, sir? I had no notion that you knew my goddaughter!'

Beth was aware of a sinking feeling as she watched Marcus bow elegantly over Lady Fanshawe's hand. She knew that her godmother, voluble as ever, was about to give her identity away completely.

'It is so delightful to see that the younger generation has ended that tiresome estrangement between the Mostyn and Trevithick families!' Lady Fanshawe burbled. 'I have never quite understood the cause of all the trouble, for it was an unconscionably long time ago and over some trifling matter such as a lost battle—'

'Or perhaps a lost island, ma'am!' Marcus said smoothly. Beth felt his dark gaze brush her face and deliberately evaded his eyes. 'In fact, I was hoping that your charming goddaughter—' there was just a hint of a query in his voice '—might tell me more about our family feud, for I confess it fascinates me!'

Lady Fanshawe beamed, accepting Marcus's other arm as they strolled slowly back towards the box. 'Oh, well, Beth will be able to tell you the whole story, I dare say! All the Mostyns are steeped in family history from the cradle!'

'I see,' Marcus said slowly. Beth could feel him moving closer to his goal, but for some reason she felt powerless to intervene and direct the conversation into other channels. And Lady Fanshawe was so very good-natured, and seemed pleased that the Earl was showing such an interest...

'You must know the family extremely well, ma'am,' he continued.

'Oh, indeed, for Davinia Mostyn, Beth's mama, was such a dear friend of mine, was she not, Beth, my love? It was such a tragedy when Lord and Lady Mostyn were killed in that horrid accident! But then Kit inherited the title and Beth married Frank Allerton...'

Beth felt Marcus's arm move beneath her fingers. She caught her breath.

'You did not tell me that you were Sir Francis's widow, Lady Allerton,' Marcus said gently, smiling down at her. She could see the triumph in his eyes. 'He was a fine man and a great scholar. His treatise on hydrostatics formed part of my university studies. I remember his work well.'

'Thank you,' Beth murmured, looking away. 'Sir Francis was indeed a fine academician.'

They had reached their box now and discovered that the second act of the play was about to start. Kit was already in his seat and looked up, startled, to see both his cousin and Lady Fanshawe escorted by the Earl of Trevithick. The two men exchanged a stiff bow, and then Marcus took Beth's hand in his.

'I should deem it an honour to call on you, Lady Allerton,' he murmured, his gaze resting on her face in a look that brought the colour into her cheeks. 'I understand that you are staying in Upper Grosvenor Street?'

Beth hesitated. 'We are, but—'

'Then I shall look forward to seeing you shortly.' He bowed again. 'Good evening, ma'am.'

Beth bit her lip as she watched his tall figure make its way back to the party in the Trevithick box. It seemed that the Earl was difficult to refuse. And now that Lady Fanshawe had told him everything he needed to know, his position was well nigh unassailable. With a sigh, Beth tried to direct her attention back to the play. She wondered what his next move would be.

'I am not at all sure about these newfangled artists,' Lady Fanshawe sighed, pausing in front of a landscape painting by John Constable. 'Only look at those odd flecks of light and the strange *rough* technique. There is something not quite finished…indeed, not quite *gentlemanly* about it!'

Beth laughed. She rather liked Constable's atmospheric landscapes and they gave her a longing for the countryside and the fresh sea air. It was pleasant to be able to escape the bustle of the London Season for a little and step through an imaginary window into another landscape, even if they were in fact in the Royal Academy and Lady Fanshawe was starting to complain that her feet were aching.

'Why do you not take the seat over there, ma'am, if you are fatigued?' she suggested, gesturing to a comfortable banquette placed over by the window. 'I shall not keep you long, but I should just like to see Mr Turner's collection in the blue room. If you would grant me five minutes…'

Lady Fanshawe nodded, sighing with relief as she took the weight off her feet. 'Take as long as you wish, my love,' she said, sitting back and closing her eyes. 'I suggest we call in Bond Street on our way home. Far more to my taste, but one must be seen here, you know!'

Smiling, Beth wandered through to the second gallery. There was quite a fashionable crowd present, bearing out the truth of Lady Fanshawe's statement on the social importance of attending the exhibition. Beth paused before a picture of seascape and gave a small, unconscious sigh. The water was a stormy grey and the clouds were building on the horizon, and far out to sea there was an island…

'Daydreaming, my lady?' The voice, deep and slightly mocking, caught Beth by surprise. She turned her head sharply to meet the quizzical gaze of the Earl of Trevithick. She could feel a vexatious blush rising to her

cheeks and looked away swiftly. It was irritating enough
that she had spent the last three days waiting for him to
call on her, with a secret anticipation that she had not
acknowledged even to herself. She had just begun to
relax and think that he had forgotten her, when here he
was.

'How do you do, my lord.' Beth smiled politely. She
tried not to notice how superbly elegant Marcus looked
in a coat of green superfine and the fawn pantaloons that
clung to his muscular thighs. 'I hope that you are enjoying the exhibition?'

Marcus took her hand. 'To tell the truth, I came here
with the sole intention of seeing you, Lady Allerton. I
called in Upper Grosvenor Street and was told that you
would be here, and I hoped to persuade you to drive
with me. It is a very pleasant autumn day and my curricle is outside.'

Beth hesitated. 'Thank you, my lord, but I am here
with Lady Fanshawe—'

'I am sure she could be persuaded to entrust you to
me.' Marcus smiled down at her. 'That is, if *you* wish
to come with me, Lady Allerton. You might not want to
break a centuries-old feud, after all!'

Beth could not help laughing. 'How absurd you are,
my lord! I believe I might take the risk, but…'

'I know!' Marcus looked apologetic. 'You are quite
out of charity with me because of my ungallant refusal
to grant you Fairhaven! But now, Lady Allerton…' he
bent closer to her '…now you have the opportunity to
persuade me! Will you take the challenge?'

Beth looked at him. There was a definite gleam of
provocation in his eye. She frowned.

'It seems to me, my lord, that you have the best of
both worlds! You have nothing to lose whereas I may

wear myself to a shred trying to convince you of my attachment to Fairhaven and still have no influence over you!'

A wicked smile curved Marcus's lips. 'Believe me, Lady Allerton, you have made quite an impression on me already! I would put nothing outside your powers!'

Beth blushed and looked away. 'Pray do not tease so, my lord.'

'Must I not?' Marcus offered her his arm and they started to walk back through the gallery. 'It is difficult to resist. So, will you take my challenge?'

Beth paused. 'I will drive with you. That would be most pleasant.'

'Very proper. You are not always so proper, are you, Lady Allerton?'

'However, I could withdraw my acceptance. Any more of your mockery, my lord—' Beth looked at him severely '—and I shall do so!'

Marcus inclined his head. 'Very well! We shall instigate a truce! You are a most determined person, Lady Allerton. It is quite unusual.'

'Unusual, perhaps. Most certainly imprudent.' Beth spoke wryly. She was thinking of Charlotte and her strictures on her conduct. 'I think it comes from being an only child, my lord. I was much indulged and given my own way. It bred stubbornness in me, I fear. And then, my late husband ...'

'Yes?' Marcus slanted a look down at her. Beth sensed that his interest had sharpened and she managed to stop her runaway disclosures just in time.

'Well, he was very kind and indulgent too...generous to me... I was most fortunate.'

'You must have been a child bride,' Marcus observed lightly, after a moment. 'After all, you are scarce in your dotage now! How long have you been widowed, Lady Allerton?'

Beth turned her head so that the brim of her bonnet shielded her from his too-perceptive gaze. Something about this man made her feel vulnerable, as though he could read into her words all the things she did not say.

'Sir Francis died two years ago. Yes, I was very young when I married. My parents had been killed in an accident and I...' Her voice trailed away. She did not want to reveal how lonely she had felt, uncertain if she was making the right decision in marrying hastily. On the one side had been security and on the other... On the other, she had felt as though she was throwing away all her youth and future by marrying a man older than her father. Yet Frank had been a kind husband, as kind to her as to a favourite niece. All she had lacked was excitement.

'I see,' Marcus said, and Beth had the unnerving suspicion that he did indeed see a great deal.

'My dears!' Lady Fanshawe had watched them approach and now rose to her feet, wincing slightly. She greeted the Earl as though he was a family friend of long standing, which Beth found slightly unnerving. She watched with resignation as it took Marcus all of a minute to persuade Lady Fanshawe to his plan.

'If you have offered to take Lady Allerton up with you I am all gratitude, my lord,' Lady Fanshawe trilled, 'for I am sorely in need of a rest! I was intending to call at Bond Street, but fear I do not have the energy! This picture-viewing is unconscionably tiring!'

They went out of the Academy, Marcus calling a hackney carriage to convey Lady Fanshawe home before handing Beth up into his curricle. It was a fine, bright day for autumn and the pale sun was warm. It was pleasant to be driving slowly through the fresh air of the Park, although it seemed to Beth that they were obliged to stop every few yards to greet the Earl's acquaintances. She knew few people in London, so had little to contribute to this social ritual, and after a while she had been introduced to so many new people that her head was spinning.

At last, when they reached a quieter stretch of road, Marcus turned to her with a rueful smile. 'Forgive me. To drive at the fashionable hour precludes sensible conversation!'

'You seem to have a vast number of friends in London, my lord,' Beth said non-committally, thinking of the elegant ladies who had appraised her with curiosity-hard eyes and the sporting gentlemen who had looked her over as though she was a piece of horseflesh.

Marcus smiled. 'I certainly know a lot of people, but as for friends—' he shook his head '—I could count them on the fingers of one hand! But I almost forgot, Lady Allerton...' His gloved hand covered Beth's and her pulse jumped at the contact. 'I cannot count you my friend, for we are sworn enemies, are we not? Will you tell me more about the feud?'

'Oh, the feud...' For a moment, gazing into those dark eyes, Beth was all at sea. She had forgotten all about it. Then she pulled herself together. This was the point of the whole exercise, after all. Somehow she had to persuade Marcus Trevithick of the importance of Fairhaven to her, and becoming distracted by his company was not going to help at all. She pulled her hand away and saw him smile at the gesture.

'I believe that the feud between the Trevithicks and Mostyns dates back to the Civil War, my lord.' Beth cleared her throat and tried to sound businesslike. 'The

Mostyns were on the side of the King and the
Trevithicks were for Parliament. When Sir James
Mostyn went into exile with Charles II, the Trevithicks
took the chance to steal—I mean to seize—Mostyn
land.'

'Steal will do,' Marcus said lazily. 'I fear the
Trevithicks always were thieves and scoundrels, Lady
Allerton! But they prospered as a result!'

'To profit by the misfortune of others is not honourable!' Beth said hotly. 'Even worse, at the Restoration,
the Mostyns regained a little of their former estate, but
the Trevithicks managed to persuade the King of their
good faith and were not punished!'

'I can see that you have a very strong sense of fair
play, Lady Allerton!' Marcus observed. 'Sadly, the way
the Trevithicks prospered is the way that fortunes are
often made—through double-dealing!'

Beth looked severe. 'That is no recommendation, my
lord!'

'No, I can see that my ancestry is doing me little service here. I sense that worse is to come as well. Pray
continue!'

Beth glanced at him doubtfully. Although his tone
contained its habitual teasing edge, he was looking quite
absorbed. She shifted uncomfortably.

'I hope that the tale does not bore you, my lord?'

'Not in the least! I am all attention!'

Beth realised that this was true. Marcus had loosened
his grip on the reins and the horses, very well-behaved
thoroughbred bays, were trotting at a decorous pace
along the path. All of Marcus's attention was focused
on her and as soon as Beth realised it she became acutely
aware of the warmth of his regard and the disturbingly
intent expression in those dark eyes.

'Well, yes…anyway… For a hundred years the Trevithicks prospered and Mostyns struggled, but they still held Fairhaven Island.' Beth glared at Marcus, forgetting for a moment that he had not been personally responsible for wresting it from her grandfather. It was easy to fall back into the stories of her childhood, the enthralling tales of Trevithick treachery. 'Then my grandfather inherited the estate and came up against your grandfather, my lord, the fifth Earl, George Trevithick.'

'Ah, the Evil Earl. I have heard much of his exploits. They say that in his youth he was in league with the wreckers and the smugglers and the pirates and anyone who could help him make an illegal profit.'

'I have no doubt. What is certainly true is that our grandfathers were implacable enemies, my lord, and had sworn to take their fight to the death. One stormy March night my grandfather was sailing for Fairhaven, not knowing that the Earl had already landed there and that the wreckers were waiting for him. There was a gale blowing and in the dark my grandfather did not realise that the shore lights were not placed there by his servants but were a trick of the enemy.' Beth took a deep breath. 'His ship ran aground and all hands were lost, along with the chest of treasure the ship had been carrying. My grandfather was the only one to escape ashore, but he was ambushed by the Evil Earl and cut down in the fight. Then the Earl stole his sword, the Sword of Saintonge, that had been in the family for centuries, and took the island into the bargain! Now, what do you think of that, my lord?'

Beth finished, out of breath, and looked at Marcus expectantly. It was a tale for a dark, stormy night rather than a bright day in the park, and it was difficult to believe that either of them were the descendants of men who had struggled to the death for supremacy only fifty years before. That conflict had been ruthless and atavistic, belonging to a previous and less civilised time. Beth allowed herself to consider the man who sat beside her, looking every inch the sophisticated society gentleman. She wondered suddenly just how much of that image was a façade, for she already knew from her dealings with Marcus that if one scratched the surface there was something infinitely more ruthless beneath. As for herself—how far would she go to regain Fairhaven? The stubborn tenacity of the Mostyns was in her blood. Perhaps both of them were true to their ancestry after all.

Marcus encouraged the horses to pick a bit of speed, then turned to Beth with a smile. 'What do I think of it? I cannot deny that it is a tale that reflects no credit on my grandfather. Yet I have some questions for you, Lady Allerton. What was Lord Mostyn doing sailing in such dangerous waters at night? Why did he have his treasure with him? Was there not something slightly suspicious about his own actions?'

Beth stared. In twenty years she had never questioned the detail of the story. She remembered Maddy, her nursemaid, telling her the tale at bedtimes, by the light of the candle in the nursery at Mostyn Hall. She had imagined the perfidious, flickering light of the wreckers' lamp on the cliff, the smashing of the ship's timbers as it broke up on the rocks, the glint of gold as the family treasure tumbled into the depths of the sea... It had never occurred to her to wonder why her grandfather had been carrying so much money on his journey, nor what he had been doing sailing to Fairhaven on a stormy night. Until Marcus had spoken, she had not even thought of it.

Beth wrinkled up her nose, looking at him thought-fully. 'I must concede that it is odd...'

'Indeed. One is tempted to go to Fairhaven to discover the truth of the whole story!' Marcus flashed her a smile. 'Would you accompany me, Lady Allerton, if I invited you to join me on Fairhaven Island?'

Beth looked scandalised. 'Accompany you? I should think not, my lord! A most improper suggestion!'

Marcus laughed. 'A pity. Yet I do not doubt your loyalty to the notion of regaining Fairhaven for your family.'

Beth clenched her gloved hands together in her lap. 'It is something that I feel I must do, my lord. My grand-father's ghost is unquiet...'

Marcus smiled at her. 'I hope you do not feel that in order to lay the ghost you must foster the quarrel!' Once again he transferred the reins to one hand and put the other over hers. 'I have a feeling, my lady, that you and I might settle this feud once and for all.'

This time Beth let her hand rest still under his. 'I hope that we may, my lord,' she said, deliberately reading nothing into his words. 'Might I suggest that you accept my offer for Fairhaven as a first step? It is a very gen-erous offer...'

'It is.' Marcus let go of her and picked up the reins again. 'Too generous. Fairhaven cannot possibly be worth such a sum.'

Beth shrugged a little. 'How does one assess senti-mental value, my lord? To me, Fairhaven is priceless.'

Marcus smiled. 'I understand that,' he said slowly. 'Fairhaven has become your passion, has it not, Lady Allerton? I wonder just what you would do to achieve that obsession.'

Beth stared at him. Despite the fact that his words

only echoed what Charlotte had said to her previously, it was disconcerting to hear them from a relative stranger. It was even more disconcerting to read the double meaning behind them. She looked at him very directly.

'I am not sure that I understand you, my lord. Are you rejecting my offer?'

'I preferred your original one,' Marcus said coolly.

Their gazes locked. The sun disappeared behind a grey cloud and suddenly the wind was chill. Beth shivered inside her pelisse, but it was not entirely from the cold.

'Are you offering me *carte blanche*, my lord?'

Marcus laughed out loud. 'You are very frank, my lady! I was under the impression that the boot had been on the other foot! You set the terms of our wager—'

'You lost the wager,' Beth said swiftly, 'and it is because you did not honour your stake that I am offering so much more!'

'You are offering more financially, I suppose. As I said, I preferred your original—more personal—offer!'

Beth could feel herself blushing and was vexed. She knew he was deliberately provoking her and was determined to stay calm. It was difficult, however, particularly as a tiny corner of her mind was acknowledging the attractions of such a course of action. To offer herself to Marcus in return for Fairhaven Island. It was immoral. It was iniquitous. And it was definitely tempting…

She frowned.

'The wager was a means to an end, my lord! It is not my usual mode of behaviour to offer myself as part of a bargain!'

'I see.' Marcus had allowed the curricle to come to a

halt under the bare branches of a spreading oak tree. 'In that case it was a remarkably dangerous wager.'

'It was.' Beth held his gaze. 'However, if I had lost, I had only to refuse to honour my stake—as you did, my lord!'

'Touché!' Marcus laughed again. 'I must confess myself disappointed, Lady Allerton. I was hoping that you might be persuaded—'

'Were you? You cannot know me very well, then, my lord!' By now there was a warning glint in Beth's eye. 'I have told you that I am no courtesan! I wish you take me home now, if you please!'

'Very well!' Marcus's tone betrayed amused admiration. 'I will not tease you any further, my lady. And if it is true that I do not know you well, time can at least remedy that situation!'

The thought gave Beth little comfort. In the first place, she had a strange and disturbing conviction that Marcus did in fact understand her very well, for all his teasing. As for his pledge to know her better, her instinct told her that that could be a very perilous enterprise indeed.

Chapter Three

Another country dance came to an end and Beth applauded enthusiastically and accepted the escort of her partner back to Lady Fanshawe's side. It was very hot in the Duchess of Calthorpe's ballroom for there were at least two hundred guests and the event was assured of the accolade of being a crush. The Duchess had chosen white as her theme to create the impression of approaching winter, and it was ironic that the temperature resembled that of the tropics. Hundreds of white candles added to the heat in the ballroom, creating such a fire risk that footmen were stationed about the room with buckets of water.

'Are you enjoying yourself, my love?' Lady Fanshawe fanned herself vigorously. 'It is such a sad crush in here, I declare there is barely a spare rout chair to be had! And all this white is quite dazzling to the eye!'

Beth giggled. As well as the white candles there were filmy white draperies that were threatening to catch fire and droopy white lilies that evidently preferred a cooler climate.

'You are in looks tonight, my dear,' Lady Fanshawe

continued. 'That lilac muslin is very pretty and stands out well amongst the debutantes. Poor girls, I fear they will melt into the draperies!'

'In more ways than one!' Beth agreed, gratefully accepting a glass of lemonade from Mr Porson, who had been partnering her in the previous dance. He was a worthy young man and he showed signs of lingering at her side, which Beth did not particularly mind. At least she felt safe with him.

'Mr Porson, do you think—?' she began, only to raise her eyebrows in surprise as the young man shot away with barely a word of farewell. Kit Mostyn came up and took the vacated rout chair at his cousin's side.

'Good gracious, Kit!' Beth said crossly. 'What sort of reputation do you have that scares away my innocent admirers? Poor Mr Porson was only indulging in conversation!'

'I doubt that it was my arrival that scared him off,' Kit said drily. 'The Earl of Trevithick has just come in, Beth. Porson won't want to be seen trespassing on Trevithick's ground!'

Beth glanced quickly at the doorway and looked away equally quickly, conscious that plenty of people were watching her. She was unhappily aware that she had become the talk of the town during the previous ten days, all as a result of Marcus Trevithick's attentions. They had driven in the park twice, attended a concert and fireworks at Vauxhall, met at a musical soirée and danced at a couple of balls. That had been sufficient to set tongues wagging and it seemed to Beth that Marcus had done nothing to quell the speculation. He had behaved entirely correctly towards her on all occasions, and yet Beth was aware of something beneath the veneer of convention, something entirely more exciting and dangerous in his attitude towards her.

The interest of the *ton* was piqued because of the family feud and also because the Dowager Viscountess of Trevithick had made her disapproval of Beth very plain. Only the previous night, the Dowager had cut her dead at the opera and Beth had decided that she would have to avoid Marcus in future. This was not entirely because of his mother's attitude but also because of some belated sense of self-preservation. Beth knew that she found Marcus all too attractive and she had heard something of his reputation and did not want to become another conquest. Now, however, her resolution put her in an awkward situation, for to shun Marcus's company at the ball would be remarked upon. Beth fidgeted, drumming her fingers on the arm of the chair as she tried to decide what to do.

She saw Marcus start to cross the room towards her. He had paused to speak to an acquaintance but Beth saw that although he was talking to the man, he was still watching her with a deliberation that was most disturbing. She got hastily to her feet.

'Kit, will you dance with me, please?'

Kit looked pained. 'Must I? If this is some elaborate charade to avoid Trevithick—'

'Kit!' Beth frowned at her cousin's lack of tact. 'How can you be so unchivalrous? Even if it is, I still need your help!'

Kit grinned at her. 'I only meant to warn you that Trevithick would not be fobbed off! By all means let us dance if we must!'

He took her arm and led her away from Marcus Trevithick, joining the set that was at the furthest end of the ballroom.

'I saw you talking to Eleanor Trevithick when her mother's back was turned,' Beth said slyly, as they took their places. 'If you seek to warn me, perhaps you will take some advice in turn? I hope you do not have a *tendre* there, Kit, for you must be doomed to disappointment!'

She had the satisfaction of seeing a hint of colour come into Kit's lean cheek. He avoided her gaze. 'Don't know what you mean, Beth! Miss Trevithick is a charming girl, but I have no interest there!'

Beth smiled beatifically. 'Of course not! How foolish of me even to imagine that you did!'

'It's bad enough having Charlotte dispensing advice,' Kit said gloomily, 'without my honorary sister joining in as well!'

They danced in perfect accord, though Beth found that she had to concentrate on her steps rather more than usual. Her gaze was drawn with tiresome repetitiveness to the tall figure of Marcus Trevithick as he threaded his way through the crowd and joined his mother and sister over by one of the long terrace windows. It seemed that some strange compulsion made it well nigh impossible for Beth to ignore him, for even when she was not looking at Marcus she sensed exactly where he was. It was only when Justin Trevithick came up to the family group and he and Marcus headed towards the card room that Beth started to relax, but by then the dance was ending. Kit bowed to her, then hastened away to claim another lady for the boulanger.

Beth was about to rejoin Lady Fanshawe, when she saw Marcus emerge unexpectedly from the card room again and start walking towards her through the crowd. She immediately dived towards the door and took refuge in the ladies' withdrawing room, where she fretted and fidgeted for twenty minutes, uncertain whether Marcus would simply be waiting in the corridor outside. He was not. Wrestling with a mixture of relief and disappointment, Beth tiptoed back into the ballroom and saw that Marcus was now dancing with Eleanor. She made her way back to Lady Fanshawe's corner of the room, only to find that her chaperon had disappeared.

Beth sat down, feeling a little self-conscious. She could see Kit, who was dancing with a plump debutante in a pink gown, but was looking over her shoulder all the time at Eleanor Trevithick. So much for his denials of an interest there! Beth smiled to herself. It seemed that she and her cousin were both caught in the same trap.

The crush in the ballroom was lessening now as some of the guests moved on to other engagements, and without the camouflage of the huge crowd Beth felt strangely vulnerable. She watched as the dance ended and saw Marcus look around and fix on her with an almost uncanny accuracy. In a candlelit room of a hundred and fifty people it seemed unreasonable that he was able to pick her out so quickly, but she did not feel she had time to stop and think about the implications. She started to edge towards the doors that led out on to the terrace, then paused, thinking that it would probably not be a good idea to wander out into the dark, especially on a cold autumn night. If Marcus decided to follow her they would end up playing hide-and-seek in the gardens and who could say where that would end. Glancing over her shoulder, Beth saw that he was getting closer to her, moving with a purposeful intent that was most disconcerting. She skittered along the edge of the dance floor, almost tripping over in her attempts to put some more distance between them. What she really needed now was someone to ask her to dance. Someone, anyone…

'Would you care to dance, Lady Allerton?'

Beth turned sharply, her grateful acceptance withering on her lips as she looked up into the smiling face of Justin Trevithick. Out of the frying pan and into the fire. She was certain that Justin had seen her trying to avoid Marcus, but she was also aware that she could not refuse to dance with him without seeming dreadfully rude.

'Oh, Mr Trevithick! I…yes…thank you, sir…'

Beth had met Justin several times in the previous ten days and had taken to him immediately, liking his sense of humour and easygoing manner. Just now, however, she was wishing him at the bottom of the sea. Dancing with Marcus's cousin was getting too close to Marcus for comfort. She looked round and saw that Marcus was now speaking to a fashionable matron in striped red and white silk. He looked engrossed and suddenly Beth began to feel rather silly. Perhaps Marcus had never intended to approach her at all and all her diversions had served no purpose other than to make her look foolish. Probably she was flattering herself by imagining that he had ever shown any real interest in her.

Justin was waiting, a look of speculative amusement in his eyes. Beth hastily wiped all expression from her face and gave him her hand. She was pleased that she managed to keep up a tolerably bright conversation throughout the polonaise, only faltering slightly when she observed Marcus and the stripily clad matron disappearing through the door together. That was that, then. Evidently Marcus had found company more to his taste and had retired to enjoy it in privacy. Beth felt even more out of countenance at the unedifying jealousy that swept through her.

At the end of the dance, Justin guided her off the floor and into the refreshment room.

'May I fetch you a glass of lemonade, ma'am?' he suggested. 'It may be a tame sort of beverage but is just the thing in a hot climate like this! If you take a seat in this alcove I will undertake to be back directly.'

Beth sank gratefully onto the window seat. It was fresher here with a pleasant draught of air that cooled her heated face. She rested her head against the stone window casing and closed her eyes. The noise of the ball swirled around her but she took no notice.

'Your lemonade, Lady Allerton.'

Beth jumped so much that she almost banged her head against the stone. The voice was not Justin Trevithick's, but the deeper tones of his cousin the Earl. Sure enough, Marcus was standing before her, a glass of lemonade in one hand, watching her with the same quizzically amused expression that he had been wearing all evening. Beth felt at a disadvantage and tried to get to her feet, but she found that Marcus was standing too close to her and that any movement would bring her into physical contact with him. This did not seem a very good idea, so she leant back instead and took the lemonade from him with an assumption of ease.

'Thank you very much. How do you do, Lord Trevithick?'

Marcus gave her his devastating smile. 'I am all the better now that I have finally caught up with you, Lady Allerton! I thought that I would never achieve it!'

'I was expecting your cousin's company—' Beth began.

'And did not want to have to tolerate mine instead? I fear I persuaded him to exchange places with me.' Marcus shrugged lightly. 'Now that I finally have you to myself, Lady Allerton, I would be obliged if you would keep still for at least a minute! I would like to speak with you!'

Beth shifted guiltily on the window seat. There was little chance of her escaping anywhere since Marcus was now leaning against the alcove embrasure and comprehensively blocking her retreat.

'In that case you had better sit down,' she said coolly, 'and cease looming over me in that threatening manner!'

Marcus grinned and sat down next to her. 'I will do as you ask on the understanding that you will not run away! What has all that ridiculous rigmarole been about this evening—dodging out of rooms, hiding away, avoiding even looking in my direction—?'

'When I did look in your direction I thought you most preoccupied!' Beth said tartly, before she could stop herself. 'I am surprised that you noticed me at all!'

Marcus laughed. 'I collect that you are referring to me stepping aside with a lady just now? That is my elder sister, Lady Grace Walters. She found the heat too overpowering in the ballroom and needed some fresh air.'

Beth looked away, feeling foolish. 'I am sure that I do not care—'

'Well, you do, or you would not have quizzed me about it!' Marcus sat back on the window seat and stretched his long legs out in front of him. 'And you still have not answered my question, Lady Allerton. What was all that play-acting for?'

Beth flushed. 'I thought it best to avoid you,' she said candidly, trying to look him in the eye. 'There has been so much speculation about our...' She hesitated, trying to think of the right word to describe their relationship.

'Our friendship?' Marcus supplied helpfully.

'Friendship. Yes, thank you. So much speculation

about our friendship, my lord, that I thought it best to subdue it by—'

'By creeping about like an actor in a bad play? You have caused so *much* speculation tonight by your strategies for avoiding me that I am amazed you are not aware of it!'

'Well, if it comes to that, you have hardly suppressed the gossip by cornering me in this alcove!' Beth said, firing up. 'It seems to me that you positively enjoy stirring up scandal, my lord!'

Marcus shrugged his broad shoulders. 'I confess that I seldom regard it. As you should not, my lady! Why should the tabbies concern you? I am minded to kiss you here and now and see what the scandalmongers make of that!'

Beth recoiled slightly. 'Do not jest, my lord!'

'Why should I be jesting? You did not object to kissing me before!'

Beth blushed scarlet. 'My lord! Kindly lower your voice—'

'Come and speak with me in private, then. I want to talk to you about your offer for Fairhaven. It is time that we settled the matter.'

Beth gave him a very direct look. 'I do not believe you, sir! This is just a trick! In fact, I do not trust you! At all!'

'Why not?' Marcus grinned. 'Because the last time we were private together we shared more than just a conversation—'

Beth waved her hands about in mute appeal. 'I believe you must be inebriated to speak thus, my lord—'

Marcus captured both her hands in one of his. 'Not in the slightest! But if you will not speak with me, come and dance with me instead!'

He had already pulled her to her feet and was steering her through the crowded room with one hand resting lightly in the small of her back. Beth was sharply conscious of his tall figure close beside her, so close that her skirt brushed against his thigh as they walked. She tried to move away a little but found that the press of people forced them together. She could feel the warmth of his touch through the thin muslin of her dress, and suddenly she felt hot and vulnerable. It was no state in which to begin a dance, and when Beth heard the waltz striking up she almost turned tail and fled.

'No need to look so terrified, sweetheart,' Marcus murmured in her ear. His voice was warm and persuasive. 'I promise to behave!'

A strange shiver went down Beth's spine. She did not dare look at him. She reluctantly moved into his arms and felt only slightly relieved when Marcus held her at an irreproachable distance from his own body and made no attempt to draw her closer.

They started to circle the floor in time to the lilting rhythm of the music. The faces of the guests spun past them, curious, avid, amused, sharp, and spiteful... It seemed to Beth that the music was whirling faster and faster and that the flickering candlelight washed over them like a kaleidoscope of black and white. Marcus's face was in shadow, his expression inscrutable, almost distant. Yet despite his apparent coolness Beth could feel a current of heat running between them, intense and strong. She shivered again, convulsively.

Beth had intended to keep a decorous distance between them and to avoid the intimacy of conversation during the waltz, but some compulsion made her glance up into Marcus's face as they completed their second circuit of the floor. His gaze met hers for a split second

and now it was dark and heavy with a passion he made
no attempt to conceal. Beth caught her breath on a little
gasp and almost lost her footing. Immediately Marcus's
arms tightened about her, pulling her into sudden and
shocking contact with his body. His cheek brushed hers,
hard against the softness of her skin, causing a feeling
of helpless, wanton warmth to flood through her. Beth
shuddered in his arms, unable to prevent her body be-
traying her with its trembling. She saw Marcus's lips
curve into a smile, felt his own body harden with arousal
against hers and thought that she might well faint with
shock and sheer, sensual delight, there in the Duchess
of Calthorpe's ballroom in front of one hundred and fifty
people. It was terrifying but also strangely exhilarating
all at the same time, and she was thoroughly confused.
She did not risk looking at Marcus again.

The music was ending, the waltzing couples slowing
down, breaking apart and walking away. The chatter rose
around her and the room suddenly seemed brighter. Beth
tried to break free of Marcus's grip, intent only on putting a little distance between them, but he held on to
her, keeping her close.

'You must give me a moment...' his voice was husky
'...if you are not to embarrass me...'

The colour flamed into Beth's face. She allowed him
to guide her skilfully to the edge of the dance floor,
where she plied her fan and desperately tried to think of
an innocuous topic of conversation. Her mind was
dazed, cloudy with desire, and all she could think of was
what had happened between them and how she was still
trembling with an echo of the passion she had seen in
his eyes.

'It is very warm,' she said uncertainly, and was relieved to see amusement replace the sensual heat in Marcus's face.

'Certainly it is very hot in here,' he drawled, 'and between us, Lady Allerton, I should say that it is almost too hot for comfort!'

Beth's gaze flew uncertainly to his face, but before she could answer, Justin Trevithick appeared, escorting Lady Fanshawe. Beth was tolerably certain that Marcus's cousin had summed up the situation with one comprehensive glance, for his gaze moved from her face to Marcus's and his eyebrows rose fractionally as he picked up on the tension between them. Fortunately Lady Fanshawe was decidedly less perceptive.

'There you are, my dear! You know that we are promised to Lady Baynton's rout and positively must put in an appearance before the night ends!' She beamed at Marcus and Justin. 'Do you gentlemen wish to accompany us, or do you have other plans?'

Beth felt Marcus's gaze rest on her. It was not difficult to imagine just what other plans he might have for her. She schooled her face to remain blank, annoyed that he seemed to be able to make her blush at the slightest provocation.

'Thank you, ma'am, but I believe we are for White's,' Justin was saying, with a smile. 'May we escort you to your carriage?'

It felt cold outside after the stifling heat of the ballroom. Beth drew her velvet cloak more closely around her and tried not to shiver. Marcus kissed her hand before helping her up into the coach, and murmured that he hoped to call on her the following day. She was almost at a loss for a reply, half-longing to see him again, half-afraid of the feelings he could evoke in her.

As she settled back in the coach, Beth reflected that

it seemed strange now, but she realised that she had barely given a moment's thought to physical passion in her whole life. She had married almost from the school-room and had considered herself happy with Frank Allerton, but he had rarely troubled her for his marital rights and had treated her with all the indulgence of a fond parent. No hint of passion had disturbed the even tenor of their relationship. From the vague comments that Charlotte had occasionally made, Beth had realised that there could be a great deal more to marriage than she had shared with Frank, but she had largely dismissed such matters as simply not for her. She had met a few personable men during her widowhood and had even enjoyed the company of some of them, but had never felt moved to indulge in a love affair. She realised now that she had even begun to believe that she was simply not very interested in love.

Then Marcus had kissed her and it felt as though a whole new side of her personality, both emotional and physical, had been brought to life. Curled up in a corner of the carriage, listening vaguely to Lady Fanshawe's chatter, Beth reflected that Marcus had awoken something she had not even been aware was sleeping: a hunger to experience emotion and passion in vivid detail.

And it was the first of these that was the problem. If she had only wanted to take a lover, matters would have been simple. Marcus was there and he was eminently suitable, eminently desirable as a lover. Beth felt the warmth steal over her again. It was a tempting thought, yet she knew that she could not accept it. Newly awak-ened, her feelings were craving satisfaction as much as her body was, and the thought was terrifying. Against her better judgement she liked Marcus. She enjoyed his company, his conversation, his humour. She knew she was in danger of loving him, too quickly, careless of the risk. It was in her nature to be impulsive, but on this one occasion she had to be more careful and protect herself against this danger. For though she knew Marcus wanted her, she could not be confident that his feelings were engaged any more deeply than that. It hurt her to think it, but she knew she was right.

'Would you mind if we do not go on to Lady Baynton's rout, dear ma'am?' she asked Lady Fanshawe in a small voice. 'I am a little fatigued and would prefer the quiet of going home.'

Her godmother shot her a concerned look. 'Of course, my love. You do look rather done up! I suppose that it is country living—you are simply not prepared for such a dizzy round of events as we indulge in here in town!' Lady Fanshawe fidgeted with her reticule. Her voice changed a little. 'Beth, dear, I do not mean to pry, but I feel I should warn you about the Earl of Trevithick…'

Beth shifted slightly on the seat. 'There is no need to warn me, ma'am,' she said sadly. 'No need at all.'

'Beth, I do declare you are in a brown study this morning!' Charlotte Cavendish put down the dress she was holding and viewed her cousin with a puzzled eye. 'I asked you if you preferred the mauve or the green and you said both! Are you not feeling in plump currant? You need only say if you wish us to stop!'

Beth shook herself. They had been wading their way through the dizzying pile of goods sent round that morning by the Bond Street modistes. There were dresses, shawls and spencers, scarves and tippets, stockings and petticoats, gloves, fans and hats. The crimson saloon looked like an eastern bazaar and Beth felt utterly unequal to choosing anything from the selection. Not that her mind was on the task in hand. Not at all. She had spent the best part of the night and most of the morning dwelling on Marcus Trevithick; on his high-handed manner and his infuriatingly mocking tone, on the dark face that could soften into a warmth that took her breath away, on the forceful attraction of a man who was quite beyond her experience. Any minute she was expecting— hoping—that the bell would ring and he would have fulfilled his promise to call on her. And at the same time she was thinking that to foster any hopes of him was the greatest folly.

'The pale blue suits you to perfection, Lottie,' she said hastily, admiring the way that the figured silk mirrored her cousin's bright eyes, 'and I would take the ivory muslin and the grey as well.'

'That is all very well for me, but what about you?' Charlotte questioned. 'You do not seem very interested, Beth, and this is the finest that Bond Street has to offer!'

Beth let a pale green scarf float through her fingers and stood up, moving over to the window. 'I am sorry. I think I am a little tired from last night. We were back very late, you know, and I did not sleep particularly well.'

Charlotte frowned a little. 'I wish I could come with you to all the parties and balls, Beth! Lady Fanshawe is the sweetest person imaginable, but I am not entirely sure she is up to snuff! Why, she told me she was hoping that Sir Edmund Netherwood might make an offer for you, when everyone knows he is the most tiresome old fortune-hunter and has been through three wives and their dowries already!'

Beth giggled. 'You need have no fears on that score, Lottie!' She sobered. 'All the same, it would be so much more fun if you could accompany me about town. I do not like to think of you sitting here on your own whilst Kit and I set the town by the ears!'

'Speaking of which, Lady Fanshawe said that you met with the Earl of Trevithick at the ball,' Charlotte said casually, examining the stitching on a fine pair of kid gloves. 'She said that he was most attentive, Beth!'

Beth blushed. She looked away, down into the street, where a flower-seller was just setting up a stall on the corner opposite.

'Yes... I... Well, I could not really avoid him...'

'Oh, Beth! Did you really want to?'

Beth raised troubled grey eyes to her cousin's blue ones. 'No, not really.' She spoke in a rush. 'I like Lord Trevithick a great deal, Lottie, but I am afraid...'

Charlotte was folding up the material, but now she let her hands rest in her lap. 'Afraid? Of how you feel about him?' she asked shrewdly.

Beth nodded, avoiding her gaze. 'He is just so very different from Frank!'

Charlotte laughed. 'I should say so!'

The doorbell shrilled, making them both jump. Carrick, the butler, strode into the room, carrying a flat packet wrapped in brown paper and tied with string. He proffered it to Beth.

'This parcel has arrived from the Earl of Trevithick, madam. There is also a note...'

Beth shot Charlotte a startled look, and then tore open the envelope. Inside was a single sheet of paper, written in the strong scrawl that she had come to recognise:

Dear Lady Allerton

I enclose your winnings. I have every intention of regaining them in time, however. Pray do not flee

London for Devon before I have time to call upon you.

Until then,

Trevithick

The note drifted to the floor as Beth slit the parcel with her letter opener. Her fingers shook slightly. Inside was a document, dated that very morning, granting the Island of Fairhaven in the Bristol Channel to Elizabeth, Lady Allerton, and her heirs in perpetuity. Again, it was signed in a strong black hand with the one word, Trevithick. There was also a bundle of other papers, some of them ancient manuscripts written in Latin on paper so old and thin that the light shone through. Beth riffled through them in disbelief, seeing the history of her beloved island so suddenly and unexpectedly in her hands.

Charlotte had picked up the note and was reading it. She looked doubtfully from the letter to Beth and back again.

'Oh, no! I cannot believe that the Earl is prepared to humour you in this mad obsession!'

Beth could not quite believe it either. 'I suppose that it does not matter to him,' she said, a little breathlessly. 'He has so many other estates more valuable. Fairhaven has only its sentimental worth, and that only matters to me!'

'I wonder what he means by saying that he intends to regain Fairhaven,' Charlotte said thoughtfully, 'and what he wants in return for his gift!'

Beth looked up, startled.

'Why, nothing! He is paying his debt, that is all! He lost the wager—'

'Do not remind me of it!' Her cousin pursed her lips. There was a twinkle in her eye. 'Sometimes you are so naïve, my love! In my experience there is no such thing as something for nothing! Ten to one, Trevithick has some kind of bargain in mind! It might be that he seeks your good opinion, which would be reassuring, or it might be that his intentions are dishonourable.'

Beth could feel herself blushing again. She had not told Charlotte that the Earl had already offered her *carte blanche*, for she knew it would only fuel her cousin's fears. 'Oh, no, I cannot believe—' She met Charlotte's sceptical gaze. 'Well, perhaps…'

'You know you suspect it yourself!' Charlotte said drily. 'What exactly happened during that wager, Beth?'

Beth felt herself blush harder. 'Why, nothing! Only…' She evaded Charlotte's penetrating gaze. 'I suppose he did…does…perhaps admire me a little…'

'Quite so. That being the case, I think you should be careful. Trevithick is not a man with whom to indulge in an idle flirtation! He is far too dangerous!'

Beth was momentarily distracted. 'Is he? I was not aware that his reputation was *so* bad.'

'You never are,' Charlotte said, with a sigh. 'Remember that fortune hunter who tried to attach your interest at the Exeter Assembly? You thought him a very pleasant fellow, as I recall—'

'Oh, but he was not in the least like Lord Trevithick!'

'No,' Charlotte said, opening the door, 'he was harmless! Just take care, Beth!'

She went out. Beth picked up all the documents and walked over to the window seat, sitting down in the mid-morning sun. Outside the street was busy with vendors and passers-by.

She put the papers down on her lap and gazed out at the jumbled spires and rooftops stretching into the distance. It felt very claustrophobic to be cooped up in

London in the autumn. It was a season in which to ride across the fields and feel the sharp breeze on her face, to stand on the cliff tops and look out across the sea, to walk along the beach and hear the hiss of the waves on the sand.

Beth looked down at the papers again. She realised that she felt decidedly odd, but could not work out why. Perhaps it was the shock of having her heart's desire suddenly thrust into her hands, or that the pleasure of owning Fairhaven had overcome her. But it did not feel like that. She realised that she had wanted Marcus to talk to her about it, to tell her what he intended. Now she felt oddly cheated. She had what she wanted but she was uncomfortable about it. And she was not entirely sure why.

The reading room at White's was very quiet that morning and it was proving a most pleasant oasis of calm for Marcus after an eventful breakfast at Trevithick House. The Dowager Viscountess, mindful of her elder son's behaviour at the ball the night before, had rung a peal over him for his lack of filial duty. It was her expressed view that the Trevithicks had not fostered a feud with the Mostyns for two hundred and fifty years simply for Marcus to disregard it by paying attention to a fast little widow, no matter how rich. Marcus, incensed to hear his mother speak so slightingly of Beth, had thrown down his napkin and departed the house forthwith, fortunately bumping into Justin in St James's. The two of them had retired to White's where Justin promptly fell asleep and Marcus buried himself in the *Morning Chronicle*.

After half an hour, Marcus stirred his cousin with his foot. 'How much did you win last night, Justin? When

I left you were ten thousand guineas up against Warrender. Did you make enough to pay off that voracious opera singer you had in keeping?'

'Twenty-five thousand, all told,' Justin muttered, without opening his eyes. He slumped down further in his chair. 'I took the money and Warrender took the girl off my hands! She was sweet, but too much of a handful!'

Marcus laughed. 'Seems you struck a good bargain! So, are you clearing your decks in order to settle down, old fellow?'

'Devil a bit!' Justin yawned. He opened his eyes and squinted at Marcus. 'Thought you were the one about to be caught in parson's mousetrap!'

Marcus raised his eyebrows. 'Are you trying to marry me off by any chance, old chap? Only last night you were singing Lady Allerton's praises!'

'No harm in marrying a fortune,' Justin said laconically, straightening up. 'Good money but bad blood in that family! Not that the Trevithicks should criticise the Mostyns! Pirates and thieves, the lot of them!'

'Call me fastidious, but I would not care to marry for money,' Marcus said slowly.

Justin bent a perceptive look on him. 'Ah, but you wouldn't be, would you, Marcus? Never seen you more smitten, old fellow! After all, you've never given away an island before, have you?'

Marcus smiled, but did not trouble to reply. Justin knew him too well to be fooled, but equally he had no intention of discussing his matrimonial plans just yet. He shifted a little in his chair as he thought of Beth. He would call on her in a little while and take her driving. He wanted to talk to her about Fairhaven, make her promise that she would not rush away from London to inspect her new property. His smile deepened as he imagined how excited she would be to have the island in her possession. It pleased him to make her happy and it was a feeling he was not accustomed to. He had always been generous in a careless, casual way, but this protective desire to take care of someone else was entirely new. He grinned. Damn it, he must be getting old, wanting to marry and set up his nursery…

A servant was approaching them with a folded note on a silver tray. The man's face wore a rather pained expression, as though he had been entrusted with an errand that was in poor taste.

'Excuse me, my lord. A person by the name of Gower is without. He asks if you might spare him a moment of your time…'

Marcus raised his eyebrows. He had seen Gower only the previous day when his man of business had reluctantly presented him with the deed of gift by which Marcus had signed Fairhaven away. Gower had begged him to be prudent, to reconsider, to wait… And Marcus, impatient to make Beth happy, had signed the document and sent it round immediately, ignoring Gower's advice. He knew that something untoward must have happened for Gower to seek him out at White's. Wondering if it was to do with Fairhaven or some completely unrelated matter, Marcus felt his own apprehension growing.

The man of business was waiting for him out in the street, turning his hat round between his hands in the gesture he always employed when he was worried or nervous. On this occasion Marcus judged him to be both of these things.

'My lord,' he said jerkily, looking from Marcus to Justin and back again, 'forgive me for disturbing you, but the matter was most urgent. I would not have troubled you else—'

'That is understood, Gower,' Marcus said shortly. 'What is the difficulty?'.

'My lord…' Gower looked unhappy. 'There are documents I feel you should see, matters that have come to light—'

'Matters to do with Fairhaven Island?' Justin interposed, his gaze keen. Marcus felt his heart sink as Gower nodded his head.

'Matters concerning Fairhaven—and Lady Allerton, I fear, sir.'

'Well, we cannot stand here in the street discussing it,' Marcus snapped. 'Gower, your rooms are more appropriate than Trevithick House. We will go there.'

They walked to Gower's rooms in Chancery Lane in an uneasy silence. Gower ushered them into his office and a clerk who had been working at the desk moved unobtrusively away. Gower carefully moved some stacks of papers from the chairs and invited the gentlemen to take a seat, but Marcus ignored the suggestion.

'Thank you, I prefer to stand,' he said tersely. 'Now, what is this matter that is of such import, Gower?'

Gower resumed his seat behind his large mahogany desk. He moved a few documents to the right, picked one up, put it down again, then moved the pile left. Marcus felt his nerves tightening.

'For God's sake, man, just get on with it—'

He saw Justin shoot him a warning glance and tried to get a hold on his temper. Shouting at Gower would do no good and the man was only doing his job anyway. Marcus knew that he needed a pernickety lawyer to attend to all the matters that held no interest for him, but when he wondered what Gower was about to tell him about Beth he felt the cold seep through him like water on stone.

'Yes, my lord,' Gower said expressionlessly. He settled his half-moon spectacles on his nose. Behind the lenses his eyes gleamed palely. He picked up the document on the top of the pile and cleared his throat.

'On the matter of Fairhaven Island, my lord… Several weeks ago, when you first mooted the possibility that you might cede the island to Lady Allerton, I instigated some investigations—' Gower's pale eyes flashed '—all in your best interests, my lord.'

'Of course,' Marcus said politely. He resisted the impulse to take the lawyer by the throat and shake him. 'Pray continue, Gower.'

'Yes, my lord. I discovered that the possibility of a sale of Fairhaven had first been suggested some twenty years ago, when Sir Frank Allerton approached your grandfather, the late Earl.'

Marcus shifted impatiently. 'What of it, Gower?'

The lawyer shuffled the papers again. 'It seems that Sir Frank was a notable mineralogist, my lord, and suspected that there might well be valuable resources on the island, mineral deposits that would justify the cost and difficulties of mining there.'

Justin gave a low whistle. 'There cannot be many substances that would be worth such an effort, Gower.'

'No, sir.' Gower permitted himself a small, prim smile. 'Naturally enough, Sir Frank did not inform the late Earl of his precise interest in Fairhaven, but information that subsequently fell into my hands…' the lawyer looked slightly shifty '…suggested that the substance under discussion was gold.'

Marcus expelled his breath sharply. He did not speak, but turned away to look out of the dusty window. There were some pigeons pecking in the gutter opposite. In the room behind him he heard Justin say carefully, 'Would you say that Sir Frank was well informed on the mineral potential of the Devon area, Gower?'

Marcus swung back round. 'Of course he was,' he said abruptly. 'Why, even I know that Sir Frank Allerton was a distinguished expert on such matters! In addition to work in his native county, he was looking to develop the Somerset coal field and held considerable concessions in the Cornish tin mines—'

'Concessions which his widow still holds,' Gower finished quietly.

Marcus leant on the desk. 'Very well, Gower. I believe you have reached the crux of your story, have you not?'

The lawyer looked unhappy. 'Perhaps so, my lord.' He took a deep breath. 'My lord, I do wish you to know that I am only looking after your best interests—'

'It is understood,' Marcus said tersely. His mouth was set in a grim line. 'Please go on.'

'Very well, my lord. As you are aware, your grandfather did not choose to sell Fairhaven to Sir Frank, claiming that he had only just wrested the place from the ''cursed Mostyn brood'', as he put it, and had no wish to give it up so easily. He had neither the money nor the inclination to explore the island's potential himself, but was content to leave it unexploited for the following years.' Gower looked up. 'There is an ancient castle there, my lord, as well as a farm and a rudimentary village. If you recall, your uncle St John Trevithick holds the living there and he and your aunt Trevithick live in the castle. I last visited it some two years ago, when your factor, Mr McCrae—'

'Please get to the point, Gower,' Marcus said wearily,

subsiding into the chair opposite Justin. He saw his cousin's look of concern and flashed him a brief smile. 'Forgive my abruptness, but what is really of concern is the nature of your allegations against Lady Allerton.' He stopped and looked at the lawyer. 'For I believe that you have some.'

'Yes, my lord,' Gower said again. The paper in his hand shook slightly. 'Some two years ago, shortly after the death of her husband, Lady Allerton petitioned the Earl to buy Fairhaven.'

Marcus raised his eyebrows. 'Yes? She has told me as much.'

'Indeed, my lord.' The lawyer's voice was dry. 'She approached your grandfather twice, in point of fact, and after he refused her offer a second time, she wrote to tell him that she would resort to whatever methods necessary to gain the island. I remember the Earl laughing and saying she was a spirited little filly with more mettle than the rest of her family put together! But for all that he thought it unbecoming that such a young lady should involve herself in business matters, for all that she brought her lawyer with her—the self-same man whom Sir Frank had always used to negotiate his mining ventures.'

Justin shifted uncomfortably. Marcus's eyes narrowed on the lawyer's face. 'I do not find that in any way surprising, Gower. If the man were acting for Sir Frank it would be natural for Lady Allerton to retain his services in matters relating to the estate. It does not mean that she retained an active interest—'

He broke off at the look on the lawyer's face. 'No, my lord,' Gower said lugubriously. 'However, when Lady Allerton was out of the room, the man apparently told your grandfather quite openly that it was their intention to pursue Sir Frank's ambitions on Fairhaven. Lady Allerton still retains the same lawyer,' he added quietly, 'a gentleman by the name of Gough, as you know, my lord. As soon as you mentioned to me the matter of the wager for Fairhaven I was suspicious, my lord, and even more so when I discovered that Gough was involved.'

Marcus let out a long breath. He could see both Gower and Justin watching him with similar sympathetic looks and felt the anger rise in him. It seemed that he had made a fine fool of himself over Beth Allerton and was in danger of appearing even more foolish by his unwillingness to believe badly of her. He remembered the passion with which she had spoken of her love of Fairhaven, the way she had related the tales of her childhood, her fervent intention to regain her patrimony. It seemed that it had all been assumed to hide a more avaricious reason, a convenient tale to make him sympathise with her, to bewitch him, as she had done so subtly, with her smoky grey eyes and her soft, sweet body and her conniving mind. He clenched his fists.

'Is there any more, Gower?'

'Only that I have heard this very morning that Christopher Mostyn has been approaching various backers for a new commercial venture,' the lawyer said slowly. 'It was then that I felt I had to lay all this matter before your lordship. I understand that Lady Allerton signed over all active interests in her late husband's business to Lord Mostyn, although she shares in the profits.'

'And the plans,' Marcus said grimly. 'Could this new venture be the mining of Fairhaven, Gower?'

'I do not know, my lord,' the lawyer said truthfully, 'but it might well be.'

There was a silence.

'It does not look good,' Justin said carefully, after a moment. He put a hand on his cousin's arm. 'I am sorry, Marcus…'

Marcus shook him off and stood up. 'There is no need. Gower, I am obliged to you for your information. Justin…' he turned to his cousin '…we have a call to make, I think. In Upper Grosvenor Street. I will take back the deeds to Fairhaven and give that devious little witch a piece of my mind!'

Chapter Four

'Excuse me, my lady.' Carrick, Beth's butler, had come into the red drawing room and was looking rather dubious. 'The Earl of Trevithick is here and is asking—rather strongly, my lady—that you should receive him.' The butler's frown deepened. 'There is another gentleman with him, a Mr Justin Trevithick. I was somewhat concerned, my lady, that the Earl was inebriated, for he was most forceful in his demands for entry.'

Beth put her book down and looked at Charlotte in some consternation. The clock stood at ten minutes to two, which seemed somewhat early for a gentleman to be in his cups. It also seemed somewhat out of character.

'I cannot believe that the Earl is foxed, Carrick,' she said forthrightly, gaining a squeak of disapproval from Charlotte at her unladylike language, 'so perhaps I should see him to ascertain the reason for his behaviour.' She turned to her cousin. 'Shall I receive Lord Trevithick in the green study, Charlotte, so that you need not be disturbed? I do not wish you to have to receive two strangers so unexpectedly.'

Charlotte stood up, smoothing her dress with nervous fingers. 'Thank you, Beth, but there is no difficulty. If the Earl is inebriated I would rather be with you to prevent an unfortunate scene—'

The words had scarcely left her lips when the door was flung open with a crash as Marcus stalked into the room, closely followed by Justin, who was looking slightly less than his usual imperturbable self.

'My apologies, ma'am,' Marcus drawled, sketching a slight bow in Charlotte's direction. 'I have no wish to discompose you, but I have an urgent need to speak with Lady Allerton and I was afraid that I would have taken root to the spot by the time your butler saw fit to return!' He turned to Beth and she recoiled slightly from the expression on his face. There was a furious light in his eyes and a very grim set to his jaw. The change from the attentive suitor of two nights before to this hard and angry man was almost impossible to believe.

As she stared at him in bemusement, Marcus said silkily, 'I am glad to find you at home, Lady Allerton, and not halfway to Devon to claim your ill-gotten gains! Will you grant me a private interview or must I rehearse my quarrel with you in front of your cousin and a host of servants? I have no difficulty in doing so, you understand, but Mrs Cavendish might find it somewhat distasteful…'

Beth drew herself up. The reference to her ill-gotten gains puzzled her, for had Marcus not sent her the deeds of Fairhaven only that morning, and with a perfectly amicable note into the bargain? She wondered briefly if Carrick had been correct and Marcus was drunk, but it took only one glance to see that he was stone cold sober. Sober but very angry. It was frightening.

'I have no notion to what you refer, my lord,' she said a little shakily, 'nor have I any wish to hear your impertinent accusations! I think you must be either drunk or mad to speak like this, and I suggest that you return when your temper has cooled!'

Justin caught Marcus's arm. 'Lady Allerton is in the right of it, old chap! Cool reason is better than hot heads! Let us retire for now—'

Marcus ignored him. He crossed the room to Beth and stopped an unnerving foot away from her. She could see the anger and dislike clear in his face.

'Well, ma'am?' he challenged softly. 'What is it to be? A private discussion or a public quarrel? The choice is entirely yours!'

Beth heard Charlotte draw a protesting breath and saw Justin Trevithick move protectively to her cousin's side.

'Beg pardon, ma'am,' she heard him say in an undertone. 'Dreadful intrusion, I know, but there is no reasoning with him when he is like this. The Trevithick temper, you know. The old Earl was renowned for it...'

Beth's gaze flickered to Charlotte and back to the compelling anger in Marcus Trevithick's face. She drew breath to give Marcus a blistering set-down, but Charlotte spoke first.

'Beth dear, it does seem that the Earl has some pressing matter to discuss with you. Perhaps you could take him into the study, whilst Mr Trevithick stays here with me? Carrick, would you bring tea?'

The prosaic suggestion seemed to restore some sense of normality. The tight rage lessened slightly in Marcus's face and he walked over to the door and held it open for Beth with studious courtesy. Carrick moved away with his customary composed tread to fetch refreshments. Beth saw Justin take Charlotte's hand and start to introduce himself formally, then the door closed behind them with a snap and she was alone in the hall with Marcus.

'If you would step this way, my lord,' she said, a little faintly, gesturing towards her book room, 'I am sure that we can resolve this problem, whatever it may be…'

The study faced south and had a warm fire burning. Earlier that morning Beth had taken the deeds to Fairhaven and placed them on the desk, intending to read them thoroughly in the evening. She had wanted to see Marcus first and talk to him about his gift. And now it seemed that she had the opportunity, but not exactly as she would have wished it…

She saw Marcus's gaze go to the pile of papers and saw a frown crease his forehead as though he wanted to snatch the deeds up and simply walk off with them. For a moment her mind was filled with the ludicrous picture of them tugging on opposite ends of the papers until they tore across and fluttered to the ground. And for what? She was still utterly confused about the nature of his quarrel with her.

Marcus drove his hands into his jacket pockets. 'Lady Allerton, I have come to ask for the return of the deeds to Fairhaven Island,' he said, in tones of measured dislike. 'It seems that you have obtained them under false pretences and so our agreement, such as it was, is null and void. The wager, the gift…' his dark gaze dwelled on her face for a moment in a look that made Beth feel curiously vulnerable '…everything. I do not expect to see you again or have any further debate about the ownership of the island.'

Beth sat down weakly in the nearest chair. She raised her eyes to his face. 'I do not understand you, my lord. You made me a free gift of the island only this morning—'

Marcus spoke through his teeth. 'It was a mistake. I am rescinding it.'

The indignant colour sprung into Beth's face. 'But you cannot do that! There is no reason— Why, how dishonourable can you be? First to renege on the wager and then to cancel your gift—'

Marcus came across and bent over her chair. His furious dark eyes were only inches from hers. 'If we are talking of honour, I would like to know how a woman who lies and cheats could possibly know anything of such a quality!' He turned away from her, his movements so full of repressed rage that Beth quailed. 'I have heard about your plans to exploit Fairhaven for financial gain! So much for your touching protestations that you were wishing to regain your lost patrimony! And to think that I believed you—' He stopped and ran a hand through his disordered dark hair. 'Well, I was richly taken in, but not any more!'

Beth got to her feet. Her eyes were wide and puzzled. 'Truly, my lord, I do not understand—'

Marcus spun round and caught her wrist. 'Not understand? Do you deny that your late husband tried to buy Fairhaven because he wanted to mine gold there? Do you deny that you went to my grandfather and told him that *you* wished to buy the island for the same reason? Do you deny that your cousin is even now looking for investors for such a project, now that you have tricked me out of Fairhaven—?'

'Yes, I do deny it!' Beth wrenched her wrist out of his grasp. 'I knew nothing of Frank's business concerns, nor do I know anything of Kit's! I do not wish to! I want Fairhaven for all those reasons I told you, my lord, and as for telling your grandfather otherwise—' she swallowed a sob '—I never said anything of the sort!'

Her gaze searched Marcus's face and saw the unyielding disbelief there. She could tell that she was wasting her breath. 'It seems, however, that you have no wish to trust me,' she finished quietly.

Marcus moved over to the writing table. 'I will take these with me—'

Beth whisked across the room before he could reach for the deeds to Fairhaven, and inserted herself between Marcus and the desk, blocking his way. She put her hands behind her and leant back against the desk's smooth surface to steady herself. Marcus looked at her for a moment, then raised an incredulous eyebrow.

'So determined to keep your island, my dear? I have not forgotten exactly what it was you offered me when we made our wager! It seems you will do anything to achieve your ambition!' His gaze swept over her with contemptuous familiarity, from the black curls piled up on her head to the kid slippers peeping from beneath the hem of her pale blue muslin gown and Beth felt as though he was stripping her naked. He moved forward until she was completely trapped with the writing table behind her and Marcus in front of her. Beth drew back as far as she could, but she felt the sharp edge of the desk digging uncomfortably into the back of her legs. A second later she forgot all about the discomfort as Marcus moved in closer, so close that Beth could feel his thigh pressing against hers through the thin muslin gown. She drew an outraged breath.

'My lord, kindly let me go!'

Marcus smiled with wicked amusement. All his anger appeared to have gone now, replaced by a devilish enjoyment that Beth suddenly found even more frightening. She tried to lean away from him, but the desk behind her blocked her path completely, and when she attempted to slide sideways Marcus simply leant both arms on the desk on either side of her, effectively pin-ning her down. As Beth tried to arch away from him she saw his gaze drop to the neckline of her dress and linger there on the soft swell of her breasts.

'My lord!' Beth's voice came out as a desperate squeak. 'This is not fair!'

Marcus leant closer. She could feel his breath soft on her heated skin. He raised a hand and traced one lazy finger down her cheek, continuing down the line of her neck to her collarbone. His eyes were dark with desire.

'Would you have honoured the bet if you had lost, sweetheart? Would you?'

'No!' Beth gasped. She felt his fingers pause at the hollow in her throat, felt him stroke the pulse there.

'Your skin is all flushed.' Marcus's voice had sunk to a husky whisper now. 'You are as hot as you were the other night. I do not believe you, Lady Allerton. I think you are as shameless as you pretended to be at the Cyprians' Ball...'

Beth's gasp of fury was lost as his mouth came down on hers. This time his kiss was hard and hungry, as demanding as the one at the ball had been gentle. He forced her lips apart and she felt his tongue invade her mouth and her senses spun under the onslaught. She brought her hands round to grip Marcus's arms, intending to push him away, but he leant his weight against her so that the table caught her behind the thighs and she was borne helplessly back, to lie amongst the scattered papers and rolling inkpot. She felt her dress gape and her hair come loose from its pins and fan out across the wooden surface, and she could neither struggle nor scream, for Marcus's weight was on top of her, holding her still, and his mouth still plundered the softness of hers.

It was only when his lips left hers, to follow the line his fingers had traced earlier and brush against the sensitive softness of her throat, that Beth realised she had no will to struggle anyway. The touch of his hands and lips was exquisite pleasure and she wanted more. She tangled her fingers in his hair and pulled his mouth back up to hers so that she could once again touch and taste him.

She had no idea how long they lay locked together before Marcus moved with single-minded concentration to strip the dress from her shoulders. Beth felt the little puffy sleeves slide down her arms to the elbow and a moment later Marcus had slid one warm hand inside the gap in her bodice and cupped her breast. Her involuntary moan was lost against his lips as he thrust his tongue deep into her mouth. His fingers found her hardening nipple and he pulled the bodice of her dress down before his mouth left hers to fasten over the pink tip he had exposed. Beth squirmed in delight and desperation as he bit down on her sensitised skin. There was an exquisite pain in the pit of her stomach and she was lost in the sensations of pleasure that he was creating. The remaining papers went flying from the desk as she writhed with excitement.

There was a sudden noise out in the hall and Marcus eased away from her with a purely involuntary movement. It was enough to bring Beth down to earth. Suddenly she was horribly aware of something digging into her back, of the papers scattered beneath her hands, the dress that had almost slipped to her waist. She wriggled again but this time in a desperate attempt to stand up, and Marcus stepped back and put out a hand to help her to her feet. Beth flinched away.

'Don't touch me!' All her horror at what she had done was in her voice. She could not believe it—could not believe her own behaviour and could not forgive him his. She saw Marcus recoil and knew that finally, she had the upper hand. She gestured towards the door. 'Lord Trevithick. Please leave. Now.'

She tidied herself with trembling fingers and watched as Marcus smoothed his hair and straightened his clothes. His eyes met hers and she saw that they were as dazed and dark with passion as she knew her own must be. Suddenly she wanted to throw herself into his arms, to make all well again between them, but she drew herself up haughtily and simply waited for him to go.

'Beth—' Marcus put out a hand to her, but Beth turned her shoulder and stared blindly out of the window. 'Beth, I am truly sorry—'

'No!' Beth's eyes filled with tears. She did not know whether he meant that he was sorry for his actions or for his earlier suspicions but whatever the case, she *did* know that she would cry in another instant. 'I do not want to hear it!'

She heard Marcus open the study door and she turned round quickly. Before he went there was something she had to say to him, something that had to be absolutely clear.

'Lord Trevithick.' Her voice shook. She could not help it. She took a deep breath and ploughed on. 'Lord Trevithick, I intend to travel down to Devon immediately. Fairhaven Island is mine and I am going to claim it.'

She watched with misgiving as Marcus straightened up and gleam of amusement came back into his eyes. He sketched an ironic bow. 'Very well, my lady. You are going to Fairhaven. I am going to Fairhaven. We shall see which of us manages to claim the island first!'

And before Beth could say another word, he was gone.

Charlotte was very good. She did not ask why Beth had ink stains on her blue muslin dress, nor why her hair, so prettily arranged *à la Greque* earlier in the day now looked as though it had been dragged through a hedge, nor even why her cousin chose to lock herself in her room for several hours, emerging pale and wan for dinner. She patted Beth's hand, told her that if she wished to discuss anything she was always happy to talk, and tactfully went off to the kitchen to confer with the cook about menus.

Kit joined them for dinner and seemed inclined to quiz Beth over her pallor and lack of appetite, but a well-aimed kick from his sister soon put paid to his questions. He was more voluble about the use to which the fine dessert wine had been put in removing the ink stains from a certain blue muslin dress, but when Beth pointed out that it was her wine cellar he did not pursue it. Beth herself felt inclined to take the rest of the bottle and drink it straight down, but her natural good sense suggested that she would soon feel the worse for it. Besides, she found dessert wine too sweet and reflected wryly that if she wished to become intoxicated for the first time in her life, she should find a more enjoyable way of doing so.

Beth felt miserable and as weary as though she had been awake for a week, but most of all she felt furious at the injustice of Marcus's behaviour. To make wild accusations and not even do her the courtesy of explaining them properly; to give Fairhaven to her only to try to take it away again; to behave in a less than gentlemanly fashion—but here she blushed hotly even in her thoughts and hastily turned her mind to something else.

After dinner, Beth sought Charlotte out in the red drawing room where her cousin was sitting placidly embroidering at her tambour frame. Charlotte was working on a piece of white muslin, sewing the hem with exquisite neatness, and Beth smiled a little as she remembered her own hopeless efforts at needlework. She plumped herself down next to her cousin, curling up and hugging one of the red velvet cushions.

'Charlotte, I have been thinking,' she began. 'I intend to leave London tomorrow and go home to Devon. I know that Kit has business to finish here, but I have no more taste for parties and balls, and it would be better to be home in good time for Christmas.'

She saw her cousin's penetrating blue gaze resting on her and blushed slightly. 'Well, there is no reason to stay…'

'I know that you are doing this to avoid Lord Trevithick,' Charlotte said calmly, cutting her thread. 'I do not really understand the nature of your quarrel, Beth, for Justin Trevithick had too much delicacy to speak to me of it, but if you wish to run away from your troubles that is your affair!' She fixed her cousin with a severe regard. 'However, running away does not generally solve anything!'

Beth hugged her cushion harder. 'No, I know you are right! But I do not believe I can resolve my dispute with Lord Trevithick, for he is utterly indifferent to my explanations! Indeed, he scarcely gave me the chance to offer any! Oh!' All her pent-up frustration came out on the word. 'He is the most arrogant and tiresome man imaginable!'

'Strange, when his cousin is so courteous,' Charlotte

observed, with a little smile. 'Mr Trevithick is all that one could wish for in a gentleman of quality!'

Something about her tone of voice struck Beth, despite her preoccupation. She gave her cousin a penetrating stare.

'Charlotte, are you developing a *tendre* for Mr Trevithick?'

Charlotte blushed. 'Certainly not!' she said with dignity. She bent her head over her tambour frame. 'Besides, we are speaking of your concerns, Beth, not mine!'

Beth had not missed the colour that stained her cousin's cheeks. She smiled. 'I would far rather talk of the impression that the *gallant* Mr Trevithick made upon you than the shortcomings of his kinsman, the Earl!'

'Humph!' Charlotte seemed put out of countenance for the first time. 'I know you are only seeking to distract me, Beth! Mr Trevithick was very charming, but I doubt that I shall see him again. Now…' she recovered herself '…you mentioned returning home to Devon, but did you intend to go to Mostyn Hall—or to Fairhaven Island?'

Beth narrowed her eyes. Her cousin's powers of perception were disturbing at times. 'Well, I confess I had thought to visit Fairhaven first… That is, the Earl granted the island to me, so it is mine now! And though he now wishes to rescind his gift, I do not see that I should make it easy for him…'

Charlotte selected another thread from the sewing box open on the seat beside her. 'I see. So what do you intend to do? Take Fairhaven by storm and defend it against him? Really, Beth! This is the nineteenth century! You are not in the Civil Wars now, you know!'

Beth got up and walked over to the window. She was not going to admit it, but there was something powerfully tempting about Charlotte's suggestion. Things must have been so much easier when one could round up an army of retainers and take the fight to the enemy. Perhaps she had been born in the wrong century but, army or not, she was determined to claim her island.

'It would not be like that, Lottie,' she said, with more confidence than she felt. 'I'll warrant that there is no tenant on Fairhaven—who would want to live in such an out-of-the-way place? And doubtless the villagers will be pleased to have someone take an interest at last…'

Feeling restless, she pulled back the red velvet curtain and looked out. It was dark in the street outside and the lamplighter and his assistant were making their rounds. The lamplighter had rested his ladder against the stand and passed the oil container down to his assistant for refilling. The boy was pouring oil slowly from the jug, his tongue sticking out of the corner of his mouth with the effort of concentration. Beth smiled a little.

'Anyway, I still have the deed of gift to Fairhaven,' she said slowly, 'signed by the Earl himself. It is a legal document and he would find it difficult to explain it away in a court of law—'

Charlotte looked horrified. 'You would not take this matter to the courts! Think of the cost! Think of the scandal, and all for what? Beth, surely you cannot mean it?'

Beth turned back to the candlelit room. 'No, Lottie. I would not go so far, but I do intend to claim Fairhaven.' She pressed her hands together. 'It is just that Trevithick's behaviour has been so *unfair* and I have the greatest dislike of being bested!'

'I had observed it,' Charlotte said, very drily. 'Oh, Beth, can you not just let it go? If you truly do not believe you can come to terms with the Earl of Trevithick, then concede gracefully and let us go home to Mostyn!'

There was a silence. The fire crackled and spat. 'Does that mean that if I were to go to Fairhaven you would not come with me?' Beth asked, after a moment. 'I know you disapprove, Lottie…'

Their eyes met. Charlotte looked pained. 'Oh, Beth! Yes, I do disapprove! Most heartily! *Why* must you go?'

Beth looked unhappy. 'Because it is a point of principle. Because I cannot let him win!'

'Those are not good reasons!' Charlotte almost wailed. 'Of course Trevithick will win! He is the Earl and he holds the island and he has all the advantage! You are tilting against windmills!'

Beth's mouth set in a mutinous line. 'Perhaps so. But I have to try!'

Charlotte screwed her face up. 'Why? Such stubbornness is so unbecoming!'

Beth laughed. 'Stubbornness, impetuosity… Oh, Lottie, you have been trying to improve me this age! I do not know why you bother, for I shall never become more ladylike!' Her smile faded. 'But if you do not wish to come with me I shall understand. There is no reason for you to have to compromise your propriety just because I am a hoyden!'

Charlotte pushed the tambour frame away and got to her feet. 'What, am I to let you go jauntering about the countryside alone and in even more of a hoydenish manner? I shall go and start my packing!'

Beth rushed across the room and gave her an impetuous hug. 'Oh, thank you!'

Charlotte hugged her back. 'Do not thank me for being as foolish as you! Why, it will take us at least six days to get there at this time of year—'

'Oh, no, only three! And the weather is not so bad at present!'

'And the inns will be dreadful and the sea will be rough and like as not we will end locked in a dungeon! Oh, Beth…'

'There will be no difficulties,' Beth said, with far more confidence than she was feeling. She did not think that this was the moment to tell Charlotte that the Earl of Trevithick had indicated that he too would be travelling to Fairhaven, so that another confrontation was inevitable. 'I have it all planned! I will ask Gough to formally register the transfer of the island from the Earl of Trevithick to myself, so there will be no questions about the legality of the situation! Gough will take care of everything!'

Charlotte looked unconvinced. 'It seems to me that there is every doubt! However, if Gough will deal with it, I suppose we may be comfortable on that score!' She brightened a little. 'Now, if we were to wait until your legal title to the estate was established…'

Beth shook her head. She knew that Charlotte was right; it was the most sensible course of action and by far the safest. She also knew that the Earl of Trevithick was eminently capable of opposing her at every turn and that the ensuing struggle might last for months. And possession was nine-tenths of the law…

'It would never serve, Lottie. I could be waiting for ever!'

Charlotte sighed, apparently accepting the inevitable. 'Very well! I suppose I shall have a few days on the road to try to change your mind!'

Beth smiled. 'I have it all planned out! Kit can keep

the house open here for as long as he has business in town and meanwhile I will send to Mostyn Hall for some of the servants to join us on Fairhaven! We shall go across and tell the islanders that the property has changed hands—it will be exactly as though I had purchased the estate!'

'Not precisely,' Charlotte said drily. She looked at Beth with deep misgiving. 'A disputed deed of gift is hardly the same as an acknowledged sale! However, I can see that there is no reasoning with you! This whole plan will go horribly awry! Mark my words!'

On the first night of their journey the inn, the Castle and Ball in Marlborough, was of good enough quality to meet even Charlotte's specifications. They had a neat private parlour, well away from the public tap, and a bedroom on the quiet side of the inn so that they would not be disturbed by the comings and goings in either the main street or the coach yard.

Charlotte had wanted to put up for the night at Newbury and had argued that there was no necessity to push on to Marlborough, but Beth had been adamant that they needed to cover as much distance as possible. Their departure had already been delayed by two days, for it had taken far longer than she had expected to make all the arrangements for their journey. Firstly she had had to discuss her plans with Gough, who had raised any number of legal queries about the deed of gift. Then she had had to send a messenger to Mostyn Hall to ask the estate manager to arrange for a group of servants to be ready to join them on Fairhaven once she gave the word. She could imagine the raised eyebrows that letter would cause when it was received. Finally she had to attend to her own packing and all the preparations for the journey, which all took twice as long as she had expected. Then, when they were about to depart, Kit had expressed his severe disapproval of the plan and all but threatened to forbid them to go. The quarrel that ensued had ended with him telling Beth that she was headstrong to the point of madness and with Charlotte telling both of them that they were as bad as each other. It had not been a good start to the venture.

Beth sighed. Downstairs in the inn parlour, a clock chimed seven. They had set off at eight o'clock that morning and had been travelling for almost nine and a half hours, with barely time to snatch a drink or something to eat when they stopped to change the horses. Charlotte had frowned at Beth's urgency and both of the girls had become increasingly tired and irritable as the day had worn on. However, when they had arrived at Marlborough, a pitcher of hot water, a change of clothes and the promise of a good meal had made them both feel much better, and Beth was looking forward to a peaceful night's sleep.

Charlotte stuck her head around the bedroom door. 'Are you ready to come down to eat, Beth? Our supper is on the table.'

The most delicious smell of roasting lamb filled the corridor and Beth's stomach gave an enormous rumble. She went gratefully into the little parlour and allowed the bowing landlord to escort her to her seat. The table was already laden with covered dishes, the candles were lit and the room had an altogether welcoming feel to it. Beth was glad to see that Charlotte seemed much happier now that they were settled and that the accommodation was everything that she could have desired.

Neither of them spoke for about ten minutes, for they were far too busy applying themselves to the food and drink. Eventually Charlotte accepted a second glass of wine and a second portion of lamb, and smiled across the table at her cousin.

'Thank goodness! I feel so much better! And this place is a most superior establishment! I was afraid that they would not treat us so well, travelling alone and without any gentlemen to bespeak rooms for us!'

Beth shifted a little on her chair. Like her cousin, she was aware that their arrival had caused some curiosity, travelling as they were with only a couple of servants and without an escort. She knew that it made Charlotte feel vulnerable and whilst she did not believe that they were in any danger, it was certainly more comfortable to have Kit's company when travelling. He had always been the one to bespeak rooms, arrange meals and deal with payment. Beth was in no way a retiring female, but she had not travelled a great deal and so had little experience to draw on. Fortunately the inns at which they planned to stay were all reputable ones and there was no doubt that her title and evident wealth were most useful in smoothing their way. She did not anticipate any trouble.

The dishes were removed and a fine apple pie brought in. Beth considered another glass of wine and regretfully decided that it would make her fall asleep at the table. Charlotte yawned prettily.

'May we travel a little less precipitately tomorrow, please, Beth?' she pleaded. 'I am shaken to pieces from the journey, for all that the coach is so comfortable! Surely we could stop at Trowbridge or Frome? There is no need for us to hurry in this madcap way!'

Beth toyed with a spoonful of pie. She had still not told Charlotte that the Earl of Trevithick had threatened to journey down to Fairhaven himself and that it was her main aim to reach the island before him. When they had left London that morning she had been reassured to know that Trevithick was still in the capital—Kit had seen him at a ball only the night before. Beth had begun to wonder if, in fact, the Earl did not intend to go to Fairhaven at all. He had never evinced any interest in the island for its own sake, and his only aim had been prevent her from claiming it. It was a matter of pride to him as well as to her. But perhaps, Beth thought, it was not important enough to him to come chasing after her. Only time would tell.

She reached for the cream jug and poured a little on to her remaining piece of pie.

'I had hoped to reach Bridgwater tomorrow night—'

'Bridgwater!' Charlotte seldom interrupted for her manners were too good. This time, however, she was staring at her cousin with incredulous eyes. 'Why, that must be all of eighty miles! Why on earth do we need to go so far in one day?'

Beth sighed. 'It is simply that I had hoped to reach Fairhaven as soon as possible.' She avoided her cousin's gaze. 'When we last met, the Earl of Trevithick indicated that he was intending—well, that he might be thinking of travelling to Fairhaven himself. So—'

'Trevithick going to Fairhaven himself?' Charlotte interrupted for a second time. She stopped eating and put her spoon down slowly. 'Why did you not tell me this before, Beth?'

Beth toyed with her food, still evading her cousin's eye. 'I thought you would only worry if you thought we were engaged in some sort of race. Matters were bad enough as they were...'

'Yes, but if Trevithick is going to be at Fairhaven that will not be so bad at all!'

Beth looked suspiciously at her cousin. For a moment she wondered if Charlotte had had too much wine, but although her cheeks were becomingly pink and her eyes bright, she did not appear inebriated.

'Whatever can you mean, Lottie? How could it possibly be a good thing for us both to be there together? We would come to blows within minutes!'

'Well…' Charlotte started to eat again. 'It will not be so much like an invasion this way, more a house visit—'

'House visit!' Beth stared. 'Good gracious, what can you mean? It will make things twice as bad!'

'Oh, surely not! For we may all sit down together and discuss the matter calmly!'

Beth stared all the more, wondering which of them was mad. 'Lottie, you saw what the Earl was like when he came to the house in London! How can you imagine that we would be able to discuss anything calmly?'

Charlotte frowned. 'Well, I realise that the Earl was suffering under some strong emotion then, but surely he is perfectly reasonable under normal circumstances!'

Beth grimaced. She could not imagine how their situation could be interpreted as normal and was afraid that Charlotte was clutching at straws. Should the Earl of Trevithick appear and throw a rub in their way, it would prove decidedly awkward. Beth's fervent hope by now was that the Earl would not care enough for Fairhaven to put himself to the trouble of going all the way to Devon in winter. The little Season was in full flow and Christmas was approaching and surely he had better things to do with his time than pursue a wild goose chase?

Before she could put this view to Charlotte, however, there was a rumble of wheels in the courtyard outside and the flare of carriage lamps in the darkness.

'Ostler!' a deep masculine voice shouted. 'Look lively there!'

Beth got up from the table and hurried over to peer through the diamond-paned windows. A curricle was standing in the yard outside, a superb vehicle in dark blue or green livery, with four elegant horses of a quality to match. As she watched, the driver handed his reins to his passenger and swung down from the seat. Beth's stomach suddenly felt hollow for all the excellent meal she had just eaten.

She turned back to Charlotte who had also started to look apprehensive.

'You may judge for yourself how reasonable the Earl of Trevithick is, Charlotte,' she said slowly, 'for I do believe that he is here now!'

In an excess of propriety, Charlotte had whisked her cousin away from the window, drawn the curtains tightly and ordered the servants to remove the dishes and to serve tea. She and Beth now sat in the wing chairs on each side of the fire, clutching a cup in their hands and looking at each other with ill-concealed nervousness. Both of them knew that good manners demanded that they make themselves known to the new arrivals. Neither of them had moved to do so.

The whole inn seemed to have come alive with the gentlemen's arrival. Beth could hear Marcus out in the yard, chatting with the grooms and ostlers and accepting many complimentary comments on the quality of his horses. Lights flared, doors banged and Beth reflected uncharitably that it was typical of the Earl to make as much fuss as possible wherever he went. She sipped her tea, wondering how on earth Marcus could have reached Marlborough that night and with his own horses. Then she told herself that she did not want to know. She did not want to speak with him and preferably she did not want him to know that she was even there. Her appetite for a confrontation seemed to have vanished completely.

Beth heard Justin Trevithick's voice in the corridor outside, bespeaking supper for two and rooms for the night. Charlotte heard it too; Beth saw a hint of colour come into her cousin's face as Charlotte busied herself pouring fresh tea. Then Beth heard the door of the taproom open and a gust of laughter flow out, and for a moment she thought that they were safe and that the gentlemen had chosen to take a drink in the bar. She was swiftly disabused.

'The ostler tells me that there are some other travellers staying tonight, landlord.' Beth heard Marcus's voice sound from further down the corridor. She realised that the maid had left the parlour door slightly ajar when she had removed the dishes. She crept towards it and put her ear to the crack.

'Yes, my lord.' The landlord spoke above the hubbub coming from the taproom. 'There are two ladies staying with us.'

'Beth!' Charlotte whispered urgently from behind her. 'What are you doing?'

'Hush!' Beth put her finger to her lips. 'I am trying to eavesdrop—'

'Real ladies or the other sort?' Beth heard the amusement in Marcus's voice. Evidently the landlord did as well, for this time his tone was scandalised.

'Beg pardon, my lord, but I don't run that sort of a house! And these are very definitely real ladies!'

'My apologies.' Marcus had erased the amusement from his tone. There was a rustle of something and a mutter of thanks from the landlord.

'It is just that some friends of ours are on the road and we are trying to catch up with them,' Marcus continued. 'We traced them through the toll houses and the posting inns and wondered if they had already arrived here…' The rustle sounded again. 'Two ladies, young… attractive… The younger is very striking, with black hair and silver-grey eyes…'

Beth felt herself warming and pretended that she was hot with indignation that Marcus should be speaking so freely of her. She had a small suspicion, however, that it was his compliments that made her face glow. She was not totally immune to his admiration. And the landlord had evidently recognised her from the description. She heard him clear his throat and speak obsequiously.

'Yes, sir. I do believe you are describing our guests… A most beautiful young lady, sir. Most striking.'

Beth drew in her breath silently. She had not suggested to the staff in any of the inns that her journey was secret, so they had no reason not to give out information, particularly if Marcus smoothed the process with the kind of tip that she could imagine had just changed hands. The landlord was still talking, evidently anxious to please his open-handed visitor.

'The ladies have the private parlour, sir, so you will find them there. I dare say they may be retiring soon though, as they've already partaken of supper and have been travelling all day—'

'Of course they have,' Marcus murmured. Beth could tell he was coming closer. 'But I am sure that once they know we are here, the ladies may be persuaded to share their parlour with us…'

Beth shot away from the door like a scalded cat. Charlotte was watching her with a frown between the eyes. 'What is it, Beth?' she hissed.

Beth closed her eyes and opened them again sharply.
'Oh, Lottie, I think we should have retired when we had
the chance—'

There was a step right outside the door, then Justin's
voice came even closer at hand. 'Marcus, can you come
out to the stable for a moment? Stephens tells me that
there is a problem with one of the horses—'

A cold draught swirled through the parlour as the door
to the courtyard opened and closed again. The gentlemen's footsteps could be heard outside on the cobbles.
Without a pause for thought, Beth grabbed Charlotte's
hand, pulled her from her chair and bundled her out of
the room and up the stairs. Charlotte, out of breath and
protesting, sank down on to the big four-poster bed as
Beth closed the bedroom door behind them and leant
against it, breathing hard.

'Beth! What on earth was all that about? Why could
you not just greet Lord Trevithick in a civilised manner?'

Beth was not sure of the answer to that. All she knew
was that she felt unequal to the task of confronting
Marcus that evening and that any such meeting would
have to wait until the morning when she would be
stronger and better prepared. She did not have the first
idea of what she would say to him or how the conflict
between them might be resolved. What she *did* know,
however, was that she was certainly not going to agree
to go tamely home just because Marcus had caught up
with them already.

There was a knock at the door and Beth's heart
jumped into her throat. The cousins looked at each other.

'Well, go on,' Charlotte said, a little impatiently. 'Pray
answer! I cannot believe that even Lord Trevithick
would beard a lady in her bedroom!'

Beth privately thought that that was exactly what Trevithick would do, but she went over to the door and peeped round. To her relief there was only the maid on the landing outside. The girl dropped a slight curtsy. She was carrying a tray with two beakers of steaming liquid, and now brought them into the room and placed them on the table by the window.

'His lordship's compliments, ma'am, and he wondered if you would both care to take a nightcap that is sovereign against the aches and pains of the road.'

Beth stared suspiciously into the cup. The smell was delicious, a mix of mulled wine and spices. Charlotte came across and stood looking over her shoulder.

'Oh, how thoughtful! Pray thank Lord Trevithick for his consideration!'

The maid dropped another curtsey and went out, and Charlotte, smiling, picked up one of the cups and took a sip. She gave a sigh.

'Oh, that is truly delicious! Beth, you must try some!'

Beth took a careful taste. The liquid was warm and soothing, easing away all the aches of the journey just as the maid had promised. Suddenly it seemed churlish to be suspicious of Marcus's motives. Beth drained the cup to the dregs.

Charlotte was yawning widely. 'Goodness, I feel tired! I am for my bed.' She gave Beth a kiss. 'Do not forget to lock your door, Beth—and I am in the next room should anything untoward happen! I am sure we can resolve this situation with Lord Trevithick in the morning. Goodnight!'

Beth closed the door behind her and after a moment bolted it. She hesitated over calling the maid but felt too

weary to bother. She donned her nightdress in a somewhat haphazard fashion, and half-climbed, half-tumbled
into the big bed. She had barely blown out the candle
before she was asleep.

Chapter Five

Beth awoke feeling warm and comfortable. The room was full of sunlight and shifting shadow, and for a moment she was puzzled until she realised that she must have fallen asleep before she could draw the bed curtains. Certainly she remembered that she had felt extraordinarily weary the night before, which she supposed was no great surprise since she had been travelling for an entire day with little rest. Now, however, she felt miraculously restored and quite capable of dealing with the problem of seeing Marcus Trevithick again. She swung her legs over the side of the bed and hurried to ring the bell for some hot water.

It was whilst she was waiting for the maid to appear that she heard the clock downstairs in the parlour strike twelve. Beth paused in the act of brushing out her hair, then counted very carefully as the faint chimes of the church clock out in the square echoed the same twelve strokes. She put down her brush and flung open the bedroom curtains.

Her window looked out on to a small kitchen garden with rows of neat vegetables and a chicken scratching in the dust. The sun was bright and high, and Beth could feel its October warmth through the glass pane. High noon. There could be no doubt. She had slept for fifteen hours.

Beth frowned. She had been intending to breakfast no later than seven-thirty and be on the road by eight. If they were to reach Bridgwater that day... But there was no possible chance of reaching Bridgwater now, or even Glastonbury. They would be lucky to make thirty miles that day and meanwhile Marcus would be halfway to Devon. No doubt he was on his way already.

Beth's eye fell suspiciously on the cup that had held the mulled wine. She picked it up and sniffed the dregs. They smelled of nothing but the same delicious honey and spice scent that had tempted her the previous night. Sovereign against the aches and pains of the road, the maid had said, but perhaps they had been sovereign against more than that...

There was a knock at the door and the maid appeared, clutching a large pitcher of water.

'Good morning, milady! And a lovely day it is—'

'Is my cousin awake yet?' Beth asked urgently, dispensing with the greetings somewhat precipitately. 'It is far later than I had imagined and we had intended to be on the road hours ago!'

The maid, a large, untidy country girl, put her hands on her hips and surveyed Beth with a certain puzzlement.

'Lords lawks, ma'am, there's no need to go hurrying about the country on a lovely day like this!' Her accent was as rich and soothing as butter. 'Mrs Cavendish only woke a few moments ago—just like yourself, ma'am!— and ten to one you'll be needing some luncheon before you set out!'

Beth fidgeted with the curtain cord. Charlotte was a

notoriously slow riser and if she had only just woken it would be at least an hour until she was ready to go. It was with difficulty that Beth restrained herself from rushing into her cousin's room and exhorting her to hurry up, but she knew there was no point in harassing Charlotte, who would proceed at her own unflappable pace.

The maid shot her a curious look, then started to pour the water into the basin. 'His lordship sends his compliments, ma'am, and asks that you join him in the parlour—when you're ready, of course.'

Beth paused. 'His lordship? Lord Trevithick is still here?'

'Yes, ma'am.' The girl lowered the pitcher. 'Some problem with one of his horses, so I'm told. Still, there's no rush, is there, ma'am? I'll tell him that you'll be down shortly!'

Beth sighed. However polite Marcus's request, she suspected it hid a rather more emphatic order and there was little point in resisting.

She came down the stairs fifteen minutes later, her travelling dress neatly pressed and her hair demurely plaited. The door of the parlour was closed and there was no sound within, and after a moment Beth decided that she had no wish to beard Marcus in his lair just now, and went out into the sunshine.

There was a busy market in Marlborough High Street and Beth resolved to take a look at the stalls that lined either side of the wide cobbled road. She was in no hurry. Charlotte would not be ready for ages and as far as Beth was concerned, the longer she put off her meeting with Marcus, the better.

Plenty of cottagers had brought their vegetables to

market and turnips, onions and potatoes spilled out of baskets and across makeshift wooden trestles. Cheek by jowl with these were the vendors of bootlaces, nutmeg graters, cough drops, corn plasters and any number of necessities that Beth had never realised that she needed. She wandered along the row of stalls, pausing to chat with everyone and admire their produce and their children. A persuasive street trader almost convinced her that she would like to buy a small, mewling kitten—her heart was broken at the thought of it ending up in a drowning sack—but common sense suggested that it would not make a comfortable pet, particularly on a journey. It was whilst she was explaining to the trader that he must on no account sell the kitten to a bad home, that a gentleman paused beside them and Beth realised with a sinking heart that Marcus Trevithick had caught up with her at last. Her authoritative instructions wavered and faded away as she completely forgot what she had been talking about.

Marcus was watching her with an expression of amused indulgence in his eyes. He was bare-headed and in the bright sunlight his thick dark hair gleamed a glossy blue-black. He was immaculately dressed in buckskins and an elegant coat of blue superfine, and his Hessians had a mirror-polish that reflected the sun. As Beth watched, he handed the kitten's owner a coin and said gravely, 'Take the little creature to the Castle and Ball Inn. It can earn its keep catching mice in the stables.'

He offered Beth his arm. 'Good morning, Lady Allerton. Have you completed your purchases, or are there more desperate animals that you wish to rescue? I noticed a small piglet at the stall on the left—if you do not buy it, it will surely end in the pot...'

Beth took the proffered arm a little gingerly. 'Thank you, my lord. I am not in a position to establish a sanctuary for animals at the moment and I do not believe I require any more candles, or bootlaces—'

'Or corn plasters or tin trays!' Marcus finished for her. He smiled down at her. 'It is tempting though, is it not? I have purchased a box of cigars and a carved walking stick and have no clear idea of how I came to part with my money!'

They were walking away from the bustle of the market now and down the hill towards where the river curled its lazy way through the fields. The water sparkled in the sunlight. Beth wondered how long it would be before one or other of them came to the point. After all, they could scarcely pretend that this was a chance encounter. Yet Marcus did not speak, and when she risked a glance at his face she saw that he was watching her with thoughtful consideration.

She paused on the bridge and looked down at the ducks splashing in the shallows beneath.

'Oh how pretty it is here!' she said impulsively. 'I would almost like to stay...'

She looked up, caught Marcus's eye, and bit her lip. She had no wish to give too much away.

Marcus leant back against the stone parapet and smiled at her.

'Is your journey too urgent to let you linger here?' he asked. 'Tell me, Lady Allerton, are you making your way home to Mostyn Hall—or, as I suspect, to Fairhaven Island?'

Beth held his gaze. 'We are travelling to Fairhaven!' she said. She raised her chin. 'Now that I have the deeds to the island I consider it my own! I told you that I would not give in easily, my lord!'

Marcus straightened up. 'Truth to tell, I should be immensely disappointed if you did,' he said softly.

The breeze rippled along the river and raised an echo of a shiver along Beth's nerves. A few dead leaves swirled down onto the water and floated away. She found that she could not look away from Marcus's compelling gaze, could not break the contact between them. Then Marcus shifted slightly.

'However, there are difficulties in your way,' he said. 'Did you expect that I would just let you sail to Fairhaven and stake your claim? I warned you that I would be travelling there myself!'

'I thought to get there first,' Beth said defiantly. The cold autumn wind had whipped the colour up in her cheeks. 'And I was not sure that you cared sufficiently for Fairhaven to put up a fight, my lord!'

Marcus laughed. 'But I have to defend my property against invasion—'

'Oh, do not be so melodramatic!' Beth snapped. She turned away from him, frowning down at the eddying water. 'The truth is that you do not wish to be bested, my lord! You care nothing for the island, but you have some cock-and-bull notion in your head that I cheated you in some way and you do not wish me to win!'

Marcus drove his hands into the pockets of his coat. 'It is true that at first I thought you had lied to me, Lady Allerton—'

An angry sparkle lit Beth's eyes. 'You have such a way with words, my lord! Pray do not spare my feelings! You made your opinion of me quite plain before!'

'And the evidence against you is very strong...' Marcus's gaze was thoughtful on her. 'If it were not that my own instinct is to the contrary, I should say that you had to be guilty.'

Beth turned her back on him. 'I do not wish to discuss this with you, sir. There is no point in doing so! You did not do me the courtesy of presenting your apparent evidence to me before, so I do not feel I need to listen to you now!'

Marcus shrugged elegantly. 'That is only fair, I suppose! So, how do we resolve this conflict, Lady Allerton? You wish to claim Fairhaven. I wish to prevent you from doing so. We are here together. So…'

Beth pressed her lips together. It seemed a frustrating and faintly ridiculous situation in which to find herself. She could rush back to the inn and leap into her carriage, but she could not prevent Marcus from following her. Similarly he could hardly force her to go home to Mostyn. It seemed that they had reached deadlock.

'This problem would never have happened if you had not got here so quickly!' she burst out. 'You were in London only yesterday morning, and yet you were here in Marlborough by nightfall and with your own curricle and team! It is not possible—' She broke off and looked at Marcus stormily as he started to laugh.

'I fear that your information is faulty, my dear! I was *not* in London yesterday morning.'

Beth frowned. 'But Kit said that you had been at Lady Paget's ball the night before!'

'That's true. After the ball, Justin and I drove through the night to Bradbury Park, a place I have close by Reading. We rested the horses for a few hours before pressing on to here. We did not wish you to get too far ahead of us, you see!'

Beth stared at him, anger and indignation warring within her. 'But how did you know where to find us?'

Marcus took a step closer to her. 'We could not be sure, of course, but when we asked at the post houses they were able to tell us of two ladies, travelling alone, who were anxious to press on with their journey.' He shrugged. 'It might not have been the two of you, of course, but given that you had told me you would be travelling into Devon and I knew you would not wish to linger, it seemed likely.' He raised a hand and touched Beth's cheek. His voice grew softer. 'Besides, you are very memorable, you know, sweetheart. At least three of the landlords knew exactly whom I was describing when I spoke of the beautiful lady with ebony black hair and smoky silver eyes!'

Beth gazed at him, trapped equally by the warmth of his regard and the softly mesmerising tone of his voice. In all her life she had never ever considered herself to be beautiful and had certainly never imagined that anyone else would think so. She broke the contact with an effort and turned away, resting her clasped hands on the parapet of the bridge and feeling the chill of the cold stone through her gloves. She did not want this confusion of her senses. It undermined her resolve to oppose Marcus and made it so very difficult to be angry with him. It simply was not fair. She deliberately recalled his behaviour in London, his lack of trust and his unfair accusations, and then she felt able to harden her heart.

'I do not believe your compliments sincere, my lord!' she said coldly. 'Indeed, I have the gravest suspicion that you are not to be trusted at all! That mulled wine that you sent up to us last night—can it be a coincidence that both Charlotte and I slept the clock round?'

Marcus was laughing again. 'I can only assume that you slept so well because you were tired, Lady Allerton, and no wonder if you will dash about the countryside at such speed!'

Beth smiled sweetly in return. 'And what a fortunate

thing for you, my lord, when one of your own horses had gone lame and needed a rest! On your own admission you would not have wanted us to get too far ahead of you!'

'Indeed,' Marcus agreed affably, 'for how could we escort you if that were the case?'

Beth stared at him. The breeze was ruffling his silky dark hair and there was the beginning of a smile curling the corners of his mouth. She frowned a little. 'Escort us? What new nonsense is this?'

'It is an idea I have just had.' Marcus's smile grew. 'Would you not be far more comfortable on your journey with Justin and myself to smooth out any difficulties?'

Beth raised her eyebrows. In some ways the answer was a definite yes, but in others there was no doubt that Marcus's company was the last thing she sought, the most unsettling thing imaginable. Besides, it was simply not possible when they were adversaries.

'Well, it is most kind of your lordship to offer us escort, but—'

Marcus's hand covered hers on the stone parapet. 'Please don't refuse me, my lady. It would be my pleasure.'

Beth looked up at him and away quickly. The conventional words were given a completely new meaning by the sensual intensity in his eyes. She tried to slide her hand from beneath his.

'It would not be appropriate, my lord. How could you escort us? After all, we are in competition to reach Fairhaven first and can hardly travel together!'

'Need we be rivals?' Marcus queried softly. His fingers tightened over hers. 'I am sure we can find another solution…'

Beth held her breath. 'Such as?'

'Well…' Marcus looked thoughtful. 'With autumn so far advanced you might reconsider a sea voyage. Then we could escort you home to Mostyn for Christmas—'

Beth wrenched her hand from his. 'Oh, I understand your motives very well, my lord! You wish to persuade me to give up my quest! Well, I have already told you I shall not! Nor have I forgotten the slighting way you spoke to me when last we met! You are the last person whose escort I should accept on any journey, I assure you!'

She whisked past him and took the path up the hill towards the High Street, trying to hurry without the indignity of slipping on the cobbles. She was all too aware of Marcus's step close behind, his hand steadying her when she nearly lost her footing on some damp leaves, as she had known she would. By the time she reached the road, her cheeks were flushed with exertion and she felt hot, bothered and cross. Marcus, in contrast, was sauntering beside her, looking cool and infuriatingly amused.

Beth stalked across the road, narrowly missed being crushed by a cart that was clattering between the market stalls, and shot in at the door of the Castle and Ball with the intention of sweeping Charlotte up and driving off immediately. As she paused briefly in the corridor, she heard Charlotte's voice and pushed open the door of the private parlour.

Charlotte and Justin Trevithick were seated at the table partaking of luncheon. There were two other places set and an array of cold meats, cakes and fruit on dishes before them. As Beth burst through the door, Charlotte looked up and smiled at her. She looked pink and pretty and turned her glowing face to her cousin.

'Beth! And Lord Trevithick! Pray join us for some

luncheon!' She drew out the chair beside her and smiled at Beth. 'The most excellent news, Beth! Mr Trevithick and his cousin are to escort us for the rest of the journey! What do you think of that?'

'This is ridiculous!' Beth grumbled, leaning back against the carriage's comfortable green velvet cushions and glaring out of the window at the passing scenery. 'How can we possibly be involved in a race to claim Fairhaven Island if we are accepting the escort of the very gentlemen we wish to outrun? Really, Charlotte! I never heard anything so foolish!'

Charlotte surveyed her placidly. She suddenly seemed much happier and Beth sighed inwardly with resignation. Charlotte did not have the temperament for risk or competition and now that she had the Earl and, more importantly, Justin Trevithick, to take care of all arrangements, she was much more comfortable.

'I do not see why we needed to become involved in a silly race in the first place,' Charlotte said comfortably. 'Everything will be so much better now!'

Beth wriggled crossly. 'Certainly it will, for unless we can shake off the Earl we shall not be going to Fairhaven at all and shall end by going quietly home!' She looked out of the window, saw Marcus pull alongside on a raking black hunter, and hastily looked away. She wished that she had selected a book to pass the time, but it was such a lovely day that she had wanted to look out at the view. Unfortunately, the view seemed to consist of Marcus most of the time.

Justin Trevithick had taken the reins of the curricle for the time being and Marcus had chosen to ride. It was impossible for Beth not to observe that he had a magnificent seat on the horse and that he rode with an authority and elegance that was instinctive. She turned her gaze away from him and concentrated rather fiercely on the pretty Wiltshire scenery. Even though most of the trees had lost their leaves by now, it was still an attractive scene. It was a fresh day with a pale blue sky and the countryside shone in the weak warmth of the sun. It had not rained for several weeks, so the road was dry and the going good. The cows grazed in the fields and they rolled through several villages where the children played at the cottage gates. Charlotte dozed on the seat opposite. Beth reflected that she was the only one who seemed to be sitting underneath a private rain cloud.

They passed another tollbooth and drew up at the next inn to change the horses. Marcus appeared at the carriage door.

'Lady Allerton, it is such a fine day that I wondered if you would care to drive with me? I am leaving the hunter here—it belongs to the Castle and Ball anyway, and Justin is happy to take a turn in the carriage. What do you say?'

'Oh, do let Lord Trevithick take you up, Beth!' Charlotte said, before Beth could decline. 'You know you would prefer to be out in the fresh air and you are well wrapped up.'

This was true, but Beth could not help wondering how much Charlotte's eagerness owed to the prospect of spending some time with Justin. Marcus was holding out a hand to help her descend from the carriage and appeared to have taken her acquiescence for granted. Beth could not be bothered to argue, at least not for the time being.

They had some steaming hot coffee to warm them, but Charlotte declined a hot brick for her feet, saying that the day was mild enough for it not to be required.

Nevertheless, when Marcus handed Beth up into the curricle, he was solicitous for her comfort, wrapping a blanket around her and ensuring that she had scarf, gloves and hat to keep her warm. Soon after they set off Beth realised that there was a great difference from travelling in the carriage; the speed was exhilarating, but it did generate a breeze, and because there was no shelter in the curricle it was considerably colder.

They had gone several miles when Marcus broke the silence and turned to her with a smile. 'I hope you are enjoying the journey, Lady Allerton! If you are too cold you need only to say, and I shall hand you up into the carriage again.'

Beth turned her glowing face to his. 'Oh, no, indeed, this is most enjoyable!' She looked around. 'Everything is so much more immediate, somehow, when one is in the open air! And Wiltshire is such a very pretty county...'

'It is,' Marcus agreed gravely. 'Do you know this area at all, Lady Allerton?'

'Oh, no, for I have travelled little and then only on the way to London and back.' Beth looked with lively interest at some curiously shaped little hills that lay close to the road.

'Only look! What odd-shaped mounds! I believe that these must be the mysterious barrows and hills that I have read about! They date from...oh, thousands of years ago! Is that not intriguing!'

Marcus laughed. 'It seems that history must be your subject, Lady Allerton! Was it an interest that you shared with your late husband?'

Beth turned her face away. For some reason she felt vulnerable when she spoke to Marcus about her marriage to Frank Allerton. It was as though no matter how little she said, Marcus could always see what lay beneath her superficial answers. Not that she had anything to hide, she told herself sharply. Her marriage had been no worse and no better than many others, May and December perhaps, but developing into mutual respect, if not love.

'Oh, Frank had little interest in the arts,' she said lightly, 'whilst I had no aptitude for mathematics or the sciences!'

'Complementary interests can be stimulating, however,' Marcus observed. 'There is much to talk about.'

'I suppose there could be.' Beth knew she sounded uncertain and for some reason honesty prompted her to add, 'Frank was too wrapped up in his studies to have much time to discuss matters with me.'

'Did you not find that disappointing?' Marcus enquired. Although Beth was not looking at him, she sensed that he was watching her rather than the road.

'Not particularly. A lady does not expect...' She glanced at him and her voice trailed away at the look in his eyes, for she was sure that she could see pity there.

'Surely it is reasonable—desirable—to hope for a certain sharing of interests? Life would be damnably lonely otherwise.'

Beth felt a strange pang inside her. She *had* been lonely at Allerton during the long weeks when Frank was absent, and even when he had been at home they had shared nothing more than an undemanding companionship. Marcus's words had given her a sudden glimpse of a different world, an existence where ideas were discussed and shared, giving mutual enjoyment. It was the sort of relationship that Charlotte had once described, something far beyond Beth's experience. Suddenly she felt as lonely as she had ever done at Allerton and she tried to cover it with a light laugh.

'Your ideas are somewhat unconventional, my lord! I can think of any number of married ladies and gentlemen who would be appalled by your suggestion that they speak to each other!'

Marcus smiled. 'Perhaps I ask a lot of the lady I would marry... An elegant and informed mind as well as gentleness, wit and charm! Am I then unlikely to find such a paragon?'

'Impossible!' Beth looked away. Marcus's references to his future wife made her feel peculiarly out of sorts.

'And since Sir Francis's death have you not felt inclined to remarry, Lady Allerton?' Marcus persisted. 'Doubtless you must have met plenty of gentlemen eager to persuade you?'

Beth shrugged, trying to hide her discomfort. 'Oh, I have no inclination to wed! I have my home and my cousins and plenty to interest me! What else could I want?'

It was a rhetorical question, but Beth wished she had not asked it when Marcus answered quite seriously.

'Companionship? Love?' His voice dropped. 'Passion?'

Beth shifted a little. 'Oh, love and passion are the most ephemeral and unreliable of things!' she said, with what she hoped was a worldly-wise air. 'I do not look for happiness there! Besides, I believe my nature must be cold—'

She saw Marcus raise his eyebrows in disbelief and almost immediately regretted her words. The memory of the kisses that they had shared seemed burnt on her mind. She looked about quickly for a distraction.

'What town is this that we approach, my lord? Can we be in Trowbridge already?'

They chatted easily until they reached the next stop,

when Marcus insisted that, as darkness was falling, Beth should resume her place in the carriage to avoid becoming cold. She did not demur, changed places with Justin, and an hour later they arrived at the King's Arms in Shepton Mallet.

The King's Arms was much smaller than the inn in Marlborough, but it was a handsome building, clean and well cared for. Beth saw Charlotte nodding her approval as Justin escorted her inside, but then Beth thought Charlotte was wont to approve everything at the moment. Beth herself found that her earlier good mood had vanished as they settled into their room. She had wanted to press on to Wells, but Marcus decreed that they had gone far enough; she wanted to set off bright and early the next day whilst Marcus had already observed cheerfully that there was no hurry to be away in the morning.

During dinner, the other three chatted whilst Beth sat quietly and mulled over the frustrations of the situation. She could see no way of shaking off Marcus and Justin and getting ahead of them again, but on the other hand it seemed nonsensical to accept their escort all the way to Fairhaven. Such a course of action could never result in her claiming the island, for she would be there as Marcus's guest and not as the new owner. That was assuming that they had not worn down her resistance in the meantime, of course—Beth was determined that not even the combined persuasion of the other three would persuade her to go tamely home to Mostyn Hall.

She had to admit that Marcus had outmanoeuvred her, but only for the time being. She would think of a plan to escape him, of that she was quite determined.

The idea came to her after dinner, whilst she and Charlotte were waiting for the gentlemen to rejoin them to partake of tea. Charlotte had been asking idly how it was that Marcus and Justin had caught up with them so quickly and Beth had explained that they had travelled through the night. And whilst she was speaking she had suddenly thought that if Marcus could do that, so too could she… All that was required was that Fowler, the coachman, should be ready—and should keep the secret.

Beth had considered asking Charlotte to come with her and had reluctantly rejected the idea. Her cousin was so much happier now that she had Justin Trevithick's escort and Beth knew that she would kick up such a fuss at the plan that it would not be worth mentioning. It was in no way desirable to plan to travel alone, without either escort or companion, but Beth argued to herself that she would be able to reach the coast the following day, take ship for Fairhaven, and that would be that. She would have Fowler to protect her and plenty of money to ease her passage, and Marcus would not find out until it was far too late. The plan was perfect.

Before retiring, she went out to stables to apprise her coachman of the new arrangements and the need for secrecy. Fowler had been in the Mostyn family for many years and was accustomed to receiving orders unquestioningly, but even he commented that it was a powerful bad idea to be travelling at night in winter, and it took a lot of persuasion on Beth's part to convince him. Eventually he went off to the tack room, muttering under his breath, and Beth crept back inside the inn intending to sit out the night until two of the clock.

Although it was not yet late, Beth could discern a certain change of atmosphere in the inn. The gentility that had been so apparent during the early evening had now vanished. Earlier the corridors had been cleanly swept and bright with lamplight. Now they were gloomy and full of smoke, the stale smell of beer hung in the air and the sound of loud voices and coarse laughter, both male and female, roared from the bar. Beth scuttled in from the courtyard and made for the stairs, taking care to keep in the shadows, for she was not sure where Marcus was now and she had a particular reason for not wishing to draw attention to herself.

She had only ascended three steps, however, before she saw the shadow at the turn of the stair and checked as a man came down towards her. Her heart sank. Naturally it had to be Marcus Trevithick. It really seemed that there was no escaping him.

Marcus and Justin had evidently settled down in privacy to enjoy their port, for Beth registered that Marcus had discarded his jacket and loosened his stock. The pristine whiteness of his shirt seemed only to emphasise the bronze of his face and the unreadable darkness of his eyes. Beth felt her heart start to race as a mixture of guilt and some other more disturbing emotion stirred within her. She swallowed hard. She considered trying to slip past Marcus without having to stop for tiresome explanations, but knew it was a vain hope. Sure enough, as they drew level, Marcus put out a hand to block her escape up the stairs.

Beth instinctively stepped back and felt the hard wood of the banister against her back. In the dim light she could see nothing of his expression but felt rather than saw the intensity with which his gaze rested on her flushed face. She wondered if he and Justin had been drinking copiously. Not ten minutes previously she had hoped that they would be so sunk in their cups that they would not notice or suspect her escape. Now it seemed that that was all too likely—and rather dangerous.

'A moment, Lady Allerton.' Marcus spoke silkily. 'I

have just been up to your room to check that you and
Mrs Cavendish had everything for your comfort and I
was concerned to find you absent. I cannot believe that
it is appropriate for you to be wandering the corridors
of an alehouse alone at this time of night! Whatever can
have prompted you to venture out like this?'

Beth raised her eyes to his face in a look that she
hoped was innocent. 'I was merely checking that all was
well with my servants and carriage for the onward journey, my lord,' she said.

There was a pause. Marcus was still looking at her
quizzically and Beth had the unnerving feeling that he
was not convinced.

'I see. Well, I shall be very happy to attend to such
matters myself and spare you the trouble.' Marcus
shifted slightly and Beth backed away as far as she
could. It had the reverse effect from the one she was
trying to achieve, for Marcus took hold of her arm and
drew her closer to him. 'Be careful that you do not fall
over the banisters, my lady. They are a little rickety.'

Beth pulled her arm away. 'I am perfectly safe, I thank
you, my lord.'

'I would dispute that,' Marcus said, giving her a smile.
His gaze appraised her with disconcerting thoroughness.
'I think I should see you to your room, Lady Allerton.
This inn is no place to be loitering alone. It has a somewhat…raffish…clientele in the evenings.' As if to un-
derline his words the taproom door opened and a couple
fell out into the corridor, laughing and amorously entwined. Beth looked away.

'There is no need to come with me,' she said a little
abruptly. 'I can find my own way! Goodnight, my lord!'

Marcus stepped back and she brushed past him and
hurried up the remaining steps. When she looked down,

he had reached the bottom of the stairs but he was still watching her and the mocking light was back in his eyes. He raised a hand.

'Goodnight, then, Lady Allerton! Sleep well!'

'And you, my lord!' Beth said politely.

Marcus's grin widened. 'Oh, Justin and I will no doubt sleep like tops once we have polished off our brandy!' He disappeared down the passage and Beth heard the parlour door close behind him.

She let out the breath she had been holding, and slumped against the banister, moving quickly away as it creaked protestingly under her weight. What to do now? She was certain that Marcus suspected something, but there was no chance that she would give up her scheme. It was tonight or not at all. Beth sped away up the stairs to pack her trunk and put her plan into action.

It was pitch black. Beth crept down the stairs, feeling for each tread and clutching the banister tightly so that she should not fall. Every creak of the steps sounded like a thunderclap and she was sure it was only a matter of moments before a door was thrown open above and she was discovered. Her trunk seemed very heavy and she could feel it nudging against her leg and threatening to push her down into the darkness beneath as she tried to steal silently down to the hall.

There was no sound in the passage but for the scratch of a mouse in the wainscot and the uneven tick of the parlour clock. Beth tiptoed to the door and drew back the bolt stealthily. She could see a faint light shining in the stables but there was no sound and the carriage was certainly not waiting in the yard for her. Perhaps Fowler had decided it would cause less of a stir to set off only when she was ready. Beth shivered. The moon was riding high amidst the stars and a cold breeze was swinging the weathervane on the stable roof. It was a frosty night.

Beth slipped out of the door and across the yard. The moonlight was very bright and it was easy to pick her way past the water trough and in at the darkened stable door. One torch still burned at the far end of the stables. A couple of the horses heard her approach and shifted in their stalls, bumping against the wall. There was the chink of harness. Beth paused, then went through the wide doorway into the coach house.

Here also a torch still burned, high on the wall. Her carriage was standing in the middle of the cobbled floor, exactly where it had been five hours previously when she had come to give Fowler his instructions. The door was open but of the coachman there was no sign and it was quite evident to Beth that she would be going nowhere other than back upstairs to bed. Fury and disappointment swept over her. It had been such a good opportunity to get ahead, with Marcus and his cousin no doubt dead to the world and unlikely to wake for hours. For a moment she toyed with the idea of harnessing the carriage horses herself and driving off, but she knew it would not serve. She had taken a gig out alone on more than one occasion but the idea of driving a coach and four was clearly unworkable. She almost stamped her foot in frustration.

Just as she was turning to leave the coach house Beth heard a sound emanating from inside the carriage itself. She froze, staring into its dark interior. There was no movement, but then the sound came again, a soft scraping that turned her blood cold. Someone was inside.

For a moment Beth wanted to turn tail and flee, but then she was seized by the conviction that the unfortunate Fowler must have fallen asleep about his work—

or, worse, was dead drunk and was even now sleeping off his excesses in her coach. She marched up to the carriage steps and peered inside the open door.

'Fowler! Wake up at once! How dare you sleep when I require you to be working—?'

Strong hands grabbed her and pulled her inside the coach before she even had the chance to finish her sentence. All the breath was knocked out of her so that she could not have screamed even had she wished. In a hair's breadth of time she found herself tumbled on the velvet seat, pinned under a hard masculine body. She struggled and the cruel grip tightened, forcing her back against the cushions until she could not move. It was too dark to see anything of her assailant and her hair was blinding her anyway as it came loose from its plait and fell about her face. She drew a ragged breath, intending to call out or at the very least make a small yelping noise, but she suddenly froze, overwhelmed by the message that her senses were passing to her. Her assailant was none other than Marcus Trevithick.

Beth could hear him breathing and could smell the faint aroma of smoke and brandy that overlaid the more elemental scent of his skin. As soon as this impinged on her she felt herself weaken hopelessly in a way that was both inappropriate and unhelpful to her current circumstances. She let her breath out on a shaky sigh.

'Lord Trevithick!'

Immediately the ruthless grip eased and Beth heard the sound of flint striking sharply. A flame flared, then settled to a warm glow. Beth sat up and looked around.

The interior of the carriage, which was not particularly large in the first place, looked even smaller and oddly intimate in the glow of the lantern. Marcus adjusted the wick, then sat back in the corner. He was watching her with a mixture of amusement and calculation.

'That was…interesting, Lady Allerton. How did you recognise me?'

Beth had no intention of telling him, just as she had no intention of allowing him to gain the advantage. She edged towards the doorway and his hand immediately shot out and took her by the wrist.

'Not just yet. I believe you have some explaining to do!'

'I!' Beth looked him straight in the eye. 'It is your actions that require explanation, Lord Trevithick! Lurking in darkened stables, attacking innocent women…'

'And all in the middle of the night!' Marcus finished laconically. 'You start, Lady Allerton! Or perhaps I can help you?' His voice took on a sardonic inflection. 'When we last met you had apparently been checking on the welfare of your coachman. Perhaps you are repeating the exercise? To my mind it shows an unconscionable consideration for one's servants to come out to visit them at two in the morning!'

Beth sighed angrily. 'That was not my intention, as well you know.'

Marcus shifted on the seat. He was still holding her wrist and Beth had the unnerving impression that he would not let go of her until she came up with an adequate explanation. It was likely to be a long wait.

'So your intention was—what, precisely?'

Beth flushed at his tone. She was conscious that her hair was tumbled about her face and that Marcus was looking at her in a speculative manner that just made her feel all the more self-conscious.

'By what right do you quiz me anyway, my lord?' she demanded. 'It is not your place to question my conduct!'

There was a loaded silence, then Marcus shrugged. 'I suppose not, Lady Allerton. And as a matter of fact I do know the reason for your appearance here. You had asked your coachman to be ready to depart in the early hours, no doubt wishing to gain a march over us!' He smiled politely. 'I am sorry that your plan has failed, but, you see, Justin and I felt that Fowler was deserving of several glasses of the best brandy as a reward for the work he had done today, and alas…' He shrugged. 'It has such a detrimental effect on one's ability to drive a coach in the dark!'

Beth's eyes narrowed furiously. 'I see that you are intent upon corrupting my servants, my lord, as well as laying violent hands upon my person!'

Marcus was still smiling with infuriating calm. 'It was in your best interests, Lady Allerton! Driving in the dark is not a good idea and I was anxious to save you from harm. I believe that there is a frost tonight and the going might have been slippery. As for laying hands on you, well—' his gaze swept comprehensively over her '—I confess that it is tempting…'

Beth tried to pull away from him. 'I did not mean now.'

'I am well aware of what you meant.' Marcus looked rueful. 'However, you have put the idea into my head…'

Beth tried to draw away. The thought of Marcus fulfilling his threat gave her a feeling of nervous excitement that she tried hard to quell. She summoned up her most severe tone.

'This is foolish, my lord! We are in a carriage in a stables in the middle of the night…'

'True,' Marcus said, sighing. 'By all means let us be sensible and go back inside the inn.' He let go of Beth's hand and she immediately felt both disappointed and cross with herself. Marcus picked up the lantern, jumped down from the carriage and held a hand out politely to help Beth descend.

'Take care, Lady Allerton. It is dark and the steps are steep.'

Beth was never sure whether she slipped first or if he tugged on her hand, but as soon as the words were out of his mouth, she lost her footing on the carriage steps and fell into his arms. This did not appear to cause Marcus any problems; he held her pressed close against him for a second, a second during which Beth became acutely aware of the strength of his arms and the hardness of his body against hers. Then he slowly let her slide down the length of him so that her feet were once more on the cobbles but the rest of her body was still in startling proximity to his. Beth tried to step back and regain her balance, but Marcus simply moved closer so that her back was against the side of the carriage and he had a hand against the panelling on either side of her.

'My lord!' Beth's voice came out as a squeak.

'Yes, my lady?' Marcus's voice was barely above a whisper. His lips grazed the skin just beneath her ear, sending shivers rippling all over her body. He raised one hand to brush her hair gently back from her face.

'You said you would not!' Beth tried to sound authoritative but knew she simply sounded dazed. 'You said you would not lay a finger on me—'

Marcus stepped back a little and spread his arms wide in an exaggerated gesture of surrender. 'I am not doing so.'

Beth frowned slightly. 'Then…'

Marcus bent his head and kissed her.

It was like putting a flame to tinder. Beth's lips parted instinctively as his mouth came down on hers, its first light and persuasive touch deepening swiftly into passion. She reached out to him and his arms closed about her, holding her tight and fast. Beth gasped at the sensation of sensual pleasure that swept through her and Marcus took immediate advantage, tasting her, teasing her, exploring her with a languorous expertise that left her weak with delight. A wave of heat washed over her that had nothing to do with shame and everything to do with a more primitive emotion.

Beth struggled against the compelling demand of the kiss, the invitation to lose herself in the intense web of desire that surrounded her. She had almost forgotten that they were in a stables in the middle of the night; almost, but not quite. She had no intention of allowing Marcus to seduce her in the hay, which she was sure he would do without any compunction at all. She freed herself and Marcus reluctantly let her go.

'What is it, sweetheart?'

Beth frowned. 'It is just that it is not right, my lord!' She cast him a fulminating look. 'We are meant to be at odds—we *are* at odds—over Fairhaven and it is simply not appropriate for you to—' She broke off hopelessly. In the torchlight she could see a faint smile curving Marcus's mouth and it quite made her forget what she was talking about.

'To kiss you?'

'Yes! To kiss me and to make me forget…things.'

'Things?'

Marcus stood back for her to precede him through the coach house door.

'Things such as the reason why I was angry with you in the first place—apart from the matter of Fairhaven, I mean.'

'Ah.' Marcus sounded pensive. 'I think we may put that behind us now.'

'Well, I do not! If I could remember what it was…' Beth tried to marshal her scattered thoughts, but they remained obstinately elusive. 'When I do remember—'

'Beth? What on earth is going on?'

It was Charlotte's plaintive voice, emanating from the back door of the inn. 'I woke up and found you missing—'

She broke off as the light from Marcus's lantern illuminated their little group. 'Oh! Lord Trevithick! Good gracious! Whatever is going on?'

'I am sure your cousin will explain all to you, Mrs Cavendish.' Marcus politely held the inn door open for them. 'May I encourage you both to return to your chamber? And do not worry about an early breakfast! There is no hurry to depart in the morning.' He turned to Beth. 'Goodnight—again—Lady Allerton!'

'Whatever happened?' Charlotte whispered urgently, once they were back in their chamber and the door closed behind them. 'Beth, you are chilled to the bone and trembling! What were you doing in the stables—and with Lord Trevithick? I can scarce believe it!'

Beth told the story as concisely and unemotionally as possible, pausing only to allow for Charlotte's unavoidable exclamations.

'Fowler was apparently in his cups,' Beth said bitterly, as she reached the end of her tale, 'as a result of Lord Trevithick's generosity! And Lord Trevithick was in the coach, waiting for me!'

Charlotte gasped and pressed a hand to her mouth. 'Oh, Beth! What happened?'

'Nothing!' Beth said, shortly and untruthfully. 'Damnation! It was such a good idea.'

'Well, I do not think so,' Charlotte declared, 'and I can only be grateful that it has not come off! Driving off in the middle of the night! Whatever next!' Her gaze softened. 'Oh, let us talk about this tomorrow, for we are both tired and upset!'

Within ten minutes she was asleep again, but Beth lay awake for much longer. In part she was preoccupied with the infuriating failure of her plan, for she could not see how she would get another opportunity to get away. Her predominant thoughts, however, were of Marcus and of the devastating effect that he appeared to have on her. It made it even more imperative that she should escape him, and soon. She could not trust him and she could not trust her own reactions. Beth stared into the darkness of the bed canopy. Her body ached with an echo of the need that Marcus had aroused in her, a need that was both new and powerfully demanding. With a suppressed groan, Beth turned on her side and curled up. She was not accustomed to lying awake and suffering the pangs of frustrated desire and at that moment it was an experience she would happily have done without.

Chapter Six

The weather changed later that morning. The skies were grey when they set off from Shepton Mallet and by the time they reached Glastonbury the rain was falling and a strong westerly wind was blowing.

'I do not envy the gentlemen,' Charlotte said, peering out of the carriage window through the squally rain. 'Their curricle will be full of water! If the weather becomes much worse, I believe the roads will become waterlogged and we shall have to stop at the next inn.'

Beth did not reply. She had only had a couple of hours' sleep and was convinced that Marcus had roused them to set off at a particularly early hour because he knew she would still be half-asleep. Despite telling them that there was no hurry to depart, he had been knocking on the door at seven-thirty.

Beth felt tired and cross-grained but she did not want to vent her bad temper on Charlotte, who did not deserve it. They had already had one difficult conversation that morning; Charlotte had been hurt and reproachful that Beth had even considered leaving her behind. Once they had patched up that quarrel, Charlotte had almost undone all the good work by trenchantly expressing the view that Beth's plan had been foolish, impulsive and utterly unworkable and Beth had had to bite her tongue hard to keep silent. It did not help that she knew there was a lot of truth in Charlotte's words. She knew she could be rash and impetuous, and that Charlotte considered her conduct unbecoming to a lady. She even accepted that she was thoroughly obsessed with Fairhaven and that that might also be considered inappropriate.

Beth wriggled crossly on the cushions. Today, for some reason, the carriage felt so much more uncomfortable. Her hours of insomnia the previous night had not led to any useful thoughts, either—she was still completely baffled as to how she might shake Marcus off and reach Fairhaven before him. Beth looked out at the pouring rain and sighed. Matters were not going at all to plan. The journey to Fairhaven, which had appeared so romantic and exciting to her only a few days earlier, had assumed a resemblance to a farce. Marcus held all the cards and she might as well give up now, which was no doubt what he intended her to do.

Then there was Marcus himself. She knew that the longer she was in his company, the greater her danger. She was as untried in love as a young debutante and no matter how fiercely she tried to defend herself against him, she was fighting her own feelings as well as him. She found him all too devastatingly attractive but, whilst she was certain he might try to seduce her, she had no confidence about reading his feelings. She stared glumly out at the rain. Perhaps Marcus even viewed her seduction as part of the challenge of the situation.

Just as she was thinking of him, the coach lurched to a halt and Marcus appeared at the window. His strong brown face was dusted with raindrops and his dark hair was plastered to his head. The rain was running in rivulets off his caped driving coat. Beth pushed the window down.

'Lady Allerton, Mrs Cavendish—the weather is far too inclement for us to continue. I have a friend living a short distance away in the village of Ashlyn. If you are agreeable, we shall call at the vicarage and beg shelter, at least until the storm stops.'

'Only fancy Lord Trevithick having a friend who is a clergyman!' Charlotte commented when the plan had been agreed and the carriage was in motion once again. 'He cannot be so dreadfully wicked if he keeps company with a man of the cloth!'

Beth laughed. 'Really, Charlotte! I sometimes think you are thrice as naïve as I, despite your greater years! There are plenty of clergymen far more wicked than Lord Trevithick will ever be!'

Charlotte looked affronted but did not argue. The coach had turned in at a neat entrance gate and was making its way up a drive to a substantial stone house, far grander than most of the vicarages Beth had known.

'I believe Lord Trevithick's friend keeps a certain style,' she commented, as they drew up outside the pedimented front door.

This impression was reinforced once they were inside the house. A neat housekeeper had gone to alert the Reverend March to their arrival and the visitors had time to admire the marbled hall, the sweeping stairway and the fine family pictures on the wall. Beth was just looking at a gold-framed portrait of a winsome child, when there was a step along the passage and a small gentleman hurried towards them, blinking myopically through thick reading glasses. His face broke into a smile of great sweetness as he saw Marcus, and he held out his hand.

'Marcus, my boy! How delightful to see you again!

And Justin!' The Reverend March swung round on Justin Trevithick and shook his hand with equal enthusiasm. 'Your dear mother will be so delighted to see you! I was taking tea with her only the other day and she said it was high time you were bringing home a wife—' The Reverend broke off and peered at Beth and Charlotte. 'Upon my word, how remiss of me! Forgive me, ladies, I scarcely saw you there! My tiresome eyesight, you know… How do you do?'

Marcus stepped forward, smiling slightly. 'Lady Allerton, this is the Reverend Theophilus March who, for his sins, was once my tutor! Sir, may I present Lady Allerton and her cousin, Mrs Cavendish? We are travelling to Devon and have been in some distress from the weather, so thought to throw ourselves on your mercy…'

'Of course, of course!' Theo March seized Beth's hand and shook it firmly. 'Allerton? Cavendish? No relation of Hugo Cavendish, I hope, ma'am?'

'A distant cousin of my late husband's, sir,' Charlotte confirmed, looking slightly bemused. 'I have never met him myself.'

'Another of my tutees, I fear!' The Reverend Theo wrung his hands. 'A hopeless case! Quite wild and ungovernable as a boy and set fair to ruin himself as a man! You are to be congratulated on the fact that there is no close acquaintance there, ma'am!'

'I am sure that all your tutees drove you to distraction at times, sir,' Marcus said feelingly. 'I know that I was a sadly lacking in any academic ability!'

'Good at mathematics, but no application in Greek!' the Reverend Theo observed. He turned to Beth with a smile. 'I believe I knew your husband, Lady Allerton. A man of ideas, devoted to his studies. We were all very surprised when he married. Now, may I ask Mrs

Morland to show you to your rooms? I am sure you will want a little time to rest before dinner.'

'I am sorry if you were offended by Reverend Theo's remarks,' Marcus whispered in Beth's ear, as Theo went off to call the housekeeper. 'He is tactless, but his heart is in the right place.'

Beth laughed. 'I did not take any offence and I am sure that Charlotte feels the same. Reverend Theo is quite a character, and more than generous in offering us all shelter!'

She saw Marcus relax slightly. 'I am glad you see it that way. He has offended many people from his pulpit, but the family is rich and owns the benefice and those who take him in dislike can find no way to remove him!'

Mrs Morland arrived then to show them all upstairs, and Beth found herself in a prettily appointed bedroom that faced south towards the Quantock Hills. The clock showed that there were several hours before dinner, and with a sigh of relief Beth removed her damp clothes and lay down to catch up on some sleep. The bed was soft and downy and before long she had drifted into a feverish dream where Marcus was pursuing her along a beach and into the sea itself. She woke up feeling hot and bothered and found herself tangled up in the bedclothes and feeling very little refreshed. It was now only a half-hour before dinner, and Beth forced herself to get up, wash her face and prepare to go downstairs. She had only brought one good evening dress with her, a confection of silver and lace, and though it was a little crushed it lifted her spirits to wear it. She called the maid to press the worst of the creases from the dress and arranged her own hair in a simple matching silver bandeau.

Everyone was already assembled in the drawing room and Beth was glad that she had taken trouble to repair as much of the ravages of the journey as she could. The gentlemen were elegant in their black and white evening dress and Charlotte always had the ability to look as immaculate as though she had just stepped out of a Bond Street modiste's. At her side, Justin Trevithick already looked proud and proprietorial and Beth smiled to herself. No matter what the other outcomes of the journey, that was one romance that she would wager would reach the altar.

Marcus came across to her side and took her hand. His gaze was admiring and Beth felt doubly glad that she had made an effort.

'Lady Allerton, you look very beautiful tonight. May I offer you a glass of Theo's excellent ratafia?'

It became apparent during dinner that the Reverend Theo kept an excellent wine cellar as well as a very good table. As dish succeeded dish, all accompanied by the most exquisite wines, the clergyman kept up an entertaining flow of conversation about parish life, then started to reminisce about Marcus's exploits as a youth. By the time that the gentlemen retired to take their port everyone was fast friends, and even Beth had almost forgotten that they were engaged in a contest for Fairhaven. The thought popped into her head as she was preparing for bed, but for once she dismissed it and as a result slept soundly and dreamlessly, leaving her worries to be confronted in daylight.

'I feel wretchedly sick!' Charlotte said miserably, the following morning. She was sitting up in bed and her pretty face was creased with pain and distress beneath her lace cap. 'It is all my own fault, for I knew I should not have had the sherry trifle last night! And now it has brought on the megrims and I have the most dreadful headache—' She winced as Beth pulled back the curtains a little and a bar of sunlight fell across the bed. 'Oh, Beth, pray do not! I fear my head will burst!'

Beth hastily pulled the curtains together again and went across to sit on the edge of the bed. It was a beautiful morning and she wanted nothing more than to be out in the fresh air, but she knew that Charlotte could not bear the light when she had one of her headaches. Besides, Charlotte was being more than generous in blaming the trifle. Beth suspected that it was the strain of the journey and the necessity of meeting new people that had done her cousin up and she felt more than a little guilty.

'Can I fetch you anything, dearest Charlotte? Some rose water or something to drink?' She saw the spasm that went across Charlotte's face as she shook her head. 'No? I shall leave you in peace, then.'

Beth went out and closed the door softly. When Charlotte was poorly it usually took at least a day for her to recover, so there would be no travelling to Devon that day. Beth knew that she would just have to be patient. It was not one of her usual virtues, but under the circumstances it was the only course. She hoped that the Reverend Theo would not mind prolonging his hospitality.

The house was very quiet. Beth went downstairs and into the breakfast room. Marcus was alone, sitting by the fire and reading a newspaper. He put this to one side immediately as Beth came in and stood up to hold her chair for her, his dark eyes intent on her face.

'Good morning, Lady Allerton. I trust that you slept well?'

'Exceptionally well, thank you,' Beth said truthfully.

'I am afraid, however, that my cousin is in poor health this morning and will be staying in her room.'

'I am sorry to hear it.' Marcus looked grave. 'It is a relief for me to find that you do not expect to move on today, however. Justin has gone to visit his mother over at Nether Stowey and the Reverend Theo has been called to the sickbed of a parishioner whom he assures me thinks himself at death door at least twice a month! It has become a ritual for them, I believe. Theo takes a couple of bottles of claret and the two of them sit drinking 'til the cows come home! I doubt we shall see him again this side of dinner!'

Beth looked at him a little uncertainly. 'Then we are…on our own?'

'To all intents and purposes.' Marcus's smile was faintly mocking. 'I will not inflict my company on you, Lady Allerton—not unless you wish it! Is there any possibility that you would like to spend the day with me?'

Beth hesitated, trying not to smile, but she could not prevent herself. It sounded a most attractive option. She reached for a piece of toast and buttered it slowly. 'Well, I could be persuaded…'

'Excellent!' Marcus smiled broadly. He handed her a cup of tea. 'Theo keeps as excellent a stable as he does a wine cellar, if you would like to ride!'

Beth's eyes sparkled. It was indeed too fine a day to sit inside and she relished the thought of a ride across country.

'Very well, then. I am sure we shall get on splendidly, my lord, provided that we do not quarrel over Fairhaven!'

Marcus smiled and got to his feet. 'Then we shall not mention it for the whole day!' He walked over to the door. 'Excuse me. I shall go to see to the saddling of the horses.'

As soon as Beth had finished her breakfast she hurried upstairs to change into her riding habit. The anticipation was buzzing through her body, as light and bright as the sunshine.

To spend a day with Marcus without the tension of Fairhaven between them seemed almost too good to be true. Maybe it was a temporary truce rather than a resolution of the conflict, but whatever the case, she intended to make the most of it.

They rode out all morning, taking an old green lane from Ashlyn towards the sea at Holford. They did not speak much. There was no need, for the sun was warm and the birds sang and the colours and wood smoke smell of autumn was all around them. Beth felt curiously content, more tranquil than she could ever remember. Her enjoyment sprang from the pleasure of Marcus's company, the warmth of his smile, the cadence of his voice and the light touch of his hand on her arm whenever he pointed out a view or something of interest. It was a more gentle feeling than the disturbing awareness that Marcus's presence habitually engendered in her, but Beth knew that under the calm surface ran the same attraction that was always between them.

After a while they started to speak more and Marcus told her a little about how he had felt when he had had to give up his diplomatic career to take over the responsibilities of the Trevithick estate. In return, Beth told him about Mostyn and her relationship with Kit and Charlotte. The time passed all too quickly and soon Marcus suggested that they return to Ashlyn for luncheon. It seemed a shame, but the exercise had given

Beth an appetite and she reflected that they could always go out again in the afternoon. Or perhaps she might challenge him to a game of billiards, for she had spent many a long afternoon alone practising when Frank had been away from home and was tolerably certain that she could beat Marcus. She sighed. No doubt that was considered unladylike too.

Mrs Morland had set out a simple meal for them of bread, cheeses and Somerset cider; and as Charlotte was still prostrate with the migraine, Beth and Marcus ate alone. Marcus seemed preoccupied and quiet, and when Beth looked at him she thought he seemed rather stern. The thought was quelling. Perhaps the delightful morning had been a prelude to something more unpleasant—perhaps Marcus had only been kind to her because he was about to spring on her the fact that he was prepared to fight her through the courts before he let her have Fairhaven...

'Lady Allerton?' Marcus's quizzical tone recalled her to the present. 'There is something I wished to say to you. I know we agreed that we would not mention Fairhaven today, but—'

Beth jumped to have her suspicions confirmed so promptly. She closed her eyes to ward off the blow.

'But I wanted to tell you that I will not oppose your quest to regain the island,' Marcus continued. 'You won Fairhaven in a just, if unorthodox, fashion...' there was an undertone of amusement in his voice '...and I know it means a great deal to you.'

Beth realised that she still had her eyes closed and opened them now, to see that Marcus was watching her with quizzical humour.

'Lady Allerton? Are you quite well?'

'I... Yes, indeed...' Beth floundered. It was the last

thing that she had expected and it left her quite lost for words.

'That being the case,' Marcus continued, his tone steady, 'I would still like to escort you to the island in order to arrange a smooth transfer of the estate. I trust that that will suit you?'

'Oh, yes, of course…' Beth knew she sounded totally bemused. She simply could not believe that he had capitulated in such a way.

'Good!' Marcus smiled, getting to his feet. 'Please excuse me for a moment. I believe that Mrs Morland has a message from Theo…'

As he closed the door behind him, Beth sat staring at the panels, a lump of cheese still clasped unnoticed in her hand. Marcus's statement had been so unexpected that she had not gathered her wits to question him properly and already the doubts were creeping in. Could he be in earnest or was this just another cunning ploy to set her off her guard? She had been so certain that his tactic would be to try to persuade her to relinquish her claim and go home. Now she was thoroughly confused.

Beth nibbled the cheese absent-mindedly. Did she trust Marcus? He had played her false before. Yet she wanted to believe him. Her instinct told her to let go of her doubts and have faith in him, but that was dangerous, too dangerous for her to contemplate at the moment. It involved admitting to other emotions that made her feel totally vulnerable. Beth suddenly felt as though she was on the edge of a precipice where her own intuition was prompting her to step into the unknown but her natural caution was holding her back.

She sighed. If only Charlotte were not feeling ill she would go and ask for advice, but what was the point of that anyway, when she already knew what her cousin would say? Charlotte had never liked their escapade and would fall on Marcus's suggestion with cries of relief. Her advice could not be impartial. And there was no one else whom Beth could ask.

Still mulling over the problem, Beth went upstairs to see how her cousin was faring. Charlotte was asleep, so Beth came back down again. Mrs Morland was just crossing the hall as she reached the bottom step.

'Oh, Lady Allerton,' the housekeeper said, 'there is a message from the Reverend March. He anticipates being at Hoveton for the rest of the afternoon and begs your pardon.' She smiled. 'He especially asked that Lord Trevithick go down the wine cellar to select a particular claret to have with the dinner, plus a dessert wine and some more port! His lordship is down there now, if you were wondering where he had vanished to, my lady!'

'Thank you, Mrs Morland,' Beth murmured. She watched the housekeeper hurry off back to the kitchens and wandered slowly towards the drawing room, still turning the problem of Fairhaven over in her mind. It was as she reached the drawing-room doorway, when she actually had her hand on the door frame, that she was struck by an idea; an idea so outrageous, so daring, that she was not sure that even she would put it into execution.

There was Fairhaven and there was Marcus. She might trust him, or she might not…

Beth tiptoed down the corridor to the wine cellar. The heavy oak door was wide open, the cellar steps yawning below into darkness. Beth could faintly discern the flicker of a candle flame far in the depths of the vault and she heard the dusty scrape of glass on stone. Marcus was evidently engrossed in the task that Theo had set.

Only the previous night, when Theo March had been

extolling the virtues of his wines, Beth had heard him joke that there was only one key to the cellar to prevent envious friends sampling his collection. That key was now in the door...

Beth stared. She crept forward and swung the door closed. It shut silently on oiled hinges. Beth turned the key, extracted it from the lock, and put it in her pocket.

A strange kind of madness took her and she almost laughed aloud. She ran up the stairs—she had not unpacked her trunk completely and now she threw her possessions in at random, squashing them down and slamming the fastening closed. She paused only to pen a hasty note to Charlotte and all the time she was listening intently, waiting for the inevitable shout from below that would show that she had been found out. None came. She hurried back down the stairs, her trunk bumping clumsily on every step, and shot out of the front door.

And all the while she was exulting in her escape and the fact that she had won.

It was only a step into Ashlyn village, but Beth hurried, glancing over her shoulder all the time, convinced that someone was watching her and about to ruin her plan. She had quickly considered and discarded the idea of asking Fowler to harness the carriage horses—that would take too long and be too noisy. Instead she was banking on the fact that there was a carter in Ashlyn who would be able to take her to Bridgwater.

At the forge she found exactly what she was looking for. An old cart was already standing waiting, half-loaded with sacks, the piebald cob chewing placidly on some hay whilst the carter chatted to the smith. Both of them looked up curiously as Beth hurried forward.

'Excuse me, sir! Can you take me to Bridgwater, if you please? I can pay you well…'

The carter was an elderly man and he was not to be hurried. He looked at the blacksmith, who gave him a significant look in return. He took off his hat, scratched his head, and put his hat back on again. Beth was almost dancing with frustration.

'Aye,' he said, after a long moment. 'I can take you there, missy.' He threw her trunk in the back, climbed slowly into the seat, leant down to give Beth a hand to scramble up beside him, then flicked the reins for the horse to set off. It seemed to Beth that the big cob was resentful of the sudden departure and moved with deliberate, agonising slowness.

'I believe it is but five miles to the sea?' she ventured, as they turned on to the road.

'Aye.'

'And we can go straight there?'

'Aye.'

Beth glanced over her shoulder. The village was receding, slowly, and no one was running down the main street and shouting after her. She started to relax a little. After all, there was only Charlotte and the servants at the vicarage. Charlotte was so poorly that she would not wake up for hours and the kitchen was well away from Theo's wine cellar. It could be some considerable time before anyone realised Marcus's predicament and even then she had the only key. It was heavy in her pocket.

As the cart lumbered down the country lane, Beth sat back with a sigh. The moment of exhilaration had gone, leaving her feeling oddly empty. She told herself that it was only because she felt so nervous at venturing off on her own, but her heart gave her another answer. They had been in complete accord, she and Marcus. It had been such a perfect morning. He had told her that he would not oppose her in the matter of Fairhaven. But…she had not trusted him. And she had ruined everything with her impetuous flight.

Beth gritted her teeth. She had won now. That was the important thing. The Reverend Theo would not return for hours and, even if he did, the door to the cellar was stout and could not easily be broken down. Marcus was trapped and she would definitely reach Fairhaven before him now. It did not matter if he had genuinely intended to give her the island or not, for she had won.

Beth swayed backwards and forwards with the movement of the cart and wondered what would happen next. In all likelihood Marcus would not even trouble to follow her. Probably he would never wish to see her again. Certainly he would never speak to her, unless to haul her over the coals for her appalling behaviour. And it had been appalling; Beth could see that, now that she had plenty of time for reflection. To have locked him in the wine cellar was bad enough, but to somehow betray the memory of their happiness that morning, to distrust him, that was her real offence. She reminded herself that she had finally outwitted him, but all she could think of was that the price had been so very high. She found that she was totally confused by her conflicting feelings and was almost in tears.

They lurched their way along the country roads towards the sea. It became clear to Beth that her idea of a direct journey and that of the carter was slightly at odds—he detoured to several farms on the way to unload his sacks and stood around chatting for what seemed like hours to Beth. After a while the sun dipped behind the clouds and a sharp wind sprang up, bringing with it the first hint of rain. Beth huddled down on the seat of the cart, but there was no shelter. She was cold, for her gloves, hat and scarf were in the trunk and the wind seemed to blow right through her coat. By the time the carter dropped her on the quay in Bridgwater it was getting dark and Beth felt more miserable than she had done for a very long time.

'How could she do such a thing?' Charlotte Cavendish wailed, pressing a small and inadequate lace handkerchief to her eyes. 'I know that Beth can be rash and impulsive, but she has never behaved like this before! Never!'

'Your cousin, madam, has all the self-restraint of a wayward child!' Marcus said, through his teeth. He was trying to remove some clinging cobwebs from his jacket and was tolerably sure that it would never be quite the same again. Certainly it was no longer a glowing tribute to Weston's tailoring.

'It is this absurd obsession with Fairhaven!' Charlotte lamented. 'I fear that it has quite taken over Beth's thinking! If only we could find some way to distract her attention—'

'I will give her something else to think about when I catch up with her!'

Marcus's gaze fell on Charlotte's apprehensive face and his own hard features softened a little. Mrs Cavendish had only risen from her sickbed a half-hour previously, and to find that her cousin had abandoned her and locked him in the cellar into the bargain was a shock that might have justifiably sent her into a fit of the vapours. Yet she was quite resolute, if pale, and Marcus admired her for that.

'Have no fear,' he said, in a gentler tone. 'I will find Lady Allerton and I will escort her to Fairhaven just as

I had intended and I will also marry her! So you need have no concerns for propriety, Mrs Cavendish…'

Charlotte looked slightly winded at this rush of events. '*Marry* her! I cannot conceive why you would wish to do so, my lord—'

'Neither can I at this moment!' Marcus said feelingly. 'But it is inevitable, I fear! Would you be so good as to pass me those scissors, ma'am? There are several loose threads…'

Charlotte snipped assiduously for a moment. 'How did you remember the other entrance to the cellar, my lord?'

Marcus laughed. 'A relic of my misspent youth, I confess, ma'am! I remembered Reverend March once telling us that there was a passage from the cellar to the icehouse in the garden and one day when I was about fourteen I had sought it out. This time it seemed much smaller!'

Charlotte shuddered. 'Reverend March! Whatever will he say when he returns and finds the key to his wine cellar missing?'

'I leave you to smooth that over, ma'am!' Marcus said cheerfully. He looked up as Justin came into the drawing room. 'Is the curricle ready, Justin?'

'It's waiting for you,' Justin said, with a grin. 'I've sent a messenger to meet McCrae in Bridgwater, so he will be expecting you and will also have started to instigate a search. Don't worry, ma'am—' he turned swiftly to Charlotte '—I am sure Marcus will find Lady Allerton before she comes to any harm!'

Marcus clapped his cousin on the shoulder. 'Sorry to leave you so precipitately, old fellow, but I know you will deal admirably with Theo, and see Mrs Cavendish safely home.' He did not miss the look of guilty pleasure that passed between the two of them and smiled a little to himself. 'Mustn't let the horses chill! Oh, and Justin...' he paused in the doorway '...I'll wager that Theo will be more distraught at being debarred from his own wine cellar than by aught else! Pray tell him that I will send his key back to him as soon as I have wrested it from Lady Allerton's grasp!'

Although it was late afternoon and growing dark, Bridgwater quay was still busy with traffic from the river. Beth picked her way between barrels of herrings and piles of coal, trying to ignore the curious stares of the sailors and their occasional coarse remarks. She had thought that it would be a relatively easy matter to charter a boat to take her to Fairhaven, but now she realised that she had no idea where to start. There were plenty of ships tied up at the quay, but she knew she could not simply pick one, go aboard and ask the captain if he would take her to Fairhaven Island. Her trunk was weighing her down and seemed twice as heavy as it had done earlier. Eventually, when she had walked all the way down the North Quay and was wondering what to do next, she came to a brigantine whose captain was busy coiling a huge jute rope whilst his crew unloaded a cargo of lemons in big panniers. The captain looked up, smiled at Beth and touched his cap; emboldened by his courtesy, Beth hurried forward.

'Excuse me, sir. Could you tell me if there is a ship sailing past Fairhaven that might be prepared to land me there?'

'There's a ship sailing for Fairhaven on the morrow, ma'am,' the captain said, peering through the dusk. 'Moored just down the quay, past the square rigger. Over there, see—' And he pointed to a ship that was tied up some fifty yards away. 'Tidy craft, is that,' he said approvingly. 'Lovely job. Built originally as a French privateer, they say, and quite old now but as neat and as quick as they come...'

Beth stared, transfixed. The ship was very trim indeed and on the port side could be read the name *Marie Louise* next to a painting of seagull in flight. At the back of Beth's mind a voice echoed, the voice of her nursemaid all those years ago at Mostyn:

'Your grandfather had a beautiful ship called the *Marie Louise*, named for his French mother... It has a drawing of a seagull on the side, *La Mouette*, in French...'

So the evil Earl of Trevithick had stolen the ship along with the island and the sword. Beth let out a small gasp of shock and the captain looked at her in some concern.

'Are you feeling unwell, ma'am?'

Beth did not—could not—reply. She had seen two men, who were standing on the quay beside the *Marie Louise*, deep in conversation. One was thin and almost concave, dressed in an old-fashioned brown waistcoat and serviceable dark trousers. The other was tall and elegant despite his working garb of a rough frieze coat over his white linen shirt. The sea breeze ruffled his black hair. Beth pressed one hand to her mouth and took an instinctive step backwards, almost tripping over the coil of rope. Her movement caught the eye of the thin man, who caught his companion's arm and swung him round.

It seemed impossible to Beth that the man whom she had locked in a wine cellar only a few hours ago could be here on the quay at Bridgwater, seeing to the provisioning of what could only be his own yacht. How could Marcus possibly have escaped in the first place, let alone reached the port before her when she had a head start? All this went through her mind even while she spun around, ready to run away. Marcus was too quick for her. He had already halved the distance between them and when she bumped clumsily against a stanchion and nearly fell, Marcus's arm went around her, scooping her clear of the ground.

Beth gave a small sob of mingled fear, annoyance and strangely, relief. 'Lord Trevithick—'

'Lady Allerton?' Marcus sounded savage.

The thin man came running up, panting. 'My lord...'

'All right, McCrae.' Marcus's tone was clipped. He did not put Beth down. 'Would you call off the search, please? And take care of Lady Allerton's luggage. I will see you in the Sailor's Rest later...'

He looked down into Beth's face and she saw that his eyes were blazing with fury. She instinctively shrank back from the anger she saw there.

'As for you, Lady Allerton,' Marcus said smoothly, 'I will settle with you now! And in private! You are about to wish you had never been born!'

The inn was not like any that Beth had previously encountered in her travels. Although it was only late afternoon it was already full and smelled overwhelmingly of ale and tobacco. The noise was deafening— there was raucous laughter and loud conversation that quickly became lewd repartee when Marcus pushed his way thorough the throng, still carrying her.

'That's a pretty little moppet you have there, my lord, and no mistaking! When you've finished with 'er, pass 'er on...'

Beth struggled in Marcus's arms. 'Put me down at

once, Lord Trevithick! How dare you subject me to the comments of these people—?'

'You have brought all this and more upon yourself through your own behaviour,' Marcus said, through shut teeth. 'You will oblige me by keeping still, my lady, or I shall drop you into the nearest lap and let them have their way!'

This dire threat led Beth to turn her face into Marcus's shoulder, close her eyes and try to blot out the coarser comments of the crowd. In a moment the noise faded and Beth realised that they had left the taproom and were going upstairs. Marcus was carrying her with about as much consideration as a sack of potatoes—her feet bumped against the wall and she scraped one elbow painfully on the banister. She opened her mouth to protest, saw the look in Marcus's eye and closed it again.

Marcus pushed open the door of a tiny chamber and dropped her unceremoniously on to the bed. Beth bounced on the mattress and came to an undignified rest with her skirts all tumbled about her and her hair falling from its pins.

'Oof! Is it really necessary to treat me with such lack of consideration, my lord? And what can you mean by bringing me to this low place? I demand to return to Ashlyn at once—'

'No, madam,' Marcus said, still through gritted teeth. 'You were the one who was so determined to be here that you would take any steps to achieve it!' He kicked the door closed and turned to survey her, his glittering dark gaze raking her ruthlessly.

'I have no real wish to speak to you now, but there are a few things that I must say. Leaving aside your inexcusable behaviour in locking me in Theo March's wine cellar, you have the gross folly to try to run away

and arrange passage for yourself to Fairhaven! Alone!'
Marcus ran a hand through his hair. 'Have you any idea
of the distress you have caused your cousin? Do you
even care? You have no more sense than a spoilt brat
and you deserve a good spanking!' Marcus drove his
hands into the pockets of his coat as though to prevent
himself from doing her an injury. 'I would administer
one myself were it not for the fact that I should probably
enjoy it far more than I ought!'

Beth blushed bright red. 'My lord!'

Marcus shot her a furious look. 'My lady? It is about
time that someone told you a few home truths! You are
easily the most infuriating and exasperating woman that
I have ever met! Now, I am going to meet with McCrae
to arrange tomorrow's sailing, and I shall be locking you
in here for your own safety! Do you object?'

Beth stared at him, quite cowed into silence. 'I...
Marcus, I am sorry—'

'I do not wish to hear it!' Marcus stalked over to the
door, then turned back to her. 'Speaking of keys, I
should be obliged if you would hand over the key to
Theo's cellar—at once!'

Beth fumbled clumsily in her pocket, aware that
Marcus was watching her efforts with the same angry,
implacable regard. When she put it into his hand she
heard him make a noise of disgust, and he took it from
her without a second glance.

'We shall speak later, if I regain my temper sufficiently to do so without shouting!' he said, over his
shoulder. 'In the meantime I suggest that you draw as
little attention to yourself as possible. No leaning out of
windows and begging for rescue! Do you really wish for
that pack of villains to come upstairs for you? It is about
time you learned some sense, Lady Allerton!' And, so

saying, he slammed out of the door and Beth heard the key turn with finality in the lock.

Marcus had not returned by eleven o'clock that night. Shortly after his departure a slovenly maid had appeared with a tray of greasy beef stew and Beth ate some half-heartedly whilst she listened to the noise swell downstairs as even more seafarers joined the throng gathered below. The tiny room was cold and dirty, but she had absolutely no wish to effect an escape and go straight from the frying pan into the fire. It was unnerving not knowing what Marcus intended. She did not believe that he had locked her in in order to take advantage of her, but she felt uncomfortably vulnerable.

She still could not understand how Marcus had reached Bridgwater before her, but then it seemed that there was a lot that she had overlooked. It was apparent now that Marcus had intended to sail for Fairhaven right from the start, either with or without her, for he had had a boat and a crew waiting. Beth stared miserably into the meagre fire. He had told her only that morning that he intended to escort her to the island, but she had only half-believed him. Yet perhaps his intentions had been honourable all along. She had already begun to regret her impetuous flight and particularly her lack of trust, and now she felt ashamed. But the damage was done. Marcus was deeply angered by her behaviour, and with good reason.

Beth shivered miserably. If Marcus had been acting honourably all along, her lack of trust would have been particularly wounding to him. Locking him up would hurt his dignity but distrusting him went deeper, much deeper. And just at the moment he was so angry he would not even let her apologise.

The fire had burned out and Beth slowly prepared for bed by the light of the one candle. The bedding looked none too clean and she was almost certain that she saw a flea jump from the mattress when she turned the sheets down, so she decided to lie under the bedspread and try to keep warm as best she could. This proved none too satisfactory; even fully dressed she was cold and uncomfortable, and had only drifted into a light doze when the door opened and Marcus came in.

'Lady Allerton? Are you awake?'

Beth opened her eyes and tried to discern whether or not Marcus was drunk. Certainly a strong scent of spirits had entered the room with him, but when the candle flame flickered briefly on the expression in his eyes, she saw that he was frowning and looked sober enough. His tone of voice was as abrupt as when he had gone out hours previously and Beth's heart sank as she realised that his temper had not improved. She struggled to sit up as Marcus sat down on the edge of the bed and started to pull off his boots.

'Oh, what are you doing—?'

Marcus shot her an irritated look. 'What does it look as though I am doing? I am coming to bed!'

Beth clutched the bedspread to her. 'Here? But what will people think?'

This time the look that Marcus gave her combined exasperation and a certain grim amusement. 'Believe me, Lady Allerton, none of the occupants of this alehouse care a jot for your reputation! They already believe that I have ravished you thoroughly and have been pressing me for the details!' He threw his boots into the corner of the room and started to unbutton his jacket. 'Besides, it seems a little late for you to be worrying about such things! A hoyden who dashes about the countryside barely chaperoned, who tries to run away in the middle of the night, locks gentlemen in wine cellars and wanders about a port alone after dark clearly has no consideration for propriety!' His frown deepened. 'Just tell me one thing—do you have so little faith in me that you disbelieve everything I say to you? I had thought that there was more trust between us than that!'

Beth stared at him in the candlelight. His face was set in hard, angry lines, but behind that she thought she glimpsed another emotion: hurt perhaps, or disappointment. It made her feel wretched, doubly so for mistrusting him and for causing him hurt. A big lump came into her throat and she looked at him, unable to speak. For what seemed like a long moment they stared at each other, then Marcus turned away with a sigh.

'Just why are you fully dressed and why are you *on* the bed rather than *in* it?'

Beth let out her breath on a sigh. Marcus was evidently so cross with her that he would find fault with anything.

'It is cold and there are fleas in the bed! Not that it is any concern of yours, Lord Trevithick! Why do you not sleep on your ship?'

Marcus laughed abruptly. 'What, would you have me leave you here all night unprotected? Is that the lesser of two evils?'

Beth turned away from him. 'Well, if you must stay, I am persuaded that you will find the chair comfortable enough.'

Marcus made a rude and derisive noise. 'Do not be ridiculous! And kindly move over! You are taking up all the space!'

Beth squeaked and rolled away quickly as the mattress sank under his weight. He was still in shirt and pantaloons, but he suddenly seemed too big and far too close. He was even closer once he had put out a lazy hand and pulled her back to his side. The treacherous mattress tumbled her into his arms.

'Why, you *are* cold…' Marcus's voice had softened as he felt the chill in her body and tucked it closer to his. He pulled the bedspread over the two of them. 'There, we shall warm up soon enough and be asleep…'

Beth was warming up far too quickly. Her head was on his shoulder and she could feel the heat of his skin through the thin shirt where the palm of one hand rested against his chest. His breath stirred her hair. The prospect of sleep now receded as she became acutely aware of every line and curve of Marcus's body against hers and felt the beat of his heart strong and steady against her ear. She had never gone to sleep in such a position before. Frank had never shared her bedroom and seldom her bed. On the infrequent occasions he had troubled her for his marital dues, he had left immediately afterwards.

Beth lay still, torn between arousal and comfort. She was keenly aware of Marcus's arm about her, his hand resting just below her breast. The awareness kept her awake whilst the corners of her mind started to cloud with warmth and drowsiness and comfort. Marcus turned his head a little and spoke drily.

'Try to breathe a little, Lady Allerton, or you may find yourself in difficulties. Unless…' his voice changed subtly '…your clothing is too tight to allow ease of breathing? If you wish to take anything off—'

Beth gave a protesting squeak and tried to pull away, but he held her tightly. 'Never fear. I do but tease you. But you should try to get some sleep, for the voyage tomorrow will take the best part of the day.'

Beth's eyes flew open. 'Tomorrow? So we do sail for Fairhaven?'

'Of course.' Marcus sounded sleepy. 'I said we would and so we shall.'

'But—'

'No buts…' He shifted slightly so that Beth's head was more comfortably pillowed on his shoulder. 'And no more discussion. I am exhausted, even if you are not. Talking can wait until tomorrow.'

Beth heard his breathing deepen almost immediately and realised that he had fallen asleep. Part of her, a very small part, was affronted that he could so easily ignore the fact that she was in his arms. Evidently he was used to being in such a situation, whereas she was tormented by his proximity. Another part of her mind was grappling with the implications of sailing for Fairhaven in Marcus's company the following day. She tried to think about it, but she was so weary with the events of the day that drowsiness overcame all resistance. At last she was warm, comfortable and safe, and she soon fell asleep.

Marcus awoke as the grey dawn light started to filter in through the bedroom window. The quay below was already noisy with the business of the new day. He opened his eyes and saw that they had both moved in the night; Beth was now tucked in front of him and they were lying very close and snug, like spoons. Her silky black hair was spread out on the pillow and in sleep her face was as clear and untroubled as a child's. Marcus smiled to himself. He had to admit that he had treated her very badly indeed.

When he had first seen Beth on the quay he had been so angry that he had not cared a jot about her feelings.

As soon as she had tricked him and run away from Ashlyn he had known immediately what she intended and at first could not believe that she could be so foolhardy. He had thought that he had made it clear that he would take her to Fairhaven, yet clearly she had either disbelieved him or simply not wanted his company. Either way he was hurt and angry, but he was also worried. Very worried. A woman alone wandering around the quay at Bridgwater would soon find herself receiving several offers, none of which would be passage to Fairhaven. Passage to the nearest whorehouse, perhaps, and the invitation would be phrased in a way to brook no refusal.

He looked down at Beth's sleeping face. He wondered if she had even considered such a possibility or whether her obsession with reaching Fairhaven had blinded her to all good sense. She was no child to be unaware of the perils of journeying alone, though perhaps she had been so sheltered that she did not truly know what could so easily have happened to her. He had known it, and he had had men on every corner, in every inn, looking for her. He had been terrified that he would not find her in time, or that some accident had already befallen her on the way to Bridgwater.

Then he had seen her and his anger had increased tenfold because she was so obviously unharmed and still unaware of the danger she was in. He had wanted to take her and shake her hard, to force her to recognise her own folly, to punish her for the fear and misery she had made him suffer. He had wanted to kiss her and make love to her despite the hurt of her betrayal. So he had locked her in and left her until his anger had subsided, and then he had come back and seen her and wanted her all over again…

Chapter Seven

Beth sat in the shelter of the wheel-house, out of the wind, a blanket tucked about her legs. Marcus had suggested that she stay below in one of the cabins and at first she had complied, but once they were clear of the land the wind had picked up and the boat had started to pitch alarmingly. Beth had soon started to feel nauseous and had moved out into the fresh air, where one of the crew had taken pity on her and arranged the makeshift seat from a few wooden crates. Now, although the horizon still dipped and soared with sickening regularity, Beth could at least feel the refreshing spray on her face and breathe deeply of the salty air.

She had quickly noted that Marcus seemed quite unaffected by the movement of the boat. He had been in the wheel-house for quite some time talking to the helmsman and he had also taken his turn at doing whatever job was required; casting off, trimming the sails or simply giving a hand to the other members of the crew. And she saw that the men appreciated it. There had been a quick compliment for his skill from one of the hands, and at least one glance between the crew that showed

Marcus shifted uncomfortably. Beth was pressed against him, very soft and sweet, the curve of her buttocks resting tantalisingly against his thighs. Marcus was already half-aroused and now felt himself harden further as he considered their relative positions. He reminded himself sternly that there were several layers of clothing between them but this did not help as it simply made him think of removing them all. Then there were the fleas… That was better. His tense body relaxed slightly. He had locked Lady Allerton in a flea-ridden room in a rough alehouse on the quay in Bridgwater and had spent the night with her there. He smiled a little to think of the reaction of the society gossips to such a story.

He smoothed the hair away from Beth's face with gentle fingers and she turned her head slightly, snuggling closer to him. Marcus obligingly adapted the curve of his body to hers. He knew there could only be one ending to Beth's adventure now, now that she was so thoroughly disgraced. It did not disturb him, since it was what he had intended almost from the first moment he had met her. How Beth would react to his proposal was a different matter, however. Marcus frowned. He was not at all sure if she would accept him. Most importantly, she was still obsessed with Fairhaven and he did not want to have to contend with such a rival. So they had to go to the island and Beth had to find out the truth about her grandfather and then perhaps she could put the whole matter behind her and concentrate on the future. A future with him. Marcus sighed. It should have been easy but he had the deepest suspicion that it would not be. Where Beth Allerton was concerned, nothing was that simple.

their approval. It was a side of Marcus that Beth had not seen before.

Unfortunately his attitude towards her was in stark contrast. She and Marcus had barely spoken that morning, except for one humiliating conversation over the stale bread and porridge that had constituted their breakfast in the inn. Beth had requested to be taken back to Ashlyn. Marcus had looked at her stonily and said that she could return there if she wished, but that he was travelling to Fairhaven and she might as well accompany him since she had gone to such an unconscionable amount of trouble to get there. That had been the end of the conversation and Beth did not dare question him further about the trip. His face had assumed the same forbidding expression that it had worn the previous night and she knew that she was still in deep trouble. When the meagre breakfast was over she had gone with him out on to the quay where the boat was waiting. They had cast off and now turning back was impossible.

Beth shivered a little within her fur-lined cloak. Ahead of them there was nothing to see but the grey of the ocean, and on the port side the land was slipping away, the hills of Devon growing smaller all the time. Marcus had said that it would take them the best part of the day to reach Fairhaven. To Beth that seemed as nothing after so many years of waiting.

After an hour or so she fell into an uneasy doze and woke feeling queasy and a little befuddled. The sun was peeping through thin cloud overhead and the wind was strong. A rich smell of stew filled Beth's nostrils and her stomach lurched. She turned away as Marcus appeared before her, his bare feet braced on the wooden deck, a plate of food held in one hand. He took one look at her face and smothered a smile. Beth glared at him.

'Oh, dear, you look distinctly sickly, Lady Allerton…'

Beth tried to ignore the persistent smell of the stew but was forced to resort to holding her nose. She spoke with a distinct lack of dignity.

'Lord Trevithick, I would be obliged if you would go away! Now! And take that repellent plate of food with you!'

Marcus sauntered away, grinning. 'Pray call me if you require a bowl, ma'am!'

Within a half-hour Beth was too chilled to sit still any longer. She was tempted to go down to a cabin and try to sleep, but the thought of the enclosed stuffiness below decks made her feel even more seasick. Instead she wandered over to the rail and leant against it, staring into the flying spray below. She felt cold, sick and lonely, and it was a far cry from the way she had imagined arriving on Fairhaven Island.

Now that she thought about it, she realised that she had given very little thought to the practicalities of the journey. Her imagination had flown ahead of her, skipping over the difficult bits like a rough sea crossing, and had pictured some triumphant return to her grandfather's castle. She felt a little foolish. It did not help that Marcus had ignored her for the best part of the day and that his crew, apart from a few sympathetic glances, had left her to her own devices.

As much to occupy her mind as to keep warm, Beth wrapped her cloak closer and strolled around the deck, watching the seabirds that whirled and screamed in the ship's wake, scanning the horizon for land or for any other passing ships out of Bristol. The afternoon dragged by.

'Land ahoy!'

Beth had been staring at the sea for so long that she

felt almost mesmerised by the time the call came. She swung round. Marcus was strolling towards her across the deck, a telescope in his hand. 'Fairhaven is visible from the starboard bow, Lady Allerton. Would you care to see?'

Beth went with him across to the rail, took the spyglass a little gingerly in her hand and searched the horizon. Sure enough, the great granite cliffs of the island were visible above the tossing of the waves. Everything looked grey: sea, sky, land. The clouds were lowering and clung to the island like a veil. But it was beautiful.

'Oh!' Beth handed the telescope back to Marcus, her eyes shining. 'I can scarce believe it! It looks very beautiful, my lord!'

There was a strange expression on Marcus's face, part amused, part rueful. 'If you think that, Lady Allerton, you must love Fairhaven very much indeed! To my mind it looks a damnably lonely place!'

He turned away to issue some instruction to the helmsman about avoiding the shoals around Rat Island and anchoring in Fairhaven Roads. Beth hardly paid attention. She was clinging to the rail as the island slowly grew bigger in front of her. Within minutes she was soaked by the spray and the drizzle that was falling from the grey sky, but she barely noticed. She was so close to achieving her dream of reaching Fairhaven that she had no thought for anything else at all.

As they grew closer the island took on a clearer shape and Beth could even distinguish the chimneys of the castle and the roofs of the houses in the tiny village that huddled at the top of the cliff. The whole of the eastern side of the island was now spread out before them and Beth could see what Marcus meant—there were no trees, no shelter, only the plunging cliffs and the screaming seabirds.

'There are no trees...' she murmured, when he came back to her side. 'Does nothing grow here?'

'Colin tells me that the crops grow well enough,' Marcus said, nodding in the direction of Colin McCrae, 'and my aunt tends a small garden in the shelter of the castle walls. She always complains that the sheep take the greenest shoots!'

Beth frowned. 'Your aunt?'

'Why, yes.' There was a mocking smile curling Marcus's mouth. 'Did you imagine Fairhaven quite uninhabited, Lady Allerton? My uncle, St John Trevithick, has been the vicar of Fairhaven for donkey's years and his sister Salome keeps house for him at Saintonge Castle.' He gave Beth an old-fashioned look. 'Did you imagine that I was bringing you to a place quite beyond the pale? The truth is rather more prosaic, I fear!'

Beth looked away. She was not entirely sure what she had imagined, but her thoughts had not encompassed meeting any of Marcus's relations. She doubted that they would be pleased to see her. Certainly she had not supposed that she would be evicting a vicar who had served the community for decades, nor supplanting his spinster sister. It looked as though her image of Fairhaven as a bleak and neglected place had been embarrassingly at fault.

By now they had reached the shelter of the island and the sea swell abated a little as they anchored in the lee of the great cliffs. A rowing boat was lowered and Marcus and Colin McCrae assisted Beth down the ladder to a place in the stern. It seemed the work of moments for two burly seamen to row them ashore and pull the boat up on the shingle of the beach. A cart was already waiting at the bottom of the cliff and they lurched up a rough track that seemed carved into the face of the rock, Beth clinging to the sides of the cart whenever they turned a corner and the wheels seemed to skim the thin air. Suddenly the walls of the castle rose before her, Saintonge Castle, built by her forebears so many years before. A lump came into her throat and for a moment she was afraid she would cry.

There was a reception party waiting for them at the bottom of the castle steps. It seemed that every man woman and child on the island had assembled to greet the new Earl. Beth became suddenly and devastatingly aware of the figure she must cut as she crouched in the back of the cart, her hair straggling from her bonnet in rats' tails and her soaking dress and cloak clinging to her body in a manner far too voluptuously revealing. No doubt the good villagers of Fairhaven would think the sailors had brought their concubine with them! As for what Marcus's relatives would make of her... Uncharacteristic reticence made her hang back, but it was too late, for Marcus was climbing down from the cart and had cheerfully swept her up in his arms, to deposit her right in front of the curious crowd. Beth suspected that he had done it on purpose.

'Marcus, by all that's holy!' A voice boomed from behind them. 'I never thought to see the day! The lord moves in mysterious ways!'

Beth and Marcus both spun round. An elderly woman was descending the steps from the castle entrance. She was not fat so much as large, and recognisably a Trevithick from her very dark brown eyes, high cheekbones and the luxuriant dark hair that was coiled in a huge chignon in the nape of her neck. She was improbably dressed in pink satin with matching embroidered slippers, and a scarlet cloak was thrown carelessly about her shoulders and was now flapping in the strong wind. Beth found that she was staring.

'A plague upon this weather!' the woman said cheerfully, grasping Marcus to her and kissing him enthusiastically on both cheeks. 'Seven plagues upon it! My, my, how you've grown!'

'Aunt Sal,' Marcus said, grinning, 'it is such a pleasure to see you again!'

'And you, dear boy!' Salome Trevithick looked round and her bright brown gaze fell on Beth. 'Bless me, a stranger in the desert!' Then, at Beth's look of puzzlement, she added, 'Isaiah thirty-five, verse six, my dear.'

'Aunt Sal, this is Beth Allerton,' Marcus said formally. 'Lady Allerton, my aunt, Lady Salome Trevithick.'

'Welcome, my dear!' Salome Trevithick extended a hand sparkling with diamonds. She looked Beth over approvingly. 'A veritable angel, Marcus, albeit a rather sodden one!'

Beth blushed.

'Aunt Sal writes all my uncle's sermons,' Marcus explained in an undertone, 'so her conversation is always peppered with Biblical allusions! Indeed, she quotes the Bible at every available opportunity!' He raised his voice. 'Is Uncle St John not with you, Aunt? I was hoping—'

'Alas, St John has taken a journey into a far country,' Salome said, beaming. 'He has been called to the Bishop at Exeter, my dears. Apparently the poor man had heard that St John was drunk in the pulpit last month and demanded an explanation!'

'Nothing else to do on Fairhaven!' a voice from the back of the crowd shouted.

Marcus turned back to the villagers, who had been waiting with good-humoured patience. 'Thank you for such a warm welcome to the island!' His voice carried easily to everyone. 'It is good to be here at last, even on such an inclement day!'

'You should see the place in really bad weather!' the voice at the back of the crowd responded.

Everyone laughed. 'I am sure I shall!' Marcus said, grinning. 'For now, I am happy to see you all and to introduce Lady Allerton, who is to be the new owner of Fairhaven.'

To Beth's horror, Marcus pulled her to his side. 'I know that many of you will remember Lady Allerton's grandfather, Charles Mostyn, and be glad that the days of a Mostyn landlord are to return!'

A curious murmur ran through the crowd. Beth's smile faded as she saw the looks on the faces of the people in front of her. From smiling good humour they had moved to uncertainty and even sullenness. Some were muttering to each other and a few were watching her with undisguised hostility. Even Salome Trevithick looked stern. Beth bit her lip, conscious of their resentment but taken aback by the suddenness with which it had sprung up.

There was an awkward pause, then a woman who had been standing a little apart from the crowd bent down to murmur in the ear of the small blonde child beside her. A moment later, the girl had trotted forward and held out a wilting posy to Beth.

'Welcome to the island, my lady,' she whispered.

Beth forgot about the strange hostility of the crowd and her own dishevelled state. She smiled at the child, then crouched down to take the flowers and give her small admirer a kiss. The little girl looked at her with huge, considering blue eyes for a moment, then smiled back, stuck her thumb in her mouth and ran back to her mother. Another murmur ran through the crowd, this time of guarded approval.

'Prettily done,' Salome Trevithick said gruffly, grasping Beth's elbow and helping her to her feet. 'Suffer the little children to come unto me! Matthew nineteen, verse fourteen! Let me show you to your room, Lady Allerton. You look in sore need of some refreshment!' She linked her arm through Beth's and steered her up the castle steps. 'Some of the islanders have long memories, I fear, Lady Allerton. But ashes to ashes, I always say, and never speak ill of the dead!'

Before Beth could ask her to explain this strange pronouncement she found herself inside the castle and forgot everything in admiration of the sheer splendour of it all. Saintonge Castle had originally been built in the thirteenth century, but within the huge, windowless walls, a more modern dwelling had been fashioned. The stone-flagged entrance hall was neither as shabby nor as bare as Beth had imagined it, but was hung with rich tapestries and decorated with polished silver. Salome ushered her upstairs, to an opulent suite of rooms set into the southern wall of the castle. There was a huge bedroom with a wide window that looked out over the sea, a sitting room with a most comforting fire, and a modern bathroom with the biggest bath Beth had ever seen. She went back into the bedroom and walked over to the stone casement, standing by the window to look at the huge sweeping panorama of the sea. She gave a little sigh.

'Oh, how beautiful!'

'Bless you, my child!' Lady Salome said, moist-eyed. 'It is indeed a lovely place! Now, I shall send Martha McCrae to you in a little while to see if you need anything. She is the mother of that delightful child who greeted you outside!' She paused. 'Martha will bring you dinner in your room tonight, for we do not eat *en famille* until tomorrow. I thought you might be too tired for company!'

'Thank you!' Beth said gratefully. She did indeed feel worn out with travelling and trying to absorb new experiences. Lady Salome smiled and went out, red cloak flying, and Beth sank down on to the window seat to look out, entranced, across the bay.

She was still sitting there half an hour later, when Martha McCrae knocked at the door and came timidly into the room, bearing a supper tray.

'Is everything to your liking, my lady?' The housekeeper sounded a little strained.

Beth turned to her with a smile. 'Oh, of course! It is entirely delightful! I am just so taken aback by the beauty of the whole island!'

Martha McCrae smiled shyly. Unlike her blonde daughter, she had soft brown hair and kind brown eyes. Her complexion was very pale and freckled, and her face wore an unmistakably worried air. Beth wondered what could be making her so nervous.

'Have you lived on Fairhaven for long, Mrs McCrae?' she asked, anxious to put the woman at her ease.

The housekeeper nodded. 'A little while, Lady Allerton, but not as long as Lady Salome and the vicar. I came here as a bride six years ago, when the old Earl took Colin on as his estate manager here.' She wiped her hands down her apron in a sudden, nervous gesture. 'It has not always been easy—the winters are hard and the Earl—well, I believe that he forgot about us being here sometimes.' She sighed. 'That is why we thought…

When we heard that the new Earl was finally coming here, we hoped—' she broke off and resumed '—we hoped he might have the good of the island at heart. But it seems he intends to give Fairhaven away—'

She broke off and her pale face flushed bright red. 'Forgive me, my lady. I was thinking aloud! Excuse me. I will send a maid up with some water…'

And before Beth could say another word, she had turned and fled.

Beth sat down a little heavily on the edge of the big tester bed and pecked half-heartedly at the food on the tray. Now she understood—in part, at least—the hostility of the villagers. Like the McCraes, they had believed that Marcus's arrival on Fairhaven must herald a better time ahead. They had flocked to welcome him, buoyed up by hope and expectation. And almost the first thing that he had done was tell them that he was giving Fairhaven over to her. Worse, her arrival threatened the future of St John and Salome, the only members of the Trevithick family who had ever shown any loyalty to the island and its inhabitants…

The water arrived. Beth stripped off her sodden clothes and washed the sticky salt from her skin. She felt tired and light-headed. The seasickness had gone now, although the floor still showed a disturbing tendency to rock beneath her feet. She donned a fresh petticoat and was about to lie down when she heard the echo of a door closing below and footsteps ascending the stairs.

'All I am saying, my lord, is that the Fairhaven estate is no plaything for a girl—'

The voice was that of Colin McCrae, pitched somewhat louder than his customary soft burr because of the passion with which he spoke. Marcus replied, but Beth could not hear his quieter tones.

'And with the current threat from the sea, it would be the greatest folly—'

'That will be short-lived.' Marcus's voice was clipped. 'We land Marchant's cargo tomorrow night.'

Beth's curiosity was caught. Where previously she had tried not to overhear, now she strained closer. The men had paused on the landing, a little away from her room. They were speaking quietly, but she caught the odd phrase here and there and pressed against the door to try to hear more.

'Will you tell Lady Salome?' Colin McCrae was asking now, his voice amused. 'I can imagine her reaction...'

'Oh, Aunt Sal is up to all the rigs!' Marcus laughed. 'There can be no harm in telling her about the business with Marchant!'

'And Lady Allerton?'

Marcus's voice had sobered. 'No. There is no need for that. Now, Colin, you were telling me about the need to build a new barn up at Longhouses...'

Their footsteps and their voices blurred as they passed Beth's door and moved on. She expelled a sharp breath and leant against the panels, pushing the door closed. Her head was spinning.

The threat from the sea...Marchant's cargo...and the fact that Marcus did not intend to tell her... Her imagination raced. Could it be—was it possible—that Marcus was using Fairhaven Island for smuggling, as his grandfather had done before him? Certainly the island was perfectly placed for such a venture and she knew that Marcus needed to make money.

Beth lay down on the bed and stared fixedly up at the

vast canopy. It all seemed to hang together. She had suspected from the first that Marcus intended to travel to Fairhaven. Her presence had provided the perfect excuse and the perfect camouflage. His ship had been ready and waiting in Bridgwater, so clearly his men must have received their instructions some days before. Lady Salome and all the villagers had been expecting their arrival. There was evidently a plan.

And who knew what cargo the *Marie Louise* had been carrying today. Marchant's cargo, Marcus had said. Perhaps Marchant was the free trader with whom Marcus was in business... Beth turned over restlessly, wondering if she should confront Marcus straight away or wait until she had some evidence. Her instinct was to challenge him at once, to demand an interview now and have it out with him, but she reluctantly decided to wait. It went against her nature but Marcus had been so sparing of the truth up until now that Beth had no doubt he would think of some plausible excuse. Better to keep quiet and watch what happened. And she would not have long to wait, for if Marcus was correct, tomorrow night would reveal the truth.

Dinner the following day was an entertaining meal. Beth had spent much of the day resting and felt quite restored by the time she joined Marcus and his aunt in the castle's impressive dining room. Lady Salome was resplendent in purple satin, orange turban and pearls, and Beth felt supremely dowdy in her practical grey gown. She remained quiet whilst Marcus and his aunt covered all the family gossip, but then Salome moved on to ply her with eager questions about London, the fashions, the scandals and the entertainments, and Beth soon forgot her reserve. They chatted through to dessert, when Lady

Salome started on a series of outrageous anecdotes about her own Season some thirty years before, looking from Beth to Marcus with sparkling brown eyes.

'I did not *take*, my dears. The style was for plump girls with fluffy blonde hair—rather like those little dogs that Lady Caroline Lamb is said to favour—so I was utterly unfashionable! I was in despair of ever finding a rich husband and even considered running off with my piano teacher, but he always smelled of mothballs and that was quite quelling to passion!' She popped a sugared plum into her mouth and pushed the dish in Beth's direction. 'Where was I? Oh, yes... Well Papa was a man of little patience and when I had not caught a husband after a few months he decided to despatch me to Fairhaven! St John had lost his housekeeper here—she fell from the cliffs in strange circumstances—and so Papa thought to save some money by sending me in her place!'

Beth smiled. 'Have you lived here ever since, Lady Salome? It is a very long time!'

'Oh, yes, my dear, but then it is my home. Home is where the heart is. Now is that St Mark's Gospel or the Book of Proverbs?'

'Neither, I believe.' Marcus laughed. He stood up. 'Excuse me, ladies. I will take my port and rejoin you in the drawing room shortly.'

'Take your time, dear,' Salome said absently. 'Lady Allerton and I have much to talk about! Ah, the sweetness of a friend!' She looked triumphant. 'Now, *that* is the Book of Proverbs!'

Marcus bowed and went out, a twinkle in his eye, and Beth sighed unconsciously. For all the relaxed atmosphere of the meal and the entertaining company of Lady Salome, she did not delude herself that she was forgiven.

Marcus had barely spoken to her directly during the evening, except to ask if her room was comfortable and if she had everything she required, and she felt uncomfortable in his presence. Once or twice she had caught his gaze upon her, expressionless or stern, but when she had looked up at him he had not smiled in return. There was so much that needed to be said between them, yet she did not know where to start. Last night he had been too angry to listen to her. Now she hardly dared approach him, particularly if it were only to stir up more trouble on the matter of smuggling.

'You look sad, my dear,' Lady Salome said comfortingly, when they were ensconced in front of the drawing-room fire and had a big pot of tea between them. 'I suppose you must be tired from your travels and all the excitement of reaching Fairhaven at last! Marcus tells me that it has long been an ambition of yours to regain the island for your family!'

'Yes, I suppose so.' Beth said dolefully. Suddenly, sitting here under Lady Salome's bright gaze, it did not seem such a worthy thing to want to reclaim Fairhaven. 'Ever since I was a little girl I wanted to come here, but...' she looked up, troubled '...I did not think... What will you do, ma'am, if you leave the island?'

'Oh, I shall travel to the fleshpots of Exeter!' Salome said enthusiastically, ladling three spoonfuls of sugar into her tea. 'Or perhaps to London itself—Sodom and Gomorrah rolled into one! You have no idea, my love, how frustrating it is to receive six-month-old copies of the *Ladies' Magazine* and never to have the fashionable clothes to wear when one goes out! And then there is the food—salted, pickled but seldom fresh! Unless one likes turnips, of course, but I never have! Indeed, I am *aux anges* to be thinking of escape!'

Beth smiled, but she was not convinced. She knew that Lady Salome thought of Fairhaven as home and suspected that the redoubtable spinster was just putting a brave face on things. Besides, there was St John to think of as well—how would an elderly cleric cope with a new parish when he had become so attached to his eccentric islanders, and they to him?

'Besides—' Lady Salome leant forward a little arthritically to put another log on the fire and Beth hurried to help her '—you are so rich, my dear! You may give the island all the things it needs!'

'Materially, perhaps,' Beth murmured. She smiled at Lady Salome. 'Surely there are other things more important? The love of money is the root of all evil, after all! The Book of Timothy, I think!'

'Very good!' Lady Salome clapped her hands. 'But, oh, to be the one camel that passes through the eye of the needle! Matthew nineteen, verse twenty-four!' She happily capped Beth's quotation, then fixed her with her perceptive dark gaze. 'Tell me, do you like Marcus, Lady Allerton?'

The abrupt change of subject took Beth aback a little. Normally she would have prevaricated, particularly on so short an acquaintance. Yet there was something about Lady Salome's open friendliness that made her reply truthfully.

'Yes. Yes, I do. I like the Earl of Trevithick a lot, but…' A tiny frown wrinkled her brow.

'But!' Lady Salome said sonorously. 'There is always a but!'

Beth laughed. 'Oh, Lady Salome, there are difficulties. We do not know each other very well—'

'Love conquers all!' Lady Salome said grandly. 'The Book of Kings—'

'Quite,' Beth said, thinking it unlikely. She saw that Marcus had come in and hastily changed the subject. 'Are there many tales of smuggling in these parts, Lady Salome?'

Lady Salome gave her a penetrating look. 'Not since the time of your grandfather, my dear! There's no money in the trade these days and little interest in it!'

Beth could feel Marcus's gaze resting on her thoughtfully. She gave him a dazzling smile. 'I was asking your aunt about smugglers' tales, my lord—'

'I heard you.' Marcus took a cup of tea from Lady Salome and sat back, stretching his long legs out to the fire. 'The profession has almost died out, has it not, Aunt Sal?'

'Along with piracy and wrecking!' Lady Salome agreed. 'Life on Fairhaven is nowhere near as exciting as one might imagine, my dear! Why, even the American War scarce touches us here!'

'That reminds me,' Marcus said. 'McCrae has given me the direction of one of the islanders who knew your grandfather, Lady Allerton. I am sure he will be pleased to talk to you! Jack Cade, I believe his name is, up at Halfway Cottage. Perhaps you may choose to walk up in the morning?'

'Perhaps I shall,' Beth agreed. 'Thank you, my lord.' She was not sure why she did not feel more exhilarated at the news, but for some reason she could summon up little enthusiasm. It was all very odd. She had been wanting to come to Fairhaven for years, with an intensity that had eclipsed all else, yet now she was here it was all falling oddly flat. Beth wondered if she was one of those tiresome people who, once they had achieved something, had no use for it any more. She hoped not.

She stood up and smiled at Lady Salome. 'Pray ex-

cuse me, ma'am, Lord Trevithick…' she gave Marcus a
distant nod '…I am tired and would like to retire. There
is no need to accompany me,' she added sharply, as
Marcus rose from his chair with some reluctance, 'I can
find my own way. Goodnight!'

As she went up the stairs, Beth reflected that there
was nothing more insulting than Marcus's pretence of
courtesy towards her, no doubt assumed for Lady
Salome's benefit. She hated this coldness between them
that threatened to harden into indifference, then plain
dislike. Already she felt absurdly distanced from
Marcus, as though their earlier intimacy had never been.
It seemed almost impossible to believe that Marcus had
once held her in his arms, had kissed her, had evoked a
response from her that she had not even known could
exist. Yet all that was in the past. From now on a slightly
bored courtesy was probably all that she could expect.

Beth sat on the window seat in her bedroom and
looked out at the moonlight skipping across the black
water. The poor weather that had dogged their crossing
the day before had vanished and it was a clear night
with the stars showing bright and hard in the heavens.
Somewhere in the depths of the castle, a clock struck
one. The chimes echoed through the stone walls and died
away. Beth shivered a little. She had been waiting for
four hours and was thoroughly tired and chilled, but she
had been determined not to miss whatever it was that
Marcus and Colin McCrae were up to that night.

The sound of stone on stone far below cut through
her boredom. Someone had opened the door of the castle
and was even now setting off down the twisting track to
the beach. Beth pressed her nose to the cold window
glass. Her bedroom looked out on a short stretch of grass

that ended abruptly where the track began its descent of the cliff. She could hear nothing, but she could just see the dancing flame of a torch as someone picked their way down towards the harbour. Beth slid off the window seat, reached for her cloak, and made for the door.

She drew back the bolt, turned the huge knob and pushed. The door did not move. Beth pushed again but it remained shut fast. She stood back, frowning.

The door had not stuck earlier in the evening. Then, it had swung smoothly on oiled hinges. Which meant that now it could only be locked—on the far side. She pushed the door again, sharply. Nothing happened.

Kneeling down, Beth peered through the keyhole. She could see the key still in the lock on the other side of the door. Indignation swelled in her, confirming her suspicions. Marcus had locked her in, and she knew why.

Beth went to her trunk and took out the enamelled box that held her hairpins. Near the window stood an old wooden writing desk and she was almost certain she had seen some thick blotting paper there earlier. She whipped it up and hurried back to the door. There was a gap of at least an inch between the smooth stone step and the bottom of the door and Beth bent down, stealthily inserting the paper into the space. The first hairpin bent when she pushed it into the lock but the second loosened the key and after a little jiggling, it fell to the floor. The blotting paper muffled the sound and all Beth heard was a soft thud.

Holding her breath, she drew the paper towards her. The key caught on the bottom of the door and she bit her lip, trying to manoeuvre the paper through the gap without making any noise. After a few nerve-racking seconds, it slid smoothly into her grasp.

Dusting her skirts down, Beth turned the key and

opened the door a crack. The corridor outside was faintly lit by lamplight and was quite empty. She pulled the door closed behind her and tiptoed to the top of the stairs.

It took her several minutes to negotiate Saintonge Castle's dark corridors and stairs, for she was anxious to make no noise and draw no attention. At one point she was obliged to dodge into the Great Hall when a servant came out of the kitchens with a pile of clean crockery, and she had almost reached the front door when Martha McCrae came hurrying down the nursery stairs, a candle in her hand. By the time that Beth slipped out into the night, her heart was in her mouth and she had to stop to rest for a moment in the lee of the castle wall.

It was a fine night, but there as a strong wind blowing. Beth quickly realised that it would be the utmost folly to try to descend the cliff path without the aid of a light, for even in the daytime the track was treacherous. It was also the perfect way to walk directly into the smugglers' path before she had realised it. She had just resigned herself to another long wait out in the cold dark when she saw the glint of torchlight below and heard the crunch of footsteps on shingle. They were already coming back. She dived for shelter behind the nearest wall.

She was just in time and the sight that met her eyes was a curious one. A torch-lit procession of men was coming up the cliff path, but where Beth's imagination had supplied all the trappings of a smuggling operation—the donkeys, the panniers full of bottles, the packets of lace—they were carrying two coffins high on their shoulders. Beth recognised the crew of the *Marie Louise* and some of the village men she had seen earlier in the day. Amongst them, Marcus was carrying the corner of one coffin and Colin McCrae another. Beth crouched behind the wall and watched them pass by, and stared after them into the darkness.

She had not been aware that the *Marie Louise* was carrying any men home for burial, but then she supposed that Marcus would not necessarily want to distress her with the fact. Perhaps this was what McCrae had been referring to when he had asked Marcus if he would tell her, and Marcus had said that there was no need. Perhaps so, perhaps not. The whole thing was odd in the extreme.

The more Beth thought about it, the odder it became. The men had been smiling and chatting amongst themselves and there had been none of the grim-faced respect that she would have expected on such an occasion. She pulled her cloak about her and tried to huddle more closely into the shelter of the wall. Where did Marcus's reference to 'Marchant's cargo' fit in? Were the coffins the cargo, and if so, were the deaths suspicious? Why not wait until daylight to bring the coffins home to rest? And why lock her in her room to ensure that she knew nothing of the night's activities?

Beth scrambled out onto the track and set off towards the village in the direction that the men had taken. She could just see the flickering of the lanterns up ahead and the moon cast enough light on the track for her to pick her way. All the same it was an uncomfortable walk and she almost slipped and fell several times. She resolved that the road was the first thing that she would spend money improving when once she was the official owner of Fairhaven.

By the time that Beth reached the first cottages, the pallbearers were entering the church, which, Beth thought, was entirely appropriate if they had a couple of dead men for burial. She felt cold, stiff and rather silly to have become so wrapped up in her own imaginings, and she was about to turn back when she heard a crash in the church porch and Marcus's voice carried to her on the wind.

'Careful there! Marchant will not be pleased if the goods are damaged...'

Curiosity aroused once more, Beth picked her way across the graveyard and peeked around the church door. She knew she was taking a big risk, but it was dark and the men were safely inside the church, so it seemed safe to take a look.

Fairhaven's chapel was small and ill lit and though she could just make out the shapes of the coffins laid out before the altar, a huge pillar obscured the rest of her view. The smell of musty cloth and dust hung in the air. Taking care to remain unseen, Beth slipped behind one of the Mostyn family memorials and peered round.

Two lanterns had been placed at either end of the altar and in their flickering light Beth could see the men from the ship busy with the coffin lids. They were showing little respect for the dead now. One man had a crowbar that he was wedging under one corner. There was a creak of protest from the wood and then a splintering noise as the lid came free. Beth smothered a gasp.

'Fine workmanship on these,' she heard one of the sailors say appreciatively as he leant over the coffin.

'Aye...nothing but the best...' One of his colleagues was lifting something from inside. The lantern light glinted on steel. Beth drew back sharply as she saw the rifle in his hands and the pile of guns spilling over the top of the coffin.

Suddenly there was a prickling feeling on the back of her neck, a warning instinct that was as ancient as it was inexplicable. Beth froze, her eyes still on the scene be-

fore her. Several of the crew had guns in their hands
now and were inspecting them with admiration. Colin
McCrae was exchanging a few words with one of the
sailors as they fastened the lids back down. But of
Marcus there was no sign.

Beth turned slowly. The empty ranks of pews and the
rows of memorials stared back at her, cobwebby and
dark. There was nobody there. She started to back towards the door, stepping silently, pausing to check every
few seconds that she was unobserved. She could see no
one at all but the feeling of being watched persisted. And
then someone moved.

Beth caught her breath on a gasp that seemed to echo
around the chapel's rafters. She saw the sailors put down
the guns and look in her direction and then Marcus
Trevithick stepped from the porch directly into her path.

'Good evening, Lady Allerton,' he said politely.
'What an unexpected pleasure to find you here!'

For a moment Beth seriously considered trying to
push past him and run, but then Marcus put out one hand
and took her arm in a grip that was not tight but that
she could not have broken without a struggle.

'Do you know,' he said conversationally, 'that you are
forever running away from me, Lady Allerton? On this
occasion I do beg you to reconsider. I would be put to
the trouble of trying to catch you and you would probably go straight over the side of a cliff in the dark!'

They stood staring at each other, then Beth let go of
the breath she had been holding. 'Oh! I might have
known that you would find me here! Though why you
did nothing to prevent me seeing the rifles—' She broke
off as she tried to work out what was going on. She saw
Marcus grin.

'Why should I prevent you? There is nothing illegal

to hide and if you wish to wander about Fairhaven in the middle of the night, that is your choice!'

'Nothing illegal?' Beth's voice had warmed into indignation. 'You smuggle munitions in here, no doubt intending to sell them on—' Once again she stopped, this time as he laughed.

'Is that what you think? My dear Lady Allerton, I am always astounded by your fertile imagination! This is no Gothic romance!' His voice changed, became grimmer. 'I am less flattered by the fact that you always suspect the worst of me!'

Beth felt suddenly ashamed. She freed herself from his grip and stepped back, smoothing her cloak down with a self-conscious gesture.

'Yes, well you must admit that your actions were of the most suspicious! If I have been mistrustful of you it is only because I found myself a prisoner in my own room!'

'Let us discuss this back at the castle,' Marcus suggested. He drew her through the doorway and into the porch, picking up his lantern as they went. The light skipped over the gravestones and illuminated the uneven stone path to the lych-gate. Marcus took Beth's arm again, this time in a gentler grip as he guided her back to the road.

'Stay close to me,' he said abruptly. 'I am amazed that you did not break an ankle creeping about in the dark!'

They walked back to the castle in silence. The moon was high and the combination of that and the torch lit the way well enough, but by now Beth was shaking with cold and reaction. She was glad when they reached the huge oak front door and Marcus ushered her into the hall.

'Please join me in the drawing room, Lady Allerton.'

Beth, who had been nursing a craven desire to run upstairs and hide in her room, realised that this was not an invitation so much as an order. She reluctantly allowed Marcus to take her cloak from her, noting that the once-smart black velvet was now crushed and stained from its travels and would never be the same again. Marcus held the drawing-room door open and Beth went in. She watched as he kicked the embers of the fire into life before moving over to the silver tray on the sideboard.

'A nightcap, Lady Allerton, to accompany our discussions? The brandy will warm you.'

He put what looked like a huge quantity of amber liquid into the glass before passing it to her. Beth risked a taste and felt the spirit burn her stomach. But Marcus was right. It was warming and in a little while she had stopped shivering.

Marcus gestured her to a chair by the fire and sat down opposite her. In the faint light his face looked brooding, severe. He looked up and their eyes met, and Beth's heart skipped a beat. Marcus smiled faintly.

'I see that the small matter of a locked door cannot stand in your way, Lady Allerton! I have seldom met anyone so indomitable!'

Beth shrugged, avoiding his gaze. ''Tis simple to open a locked door, my lord, when the key is still on the other side!'

Marcus laughed, a laugh that turned into a yawn. He slid down in the chair and stretched his legs towards the fire. 'Excuse me. It has been a long night. I blame Colin McCrae for leaving the key in the lock. I warned him to make sure that all was secure but, unlike me, he underestimated you!' He looked at her and his smile faded. 'Believe me, Lady Allerton, it was for your own good.'

Beth took a mouthful of brandy. 'I do so detest it when people say that,' she confided, 'for generally it is not true at all! From what were you protecting me, my lord? My own curiosity?'

Marcus inclined his head. 'That, and the vivid imagination that has already led you to invent wild stories this night!' He grimaced. 'But your reproof is fair, Lady Allerton. I should not have had you constrained in your room. Indeed, I should have trusted you with the truth and I apologise that I did not.'

Beth took another sip of brandy. The fiery taste was growing on her and the warm feeling it engendered even more so. She could feel the colour coming back into her face, the relaxation stealing through her limbs.

'And the truth is—what, precisely, my lord?'

Marcus shifted in his chair. 'The truth is that there is a certain Dutch privateer by the name of Godard, who has been taking advantage of the hostilities between our nation and America to prey on the ships trading from Bristol.' He leant forward and threw another log on the fire. 'The guns that you saw were entrusted to me by Captain Marchant of his Majesty's navy. Marchant wanted an arsenal for the navy to draw on locally if they find themselves within striking distance of the enemy. There is more to unload from the *Marie Louise* tomorrow.'

He looked across at her and smiled. 'That is the explanation for tonight's activities, Lady Allerton!'

Beth frowned. 'Do you think this privateer is likely to threaten Fairhaven, my lord?' she asked after a moment.

'It is most unlikely.' Marcus stood up to refill her glass. 'Godard would gain little from taking Fairhaven, for then he would have to defend it. It is more likely that he would stage a raid in order to gain fresh supplies, but even that is improbable. I confess that it was that aspect of the case that held me silent, however, for I did not wish to disturb you with the knowledge unless the threat became real.'

Beth drained her glass. 'I see. But Lady Salome has a stout enough constitution to be told the truth?'

Marcus grinned. 'You heard that, did you? McCrae and I should be more careful of speaking behind peoples' backs!' He shrugged. 'The truth is that Aunt Sal, for all her disclaimers, has dealt with everything from smugglers to pirates in her time here on Fairhaven and is quite up to snuff! Whereas you, Lady Allerton…' his smile robbed the words of any sting '…you are young and have led a more sheltered life!'

Beth decided to let this go. It was indisputable; anyway, there were other matters she wanted to pursue.

'Why go to such an elaborate charade with the coffins, my lord?'

'It was all for show.' Marcus laughed. 'It is, in fact, a convenient way of carrying a large quantity of guns and Marchant and I thought it might confuse any spies…'

'Such as myself,' Beth said ruefully. She had begun to realise just how much she had built up on so little. What was it that Marcus had said—that she always suspected the worst of him? That, and the fact that she was always running away from him. She bit her lip. Perhaps both charges were true and the thought made her feel uncomfortable. She put her empty glass down carefully on the walnut table, suddenly aware that she was feeling rather light-headed from unaccustomed liquor.

'I am sorry, my lord…'

'For what, Lady Allerton?'

Marcus was sitting forward, his own glass held between his two hands. His dark eyes were fixed on her face. 'Are you apologising for suspecting me unjustly, or for running away from me or even for locking me in a cellar?'

Beth looked up at him, then away quickly. There was something in that intent gaze that disturbed her and though his tone was light she had the oddest feeling that he had been hurt by her behaviour.

'For all of those, I suppose, my lord. I did try to apologise to you before about the cellar incident...' Beth groped for words. 'It was...very bad of me and I truly regret it...'

'Do you?' Marcus's face was unyielding. Beth, who had hoped that time would have softened his anger towards her, felt her heart sink. She had not thought him a man who bore grudges, but perhaps she deserved it.

'It is just that I thought I had to do it in order to reach Fairhaven first!' she burst out. 'That had been my intention all along and I did not think I could expect you to help me.'

'You mean you did not think you could trust me to keep my word even though I told you I would give Fairhaven to you.' Marcus's quiet tones cut through her excuses and silenced her. He looked at her, a hint of amusement coming into his eyes. 'Well, perhaps you had good reason, my lady. I had broken my word to you twice and you have no reason to suppose I would not do it a third time.'

'No, I...' Beth frowned. That seemed all wrong, but she was tired and light-headed and unable to frame her thoughts properly. She knitted her fingers together in her lap and stared fixedly at them.

'I do not think that is fair, my lord.' She spoke very quickly, before her courage deserted her. 'I do trust you and it was very wrong of me to behave as I have and, if I have hurt—offended—you in any way, I am truly sorry.' She looked up swiftly and gave him a watery smile. 'At least we are speaking to each other again!'

Marcus moved so that one of his hands was covering her clenched fingers. 'Did it trouble you that we were at odds?'

Beth stared at him, unable to tear her gaze away. There was warmth and tenderness in his eyes and she felt such a rush of relief that the tears came into her eyes and she almost cried.

'Oh…' She cleared her throat, embarrassed. 'Well, it was decidedly uncomfortable…'

Marcus smiled. He raised his hand and turned one of her curls absent-mindedly about his fingers, but his eyes never left her face. 'I thought so too.'

'Then—' Beth held her breath '—are we to be… friends…again, my lord?'

'Friends?' Marcus's gaze became thoughtful. 'I do not think so, Lady Allerton. Of all the things we are or could be, that is far too tepid a description! Passionate enemies or equally passionate lovers, perhaps, but nothing less than that!'

His fingers brushed her cheek and he took her chin in his hand. His gaze dropped to her lips. 'Are you sure that you trust me?'

'Yes,' Beth whispered.

Marcus laughed. He bent his head and kissed her, a brief, hard kiss, before allowing his hand to fall to his side.

'What a way you have of taking the wind from a fellow's sails, Lady Allerton!' His tone was rueful as he pulled Beth to her feet and steered her out into the hall. 'If you could see yourself, ever-so-slightly drunk and more than a little tempting…' He shook his head. 'And for the first time, you are looking at me with utter trust in your eyes! Your sense of timing is immaculate!'

He lit a candle for her and handed it over with a quizzical lift of his brows. 'I hope that you can find your own way to your room? It would be a mistake to trust me to deliver you there safely!'

Beth took the candle and scurried away up the stairs. She was aware that she was indeed more than a little tipsy, although the blame for that could be laid squarely at Marcus's door for giving her so much brandy. She was more concerned, however, about that casual kiss and the promise behind it. For although Marcus had behaved as a perfect gentleman, there had been an assurance in his tone that Beth was certain would be fulfilled. Enemies or lovers; she knew which she would secretly prefer and it was not just the brandy in her blood that was speaking. She closed her bedroom door behind her and locked it carefully. For now it was enough to know that she and Marcus were reconciled as friends, but for the future… Beth undressed quickly, lay down and blew out her candle flame.

Chapter Eight

It was in fact a little over a week before Beth found the time to visit Jack Cade and ask about her grandfather. Salome Trevithick had seen it as her duty to show Beth the island and had bundled her into the gig every day, taking her to meet the farmers and cottagers, and to view all the places that Salome whimsically referred to as 'the sights'. By the end of the week Beth's head was spinning with names and faces, but her overriding impression was how deeply Salome was involved in the life of the community and how much the islanders loved her. Beth they greeted with a guarded respect that was cold in comparison, but she knew that love and loyalty had to be earned and were not given for nothing. She set about following Salome's lead and spent hours at the school or in the different houses, chatting to the villagers, reading to the children or playing outside with them when the weather was fine. In the rare moments when she was left to her own devices, Beth would wander for hours along the cliff tops, admiring the view or just watching the clouds chase across the sea.

Meanwhile, Beth could not help but notice that Marcus was setting out to make a particularly good impression on his tenants. Not only did he spend a great deal of time with Colin McCrae, discussing his plans for the farms and the harbour, but he did not scruple to get his hands dirty. A new barn was being built alongside the five-acre field, and Marcus could be seen there every morning, stripped to the waist and lending a hand.

When Salome had stopped the gig by the gate one day and called Marcus over to tease him about his industry, Beth had tried to look away—the sight of Marcus's bare brown torso and firm muscles had been curiously disturbing. But instead of fixing her gaze on a nearby flock of sheep, she had found herself staring, until Marcus had looked at her with raised eyebrows and asked if she was feeling quite the thing. And certainly Beth had *not* been feeling at all well. Her face was flushed and her pulse was racing and she wondered if she had contracted a fever. Salome had taken one look at her, smiled, and said that she thought Beth was suffering from a certain affliction, but had not said which.

Marcus had sought Beth out one evening and explained that he did not wish to leave Fairhaven until he had had the chance to discuss the future with his uncle St John as well as with Salome. This was clearly impossible with St John in Exeter, and Beth, anxious not to appear to be pushing the Trevithicks from their home, made no demur about extending her time on Fairhaven. She sent a letter to Charlotte, explaining what was happening and saying that she intended to be back at Mostyn Hall for Christmas, then, when she finally had a spare morning, she set off to find Jack Cade.

Jack Cade's cottage sat about a mile away from the main village, on a small hill that looked out westward across the harbour to the coast of Devon. Marcus had said that Cade had been a fisherman all his life, but that he was too old to go to sea any more and had retired to live alone. The other villagers considered him something of an oddity, but as one of the longest-lived inhabitants of Fairhaven he was given grudging respect.

Beth trod up the shell-lined path to the cottage door. A few straggling plants huddled in the shelter of its white-painted wall and there was a collection of floats and old rope tumbled amidst the grass of the headland, with a sheep grazing placidly nearby. Beth knocked tentatively at the door. Now that the moment had come for her to meet one of her grandfather's contemporaries, she was almost sick with nerves.

The door creaked open to reveal a bent old figure in the aperture. Beth's smile faltered a little.

'Mr Cade? I am Beth Allerton. I heard that you knew my grandfather, Charles Mostyn, and I wondered if you would be able to tell me about him, please?'

The old fisherman looked at her. His eyes were as sharp and bright as a hawk's in a face of old leather. He smiled, showing the stumps of blackened teeth. 'I thought you'd be a'coming, my lady. Yes, I knew Charles Mostyn. I could tell you about him.'

A trickle of anticipation crept down Beth's spine, making her shiver. She was shaking at the prospect of being so close to the truth at last and hearing directly what had happened to Lord Mostyn on the night he had died.

'Take a seat, ma'am,' the old man said courteously, stepping back to allow her to precede him into the cottage. He swept a pile of floats and nets from the armchair nearest the fire and Beth sat down, looking about her with interest.

There was only the one room but it was snug and

wood-lined, with a roaring fire in the grate. Various bits
of flotsam and jetsam adorned the walls: a set of antlers,
a brown glass bottle, a twisted piece of bleached wood—
all the bits and pieces that Cade must have picked up
throughout his life at sea.

The old man sat down on the settle opposite Beth,
groaning and creaking like the old wood as he found a
comfortable position. He pulled a bottle of whisky towards him, knocked his pipe out on the arm of the chair
and stuffed it full of fresh tobacco. He did not speak
until it was lit and he was puffing away, with several
clouds of evil-smelling smoke adding to the alcoholic
fug in the room.

'Charles Mostyn...' he said, thoughtfully. 'He was the
one before the old Earl. The Evil Earl.' He cackled suddenly. 'Not like this young 'un, for all his London ways.
Seems like some good can come out of the old stock
after all!'

Beth held her tongue and kept her patience. There was
no point in hurrying the old man and she had heard
plenty of people sing Marcus's praises over the past
week.

'The Old Earl,' Jack Cade said again. 'Aye, he were
a bad 'un and no mistake. And Mostyn too—as alike as
two brothers, with nothing to choose between them!'

Beth sat up straight in her chair, frowning slightly.
This did not sound right. 'Nothing to choose? But, Mr
Cade—'

Jack Cade puffed hard on the pipe. 'Trevithick had a
violent temper, but Mostyn was cruel hard—cold and
vicious where Trevithick was loud and brutal. But
Mostyn was clever, see?' His sharp gaze pinned Beth to
her chair. 'He brought the trade in here, though we said

as we wanted no trouble. But he wouldn't listen. Needed the money, I reckon, and the silly lads with him.'

'The…trade?'

'Smuggling!' Cade said triumphantly. 'Smuggling, m'lady! Big business here in the straits it was in them days. Trevithick and Mostyn at each other's throats, allus a struggle to control the trade along the coast. That's all! No more to it. But Mostyn held Fairhaven, see, so he had the advantage and a hard landlord he was, into the bargain.'

Beth swallowed hard. This was not at all as she had imagined it, nor indeed how the old stories had been spun to her in the nursery at Mostyn Hall all those years ago. She cleared her throat.

'Mr Cade, are you sure? I mean—' she saw his piercing gaze resting on her '—it is simply that I was told a vastly different story.'

'Bound to tell you something different, weren't they!' Cade said simply. 'Little lass wi' no family to speak of! Who'd want to tell the truth? Plenty to hide, that family, plenty to hide!'

Beth took a deep breath. She was shaking so much that she had to lock her fingers together to still them, but it was not with anticipation now. There was a pain lodged somewhere in her chest and another that blocked her throat until she could barely speak. But she had to know the truth now.

'What happened?' She whispered. 'In the end, I mean.'

There was pity in Cade's face. She could see it there and it struck another blow to her heart.

'In the end there was so much rivalry for the trade in these waters that Trevithick and Mostyn came to blows.' The old man coughed. 'Trevithick won and he took the island, and no Mostyn has been here since. 'Til now, my lady.'

'How did Trevithick take Fairhaven?' Beth asked. She stared as the old man took a deep swig from his whisky bottle, wiped his mouth on his sleeve and smacked his lips.

'Ah! The last quarrel. It was all over a load of brandy Mostyn was waiting for, see? The free traders brought it in, but Mostyn was late for the meet and Trevithick got here first. Offered to double the payment for the men if they traded with him, not Mostyn, and helped him take the island into the bargain.' Cade shook his head. 'Didn't need much persuasion. Everyone hated Mostyn. Trevithick was little better, but at least he was paying well. So when Mostyn came they ambushed him and cut him to pieces—saving your presence, my lady.'

'But I thought—' Beth stopped, swallowed hard, and started again. 'I had heard that he was ambushed by the Earl of Trevithick's men, and the Earl stole the family silver.'

Cade cackled with laughter. 'Weren't no silver, m'lady. Mostyn was too mean to pay his dues! There was just the sword and the ring.' He got to his feet and hobbled over to an old sea chest in the corner, rummaging about inside. 'I've never worn this. Didn't seem right, somehow, after Trevithick had cut it from his finger! Best for you to have it now, perhaps, seeing as he was your grandfather!'

Beth held out her hand automatically and Cade dropped the signet ring into it. Through the blur of her tears, she saw the arms of Mostyn cut deep into the gold, the motto that was barely legible after all these years: *Remember*. She closed her fist tightly about it.

'What happened to the Sword of Saintonge?' she

asked, marvelling at the steadiness of her own voice. 'Did Trevithick take that too?'

Cade was shaking his head. 'The sword broke in the fight, my lady. I have the stump of it here, but it's nothing but rust now—'

Beth was suddenly, devastatingly aware that she was about to cry and she had absolutely no wish to do so in Cade's cottage. She stood up abruptly.

'Excuse me. You have been more than kind, Mr Cade, but I fear I must go.'

The old man patted her arm clumsily. 'Forgive me, my lady. I did not know what to do for the best, but his lordship said that it was important I tell you the truth.'

Beth paused, her tears suddenly forgotten. A ray of sunlight struck across her eyes from the open door and she moved impatiently into the shade. 'His lordship said so? Lord Trevithick? When?'

Cade shifted awkwardly. 'When he came to see me, ma'am. Said you were looking for someone who knew your grandfather and that I was to tell you everything, honestly. Imperative, he said it was—'

Beth wheeled round and ran out of the cottage door, scaring the sheep that had been calmly grazing by the gate. She plunged down the village street, conscious that people were looking at her curiously, and practically crashed into the farm gate where she had last seen Marcus helping to stack some hay. He was still there. The last of the bales had been moved into the barn and he was standing nearby, talking to Colin McCrae.

'Lord Trevithick!' Beth had intended to sound imperious, but her voice came out with a desperate wobble in it. She tried to steel herself. 'Lord Trevithick, I require to speak with you! At once!'

Marcus exchanged a few quick words with Colin

McCrae, then came across to her, vaulting over the gate and taking her arm. His gaze was searching.

'You have seen Cade, then, Lady Allerton? Are you all right?'

'No, I am not all right!' Beth said stormily. Two bright spots of angry colour shone in her cheeks. Despite the chill of the day, she felt feverishly hot. 'How dare you, Lord Trevithick!' Her voice rose. 'How dare you let me go to speak to that old man when you knew the truth about my grandfather and could have told me yourself and spared me the pain!'

'Not here,' Marcus said. His grip tightened on her arm. He was looking over her shoulder at the crowd of farmworkers and villagers who were now providing an embarrassed but none the less interested audience. Beth shook herself free. At that moment she would not have cared if the entire island had gathered for the entertainment.

'Let go of me!' she hissed. 'I detest your behaviour, sir.'

There was the flash of something elemental and angry in Marcus's eyes. This time his grip bruised her skin. 'And would you have believed me if I had told you that your grandfather was nothing but a common free trader, Lady Allerton? I think not! Your trust in me has been notable for its absence up until now! You had to hear the truth from someone else!'

Beth stared into his angry eyes for what seemed like hours. Behind her the crowd shifted and murmured and even through her preoccupation she heard one buxom lady saying to another: 'Cade has told her all about Charles Mostyn… They'd told her he was a good man, poor lamb…'

It was the pity that broke Beth. She could see it on

the faces of all those about her as they witnessed her terrible distress. It was the same sympathy that had been reflected in Jack Cade's eyes at the end. Probably they had all known the truth about Charles Mostyn, but no one had wanted to mention it to her. At first they might even have imagined her to be a chip off the Mostyn block, come to take them back to the bad times. She and Marcus both. Trevithick and Mostyn, at each other's throats, dragging their people down with them when they should have been defending them.

There was no sympathy on Marcus's face. He looked at her and his expression was carved from stone. With a cry, Beth tore herself from his grip and turned her back on all of them, running down the hill towards the castle until her legs were going so fast that she was almost falling over herself. The wind roared in her ears and her hair whipped about her face, blinding her. She slammed the castle gate open and raced across the greensward to the cliff edge.

'Beth! For God's sake! Stop before you fall!'

Marcus caught her from behind, knocking all the breath from her body as he pulled her to the ground. She was crying now, struggling and pummelling him in her efforts to get away from him, gasping for breath until he had quite simply to lean the whole of his weight on her to subdue her. Beth lay still, trying to calm her sobs, feeling the cold grass beneath her cheek and the warm tears that ran down her face and splashed onto the springy turf.

'Oh, Beth…'

There was a world of pity in Marcus's voice now and she did not resist him when he pulled her into his arms, half-cradling her as she cried as though her heart was breaking.

For what seemed like endless hours she wept into his jacket and felt his hands stroking her and his voice murmuring words that made no sense but sounded inexpressibly comforting. And at length she sat up a little, wiped her hand across her wet cheeks and said, in a small voice, 'I never cry!'

Marcus smiled, brushing the hair back from her face. 'No, indeed. I had noticed.' He got to his feet, pulling her with him. 'Come, we must get you inside. Sitting on the damp grass will not make you feel any better...'

Beth clung to him. 'Marcus...'

'I know.' For a moment Marcus's arms tightened about her in a hug before he slid one arm about her waist and guided her back towards the castle. Lady Salome met them at the door, her gardening trug over her arm, a look of distress on her face.

'I heard,' she said, patting Beth's shoulder consolingly. 'My poor girl, to have all your memories dashed in such a cruel way! Oh, the betrayal of innocent blood! Matthew twenty-six, verse twenty-seven!'

Beth hiccuped a little and smothered a giggle. 'Oh, Lady Salome, you are a very present help in trouble!'

'A glass of madeira and a hot brick are what we need!' Lady Salome said bracingly. 'Come upstairs, my dear, and I will give you rest!'

'Exodus thirty-three, verse sixteen,' Marcus said, with a sigh.

'Matthew eleven, verse twenty-eight!' Lady Salome called, over her shoulder. 'Marcus, pray ask Mrs McCrae to bring some hot soup and some physick—'

'I am not ill!' Beth objected, borne irresistibly upwards on Lady Salome's arm.

'Nonsense! You have sustained a shock and require food, drink and rest,' Lady Salome said decisively. She opened the bedroom door and pushed Beth inside. 'You mark my words—within half an hour you will be asleep!'

The sound of the sea was in Beth's ears and it was very soothing. She opened her eyes reluctantly. The room was bathed in candlelight and the long curtains were drawn. Martha McCrae was sitting beside the bed, reading a book. She looked up as Beth opened her eyes and her face broke into a smile.

'Oh, my lady! How are you feeling now?'

Beth frowned slightly. 'Have I been asleep, Martha? Good gracious! Lady Salome gave me a glass of ratafia and the next thing I remember… Why, I do believe I feel hungry!'

Martha jumped up. 'There is some fresh broth made this afternoon, my lady, the very thing! I will go and fetch some for you—'

'Stay a moment, please!' Beth put out her hand and caught the girl's sleeve. 'Martha, will you answer something for me?'

'If I can, my lady.' Martha looked apprehensive.

'Does everyone on the island know the truth of my grandfather's dishonour?'

Martha fidgeted, avoiding Beth's gaze. 'Oh, my lady! Everyone knows the old stories, of course, though it was only Jack Cade and one or two others actually remember…' She twisted her hands together. 'I'm sorry, my lady. We thought you knew, you see, until his lordship told Colin that you had been told quite a different tale! Then we were afraid, for we knew you would find out…' Her unhappy brown eyes met Beth's and there was apology in their depths. 'It has all been so difficult, my lady, what with thinking his lordship was showing an interest in the place, then hearing that you would be taking Fairhaven over, and worrying for Lady Salome, and not knowing what was really going on.'

Beth nodded. 'I understand. But Lord Trevithick *has* shown a genuine interest in Fairhaven and has done so much for the island—'

Martha smiled and it was like the sun breaking through clouds. 'Oh, my lady! Now we don't know what to think! We know you care about Fairhaven, but Lord Trevithick is a good man and has already helped us so much! If only you could both keep Fairhaven—' She broke off, getting to her feet. 'Excuse me, my lady. I will go to fetch that soup.'

Beth turned her head against the pillow. Now she fully understood the hostility of the villagers when first she had come to Fairhaven. They had either remembered the bad old days of the Mostyns or remembered hearing stories of that time. Her grandfather's legacy had gone deep and in ways that she had not even imagined. Beth sat up, reached for her wrap and propped herself up on her pillows. She had seldom had a day's illness in her life, but just for now it felt pleasantly indulgent to stay in bed and let Martha wait on her. She no longer felt tearful, but she did feel tired.

'Entirely respectable, alas!' The voice from the doorway made her jump and she turned to see Marcus strolling forward into the room. He grinned at her in the old way that she remembered and gestured to the edge of the bed.

'May I?'

'Well…' Beth frowned. 'You should not be here, my lord! Whatever would Lady Salome say?'

'I know!' Marcus looked unabashed. 'But Martha left

the door open and I was anxious to see if you were really better!'

Beth dropped her gaze. She felt curiously shy, aware of the thinness of her nightgown and wrap, even if Marcus seemed oblivious to it. Which was in itself rather disappointing... Annoyed at the direction of her thoughts, she forced herself to meet his gaze.

'Please, my lord, before you say anything else I must apologise—'

Marcus touched her hand. He shook his head. 'Beth, do not. You had sustained a huge shock and anything you said was entirely understandable.'

Beth gave him a slight smile. 'Thank you.' She hesitated. 'I do understand why you did not tell me. I had to hear it from someone who had been there, someone who had seen with their own eyes—'

'Believe me—' Marcus voice was a little rough '—if I had thought that there could be any other way...'

Beth felt her face grow warm. She was glad that there was no light but the glow of the fire. She felt a constraint between them, a tension that was due to all the emotions that were present but unspoken.

'I confess I feel rather foolish,' she said, after a moment. 'For so long, the history of the Mostyns has been like...' she hesitated '...almost like a talisman to me, I suppose. The romantic history, the feud, good vanquished by evil, or so I thought, when really...' Her voice trailed away.

'When really there were two warring families, neither of whom deserved your good opinion,' Marcus finished drily.

Beth sighed. 'The whole quest for Fairhaven was based on a false dream. I can scarce believe it! Ever since I was a child I have longed for it!'

Marcus let go of her hand and stood up a little abruptly. She could not read his expression but his voice was once more his own. 'It is not surprising. Children are most tenacious of dreams, after all, and you were orphaned young and needed something on which to hang your hopes.' He smiled down at her. 'Now I must go. Martha will be back soon with the soup and would be scandalised to find me here!'

He went out, leaving Beth staring blindly into the fire. Something in Marcus's tone had pierced her, stripping away the remaining illusions from before her eyes. Somewhere in the past few weeks she had become so intent on gaining Fairhaven and achieving her dream that she had been prepared to sacrifice anything to win it. That feeling had possessed her when she had met Marcus in London, it had prompted her to start the chase down to Devon, it had even driven her to lock him in Theo March's wine cellar just so that she could get ahead. The obsession with Fairhaven had always been slumbering, but once the island had seemed almost within her grasp, it had taken over.

Beth slid down under the blankets. It seemed extraordinary now, for she no longer felt that way. She could see clearly for the first time in years, and what she saw was that her quest had exacted a higher price than any wild goose chase. There was Charlotte, who had loyally accompanied her from London on what she had surely known was a fool's errand, only to be abandoned at Theo's vicarage for her pains. Beth had regretted her behaviour to her cousin before, but now she saw its full magnitude.

And there was Marcus… Weeks ago—it seemed like years to Beth now—she had realised that she was in danger of falling in love with Marcus too quickly, too soon. She had distracted herself by the race for Fairhaven, pretending that they were in opposition when, in fact, their conflict had only masked the growing attraction between them. An attraction that Beth now realised, with a dreadful sinking feeling, had developed on her part at least into a hopelessly deep love...

With a groan, Beth rolled over and buried her face in the pillow.

'My lady, are you feeling poorly again?'

Beth raised her head to see Martha McCrae standing by the bed with a steaming pot of soup on a tray. 'Oh, Martha! I did not see you there! No, I am very well...'

After she had finished the chicken broth, she slipped out of bed and trod across the room. Her cloak was still hanging over a chair before the fire. Beth put a hand in the pocket. Her grandfather's signet ring was still in there. She took it out and held it up to the firelight, reading the inscription once more. *Remember.* There had been too much of that. Beth opened the casement window and a flurry of snow blew in on the cutting edge of the wind. Beth gave her grandfather's ring one last glance and flung it out into the darkness.

'You look very beautiful, my lady,' Martha McCrae said with a smile, twisting the last lock of hair into Beth's chignon.

Beth looked at her reflection and smiled. 'Certainly no one would know that you had fashioned my dress out of some old curtains, Martha! You have done a splendid job!'

Martha giggled. 'But they were the best drawing-room curtains, ma'am, and you have the figure to carry anything off!' She gave Beth a sly look. 'I'll wager his lordship will think so too!'

Beth could feel herself colouring up. Now that she was so aware of her feelings for Marcus she was hopelessly self-conscious. She had done everything she could to avoid him over the past week and had been practically tongue-tied in his presence, feeling like a green girl scarcely out of the schoolroom. Fortunately Marcus did not seem to have noticed, for he was so involved in various projects of Colin's devising that Bath barely saw him. He had gone about the estate and she had helped out in Lady Salome's garden and another week had slipped by, bringing them to the date of the annual Fairhaven dance.

'I imagine that there will be plenty of young ladies vying for Lord Trevithick's attention tonight,' Beth said lightly. 'I shall not expect to monopolise him!'

Martha looked disappointed. It had amused Beth that the villagers, who had started by assuming that she was Marcus's mistress, had swiftly learned of their error and had actually seemed disappointed that she and Marcus were not in fact lovers. Beth had wondered if this was because they wanted a neat solution to the future ownership of the island. It would certainly solve the problem if she and Marcus were to share ownership of Fairhaven, but she knew this was not to be. For several days, watching him about the estate, she had felt a growing conviction that it would be wrong to take Fairhaven away from Marcus. Soon she would have to tell him so.

Beth saw that Martha was still watching her and gave her a quick smile. 'Besides, I shall want at least one dance with your Colin tonight, Martha! Now, should you not run along and get ready yourself? You have spent so much time helping me that it is almost time to go down!'

After Martha had hurried away to her own toilette,

Beth picked up her reticule and stood up to admire the clinging cherry-red velvet dress. With her black hair and silver eyes it did indeed look striking and appropriately festive since this was the island's annual dance. Beth sighed unconsciously. She felt as gauche as a debutante and hoped that the young ladies of Fairhaven would distract Marcus's attention. With his strong physique and dark good looks she knew that he was much admired, for she had seen the village girls watching him and giggling together in corners. But perhaps the good people of Fairhaven had had enough of a lord with a wandering eye. The stories of the Evil Earl's philandering had been enough to shock even Beth's strong constitution.

She realised that she could hear music playing below, the pluck of the violins and the thump of drums. That meant that the musicians had already arrived and with them, no doubt, most of the other villagers. It was time to go down and she just hoped that Marcus would be too occupied to notice her.

That vain hope died as she went slowly down the stairs. Marcus was standing in the hall, dressed in evening clothes that had certainly not been fashioned from some cast-off furnishings. He was talking to Lady Salome, who looked glorious in a dress of yellow satin with an overskirt of green sewn with lots of tiny diamonds. Her hair was dressed with pheasant and seagull feathers. Beth hoped that the birds of Fairhaven had not died in vain.

Marcus looked up as Beth came down the final flight and watched her all the way, with a disconcertingly direct gaze that made her feel totally flustered. As she reached the hall, he took her hand and raised it to his lips.

'You look very beautiful, Lady Allerton. I particularly like your necklace! It matches your eyes!'

Beth laughed, fingering the beads a little self-consciously. She had brought no jewellery with her on her journey, but the low-cut dress had cried out for something and Martha had tentatively pressed on her a necklace made of tiny grey pebbles from the beach. Beth had thought it quite as beautiful as the expensive pearls and diamonds she had locked away in London and had been touched by Martha's gesture.

'Sheba dressed to greet Solomon!' Lady Salome said expansively, enveloping Beth in a scented hug. 'I hear that the dancing has started. Excuse me, my dears, I am off to tread a measure!'

Marcus offered Beth his arm and they followed slowly. A lively country dance was striking up as they came into the Great Hall. 'It is remarkable that there are so many musicians on the island, my lord,' Beth observed, looking at the motley orchestra, 'especially with the ruinous effect of the sea air in warping their instruments!'

Marcus laughed. 'A resourceful lot, our islanders! If one asks why there are so many young children on the island or why there are so many musicians, one receives the same answer—that there is nothing else to do during the long winter!'

'My lord!' Beth laughed in spite of herself.

'Come and dance with me,' Marcus said persuasively, smiling down at her. 'I have been saving the first dance for you!'

'In the face of much temptation from other young ladies, no doubt,' Beth said, arching her brows.

Marcus gave her an expressive look. 'There is only

one lady who throws temptation in my path, Lady Allerton, and sooner or later I will fall!'

Beth had always considered the Great Hall to be a cold and bare room, but tonight it looked as she imagined it might have done for some masque centuries before. A huge fire roared in the grate and the light from a score of torches reflected off the polished shields and swords on the walls. The tapestries glowed with rich colour and between them were draped boughs of evergreen as a reminder of the approaching Christmas season. It seemed that all eighty-six inhabitants of Fairhaven were present, resplendent in their best party clothes.

As all the servants had been invited to the dance, the food and drink was very much a matter of helping oneself. A large table almost bowed under the weight of Christmas pies made of minced beef and spices and everyone was dipping into a large cauldron that held a brew that Marcus informed Beth was called Puffin Punch.

'The bird does not form the chief ingredient, however,' he added, when Beth drew back, wrinkling her nose up. 'I believe you will find it quite appetising.'

He was right. The mixture of wine, spices, oranges and lemon was thoroughly delicious and put Beth in mind of the soothing mulled wine that Marcus had sent up for her and Charlotte that night at the inn in Marlborough. The memory brought a strange lump to her throat, for it seemed that so much had happened since that night and not all of it as she had planned. Marcus was watching her, his eyes narrowed on her face.

'What is it, Beth? You look as though you've seen a ghost!'

Beth raised her eyebrows haughtily. 'My name, my lord?'

Marcus laughed. 'You think me inappropriate? After all that we have…been through together? You have called me by name before!'

'You are certainly inappropriate to remind me, my lord,' Beth said pertly, looking at him over the rim of her drinking cup.

'Yet on such an evening as this we could dispense with formality, perhaps?'

Beth finished her punch. 'Very well then, Marcus. But we must not let Lady Salome hear us, for I am sure she is a stickler for formality—' She broke off as Lady Salome whirled past them clasped in the arms of one of the sheep farmers. His face was flushed with drink and excitement and Lady Salome was roaring with laughter at whatever tale he was telling her.

'Well, perhaps not!' Beth finished.

'I hope that the Fairhaven festivities will not shock you, Beth,' Marcus said, grinning. 'They are rumoured to be quite outrageous!'

Beth tried to look cool and unshakable but it was difficult under Marcus's mocking gaze. She looked down the table, seeking distraction.

'Good gracious, what is that?' She pointed to an orange studded with cloves and decorated with a sprig of holly that stood in the centre of the table on a little tripod of twigs.

'The Calennig,' Marcus said indulgently. 'I believe it is a Welsh tradition, for here the customs of Wales and England merge sometimes. It is a symbol to bring a fertile harvest.'

Beth looked around. 'And are there any other traditional decorations here tonight?'

'There is the mistletoe,' Marcus said, a wicked gleam suddenly in his eye. He pointed to the beams above her head. 'If you would care to glance up, my lady…'

Beth evaded the snare deftly. 'Hmm. I think not, my lord. I would prefer to dance!'

The country dance was ending and the impromptu orchestra swung straight into the next tune. Beth clapped her hands.

'Oh! The Furry Dance! I have not danced this since I was a child!'

The dancing was fast and furious, and bore little resemblance to the sedate entertainment of a London ballroom. Beth managed one country dance with Marcus before he was snatched away from her and she was whirled into a jig by one of the village lads. They had no shyness in approaching her and she barely had any rest during the evening as the old folk dances of her childhood and familiar country airs intermingled. The dancing became progressively less decorous as the evening went on and finally she was swept into the lilting rhythm of something called the Brawl, and ended up face to face with Marcus, as she had begun. Dark eyes blazing, he swept her into his arms.

'A kiss under the mistletoe!' one of the village lads shouted, energetically setting the example with his own partner.

Beth saw Marcus grin. 'It is customary,' he murmured, and before she could reply he bent his head and kissed her. His lips were gentle at first, but Beth could not conceal her instinctive response and he crushed her to him, unleashing a passion in both of them that could not be denied. When he let her go and steadied her with a hand on her arm, Beth felt dizzy and confused, aware of the curiosity and approval on the faces all about her.

Marcus kept a protective arm about her as he steered her towards the refreshments and someone pressed another glass of Puffin Punch into her hands.

'This is probably a mistake,' Beth said hopelessly, aware that she was already more than a little incbriated. 'If you do not wish me to be drunk, my lord—'

'Marcus, remember?' Marcus was smiling down at her in a way that made Beth feel distinctly unsteady. 'My dear Beth, I should be delighted to see you a little foxed if it makes you more receptive to my advances! Would you care to see the castle gardens by moonlight?'

'Marcus, it has been snowing these five days past!' Beth said severely. 'If it is your wish that we catch our deaths—'

'Then perhaps we could watch the snow falling from Lady Salome's orangery?' Marcus suggested, a glint of amusement in his eyes. 'That would be most romantic and so very pretty…'

'Lady Salome would scarce approve!' Beth said lightly. The idea held much appeal but she was no green girl to fall for such a suggestion. She knew exactly what would happen once the orangery doors were closed behind them.

'Marcus, why do you not take Beth to see the view from the orangery?' Lady Salome said, appearing beside them with a huge glass of Puffin Punch clasped in her hands. 'It would be so very pretty with all the snow!'

'Exactly what I have been saying, ma'am!' Marcus agreed, whilst Beth smothcred her giggles. 'Come now, Lady Allerton, surely you cannot resist such a recommendation!'

'She is matchmaking,' Beth said, as Marcus tucked her arm through his and steered her firmly out of the hall and along the corridor to the orangery. 'Or making an alliance to save Fairhaven, perhaps!'

'I imagine all the villagers are behind her!' Marcus agreed. He held open the orangery doors. 'There…and is that not as pretty as I promised it would be?'

Beth moved forward to the big windows, feeling the cold coming from the glass in contrast to the warmth of the room behind. The bare branches of the orange and lemon trees struck spiky shadows across the floor. The snow brushed softly against the windows, melting as it ran down the glass. Outside, nothing could be seen but the soft darkness and the falling flakes.

Beth turned. Marcus was standing just inside the door, his face shadowed, but a faint smile on his lips. She felt puzzled. She had been certain that he would kiss her as soon as they were alone and she had been ready, waiting even. Such sweet pleasure could not be denied even if she was uncertain where it was leading. Yet now he made no move towards her and she felt confused—and more than a little disappointed.

'It is very pretty, my lord.' Her tone was cool as she struggled to master her feelings. 'However, I think I should retire now, if you will excuse me—'

'I will escort you to your room,' Marcus murmured.

Beth looked him in the eye. 'I am not likely to become lost, my lord.'

'No, but you are a little intoxicated—'

'I am not foxed!' Beth said indignantly, clutching the nearest orange tree for support and belying her words. 'I may be a little merry—'

'More than a little,' Marcus said, lips twitching.

'But it is a most pleasant feeling…'

'Not to be recommended on a daily basis, however.'

'Dear me…' Beth wavered a little '…you have become most censorious, my lord!' She had reached the orangery door and looked up into his face. 'Yet it seems to me that, for all your severity, you are not above taking advantage!'

'It is well-nigh impossible,' Marcus said solemnly, 'and I swear you are deliberately tempting me...'

He took a step forward and drew her into his arms. His lips touched her cheek. 'Dear Lady Allerton, have I told you how much I esteem and admire you?'

'No,' Beth said, determined to be prosaic despite the excitement racing through her blood, 'you have not.'

'Well, I do.' Marcus's mouth grazed the corner of hers. Beth stood quite still repressing the urge to press closer to him. He took her chin in his hand and brushed his thumb across her lower lip. Beth felt a shudder go straight through her. Desire swept over her in a crashing wave, leaving her thoroughly shaken.

'My lord—'

'Marcus, remember...' Marcus's voice was husky. He kissed her lightly, slowly, his lips just touching hers. Beth made a small, inarticulate sound deep in her throat and melted against him.

'Marcus...'

'Mmm...no.' Marcus drew back slightly. 'Beth, there is something I must ask you. Will you marry me?'

For a moment Beth clung to him, her senses still adrift, then her mind focused on what he had said.

'Marry you? I don't think... What...? Why...?'

She lost the thread as Marcus took her earlobe between his teeth and bit gently. 'I want to marry you, Beth. I want you very much.'

Beth's eyes, a cloudy silver grey, searched his face. 'Marcus, I cannot think properly if you keep kissing me.'

'Fortunately, there is no necessity to think. Will you marry me? Here on Fairhaven? Say yes.'

'Because of Fairhaven?'

'Devil take Fairhaven! I want you, not the island!'

Marcus was kissing her again fiercely, robbing her of breath. Beth realised that he had abandoned the idea of a gentle approach, abandoned restraint. Her whole body shook with the force of his passion—and of her own, for she was wrapping her arms round his neck to pull him to her with an urgent need that matched his own. Her body was besieged by heat and desire, desperate to be closer to his.

There was an insistent tapping on the orangery window behind them. Beth spun round.

'Marcus!' Lady Salome was peering at them through the glass. 'How much longer do you need? We are all waiting for an announcement!'

Beth laughed shakily. 'My guardian angel!'

'With the devil's own timing,' Marcus said ruefully. 'Very well, Aunt Salome. We will be with you shortly.' He took both of Beth's hands in his. In the pale, white light of the snowbound conservatory, Beth saw him smile faintly.

'So what do you think, my love? If you do not like the idea you need only say!'

Beth smiled shyly. 'I do quite like the idea—' she confessed, and got no further as Marcus swept her back into his arms again.

Chapter Nine

'I fear I must be leaving you for a trip to the mainland,' Lady Salome said dolefully to Beth, leaning on her hoe and tucking the ends of her orange and purple scarf more firmly inside her green velvet coat. They were standing in the castle garden, where Lady Salome had been using the hoe to break the ice on the fishpond, so that the golden carp could breathe. Beth could see the faint flash of a fin deep in the gloom at the bottom of the pond. She hoped that the carp were warmer than she was, or at least more able to withstand the cold.

'Drat this frost!' Lady Salome proclaimed. 'We cannot be doing with a hard winter! Not when there is so much to do about the island!'

'Why are you leaving, Lady Salome?' Beth asked, as they crunched across the fresh snow to the castle door.

'A letter from St John!' Lady Salome said. 'He has been delayed in Exeter and asks that I join him. He is worried that we may be away for Christmas and what our poor, benighted islanders will do for pastoral care in the meantime is not to be imagined! I suspect that there will be any number of christenings to attend to next autumn!'

Beth giggled. 'Surely the Bishop will send a curate to take care of your flock here?'

Lady Salome humphed. 'Very likely, but it will not be the same! And indeed, my dear—' she fixed Beth with a stern gaze '—I cannot like leaving you alone here with Marcus, for all that you are betrothed! It is most irregular!'

Beth blushed and made a little business of wiping all the snow from her boots before she followed Lady Salome into the warmth of the hall.

'You know that we intend to leave Fairhaven in a few weeks, Lady Salome!' she said. 'I have promised to join my cousins at Mostyn for Christmas and Marcus is going to Trevithick, and the wedding will probably be in the spring—'

'It is what happens in the next week that concerns me,' Lady Salome said darkly. 'It is easy to stray from the path of righteousness! And without me here to act as chaperon—well, the descent into hell is easy, but there is no turning back!'

Beth tried not to smile. To her mind, being seduced by Marcus would be heaven rather than hell, but she could scarcely express such inappropriate remarks to Lady Salome.

'I really do not think that you need to worry, Lady Salome!' she said wistfully. 'Marcus has been a very pattern of propriety these last three days since the dance!'

Lady Salome looked unconvinced. 'You mark my words, child—once a rake! Still…' her face softened '…I do believe that Marcus truly loves you! It is a blessing to see it!'

Beth was not so convinced. Although she did not think that Marcus had proposed merely to reach a compromise over Fairhaven, she was not certain that he loved her. She was even beginning to doubt that he desired her for, although he had been ardent in his pursuit of her before their betrothal, since the dance he had been positively distant. Beth knew that Marcus was deeply engrossed in the plans for the estate, even more so now that he knew there would be her money to back his projects. Even so, she thought he might have been a little more attentive as they were so newly engaged.

The week following Lady Salome's departure did nothing to change this view. Marcus either worked in his study with Colin McCrae or was out and about the island. He and Beth dined together in the evenings, took a pot of tea like any old married couple and sat chatting, reading or playing cards. When it was time for Beth to retire, Marcus would escort her to the bottom of the stairs, light her candle for her and give her a chaste peck on the cheek. It was becoming so frustrating that Beth swore to herself that she would cast herself into Marcus's arms the next night just to see how he reacted. She was tolerably certain that he would simply disentangle himself and ask her if she was feeling unwell. It was as though the passion that had flared between them had never existed at all.

Now that Lady Salome had gone to the mainland, Beth found herself taking over many of that redoubtable spinster's responsibilities towards the islanders. She would visit the sick or call in at the school and she kept a keen eye on Lady Salome's garden, knowing that her future aunt-in-law would never forgive her if the orange trees died or the fish perished. On days when the weather was crisp and fine she would sometimes walk along the shore or over the hills, delighting in the beauty of the

island and the freedom of the open air. Once, when she
had returned to her room at the castle after a scramble
over a rocky beach, Beth had looked at her reflection in
the mirror and wondered what on earth Charlotte would
say if only she could see her now; her hair was all tumbled and windblown and her cheeks flushed from the
cold air. There was a long rent in her skirt where it had
snagged on the rocks and her petticoat was stained
equally with mud and seawater. Decidedly she did not
look like a lady, or at least not the sort of lady who
flourished on the rarefied air of a London drawing room.
Charlotte would despair of her.

November slid into December. It was a full two weeks
since Lady Salome had left for Exeter and still they had
had no word of whether she and St John would be returning for Christmas or whether a curate would be sent
in their place. Beth knew that Marcus was delaying his
departure from Fairhaven until he had word, but she
had reluctantly started to think that she needed to make
her own plans to rejoin Charlotte at Mostyn. She was
thinking about it as she walked along the seashore that
afternoon, idly tossing pebbles into the water. Martha
McCrae was also on the beach; she had brought Annie,
baby Jamie and some of the village children down to
the shore to see if they could find any driftwood to fashion into decorations for Christmas. Martha had explained
that there were so few trees on the island that had to
improvise with other ideas and a fine, imaginative time
they had of it.

The tide was coming in. The water sucked at the pebbles about Beth's feet, splashing on to the hem of her
dress. Beth turned and looked back down the beach.
Martha and the children had walked a long way now and
were examining some shells that one of the girls had

picked up from the sand. The children's cries mingled
with the call of the seabirds, tossed on the wind. There
was another cry too, thin and faint, but closer at hand.
Beth stared. Martha had put the reed basket with the
baby in it on the rocks some twenty yards away, but
with the incoming tide it had slid into the water and was
bobbing about in the waves, already several yards from
the shore. Martha, engrossed in keeping her flock together, had not yet noticed.

Beth started to run. The wind was cold on her cheeks
and the pebbles slid from beneath her shoes, hampering
her. By the time she reached the rocks where Martha
had left Jamie she could hardly see the reed basket in
the dips between the waves.

Beth waded out to the rocks, feeling the tug of the
tide seize her. Even here, so close to the shore, there was
a strong tidal race out to sea. A rowing boat was tied up
there, dipping on the rising waves. Beth was already up
to her waist and her soaking skirts wrapped about her
legs so that she almost fell. The basket was bobbing
further away all the time and she knew she could not
swim out to it, knew that the tide race was pulling too
fast for her to catch up. She heard Jamie wail again as
a wave splashed over the side of the basket and it threatened to tip over. In desperation she grabbed the rowing
boat and tumbled over the side. The rope burned her
palms as she pulled it free of its mooring, then she had
grabbed the oars clumsily and turned it out to sea.

Beth had never rowed a boat before and whilst she
soon realised that the tide was carrying her in the right
direction, she had no skill to direct her course. Out of
the corner of her eye she saw the shoreline receding
with frightening speed. The children had realised now
that something was wrong; one of them had grabbed

Martha's skirts and started to cry. Several were screaming whilst one little girl, more resourceful than the rest,
was running in the direction of the harbour and help, as
fast as her small legs could carry her.

Beth was within a few feet of the basket. She could
see Jamie's crumpled little face and hear his screams
above the splash of the waves. She leant out, almost
overturning the boat in her desperation. A wave hit her
in the face and she gasped, shaking the blinding water
from her eyes. Then her fingers grazed the edge of the
wicker and she clung on and pulled, regardless of the
cold that numbed her hands and the force of the waves
that threatened to pull her arms from their sockets.

When she finally heaved the basket aboard, Jamie was
soaking and screaming and Beth was exhausted and her
clothes stiff and face sore with salt spray. She had paid
no attention to the shore for several minutes and was
horrified to discover that they were now at least a hundred yards out, with the strong tide pulling them towards
Rat Island. One of her oars was gone and she had not
even noticed. The prospects for both herself and Jamie
were looking increasingly bleak.

'Hold on!'

The shout came from behind her and she squirmed
around, collapsing back in the boat with relief as she
saw another small craft drawing close. Colin McCrae
was in the bows, his face a tight mask of tension as the
men behind him rowed like the devil to reach her side.
The two boats bumped together and Colin grabbed the
bulwark, pulling them alongside. Beth reached for Jamie
and thrust the screaming bundle into his father's arms.

Strong hands grasped her and half-lifted, half-pulled
her into the other boat. She felt Marcus's arms close
around her—she knew it was Marcus even though her

eyes were closed—and she turned her face into his neck, breathing in the warm and reassuring scent of his skin. Then she burst into tears. She could feel Marcus's mouth pressed against the salty coldness of her cheek and heard him say, 'Oh, Beth,' as he held on to her as though he would never let her go. The feeling soothed her and she lay still, paying no more attention to their rescue.

Things became even more confused when they reached the jetty. Quite a crowd had gathered, with other people coming running as word went around about the accident. Colin jumped ashore and handed Jamie to Martha. She was crying as well and squeezed the baby to her so tightly that he promptly started to scream again.

'Nothing wrong with his lungs,' Colin commented with a grin, giving his wife a hug. 'I think he has survived the ordeal with no harm done!'

Beth had stopped crying, but when she tried to step ashore her legs buckled beneath her and Marcus was obliged to pick her up into his arms. A ragged cheer went up as the crowd saw her and started to push forward to shake her hand and pat her on the back. Beth, who wanted nothing more than a hot bath and peace and quiet to recover from the shock, found it unnerving. Martha pushed close, trying to thank her, and she could see the tears in Colin's eyes now as he started to relate the details of the rescue to the eager crowd.

In the end Marcus was obliged to force his way through them all to reach the horse and cart, and she, Martha, Jamie, Colin and Marcus piled aboard. Marcus held her firmly cradled on his knee, regardless of propriety. He did not speak, however, and stealing a look at his face, Beth saw that it was set and grim, his previous tenderness replaced by what looked like anger. Her heart sank. She did not feel she could bear him to ring a peal over her just now.

'Mustard baths, steaming gruel and physic,' Martha was saying, having recovered her self-possession now that she was certain baby Jamie was safe. 'Oh, Lady Allerton, how can we ever thank you? You were unconscionably brave!'

'Unconscionably foolish!' Marcus said shortly, earning himself an indignant exclamation from Martha before she fell silent under her husband's meaningful glare.

Marcus put Beth down at last when they reached the castle entrance. She was feeling much recovered, although the wind had flattened her wet clothes against her body in a manner that was unpleasantly clinging. She could feel the water dripping from her hair and splashing on the stone floor. Martha started to fuss about her, but Beth interrupted.

'Martha, why do you not go to the nursery and tend to Jamie? All I need is a hot bath and some rest. I have taken no hurt—'

'Which is less than you deserve!' Marcus snapped. 'I shall see you to your room, Lady Allerton, lest you fall into some foolish scrape on the way!'

Beth heard both Colin and Martha gasp at his tone. At the back of her mind she knew that his short temper was probably only the product of relief, but indignation flooded through her and with it an anger that was warming.

'You shall not escort me, Lord Trevithick!' she said smartly, striding away towards the stair. 'I have no need of your further censure! I did what I thought was right—'

'Almost drowning yourself in the process!' Marcus finished curtly. 'When will you learn, Lady Allerton, that such impulsive actions lead only to trouble? There were plenty of men there eminently more capable than you of handling a rowing boat—'

'My lord—' Colin McCrae objected, only to fall back under Marcus's withering glare.

'Do not mistake me, Colin,' he said, more gently, 'I am more than glad that Jamie is safe and would have done anything to see him so.' He swung back to look at Beth, who was dripping quietly onto the stairs. 'What I object to is those who are not qualified wilfully rushing towards danger and causing more difficulties for themselves and other people—'

Beth did not wait to hear any more. She stalked off up the stairs, aware that she was making an undignified squelching noise and that there was a wet footprint on every step.

She felt cold and unpleasantly damp, and wanted nothing more than to strip off her clothes and rub herself dry. She devoutly hoped that Marcus would leave her alone, for she was in no mood to endure his condemnation. She was still shaking from a combination of shock and reaction. She slammed her bedroom door behind her. How dared Marcus! How dared he condemn her when she had been doing her best to save Jamie. Perhaps he was right in that there had been others more capable, but she could not stand by and simply watch the basket float out to sea!

She peeled off her soaking clothes, dropping them on the floor and hurrying into the closet to find a towel. Once she was dry she felt much better, although her hair had been blown into a hopeless tangle by the wind and would take hours to comb out. Beth wrapped herself in her brocade robe, picked up her comb and hurried back to the fire. She had just sat down and started to tease the tangles from her silky black hair, when there was a knock at the door.

'Come in!' Beth called. She had expected to see one of the maids there and her eyes widened in shock as Marcus strode into the room. He had evidently had time to change, for although his hair looked damp, his clothes were dry. Beth looked at him dubiously.

'Oh! Lord Trevithick! I did not think… You should not be here—'

'I wanted to talk to you,' Marcus said abruptly, closing the door behind him.

Beth fired up. 'Well, I do not want to hear any more! Ringing a peal over me when all I was trying to do was help—'

'I am aware of that,' Marcus said tightly. Beth saw that his hands were clenched at his side. 'What you do not seem to understand, Beth, is that the sea is treacherous around here and that you could so easily have been drowned yourself! Sometimes I think that you have no more sense than a child!'

Beth's eyes filled with easy tears. She had had a nasty shock and now she felt decidedly humiliated. 'Well, if I am lacking in sense, you are surely lacking in sensibility, my lord!' She made a wild gesture with the hand that held the comb. 'It is the cruellest thing to censure me when I am so upset—' She broke off as she saw that Marcus's attention had shifted from her white face to somewhere considerably lower. The brocade robe had loosened at her dramatic wave of the hand and was now falling open. Suddenly Beth was devastatingly aware that she was naked beneath its slippery folds. She gathered the material closely at her neck with a defensive gesture and fell silent. Her throat was dry and she could only watch as Marcus, eyebrows slightly raised, allowed his gaze to travel up again to rest thoughtfully on her now flushed face.

'You are correct, Beth.' His voice was husky now as he took a step towards her. 'It is quite wrong of me to reproach you. My anger arose only from a desire to protect you, for it seems to me that you plunge headlong towards danger without any thought of self-preservation...'

It seemed to Beth that she was racing towards danger at that very moment. The warmth of the fire could not account for the sudden heat that suffused her skin from her bare toes to the top of her head. The soft material of the robe seemed unbearably stimulating against her naked flesh. She cleared her throat, intending to ask Marcus to leave, but some inexplicable impulse kept her silent. Instead she just watched as he took the final step towards her. His eyes were very dark, reflecting his desire for her, but overlaid with an expression of tenderness that held her still. He took hold of her upper arms and drew her very gently towards him, and as his own arms closed about her, his mouth came down on hers.

An involuntary shudder went through Beth's body as her lips parted under his. His skin smelled clean and fresh, and without conscious thought her hands unclenched their hold on her gown so that she could tangle her fingers in the thick darkness of his hair. Marcus deepened the kiss and Beth moved closer into his arms with a tiny moan. She blinked dizzily as he lifted his mouth from hers and touched her lips with the tip of his tongue. Conventional behaviour, the dictates of society, had ceased to exist for her as soon as Marcus had started to kiss her; all Beth knew was that her pent-up fear and anger had fused into something exquisitely tender and sweet.

Her head fell back against Marcus's supporting arm, allowing his mouth to drift down the taut line of her throat to the hollow at its base. She felt his tongue flick over her skin, tasting her, and shivered beneath the caress. Her legs were trembling so much that she was afraid that she might fall, and Marcus evidently thought the same, for he picked her up and placed her gently on the big bed. Beth felt the cold air against her legs and realised with a faint shock that the brocade robe was almost completely undone; as soon as it came to her the knowledge seemed almost irrelevant, for Marcus was beside her and the warmth of his body kept out the cold.

She felt his fingers at her waist, loosening the robe so that it fell back completely. A moment later, Marcus's palm brushed the slope of her breast and his mouth closed over the tight peak of her nipple, the gentle caress becoming firmer and stronger as Beth gave a soft moan of satisfaction. She was adrift with pleasure, unaware of anything except her need for him. She reached out to him blindly, digging her fingers into his back, tugging at his shirt so that she could run her hands over the hard, bare skin beneath.

It felt cold as soon as Marcus left her side. Beth rolled over, the brocade robe crushed beneath her, and opened her eyes. There was the most extraordinary ache inside her and she had never experienced anything like it, nor the violent desire for that ache to be satisfied.

'Marcus…' She realised that he had only left her in order to remove his clothes and smiled a little. She was still smiling when he came back to her side a moment later.

'Beth…' There was a fierce desire in his face, but she could see that he was frowning. 'Beth, if you do not wish for this, you must say so—now…'

Beth opened her eyes very wide. 'I wish it more than anything...'

There was a moment of stillness and then Marcus smiled too and lay down to take her in his arms again. He kissed her gently, but not so gently that the effect did not vibrate all the way through Beth's body. He was stroking her back, a soft sweep of a caress from her shoulder to the curve of her buttocks, with a touch so sensual that Beth was almost melting. She rolled over helplessly on to her back, then squirmed with renewed pleasure as Marcus's mouth closed over her breast again.

'Oh, please...'

She felt his hand dip between her trembling thighs, parting her legs. He was still kissing her when he entered her and Beth was engulfed immediately in a violent surge of pleasure that made her cry out against his mouth. A second later Marcus followed and he gasped her name, pressing his face to her throat until the pleasure died away.

Beth lay quite still, her body quiescent, her mind floating. She could not even begin to think, nor did she feel that there was any immediate necessity to do so, for Marcus had pulled the covers over them and had drawn her close to his side. She turned her head against his shoulder and drifted into sleep.

When Beth woke again it was almost dark outside. Marcus was lying beside her, deeply asleep. She looked at him, marvelling at the black sweep of his eyelashes against his cheek, the faint shadow of the stubble that darkened his chin, the hard lines of his face that were soft in sleep. She wanted to touch them all. A piercing stab of love washed over her, so intense and poignant that it almost hurt. Smiling a little sadly, she picked up her robe and went over to the window embrasure, curling up so that she could look out at the pewter sea.

Charlotte had always said that she was too impulsive, but her impulses had never led her to such a point before. She and Marcus were lovers now and the whole castle, the whole island, must surely know it, for he had been alone with her in her room for hours. Beth frowned. She did not feel like a fallen woman, for her mind was so full of love for Marcus that it seemed to transcend everything else.

Beth supposed that she was now only one of a great number of rich widows who had taken a lover, yet that seemed too shabby, too unemotional a description for what had happened between herself and Marcus. She knew that society's rules, whilst allowing no latitude for unmarried girls, were far more understanding of ladies in her position. Widows and married women were given a certain freedom, one might even say laxity, to behave as they pleased. And after all, she and Marcus were already betrothed. So, provided that they were discreet… Beth frowned again. She knew she had never been very good at being discreet. Her temperament was too open and now she wanted to shout from the rooftops that she loved Marcus to distraction.

Beth drew her knees up to her chin. She felt warm and happy and satisfied in a way that she had never felt with Frank Allerton. He had shown her none of the physical pleasure or the tenderness that Marcus had. She smiled wryly, remembering that she had previously thought herself physically cold. She had started to discover her mistake when she had first encountered Marcus in London and the explosive nature of their attraction had made her realise there was a whole side of her character that she had not known existed. Now she realised that to the full.

'Beth?' Marcus had stirred and was leaning on one elbow, watching her. Her heart swelled with love for him. She went across to the bed and sat on the edge, looking at him. A faint smile touched his mouth.

'Are you quite well, my love?'

Beth dropped her gaze. It was very nice to be called that and perhaps it might even be taken to imply that he loved her... She waited, hoping he would say so, but he did not.

'I am well,' she said, a little shyly.

'What were you thinking?' Marcus asked. His dark gaze was very direct. Beth plucked at the bedcovers.

'I was thinking that...oh, that Lady Salome and Charlotte and everyone else would not approve, and that I am indeed a shameless creature...'

She saw Marcus smile, but his gaze remained grave. 'So you regret what has happened?'

'No,' Beth said, hampered by her honesty. 'I cannot. But Marcus—do you...I mean, do you think me—?'

Marcus raised a hand and touched her cheek. 'I think that you are lovely, Beth. We are to be married and I do not think the opinions of others matter.'

A strange feeling took Beth, part triumphant and part forlorn. Whilst reassured that Marcus thought no less of her, she could not help feeling that he could afford to be hardy about the opinions of others whereas she was more vulnerable. She watched as he sat up and wrapped the sheet about him. He was still watching her, but with a speculation now that made her skin prickle with excitement.

'I wondered if you would care to take a bath,' Marcus

said. 'After your ordeal in the sea it would perhaps be efficacious for your health…'

Beth looked at him. There was a spark of teasing in his eye, a hint of mischief and something more. The prickle of excitement turned into a tingle of unmistakable anticipation.

'Well, if you think I should—'

'I am certain.' Marcus swung his legs over the side of the bed and reached for his shirt. 'But only if you share it with me.'

Beth's eyes opened to their widest extent. 'Oh! But…could we?'

Marcus grinned. 'I do not see why not!'

He wandered over to the fireplace and rang the bell. Beth gave a squeak. 'Marcus, the servants—'

Marcus only grinned at her again. He sauntered back to her side and slipped his arms about her, dropping a light kiss on her lips. 'So shy, my love? I fear it is a little late for that…'

Beth knew this was true but, all the same, it seemed sensible for Marcus to go to his own rooms and for her to wait discreetly alone whilst the water was drawn.

It was Martha McCrae who delivered it herself, in company with two maids, and their faces were so blank that Beth almost had a fit of the giggles. Tellingly Martha did not enquire after Beth's health, but her gaze did rest for a moment on the tumbled bedsheets and Beth thought that she almost smiled.

'Martha,' she said quickly, as they were leaving, 'how does baby Jamie? I hope that he is fully recovered?'

Martha did smile then, and a wicked dimple appeared in her cheek. 'Yes, thank you, milady.' She dropped a curtsey. 'He has taken no hurt, as indeed I hope you have not…'

Beth blushed, flustered. Martha gave her an innocent smile and closed the door softly.

Beth went through to the bathroom. The water had been scented with lavender and smelled delicious. She slipped out of her robe and into the hot water, closing her eyes with a sigh.

A moment later she opened them wide with a little shriek as Marcus slid into the bath behind her. She felt the press of his body against hers and almost squeaked again when he pulled her back against him. The water rose dangerously, threatening to slop over the sides of the bath on to the floor.

'Stop wriggling,' Marcus instructed, laughing softly. 'Just keep still, or you will drown us both! We are fortunate that there is so much room in here…'

Beth complied, holding her breath as she felt his hands start to massage her shoulders gently. It felt delicious. The scent of the water, the hot, rising steam, the smell of lavender and the soapy slipperiness of Marcus's hands against her skin provoked the most delightful sensations within her. When he bent his head to kiss the side of her neck, where the damp black curls stuck to her skin, she leant back against his chest and closed her eyes. When his hands slipped lower to caress her breasts, she was certain she was about to dissolve with sheer pleasure.

So rapt was she in the desire he was invoking that Beth barely noticed when Marcus scooped her out of the bath and swept her up into his arms. He wrapped her in a huge towel and carried her through to the bedroom. They tumbled down on to the big bed together, Marcus pulling her under him. His mouth took the place of his hands at her breast and the exquisite surge of pleasure almost pushed Beth over the edge. She reached for him, gasping his name. Then all thought was lost as her mind was swamped in pure delight.

'You have been very quiet tonight, my dear,' Marcus observed, as he and Beth sat over the chessboard the following evening. 'Are you too tired to play? Do you wish to go to bed?'

They had taken dinner together and had now retired to the green drawing room, as had become their habit during the past two weeks. Although they usually played cards or talked, tonight Beth had chosen to play chess instead and had promptly lost the first game. She had been totally preoccupied because she had been wondering what was going to happen between herself and Marcus that night.

Marcus had stayed the previous night with her but when she had woken that morning he had been gone and she had not seen him for the whole of the day. The servants had told her that he was out with Colin McCrae on estate business, which was only natural, but Beth had been unable to settle all day. She had gone on a long walk to Admiral's Point, had done some unnecessary gardening and probably killed some of Lady Salome's wintering bulbs, and had undertaken any number of tasks to distract her thoughts from the night before. She wondered if their lovemaking had perhaps been an aberration, a night borne out of the indisputable tension that had built up between herself and Marcus. Perhaps neither of them would ever speak of it again and pretend that it had never happened, and she was not sure how she would feel if that was the case. Her emotions felt too raw and new for too much soul-searching.

Beth's pulse jumped as she saw Marcus's dark gaze resting on her, wickedly assessing, and she suddenly thought that perhaps the previous night had not been an aberration after all. Her face warmed as she thought about it. The room was intimately dark, shadowed and fire lit, with only one additional branch of candles.

Beth realised that Marcus was still awaiting her reply. She looked up, met his eyes and smiled demurely. 'No, I am not tired. Perhaps I do not have the right kind of calculating mind for chess.'

'But you always respond to a challenge,' Marcus murmured. 'How if we were to make the stakes higher? If you lose a pawn...' he paused, his gaze considering her '...then you also lose...a garment?'

Beth almost choked on her tea. 'Marcus! No, really! Surely you are in jest?'

'What, too afraid to take the challenge?' Marcus laughed, leaning back in his chair. 'That is not like you, my love, and this way the game is so much more enjoyable...'

Beth bit her lip. It was difficult to decide, to think clearly, for her mind was dizzy with anticipation and remembered desire. She admitted to herself that the challenge was well nigh irresistible and that she might as well be hung for a sheep as a lamb...

Marcus was still watching her with speculative amusement. She met his gaze directly. 'What if I should win, my lord? Once before I won a wager against you.'

'That's true...' Marcus started to set up the chessboard again. 'Well, sweetheart, we shall see!'

Beth stared at the checkerboard squares, concentrating hard. Frank had taught her chess, but he had never made it as interesting as this. On the other hand, he had taught her a sound strategy and she was determined to use it. The trouble was that Marcus was a very good player and she found she could not concentrate for long...

Even so, it was several minutes before she lost her first pawn. She paused, considering, then removed her spencer and folded it neatly over the arm of the chair. She did not dare look at Marcus for she knew that he would be watching her and that would put her off even more. The room was warm and from that point of view she scarcely noticed the loss of the spencer, and a quick mental inventory of her remaining clothes reassured her that there were plenty left. All the same, there were seven pawns left on the board…

Marcus lost two pawns in quick succession and shrugged out of his jacket and untied his stock. Beth glanced at him and looked quickly away. He was still wearing his blue embroidered waistcoat and beneath that, his linen shirt, but he already looked slightly dishevelled. His shirt was now open, revealing the strong brown column of his neck and the sight of the bronze sheen of his skin was wholly disturbing to Beth's senses. It certainly would not help her concentration to keep looking at him. She gazed fixedly at the chessboard and moved her castle, a little tentatively. A moment later she realised that she had made a mistake. A bad one.

She saw Marcus move a pawn and his hand close over the castle to take it off the board. He was watching her with a look of amusement.

'That counts as three items of clothing, I fear, my love. I forgot to tell you that there was a…sliding scale.'

Beth sighed. 'My slippers? That must be two items…'

Marcus sat back in his chair. 'I rather think that they should count as only one.'

Beth frowned at him. 'It seems to me that you are making up the rules as you go along, my lord!'

'Perhaps so.' Marcus smiled. 'That is part of the fun.'

Beth kicked off her slippers under the table, then after

a moment, put a hand up to unpin her lace cap. She was very conscious of Marcus watching her every move, his dark eyes never leaving her face. She tossed the cap aside. Now she had something of a dilemma. Unless she chose to unroll her stockings, it had to be her dress.

'You will have to help me, my lord…' Her voice was husky. She stood up and turned around. Marcus came round the table and a moment later she felt his fingers on the buttons of her gown, moving methodically downwards. Then his hands skimmed her bare shoulders, sliding the dress down.

Beth discovered that the potent effect of his touch on her skin, so explosive the previous night, had not lessened. With a little sigh, she let the dress fall to the ground. Anticipation was hammering through her body with each beat of her pulse, its dizzy stroke making her feel utterly light-headed. And she still had a game to complete. She had thought that the wager at the Cyprians' Ball had been perilous enough. Now she had an entirely new sense of danger. Danger and excitement, inextricably linked. She slid from under Marcus's hands and resumed her seat, focusing on the board.

When she captured his bishop she looked at him triumphantly. 'If the castle counts for three items of clothing, my lord, surely the bishop is two? Can you deny it?'

Marcus grinned. 'Absolutely right, sweetheart! What would you like me to remove?'

Beth swallowed hard. Her throat was suddenly dry. 'Your waistcoat and…your shirt?'

Marcus smiled with devilish pleasure. 'Certainly…'

The rustle of starched linen filled Beth's ears. She was not yet accustomed to seeing Marcus naked and knew perfectly well that the sight of his bare brown torso would destroy any remaining chance she had of concentrating. When Marcus sat down again she deliberately averted her gaze from him, despite the almost overwhelming temptation to stare. But it was already too late. Her attention had been fatally distracted and her next move was disastrous.

Marcus moved a pawn across the board and captured her queen. 'Check,' he said contentedly.

'Is that the end?' Beth whispered.

'Not yet,' Marcus said thoughtfully. 'That is, you need not necessarily lose the chess game, but I suspect you have insufficient clothing left to cover your debt—amongst other things...'

When Beth looked at him she saw that the devilish light in his eyes had deepened and he was watching her with undisguised desire. He got up and came round the table again, taking her hand and drawing her to her feet. Beth shivered a little, suddenly aware that she was already wearing little more than her chemise.

'I protest,' she said huskily, 'that you have changed the rules shamelessly, my lord—'

'I always play by my own rules,' Marcus pointed out.

He bent his head and kissed her. His mouth was soft and seductive, spinning a snare of delight. His fingers moved to unpin her hair.

Beth's mind cleared briefly. 'Marcus, we are in the drawing room! The servants—'

'—will not come in. They are too discreet.'

He kissed her again, moulding her yielding body against the hard lines of his. Beth ran her hands over the hard muscles of his chest and felt herself tremble, faint with the taste, touch and smell of him. She felt his hands move, deft and warm. Something gave, and she realised that her stays were gone, discarded. Marcus pulled her down with him on the rug in front of the fire.

The light was pale, bathing them both in its gentle glow. The fire felt warm through the thinness of Beth's chemise. Marcus pulled the tapes and undid the bodice, exposing her breasts. She saw desire distilled in his face as he bent his head to take one rosy tip in his mouth. Beth squirmed then, shivers of pleasure coursing through her. She could not believe that this was happening, not here, not now. She opened dazed grey eyes as she felt Marcus move to kneel between her thighs.

'Marcus…you still have your clothes on—'

'Barely.' She heard the laughter in his voice. She knew he still had his boots on and his pantaloons, and he was now undoing the fastening in a feverish hurry. There was something inexpressibly exciting in the urgency of the need that ran between them.

Marcus's hands slid under the hem of the chemise, pulled it up to her hips and lingered on the bare flesh at the tops of her silk stockings. She heard him give a rough groan against her throat.

'Oh, Beth, my love…'

She felt him shudder convulsively as soon as he came into her and she dug her fingernails into his back, exulting in the power she had over him. But it was too soon to feel triumphant, for the same conflagration swept over her, leaving her breathless and shaking. They lay still in the warm glow of the fire, then Marcus rolled away from her and for a moment Beth felt cold and bereft. Then he propped himself on one elbow and leant over to kiss her, tiny, teasing kisses that were very sweet.

'Such haste is not always a good thing, however…'

Beth felt his hand brush her thigh, moving intimately to part her flesh again, and groaned aloud.

'Marcus, I do not think I can—'

'Yes, you can.' His breath was soft against her face. His fingers caressed her. 'I have won this wager, remember...'

This time he took his time, spinning out the pleasure for both of them. Beth was so lost in her feelings that she did not even realise that she cried aloud as her body shook again in exquisite torment. When she finally opened her eyes, it was to see Marcus pushing the tumbled hair away from her brow as he bent to kiss her once more.

'Checkmate,' he said.

Marcus pushed the pile of papers away from him with an exclamation of disgust and rose to his feet, stretching vigorously in an attempt to shake off some of the lethargy that seemed to possess him every time he tried to study the maps. McCrae had explained it all to him several times and yet he appeared to be utterly incapable of concentrating on the plans for the new harbour. On one sheet were the scale drawings of the building work required and on the other were neat columns of costs, timings and the manpower needed. Yet more pages gave a detailed plan of how the project would be managed and supplied. McCrae was nothing if not thorough.

Marcus poured himself a glass of whisky and wandered moodily over to the window. He knew the reason for his preoccupation, of course—Beth. All the time that he was trying to concentrate on the business of the estate, she seemed to insinuate herself into his thoughts, easily clouding out every other consideration. It was not simply her physical attributes that obsessed him, although he had to admit that he had spent as much time thinking about them as any infatuated boy. Marcus laughed with self-deprecation. It was a new experience for him to be so besotted, but not an unpleasant one. He knew that Beth was revelling in her newly found sensuality and so was he. There was no likelihood that she would consider herself physically cold ever again.

However, he had to acknowledge that there was far more to his feelings than that. He loved Beth. He loved her for her openness and her lack of artifice and pretence. He loved the innocence of character that made her give so generously of herself. He had watched her with the servants and villagers, seen her genuine interest in their lives and their concerns, and it had made him want to crush her to him and never let her go.

Marcus wandered back to his desk and picked up the letter that lay a little apart from the rest of the papers. It had come that day from Lady Salome, and related that she and St John would not be returning to Fairhaven until the spring. Church business was keeping St John occupied, Lady Salome explained, and in the meantime she was visiting old friends and making the most of a sojourn on the mainland. She finished off with many expressions of affection for him and especially for Beth, and had included a paragraph about expecting him to behave with honour, which she had underlined several times.

Marcus frowned, tossing the letter down onto the table. He had been desperately hoping that St John and Salome would be back imminently, bringing a special licence from the Bishop with them. It had always been his intention to ask his cousin to marry him to Beth on Fairhaven and he had been severely disappointed to find St John away when they had arrived. Now his final hope had been dashed with the news that St John would not return before Christmas.

Marcus took a mouthful of whisky and sat back in his chair, considering his options. Suddenly it all seemed damnably difficult and he felt a keen pang of guilt at ever getting into the situation. Lady Salome's letter, with its underlined paragraph, reproached him. He had compromised Beth and now he could not put the matter right as he had intended. The only thing that he could do was marry her as soon as possible once they had returned to the mainland, and such a hasty match seemed furtive and not good enough for her when he had intended matters to be so different. The best compromise that he could think of was that they might marry at Mostyn just after Christmas, which would give time for the banns to be read and would also be an appropriate place. Beth would probably like that but he could not be sure. After all, her first marriage had taken place there.

With a groan, he pushed the glass away before he was tempted to top it up and turned back to the map of the harbour with a mixture of irritation and grim determination. McCrae would be back to ask him for his decision within the hour and he did not want his estate manager to think he had been wasting his time. And once he had dealt with business he would turn to the pressing and more important matter of his marriage. He wanted it resolved.

Beth stood by her bed, folding her clothes and tucking them neatly into her trunk in preparation for her journey to the mainland. She had considered taking the ball gown made from the drawing-room curtains because it had special sentimental value since she had been wearing it when Marcus proposed. However, she did not have enough room, so she had hung the gown up in the closet, hoping she would return to Fairhaven before too long and wear it once again.

The previous week had passed in a whirl. During the day, Marcus was still spending some of his time out and about on the estate or talking to Colin McCrae about his plans for the island. It pleased Beth to see just how involved Marcus had become in the future of Fairhaven and how much he cared that the farm would prosper and succeed. Sometimes she rode with him about the island, exploring the rocky crags and the secluded bays with their stretches of pure white sand. Once she had been tempted to paddle in the winter sea, charmed into thinking it would not be too cold because the sun was shining and the water gleamed blue in the light. She had been frozen within a few seconds, and Marcus had laughed and pulled her to him and kissed her, and she could taste the salt on his lips and would almost have sworn that it was love that she saw reflected in his eyes. Perhaps it had only been a reflection of her own feelings, for she loved Marcus and her love for him seemed to deepen every day.

She sighed. It was that love that led her to be free and unguarded, with her feelings as well as her body. And that was another story... Beth shifted a little as she thought about it. The foolish pretence that she was nothing more than a friend to Marcus had been thoroughly disproved on the very first afternoon that he had spent in bed with her, and since then there had been several others. What the servants thought when they disappeared after lunch was anyone's guess and at first Beth had been appalled. It had never occurred to her that people might make love during the day rather than wait for the night, nor had she realised the infinite variations that might apply. Marcus had seemed amused at her naïveté and quite evidently delighted to extend her education. And there was no doubt that she had been an apt pupil.

Now, however, all that might change. Being on Fairhaven had been unreal in some ways, a paradise cut off from the rest of the world where society's rules need not apply and she and Marcus had been protected from censure. Now they were to return to the mainland, to marry and to resume their place in society. There would be their estates to visit and the London Season and the Dowager Countess of Trevithick to contend with... Beth sighed. No, matters could not be the same.

In bed in the following dawn, Beth awoke and lay still, watching the grey light filter from behind the curtains and hearing the faint rhythmic roar of the sea on the rocks far below. She knew that it would be the last time she would wake like this and she was imprinting it on her memory. When she moved a little, Marcus pulled her into his arms, his mouth against her hair.

'Why are you not asleep, sweetheart?'

'I was thinking,' Beth said. She rolled on to her stomach and lay looking down into his face.

'Marcus, I was thinking that my dreams of Fairhaven were not real at all...'

She saw that he was wide awake and watching her. A tender smile was curving his lips. 'Oh, Beth. Was it so hard to find out the truth about your grandfather?'

'Yes,' Beth said softly. She bent her head. 'At the time it was hard. But now it is not so bad after all. But, Marcus, I am afraid that everything will change once we leave here—'

Marcus pulled her into the crook of his arm. 'Do not be afraid, sweetheart. This is just the start.' He paused.

His fingers were tracing the path of her spine and it was most distracting.

'We are to be married straight after Christmas—and at Mostyn. What could be better than that?'

Beth smiled. 'I know. It will be lovely.' Despite her words, a tiny qualm of disquiet remained and she did not understand it. She wriggled a little as Marcus's fingers drifted lower and his caresses became more insistent. Her melancholy thoughts faded. The urgent touch of Marcus's hands on her body was enough to send all other thoughts spinning out of her head. He made love to her slowly, with a tender intensity that left them both trembling. And when it was over he wrapped her in his arms and pulled her close to him. Beth was just drifting off to sleep again when she heard him whisper.

'Beth, I love you.'

Beth's whole body felt soft and satisfied. A little smile curled her lips. Yet at the back of her mind the doubt returned, faint but disturbing. She tried to push it away but it would not go, not completely. With a sigh she fell asleep again, but her worries pursued her, nameless and threatening, through her dreams.

When she woke in the morning, Marcus had already gone. That was not unusual in itself. At the start of their affair he had always been sure to be back in his own rooms before the other inhabitants of the castle started to stir, then Beth had pointed out to him what an unnecessary fiction this was and he had gladly stayed by her side. This morning, however, his absence left her feeling somewhat lonely and she was at a loss to explain why.

She had barely finished dressing when there was a knock at the door and Martha McCrae stuck her head round.

'Oh, my lady, I am sorry to disturb you but an urgent letter has come from London! His lordship is about to depart—'

Beth's eyebrows shot up. 'Good God, whatever can be so pressing—?'

Marcus and Colin McCrae were in the study when she hurried down. Marcus was already dressed for travelling, booted and cloaked, and when he saw Beth his face lightened for a moment before a frown returned. Colin glanced from one to the other and withdrew softly.

'Beth.' Marcus came across and took both her hands in his. 'I am so sorry. I have to leave for London at once. A letter has come—' He gestured to the desk behind him. 'Well, you may read for yourself. My mother is in despair. She writes that my sister Eleanor has been seduced and abandoned, and begs me to return to help her.'

Beth stared up at him, shocked. 'Good God, how dreadful! But who can possibly—?' She was not sure whether her own heart provided the answer or whether she read it in Marcus's face. She drew her hands away.

'Oh, no, not Kit…'

'It seems so.' Marcus's face was grim. 'I cannot be sure of the precise situation, for the letter is somewhat incoherent. But I must go, Beth. You must see…'

'Yes, of course…' Beth stared at the sheets of paper on the desk. She knew that Kit had had a *tendre* for Eleanor Trevithick. She had observed it herself and had even teased him about it, but to ruin the girl was another matter…

'I cannot believe it!' she burst out. 'Kit would never behave so! It cannot be true!'

Marcus's face was set. 'Well, I shall find out. I am

sorry, Beth, but I must go.' He came back to her side. 'Go back to Mostyn Hall—'

'I shall not!' Beth screwed up her face, trying to think straight. 'If you are for London, I shall go too! Charlotte will be distressed and all alone—'

Marcus was controlling his impatience with difficulty. 'There is no time to talk now. I have to catch the tide. Beth, you must see that this changes all our plans! I fear our wedding cannot go ahead as we had intended, but if you go to Mostyn—'

'No!' Beth said again. 'I cannot stay quiet in the country whilst this is happening!'

Marcus pulled on his gloves. 'Then contact me as soon as you reach London. And take great care on the journey.' He took her hands in an urgent grip. 'Promise me!'

'I promise,' Beth said.

'This was not how I wanted it to be for us,' Marcus said, in a hard, angry voice. 'To have everything spoiled—' He broke off, gave her a fierce kiss and straightened up. For a moment, Beth thought that he was about to say something else, then he turned on his heel and she heard his footsteps fading away across the hall.

Beth picked the Dowager Viscountess's letter from the desk and sat down in the armchair. Five minutes later, when she had perused the contents twice, she let the letter fall to her lap and stared into the fire.

The letter had been written a week before and it was evident that its author had been in a tearing hurry as well as great distress. Amidst the invective against the Mostyn family was the core of the tale: how Kit Mostyn had tricked and seduced Eleanor, then promptly abandoned her and disappeared.

Beth frowned. She knew Kit had a rake's reputation,

but he had never stooped to seducing innocent young girls. He had never needed or wanted to. Besides, Beth was certain that his feelings for Eleanor had been sincere and he would never act dishonourably. Nevertheless, the facts appeared damning. She would have to go to London herself and find out.

She crossed to the window and looked out. It was a beautiful sunny morning and she could already see the speck that was Marcus's boat, growing smaller all the time, as it tacked across the strait to Bideford. Her heart felt heavy. She knew Marcus had not had the time to wait for her and that if the two of them had travelled together it would have slowed his journey down. Nevertheless, she felt an irrational disappointment that he had not suggested it. It felt as though he did not want her with him.

Standing there, she went over the conversation that she had just had with Marcus. Of course their wedding would have to be postponed, but… She felt suddenly chill. What was it that he had said? *You must see that this changes all our plans! I fear our wedding cannot go ahead…*

But she had not seen what he was trying to say, not immediately. She had assumed that he meant only to delay rather than to call it off. It was only now, as she watched him leave without her, that the true implication of his words hit her.

This was not how I wanted it to be for us. To have everything spoiled…

She had thought that he had been going to say something else—something more final, but at the last moment he had not. Had that, perhaps, been when he was about to end everything between them, but had decided to spare her feelings until he had time to soften the blow—when they met in London, perhaps?

Beth watched the boat until the sun on the water made her eyes ache, then she turned back to the room. It seemed darker now, depressing. She hurried out into the hall and up the stairs, determined to press on with her own departure. It was the only way to keep her fears at bay. And deepest and most unacknowledged was the growing fear that Kit's actions had ruined them all and damned forever the relationship between her and Marcus. Their engagement had not been officially announced and now, surely, the marriage would not take place. For how could Marcus wish to associate with her after her cousin had apparently brought such dishonour on the Trevithick family by ruining his sister? His parting words had confirmed as much. Kit had caused the most immense scandal and all relations between the Mostyns and Trevithicks must, by necessity, be severed once again.

Chapter Ten

'You are looking very sickly, my love,' Charlotte said, holding her cousin at arm's length and looking her over critically. 'It is all this worry over Kit and Miss Trevithick, I suppose! And travelling in winter, of course. That is never to be recommended.'

There was a certain strange hush about the house in Upper Grosvenor Street, a gloominess that mirrored Beth's own feelings most accurately. She had been travelling for four long weeks in the most dreadful conditions and had finally reached London ten days after Christmas. The capital was shuttered and silent, for everyone had left Town to celebrate the twelve days of Christmas in the country. The streets were empty and cold, the skies a dull grey and the joyful Christmas spirit most noticeably lacking, particularly in their townhouse where everyone looked pinched and fearful, waiting for information about Kit and yet dreading that it might be bad. Charlotte had been relieved to see her, but the first piece of news that she had imparted was that Kit had not reappeared and there had been no progress in finding him.

'I am sorry that you had to chase all the way to

Mostyn Hall only to find that I had come up to London,' Charlotte said, leading Beth into the drawing room. 'My letter must have passed you on the road. How was everyone at home?'

'Well enough.' Beth gave her cousin a watery smile. She stripped off her gloves and cloak, and hurried gratefully over to the fire. 'They are all very worried, of course, but there is no news from Mostyn either. Kit certainly did not go there after he disappeared.'

Charlotte wrinkled up her face. 'It was the first place that I thought he might go to if there was trouble—' She broke off. 'I am sorry! You are barely through the door and here I am regaling you with nothing but bad news! Let us at least wait until the tea is served!'

Beth laughed. 'Or let us speak of more pleasant matters! Despite our troubles you look radiant, Charlotte! I believe you must have some good news for me!'

Charlotte's worried expression immediately dissolved into a glowing smile. 'Oh, Beth, it seems all wrong to be so happy when Kit has caused so much trouble, but…yes, that is…Mr Trevithick and I are betrothed!'

Although the news was not unexpected, Beth had to fight hard to crush down an unworthy feeling of jealousy. She gave Charlotte a tight hug that left her cousin breathless. 'Charlotte, I am so happy for you! You see, travelling in the winter *can* be beneficial!'

Charlotte blushed. 'Indeed, it was all settled by the time that Justin—Mr Trevithick—had escorted me back to Mostyn Hall…'

'Just as I had thought it would!'

'And we are to be married in the spring!' Charlotte hugged her back hard. 'Oh, Beth, how can I be so fortunate when Kit…'

'You deserve your good fortune,' Beth said staunchly,

'if that is what it is! Personally, I feel that Mr Trevithick is the lucky one!'

Charlotte blushed and disclaimed, 'Of course, I was concerned that this dreadful behaviour of Kit's might put an end to our engagement, but Justin—' she blushed harder '—assured me that it did not weigh with him. He has no position to uphold within the family, of course. If it had been his cousin the Earl it would have been a different matter—' She broke off. 'All the same, it is decidedly awkward!'

Beth nodded sadly. Charlotte's words had only confirmed her own conviction that Marcus could not possibly have anything to do with her in the future. Once again his parting words came back into her mind. But perhaps it was for the best. Their relationship on Fairhaven had been decidedly irregular. Beth shuddered to think what would be said in the *ton* if it all came out—the callous seduction and abandonment of Eleanor was bad enough and the scandalous affair between herself and Marcus could only be grist to the gossips' mill. She had had plenty of time to think about it on her journey up from Devon—and plenty of time to tell herself that she had to try to learn to live without Marcus. Her heart was not listening to her head; she had missed him dreadfully and her love had not weakened but her hope had, with each hour that passed.

She sat down a little heavily.

'Let us have tea at once,' Charlotte said, ringing the bell. 'Indeed, dearest Beth, you look worn to a thread! Tell me what has happened to you! I have been so selfishly full of my good news—'

'Nonsense!' Beth said. She was finding it very difficult to remain bright when she found that all she wanted to do was to cry. 'Besides, I have nothing to tell you! I have agreed that Fairhaven Island should remain the property of the Earl of Trevithick and that is the end of the tale!'

Charlotte looked startled. 'But, Beth... After you were so anxious to claim the place—'

'I know!' Beth clasped her hands together. 'Well, now I have been there I realise how different from my imaginings was the reality! I will tell you about it all some time, Charlotte, but not now if you will forgive me. I am a little tired.'

'Of course.' Charlotte frowned a little as she watched Beth's face. 'But, Beth, I thought that Lord Trevithick was intending to ask you—'

'Let us not speak of that now,' Beth said hastily. She had no desire to explain the complexities of her stay on Fairhaven to Charlotte. 'The matter of Kit and Eleanor is surely more pressing...'

The tea arrived at that moment and Beth was relieved when Charlotte appeared distracted, although sorry to bring the frown back to her cousin's face with thoughts of Kit's disappearance. Charlotte pressed her hands together distressfully.

'Oh, Beth, is it not terrible? I came up from Mostyn Hall as soon as Gough informed me, although I do not know what good I can do here! How could Kit ruin and abandon the poor child? I can scarcely believe it of him!'

'But is it certain?' Beth enquired, accepting the cup of tea Charlotte handed her. She was glad to be speaking of someone else's affairs rather than her own, even if they were so bleak. 'I simply cannot believe that Kit would seduce and desert an innocent girl!'

Charlotte looked dubious. 'Oh, but it is worse than that apparently! Eleanor claims that they are married!'

'Is that worse?' Beth asked, a little bitterly. She saw

Charlotte give her a curious look and said hastily, 'At least Miss Trevithick does not have the shame of being ruined—'

'No, but such a scandalous marriage!' Charlotte looked as though she was about to cry. 'And then to desert her and disappear only a day later! I cannot believe he could be so dishonourable!'

Beth put down her teacup and came across to take Charlotte's cold hands in hers. 'He is not! Something must have happened to him that we do not yet know—'

'That could be even worse!' Charlotte clutched Beth's hands. 'Needless to say, I have had Gough look everywhere, but to no avail! Oh, Beth!'

Beth sat down beside her. 'You had best tell me the whole story,' she said. 'I may not be able to think of anything new, but at least I can try!'

The tea had gone cold and a fresh pot had been delivered before Charlotte had finished the tale. Much of it was third-hand from Justin, who had apparently heard the whole from Marcus, who had in turn spoken to his sister. It seemed that six weeks before, Eleanor Trevithick had taken exception to the man that her mother had indicated she should marry and had foolishly fled to Kit for help. According to Eleanor, they had been married by special licence and Kit had abandoned her the very next day. Since then there had been no word from him and Eleanor had returned to Trevithick House, heartbroken and disgraced.

'The Viscountess has been most intemperate in her condemnation,' Charlotte said, with a little sniff. Her tragic blue eyes met Beth's. 'I cannot believe that she has helped her daughter's cause by speaking as she has done! Why, the entire *ton* is aware of all the intimate details, even down to why there can be no annulment!'

Beth raised her eyebrows expressively. 'Oh, dear, poor Eleanor! I suppose we must be grateful that most people are out of town now, and the scandal must surely die down through lack of interest!'

Charlotte smoothed her dress with nervous fingers. 'Justin feels that matters will improve now that the Earl has returned, for he and his sister are close. But if we cannot find Kit I cannot see what else can be done—' Her voice broke on a sob. Beth pressed her hands.

'Oh, Charlotte, do not! All will be well, I am convinced of it!'

She was not, but she knew that it would do her cousin no good to sink into a fit of the dismals.

'Excuse me, my lady.' Carrick was in the doorway. 'Mr Justin Trevithick has called.'

Beth jumped, terror coursing through her. On no account could she face seeing Justin, for he would undoubtedly bring news of Marcus and just at the moment Beth did not feel strong enough to hear it. She saw Charlotte's face brighten immediately and knew her own had lost what little colour it had. She got to her feet.

'Oh, excuse me, Charlotte! I have not yet washed the journey off and am in sore need of a rest! Please give Mr Trevithick my best wishes.'

She saw Charlotte's look of amazement as she sped from the room with just a whisper of time to spare before Justin came in. Once in her bedroom, she collapsed on the bed and tried to still her trembling. It was going to be decidedly difficult if Justin persisted in calling on Charlotte every day, as her cousin had intimated he did. Even now he would be aware that she had returned from Fairhaven and he would certainly tell Marcus.

Beth lay back against her pillows. On the journey up from Devon she had decided that she must not see

Marcus again. There were a hundred good reasons that said that this was the best course of action. Firstly there was Kit's behaviour, which had destroyed even the remote possibility of an alliance between the two families. Unlike Justin, Marcus *did* have a position to uphold within the Trevithick family and that made any link he might have with the Mostyns quite untenable. Once Beth had accepted the truth of this, any remaining hope she had harboured of marrying Marcus had died a swift death. She had only to remind herself of what he had said that last morning on Fairhaven, to know that there was no hope. Yet the irony was that there was now a reason why marriage might be even more desirable…

Beth closed her eyes. She loved Marcus too much to torture herself with seeing him when she could not have him. The thought of meeting him, talking to him and agreeing that they must part was exquisitely painful to her. She had already decided that once she had done the best she could to help with the search for Kit, and had given Charlotte the moral support she needed, she would return to Mostyn Hall. It would be a strange and lonely January without either of her cousins, but at least Charlotte had Justin to look after her now… Beth impatiently dashed away a tear that persisted in squeezing from under her eyelids. She had never felt sorry for herself in all her life and she did not intend to start now.

The following morning, rather than feeling an improvement from having a good night's rest, Beth felt so sick that she could scarcely raise her head from the pillow. Charlotte came to see her, most concerned, and Beth felt quite angry with herself for adding to her cousin's troubles.

'It is nothing serious,' she croaked, in answer to

Charlotte's anxious enquiry. 'I shall rest here today and be as right as rain by the evening!'

Charlotte was wearing a smart walking dress and confessed shyly that she had started to venture out a little with Justin as her escort. London was quiet and the crowds were small and not too frightening. Beth watched her go with pleasure and not a little envy, then turned over and fell asleep immediately.

She awoke in the middle of the afternoon, uncertain just what had disturbed her, until she heard a familiar voice down in the hall.

'I understand that Lady Allerton has returned to town?'

Marcus! Beth struggled to sit up, then changed her mind and lay very still, as though her immobility might actually convince him that she was not in the house at all. She knew Marcus was perfectly capable of walking right into her bedroom—he had done so often enough, after all, albeit in Fairhaven, not London. She held her breath as the butler replied.

'Lady Allerton is resting after her journey and has asked not to be disturbed, my lord. I will tell her that you called.'

'Please do so.' Beth could read a wealth of displeasure in Marcus's tone. 'Pray tell her that I will call on her tomorrow.'

She did not relax until the door had closed behind him, when she slid supine beneath the covers and lay trembling. So Marcus had come to find her, as she might have imagined he would do. Beth knew Marcus was not the sort of man to ignore a difficult situation and hope it would just go away. He was far too honourable for that. He would deem it his duty to see her and tell her that their betrothal must end. It was a private matter between the two of them, for the engagement had never been officially announced, or at least only on Fairhaven. She could leave the island in Marcus's care, could write to Lady Salome explaining that family circumstances prevented the marriage, and could then return to Mostyn Hall and forget the whole thing. Except that she could not. For in addition to her feelings for Marcus, which would not simply go away, there would soon be a very real reminder of what had happened between them…

Beth groaned and rolled over in the bed. In her heart she knew it was going to be hopeless to try to avoid Marcus but just at the moment she did not feel she had the strength to face him, and certainly not to keep secrets from him.

In the evening Beth managed to struggle from her bed but as soon as she joined Charlotte for dinner she realised that she could not bear to eat a mouthful and promptly retired to the drawing room. Charlotte reported that Gough had no further news of Kit's whereabouts; he had sent word to all the ports but to no avail and none of Kit's friends claimed to have seen him for well over two months. It appeared that he had vanished into thin air.

'Justin says that his cousin the Earl is most anxious to see you, Beth,' Charlotte said, when they had fruitlessly discussed Kit's disappearance for half an hour. 'Apparently Lord Trevithick called here earlier—'

'I heard him,' Beth said hurriedly. 'Unfortunately, I did not feel well enough to receive visitors.'

Charlotte was looking at her thoughtfully. 'Well, perhaps tomorrow? It may help in the hunt for Kit if we share our information.'

Beth shook her head stubbornly. 'I do not wish to see Lord Trevithick, Charlotte. I will not be at home.'

A frown furrowed Charlotte's brow. 'But, Beth, why—?'

'Please…' To her horror, Beth felt the weak tears rise in her throat. 'I do not wish to speak of Lord Trevithick!' And once again she hurried from the room before Charlotte could remonstrate with her.

On the next day she was as good as her word. When Marcus called she refused to see him and had the satisfaction if hearing him storm from the house, slamming the door behind him. Beth knew she was being cowardly in avoiding him, and when Charlotte returned from her walk with Justin, she told Beth so in no uncertain terms.

'As though things were not difficult enough as they are,' Charlotte scolded. 'Really, Beth, have you quarrelled with Trevithick again? Because, if so—'

'Please!' Beth said quickly. 'Charlotte, please do not!'

In desperation she put on her coat, hat and gloves and called the carriage to take her to Gough's chambers in Holborn. The man of business had nothing new to impart, but at least Beth felt that she was doing something useful and it took her away from Charlotte's too-perceptive questioning.

It was as she was leaving the building that she saw the Earl of Trevithick across the street, with Eleanor by his side. Beth's heart began to race. Just seeing him again was dreadful. He looked tired and worn and Beth wanted to rush across the street and fling herself into his arms.

They were taking a farewell of a gentleman whom Beth took to be the Earl's man of business, Gower. She had forgotten that he and Gough had rooms so close to one another and cursed herself for not thinking of it. Even as she made to turn away, Marcus saw her, exchanged a quick word with Eleanor and then set off across the street towards her. Quick as a flash, Beth jumped into her coach, without even pausing to thank Gough for his help. She was aware of similar looks of astonishment on the faces of both Gough and Marcus, though Marcus's look was decidedly more threatening. Before she could give the order to drive off, he had swung open the carriage door.

'Lady Allerton!'

Beth adopted her most haughty tone. It was the only way she could keep her voice from shaking.

'Lord Trevithick?'

Marcus was looking puzzled and annoyed. It made Beth want to cry.

'Will you step down and speak with me, ma'am?'

'No!' Beth snapped. 'I do not wish to, my lord!'

She saw Marcus flinch and it gave her a pain inside. He still looked more bewildered than angry, which only made Beth feel worse about the way she was treating him.

'Is this because of what has happened, ma'am?' he asked with constraint. 'Your cousin's behaviour—'

'It has nothing to do with that!' Beth said stonily. She wished that he would not persevere in questioning her, for she was sure that she would burst into tears in a moment.

'Then it must be the change in our own circumstances,' Marcus persisted, running a hand through his tumbled dark hair. He looked cross and confused. 'You have every right to be angry at the changes this has necessitated, Beth, but at the least let us discuss the matter.'

Although it was only what Beth had expected, the confirmation hit her like a blow. She tried to tell herself that it was no surprise, that she had known since Fairhaven that Marcus no longer wished them to marry, but she could not be reasonable about it. She felt herself shake with the shock and misery.

'I do not believe that we can speak with each other again, Lord Trevithick,' she said, as firmly as she could. She avoided Marcus's eye. 'It would not be appropriate!'

She saw his gaze narrow furiously on her. 'Inappropriate, ma'am? I never heard such nonsense! Shall I remind you just how inappropriate your behaviour has been with me?'

Beth shrank back. 'I would be obliged if you would leave me alone, sir! We have nothing more to say to each other!'

For what seemed like an age Marcus's gaze searched her face, then he stood back abruptly. 'Very well! You always were very attached to the idea of the feud between our families, were you not? If you are determined to pursue it, then I shall not oppose you! Good day to you, ma'am!'

The door swung closed. Beth leant back against the cushions and closed her eyes, but the tears slid out from beneath her lids. She had burned her boats now and, although she knew there was no alternative, she felt more desolate than she had ever done before.

Beth was down early for breakfast the next day, for she was intending to tell Charlotte of her plan to return to Mostyn Hall. It was the second week of January and seemed an appropriate enough time for a new start, except that it was not always possible to leave the past behind entirely. Beth needed no reminder that she would be taking a substantial keepsake of the past few months with her.

Her cousin was already at the table, looking fresh and pretty in a yellow and white striped dress, her hair confined in a matching bandeau. Her face was radiant and Beth felt decidedly wan in comparison. She slid into the seat opposite.

'Charlotte,' she began, 'I have decided to go back to Mostyn tomorrow—' She broke off as Charlotte lifted the lid off one if the serving dishes and placed it carefully on the sideboard behind. Beth stared at the devilled kidneys with fascinated repulsion.

'It always was Kit's favourite,' Charlotte was saying despondently, 'and I had no heart to tell Cook that I could not eat it. I believe that the servants are as upset as we are over Kit's unaccountable disappearance—'

Feeling an uprush of nausea, Beth pressed a hand over her mouth and got hastily to her feet. 'Excuse me, Charlotte!'

She only just managed to gain the shelter of her room in time; after she had been sick, she washed her face and peered dispiritedly at her reflection in the mirror. She looked dreadful, her face as pasty as parchment and her hair hanging damp and lifeless about her face. She still felt sick and dizzy, and went over to the bed to lie down.

There was a knock at the door.

'Beth?'

Beth closed her eyes in despair. She felt too wretched to curse the kind nature that prompted Charlotte to check up on her, but she would have given anything for her cousin not to see her just now. But it was too late. Charlotte had opened the bedroom door and was advancing towards the bed with a determined expression. She sat down next to Beth with a soft hush of silk skirts.

'Beth, how long have you been sick like this?'

Beth looked at her cousin and swiftly away. There was a knowledge in Charlotte's eyes that meant that she needed no explanations. With a sinking heart Beth acknowledged that she would never lie to her anyway, not to Charlotte, her dearest friend.

'Only a few days,' Beth said weakly. 'I feel wretched.' A tear squeezed from the corner of each eye and slid down her cheeks. Charlotte took her hand.

'You will feel better soon,' Charlotte said, in a practical voice. 'After twelve weeks the sickness generally improves—'

'Charlotte—'

Charlotte shook her head slightly. 'Oh, Beth, I may not have had any children of my own yet, but I saw many born on campaign! I know about all sorts of things, from how to deliver a baby to the best cures for the morning sickness—'

'Not just the morning!' Beth said dolefully.

Charlotte smiled. 'No, well, it takes some people that way, unfortunately! But there are remedies.' She leant forward and gave her cousin a gentle hug. 'Thank you for not trying to pretend that you had travel sickness, or had eaten something disagreeable...'

Beth burst into tears. 'Oh, Charlotte...'

'I know.' Her cousin gentled her.

'I'm so unhappy and confused! I cry all the time and I hate it!'

Charlotte laughed a little shakily. 'Yes, it is so unlike you! It was one of the first things that alerted me—that and your persistent refusal to speak of Lord Trevithick!

Beth…' she put her cousin away from her a little '…what happened?'

Beth sniffed, reaching for a handkerchief. 'I would have thought that that was obvious, Charlotte!'

'Yes, well…I mean…' Charlotte hesitated. 'But how…?'

Beth sighed. 'I am sorry, Charlotte. I did not mean to be flippant! Marcus did not seduce me, if that is what you mean.' A shade of colour came into her pale face. 'It just happened. I became his mistress… I chose to do so, there was no coercion! Quite the reverse…'

Charlotte frowned. 'But I thought—we all thought—that Lord Trevithick intended marriage! Justin was quite certain of it.'

Beth winced. 'Well, we are betrothed, or at least we were—' She stopped and started again. 'Marcus always intended that we should be married on Fairhaven, but then his cousin the vicar was absent, so it could not be. So then we planned to marry at Mostyn after Christmas—' she swallowed a sob '—but now this business with Kit and Eleanor has ruined our plans and we are not to marry after all and I certainly did not intend—' She gestured vaguely.

'Your planning does not seem very good all round!' Charlotte said drily. 'And I would venture that you have not even told Trevithick that you are increasing! *That* is why you keep avoiding him.'

Beth clutched at the bedspread. 'You will not tell him—'

'No,' Charlotte said, sounding sterner than Beth had heard her in a long time. 'You will tell him yourself!'

Beth shook her head. Her eyes sought Charlotte's. 'Oh, Lottie, I cannot. Not because I am afraid—' she spoke quickly as she saw Charlotte was about to interrupt '—but because I know he will insist on marrying me! He is too honourable to do otherwise!'

'So I should hope—'

'No, please!' Beth twitched the material between her fingers. 'I could not bear to be married to Marcus simply because of the baby! I love him so much and I would always be thinking that he had only proposed to save my reputation!'

Charlotte frowned. 'Beth, you are not thinking straight! Marcus has already proposed to you—why, you were betrothed on Fairhaven! Of course he wants to marry you! There is no difficulty—'

Beth shook her head. 'Yes, there is! The matter of Kit's dishonour—'

'Oh, fie!' Charlotte was starting to look really cross now. 'Are you to martyr yourself because of my foolish brother? I know it is the most monstrous scandal, but it is not your fault!'

Beth turned her face away. 'You said yourself that someone in Trevithick's position, with the honour of his family to uphold, could not possibly even speak with us any more, let alone consider a marriage alliance!'

'I...' Charlotte hesitated. 'I know that I said that before, but this puts a different complexion on the matter...' She fell silent.

Beth turned her head tiredly on the pillow. 'No, you were correct, Charlotte. Before he left Fairhaven, Marcus told me that the marriage could not go ahead. There is no more to be said!'

Charlotte put her hands on her hips. 'Have you discussed this properly with him, Beth? I thought that you had not even done the Earl the courtesy of seeing him!'

'I have told Marcus that I do not want to see him ever again—' Beth's voice broke on the words. 'It is better this way! I cannot see him again, for I would not be able to keep the secret of my condition from him!'

Charlotte looked stubborn, but she did not argue. 'So what will you do?' she asked quietly, after a moment.

Beth looked at her defiantly. 'I shall go back to Devon just as soon as I can manage it. Tomorrow, perhaps, if I am well enough to travel! There is nothing I can do to help find Kit, and should Marcus discover my situation…'

'Beth, he find out soon enough! You cannot hope to give birth to Marcus Trevithick's child without the most immense scandal!'

Beth looked mulish. 'I shall deal with that as and when it happens!'

Charlotte got to her feet. 'Well, we shall see. For myself, I think you are speaking a deal of nonsense, but we shall not quarrel now! I will go to fetch you some dry toast. It may sound odd, but it will make you feel better!'

Charlotte had been down to the kitchen, fetched the toast and was about to knock on the door of Beth's room again when she heard a sound from within. She paused. It sounded as though Beth was crying again, and in an intense, heartbreaking way that suggested that to disturb her would be too cruel. With a heavy heart, Charlotte retraced her steps and went to sit in the drawing room whilst she tried to think.

She sat down in an armchair with a heavy sigh. She did not doubt that Beth loved Marcus deeply, for her cousin had never shown any interest in casual love affairs. Charlotte had always thought Beth too impulsive, too unguarded, and had wanted to protect her cousin. Now she could see that Beth had given her heart and herself where she loved, and was set to be dreadfully hurt because she believed that her marriage to Marcus could not go ahead.

Charlotte sighed again. She was utterly convinced that her cousin would do exactly as she had said, and would run away to Devon without seeing the Earl of Trevithick again. Obstinate, headstrong and in this situation just plain wrong... Charlotte smiled sadly. She loved Beth for all her faults and she was determined not to allow her to make so terrible a mistake. The issue of Kit's dishonour was a powerful one, but surely not enough to keep Marcus from Beth's side once he knew the truth.

Charlotte frowned as she thought it over. Beth's obstinacy was clear, but what was Marcus's view? Surely if he had become concerned to sever all connections between the Mostyns and Trevithicks, Justin would have told her. Yet not only was Justin as ardent in his attentions as ever, but he had also brought messages from his cousin, the Earl, showing that Marcus was anxious to see Beth as soon as possible. To Charlotte's mind, that was not the behaviour of a man who wished to break his engagement.

She drummed her fingers on the arm of the chair. Beth had said that Marcus had told her the wedding would not take place, but Charlotte wondered if Beth had misunderstood. In the rush and distress of their parting it would have been all too easy to misconstrue his words, and after that they had never discussed the matter properly. And now Beth had told Marcus some cock-and-bull story about not wishing to see him again and his pride had no doubt prevented him from persisting. They were apart and unhappy. Charlotte tutted to herself. Really, they deserved each other! But she could not let them suffer...

She got up and went to fetch her cloak, bonnet and

gloves. Her conscience was troubling her a little. It was really Beth's place to tell Marcus that she was in a delicate condition and strictly none of her business at all, but she knew that Beth was too stubborn to be persuaded. That being the case, she was acting in Beth's best interests...

Charlotte had never been out on her own in London, for her agoraphobia had made her shy away from the busy streets and crush of passers-by. When she had had Justin by her side she was reassured, but now she was alone. She almost gave up on the steps and went back into the house, but the memory of Beth's white face and desperate sobs was enough to drive her on. Even so, she was shaking by the time she reached Trevithick House and could barely tell the impassive butler that she wished to see the Earl of Trevithick. It was inevitable that she should be told that the Earl was not at home.

Charlotte was trembling like a leaf. Tears of fear and abject misery were not far away, but she drew herself up and said:

'Indeed? Tell Lord Trevithick that Mrs Cavendish wishes to speak to him on a matter of the highest importance—'

One of the doors to the entrance hall opened and Marcus Trevithick came out, deep in conversation with another man. Charlotte noticed that there was a deep frown on his forehead and he looked as though he was in an exceptionally bad mood. Her heart sank.

'We have tried the Port of London and sent runners to Southampton—' The other man was saying. Both of them broke off when they saw Charlotte and after a moment, to her inexpressible relief, Charlotte saw Trevithick's expression lighten.

'Mrs Cavendish! Pray forgive me for not receiving

you sooner, ma'am! Gower...' he turned courteously to the other man '...excuse me. We will talk again later and I thank you for your help.'

Charlotte came forward a little shakily as Marcus held the door of the study open for her. 'Let me send for a glass of wine for you, Mrs Cavendish,' he said solicitously. 'You look somewhat done up! What can have put you to so much trouble as to come here in person? Has there been some news of your brother?'

Charlotte smiled a little shakily. 'No, sir, I am afraid not. This is far more important. This is to do with my cousin...with Beth—Lady Allerton.'

She saw Marcus's expression harden, felt him withdraw from her, and put a pleading hand out.

'Please...'

She was not sure what was showing in her face but, whatever it was, Marcus's own expression softened and he took her arm and guided her to a chair. 'I am sorry, ma'am. Pray do not be distressed. Now, what is it that you wished to tell me?'

Some ten minutes later, Justin Trevithick called at Trevithick House and was astounded to hear from the butler that a Mrs Cavendish was with his cousin the Earl. Another moment, and the door of the study was flung open and Marcus strode out across the hall, his face set and intent. He checked on seeing his cousin.

'Justin! The very man! Mrs Cavendish is here and I fear I must desert both of you! Pressing business! If you could escort the lady home I should be most grateful, old fellow, but pray leave it for at least a half-hour! I rely upon you to think of a way to pass the time!' And, without another word, he was gone.

On gaining the study, Justin found his betrothed sitting calmly sipping a glass of madeira and looking quite pleased with herself. There was a twinkle in her eye as she gave her hand to him.

'Good morning, Mr Trevithick! How do you do?'

'I should be considerably better if someone could explain to me just what the devil is going on!' Justin said feelingly. 'How comes it that you are here, Charlotte, and what have you said to Trevithick, to send him off in such a confounded hurry?'

He thought that Charlotte looked positively mischievous as she replied. 'I have struck a light,' she said contentedly, 'and I am certain it is about to explode into flames!'

Beth had found the plate of dry toast waiting outside the door and was astonished to discover that it had indeed made her feel better—so much restored, in fact, that she decided there was no point in delaying her preparations to remove to Mostyn. Happily, her trunk was still out since she had not bothered to unpack it from her last journey. She did not think of Charlotte's reaction to her hasty departure, nor of Kit's mysterious disappearance, and especially not of Marcus Trevithick. She knew that she would only become odiously miserable if she dwelled on any of them and she was running for home out of simple instinct.

At first she did not hear the fuss in the entrance hall and then assumed that Gough had called to see Charlotte. After a moment, however, she heard an unmistakable male voice.

'Don't be so bloody foolish, man! Of course Lady Allerton is at home!'

Then there was a step on the stair, and the door was thrown open.

'Running away again, my dear?' the Earl of Trevithick said with silky politeness. 'It is become quite a habit!'

To Beth's eyes he looked both devastatingly handsome and frighteningly unyielding. With her hands full of underwear and the half-open trunk giving her away, she decided to hold her ground. Her heart was beating uncomfortably fast, but she raised her chin defiantly to stare him out.

'Good day, Lord Trevithick! I fear that you find me on the point of departing for Devon—'

'Again?' Marcus lounged in the doorway, making it quite clear that she was unable to go anywhere. 'You rocket about the countryside like a dangerously loose cannon, my dear!' He came forward into the room. 'I fear I cannot allow it. Not in your condition!'

Beth lowered her hands slowly. She could feel what little colour she had fading from her face.

'You know!' she whispered.

'I know,' Marcus confirmed grimly. 'Your cousin had the grace to tell me, Lady Allerton, where you did not.'

'She had no right,' Beth said stiffly.

Marcus strode over to the window. There was so much suppressed violence in his movements that Beth shrank away. 'Maybe not,' he said evenly, 'but when were you going to tell me, Lady Allerton? Ever? Or was I to hear about my own child from some gossip at a *ton* party?'

Beth's eyes filled with the infuriating tears that beset her all the time. 'Oh, do not! I did not intend...I just thought that you would insist on marrying me.'

Marcus raised his eyebrows. He took a deep, impatient breath. 'Beth, I have been wanting to marry you this past age—'

Beth's tears overflowed. 'You said that we could not

be married!' she contradicted him crossly. 'You know it is impossible because of Kit's behaviour to Eleanor! You have only changed your mind because of the baby—' She broke off, crying too hard to carry on.

Marcus sat down on the bed and pulled her on to his knee. He took a clean handkerchief out of his pocket and carefully wiped her face, kissing her gently when he was done.

'This is foolish. I *never* said that we could not be married—'

'Yes, you did!' Beth burst out. 'When you were leaving Fairhaven you said that all our plans were changed and our wedding could not go ahead! You said that everything was spoiled for us...' She gave a huge gulp and fell silent.

Marcus was frowning. 'I remember. We did not really have time to talk properly, did we? I only meant that our Christmas wedding could not take place, but I had every intention of rearranging it as soon as I could! I never meant for the engagement to end!'

Beth gave a doleful sniff. Another tear slid down her cheek. 'But—'

Marcus gave her a little shake. 'Listen to me, my darling. I have had a special licence for the past four weeks—you may check the date if you wish!—and all because I wanted to marry you so much that I obtained one as soon as I arrived in London!' His arm tightened about her. 'I did that before all else—before seeing Eleanor, or enquiring into your cousin's whereabouts, or discussing matters with Gower. It was always the most important thing to me and the fact that your cousin has ruined my sister is irrelevant to our marriage! I do not intend to let him ruin my happiness as well as Eleanor's!'

Beth was so astounded that she stopped crying altogether. She borrowed the handkerchief and blew her nose hard. 'But I thought—Marcus, it is impossible for you to associate with the Mostyn family, with me—'

Marcus started to laugh. 'I have already associated with you and I intend to continue to do so at every available opportunity! I love you, Beth! You know that I always wanted to marry you—I was in a fever of impatience for St John to return to Fairhaven, and it was not because I simply wished to see him! When he did not return in time to marry us, and then all my plans were dashed again, I was frustrated and most disappointed!'

Beth looked at him. Marcus was smiling at her with a gentleness that somehow made her feel quite weak inside. She squashed the treacherous warmth and frowned at him.

'Promise me that this is not simply because I am increasing…'

Marcus pulled her into his arms again. 'Oh, Beth, do you doubt me still? I blame myself more than you could know, my darling, for damaging your reputation and exposing you to gossip through what happened on Fairhaven…' He hesitated. 'I wanted to marry you almost from the first time we met, when you challenged me to that ridiculous wager.' He brushed his mouth against her hair. 'Beth, I am more happy than I can say about the child, but I wanted to marry you long before I knew. I love you…'

Later, when she had stopped kissing him long enough to draw breath, Beth said a little diffidently, 'I thought perhaps that you would not wish to marry me because I was not suitable…'

Marcus kissed her again. 'It seems to me that you

have imagined every possible or impossible reason to keep us apart! How could you not be suitable?'

Beth fidgeted. 'Well, because I...because we—did things together that were not at all respectable—'

Marcus started to laugh. 'Oh, Beth, I can see I need to change your view of how married people behave! And you must never think I believe you unsuitable. I love you for your openness and your lack of artifice!'

This seemed to warrant another kiss. Then Beth drew back again.

'I have been so miserable without you, Marcus! It has been the most unhappy Christmas—'

'We shall make up for it, I promise you!' Marcus kissed her again.

'But what are we to do about this dreadful situation of Kit and Eleanor?' Beth frowned. 'I could not blame you if you damned the name of Mostyn forever!'

Marcus's face hardened. 'My love, I wish your cousin to the devil for what he has done but, as I told you, I refuse to let it ruin my happiness! Justin is in the right of it—we shall end the Mostyn and Trevithick feud and damn the gossips!'

'Passionate enemies and passionate lovers?' Beth asked mischievously and smiled as Marcus started to kiss her again. She freed herself for a moment. 'My lord, you mentioned the wager and, strictly speaking, I have still won Fairhaven—'

Marcus pulled her back firmly into his arms. 'Wager be damned!' he said.

* * * * *